CW00701096

The BOOKSHOP DETECTIVES

Dead Girl Gone

GARETH WARD
& LOUISE WARD

The BOOKSHOP DETECTIVES

Dead Girl Gone

PENGUIN BOOKS

PENGUIN

UK | USA | Canada | Ireland | Australia
India | New Zealand | South Africa | China

Penguin is an imprint of the Penguin Random House group of companies, whose addresses
can be found at global.penguinrandomhouse.com

Penguin
Random House
New Zealand

First published by Penguin Random House New Zealand, 2024

1 3 5 7 9 10 8 6 4 2

Text © Gareth Ward and Louise Ward, 2024

The moral right of the authors has been asserted.

All rights reserved. Without limiting the rights under copyright reserved above, no part
of this publication may be reproduced, stored in or introduced into a retrieval system, or
transmitted, in any form or by any means (electronic, mechanical, photocopying, recording
or otherwise), without the prior written permission of both the copyright owner and the
above publisher of this book.

Quote on page 58 from George Orwell's *Nineteen Eighty-Four*, first published in 1949.

Design by Cat Taylor © Penguin Random House New Zealand
Author photograph © Max Ward

Printed and bound in Australia by Griffin Press, an Accredited ISO AS/NZS 14001
Environmental Management Systems Printer

A catalogue record for this book is available from the National Library of New Zealand.

ISBN 978-1-77695-100-0
eISBN 978-1-77695-101-7

penguin.co.nz

MIX
Paper | Supporting
responsible forestry
FSC® C018684

For Vonnie

PROLOGUE

When we opened Sherlock Tomes people warned us that we'd made a terrible mistake. People warned us that e-readers were taking over. People warned us that we'd never compete with Amazon. The one thing they didn't warn us about was the murders.

CHAPTER 1

Eloise: Tuesday

There's a dry, paper-dust and furniture-polish scent in the air. I breathe it in as I make my way through the biographies and history, past the dumpbin of the frothy new political scandal, *Jokers to My Right*. I pop a copy of the new Fiona Kidman on an empty stand and retrieve an abandoned copy of *A Summery Saturday Morning* from a shelf at about a three-year-old's height. A cursory check of front and back covers reveals no sticky finger marks.

Stevie's shadowing me around the shop, sniffing suspiciously at the bottom of the New Zealand fiction; I dread to think what a toddler has done there to make it smell so appealing. We traverse the centre aisle. All appears to be in order.

The murmur of conversation that has been on the edge of my hearing becomes clearer. Garth and Rose, one of the book reps we entertain monthly, are in the event space near the counter, deep in conversation.

Stevie slips past, a slinky silver shadow heading for the safety of the stock room.

'Steve!' says Garth, but he's too late. The pupper's white-tipped tail disappears around the corner.

Garth looks disappointed but shifts his focus to smile a welcome as I find a chair at the small wooden table crafted in the shape of a book. Some people notice the genius of Garth's handiwork, some don't, which is a shame as it really is very clever.

'Ah good, you're here,' says Rose, all impatience, looking me straight in the eye with a glare worthy of Medusa.

I try not to, but I squirm just a little bit.

'We have a very important title to discuss first up.' Rose lowers her voice. 'It's top secret.'

'Cool!' Garth sits forward, sensing drama and a story. I'm faffing about, getting my laptop out of my bag, fishing around for my glasses.

'Do I have your full attention, Eloise?'

'Err . . . yes?' I do dislike being treated like a scatty five-year-old. Besides, we've been here before. Every publisher has an occasional top-secret, not-to-be-discussed-before-release-date title. It'll be another political exposé or somesuch — *Clowns to the Left of Me* perhaps.

We settle in, calm down and look at Rose expectantly.

'The reason I'm back so quickly after my last visit,' she says, 'is that I have momentous news for you.' She looks at each of us, her eyes wide, her gob firmly shut. After at least twenty seconds I cave.

'Well, go on then,' I say.

'Okay, so. Isabella Garrante.'

'Brilliant. New novel? Why the big deal?'

'It's set in Havelock North and she wants to launch it here at Sherlock Tomes.'

'Fucking hell!'

'Language, Eloise, there are children in the shop.' Garth's very much a right swear, right place person.

'Well, you can't get much more of a big deal than this, can you?' I counter, looking around. 'And it's only the one child way down by the comics.' I stretch my neck further to see who it is. 'And it's that kid that hangs outside the dairy all the time, vaping. He's a right foul-mouthed little bugger.'

'Can you try and stay on task, Eloise? This could make or break you,' says Rose.

As soon as she says it, my stomach lurches.

So little is known of Isabella Garrante, it's not even certain she's a woman. But she's bloody famous. Her *Tuatara Trilogy* chronicling the lives of a New Zealand crime family has had the world in thrall for the past eight years, and a new instalment — never mind a launch in our shop — would be epic. Still, I can't quite identify the feeling spreading through my gut: it might be the excitement of opportunity but could just as easily be terror.

'She wants to launch it in our shop? We can't fit that kind of crowd. It'd actually be dangerous.'

'That's right!' Garth comes to my rescue. 'We'll have to hire a venue. We can't possibly . . .'

'Not an option,' says Rose. 'She has specifically stated that it should be here, at this shop. And it is so super-top-secret that it has to happen early October. We have stock in Auckland already, highly guarded, of course.'

'Do you mean to say she's actually going to make an appearance? And we've only got a month and a bit to prepare?'

'Yes. In person. And, yes, because it's a drop-in title and we want to get it on the shelves as soon as possible. Now you need to sign this non-disclosure agreement and—'

'An NDA? Cool!' says Garth.

Rose glares, I giggle, she frowns more. She's starting to piss me off a bit, if I'm honest.

'—and make damn sure you don't tell a soul,' she says. 'Not a word. Do you understand?'

'Well, I'm not really sure I want to be dictated to like—'

Garth cuts me off with a nudge of his foot. 'Of course, Rose. Where do we sign?'

Trade embargo agreements add to the hype surrounding certain titles, and I hold little truck with the fuss and faff they involve: don't open the boxes before the correct time, keep copies of the work out of sight of customers and provide adequate security, ensure that no part of the work is visible to others. I mean, it's not like the autobiography of Prince Harry is going to bring down the world order if someone sees it before 9am on a specific Thursday.

'But how are we supposed to organise a launch of this size in a month?' I ask.

'It's seven weeks, so more like two months. I'm sure you'll work it out. You always pull off the spectacular with no resources, don't you?'

I'm trying to formulate a response when Rose puts a pen in my hand, slams a piece of paper onto the table and taps it, nodding at me, then back at the paper. I sign, and hand the pen to Garth who gives an old-man grunt as he leans forward, looking around for his glasses. You'd think he was in his eighties rather than his forties.

'They're on your head, love.'

'Ah, of course.'

After a bit of mucking about and attempts to make sense of the legal jargon, Garth completes his part of the deal.

'Not. A. Word,' Rose says, pointing her finger at me, then Garth, then back to me.

We move on to the rest of the new titles. I pull my head together and try to focus.

The list includes some good stuff — a new Mary-anne Scott that piques Garth's interest, an advance reading copy of something a bit different from Kate Atkinson, and one of those 'couple renovates house in Provence' books that has Havelock North written all over it. I stifle a sigh at yet another 'influencer' releasing a lifestyle book that will change our lives. I'm grateful for Rose's advice on that one; just because I think it's bollocks doesn't mean that a fair few people will not follow the latest Instagram sensation and aspire to her glowing skin and sun-bleached locks. As Rose starts to pack up her stuff, I feel a surge of affection for her. She's a pain in the arse but she's just trying to look after us.

'That vegan travel book you made me take is going really well, so thank you for that,' I tell her.

'*Plant Based Meandering*? She's unstoppable, that woman. Currently in India researching edible grasses.' She shrugs her coat on. 'I'll be in touch. I can't stress how big of a deal the Garrante is. Brace yourselves.'

And with that, she's gone.

'Bloody hell,' I offer.

'Yeah,' says Garth.

I tidy up cups and papers, and try to focus on the more manageable mundanities of the day ahead.

'Have you finished the mags yet?' I ask.

Garth huffs, then off he shuffles like a wounded martyr, trying to pretend he's not just going to ask Phyllis to sort the magazines out when she arrives.

Soon there's a bustle in the shop. A couple of women are down by the Dalek, a display case we had built for new releases that bears a slight resemblance to the bane of Doctor Who's existence. They're discussing the Booker longlist and speculating on who'll make the next stage.

'I couldn't bloody read it. I mean, who is even talking? Is it a tree, or a spirit or what?'

'I think it's an old spirit. You know, omniscient or something. The writing's exquisite, though. I reckon we keep going and just enjoy her skill with words and it'll end up making some sort of sense. It's supposed to be innovative, right?'

Her friend emits a non-committal 'hmm'.

I leave them to browse and head up to the till. There's a present to wrap and a wee girl who wants to choose the paper. Garth is poking at the magazines.

'It's for my friend Oriana and it's a Very Secret Thing,' says the girl, swooshing her sparkly pink frock.

'Well, I think she'll love it. Are you going to the party now? That's a lovely dress,' I say.

'Yes, it's a unicorn party and Ori will be four like me and I have unicorns on my socks, too, and that's another secret.' She shushes me, finger on lips.

I wrap the unicorn sticker book in unicorn paper and hand it to the little girl in the swooshy unicorn dress with secret unicorn socks. It's a day for secrets, I muse, thinking about Rose and the secret-squirrel Garrante title.

An embargoed title is not unusual; the hype can be a lot of fun and a good opportunity for a release-day party. The threat of litigation is intriguing, though; we don't get that so often. Jeez, this really is massive — and such a lot of work if we're going to pull off a launch. I think I'll have a five-minute pat with Stevie.

CHAPTER 2

Garth: 50 days until Isabella Garrante book launch

Dinner is a seafood lasagne ready meal for me and Eloise, and for Stevie biscuits and Possychum, which is dogroll made from possum, garlic and semolina. It's not as bad as it sounds, and Stevie loves it. To be honest, I've been tempted myself, even considered frying up a slice of Possychum with a couple of eggs and pretending it's bacon. Possibly the only thing that's stopped me is the semolina.

I carry two bowls into the lounge and offer one to Eloise. She is relaxing in a battered armchair, her pink hair bright against green leather. In one hand she grasps a glass of syrah, in the other the latest Catherine Chidgey. Finishing her sentence, Eloise necks her wine, deposits the glass and then places a scrap of paper between the book's pages; we're booksellers but for some reason never seem to have any bookmarks.

'How's the Chidders reading?' I ask, using our pet name for the author that allows us to feel like she is an actual friend rather than a goddess of literary genius.

'Brilliantly, obvs.' Eloise slides the book onto the coffee table out of Stevie's reach, just in case he feels it would make a satisfying palate cleanser after his Possychum.

I choose one of the three sofas so that I'm next to Eloise but get a wide view to the twinkling lights of Havelock North and Hastings beyond. The Heretaunga Plains with their patchwork orchards and vineyards stretch to the distant Kaweka Range that are like the hackles on Stevie's back when he's spotted the neighbour's cat. I'm reminded of rural Lincolnshire, too, only here there's sunshine, mountains and less interbreeding.

'What are we going to do about the launch?' asks Eloise through a mouthful of cheesy garlic sauce and pasta.

It's the thought that has been bouncing around my head all day and one about which I have failed to come to any firm conclusions. 'Well, we've got to hold it in the shop, so that's a starting point, I suppose.'

'The shop's not big enough. This is Isabella Garrante. We're going to get hundreds, maybe even thousands turn up.'

Good grief, did she need to say it out loud? I still can't make sense of why we've been chosen. Our bookshop is fantastic, if I say so myself, and two years ago we won New Zealand Bookshop of the Year, but even so, why does Isabella Garrante want to launch here in the provinces and not Auckland or Wellington? Hell, why doesn't she want to launch in New York, London or Paris? She's a big enough name with enough mystery around her to warrant it. So what if the novel is set in Havelock North?

'We could close the street and put up a giant screen on the shop's awning like you get at concerts? Livestream the event to the gathered crowds and our Facebook page.'

'Sounds expensive.' Eloise rubs Stevie's head. He's finished his dinner and is now angling for some of hers.

'The publisher might stump up for some of the costs. They see our figures, they must know we can't afford to do this on our own.'

'Rose can talk to marketing, see what they can bring to the party.'

A moment of self-doubt grabs me. I sometimes forget that not everyone shares our obsessive love of books. If I went into the street now and said 'Isabella Garrante's coming' how many people would get excited and how many people would just look at me blankly and say, 'Who?' We like to think that the provinces are as culturally well versed as the big cities, and perhaps the bookshop means that in our local sphere of contacts they are, but I can't push away the niggling thought that the latest and greatest sheep drench might have better brand recognition than Isabella.

'You don't think we're getting ahead of ourselves? Will it really be that big?' I ask.

Eloise puts her bowl on the floor for Stevie to lick and grabs her MacBook. 'Are you kidding? It's going to be massive.' With an expression that I recognise as her 'you're being a total idiot' face, she opens our stock management system and taps a few keys. 'We sold nearly two hundred copies of *The Sins of Smythe*.'

'Two hundred?' Even I'm amazed. We sell fewer than five copies of most fiction titles. Even with a well-known author like Lee Child or John Boyne we may only sell fifty or sixty.

'Yeah, in trade paperback. Another sixty-three in B format.'

A jolt of adrenaline chills me. The authors we normally deal with, even the big New Zealand names, are usually pretty laid back, and turn up on their own or with maybe just their publisher or a PR person. This isn't going to be the case with Isabella. Will she travel with an entourage, security, personal assistants, publicists? Will there be a press corps, TV, overseas media? The NDA enforces a publicity blackout until a few days before the launch, which will go some way to limiting the numbers. Even so, Eloise is right: we can expect a massive crowd. We have only a handful of staff and we're not allowed to disclose full details of the event to them till the last minute, so the planning, preparation and organising are all going to fall entirely on our shoulders. And September's when we traditionally host our Battle of the Book Clubs charity fundraiser, our biggest event of the year. The whole thing is bonkers. I feel like Stevie after he's been terrified by a loud noise. I just want to go and hide with my head under a blanket.

Eloise reaches out and puts a hand on my knee. 'It's okay, love, we'll do it together, just like everything else we've ever done.'

She's right, of course. She could be talking about the opening of the bookshop or our semi-forced emigration to New Zealand, but she isn't. We've done some darn serious stuff in the past, stuff that never quite leaves you.

'I guess,' I say, trying to be positive the way our PTSD counsellors encouraged. 'It's not like anybody's life's at risk.'

'Exactly.'

'But what if we stuff it up? It's Isabella Fucking Garrante!'

'She's just a person, and she's chosen us,' says Eloise calmly. 'Rose knows us, the publishers know us and by extension Isabella will know us. If she wasn't happy with the arrangements, we wouldn't even be having this conversation.'

I take a deep breath and hear Stevie inhale three times in quick succession — his particular sign of contentment.

'See, Stevie's not worried,' says Eloise.

'Stevie has a very limited knowledge of the bookselling world.'

'True enough.' Eloise smiles and gives my leg another squeeze. 'But soon he'll be the only dog in the world that has launched Isabella Fucking Garrante.'

CHAPTER 3

Eloise: 49 days until Isabella Garrante book launch

I'm daydreaming, reflecting on the paradise that is our little corner of New Zealand, when my reverie is broken by Garth powering on Philip, our vacuum cleaner (a Pullman). I hate doing the vacuuming and Garth hates doing any admin, so it's a useful arrangement when I'm looking at web orders and faffing about in the emails.

'So I reckon we get Hungry Havvers Catering in. I don't think a couple of bags of chippies is going to cut it,' says Garth as he emerges from the stock room ten minutes later.

I don't need to ask what he's on about. It's all we've been talking about since Rose's visit. Isabella. Fucking. Garrante. Or IFG as she's now known.

'What kind of numbers do we give them? I know I always say book launch food is only a gesture, but how many gestures are we talking here?'

'Shall we approach a local winery for help with the drinks?

Amelia's Chris could sort us out, couldn't he?'

Our colleague Amelia is a bookseller with a deep commitment to her art. If she loves a book, every customer will know about it and many of them will be convinced to make a purchase. If she hates it, watch out. Her husband is a winemaker, a generous bloke who gets roped into many of our events.

'Saved by the customer!' I all but yell as a woman about my age comes up to the counter. She's clearly taken aback by my welcome.

'Don't worry,' I say. 'We're trying to plan an event and it's proving more complicated than we thought.'

Her face relaxes and she smiles, proffering two books: *Looks to Die For*, the latest god-awful 'romance' doing the rounds on TikTok, and a more niche non-fiction on Adlerian psychology that I bought in because I liked the look of it. An eclectic reader then.

'Isn't that always the way? I'm in charge of planning my mother's ninetieth and I had no idea what a nightmare it would become. She's adamant that we order in some weird cheese she had in Italy in the fifties. That would be fine, but all she knows is that it was hard and smelly. I mean, like, what?'

'Ha. That sounds like when someone wants the book with the blue cover they saw last week but we've moved it.'

'I'm just terrified I'll muck it all up. I mean, not to be morbid but she is ninety — she might not last another year and this could be my last chance to get it right for her.'

'You can only do your best.'

The woman smiles half-heartedly and I try to squash the thought that if we don't get it right for IFG, we might not last another year either. Rose intimated as much.

The customer is not in our loyalty scheme, just passing through, but our moment of connection is valuable all the same. IFG is not my close relative, I will do my best for her, but at this late notice and in such strange circumstances, the bestselling literary megastar will get what she's given. The more I think about it, the more I reckon the publisher can help out. I'll get on to the publicist, Georgia. I've had dealings with her before and she's a good sort.

Garth has got the ancient computer that we use for stock input up and wheezing, and is filling the kettle, a marvellous idea.

'What about glassware? Think Gordon will lend us some?' he asks.

'He definitely would but I reckon we email Georgia and get them to stump up for all of this. It's going to spill out on to the street, so let's have tables outside and pray for good weather. It's the only way we can do it.'

'Who's Georgia?' asks Garth.

I tell him to leave it with me. I open the emails to get on to it, and just as I'm about to click 'new email', a reminder pops up:

Havelock North Business Association Meet and Greet tonight!

Bugger. I'd forgotten. Garth's got a writer's group meeting this evening, so I'll have to go it alone and do mingling and small talk.

Phyllis has come in to cover our lunch breaks and start riffling through the children's section for overstocks that we could return for a credit.

'Are you going to stop messing about on that computer and eat your lunch now, Eloise?' she asks. She a Dubliner, full of energy and bossy with it.

'Yes, Mam.'

'And drink some water. You're starting to talk shite.'

I move from the email to Georgia to trying to write a newsletter without mentioning Isabella Garrante, to worrying about Isabella Garrante, to fussily wiping pollen from its favourite hangouts: the lower shelves of the Dalek-shaped book table, and the face-out covers of every single book within wafting distance of the door. I do such a good job of getting in Phyllis's way all afternoon that she skedaddles bang on time rather than hanging around for a chat as is her usual habit. At 5.30pm it's just Garth and me in the shop.

'I'm off to this business thingy then. You don't mind cashing up, do you?' I ask.

'Not at all. Have a wonderful time talking to people you don't have anything in common with,' comes Garth's reply.

'Are you implying that I'm not a dynamic, thrusting business sort with, I dunno, growth figures and economic forecasts and shit on the tip of my tongue?'

'Shit on the tip of your tongue. You really are a fine and rare lady, my Eloise.'

I laugh, flip him the bird, and head out of the back door.

It's a two-minute walk across the car park and around the corner to this evening's host venue, one of the shiny restaurants in the ground floor of a new build that's recently graced the Village. Even as I enter the alleyway leading to the garden bar I hear a booming male voice; it seems the talking part has begun.

'So with establishments like this one providing such a draw card, what this Village needs is a bow-tique hotel that will offer the standard of accommodation and care we need to attract and retain high-quality consumers. My plan is to—'

The boomer is a handsome man with the air of a private school rugby boy all grown up: fifties, full head of hair, still fairly athletic. Several things immediately irritate me: his pronunciation of boutique, the word *consumers*, like we're trying to attract posh cattle to nom everything up, and the fact that everyone else has a drink and I don't.

Fortunately, a delightful young person carrying a tray of wine notices my distress and saunters over.

'I'll nab one of those please, darling,' whispers a voice at my shoulder.

I turn to see a tiny, beautifully put-together woman I recognise from one of the Village's /buːˈtiːk/ dress shops.

The woman passes me a glass of red. 'What's Franklin blathering on about? Always hustling, that man. Can't stand him.'

'He just said he's going to develop a piece of land near the Redwoods up by Te Mata Peak Park. Isn't that protected by an open-space covenant or something?'

'That wouldn't stop him. Has half the council in his back pocket. Odious little man.'

Franklin, who is not little at all, is waving a champagne flute around in front of a PowerPoint slide showing a celestial-looking glade of towering redwoods, the sun filtering through their canopy; a caption, fading in and out, announces *Redwood Ridge: Luxury in the Pines*. Atop the hill in the background there's a two-storey building with large, open bifold doors and a stone chimney. The screen gently dissolves into a new, revolving slide of the interior: gabled ceilings, many shades of white, large couches drowning in cushions of pale blue and green. It's utterly luscious and has my full attention.

The screen freezes.

And Franklin goes from charming to incandescent in about 1.8 seconds: 'Vanessa! Fix this.'

A young blonde woman almost as tall as Franklin, but rather less nourished, scurries forward and fiddles with a laptop.

'You just can't get the staff these days,' Franklin ventures, and the audience titter, as they are expected to do. They're with him, hanging off his every word and gesture, drenched in his well-honed charm, delighted when Vanessa gets us whirling around Redwood Ridge again.

'Who's that poor woman?' I ask my new friend.

'The latest squeeze, darling. Vanessa Goldsworthy-Bowles. About twenty years younger than him and twice as clever. I hope she has a long-term plan, because I heard he's wooing the Ponsonby-Forbes gal. Barely legal. It's revolting.'

'I've heard all about Franklin White but I've only ever seen him from afar,' I say. 'He's quite something, isn't he.'

The eyebrows raise without causing a hint of a wrinkle. The brown pools beneath them look me up and down with a rather saucy smirk. 'I wouldn't have thought you move in the same circles, darling.'

'Cheeky bitch,' I reply, and she tips her head back, inhaling a silent, delighted guffaw.

I quite like this woman. Franklin, not so much.

CHAPTER 4

Garth: 44 days until Isabella Garrante book launch

Eloise is taking Stevie for a run up Te Mata Peak and apparently needs the Tomato, our much-hated bright-red Ford Fiesta. My sensible, logical suggestion that they would get more exercise if she ran there from home was ignored, and so I am being unjustly forced to walk.

I am nearing the large floral roundabout decorated with alienesque pod sculptures that is a focal point for the Village, when the invigorating aroma of coffee wafts over me; Oddbeans must have fired up the roasters early this morning. I inhale deeply, like a freebasing addict, hoping to somehow absorb caffeine into my system.

Across the street, a woman dressing the window of Sell Your Sole, a new boutique shoe shop, waves to me. She's a customer of ours and I can never remember her name. I wave back; I hope the shop works out for her. It's a bit of a cursed position, having been through a diverse number of iterations in the last few years: Thai

Tanic, Pita Pan, and my personal favourite Florist Gump. Maybe punny names just don't work in the Village, although we've done all right as Sherlock Tomes. We didn't really have a choice. When you're an ex-copper with the surname of Sherlock, your bookshop is always going to have a Holmesian vibe to it.

My heart sinks as I reach the front door and a painfully thin figure with greying dreadlocks tied up with a ribbon emerges from the shadow of our exterior bookcase. Now don't get me wrong: as a person Meryl is kind-hearted and generous, if a little away with the fairies, as Phyllis might say. However, as a customer she is taxing, especially when it comes to the question of calendars.

'I got a message that my Scotch Terrier calendar is in,' says Meryl.

It's Scottish Terrier or Scottie, but I let this go; linguistic pedantry is Eloise's domain. 'Yes, they've come early this year,' I reply, trying my best to sound upbeat as I unlock.

Meryl pats the pockets of her overly baggy patchwork dungarees. 'I can't buy it today, I'm waiting on a commission.'

Meryl is an artist, as she's told us often, although I've never seen any of her work in Havelock North's galleries or that other purveyor of fine art, the local coffee shop. She barges past me pulling a granny trolley, which she is far too young to be using. 'What other calendars have you got?' she asks, seeming indifferent to the fact that I haven't set up for the day, or even yet switched the lights on.

Despite having been ordered from the reps in February, the main drop of calendars hasn't arrived yet. They get later each year and the shipping issues we've had thanks to Covid have only made matters worse. 'They're in a box up at the counter,' I tell Meryl. 'We've just had a couple of the smaller suppliers so far.' I grab two piles of magazines banded with plastic strips from outside the door and hurry after her.

'What about "Nice Jewish Guys"?'

When we first opened the shop, and didn't know what we were doing, we got an eclectic mix of calendars of which perhaps the most bizarre was 'Nice Jewish Guys'. We put a photo of Eloise swooning over it up on Facebook as a bit of a giggle and sold all four copies the same day. Ever since it has been a firm seller every year, though the calendar rep told us we're the only retailer in New Zealand that stocks it.

'Not yet, I'm afraid, Meryl. It's mostly just the dog ones and New Zealand art.'

I dump the magazines behind the counter as she rummages through the meagre calendar selection. While she's looking, I fish out 'Scottish Terriers' from our order holds shelf, knowing what's coming next.

'Can you keep this one, too?' Meryl hands me a calendar of Black Labradors. 'Oh, and this one as well.' She passes over 'New Zealand Bird Paintings'. 'I'm an artist.'

'Of course,' I say.

Meryl heads back down the accessibility ramp that descends from the raised area in front of the shop's counter down to the main shop floor. 'I'll come in for the Scotch Terriers next week,' she calls.

'Great. See you then.'

Force of habit causes me to quickly scan the area where Meryl's been. Sure enough, she has left her keys and purse behind. I scoop them up, hurry after her and catch her up at the front door.

'Meryl, you forgot these.'

'Oh, thank you, you're a darling. Now, do you know where I parked my car?'

'Can't help you with that one, I'm sorry. Good luck!'

I'm halfway back to the counter when I'm startled by a deep voice from behind the card stand.

'Is this any good?'

Dead Girl Deirdre emerges like Bela Lugosi rising from a coffin and runs a black-polished nail over the cover of a book: *Hangman* by Jack Heath. Her deep-brown eyes are cast in shadow by a wide-brimmed black hat which, if not fashionable, certainly complements her long black dress and thick, platformed, many-buckled boots. Tucked under her arm is a black lace parasol in case the Hawke's Bay sun is a little too harsh.

I switch instantly into bookseller mode. 'We love Scary Timmy. Everyone in the bookshop loves Scary Timmy. You'll love Scary Timmy.'

'But do any girls die in it?' asks Deirdre.

'Well, they're certainly in mortal danger. You know I can't give any spoilers.'

It's a foible of mine, but I detest spoilers in any form. Eloise says it's because I'm on the spectrum, to which my counter-argument is that it's because my mind is full of story and I see connections where others don't, to which she will just roll her eyes and say 'Whatever', proving another point of mine: that arguing with Eloise is like eating custard with chopsticks — possible but generally not worth the effort.

Deirdre drifts to the counter, reading already. Her face is abnormally pale and made more so by an application of white powder that when combined with her violet wig makes her age hard to ascertain. I think she's about thirty-five, although I'm shocking at this sort of thing; Eloise says she's older.

While she reads, I cast my gaze over our lovely little bookshop, the burgundy and gold bookshelves brimming with literary and not-so-literary marvels, the chalkboards with amusing handwritten witticisms, the publishers' posters, the weird and wonderful touches of our own, like the Invisible Dragon cage.

Dead Girl Deirdre tilts her head. 'I'm not convinced.'

'Have we ever set you wrong, Deirdre?'

'No. But ink on a page is like black blood in my veins. I have to be sure.'

And ink on Deirdre's fingers suggests she's a writer, or possibly an artist. I'm going with writer; I picture her with inkpot and quill, filling loose sheets of parchment with prose as purple as her bobbed wig. I tried once to broach the subject, but Deirdre enjoys her privacy and rarely talks about herself, other than discussing tattoos with Eloise.

Deirdre opens the back cover and looks at the author photo. 'Is it a series?'

'A trilogy, with possible further spin-off books.'

Because it's first thing in the morning and the shop is quiet, I'm happy to talk crime fiction with Deirdre. It also keeps me from the chore of sorting out the magazines — checking the magazine company has sent what they claim to, removing the old mags that always manage to hide behind more recent issues, contacting the customers who have made special orders with us and filing those in the appropriate pigeonhole behind the counter.

'I'll take all three.'

'You'll thank me, you're in for a treat.' I fetch books two and three from the shelf behind the counter and ring up the sale.

Deirdre teases a hundred-dollar note from a velvet purse embroidered with a pentagram and hands it over. She always pays in cash and always with hundreds. This one is pristine, not one of the modern plasticised notes but an older paper version. To be more precise, it's one of the series five bank notes which were replaced in 1999. I know this, as I checked the first time she passed me one.

I also know that they are still legal tender.

Deirdre holds open the top of her velvet purse and I drop her change directly into it. She doesn't like to handle the money, which begs the question what she does with it when she gets home. I'm imagining rubber gloves and bleach, but perhaps she just gives it to charity, possibly the SPCA. I suspect that she has cats, black of course.

'See you next week,' I say.

'If the Reaper spares me.' Deirdre dons a set of overlarge sunglasses and, with a dramatic twirl that makes her dress flare magnificently, stalks from the shop.

Inheriting a sense of Deirdre's gloom, I turn my attention to the piles of malevolent magazines that sit brooding on the counter. Perhaps I can leave them for Phyllis, who loves everything about the bookshop. It would almost be cruel to deprive her of the opportunity of seeing what new titles have come in — and there are always new titles, even if a bunch of them won't sell.

I scan the piles. The TV mags are missing again; it's easy to tell, because they're wrapped in plastic. I start to compose another email of complaint as I wander to the front of the shop to double-check that I didn't miss them when I was waylaid by Meryl: *Re: my last two emails which you seem to have somewhat cavalierly ignored . . .*

My train of thought is broken by the sight of a large brown padded envelope placed with geometric precision on the welcome mat in the doorway. I pick it up and stare at the thick Vivid writing on the front.

FAO PC 60 SHERLOCK.

It's a long time since I've seen or heard that name, and never in this country. It's no secret that both Eloise and I were coppers back in the UK — that's how we met. However, the identifying collar number is far from common knowledge.

With a vague sense of unease I take the package back behind the counter, feeling it as I go. It's bulky, like it contains a book, not unusual for us. I turn it over and examine the back and flaps for clues as to the sender. There are none. But the manner of address and delivery is strange — and unnerving. The past seldom intrudes here.

I hold the parcel to my ear to ensure it isn't ticking. I know I'm being paranoid, but when for years the first thing you did before getting in your car was to check under it for bombs, you become overly cautious. I hear nothing. It was probably a pointless exercise anyway: I'm somewhat deaf and an improvised explosive device these days would have an electronic timer or be remotely detonated by phone.

For the next hour I don't achieve much other than looking at, but not opening, the parcel, checking the emails and deleting an excessive amount of spam. It's a relief when Phyllis arrives.

'I'll get the kettle on,' I say, refusing to use 'jug' which in my parlance is an object for holding milk or Pimm's and lemonade, and certainly not an item for boiling water.

'You do that.' Phyllis fishes inside her striped woven bag and pulls out a napkin-wrapped package. 'I made scones.'

This was exactly the response I was hoping for; unlike use of the term 'jug', morning tea is a Kiwi-ism I'm only too willing to accept. I put the coffee in the mugs first and then add the milk, because like me Phyllis agrees that this is the correct order of things. 'Coffee and scones,' I say, 'then if you're going to be all right on your own, I've got to pop out for a bit.'

'Sure, I'll be fine,' answers Phyllis.

I take another look at the suspect package. I desperately want to open it, but I can't. PC 60 wasn't my collar number, it was Eloise's.

CHAPTER 5

Eloise: 44 days until Isabella Garrante book launch

Where the bloody hell has Garth disappeared to and, more importantly, where has he put the stapler? Not in its one true home, that's for sure. I swallow down a stab of frustration as I search the nooks and crannies beneath the ancient counter.

Garth's not a bad fella, just extremely absent-minded with a side dose of not giving a shit. And he's left the magazines for Phyllis to sort again, the bugger.

Phyllis, bless her, is unfazed. She bustles about, finding space for new stock where none should be found, like a book physicist, all the while telling me about the novel she read last night. Yes, the whole book — she's voracious.

'And of course he feckin' killed her, but I can't tell you the next bit as it's to do with the dog, so.'

I tune back in at the word 'dog', as does the actual dog, who is lurking in the stock room, perhaps hoping the word 'treat' will follow.

Phyllis is one of his peanut-butter suppliers, and he loves her dearly. Lurking is one of the things Stevie does best. We adopted him at one year old and he wasn't used to the finer things in life. Since we've had him he's learnt about lounging on a bed, scoffing frozen peanut butter, and gambolling through the hills of Te Mata Peak Park and the sandy paradise that is Ocean Beach. He's also learning that not every swift movement or loud noise means danger, though that's taking a lot longer to sink in.

Before I get a chance to ask about the fictional dog, Phyllis continues. 'Dafydd wafted by this morning. It's so hot you could smell him about twenty minutes before he came past.'

'How did he look?'

'Sure he looked the same as ever. I just hope he'll dump that big old coat when we head into summer.'

Dafydd visits a bit when he's in the Village. He disappears every now and again, presumably when he's been housed and is taking his medication and doing whatever society deems he should be. But he'll be back, unshaven, sunbathing on the Village Green, in that huge dirty coat that could do with burning, and camping out behind the shops along the road where there's a service alley. It's not ideal for anyone, but it is what it is.

He's a bit of a conundrum, our Dafydd. I sometimes give him old copies of magazines he's shown an interest in. One time it was *NZ Art News* that had an article about Toss Woollaston in it. Dafydd muttered on about his old mate Toss, and how they should catch up over dinner and a show. I didn't have the heart to tell him that the artist died in 1998. It seemed like the least of his problems.

'He was talking to someone about sub-atomic particles or somesuch,' Phyllis continues.

'Someone?'

'Ah well, you know, someone or something not of this realm.

Invisible. Which is just as well, as I'm not one to be engaged with quantum physics of a Friday.'

I'd love to know what Dafydd sees that we can't. He quite often appears sad — and yes, I know not having a home or a family might seem the obvious reason for that. But there's something deeper going on behind those blue eyes and bushy ginger brows. I'm pretty sure he has a photographic memory — I gave him a copy of *Pounamu Pounamu* to read about seven years ago and he mentioned it the other day, referencing the (free) transaction and the chipped nail on my right little finger as I passed it to him. Fascinating bloke. Pungent, but fascinating. I'll try and catch up with him later, see if it's angels or demons visiting him today.

I turn back to my stationery search and tune in to Phyllis as she hand-sells her latest favourite to a woman shopping for her book club. Her accent weaves its magic, and I watch as her victim's head begins to tilt like a dog tuning into a 'treat' reference and a beguiled smile plays about her lips. She's sold.

Phyllis's voice drops a little: 'There's this book I just finished but maybe it's not for you. The dog scene makes that puppy bit in *John Wick* look like the happy bits of *Marley and Me*.'

The colour drains from the customer's face as she follows Phyllis to the counter. I have a moment in which I feel such gratitude for my life and the people in it that, if I was a crier, I would cry. We've absolutely landed on our feet in this country, this wee Village, with this bunch of people, even stinky Dafydd. I never take for granted what we survived and what we've made here.

My cell phone tings. I ignore it, determined not to be its slave. After about three seconds I wake the screen. It's a text:

Garth: Loo roll. Garth.

This is not unusual. He's noticed something needs replacing at home, but his responsibility ends as soon as he tells me about it. He also signs his name at the end of every text, even though I have him saved in my phone and, perhaps more significantly, we've been married for nigh on thirty years. Weirdo. Okay, I'll pop into the supermarket on the way home.

I'm just about to lock the screen when another message appears:

Garth: Oddbeans. 5 minutes. Come alone.
Or bring Stevie if you want. Garth.

Weirdo all right.

CHAPTER 6

Garth: 44 days until Isabella Garrante book launch

The bookshop is too small for any private discussions, the only secluded area being the stock room, which is cramped, cold and gloomy, so with the suspicious envelope tucked under my arm I head to Oddbeans, a café far enough from the shop to mean we might not be disturbed.

I order two coffees from the counter and refrain from buying any slices, though the ginger crunch looks like it is to die for; according to my doctor after my last cholesterol check, it probably is.

I select a table in the corner with a good view of the entrance and easy access to the staff-only door in case things go sideways and I need a secondary exit. Not that I'm expecting any trouble, just Eloise. However, as my old DS used to say, the trouble you're expecting isn't the trouble. I position the padded envelope at the table's corner so that the sides align with the straight edges of the varnished pine. Then I text Eloise and wait for my drinks.

I vaguely recognise a couple near the window, who I think are estate agents; they are both on their phones, ignoring each other and their coffees. The only other customer in this part of the café is sitting near the espresso machine. I've never seen him before. His shirt is nondescript but has expensive-looking silver cufflinks in the shape of anchors. Covering most of the shirt is what I would call a bodywarmer but in Havelock North is probably a gilet. The baseball cap that largely hides his face seems a little incongruous for his age. His back is to me and he seems uninterested in my presence but the huge gilt-edged mirror behind the counter would afford him a sneaky view of my table.

Kim, the waitress, delivers my latte and flat white. She is a regular customer at the bookshop and is valiantly working her way through the Popular Penguins.

'There's a copy of *Perfume — The Story of a Murderer* put to one side for you,' I say.

'Sweet as.' She rests her hands on her hips. 'I'm over Dickens. So gloomy.'

'You didn't enjoy *Great Expectations*?' I ask, arranging the coffees so that they sit symmetrically on the table.

Ever thoughtful, she takes a moment to consider. 'It wasn't as good as I thought it was going to be.' She winks and grins before hurrying away.

At last I spot a splash of bright-pink hair through the window. Moments later Eloise hurtles though the door, dragged by Stevie. He disappears under the table; Eloise sits. She is wearing one of our new Sherlock Tomes tee-shirts emblazoned with a screenprinted gold magnifying glass and feathered quill resting on a book, a pair of truly hideous trousers and sparkly Doctor Marten's boots. I wonder if the boots are some sort of cosmic sign, Doc Marten's having been invented in Wollaston, Northamptonshire, where

Eloise and I policed before being seconded elsewhere.

'This is a pleasant surprise,' she says.

'It's certainly a surprise, but whether it's a pleasant one or not remains to be seen.' I slide the padded envelope between us. 'This was left at the shop. I don't know who by.'

'By whom,' Eloise corrects, and pulls the envelope towards her. 'What is it?'

'I have no idea. It's addressed to you, so I didn't want to open it.'

Eloise's brow furrows as she clocks her name and collar number. In the police you develop a sixth sense, the copper's gut they used to call it; by the tilt of her head and her narrowing eyes I sense hers is working overtime. She turns the envelope over. Written on the back in the same Vivid is **PLEASE LOOK INSIDE THE ENVELOPE.**

I take a sip of my latte. 'It's not ticking and there are no waxy stains or powder residue, so it's probably not a bomb or anthrax. Other than that, your guess is as good as mine.'

'You're joking, right?'

'About the anthrax and the bomb, mostly. It is a bit odd, though, don't you think?'

'Probably just another self-published author trying to get our attention.'

'Well, they've certainly done that, and fair play to them. Finding your collar number can't have been easy. I hadn't even remembered it until I saw it written there.'

'Yeah. A self-pub author, that'll be it.' Eloise fiddles with the corner of the envelope, a nervous gesture rather than a serious attempt to open it. 'So why am I feeling so uneasy?'

'Because you hate having to reject self-pub authors.'

'You know that's not the reason.' Eloise raises her cup, then returns it to the table without taking a sip. 'That's why you lured me here.'

'It can't be him.' I do some quick mental arithmetic. 'He's still locked up.'

'Fuck it!' Eloise rips the top of the envelope open. 'He's not getting inside my head again.'

She upends the envelope over the table. Nothing comes out. She shakes the envelope, hard this time, and a book drops onto the table. *See You in September* by Charity Norman. The title has been circled in more Vivid. Several pages have had their corners folded over — a crime in itself.

On the first marked page, a section of luminous yellow stands out. We look more closely. The words 'you must' have been highlighted.

'Well, that's strange.' I keep my tone upbeat.

'Creepy more like.' Eloise flicks to the next marked page where 'investigate the' is similarly illuminated.

Her hands are shaking as she fumbles her way to the third overturned corner: 'disappearance of'.

'You must investigate the disappearance of . . .' I look up at Eloise, who looks as spooked as I feel. 'Who?'

Eloise turns to the last marked page. Written at the top in red Biro is: **TRACEY JERVIS**.

CHAPTER 7

Eloise: 44 days until Isabella Garrante book launch

'Who the fuck is Tracey Jervis?' I take a sip of water, trying to control the nausea and the adrenaline spike. I haven't thought about being PC 60 for a long time.

'I have no idea,' says Garth, beginning to fumble a search into Google on his phone.

I can see he's fat fingering the spelling and it's taking far too long. 'Give it here, you're doing my head in.' I grab the phone, correct the search and hand it back.

'You okay?' His hazel eyes blink at me in concern.

Am I? I look at the line of people making their way into the café. It's all so normal, and safe.

'Yes yes. Go ahead,' I say as if I'm talking to control back in the police.

Garth looks back down at his phone and clears his throat.

'Well, ruling out the freelance trombonist, the Bristol University

Professor in Knowledge Exchange and Innovation, and the LinkedIn accountant and business administrator, I suspect it might be referring to a missing Te Mata High schoolgirl.'

'Really? I've not heard anything on the news.'

Garth scrolls through the webpage. 'You wouldn't have done. She went missing in 1999. Bit before our time here.'

'Wow.' I risk a sip of my flat white. 'Is it just me, or have we somehow walked into a *Thursday Murder Club* novel?'

'We're not that old and we don't live in a retirement village, although some days I feel a bit like Ron Ritchie.'

'Bung knees?'

'Indeed,' Garth concedes with a nod.

'It's all a bit weird though, isn't it? Which is why we should ignore it. We've got enough going on with the IFG launch. That's quite enough stress, thank you.' I hand him the chocolate fish from my saucer.

'Ta. But you can't tell me that you're not a little bit intrigued by a real-life murder mystery.'

'She's missing, not murdered,' I counter.

'If she's not turned up after twenty-plus years, she's murdered, or dead by misadventure at the very least.'

'You're cheery today.'

'Just being realistic. Ninety-four percent of recovered children are found within seventy-two hours.'

'And you know this how?'

'I was a cop, too.'

'Yes, but you just raced around with the blues and twos blaring and got into fights. Back in the day you would have done anything to dodge a misper case.'

'True, but I'm older and wiser now.' Garth strokes his goatee. He thinks he looks sage but he just looks a bit pretentious, bless him.

'Well, certainly older.'

'Harsh.'

I pat his hand to soften the blow. I'm shaken by the morning's events, but I shouldn't be taking it out on him.

'So, you want to look into it?' I ask.

'Not a chance. I'd still rather race around in fast cars.'

'And get into fights?'

'Not so much.' He stretches his shoulders back. 'I find one of the most enjoyable aspects of being a provincial bookseller is that in the ten years we've owned the shop, not once has anybody tried to kill me.'

'I've considered it a couple of times,' I say, draining the remainder of my coffee. 'And I swear, if you don't put the bloody stapler back in its one true home I'll do it next time.'

Garth laughs as if I don't mean it. 'Would you like a doughnut, for the shock? I don't mind joining you if it would be helpful,' he says.

'No, I do not need a doughnut for the shock, thank you. Nor do you. I know you had a scone. Phyllis told me.'

'What a snitch!'

The shock. The shock is the past coming back to haunt me. I'm yanked from my nice safe provincial New Zealand life back to the late nineties, seeing myself as vividly as if young Eloise had just walked into Oddbeans. My youth, energy and the English Literature degree that had hitherto shown no sign of being useful to my policing career had made me the obvious choice to go undercover. I was to try to lure a killer whose modus operandi focused on punishing writers.

I arrive at the Criminal Investigation Department, a series of freezing cold concrete-floored offices in a freezing cold concrete box of a nick. It's 9am and I'm dressed in the new pale-pink wool jacket I'd bought that weekend, my uniform abandoned in my locker downstairs. My hair is bobbed, black and shiny, and all 55kgs of me is neat as a pin and bristling for action.

I push open the military-grey door. The secondary smoke that pools from the room smells like the start of something, an opportunity to test my limits, to use the ambition that's been languishing in a patrol car, sorting out neighbours' disputes and shoplifting cases.

Three men are seated at desks. Unlike the squad room, it's quiet, as though the haze is dampening any sound. I approach a bald guy with a couple of chins, white shirt straining over a barrel chest and belly, jacket slung over the back of his seat, cigarette slung behind his ear. The whole scenario is so cliché it feels like something from a seventies cop show. I'm already worried about how I'll get the smell of smoke out of my new jacket.

'Eloise Sherlock reporting for duty,' I say jauntily.

Baldy looks up and squints at me. 'What?'

'PC Sherlock. I'm on secondment.'

'Sherlock? Are you having a laugh?'

'Err, no. I'm on secondment. You need me for the Agent case.'

'Do we now. Talk to Kev.' He turns back to his desk where he's ostensibly been poring over a thick folder.

'Who's Kev?'

'The guv'nor,' he says, without looking up. 'Make yourself useful while you wait and get the kettle on. I'd love a cuppa tea.'

A halo of tight dark curls pops up from a desk behind Baldy.

'Make your own fucking tea, John. It's the nineties, mate, not the fifties.'

'Sorry, Sarge, didn't know you were there.'

'Head down working, mate, you should try it sometime.' The

woman stands up and walks around her desk, warm black hand reaching for my freezing cold white one. 'DS Taylor, Paula. Good to have you with us, Eloise.'

She's large, a Londoner by the sounds of her and remarkably youthful for a Detective Sergeant; I'd guess early thirties.

'Don't mind John. He's a twat.'

I wait for a 'but' that doesn't arrive. John's just a twat.

'Come with me. I'll start getting you up to speed.' Her navy-blue nylon trousers hitch and zizz as she strides towards the window. She opens it a crack and I'm grateful for the crisp air that pierces the fug. She gestures to an incident board with its back to the window. On it are photos of victims, their names, ages, locations of death.

'I stick everything up there,' says DS Taylor. 'Helps me see connections when they pop up.'

This is it, the case I'll be working on. It's the first time I've seen a link chart, and my brain is already seeking out its patterns.

'They're all writers? Novelists?' I ask, taking in the titles written beneath the name of the victims: *Pride and Extreme Prejudice*, *A Sale of Two Titties*, *The Fax Machine of Dorian Gray*.

'Yep. Unpublished,' says DS Taylor. 'We're in possession of several typed manuscripts sent to us covered in red pen annotations, one for each victim. Whoever scrawled on them is not a fan. Latest received yesterday, which is why you're up here first thing this morning.'

'Oh, right. And what will I be doing, exactly?' It's becoming real now I've seen the victims' faces.

'You, Sherlock, are to be our silk stocking, our Sir Henry Baskerville, our Irene Adler.'

'I'm not with you, Sarge.'

'The bait, sweetheart.'

CHAPTER 8

Garth: 43 days until Isabella Garrante book launch

My home office is small and messy, which Eloise says is a metaphor for my head — although she also claims it is incongruent with my obsession with symmetry. Which just goes to show that even after more than twenty-five years of marriage she still doesn't fully understand me. I don't have an obsession. It just makes sense that if you are laying out two place settings for a meal you need to make everything align neatly, and who doesn't take pleasure from a tessellating pattern? Also, a messy desk is not anti-symmetry but an obfuscation of a lack of symmetry. A tidy desk with a holepunch carefully placed in the midpoint is a thing of beauty but also impractical, and buying two holepunches so that they can be equally spaced either side of the desk is clearly an excess.

I sit at my keyboard, my PC's three identical screens positioned ahead of me, and begin a quest to find out more about Tracey Jervis. I'm soon down a rabbit hole.

It appears that on 5 November 1999 Tracey Jervis told her parents that she was going to a fireworks display with her best friend, Prudence Ballion. When she didn't return by 11pm her parents contacted Prudence, only to discover that no such arrangement had been made. So far, so teenage, and if the story ended there it would have been a case of no harm, no foul. Only it didn't end there. It has never ended. Tracey was never seen again.

I spiral deeper, following link after link, any hope of extricating myself from the mystery fading with each newly opened tab. By the time I close the three screens' worth of photos, articles and reports, my head is a jumble of facts, theories and wild speculation pertaining to the vanished girl. Perhaps Eloise is indeed correct in her office-brain analogy.

Ruling out the most bizarre suggestions, which are alien abduction and ritual sacrifice by witches, there seem to be three prominent theories: stranger abduction; abduction by a secret lover; or Tracey quite literally ran away with the circus that was encamped on the Village Green at the time of her disappearance.

If it is stranger abduction, there is virtually no point in us looking any further; you're relying on eyewitness accounts, CCTV and phone records, and after all these years the chances of us discovering something that the original investigation didn't are minimal. Fortunately, true stranger abduction is rare — from memory, it was only about 4 percent back in the UK — so I'm tentatively ruling this out for now, unless it does relate to our past. And that's a rabbit hole I don't want to go down.

The fact that Tracey lied to her parents about where she was going that night suggests a more furtive liaison, lending weight to theory number two, and to the fact that whoever she was seeing was more than likely to be the culprit. The internet suggests a variety of possibilities. Again, ruling out the most bizarre suggestions — Elvis and Aleister Crowley: what is it with Havelock North and the occult? — there are three main contenders. First, Trent Meek, Tracey's English teacher who appeared unduly upset by her disappearance. Second, an unknown suitor from the travelling circus. And third, and of some note given Eloise's recent tales from the Business Association meeting, Franklin White, property developer extraordinaire.

My mulling of these possibilities is interrupted by a text.

Eloise: Home early, Kitty to close.

Perfect, an early tea suits my needs. I drift into the kitchen. We are fortunate that our house is of a reasonable size, but for some reason the kitchen is tiny, little more than a galley. Without exception, everyone who visits tells us that we should knock down one of the walls to make it open plan. I always reply politely, as if this is the first time it has ever been suggested, and agree that it is a good idea and we should look into it. It is never going to happen. Maybe it's the English in me but I simply don't understand the Kiwi compulsion to have the food-preparation area extend into the front room. They are two distinct locations with two distinct purposes and should quite clearly remain so. Eloise does not entirely agree; in fact, she says I'm a weirdo.

I examine the contents of the fridge, freezer and cupboards, assessing what I should make for dinner. It is not a taxing decision; we are out of the ready meals that we get from a local café, and that means I'm going to have to rustle something up. Despite our bookshop boasting an incredible cookbook selection, I only ever cook two things: Bolognese or tortilla wraps. And to be honest, there isn't a huge difference between the two of them: substitute the olives for beans and the oregano for chilli and you're pretty much done.

The tortilla wraps, purchased by Eloise, are wholemeal and

so my decision is made for me: Bolognese it is. I start chopping onions. Stevie pads into the kitchen like a ninja and lays down right behind me in the hope of stealing some human food. For thirty-plus kilograms of muscle-packed dog, he is exceptionally sneaky, and I suspect that in his previous home he had to slink by unnoticed to avoid the bash. His only danger at our house is being hugged to death.

Stevie holds vigil until I put the garlic bread in the oven, then his ears prick up and he lifts his head from his paws. Now I, too, hear the Tomato, its automatic gearbox indecisive about how best to negotiate our drive. Stevie trots from the kitchen to greet the driver.

'Ay-up, something smells good,' says Eloise as she tramps up the stairs, her arms full of books. She is not wrong: my Bolognese is exceptional and when combined with the aroma of baking garlic bread suggests a trattoria overlooking the Arno rather than a homely, slightly shabby house in Havelock North.

'How was shop?' I ask, giving the pan of fusilli (not wholewheat) a stir.

'Good. Got some readers from Natalie.' Eloise dumps the books on the table.

One of the benefits of owning a successful bookshop is that the publishers provide you with advance reading copies in the hope you will champion them in the shop and on social media.

'Anything I'd like?'

'Not much.' Eloise hesitates. 'Just the new Ben Aaronovitch.'

'What!' I abandon my pasta-stirring and rush from the kitchen. Out of the thousands of titles in our shop, Ben's *Rivers of London* is my absolute favourite grown-up series. I say grown-up because I also have a favourite children's book series, *Lockwood & Co*, and because when you say adult books it tends to conjure entirely the wrong image.

'You can't do anything on social media until it launches.' Eloise passes me the book. 'I'm not even sure that you're supposed to have it, but you know Natalie.'

I clutch the book to my chest like Gollum with the Precious and stroke it. I don't peek inside, because this is a treasure and every sentence needs to be savoured.

'Bolognese?' prompts Eloise.

I hide the Aaronovitch high on a bookshelf out of Stevie's reach. We discovered that he, too, is a book lover after a Nicky Pellegrino stolen from the bedside table turned up with a missing cover and shredded pages in his bed. He'd clearly enjoyed it, although not in the same way that Eloise had savoured the rich Italian settings. Purely out of scientific interest I tried leaving a Dan Brown in easily accessible places and was equally gratified and disappointed that he wouldn't touch it, which I believe shows a degree of taste.

Eloise drops into her green leather chair.

'Any news?' I ask, bringing over her meal.

'Not really. Natalie was her normal self. We haggled over numbers and I won.'

I refrain from commenting, mainly because the arrival of the Ben Aaronovitch book means Natalie can do no wrong, at least until I have finished reading it.

'How about you?' Eloise dabs at Bolognese sauce with a crust of garlic bread.

'I've been digging into the Tracey Jervis case.'

'You were supposed to be working on prep for the IFG launch.'

'I couldn't concentrate so I did some googling.'

'And what did you find?' Eloise's clear exasperation is tinged with a hint of fear.

'It's an odd one, all right. Speaking as an ex-copper, certain things just don't add up.'

She lowers her plate to the carpet for Stevie to clean. 'Like what?'

'I'll show you after tea.'

'I thought we were taking Stevie for a walk after tea?'

'We're going to do both.'

CHAPTER 9

Eloise: 43 days until Isabella Garrante book launch

It's suspicious that Garth wants to go up Te Mata Peak with Stevie and me. He'd usually do anything to avoid walking up a hill.

We pull into the car park and I choose a space about 20 metres from the start of the walk. Steve hoofs out of the door and bounds up the track, disappearing into the long grass. He'll appear later further along the path, magically popping up, crocodile mouth grinning and panting.

'What's up with that face?' I ask, glancing at Garth's expression as we begin the ascent up Chambers Walk.

'There's a parking space right there, look. Right there next to where the path begins. If you were going to park that far away, we might as well have walked from home.'

'What? You're about to walk four kilometres up a great big hill. How is another twenty metres going to make any difference?'

Garth continues to moan under his breath, clearly thinking he's being smart and funny.

'All right you can stop that whinging now. Tell me what this expedition is really about.'

Garth gives me his rundown on the three main suspects and outlines his initial research into Tracey Jervis. Tracey was smart, expected to be Dux at Te Mata High School at the end of 1999. Her big passion was literature and she was planning on going to Victoria University in Wellington to study. She was one of those all-round good kids, the classic over-achiever. Her most recent moment of glory had been publishing a poetry book to raise funds for youngsters less fortunate than herself. She'd managed to rope in the coolest kids on the local and national poetry scene, and the result was by all accounts an astounding piece of work.

'What, *Caged Birds*?' I ask. 'That's an awesome book! We still get people asking for it, but it's been out of print for years.'

'Yes, that's the one. I've not heard of it.'

'Not really your thing though, is it, poetry?'

Garth shudders. Many years ago he was a member of a writing group in Northampton. A few successful writers would turn up and drop pearls of wisdom, but to reap the odd benefit it was necessary to politely sit through rambling epics or, Garth's worst fear, haikus. He really doesn't like to talk about poetry.

Clearly attempting to move on from verse, Garth continues. 'She also had a part-time job after school and on the weekends at, wait for it, FW Construction.'

'Why is that a grand reveal?'

'Franklin White Construction,' Garth says between gasps.

'Oh! The dickhead from the business meeting? Yuck.'

'Exactly. Hang on, where's Stevie?'

He stops, hands on hips, clearly using the absent dog as an excuse to have a breather. I run on ahead and find Stevie where I thought he'd be, lapping from the cool, clean stream trickling through the Redwoods. Garth catches up, puffing downhill and coming to a sweaty stop in the shade of the massive trees. He looks as though he'd like to join Stevie and stick his face in the water. We take the opportunity for a rest.

'This is it actually,' says Garth, looking around. 'Over there, I think.'

He heads down through the trees, following the stream to a picnic shelter.

'It? Are you being deliberately sketchy with the information flow?'

'This was where the only clue to Tracey's disappearance was found.' He looks slowly up, down, all around, like some deep-fried Sherlock Holmes.

'And are you going to tell me what that was?'

'Oh yes, sorry. Her stuff. Her school things.'

'Like what?'

'I couldn't find a very detailed report — it just said her school stuff, English books and such, which I thought was a bit odd seeing as it was November and she'd already gone on study leave.'

'Bloody hell. I'd love to have a good rummage through all that. So either she was here and left it behind her, or she was interfered with in some way so as to have left it behind unintentionally.'

'Or someone else dumped it here.' Garth pauses and his eyes cloud, a clear indication he's temporarily left our mortal plane.

'Meek,' he mutters. 'Mr Meek. Trent. English teacher devastated by Tracey's disappearance. School bag. English study books. *To Kill a Mockingbird*.'

Although his ramblings are telegraphic, I get the gist. 'Don't Stand So Close to Me' starts up in my head as I consider Mr Meek and Tracey: the schoolgirl on the cusp of womanhood attracted to the apparent power and intellect of the authority figure; the ageing scholar flattered by the attention of the shiny, youthful student. It's a common enough story. He's definitely earned a place on the list of suspects.

'Let's press on. Are you coming up the track, or do you want to meet us back at the car park?' I ask, aware that when Garth has retreated to his favourite place, his head, his body may not be willing to climb any further.

'I'm coming of course. I'm no quitter.'

True, he's not. Once committed, he won't back down, even if he'll suffer for it.

We head after Stevie's retreating haunches, the tip of his tail waving at us through the bushes. It's heading towards 6pm, dusk for this time of year.

'November,' I muse. 'It would have been a bit lighter than this in the evenings. Did anyone see Tracey anywhere in here around the time she disappeared?'

'I don't know but it would be worth digging into a bit.'

'Hang on a minute. We're not police anymore, Garth. It has bugger all to do with us. Also, we don't have those kinds of contacts in this country. We'd only have Google to help us investigate. And have you forgotten IFG?'

'It's intriguing, though, isn't it? You want to know what happened to Tracey as much as I do. And I had a thought . . .'

'Oh here we go . . .'

'There's that lady at book club that you're quite friendly with. Her husband's a Detective Inspector, isn't he?'

'Chloe?'

'Probably. Slim, kind of orangey hair.'

'It's called strawberry blonde and yes, that's Chloe. She's a doctor in the ED at the hospital.'

'Useful.'

'How did you ever describe people in police reports? You're crap at recognising faces. I have to go through, like, twenty steps before you know who I'm talking about.'

'I don't know what you mean. Anyway, we had codes. IC1 and such.'

'So, you know Dave Meehan, right?'

'Who?'

'Dave, the guy who orders the tractor magazine.'

'Errr . . .'

'IC1, quite short, swarthy. Wrinkly, you know, from spending so much time in the sun.'

Garth sticks his bottom lip out and shakes his head slowly.

'Wears camo a lot of the time. Lent you that book about Malta in World War Two.'

'Oh yeah, Dave! I really like him. Good bloke.'

I smirk, but it's lost on Garth who is smiling and beginning a monologue on Operation Pedestal. I know I proved my point.

We're silent as we tackle the last ascent, and I catch up with Stevie to get him back on the lead before the road.

'This is my favourite bit, this last steep bit,' says Garth through ragged breaths, sweat soaking his face. 'Gives me a sense of achievement.'

'It's all downhill from here,' I say, and we trudge on and Stevie strains homeward as the light fades. I watch my feet, negotiating tree roots and rocks, glancing up only occasionally to where lights in the distant Village are beginning to appear. Someone over there knows what happened to Tracey. I shiver. It must be the cool of the evening.

As we re-enter the Redwoods, I hear a blunt crunch from the direction of the boundary where the land gently rises to a hill.

'What's that, just through the trees?' I whisper. 'Is that a person?'

I weave carefully among the tree roots and pinecones, Garth instinctively knowing not to ask any of his silly questions and just follow.

A new fence has been erected and a sign reads: 'Danger. Construction Area. Keep out.' I spot Stevie happily snoofling in the leaf mould. The site hasn't progressed much; there's a modular unit in place as a site office, and a digger-type thing presumably responsible for the large swathe of cleared ground. A number of trees have been wrenched up, and trunks, branches and roots litter the edges of the site where survey pegs have been pounded into the earth.

Garth taps my arm. He raises his hand to his brow, then puts his finger to his lips. He points.

There's a man digging with a spade, but he's not a construction worker. He's tall, athletic, wearing a royal-blue suit. His brown Chelsea boots are caked in mud, and as he turns in our direction I see he's wearing a pale-lilac shirt and violet tie, completely incongruous for his task. He looks right at me through the deepening gloom. Instinctively, Garth and I make to fade back further into the tree cover. He slams his spade to rest upright in the dirt, pivots and walks unhurriedly over the hill.

It's Franklin White.

CHAPTER 10

Garth: 42 days until Isabella Garrante book launch

I'm back in my favourite corner at Oddbeans waiting for local historian and city councillor Nick Feather. He's published a number of coffee-table books on the history of Havelock North, Hastings and Napier which have been good sellers in the shop, and I figure if anyone can give me some insight into how to do some digging around the Tracey Jervis case, it will be him.

My phone beeps. It's a text from Nick saying he's going to be a little late, some problem with a client's IR330, which I presume is a tax form and not some new type of Mercedes. Nick's also an accountant.

'What do you think of Nineteen Eighty-Four?' asks Kim as she sets down my latte.

'The book or the year?' I have no idea how old Kim is, certainly much younger than me and definitely not alive in the eighties.

'The book.' She gives me a quizzical look and I hear Eloise's voice in my brain, 'Weirdo', which is a fair comment. I try to redeem myself by saying something eloquent about the surveillance state and Big Brother, but I haven't read *Nineteen Eighty-Four* since I was in school and I don't sound convincing even to myself. I was fifteen or sixteen and the main thing I remember is Winston and Julia shagging.

Kim departs, leaving me with thoughts of my English teacher. He's drumming nicotine-stained fingers on an old school desk that still has proper ink wells. His fingernails tap the graffiti-scarred wood as he drills quotes into us by rote: '*Who controls the past controls the future; who controls the present controls the past.*' I take a sip of coffee, savouring the bitter milky taste, and muse on how apposite those remembered words from thirty-odd years ago now seem. Who might be trying to dig up Tracey's past to control the future? And should we really be a part of it?

I am nearly done with my latte by the time Nick arrives. He is in his late fifties, wisps of grey hair clinging to the sides of his head. He sits opposite and I order more coffees.

'You'll get the jitters,' says Nick, staring at my second cup.

'I think I'll be good.'

'So, how can I help?' he asks.

'Long story short, I've become interested in the Tracey Jervis case and I wondered what you know about it.'

'Not much, I'm afraid. It's too recent history for my interests.' Nick rubs a hand over his pate. 'Ruined Franklin White's chance of election, I remember that.'

'Election?'

'He was standing for Action Now that year. Had a good chance, too, until the rumours started flying.'

'To do with Tracey?' I ask, not entirely sure that I'm managing to keep up.

'She was helping him out with the campaign, and rumours were she was helping out in other ways, too. Many reckoned that was why Franklin financed her poetry book.'

I take a moment to process. I knew that Franklin was a suspect, but now I see why.

'Of course nothing was ever proven,' continues Nick. 'But politics is a fickle friend, no smoke without fire and all that. Action Now, big on law and order, and it just didn't look good.' He glances about as if to be sure we're not overheard. 'Funny you should mention it. I hear he's intending to run for council this year.'

'Is he still affiliated with Action Now?'

'I heard that he bankrolled the local candidates at the last election, although he can't be seen to be officially connected. Not yet at least.'

'You reckon being a local councillor is a stepping stone?'

'It's worked for plenty of others and he's desperate to get signoff on his new development, which will be a damn sight easier if he can' — Nick makes air quotes — 'bargain from inside.'

'Tracey's disappearance doesn't taint him for that?'

'It was a long time ago and he's shrewd. Makes donations in the right places, has the local press onside, and some would say greases the right palms. I reckon he's in with a chance.'

In with a chance unless someone digs up the past as a smear campaign. From what I've heard of Franklin White I'm no fan, but I don't want to be played for a fool doing someone's dirty work for them either. That said, I'm becoming more and more intrigued with the vanishing of Tracey Jervis.

'Say I wanted to research the local papers from the time. How would I do that?'

Nick places his hands on the table and locks his fingers together as an almost miraculous transformation occurs. He changes from councillor and accountant to historian: his eyes sparkle, his shoulders lift, and he launches forth into the subject which he is clearly most passionate about.

By the time he finishes, his latte is still untouched; mine is empty once more and I'm infected with his enthusiasm. I'm all set to dash off to the library and riffle through the drawers of microfiche.

Nick takes his first sip of coffee and looks through to the giant coffee-bean sculpture outside. 'It's funny that you chose to meet here. Or was that deliberate?'

'Deliberate, why? I just like their coffee.'

'So not because Oddbean went missing at the same time as Tracey?'

'Oddbeans went missing?' I feel there is some vital fact I am lacking for this exchange to make sense. How can a café go missing?

Nick picks up on my confusion. 'Back in the late nineties Oddbean, the person, was a local entrepreneur and artist of sorts. He had a studio and workshop down on Cooper Street.'

'What do you mean "of sorts"?' I glance enviously at Nick's barely touched drink.

'Well, he was a bit of a hell-raiser. The local lothario, if you believe the gossip.'

'And he went missing when Tracey did?'

'He did, but no one seemed that bothered. It didn't make such a good story as the disappearance of a Dux student schoolgirl, and to be honest most people were glad to see the back of him.'

'Why? What had he done?'

'Well, if the rumours were true, most of the female clientele of The Clubhouse in the Village.' Nick glances sideways and lowers his voice. 'And some of the males, too.'

Pretty much everyone in the Village has heard rumours about The Clubhouse being a swingers' bar, but I've always been sceptical, putting it down to idle gossip and the need to make Havelock North seem more cosmopolitan. Maybe I'm wrong and there's a historic basis for the speculation. 'Do you think he was involved in Tracey's disappearance?'

'Really, I have no idea. I didn't mix in those circles.' Nick sits back as if distancing himself from any suggestion of impropriety. 'But lady-killer by name . . .'

'The police must have looked into it.'

'I suppose so, but if they ruled out any connection with Tracey, they may have been happy to let it slide.'

The police never have enough resources to do everything properly, so I can understand that the case of a missing lothario is likely to be considered less worthy of attention than that of a missing schoolgirl. However, the expression 'happy to let it slide' is an odd one and suggests there's something more, something Nick's not telling me. I fish for more detail. 'The police were happy to see the back of Oddbean?'

Nick leans closer. 'The other rumour about Oddbean and The Clubhouse was that he hung out there because he could fix you up with whatever drugs you wanted. Some said that was how he got the ladies, because he certainly wasn't a looker in the traditional sense. Quite effeminate really.'

I'd encountered similar attitudes in my own policing career — hell, I was probably guilty of thinking the same when one low-life pusher murdered another. 'One less dealer on the street wasn't a problem they were too concerned about, then? A bit of summary justice saving them a job.'

'It's just conjecture. As I said, I didn't really follow either case at the time.'

I look down at my empty cup and realise that I have missed the whole point that started this thread of conversation. 'So, the café is named after this character Oddbean?'

'He'd started to roast coffee at his gallery and had generated a good following. I'd heard from another accountant that it was making more money than his art. Franklin White had heard that, too, and bought this place with the intention of going into partnership with him. When Oddbean disappeared, Franklin found another roaster and went ahead anyway.'

'But he still named it after Oddbean?'

'Franklin and Oddbean were old school buddies. At one point they were thick as thieves. I guess he felt like he still owed him. That's why they have that concrete monstrosity outside.'

'The giant coffee bean? I quite like it.'

Nick dabs at his lips with a napkin. 'It was Oddbean's last creation before he disappeared.'

CHAPTER 11

Eloise: 42 days until Isabella Garrante book launch

I'm ringing up the transaction for Sharon's usual *TV Guide* when the back door slams and a voice calls 'Only me!'

Kitty comes through dragging a veggie bag with her. Celery leaves wisp from the top, mirroring Kitty's tawny hair, long strands of which have escaped from her scrunchie. A lovely fresh smell emanates from the bag; it makes me feel healthy by association.

Kitty is a fabulous bookseller whom we recruited from book club. Though naturally quiet and contemplative, she is able to infect customers with her love of reading and willingness to talk plot and character at length. She's also quite tall, which comes in handy for reaching books on the high shelves behind the counter.

'Oh, lovely pants,' says Sharon, alluding to Kitty's blue cords adorned with sunflowers and an orangey bloom I don't know the name of. 'I was just telling Eloise about my hyacinths. I'm growing them indoors and the smell is amazing, but they keep flopping over.'

'Ah,' says Kitty, dumping her bag in the general dumping zone in the stock room, retying her hair up into a ponytail as she emerges. 'It must be too hot for them.'

That's my cue to pass the talking stick to Kitty and wander off. I tinker with the emails and call out to a couple of other customers. They're happy to browse.

Sharon's leaving and Kitty, now armed with her little watering can, walks with her, clearly intending to give her flower box outside the shop window the necessary motherly love. I've only just turned my back to put the kettle on when I hear a shriek from the front door.

'What is it, Kitty?'

'My babies,' she whispers, pointing.

I hurry outside, and my heart sinks. Her latest display of marigolds have had their heads chopped off. Same thing happened a couple of weeks ago to the pansies. Once is mischief; twice is beginning to look like a pattern.

I survey the scene carefully. It's neat and tidy; the blooms having been lopped with surgical precision. Hmm. So the perp is someone who knows how to use a sharp blade — maybe a doctor or a butcher. Still, there's no clue at all as to motive.

Kitty and I wander back inside the shop.

'Anything on the CCTV?' I ask.

Kitty scrolls through folders, trying to find the overnight footage.

'It wasn't recording,' she says, throwing her hands up in frustration.

'Damn it.' I fiddle with the buttons, but she's right; there's nothing. Garth was supposed to have looked at it last week but clearly he's forgotten. I'm going to have to nag him until he's fixed it. No more flower babies will fall victim unrecorded. A functional CCTV might also, I realise, have picked up the person who dropped the mystery envelope on the doorstep. Double damn it.

A sniff from Kitty pulls me back to the present.

'I'm so sorry for your loss, Kitty. Do you want to pop up to the garden centre now and get some more?'

'No. I need time to grieve. I'll go tomorrow morning on my way in.' As she walks away, I notice there is one golden petal laid gently on the book she's been reading. It makes my throat tighten.

Our CCTV is great for the inside of the shop and has proved invaluable. Last Christmas a lady swore blind she'd left a bag of expensive cashmere stuff at the counter and made me check our footage. In she came with the bag, and out she went with it 15 minutes later — no abandoned cashmere in the bookshop. Another woman had a whale of a time shoving board books down her coat until I leapt around the corner yelling 'Put them back!' She did, and ran off, and then I spent too long overthinking why she would want to steal books for babies and feeling terrible for being a capitalist pig.

I get to wondering what CCTV evidence was found when Tracey went missing. It should have been able to track her if she was in the Village. How many cameras would there have been in Havvers? Some at least, surely? There are even cameras at Te Mata Park now.

A familiar scent wafts my way. Dafydd is over in the art section. He's flushed and sweaty, probably been sunbathing on the Green. There's a pie wrapper sticking out of his pocket, so at least he's had something to eat. He's addressing an incorporeal friend as he peruses the shelves. 'Working knowledge of plant morphology . . . observation of the growth habit . . . ontogenetic transitions . . .' Dafydd accentuates his words with gestures, waving his remarkably slim, elegant fingers around like tendrils on the breeze, albeit quite earthy ones.

He stops, mid-flow, tendrils frozen, and looks over at me.

'Morning, Dafydd. Did you notice that Kitty's flowers have been damaged?'

'Desecrated. She should just buy some.'

'Yes, she's getting a fresh lot in the morning.'

'Hmm. Art is theft though, I suppose.'

He turns back to the art books, hands now still by his sides, cryptic conversation over. That's all I'm getting out of him today.

A golden and glossy young woman strides down the centre aisle of the shop, stopping short and coughing when she gets a whiff of our other patron's special scent. Staring at Dafydd, she opens her mouth to speak, and to save any awkwardness I hop down the steps towards her.

'Mōrena. Do you need a hand with anything?'

She aims her glittering smile at me and asks for the new book by a popular Instagrammer who has apparently been blabbing about it on her page. I explain it's not in the shops until October and Ms Golden says she would like to pre-order it. I grab the folder, take her details, and notice her looking at Dafydd; my over-protective hackles rise. Her face relaxes and she calls a soft 'Good morning, Dafydd.' He offers a shy smile and bolts for the door. I check my prejudices and mentally re-christen Ms Golden, Ms Heart of Golden.

Next in is our favourite courier, Fetu, dumping about ten boxes of what look like new releases. That'll perk Kitty up. He peers into the lolly bowl Amelia leaves for him and him only, and finds treasure. He lets out a whoop and grabs a mini-Crunchie.

I sort the boxes into which goes with what and lug the first three through to make a start. There's another bloody split delivery and I'm pretty sure it will match up with yesterday's. As predicted, Kitty spots the 'new release' sticker.

'I'll do stock. I'm in no mood for people after the morning I've had,' she says.

I leave her to it and turn to address the family who have just poured in, some instinctively flowing right to Children's, laughing at the quotes on the chalkboards and staring up at the Invisible Dragon currently in her birdcage on top of one of the card stands (she's quite a small dragon).

Aha, they're marvelling at things. I smell fresh blood and wander forth to beguile them.

CHAPTER 12

Garth: 41 days until Isabella Garrante book launch

The steel tape measure retracts, rattling along the length of the bookshelf as Liam scribbles more numbers into his dog-eared notebook. He's the owner of Village Timber and a good customer of ours, which is why I've asked him to quote for getting our bookshelves put on castors. I reckon we're about the same age, late forties, although he wears it better, his stocky frame showing no signs of a paunch, and not a single grey in his curly black hair.

'What do you reckon?' I ask. We need to be able to move the bookshelves for the IFG launch to create as much floorspace as possible.

'It's doable.' Liam grimaces: never a good sign before a quote. 'It's more work than I figured. With the weight of the books, castors are going to rip clean out of the MDF. I'll have to build a subframe for each unit.'

'Expensive?'

Liam nods. 'Just because of the time involved. I reckon you could do it yourself though.'

'Yeah, well, Eloise reckons if I haven't managed to do a single bookcase in ten years I'm not going to get them done in a couple of weeks.'

'Ah. Boss's orders?'

'Boss's orders,' I confirm.

'Thing is, mate, we're flat tack. Earliest I could drop onto it is October.'

Damn it. The whole launch gets more and more complicated by the day. I guess we could just lift all the units to the side of the shop for the launch and then lift them back after. We'd lose a day of sales but the number of IFG books we'd shift would more than make up for it, and the kudos of hosting the reclusive author in person would do wonders for the shop, so long as we don't stuff it up. But therein lies the rub: so long as we don't stuff it up. I've crawled up to unexploded grenades with an improvised PE4 bomb, not knowing if it's going to blow up in my face; I've stood behind riot shields being petrol bombed; and I've walked into a pub full of criminals, pretending to be one of them. All of those I was trained for. The IFG launch is something else. We've never done anything like this. Hell, I'm not sure anyone has.

'Email us a ballpark figure, Liam, in case Eloise wants it done anyway.'

'Will do.' He tucks the stub of a pencil behind his ear. 'I don't suppose Lars Mytting has anything new out?'

'No. We're still waiting. We've got a non-fiction called *Elderflora* which looks fascinating. It's all about the world's oldest trees and our obsession with them.'

'Have you read it?'

'Not had a chance.' Despite an O-level in woodwork and

a grandfather who was a genius with wood, I don't share Liam's obsession. 'Maybe you could have a read and let us know what you think?'

'Sure, I'll give it go. I need something new.'

I grab a copy of the book and ring up the transaction, which isn't so much ringing it up as scanning it into the POS system. 'Hey, I don't suppose you've had any dealings with Franklin White in your line of business, have you?'

'Why?' There's an immediate cooling in Liam's manner: not necessarily hostile but wary.

I smile as if I haven't noticed the change. 'Eloise was at a Business Association meeting and said he was talking about a new development up at the Redwoods,' I say, because it seems like a better explanation than we're trying to discover if he murdered Tracey Jervis.

'I wouldn't touch him with somebody else's barge pole. Steer well clear is my advice.'

'Really?'

Liam leans in. 'Look, mate, this is between you and me, right?'

'For sure.' I hold a hand over my heart. 'Booksellers' honour.'

'Back in the day, Franklin started a concrete company and I was stupid enough to do some work for him. He was a shoddy payer and I wanted to get my lads sorted for a timber framing job we'd done. It ended up in a bit of a barny, and next thing I know I've got a couple of heavies turn up at my business threatening to put me under the foundations if I don't back off.'

'Fark!' I rest my hands on the counter. 'What did you do?'

'I backed off, of course. These were serious guys. Wasn't worth the risk. We got paid in the end and I've never worked for him since.'

'Good to know. Steer clear of Franklin.'

'I mean he's not John Gotti or nothing.' Liam makes a

half-and-half gesture with his hand. 'But he's a wrong-un and the cops never managed to pin anything on him.'

'Thanks for the heads-up. Enjoy the read.'

'Will do.' Liam waves the book at me and heads out to his truck.

I gaze at the magazine pile, then slink away like Stevie with a slipper. Wandering between the shelves I straighten books and check for any new arrivals. My two great passions are crime and fantasy, but we are not big enough to have a dedicated Crime section, or indeed to subdivide our fiction into genres, although we have recently made a Fantasy and Sci-fi corner. It used to be the Harry Potter corner but after J.K. got more radical in the expression of her views we felt uncomfortable about the HP corner. Kitty, who runs our sci-fi and fantasy book club, used the disquiet to her advantage and commandeered the space for speculative fiction, relegating poor old Harry and friends to a single small bookcase. So now the only HP in that specific corner is Lovecraft, who one could argue has committed greater crimes, but that's a conversation for another time.

'Morning men, starboard ten,' comes a shout from the front door as the Admiral strides in, his silver-topped cane tapping against the floor. His neatly trimmed white hair and beard glow under the shop's fluorescent lights, as do his cheeks which have perhaps seen too many years of port and Pusser's Rum. He's not actually an admiral, although he's certainly been in the Navy. Also, I am the only man who works at the bookshop, so men is not entirely accurate. Nevertheless, I emerge from General Fiction and throw up a salute.

'Very good, carry on, please,' says the Admiral, acknowledging my gesture. 'What's new in?'

The Admiral reads only military non-fiction, so I gravitate in that direction.

'There's a new Max Hastings, and we're waiting on the latest from Damien Lewis.' I don't mention the Peter FitzSimons; it's about

Vietnam, which for reasons best known to himself the Admiral doesn't count as a proper war.

'I met Max Hastings. The Falklands.' The Admiral's gaze drifts into the distance. 'Didn't like the man.'

'We have some new books on the Balkan situation,' I venture. This is untested waters.

The Admiral takes one of the books I offer him and flicks it open. 'Ah, yes. You can't trust Johnny Russian,' he says. 'I went to Russia once.' His blue eyes are full of mischief. 'I was supposed to meet a possible defector at the Moscow State Circus.'

'What happened?'

'Blighter never showed up.' The Admiral raises his cane, a hand at each end, and motions it back and forth. 'So, I ended up spending a rather fine evening with a bottle of vodka and a trapeze artist.'

For the briefest of moments I see the Admiral not as an eccentric old man with a gammy leg but as Sean Connery in *From Russia with Love*. 'What about the defector?'

'Our spooks could find neither hide nor hair of him.' The Admiral's smile turns downwards. 'Not until three days later when the remains of his leg turned up in a tiger's cage.'

CHAPTER 13

Eloise: 41 days until Isabella Garrante book launch

The shop feels like a different place when it's closed, as if it breathes deeply and settles itself, encouraging its people to do the same. No wonder Kitty loves pottering about way after closing; it's lovely to be alone but not alone, surrounded by words and stories and ideas and concepts quietly doing their thing whilst you're doing yours.

I settle myself behind the counter, shop's lights off, secret-squirrel style. Opening my laptop, I see that my old Detective Sergeant, Paula Taylor, is already in the Zoom waiting room. I leave her there for just a few seconds. I'm excited to catch up but afraid of what she might tell me.

'Ma'am,' I say when a beaming face full of cheek and teeth fills my screen. My old DS is now DCI Taylor, Detective Chief Inspector. Her round face is still smooth, just a few crinkles around her deep-brown eyes. Lots of grey in her buzzed hair though.

'Hahahahaha look at your pink hair, you silly old bitch. How are you doing, luv? Long bloody time no see!'

She's already at work, though it's only about 6.30am in the UK. She's in a bland grey and white office with cubicles and a withered peace lily behind her. The air quality looks about 100 percent cleaner than on the first day I met her.

'It's been a while all right. I googled you. Major Crime no less,' I say.

'Yeah, East Midlands Special Ops Unit. Keeps me out of trouble. Googled you, too. Bookshop, punk hair and tattoos. Living the dream, mate.'

I feel such gratitude and affection towards this woman, and I'm so pleased to see her.

She cuts to the chase. 'What do you want? I've got to get to work soon. Someone's chucked a geezer full of stab wounds in a wheelie bin in Blackthorn.' She seems remarkably cheerful at the prospect of a scene examination. In the swill of emotion lapping at me, I identify relief that I don't have to attend it.

'Pinter. Is he still inside?'

There's a pause. Paula takes a swig from a mug emblazoned with the phonetic alphabet. It only takes a second for me to decode the message: foxtrot uniform charlie kilo oscar foxtrot foxtrot.

'Yep, still inside. He ain't going anywhere, is he. What the fuck you asking about him for?'

'Something weird's happened. A book was delivered to the shop . . .'

'Lol, I know you've been out of the job a while but that doesn't seem so unusual to me. It's a bookshop, right?'

Cheeky bugger.

'It came with a message for PC 60 Sherlock.'

'Oh.' This information shuts her up for a minute.

'Paula, can you find out if he's been contacting anyone out here in New Zealand? I know it's not likely after all this time but . . .'

'It's fucking with your head, yeah? I'm on it. Look, I really have to go but I'll be back to you asap, all right?'

We end the call and I'm not reassured by the speed at which she agreed to my request. Does that mean she thinks there could be something in it, or is she just trying to put me at ease?

❧

It's book club tonight, so I fluff about trying to get my head back into the present whilst simultaneously fretting about my old life coming to bite the arse of my current one. I get the chairs out and put the kettle on, doing my breathing exercises, staving off the sense of impending doom that I know full well is a symptom of anxiety. It will pass. It always does.

There's a loud bang at the door: Lisa's here, very early, as usual. For once, I'm thankful for the distraction.

I love Lisa, and she won't mind if I carry on with what I'm doing whilst she puffs about, complains that it's too hot or too cold, that she's sore. She hasn't missed book club in years, and she hasn't read the book club book in years either. She's loyal, voices gentle opinions on the conversation, and offers surprising insights every now and again.

'Evening whānau,' she shouts just as Garth and Stevie come in the back door with the wine and biscuits for the evening's refreshments.

'How's life, Lisa?' I ask, then direct, 'Pour me a glass of that, will you?' to Garth.

'Ah, same old same old. I just went to the lad's for tea and he's starting a new job out at the port next week.'

We chat about family, mutual friends and acquaintances, and I make Lisa a cup of tea, white, one sugar.

Eventually, other book club members wander in.

Garth hands me the wine. 'All good?' he asks.

'Yep. Still inside. Fill you in later.'

He ruffles my hair affectionately and in the knowledge that it will irritate me enough to distract me from worrying about the past infiltrating our perfect present. I give him a shove, and he laughs.

Most of the usual suspects drift in and I'm starting to worry that Chloe's not coming when I see her ponytail flick round the door and swing through Non-fiction.

We're discussing Catherine Chidgey tonight — *The Axeman's Carnival.* I set the book confident there would be a great deal to discuss. The protagonist is a magpie, flitting, via a cat door, between human and bird worlds, watching, making sense of things, stealing as magpies do. Our conversation is animated, covering social media and the way it distorts the truth at the same time as exposing it, the way non-humans are a wonderful device for observing human behaviour, how the ending was deeply satisfying (me) or a tad harsh (Garth). Now it's the bit where we go around the circle and talk about other books we've been reading. Notebooks come out, Google is made use of for forgotten author names and details. Hilda, a voracious reader, mentions a recent release about closed adoption in New Zealand.

'I'm adopted,' says Lisa.

There's a lull whilst we all process what she's said. I rapidly overthink my response and decide that as Lisa's brought it up she's okay talking about it.

'Did you always know that, Lisa? Growing up?' I ask.

'Nah, I found out when I was in my teens. All Mum and Dad knew was that my biological mum was a young woman from Fiji and couldn't afford to keep me. Probably pregnant when she got here.'

'That sounds really hard, Lisa,' says Chloe.

'It is what it is. I would like to have known more but it's not easy getting information out of authorities like that.'

There's a bit of thoughtful quiet and a few noises of agreement. Lisa sniffs as if to end the conversation and it duly meanders elsewhere, but we collectively wrap Lisa in extra love for the rest of the evening. We all have our secrets and our hurts, and they quite often come out at book club. That's books for you.

The meeting officially closes at about 8.45, once the next book has been set. *Poor People With Money* by Dominic Hoey, a shocking omission from this year's book awards, in my opinion. We'll see what the rest of the club think next month.

Garth potters about stacking chairs, Chloe gathers glasses and cups. I'm keen to corner her before she leaves.

'How's work going?' I ask.

'It just doesn't stop really. There are a few quiet moments in ED, I'll get called away for something and then boom! It'll all kick off again. Everyone's so exhausted . . . and I want to say "after Covid" . . . but really it hasn't gone anywhere.'

'So it's as bad as the media give out?'

'Sometimes not, but mostly yeah. I'm getting too old for this shit.'

We laugh at Chloe's terrible Danny Glover impression and I notice she is carrying an extra weariness about her.

'It must be the same for Tama though, eh? Police never get a break. I'll bet you're ready for a holiday, the pair of you.'

'Oh yeah, Tama. I don't know if he's been in the force too long or something's happening at work, but he's been a bit low, to be honest. He'll snap out of it. It blows hot and cold, bit like my job.'

'It's got to be tough. I only did ten years but that was enough.'

I hesitate, not wanting to exploit Chloe's easy confidence but, as usual, my sticky beak wins out.

'Hey, I was wondering if Tama, or you for that matter, could tell me about Tracey Jervis? You know that teenager who went missing back in the day? Her name came up and, I know it's morbid, but my interest was piqued.'

'Gosh, I haven't heard that name in a while. Tama did work that one, yeah, just before he was promoted to Sergeant, I think. It really sat with him when they couldn't figure out what had happened.'

'Is it still an active case, do you know?'

'I'm not sure, I haven't thought about it for so long. I've been meaning to invite you and Garth over for a while now. How about you come for dinner and you can needle Tama about it? He needs something to pick him up — he's been so flat.'

I can hardly believe our luck.

'That would be great! I promise to keep it light, though. Sounds like he has enough on his plate.'

We all have cases like that, the ones that got away. My thoughts, never far from Pinter since that bloody envelope appeared, shift his way once more. After all this time he's still controlling, still manipulating, revelling in his mind games. But only if I let him.

CHAPTER 14

Garth: 40 days until Isabella Garrante book launch

Hastings Library is bright and welcoming, assuming you're not a gang member. No, that's unfair, I'm sure they are equally welcoming to everyone; however, since a recent spat between the East Kings and the Black Dogs where someone got thrown through a window, or defenestrated as Eloise informed me is the correct term, they've enforced a ban on gang patches being worn in the library. Fortunately, my burgundy hoodie with gold magnifying glass and Sherlock Tomes insignia does not fall into that category.

I am no stranger to the library, having worked with its staff on many joint ventures. Some people think this is odd, and that the bookshop would be in competition with them, but I believe we are kindred spirits, both serving our community of readers. I am, though, at a bit of a loss when it comes to the subject of doing research in the library.

My incertitude must be evident. A librarian in purple creepers and a cold-shoulder dress that could have come straight from Dead Girl Deirdre approaches. She has jet-black hair with a Mallen streak, heavy eyeliner and two sleeves of tattoos that would make Eloise envious. 'Sherlock, how can I help?'

I have long got over the fact that people think Sherlock is my first name and have given up trying to correct them.

'Is Agatha Hogan here?' I ask, making an assumption, based on stereotypes, that the woman in front of me doesn't look like an Agatha or a research librarian.

'Sorry, she's not in until later. Can I help?'

'I hope so. I want to look at old copies of *Hawke's Bay Today*, ones from 1999. I believe you have them on microfiche?'

Not-Agatha points to a small green cabinet on the second level. 'They're all in there. I've not used the microfiche reader myself, but I can get someone to help you when they're free.'

I'm impatient to get started and don't want to wait. Also, like many men, I see reading instructions or being shown what to do as some sort of failure. 'I'll probably be fine. I mean, how hard can it be?'

I'm somewhat sceptical that the green cabinet can actually house copies of all of the newspapers for the last twenty-five years, but I find a drawer labelled 'HB Today 1995–1999' and haul it open. Wedged inside are numerous white plastic boxes labelled with months and years. I find 'November 1999' and, after a minor struggle to pry it free, head to the microfiche reader, which is not of the ilk I used in university thirty years ago. It is in fact an optical scanner attached to a computer, and when I open the box it is not filled with individual microfiche negatives but a long spool of film.

Having attached the spool onto the scanner and fed it through the optical window to a take-up wheel, I open the app on the computer. A grainy image of the front page of *Hawke's Bay Today* appears on the screen, albeit upside down and back to front. I suspect that I have attached the film incorrectly but see that this must be a common occurrence because the software has a flip and mirror function. With two clicks the image is readable.

Even though most information I could ever want is on the internet, and has been for years, it is an unexpected thrill to click an icon on a screen and watch the film spool forward through the pages. With a second click I stop the film — and realise I have gone too far. I depress the back icon and discover I have in fact attached the spool incorrectly, because the motor reverses and a great loop of film shoots into the air rather than back onto the spool.

Hand-winding the film back, I notice a small diagram attached to the scanner that details the correct threading of the film; maybe I should have read the instructions after all. I reset the machine and, considering myself now expert in its operation, lose myself in the stories of the day from twenty-five years ago.

Several hours later I have covered five pages of my notebook with scribblings that recount everything from the elections to local retailers' concerns about an upsurge of counterfeit currency through to the main event, the disappearance of Tracey Jervis. There isn't too much that I don't already know, but reading the unfolding events day by day in the newspaper gives me a much better understanding of the context and chronology of her disappearance.

There is also one pertinent new detail. The last confirmed sighting of Tracey is a long-range shot on a garage-forecourt CCTV as she headed into Donnelly Street. For obvious reasons there is no mention of Prudence Ballion's actual address, which was where Tracey told her parents she was going, but the newspaper piece does remark that this would not be the most obvious route to take. It's hard for me to judge whether this was completely out of the way or a minor deviation that might just have been Tracey's preferred route. When

Eloise and I walk into Havelock, Eloise insists on taking a shortcut that patently isn't a shortcut, whereas I will walk via Joll Road which is quite clearly a better way to go.

My self-distracted train of thought is broken by a librarian in a brightly coloured floral dress and lavender-coloured cat's eye spectacles on a chain. 'Did you find everything you want?'

Doubling down on my earlier stereotype misdemeanour, I assume that this is Agatha. 'I don't know if I found everything I wanted but I think I found everything there is.'

'What are you researching? Maybe I can help.' She eases onto a chair alongside me. 'I'm Agatha. I believe you were asking for me?'

I had intended to make up some story about how I was researching for a short story set in the late nineties if anyone asked what I was up to. Having been here for several hours I feel I have exhausted all current avenues of research and so decide to come clean. 'I'm trying to find out about the Tracey Jervis disappearance. I've read the papers from back then and now don't know what else to look at.'

A strange expression passes over Agatha's face before she answers. 'Tracey Jervis? What makes you interested in her?'

Something in her response makes me wary, and I decide to revert to my cover story. 'We emigrated here in 2007, so I had no knowledge of the case until a few days ago when someone mentioned it in passing. Our writers' group is running a short story competition, and I was loosely planning a crime short story set here in the Bay, so it got me interested.'

Agatha doesn't respond immediately. At last she says, 'I went to school with Tracey. I wasn't a friend as such, she didn't really have friends. I think her father scared them all off. Well, all except Prudence who was either too weird or too stubborn to be bullied.'

I sense that Agatha has more to tell, and wish Eloise was here; she'd know what to say and her natural charm would put Agatha at ease and make her more likely to gossip. In the end I opt for silence, something I am good at. Agatha takes it as a cue to continue.

'Tracey and I both had a love of the school library and on the many days when Prudence had been sent home for breaking the uniform rules we'd sit together. I got the impression that she was fed up with her dad hothousing her and curtailing her freedom. She'd always choose the trashiest library books, said she was done with the classics. It was her small rebellion. I reckon that's why she had a thing with Trent Meek — to stick two fingers up at her dad.'

'Trent Meek?' I may not be getting any additional information from the spools of microfiche, but it appears that Agatha is a treasure trove in her own right.

'Well, no one was sure, that was just the rumour. One of the girls in her class saw him kissing her, and all that time she was spending with him doing the poetry book, it seemed like something else was going on.' Agatha removes her glasses and gives them a polish. 'Mind you, we were bitchy, hormone-ridden teenagers so it could have just been malicious gossip.'

'What do you think happened to Tracey?'

'I don't like to dwell on it. After she went missing it was all the talk at school. The stories were of some perverted predator picking off schoolgirls and they got more and more outlandish with each retelling.'

It feels like Agatha is deflecting. She's a witness from the time and I want to know what she really thinks. 'Stranger abduction is pretty rare,' I prompt.

'It seems wrong to speak ill of the dead and I don't think the police ever came up with any real evidence against her dad, but I do know that the black eyes Tracey sometimes came to school with weren't from hockey practice as she claimed.'

'And no one at school looked into that?'

'She was the golden child, the perfect student, the Dux-in-waiting, so none of the teachers seemed inclined to interfere. She was destined to be Te Mata High's poster girl. In the end her face ended up plastered on different posters, the ones the police put out.'

CHAPTER 15

Eloise: 36 days until Isabella Garrante book launch

I've just finished vacuuming the shop ready for opening when I notice glitter all over my jumper. The sparkly devil dust is courtesy of a wonderful visit to Time to Quill last night. I do love a stationery shop. I bought a whiteboard, all the colours of pens available, glittery string (why have plain when you can have bling string?) and many other items that I'm bound to need at some point. Oh, and the biggest tin of coffee you've ever seen. I didn't realise they did kitchen supplies.

Seeing as we're unable to stop tinkering with the Tracey Jervis case, I've set up an analogue edition of the old HOLMES information technology system that was used in murder and other big cases in the UK. It stands for *Home Office Large Major Enquiry System*. I love it. Garth thinks it's dumb. HOLMES was developed after the Yorkshire Ripper case; Peter Sutcliffe got away with murder for so long because there was so much data and so many coppers on the case that the threads didn't get connected as they should have. I'm convinced there's nothing that computerised system can do that I can't achieve with magnets and pins and string, especially as there's only Garth and me investigating. So far, I have no source documentation, just a few Post-It notes with actions on them. A1 is dinner with Tama. A2 is the teacher, Trent Meek. Pinter should probably go up there, too, but I'm loath to have that man's name displayed in my home and, anyway, there's no evidence he's connected to Tracey's disappearance.

For now, it's back to bookshop business as usual in our clean, slightly glittery shop, and Garth is talking to Stevie in the stock room: 'Who's the best boy then? He's so handsome, yes he is . . .'

'What am I supposed to be doing?' he asks when at last he emerges.

'You could start weeding out this month's returns if you like, then you can head off home when Kitty gets here.'

'Cool cool cool.'

He starts organising boxes, picking old stock from the shelves, the stuff we're allowed to send back for a credit so we can buy new stuff. I immediately distract him by verbalising thoughts about Tracey.

'Who do you think put us on to Tracey's disappearance? That's what's bothering me. I mean, what's in it for them?'

'Well, let's start at the beginning,' he says. 'A child goes missing, it's the parents who are frantic, right? Then there's the creepy teacher angle — if it wasn't him, I'm sure he'd want his name cleared. After that, maybe a political motivation, seeing as Tracey was friendly with Franklin White.'

'How do you mean, friendly?'

'From what I've gleaned there were no outright accusations but a lot of gossip that Tracey had maybe got a bit too close to Mr White whilst helping out on his campaign. That's why he pulled out of the race in 1999. The waters were too muddy for him.'

'What, so not only is she having an affair with her English teacher but she's got something going on with Franklin, too? Bit of a stretch, don't you think?'

I can't help but start to get a bit angry about the men swirling around Tracey. She was seventeen, for goodness' sake, just a girl. It won't matter if Messrs White and Meek turn out to be completely innocent, I'll still be riled because they're the ones in positions of authority, and she's gone, with no voice to shout for her. Even if she was involved with either of them, it's not the fault of the child, is it?

'And he's running again this year,' continues Garth. 'For council. So an opponent could want those waters re-muddied to get rid of him. He has some dodgy opinions, but he's quite charismatic by all accounts. A serious contender.'

'I saw that charisma — he had people eating out of his moisturised, entitled hand at that Business Association meeting. Turned my stomach. But you're right. If he's funding Action Now, that's going to be a threat to Danielle Bright. She'd certainly have motive to play a bit of dirty politics. Franklin White's party is saying all the things people want to hear.'

'You know her, don't you? Danielle Bright?' says Garth.

'Kind of. She pops in occasionally to ask how things are going.'

'You could have a chat with her. See if she'd be willing to dish the dirt.'

I start composing an email, keen to get my thoughts down before they fade. Just a general *Hello, you must be busy, haven't seen you in a while, how's the campaign going?* With luck, she'll take the bait and see the opportunity for some relationship-building with local business; that always looks good at this stage of the game.

Herb, one of our regulars, saunters up to the counter.

'What about that new book then?'

'You'll have to narrow that one down a bit for me,' I reply.

'The one that bloke wrote.'

'Oh that one. No, I haven't got it.'

'Oh. Can you get it?'

'Herb, love, I have no idea what you're talking about. Give me some clues.'

We eventually figure out it's the new Paul Cleave he's after, and yes, we do have it.

'Paul Cleave came to our Writers Festival a couple of years ago,' I say, 'and told this story about a young writer who was reading one of his novels on a plane and was so terrified by it that he puked and passed out.'

'Good grief!'

'Yeah! It gets better, too. The writer he was talking about is Jack Heath — you know, the guy we're always on about who writes the *Hangman* series? And Jack was on the panel with him. Garth was chairing. It was hilarious.'

Herb is delighted by this. 'Have you got a copy? I'll take that, too.'

There's always a lunchtime lull and while Garth is at the café down the road contemplating which pie he's going to buy, a woman comes in, older than me, perhaps mid-sixties, weary, head down like she shouldn't really be here. She's familiar, not exactly a regular, but definitely a face and a demeanour I recognise.

'Eloise, isn't it?' she says at the counter. 'I'm Janet.'

'Ah yes, of course! I was trying to dredge your name out of my old brain as you walked in. You bought the last Isabella Garrante novel. How was it?'

'Oh, yes, right, fabulous, of course. But the thing is, I'm Janet Jervis. Tracey's mum.'

CHAPTER 16

Garth: 35 days until Isabella Garrante book launch

Janet Jervis's house is a large, traditional villa with white weather-board, covered veranda and neat garden. Pink, yellow and orange tulips blossom from pots near the front door. The inside is as well kept as the out, recently modernised but in keeping with the villa aesthetic. Eloise and I sit on a velvet China-blue couch that is so ghastly it makes me want to puke. Eloise rubs a hand over the material in a way which tells me she absolutely loves it.

We're in what Janet refers to as the family area, although there is only her since her husband passed earlier in the year. I suspect they hadn't been a family since Tracey vanished, and possibly not a happy one before that.

The centrepiece of the room is a large stone fireplace in which squats a cast-iron log burner. Flames lick around a slab of gum, throwing a warm glow through the glass. On the mantelpiece rest a series of pictures of Tracey. They seem to document her entire life, from a gap-toothed pre-schooler to receiving a trophy in her Te Mata High blazer. Her entire *family* life, I check myself, trying not to dwell on what might have happened after she disappeared. More framed photographs adorn the walls and the shelves of two large bookcases either side of the fireplace. I wonder how Janet copes with all these memories. We have a few photos of our previous dog Tonks dotted about at home; when I stop to truly concentrate on her smiling face and big brown eyes, sorrow brings me to tears.

Thinking of Tonks makes me look more closely at the photographs: Tracey at ballet, Tracey in the orchestra, Tracey on the debating team, Tracey in school colours playing netball and hockey and tennis. What there don't seem to be are any pictures of Tracey enjoying herself. Well, perhaps that's unfair, she may have enjoyed all those activities, but there are no pictures of Tracey with her friends, Tracey being stupid on the beach, Tracey with her face covered in ice cream.

Janet busies herself making a pot of tea in the open-plan kitchen area. In the police, it was always a hard call on whether to accept the offer of a cup of tea, given that many of the houses you attended were ones where you'd wipe your feet on the way out. On occasion, both Eloise and I were served tea in jam jars. Often it was safest to say no, but when delivering a death message or comforting a victim of crime, tea always seemed to help. And yes, I know how English that makes me sound. I'm a New Zealander by citizenship now, but perhaps I'll never lose the effects of thirty years of Blighty.

Janet emerges carrying our tea. 'Would you like biscuits?' she asks.

'No, thanks,' Eloise and I answer in unison. Don't even get me started on the perils of policing and accepting food.

Janet takes the armchair to the sofa's side, putting her at a ninety-degree angle with us. It is an ideal position for our chat, making it less confrontational than sitting opposite her. She takes a sip of tea, then looks up at us. 'I heard from Nick Feather that you were asking about Tracey.'

Eloise and I have not planned what we are going to say, and I realise now that this is a mistake. As police officers we always followed a model called PEACE when conducting interviews, and although I can no longer remember what all of the letters stand for, I do know that the P is for planning and preparation, something I feel we have let ourselves down on.

Perhaps taking my silence as a sign that she should start, Eloise launches in. 'Thanks for inviting us and we must apologise for engaging you in such a difficult subject. Until a few weeks ago Garth and I were unaware of your loss, so please accept our sympathies.'

Out of respect, and perhaps a degree of awkwardness, I want to look down, but I force myself to keep my eyes on Janet. Another aspect of interviewing that was drummed into us was that seventy percent of communication is non-verbal, and how a subject reacts to questions can often be more telling than their answers. Not that we necessarily suspect Janet of foul play, but we have to keep an open mind — or at least a suspicious one. Generally, everyone was treated as a suspect by the police until proven otherwise. Innocent until proven guilty was for the courts, not us.

Janet's jaw tightens — in my view, a reasonable response given that we are raising such a traumatic subject. 'Thanks, but I stopped needing sympathy a long time ago.'

It's a curious answer. However, there is no correct response to grief. Too many false convictions have been based on a suspect's odd demeanour. Sure, a strange response can give you pause and grounds for taking a closer look, but it shouldn't be treated as evidence. Eloise herself rarely cries when grieving, whereas I tend to blub like a baby.

I decide to cut in now. We're not exactly doing the good cop, bad cop thing, more the sympathetic cop, blunt cop routine, which probably requires no acting from either of us. 'Two weeks ago,' I say, 'we received a parcel containing an anonymous note suggesting that we should investigate Tracey's disappearance. We wondered if you had sent it?'

'A parcel?'

Her surprise seems genuine, but she hasn't answered the question. Could she be deflecting?

'Yes. It was left anonymously at the bookshop.'

'Well, not by me.' Janet sits back in her chair. Which could just be her getting more comfortable or a subconscious attempt to distance herself from the accusations. 'I've accepted what's happened with Tracey.'

I hesitate, wanting to ask what she thinks has happened to Tracey but uncertain if this would be too indelicate even for me. In the end my copper's curiosity wins out. 'You think she's dead?'

Janet swallows and twists her hands in her lap. 'If she wasn't, she would have contacted me.'

Eloise shoots me a *I can't fucking believe you asked that* look and picks up the questioning. 'Can you think of anyone else who would want us to look into Tracey's disappearance?'

'I really can't.' Again, her jaw tightens. 'Even Tracey's father gave up on discovering the truth once the cancer took hold.'

'Yes. We're sorry to hear of his death, and for your loss,' says Eloise.

'Don't be. He was a complete bastard. It was his fault Tracey . . .' Janet falls silent, her lips tightening as if she's determined to keep the words she was about to say from spilling from her mouth.

Eloise nudges my foot with hers, and I take over. 'It was his fault that Tracey what?'

'That she lied to us that night.' Janet crosses her arms in a gesture that could be attributed to cold were the log burner not throwing out a pleasant warmth, so I'm reading it as defensive, putting a barrier between us.

I don't respond, and neither does Eloise. It's an old interview trick: most people don't like an awkward pause and will usually feel obliged to fill it. The silence draws out, uncomfortably so, then Janet cracks.

'He didn't let her have friends, except Prudence, who was too bloody stubborn to be scared away. It's no wonder she kept secrets from us.'

There's a visceral truth to Janet's words but something niggles me. I can't help but feel she's somehow hiding behind the truth, behind her anger. I'd love to see her witness statements from the time. Newspaper articles are all well and good for the general feel, but they don't contain the precise details, the witness's or perpetrator's own words that so often conflict and can be used to drive a wedge between the lies.

Eloise leans forward. 'Who do you think Tracey was really meeting?'

'It doesn't matter what I think, does it? Not now.'

'It matters to us,' says Eloise.

'Why? Because someone sent you a stupid box?'

That's interesting. It could have been a deliberate error to mislead us, but I don't think so. 'It was an envelope, actually.'

'Can I see it?' For the first time Janet seems genuinely curious. I know we're unlikely to fare any better than anyone else in finding out what really happened to Tracey, so why are we giving her false hope of a fresh lead? I feel like a grave ghoul digging up bodies for my own grim satisfaction.

'Sorry. We didn't bring it with us,' says Eloise. 'We'd be happy to come back another time. If that's okay with you?'

Janet pauses, and now it's me who finds the silence awkward. Then her face brightens. 'Yes, I'd like that.'

CHAPTER 17

Eloise: 34 days until Jsabella Garrante book launch

I'm in my incident room, otherwise known as the spare room, staring at the scant information on my board. It's all glitter string and fluff, and not much to go on. My job today is to see what I can find out about Prudence Ballion, Tracey's best and perhaps only friend. Garth and Kitty are on shop duty, so I've set up my space on the bed: laptop, specs, notebook and pencil (sharpened), bag of cheesy pea snaps, Stevie. Stevie is snoring, apparently less enthralled by the prospect of a research task than I am.

I open the laptop's browser and type in 'Prudence Ballion'. The first few hits are about the song 'Dear Prudence', and I am astonished to learn that it was a Beatles song, not a Siouxsie and the Banshees original. It was penned by John Lennon no less. How did I not know that? I'm quite the muso when I'm not selling books and getting roped in to cold case investigations, and am ashamed at this gap in my knowledge. I resist getting too distracted by the internet (oooh,

Prudence Farrow? LSD and transcendental meditation?) and refine my search to 'Prudence Ballion Tracey Jervis NZ'. That gets a few more hits.

There are some newspaper articles from the time Tracey went missing, all mentioning that she was supposed to be with Prudence the night she disappeared. I flick through them, but there's nothing new. Then, a tiny nugget of gold. Interest in Tracey's case was clearly waning when a dogged local paper published what seems to be one of the last articles on the subject about a year after the disappearance:

> With no new leads it looks as though the police are set to scale down enquiries into the disappearance of Tracey Jervis. Hawke's Bay Gazette understands that Prudence Ballion, best friend of Tracey Jervis, has recently left New Zealand for England with her family. A source at Te Mata High School who wishes to remain anonymous stated that Prudence gained her University Entrance and was awarded a scholarship grade for English Literature. She was determined to make a fresh start and intended to study English Literature or Creative Writing at tertiary level.

Apart from that there's just a passing mention of Tracey in a fairly recent Kiwi true crime podcast called *No Trace*. My search is looking like a dead end.

I open the bag of pea snacks and click on the podcast link whilst I have a break. Stevie opens an eye and sniffs in my direction — he's a fan of the cheddar pea snack. I shove one into his gob; he has a quick crunch and settles back down. I wipe my cheese-powdery hands on my trousers (they're due a wash anyway after a mishap uncorking a bottle of merlot) and stare at my incident board, considering in which colour whiteboard marker to update it. A word seeps into my subconscious and I tune in to the podcast conversation. The voices are young, languid, low and creaky in the way that seems to be a thing these days.

Female voice: Yeah, like, this is soooo many years ago now and the police didn't ever find out what happened to Tracey.

Male voice: What was the goss though?

Female voice: Oh yeah, like, the word on the street was that Prudence was the last to see Tracey and then she did a bunk to England and went off grid. Like, suspicious or what?

Male voice: What are you saying? That Prudence did something creepy to Tracey?

Female voice: There's no evidence for that, it's just me making connections, but it's a bit sus that there's no trace of Prudence Ballion now either. And I spoke to an old classmate of Prudence's who wouldn't go on the record with what he told me so I can't say what it is but — just wow!

Male voice: Hmm. It's all a bit circumstantial though, like the Forrest Dipper case.

Female voice: Totally . . .

I listen to the end of the podcast, which is mercifully short, and skim through the first part again. But there's no more on Tracey or Prudence, or what the *just wow* moment was; the disappearance of Forrest Dipper takes up the rest of the episode. *No Trace* only did five episodes. I suspect they ran out of steam pretty quickly, seeing as it's just two people — high school kids, as it turns out — speculating; they don't even link in police reports or witness statements. The most interesting thing is that they've managed to get hold of a school photo of Prudence. It's a head shot, kohl-rimmed bright-blue eyes scowling at the camera. Wherever it was taken, it doesn't look like she wanted to be there.

Okay, on to a search of universities and tertiary institutions in

England. I get momentarily excited when I see something on the University of Nottingham site, but on a proper click through it goes on about ambiguity prudence which is something to do with economics that's beyond me. There's nothing else that looks remotely relevant to Prudence Ballion.

Creepy little Prudence, huh? She seems to have maintained a remarkably low profile given this age of oversharing. I wonder what the police made of her all but disappearing, too. If only we could get hold of the case files and have a good rummage. Still, I update the incident board with my meagre findings. I can't class a high school podcast as an interview, so I'll code it X for Exhibit: in black pen I write *Prudence Ballion went to England.*

Stevie stands up and stretches, licking his chops as he, too, stares at the board.

'Not much to go on yet, eh Stevie boy?'

He blinks, his crocodile mouth widening, letting out the satisfyingly squeaky groan particular to a dog yawn.

'Bored huh? Want to go for a walk?'

He hops off the spare bed and trots at speed into our bedroom, slinking underneath the bed. Unless he knows he's going in the car first, he is highly suspicious of the word 'walk': it means the great wide outdoors, where danger lurks. He will need to be tricked into coming outside, quite like his dogfather.

As if he senses a disturbance in the force, my phone pings with a text from his nibs.

Garth: I am making progress with the IFG event planning. Garth.

Oh no. What's he done?

Me: What have you done?

Garth: Just had some magnificent thoughts. I shall run them by you.
Garth.

A familiar tingle in my lips tells me my breathing has become shallow. By daylight I've mostly managed to tell myself that a book launch shouldn't really be able to trigger Armageddon, but when I find myself awake at 2am there are far too many bizarrely believable speculative fiction plots. I take a couple of deep breaths to stem the panic and decide to pander to Stevie's and my lower inclinations. He can stay under the bed and I will head to the kitchen and open a bottle of wine, this time without emptying half of it on my trousers.

CHAPTER 18

Garth: 33 days until Isabella Garrante book launch

'I'm just popping to the galley,' says Eloise. We learnt at one of the Booksellers Conferences that in America the advanced reading copies are called galleys and some bookshops even have 'galley rooms'. We keep all our readers in the shop's broom cupboard of a toilet, so going to the galley is our way of saying we need to sit on the porcelain throne.

From behind the counter I cast my eyes over the 'events' space, which currently houses our ever-expanding selection of graphic novels. It's a growth area we've worked hard to develop. Two years ago, if someone had come in and asked if I had any *One-Punch Man* I would have looked at them blankly. Now, I can confidently point to a stand and say, 'Absolutely, they're next to the *Attack on Titan* and *Tokyo Ghoul.*'

Pinter, he was a ghoul, not in the Western sense of a monster that hangs about graveyards and feasts on human flesh but more in the classic Middle Eastern tradition: a ghūl, a diabolical class of jinn, a demon. He lured his victims with promises of publication and — no, leave it there. Even the more graphic of the graphic novels wouldn't portray that.

My hands tremble. *Push the images away. Focus, breathe. He's banged up and you're in a lovely bookshop. Eloise and Stevie are here, all is well.*

Getting my breathing under control, I glance up at the clock. It's near closing time and the day has gone by in a blur. Despite Eloise thinking I'm crazy, I've been up on the shop's flat roof to look at the possibility of rigging up a large screen to broadcast proceedings to the anticipated crowds. In late September there's no guarantee of the weather being kind, so I reckon a projector and white sheet as a screen are going to be our best bet. We don't have and can't afford a projector, so I'll have to try and blag one from a local business. With the kudos that launching IFG will bring to the Village, that shouldn't be a problem.

I've also completed what Eloise refers to as more 'realistic' tasks, enquiring with the council about how we would arrange the closure of the road outside the shop and ordering two cases of unusually upmarket bubbles from our local wine merchants. The publishers have yet to come back with any agreement to help finance the launch.

I look behind the counter where we keep our wine glasses. Over the years we've acquired about fifty to sixty, of various shapes and sizes, purchased sporadically from Crockery King when their sales have coincided with us having some spare cash. I'm not sure that they'll suffice for the IFG launch and doubt even Gordon at The Uncommon Room will have enough to lend us.

'We're going to have to hire more glasses for the launch,' I say as Eloise returns from the galley. 'Should we use ours and hire the extra or just hire enough to cover everything?'

'It's IFG, it would be nice to have them all the same for once. What will it cost?'

I google local glass hire. 'About a dollar a glass.'

Eloise does the math. 'Perhaps just order the extra.'

'Are you sure? We're going to sell a lot of books.'

'She asked for us.' Eloise shrugs. 'She can take us as she finds us.'

That's always been Eloise's attitude. There's no pretention. What you see is what you get, and if you don't like it that's your problem, not hers. Me, I'm more of a worrier. I always fret that no one will turn up to a launch, though that's happened only once. It was in our second year when we were still building our reputation, and a self-published author, who I would describe as full of hubris and Eloise would describe as a cock, approached us. We tried to dissuade him, because to be honest the book was dire, but he was convinced of his genius and just wouldn't take no for an answer. We gave him our standard talk that generally the only people who turn up are friends and family and that he should try and get it in the papers and on his social media, but our advice fell on deaf ears — the same deaf ears that had clearly not listened to any editing advice. On the evening of the event he arrived with four cartons of books, three boxes of wine and completely unrealistic expectations. Launch time rolled around and no one had turned up, so we waited in case guests arrived late. After fifteen painful minutes of small talk interspersed with dings to the author's phone, which we could only assume were people making excuses for not coming, we all packed up and went home, me feeling terrible for the author, Eloise feeling vindicated in her opinion of him.

I glance up at the clock: 5.25. It's too late in the day to be phoning anyone about glasses or catering. There is, however, time for a quick email. I log onto the website for the *No Trace* crime podcast and bring up the contact form. I'm likely only to get one chance at this, so I need to name drop and job drop. Pinter can be bloody useful for once.

> Hi, I'm an ex-copper from the UK that worked on the Arthur Pinter investigation and I love your podcast. The Tracey Jervis case is a particular interest of mine and I am hoping that you might be willing to share your research and put me in contact with Prudence's classmate that you mentioned on your show. I look forward to hearing from you. Kind regards, Garth Sherlock.

I click send, then check the clock again: 5.27. 'Stuff it, shall we close early?'

'Let's. Magnum ice creams and wine for tea?' suggests Eloise.

'You're on.'

I'm just moving to the door when a customer walks in. For goodness' sake. Who walks into a shop three minutes before closing? Someone who's never worked in retail, that's who.

She is smartly decked out in a little black dress, and wears high-heeled shoes that look expensive, not that I'd know — Eloise mostly wears dockers. I guess she's probably in her late forties.

'Welcome,' I say, keeping inside the fact that I don't feel very welcoming. 'Can I help at all?'

The woman dismisses me with a cursory glance. 'No. I'm just browsing.'

Yeah, you're just browsing at closing time, I don't say. Instead, I head out and noisily bring in the magazine billboards and doormat, the shopkeeper's passive-aggressive trick of signalling that they want to close. The woman ignores me.

'Well, that's another day done,' I say loudly, as I shake the welcome mat outside and then drop it out of the way so that I can pull the door half closed. Still the woman pays me no heed. I head up to the till and start to surreptitiously tot up the contents.

By 5.40 the woman is still floating around by the fiction. I've had enough and glance at Eloise, whispering, 'Shall I?'

She gives me the nod.

I plaster on a friendly smile and approach the browser. 'I'm terribly sorry, we're closing now.'

Barely acknowledging my presence, she looks at her gold wristwatch. 'But I'm not meeting my friends at Ki-ko for dinner until six.'

I force down my ire. Eloise and I are now ticking towards a ten-hour day. I really don't feel obliged to stay open for another twenty minutes so this lady, who clearly has no intention of purchasing anything, isn't bored.

'I'm sorry, but we have to cash up before our Eftpos machine cuts over to the next day.' This is at least partially true, although the cutover is at 6pm.

'Well!' she says and bustles out of the shop as if I have just been incredibly rude.

I guess that's one person we don't need to worry about coming to the Isabella Garrante launch.

CHAPTER 19

Eloise: 31 days until Isabella Garrante book launch

It's been a glorious Sunday morning. Stevie is knackered after our early jaunt around the reserve and is now sleeping soundly. I've been looking forward to catching up with Paula on Zoom.

I log on only just before she does.

'Watcha babes,' says Paula.

'Mōrena e hoa,' I reply.

'What?'

'Good morning, my friend.' I give a teasingly sweet smile. She's always been prone to irritability when she doesn't understand something.

'Yeah whatever. It's evening anyway innit.' She sniffs.

'How's your dustbin death hunt going?'

'Yeah, all right. Dead lad was a dealer. Intel says it was a couple of upstarts giving it all that trying-to-be-like-the-Krays or something.' She takes a swig from a brightly labelled bottle. 'Bloody gangs.

Anyway, I have news for you from Belmarsh.'

I go cold as sweat breaks out on my forehead. I can't speak.

'You wanted me to find out what Pinter's up to, right?' says Paula.

I nod, get myself together. 'Yes, absolutely. Go ahead.'

'He's nicely banged up, regular stints in separates for winding up other inmates, playing 'em off against each other. Idiot. Still likes to think he's brainier than everyone else.'

'Any comms in or out?'

'Bits and bobs but nothing relevant to our interests.' She pauses. 'There was one odd thing, but I can't link it directly to Pinter.' She shuffles through a notebook. 'I got my man to run a random search for calls and texts to New Zealand pinging off carrier towers in Greenwich. Someone in or very close to Belmarsh used a burner phone to make a call to a shop in . . . err . . . Pee-tone.'

'Petone? Near Wellington?'

'Yeah. To a bookshop, weirdly. Name of Mary's Cat.'

'I know it. So, Pinter's in Belmarsh, I own a bookshop in New Zealand and he's ringing a bookshop in New Zealand. What the fuck?'

'Calm down. We don't know it was him. Could be Julian Assange organising a Christmas present for his nephew or summin.'

'Julian Assange has a nephew in Wellington?'

'How the fuck do I know?' Paula's getting ratty now. 'Point is, don't go having kittens just yet. I'll keep an eye on him, and you let me know if anything else weird crops up.'

'All right. Hey, I really appreciate your help with this.'

'So you should. Right, I'm off. I need another beer.'

And with that she leaves me with a great deal to think about, most of which I don't want to think about. On the other hand, someone walking past Belmarsh could just have been messaging New Zealand, right? There are loads of Kiwis in London.

I have an appointment, or 'coffee date' as she calls it, with Danielle Bright, MP for the local area. She wants to know how things are going in the book trade in general and the retail vibe of the Village in particular. Havelock North is a high-end boutique shopping and restaurant destination, a draw card for the Bay and a high hitter in our tourism industry. Danielle wants what she calls 'the word on the street' and I call gossip.

We've arranged to meet at Oddbeans. I make sure I have a poo bag in my pocket and coax Stevie from his curled-up position on the green chair. We set out down the hill, and for once Stevie trots by my side. We pass the entrance to the boarding school, the landscaped grounds curving up towards a spectacularly designed arts centre. It's a beautiful shape, like the rolling hills of the Bay, and is just as impressive inside: great acoustics, lovely auditorium, spaces for conferences and workshops. Today, there are girls in old-fashioned long skirts and boaters milling about fresh from chapel. One group of three are all teeth and ponytails, shoving and squealing, full of energy and confidence — they're teenagers, though, so anything could be going on in their heads. A couple of loners move in and out of the centre like worker ants, quietly getting on with whatever they're supposed to be doing. Which sort of kid would Tracey have been? She didn't go to this private school with all its advantages, but she was in line to be Dux of the local high school. A worker, I reckon, keen to get on, make a difference.

As we get towards the Village centre I feel my blissed-out pupper tense up: he's not a fan of crowds. 'Good lad, Steve, that's it,' I say matter of factly, knowing that any sympathy will only double down on his conviction that there's something to fear. If it was just Stevie and me, I'd probably have said 'Don't be a twat, Steve' but we're right in the Village and the shop has a reputation to uphold.

Danielle is already seated at one of the tables outside Oddbeans — I spy her as I'm dragged across the road. She's impeccably turned out in a sharp suit and jacket, makeup, earrings, the lot. How do people do it? If my clothes are on the right way round, I'm happy.

She waves, tells me she's 'taken the liberty' of ordering for me already, says all the right things to Stevie, who's under the table, then dives straight into 'the word on the street' questions. I can only assume she has other sources of information, as I'm pretty useless on meaningful updates.

'What about that homeless man? I hear he's been getting a bit aggressive?'

'Which homeless man?' She means Dafydd, but I want to know if Danielle knows his name.

'The one with the big coat. I spoke to Biffy at the homeware store and she's pulling her hair out, says he's been sleeping in the alley behind her shop and leaving, err, things behind.'

'I think you mean Dafydd. Yes, I did hear that he'd made a nest in the alley. I think the police had a chat with him and got him to clean up a bit. What do you mean he's been aggressive?'

Danielle goes on to describe Dafydd's standard conversational behaviour in which only one of the participants is visible and audible. Various shopkeepers have complained to the police, and apparently to their local MP, that he's lowering the tone and putting off customers. Danielle has the good grace to look a bit uncomfortable as she relates this.

'I don't mean to sound all self-righteous,' I say, 'but Dafydd's a member of our community just as much as a person who lives in a big house up the hill. We have to take the slightly stinky with the perfumed, and I don't think talking to yourself is a crime — if it was, we'd all be locked up, wouldn't we?'

Danielle smiles and I see understanding in her eyes. For a politician she's not a bad sort. But she's starting to fidget. I leap in before she can scarper.

'Hey Danielle, while I have you, I'm just wondering what you know about Franklin White?'

I'm rewarded with a small but visible shudder. Her pleasant smile freezes a little.

'He's running for council. He's been out of the game for a while, so he'll have his work cut out,' she manages stiffly.

'Do you like him? I know you don't like his politics, but what's he like as a person?'

She sighs and fixes me with her baby blues.

'Off the record?'

I nod, hardly daring to breathe in case she spooks and dives under the table, à la Stevie.

'The man makes my skin crawl. There's never enough to pin anything on him but he'll shake your hand and hold it too long, or make comments that you can't prove are double entendres but clearly are. I've watched women who work with him, and they hold themselves differently, you know, all buttoned up and wary.'

'Do you think that's to do with Tracey Jervis going missing and his involvement with her?'

'Gosh, that's a long time ago. Maybe. There was talk, of course. Older man taking an interest in a teenager. He wasn't one known for his philanthropy before he sponsored that poetry book . . . you know about that? . . . so tongues were wagging even before Tracey went missing. Then there were his extra-curricular business deals.'

'What business deals?'

'For years before he ran for office the first time, he was a source of, I don't know, frustration, maybe? Intrigue? When his name came up at business group meetings I attended, there'd always be a bit of a cold breeze blow through, you know? Like people knew things about him and he made them uncomfortable.'

Like a Stevie with a bone, I push her a little further.

'What sorts of things? More sleazy stuff?'

'Yes and no. Rumours that if you wanted any illegal substances you'd best see what Franklin could do for you — just pop down to The Clubhouse, he's bound to be there with his car keys in the pot, swinging. That kind of thing.'

'Eww.'

'Exactly. But of course it was never Franklin with the coke in his pocket. He left that to his mate, Oddbean. Why are you so interested anyway? Not thinking of voting for him, are you?' Danielle lets out a laugh bordering on the maniacal, but manages to rein it in. Her eyes are wide and wary, though. I think she knows more but fears she's already said too much.

'Not my type of bloke in any way, shape or form, Danielle, don't you worry. I'm just being nosy. Someone mentioned him in the shop, and I thought I should be better informed. I knew you'd set me straight.'

'Yes. Well, for god's sake don't quote me on any of that.' There's the strained laugh again. I decide to put her out of her misery.

'Not my style to drop people in it, Danielle. I appreciate the info.'

Her shoulders relax a little. What must it be like to have to watch your every word and thought in case someone uses it against you? Bloody exhausting.

Danielle stands to take her leave, mucking around with her handbag, smiling fondly at Stevie. Then she stops and looks at me.

'Be careful around Franklin White. Bad things happen to people in his orbit.'

CHAPTER 20

Garth: 30 days until Isabella Garrante book launch

It's Dungeons & Dragons night, a chance to escape into a world of fearsome monsters, dangerous dungeons and evil necromancers as a bit of light relief from the worries of the IFG book launch, the mystery of Tracey's disappearance, and the pervasive seeping shadow of Pinter. I actually play in several D&D games and run a D&D podcast, *Kiwis and Dragons*, but tonight's game is one of the most chill. For a start it takes place in my favourite pub, The Uncommon Room in Hastings; even better, the pub is closed on a Monday night, so we get it all to ourselves, courtesy of the manager Gordon who is also our GM (Games Master). In more innocent times, when I first started playing, the GM was referred to as the DM (Dungeon Master).

The Uncommon Room is long and narrow with high ceilings, mural-painted walls and long velvet drapes to the rear of a small stage where bands often perform. Arches of rebar mesh held up by industrial-looking brackets and interwoven with fairy lights festoon the ceiling, and a faux skeleton left over from last year's Halloween reaches through the metal grid as if trying to escape. Above the bar, stained-glass windows reclaimed from salvage yards hang on chains. With the lights turned down low, the place has the feel of a bohemian private club.

On the stage a long table and chairs have been set up. Running down the middle of the table is a map of a medieval fantasy village, with blacksmiths, herbalist and the all-important tavern. At the edges of the map stand painted miniature figures that will represent the players in the game and serve to mark their locations. A cardboard screen decorated with magical sigils is at the far end of the table to hide the GM's notes. This is the domain of Gordon.

There's a theory that there are only six degrees of separation from you and anyone else in the world. In New Zealand, it's probably about two. Before The Uncommon Room, and before I even knew that Gordon played D&D, I worked with him at Corn Evil, a haunted maze where actors dressed as horror-film characters lurked in the corn and frightened all who dared to pass through. I was a 'stalker', the nickname for the maze's security. Dressed from head to foot in black and with our faces covered in black face paint, we'd slink between the stalks, keeping an eye on any potentially troublesome groups and ensuring that the other actors were safe. Gordon played a crazed psycho with a pair of machetes, and it was a thing of beauty to watch the punters run screaming along the dark paths, chased by the faux-blood-covered Gordon scraping metal blades together with vengeful glee.

'What can I get you to drink?' Sim stands behind the bar pouring himself a craft beer from one of the taps. He is one of The Uncommon Room's bar staff but tonight his main role will be as Pan, a gnome bard with questionable decision-making skills.

'I'll just have a water.' I grab a glass from the bar and fill it from an urn in which float mint and lemon slices. I'm not a big drinker and generally won't drink anything at all if I'm driving, having witnessed the life-ending carnage caused by drink drivers first-hand. Telling an expectant mother that her husband and firstborn have been killed by a drunk driver is something that sticks with you.

I take my place at the table and greet Nelly, who works in PR for Hard Core Apples. 'How's it going?' I ask.

'Great. I've got some new dice.' She upends a small velvet bag, spilling a selection of brightly coloured dice ranging from four- to twenty-sided. I'm not a superstitious person — my education is science based, so I tend to look for the rational, logical explanation in any situation — but I swear that Nelly's dice are cursed. And it's not just me. None of the other players in the group will let Nelly even touch their dice.

'Cool. You think these ones will roll better?' I ask.

'Doubtful,' she says, and gives one of the dice an experimental roll. It shows a two.

The final member of our party hurries in and dumps a fast-food bag onto the table. 'Sorry I'm late. Server glitch.' Noah, the youngest of our group, works in IT, doing something complicated with network security that none of us understands.

'Right,' says Gordon, 'let's get started.'

We all lean closer.

'As adventurers of local renown, you have been summoned by the Captain of the Guard in the small town of Nadbury.' Gordon holds up a map and points out Nadbury. 'With a serious look upon his battle-scarred face the dwarven captain welcomes you into his office at the guardhouse and bids you to take a seat. Once you are all settled, he closes the door, locks it behind him then addresses you.' Gordon takes a swig of beer to lubricate his vocal cords, then puts on an accent that meanders somewhere between Welsh and Pakistani: 'Three days ago the mayor's daughter went missing. She was supposed to meet a friend at the harvest festival celebrations but never showed up . . .'

I miss the next details, my mind immediately drawn back to the disappearance of Tracey Jervis. It seems that even in the sacred escapism of my D&D game I am not, in fact, going to be allowed to escape.

Our characters spend the next hour bumbling around the town of Nadbury looking for clues and getting into fights with the local thieves' guild, who seem to have an unhealthy interest in the fate of the mayor's daughter. And proceedings go even more off track when we visit the local herbalist.

'Wi wa sum herb?' says Noah, who plays a more or less permanently stoned druid who tends to drop in and out of patois.

Gordon puts on a high-pitched voice for the bemused elven herbalist. 'Ah yes, I have wolfsbane, belladonna, mugwort, sweet wood—'

'No. Di special herb.' Noah pretends to hold a blunt to his mouth. 'Ya feel me?'

'The touching of clients is never part of the transaction.' Gordon holds his hands to his chest as if mortified. 'You want the Naughty Nymph in the Sinner's District.'

'Aye. That sounds like fun,' I say in a Yorkshire accent. 'My axe needs a polish.'

Noah reaches out an arm, his fist clenched. 'I grab the front of the elf's jerkin and haul him over the counter.'

Gordon smiles, which is generally never a good sign for our characters. 'From a back room emerges the largest orc you have ever seen. His muscles have muscles and they all bulge as he unsheathes a wickedly serrated sword the size of an ironing-board.'

'I strum my lute,' says Sim, doing a fine impression of playing an imaginary instrument. 'Magic swirls from the strings as I cast a spell over the orc, charming it to do our bidding.'

Dice clatter behind Gordon's GM screen and he smiles again at the result. 'Well, we'll see whether that works after we've had a break.'

I push my chair back and stand. Beers and water are refilled, and conversation turns to the more mundane matters of work and everyday gossip. I wonder whether to broach the subject of Tracey but decide against it: D&D is creative fantasy. Then Nelly says, 'This quest reminds me of that girl who went missing back in the day.'

'What girl?' Noah probably wasn't even born when Tracey disappeared.

'Can't remember her name, which makes me feel a bit shit.' Nelly takes a sip of her beer. 'I was in my first year at Havelock High and it was a big deal.'

'Tracey Jervis,' I say, grateful that in our quiet corner of New Zealand there isn't a slew of missing girl cases to choose from.

'That's right. Tracey Jervis,' says Nelly. 'It proper gave me the creeps at the time. I wonder whatever happened to her?'

'They thought it was her schoolteacher, didn't they?' says Sim.

'That was just goss.' Nelly absent-mindedly rolls a couple of dice: a one and a three. 'My older brother was going out with a girl in her class. He reckoned her friend had something to do with it. She was a weird emo chick, and she packed a sad about Tracey seeing some older guy.'

'Yeah, the schoolteacher,' says Sim, apparently unwilling to let go of the idea.

'Bent Trent? I don't think so.' Nelly flushes red and holds a hand to her mouth. 'Sorry, it's what everyone called him at school,' she says between her fingers. 'I know it's inappropriate now, but this was twenty years ago.'

'It was probably inappropriate then, too,' says Sim.

'Yeah, but we were teenagers and therefore horrible,' says Nelly.

'Her English teacher was gay?' I query, just to make sure I've not got the wrong end of the stick and Trent hadn't got his nickname because of some inconsistency with the English department's funds.

'Well, we didn't know for sure, but he was totes effeminate, always wore floral shirts and he had a ponytail and a man bag,' says Nelly.

'Sim's got a man bag.' Noah smiles through his beard.

'Yeah, but I pull it off, darling.'

I zone out from the banter about Sim's choice of accessories and how many floral shirts is too many. Eloise and I need to do some more digging into the teacher. It's not the first time his name's come up, although it's the first mention of his possibly being gay. Mind you, that could just be teenage vitriol. Nearly a quarter of a century ago if you didn't eat raw steak and drink pints you were considered a poof.

Gordon calls us to order, and the game continues, our fantasy investigations proving easier than our real-life ones. The mayor's daughter is successfully rescued after we've destroyed a goblin statue in the village square during a horse and cart chase.

CHAPTER 21

Eloise: 29 days until Isabella Garrante book launch

Poor, poor Kitty. The new pansies are gone. Well, the flowery bits are — the stems are left but they're just wee nubs of neatly sliced greenery.

'Who could be doing this? Do you think it's personal? Am I being watched? Oh my god, that must be it. They see when I go to pick up new plants and when I plant them, and then wait a bit and sneak here in the night and murder my babies.'

We're standing outside the shop surveying the latest damage. It's grey and drizzly, adding to the sense of gloom and a certain amount of rising panic. I'd better find some reassuring words smartish or Kitty's going to have a proper meltdown.

'It's not personal. We're not here when it happens. The perp doesn't even think about other humans being involved. They have their own agenda. Probably a psychopath.'

'A psychopath?'

I realise I may have said the wrong thing.

'They're not all evil, just detached from emotion so they're not actually thinking of you at all, just their flowery agenda. Anyway, ignore me. You know we both read too many stories.'

I'm not sure if that helped or not. The drizzle drizzles and we gaze mournfully at where the flower heads should be. It's not mindless kids having fun, or 'youth violence', as some members of the media would posit; it's too neat and tidy. For the same reason, I don't think it's personal either — no customer we've pissed off when their order has been delayed, or because we've 'cancelled' Jordan Peterson by not stocking him, or whatever.

I'm distracted by a familiar rolling, squeaking sound and look across the road to the war memorial garden. It's a pleasant communal area that also, excitingly, houses the Village Christmas tree each year. The trundling continues, eerily wafting through the drizzle.

'Meryl's getting soaked,' I murmur. I've run out of reassurance for Kitty, if I ever managed to offer any.

'I think she's lost her car again. I'm not going over there in this. If she needs a hand, she'll have to come and ask.' With that, Kitty heads back inside and makes purposefully for the kettle.

The trundling gets louder.

'Bloody hell,' Kitty mutters as I follow her in.

'Excuse me, excuse me, I think my car's been stolen, can you help me please?'

Further rushed exclamations of oh dear and generalised panic follow as Meryl reaches the counter and starts fussing with her trolley and her umbrella, now dripping all over the comfy chair.

'Meryl. Your car has not been stolen. Give it five minutes and when you've calmed down you'll remember where you left it.'

Kitty's tone is so uncharacteristically sharp that Meryl is shocked out of her hyperventilation.

'I'm sorry Meryl it's just . . .' And Kitty snaps the pencil she's been fiddling with. I hadn't realised quite how much the flower mutilations were getting to her.

Meryl's pink rain poncho sags a little, as does her lovely narrow face, splattery bits of dreadlock sticking to her cheeks.

'Kitty dear, whatever is the matter?'

I explain that the phantom flower thief has been at it again, spiriting away Kitty's babies in the night or early morning or whenever. I mention that we haven't been able to identify the shadowy character on our CCTV, but the council's system may pick them up further down the street.

'CCTV? Flowers?' Meryl looks taken aback, then gathers herself. 'Oh, Kitty. I'm sorry you're so upset. Let me pay for the flowers, then you can go and buy some more and everything will be okay.'

I make the coffee, including one for Meryl. I'll live to regret this if she comes to expect it. I usher the pair of them to the comfy chairs and Meryl chats in surprisingly soothing tones about flowers, and her paintings of them, some of which I've seen and aren't half bad. Incredibly, Kitty is getting some kind of comfort from this gentle conversation, and I silently give thanks for the colourful, kind people attracted to bookshops. I leave them to it. I have twenty-five emails to address.

Among the messages that claim to have recorded me (doing what? reading my emails?) or offering the latest list price for weighing scales, there's one screaming at me like blues and twos racing through traffic lights:

From: Mary
To: books@sherlocktomes.co.nz
Re: Arthur Pinter

Kia ora Eloise! Good to hear from you.

Yes we do have an Arthur Pinter in our database. Looks like he's ordered a book via PayPal to be sent to an address in Waipukurau, 32 Pikitea Street — *The Cause of Death: True Stories of Murder from a New Zealand Pathologist*. That's near you, isn't it? Sorry you didn't get the business!

You going to conference? Catch up then.

Mary x

What the hell is this demon up to? Coincidence is unlikely — it wouldn't be hard for Pinter to find out where I went after I left the police. This has officially become A Problem, and I need to pick it apart and rationalise its pieces. Right now, I have a distressed member of staff, an insanely huge book to launch and a missing girl to investigate. What the fuck happened to running a cosy wee bookshop in quiet old New Zealand? Like England in the fifties, my arse.

Meryl eventually leaves, having remembered where her car is and done a decent job of distracting Kitty.

'Time for your lunch, Eloise,' says Kitty.

'Oh, not yet. You have yours, duck.' The inside of me feels like its tissues and fibres are plaiting and unplaiting themselves, my heart thrashing, my head desperately trying to dissociate past from present.

'Not yet,' she says, and we share a wry smile. She clearly thinks my dismay is about the flowers. It's such a daft thing to be upset about that it calms me. I look around to identify three solid things, as the police counsellor recommended. Eftpos machine, orders book, kettle. Eftpos machine, orders book, kettle. Head starts to win.

The day continues. I potter between emails from customers wanting hard to find titles and requests from authors that I review their books, some of which sound fabulous, some of which I'd rather dust every leaf of my seventy-four house plants than read. I used to agonise over how to reply. These days a no, thank you has to suffice.

'Oooo, this looks good,' says Kitty, waving a newly arrived paperback entitled *The Lace Market Hauntings*. Nothing like a gothic horror to cheer her up. A few moments later I hear a sigh followed by some violent pricing-gun action. A pile of *Colour Vibes for Flower Pots* is getting a bit of a thwacking.

At about half past two, the light seems to darken further from the persistent gloom, but it's fleeting and caused by a giant of a man taking up the entire expanse of doorway as he comes in. Thank gods. This'll distract the brooding Kitty. The light and shadow move with him as he wanders towards the counter, and Kitty and I turn to meet him. He's well over six feet tall, broad, tattooed, and magnetic in his unassuming warmth and cheer. He's also a massive fantasy fan, so he and Kitty are special friends.

'Kia ora korua. Kei te pehea koe?' he booms.

'Ayup, Bernard. Kei te pai mate. What's the haps?'

'Boy needs a book. I'll get him out for a walk this arvo but then he'll be straight back on his phone when I drop him home.'

Bernard mentors a young lad of about twelve. He's got him into reading and is keen to keep the momentum going.

'I might just have a nose in the Sci-fi whilst I'm here. Much new in, Kitty?'

Kitty's Sci-fi/Fantasy corner nestles in an alcove next to the counter, a security nightmare but a secluded spot for the kind of reader who likes to escape into far-away, parallel or fantasy realms. It's small but houses hundreds of worlds in its collection of pages; its upper shelves boast wizards' hats, an owl, a broomstick, and the

Horror Chicken, a plastic fowl with a screaming maw and the ability to let out a bone-curdling shriek when squeezed.

Kitty noodles over to chat books with Bernard; she's back in her physical and mental happy space.

It's staff meeting tonight up at our house, a pretty casual gathering of booksellers with many, many stories to tell: of customers, of ordering biff-ups, of books recently read and loved or hated. It has been known to descend into chaos when one bookseller loves a book with all her heart and another really does not. We can't all help but take our stories personally — a well-loved novel becomes real in our minds, the characters our friends or enemies. To have it dismissed can seem a personal slight, and sensitive bookish souls must be handled with care. For the most part, our meetings are full of laughter, chatter and Garth's vegan Bolognese, which I suspect is the main draw card. It's just what Kitty and I need.

I serve a few customers buying cards and magazines or asking for a book they've read a review of: all easy stuff with pleasant people that doesn't take up any brain power. Most conversation concerns the weather, as it often does. The nerds emerge from the Sci-fi/Fantasy corner and Bernard picks up the book I've set aside for him about a creature that's half pig, half bat.

'An unstoppable super-swine hero? Perfect!'

Lucky kid, I think. That bloke's a bloody gem.

CHAPTER 22

Garth: 28 days until Isabella Garrante book launch

I'm cooking my signature Bolognese again but this time I've busted out the large pan. Staff meeting sounds formal, as if we know what we're doing running a business. The reality is somewhat different: it's more like a get-together with bookish friends/evil geniuses, melding minds and plotting world domination for the bookshop.

Slinky Stevie has slunk into the kitchen and lain down directly behind my feet. Fortunately, I spotted him before I stepped back, otherwise he might quite literally have made a dog's dinner of tonight's meal. He lets out a low, quiet 'gruff' like he wants to bark but doesn't want anybody to hear him. It's enough to let me know that the first of our guests has arrived.

I hurry down the stairs, Stevie hot on my heels. He suffers from both FOMO and FOBI (Fear of Being Involved), so as soon as I open the door and he sees that it's Phyllis he speeds back upstairs and hides under our bed.

'Welcome,' I say. We don't hug, partly as a hangover from Covid but mostly because I am socially awkward and can never judge whether a hug is appropriate.

'I brought cheesecake.' Phyllis hands me a foil-covered platter, easing over my social ineptitude.

'Great. Thanks. Go on up.'

Kiwis! Even when you explicitly say don't bring anything, they turn up with food or drink. I suspect Phyllis still considers herself Irish, so she gets a pass on this one.

'Has the savage beast gone?' she yells as I wedge the door open for the other guests.

'Yes, he's back in the dog-cave. He'll probably venture forth at the prospect of food.' I hurry back upstairs and put the oven on to preheat for the garlic bread. 'What can I get you to drink?'

'A glass of red would be grand.'

I'm pouring the wine when the rumble of the automated garage door and the screeching of the Tomato coming to a halt mark Eloise's return. 'Ah, I think the readers have arrived.' I hand the glass to Phyllis and hurry back downstairs.

'How was shop?' I ask.

'Good. Kitty's just cashing up.' Eloise hauls a big box of reading copies out of the boot. 'Fuck. That one's heavy.'

As I take the box from Eloise, my back twinges. 'Did you tell her to hurry?' Kitty does have a tendency to get distracted, especially at the end of the day when she savours being in the shop with the doors locked and no customers disturbing her.

'I said all the chippies would be gone if she wasn't on time.' Eloise lugs a second box of books from the car. 'I've been thinking. I want to tell the staff about the book and Tracey.'

'What? Why?'

'It involves the shop.'

'No, it doesn't.' I adjust my grip on the box. It does little to help my back.

'What if another package arrives?'

'You going to tell them about Pinter, too?' The box weighs a bloody ton and I want to get upstairs.

'That's different.'

'I don't see why.' I stomp up the stairs. 'Do what you want.'

After dumping the box on the coffee table for Eloise and Phyllis to sort out, I retreat to the kitchen to fume. Why does she always have to overcomplicate things? There's enough going on with the IFG launch; we don't need the staff involved with this, too.

By the time the garlic bread is done, Kitty and Amelia have arrived. I take a deep breath, lay the slices onto a serving board in two neat rows, add it to the symmetry of bowls and spoons on the table, then we all tuck in.

'This is great.' Amelia dips her garlic bread into the bowl.

'It is. You'd never know it was vegan.' Kitty spoons more pasta and blood-red sauce into her mouth.

'Vegan?' I say.

Kitty drops her spoon in horror.

'Oh, Kitty. He's just fucking with you,' says Eloise.

I shoot Kitty my cheeky-chappy grin which she returns with what is meant to be a hard stare, but she has a Bolognese sauce moustache that only makes my grin wider.

The clatter of bowls being cleared into the kitchen brings Stevie from under the bed. He is rewarded with sprinkles of mozzarella from the floor. After this, it's Phyllis's cheesecake.

'It's fabulous. What recipe did you use?' asks Amelia.

'It's out of the Ottolenghi book,' says Phyllis. 'And the best thing about it is that you don't even have to cook it.'

The actual best thing about it is that I didn't have to not cook it.

I grab a second slice. Maybe I shouldn't be so hard on Kiwis bearing gifts.

'Right. Now that we're all full of kai, down to business.' Eloise opens a notebook in which she's scribbled a few items we want to go over — the closest we're going to get to an agenda. Despite our laid-back approach, Eloise and I do actually discuss the subjects we want to broach beforehand, and thrash out exactly what we need to address and what isn't worth raising as an issue. Our pre-meeting meeting is also when Eloise gives me the firm word on what I can and can't say. For some reason she thinks my more forthright approach might upset the staff, so for the duration of the meeting I generally keep quiet, taking on the role of comedy sidekick.

'This is a little bit weird,' says Eloise. 'We are going to need you all to work an evening event in a few weeks, only we can't tell you anything other than the date and time yet.'

'Oh. Exciting,' says Amelia. 'Why can't you tell us?'

'We had to sign an NDA.' I raise my eyebrows. 'One of the super-serious ones. We forfeit the soul of one of our booksellers if we break it. I voted for Kitty.'

'Garth!' scolds Eloise.

Kitty pokes her tongue out at me.

'It's a drop-in title,' continues Eloise. 'And we're going to be launching it. All very hush, hush.'

'Is it the new Patrick Rothfuss?'

'Kitty, mate, you're dreaming,' I reply.

'Colm Tóibín?' suggests Phyllis.

'Oh! Oh! Oh!' Amelia bounces on the sofa's edge. 'It's *Heart Starter*, the new gay zombie romance.'

Eloise holds up a hand. 'Look, we can't say any more. We will tell you as soon as we can, and it is going to blow your minds.' Seamlessly, she moves to the more mundane bookshop business:

ongoing issues with shipping, the importance of checking that stock levels on the computer are correct, and the troubling theft of flowers from the front of the shop.

'And finally—' Eloise gives my knee a placating squeeze. 'Garth and I are investigating the disappearance of Tracey Jervis. It doesn't really have any bearing on you or on our day-to-day business, but the way in which we were *contacted* does come back to the shop, so I thought you should all be aware.'

'Oh, wow, it's like you're in your own crime novel,' says Amelia after Eloise has explained about the arrival of the package. 'But in a good way,' she adds. 'It's not like I'm expecting to find one of you horribly murdered in the shop or anything.'

'Thanks,' I say.

'Can we have a gander at the book?' asks Phyllis.

Eloise fetches the padded envelope containing the book from our incident room and hands it to her. For some reason it makes me uneasy. Maybe it's because if we were still in the police, the envelope and book would be safely packaged in secure evidence bags, each inscribed with a chain of custody. They certainly wouldn't be passed about willy-nilly. I imagine standing in the witness box of a courtroom while some smug barrister gets the notional case dropped due to breaches of procedure. It does nothing to ease the anxious tingle of adrenaline in my fingers.

'Do you think the choice of book is significant?' asks Kitty.

'*See You in September*? Tracey didn't seem like the type to join a cult.'

'Why do you think they chose you?' asks Amelia, who then goes on to answer her own question. 'It has to be someone who knows you were a cop, and who comes into the shop and knows that you're the type of person who would care enough to take an interest.'

'Tracey's mum. Janet,' says Kitty.

'You knew Janet was Tracey's mum?' I ask.

Kitty flushes and shrugs. 'I thought everybody did.'

'No,' say Eloise, Phyllis and I.

'Even I didn't know that,' says Amelia, who normally has her finger firmly on the pulse of Village news.

'She's been coming to Forest and Bird meetings for years,' says Kitty by way of an explanation. 'She's a big fan of the kākā. She's got a bach in a forest, Raglan way, where she goes on writers' retreats, and they come right onto her deck.'

'She's a writer?' says Eloise.

'Poetry, I think. Writes about nature, although she's never read us any poems at the group, or told us exactly where her forest bach is. Says she doesn't want other visitors scaring the kākā away. She should really log it in the database, as it's rare to get kākā that far west.'

I've never been to Raglan and have only a vague idea of where it is — somewhere up the coast beyond New Plymouth, I think. I must ask Janet about it when we next visit. Could she be behind Tracey's love of poetry, or was her father not the only one hothousing her?

Eloise interrupts my thoughts. 'Garth's got a game to finish the meeting. He wouldn't tell me what it is, so let's hope it's not completely inappropriate.'

'Harsh! This game is called Shout-outs. You know how publishers love putting shout-outs on the front of books, either from an author or from their marketing department: *the new* I am Pilgrim, *the next* Hunger Games—'

'It never is,' says Kitty who is the biggest *Hunger Games* nerd I've ever met.

'Absolutely, they never are, so the object of this game is to come up with a comical shout-out that you'd never see on the front of a book.'

'This'll be gas,' says Phyllis.

'Right, I'll start so you get the idea. *For fans of* The Seven Sisters, except they're brothers and there are only two of them.'

Eloise deposits her wine glass on the table. '*The book Stephen King would write if he were a woman and wrote romantic fiction.*'

'Ohh, ohh, ohh.' Amelia clasps her hands to her chest. '*More gay than* Heartstopper.'

'Is that even possible?'

'Sooo possible,' answers Amelia.

'*Like Patrick Rothfuss except the trilogy is complete,*' says Kitty. 'Or, *not better than* The Hunger Games.'

'All very good, but I have the winner here.' Phyllis quaffs her wine, then deepens her voice like a movie trailer. '*Move over Jack Reacher, here comes Jill.*'

CHAPTER 23

Eloise: 26 days until Isabella Garrante book launch

Chloe and Tama live on what is colloquially known as The Hill in Napier. It's a much sought-after location. The driveway is practically vertical, so I find a parking space further down the road and we puff up on foot. There's a set of steps to climb, too. At least, up here, we should get some stunning views over the Bay as the sun sets.

We arrive at a large wooden door complete with iron knocker in the shape of a fantail. Tama answers, and there's a moment of hesitation about the handshake/hug thing; we've only met in passing a couple of times. I bite the bullet and give him a clumsy hug. He's a big guy, black hair greying in the usual places but still thick and shaggy. He radiates warmth. I wasn't expecting the baggy jeans and slipper boots, but I'm glad it's a casual affair. I instantly feel more relaxed.

Garth follows us into a rimu-floored hall lined with family photographs, one side older photos, the other newer ones with the latest chubby-cheeked family additions. Tama invites us into a lounge room on the left, and I'm immediately struck by how light it is — there are large picture windows with bifold doors leading out onto the deck. The views are as spectacular as I'd hoped. The glimmer of sea lures me in, and as I get closer Chloe, chopping knife in hand, emerges from the adjacent kitchen area.

We open the bottle of Birdsong pinot gris I brought with us, I ask if I can help, the men do that awkward 'how are you mate, lovely place you have, been here long' chit-chat. I hop up on a stool at the breakfast bar and watch the preparations for dinner, keeping an ear on the blokes' conversation, ready to rescue Garth if he falls into the black hole of social awkwardness.

'How long since you were in the job?' asks Tama.

'Oh, it's a while since we left. Seems like another life.' I can see Garth is struggling to count the years since we were in the police. 'How long have you been in?'

'Coming up for thirty years. I can't believe it. So what were you, general patrol or . . . ?'

They drift into the kitchen, Tama cracks open a beer and grabs a Coke for Garth. We have a bit of back and forth about the job, some anecdotes, Garth reminisces about my addiction to the cake and fried eggs at the Campbell Square canteen at the nick in Northampton. It relaxes him if he can take the piss out of me.

'I imagine the Tracey Jervis case was pretty frustrating,' I venture.

'Oh yeah, Chloe said you were interested in Tracey. What's got you into that case?' Tama takes the stool next to me, and Garth hovers, not sure where to put himself. He decides upon a lumbersome lean against the bench next to where Chloe is now on to capsicum dismemberment. He's slightly, obliviously, in her way.

I explain about the note sent to the shop. 'Weird, eh? Who on earth dug up my collar number from a million years ago?'

'I suppose there are ways to find it out if you're determined. I mean, I could, but I have contacts.'

I pour Tama a glass of wine, then launch in. 'What do you think happened to Tracey?'

A pained look crosses his face; he blows out his cheeks and sits forward, elbows on the bar.

'Oh man. I had so many leads, so many theories, and nothing came of any of them. So, here's the thing.' He takes a healthy gulp from his glass. 'The circus was in Havvers at the time of Tracey's disappearance. It was a beauty of a spring and a lot of the older school kids were hanging around the fairground, spending their parents' money, getting sneaky tattoos with fake ID.'

'Sounds like Eloise's misspent youth,' interjects Garth.

Tama laughs. 'Yeah-nah, I remember this clear as a bell. You know about Prudence?'

Nods all round.

'We gave her a good grilling about what she and Tracey had been up to, and it came up that they'd been spending a bit of time on the domain at the circus, eating candy floss, soaking up the sunshine.'

I have a vision of Prudence, her black-on-black garb swallowing the light from her golden friend. I shiver despite the warmth of the kitchen and take a swig of wine for medicinal purposes.

'Tracey had a bit of a thing for one of the fairground boys. Prudence remembered floppy hair and a big smile but not much else, said it was just harmless flirting.'

'Do you think she actually ran away with the circus?' I ask.

'It was a theory for a while, and we never totally discounted it. We tracked down the circus crew and found the boy. He said he thought he remembered Tracey but that being the handsome lad he was, she could have been any number of blonde, ponytailed schoolgirls hanging around.'

'Did you believe him?' asks Garth. What a cracking question. I get a glimpse of the talented young copper I married. He's still in there, sharp as a tack.

More cheek-blowing and a bit of scowling this time, then Tama raises his eyebrows and grins at Garth's cross-examination. I feel a bit bad that we're bringing this all back up for him, but not bad enough to let him off the hook.

'That I don't honestly know. I mean the WOF on his car was out of date and I'm pretty sure I caught a whiff of blow, but I didn't get the sense he was a particularly bad kid. He actually spoke of the girls he met quite respectfully, said he had a sister around their age.'

Dinner is ready, and the waft of onions, garlic and something herby and fragrant takes us away from tragic missing-girl talk for a bit. The conversation turns to books, films and politics, and the four of us find enough to agree and disagree upon, as well as a similar warped sense of humour from working in emergency services. Over pudding — a homemade fig ice cream, as if Chloe wasn't talented enough — I decide to bring up our favourite creepy guy.

'Did you see Franklin White's running for council?'

'That guy. Slippery as they come.' Tama scrapes his chair back and folds his arms. 'I'm pretty sure he was right in with the Black Dogs. We had an informant say there was serious money passing between him and the gang, but we didn't have enough evidence for a warrant. I reckon it was drug related but we couldn't get anything concrete. I won't be voting for him, that's for sure.'

'Do you fancy him for Tracey's disappearance?' I ask.

He pauses, rubs his face with both hands. 'You're a bugger, you are, plying me with drink and getting my tongue loose.'

'Interviewing 101,' says Garth. 'You deflected but didn't answer the question.'

'Not you as well.' Tama drains his glass. 'Prudence intimated that there was something going on between Tracey and Franklin, and that's why he sponsored the poetry book. Like so many elements of the case, there were rumours but no evidence. Franklin denied it, and although it was obvious that his employees were uncomfortable about it, no one had actually seen anything. You can't arrest someone because Hana in accounts is getting "creepy vibes".'

I can see why the case has lain heavily on Tama. He'd just made detective, and the lack of any outcome, never mind a positive one, has sat with him. Every copper has cases like this. They aren't all as serious as suspected murder, but there are always victims you never feel you achieved justice for.

'Do you know what happened to Prudence?' I ask.

'Not sure. I know it broke her heart. She became convinced her only friend in the world was dead.'

Oh god. The tragedy that keeps giving. My brain is fizzing with lines of enquiry. But Tama yawns and I suggest to Garth that we leave these good generous people be.

He nods and stands, then turns, Columbo-like. 'I have one last question. You said Prudence believed her only friend in the world was dead. Do you believe she is?'

'Yes, mate, I do. After all these years, she has to be.' Tama's face is serious. 'Talk to Franklin White. He's always been the key to what happened to Tracey.'

CHAPTER 24

Garth: 23 days until Isabella Garrante book launch

It's heading towards closing time. Kitty has dipped out early for a Forest and Bird meeting, so I'm on my own with Stevie snoring gently in the stock room. It's a pleasant moment's quiet, more what I envisaged owning a bookshop would be like, rather than investigating dead girls, stolen flowers and launching superstar authors whose fame is clearly beyond our means.

Between trying to contact Franklin White, who seems unresponsive to our emails, phone messages and texts, I've been working on a plan to shift the IFG launch to a local winery. This would have two advantages: first, they're more likely to be able to accommodate the crowds and, second, wine. Wine and books are a natural pairing. We're spoilt for choice here, but it would be nice to use a winery with links to the Village — Red Vines maybe.

I catch a movement on the CCTV and look up. Two thickset patched gang members are sauntering through the door.

Now, I try not to judge a book by its cover, but this can be hard to do when to be a recipient of that cover you have to have done something quite heinous. That said, a few months ago we had a patched gang member, a huge guy, come into the shop every Sunday to buy board books to read to his new baby. He was polite, asked sensible questions and listened thoughtfully to my suggestions, and fair play to the guy, he was reading to his kid.

I recognise today's two men as Black Dogs, and from their scowls and swagger I somehow doubt they're here to buy a copy of *Each Peach Pear Plum*. Surely it can't be a robbery: we're not a cash-heavy business, and the dairy next door would make a much better target with its cabinets full of smokes and vapes.

'Evening gents, how can I help you?' I ask.

'This your place?' says the larger of the two. He has dark slicked-back hair, a black bandana around his neck and BD tattooed on each cheek.

For the first time ever, I contemplate denying my stewardship of Sherlock Tomes. However, it is my name over the door and whatever this is about it's up to me to deal with it. 'I am.' My voice is higher pitched than normal.

'We've got a message.' The guy places a many-ringed hand on the counter. 'Youse gotta stop.'

Have they got the wrong bookshop? Maybe they're supposed to be in the Lotto Plus a couple of doors down. Or they've been sent by Lotto Plus to shut down the competition. No, get a grip; we had a feud with the previous owners, but the new staff are quite amiable. Besides, since when have the gangs been involved in bookshop wars?

'I'm sorry. I don't understand. Stop what?' I hold out my hands in a friendly and non-threatening gesture, which also puts them in a good defensive position above my waist.

The second gangster, whose face is cast in shadow by the hood of his sweatshirt, sweeps his arm along a shelf, spilling magazines across the floor.

'You stop with the Tracey Jervis shit, or next time it won't be just books we're breaking.'

'They're magazines, not . . .' I stop myself mid-correction, suspecting he's neither interested in the ISBN system nor in need of explanation that the magazines aren't broken and just need picking up and a bit of a tidy. Out of the corner of my eye I catch another movement on the CCTV. Could I be lucky enough for it to be Bernard? He's about our only customer bigger than the two thugs in front of me.

'Tracey Jervis?' I stammer, buying time.

'She went missing.' The first guy lands a second massive hand on the counter and leans closer. 'She needs to stay missing.'

My gaze falls on the box cutter and scissors behind the till. Neither is sufficient to turn the odds in my favour if it comes to blows, not that I have any intention of fighting. Even in my younger days when I was a steely-eyed commando, I couldn't have taken these guys. You can have as much fighting spirit and esprit de corps as you want, but if you're outnumbered by thugs who have a hundred-plus pounds on you, you're going to take a beating.

'Evening team, port fifteen,' says the Admiral as he hobbles up the indoor accessibility ramp, using his cane for support. 'I saw these two pirates enter the shop and thought you might need some naval fire support.'

Damn! Not Bernard.

'Beat it, old fulla, or I'll beat it for you,' says Hoodie.

I've always considered the Admiral to be eccentric rather than truly mad, but I'm hastily reconsidering my assessment. There's a joyful wildness in his eyes as he brandishes his cane and pulls a stiletto-like sword from the wooden scabbard. 'Naval fencing champ

1963 to '67. Keep at it, laddie, and I'll skewer your eyeball like a cocktail olive.'

The bigger guy reaches over the counter to grab my tee-shirt. Out of nowhere, a fur missile explodes from the stock room, then Stevie has his paws up on the counter, barking like I've never seen before. Saliva flies as he snaps and snarls with the savagery of a hound from hell.

The gangster quickly withdraws his hand, pointing a finger at me instead. 'Don't make us have to come back.' He lifts his chin, then stomps from the shop, trailed by Hoodie, who knocks over a display of books on his way out. It's David Walliams, so I don't much mind.

The Admiral is still waving his sword like Zorro. 'Borders repelled, Captain.'

'Thanks, I owe you, Admiral,' I say, my heart still pounding.

'Not at all. Pirates are pirates and need hanging from the yard arm. And besides, it is we who owe you for creating this wonderful unique sanctuary in a world of corporate homogenisation.' The Admiral fishes a hip flask from beneath his jacket and unscrews the cap. He takes a swig and then hands it to me. 'Pusser's Rum, excellent for the nerves after a battle.'

I take a swig, swirling it around my mouth before swallowing. The rum's warmth lines my throat and spreads into my tummy, at least partly countering the post-adrenaline sickness and sending me a little lightheaded.

Stevie, who has dropped down from the counter, brushes against my legs. I crouch and press my face into his fur. 'And thank you. I think there is a high probability of steak in your future.'

Stevie licks my face and gives my ear a friendly nip, all signs of the hell hound vanished.

CHAPTER 25

Eloise: 22 days until Isabella Garrante book launch

Technically, it's just Garth, Kitty and me on duty today, but Amelia and Phyllis have materialised with coffee and doughnuts.

'You can have the one with the pink icing and the jam, Garth.' Amelia looks at me, anticipating the objection that withers in my throat. 'He's had a shock.'

'A wee bit of sugar is good for the soul,' adds Phyllis, and Garth smirks, safe in the knowledge that if I mention 'pre-diabetes' today I will be nothing but a curmudgeon.

Thank goodness for our bookshop whānau, this assembly of angels and the regulars who call the place their second home. There's usually someone around we know well enough to guard the till whilst we pop out to the loo, or help bring the magazines in of a morning, or wield a fencing sword at patched gang heavies. The Admiral is currently my favourite customer, especially now I know the contents of his flask.

'Oh my god. The Black Dogs have been murdering my flower babies,' whispers Kitty. 'You have to stop whatever you're doing, or they'll get the tiny baby pansies!'

I stifle a guffaw. 'I don't think it was them. I doubt they even noticed the flowers.'

'But why wouldn't they?'

'Only because they're philistines and I doubt they would stop to appreciate the mathematical precision with which they're planted and the aesthetic placing of the . . . err . . . purple ones and yellow ones?'

Kitty stares at me, trying to gauge if I'm taking the piss or not.

'Exactly,' she says slowly, and there are wise nods all round.

'Seriously, though, even if they didn't kill the flower babies, we don't need that kind of drama going down. It's going to put people off coming in,' says Amelia.

She's absolutely right. The thought of gang members turning up at the launch of the century doesn't bear thinking about.

'Do you need us for muscle or shall we leave you to it?' Amelia licks sugar dust from her fingers.

Garth peers into the box. 'Are there any doughnuts left?'

'Nope. That was the last one.' Phyllis nods at the golden curve of crispy dough disappearing into Garth's mouth. He chews, swallows and wipes his hands on his trousers, magical sugar dust falling to the floor.

'Then you may decamp,' he says.

The doughnut fairies take their leave, Kitty starts the involved process of inserting a new roll of stickers into the pricing gun, and Garth disappears in the direction of the loo, leaving me to the racing thoughts of a sugar rush.

How the hell did the Black Dogs get involved? Has someone paid them to rattle us, or were they involved in Tracey's death? If they came with the intention of putting me off, their visit has only made me more determined to find out what happened. We're going to have to be a bit more discreet, though. The last thing we want is a bunch of heavies ruining the IFG launch. The question is how, when we don't know who told them?

Fetu bowls in the front door, bearing a large box. 'Talofa, Sherlocks! Just one today!' I catch a whiff of Lynx Africa in the air and register his beaming smile as the box lands in my arms. It's heavier than it looked when he was handling it.

'Manuia le aso,' I wheeze at his retreating back, and am rewarded with a laugh and a 'Nice one!'

I hope he sticks around a while, courier turnover being generally high. He's a breath of fresh, Lynx-scented air, that one.

'It's extraordinary, the variety in quality of visitor we've had in the last twenty-four hours,' Garth muses as he watches Fetu leave, not thinking to relieve me of the box. He still sees me as the gung-ho twenty-year-old he met at Police College who would have bitten his head off at any suggestion of female inferiority. I am not in a hurry to show any old-ladyness, so take it as a compliment.

I plonk the box down on the bench where we do the stock, and Kitty gears up to attack it with the box cutter. Garth is running minor repairs, sticking down peeling carpet corners, fixing wobbly card-stand wheels, and I'm in the middle of emailing book club about the next meeting when Tama strolls in. This is unusual; Chloe chooses his books and buys them on book club night roughly twice a year — Christmas and birthday.

'Kia ora e hoa,' I call. He's in plain clothes, of course, so I'm not sure whether this is business or pleasure. We didn't call the police after the Black Dog muppets incident, not seeing how that could move us forward in the investigation that we probably shouldn't be investigating, but word gets around and he may have got wind of it. 'Nice to see you again so soon.'

'Mōrena. I've come to thank you for my shabby head. It still hasn't recovered after you plied me with your fancy wine.'

'Hey, you can lead a horse to water and all that,' I shoot back, not prepared to take responsibility, although I was trying to loosen his tongue so maybe I should.

'I've actually come for a browse. I'm sick of reading detective novels that make my job sound exciting. I'm about ready to try something out of my comfort zone. How about fantasy or science fiction or something?'

I hear the pricing gun clatter to the bench top and Kitty shoots past me.

'Come with me,' she commands. Tama raises his eyebrows at me, grins, and does as he's told.

The daily book review has just aired on RNZ and it was obviously a bloody good one judging by the barely contained excitement of the woman on the phone upon hearing we have it in stock. By the time I've grabbed a copy and reserved it for her, Kitty is ringing up Tama's purchase: *Tarquin the Honest, Ocian's Elven* by Gareth Ward, a fantasy heist movie in a book.

Garth comes up to the counter to exclaim over his excellent choice of book. 'That's my favourite fantasy series at the moment. It's brilliant and funny, I wish I'd written it.'

'Do you write, Garth?' asks Tama.

'No, no. I mean, I try a bit. I'd like to do more but time is an issue and, well, you know how it is.'

Tama nods. 'Looking forward to getting stuck in. Got a couple of rest days coming up and I actually feel like a rest, so . . .'

He starts to raise his arm in farewell when I have a thought.

'Er, Tama? I'm wondering if you could do me a favour.' I look over to Kitty but she's back into the stock, captivated by the blurb of a bright-pink book with a yellow banana on the cover.

'I'd like to say yes but now I know you a little better I'm not sure I should be so quick to commit,' he says.

'Ha. Fast learner. Hey, back in the day I had a bit of bother with a crim in the UK and, long story short, he ordered a book from a shop in Wellington to be delivered to an address in Waipukurau. It's a bit close for comfort and I was hoping you might just look up the address for me, off the books, see if it's got any flags on it.' I smile my most ingratiating smile, the one that convinces nobody.

'Huh. Unsettling. Like I said, I'm off for a few days, but I could have a look next week unless you think it's urgent?'

Is it urgent? I don't bloody know but I don't want to make a deal of it and spook anyone, least of all myself. 'No, next week is fab. It's 32 Pikitea Street. I owe you more wine.'

'Ah, that can wait until next week, too,' says Tama. 'Ka kite,' and he finishes his wave and heads out, Garth still wittering on in his wake about how cool Tarquin the Wizard is.

Back behind the counter, I shift the computer mouse, ready to get into the emails, and nudge something metallic.

'Wait up, Tama! You forgot your keys,' I shout, waving them at him.

'No I didn't,' he replies, neither looking back nor breaking the stride that takes him right out of the shop and off in the direction of the library.

'That's strange,' I mutter.

Garth comes to have a look. There's a generic freebie keyring on a set of two keys: a padlock key and a double-sided key. I hold the fob up to him.

'There's an address on the plastic label bit, look.'

Garth narrows his eyes in what I assume he believes to be a Holmesian attitude. He might as well hold forefinger and thumb to chin and say, 'Hmmm.'

'Curiouser and curiouser,' is what he actually says.

'Yeah. Weird.'

'Is that . . . singing?' asks Garth.

'*Are you gooooing, to Saaaaan Fraaaan-ciscooooo. Dooby doooooo, with flowers in your hair . . .*'

It's Dafydd, and he's crooning to Kitty's flowers.

CHAPTER 26

Garth: 22 days until Isabella Garrante book launch

Eloise tugs sharply on the Tomato's steering wheel, taking the St George's Road roundabout at what in the police we might have referred to as *excessive speed*.

We've shut up shop early in an attempt to thwart any further visits from the Black Dogs, and are heading into Hastings and deeper down the rabbit hole.

'It doesn't make sense.' Tama must have left the keys with us. A Google search of the address on the fob has revealed it to be that of a secure self-storage facility. What we'll find there we have no idea, but we're certain it's Tama's intention for us to visit. 'Why a lock-up in Hastings?'

'How do you mean?'

'Well, he lives in Napier. It makes more sense to use one of the storage places over there.'

'They might not have always been on The Hill.'

'Perhaps. If he was involved in Tracey's case, he probably would have been working out of Hastings nick back then.'

'It's only a fifteen-minute drive between Hastings and Napier, anyway.'

'It's actually twenty-five minutes.'

'Are you sure?' Eloise frowns and swerves around a parcel courier van that was apparently going too slowly. 'I expect there's a fair bit of transfer between the nicks in the two cities.'

I smile, because neither 'city' would be considered anything other than a moderate-sized town in the UK. Northampton had a population approaching a quarter of a million. It's sobering to think that for a town that size there would sometimes be as few as twenty-five police officers working a night shift, or one officer for every ten thousand people. The thin blue line was often stretched very thin indeed. You only needed for the shift to make a handful of arrests for officers to be so committed in the cells you'd be down to single figures patrolling the streets.

The awning on a wire-mesh security fence surrounding a patch of waste ground catches my attention: 'Franklin White Construction'. They've been threatening to build a new supermarket on this site for years, but today the gate is unchained and partially open. Parked inside is a menacing black SUV with the personalised plate FWC. Alongside it are two meaty motorcycles. I think they might be Harleys, but I've never been into bikes and wouldn't really know a HOG from a Honda.

'Seen something?' asks Eloise.

'I'd never noticed that Franklin White owns that land where Fresh World want to build.'

'Doesn't surprise me. He seems to own bloody everything around here.'

I grab the car door's handle as Eloise slings the Tomato down a side street and into a small industrial estate surrounded by houses. We zip past an auto shop, a plumber's merchant and an electrical wholesaler's before a bright-yellow warehouse surrounded by substantial razor-wire-topped fences looms ahead of us.

Eloise screeches the Tomato to a halt. A high, steel-barred gate topped with rotating anti-climb spikes prevents entry. A pair of huge halogen spotlights burn to life, casting us in a dazzling pool of illumination. Alongside Eloise's car door stands an RFID entry post with a red-blinking LED. Perhaps the security here is the reason Tama chose it: many secure storage facilities really aren't that secure. This place certainly seems to be taking its responsibilities seriously.

Eloise winds down the car window.

She reaches her arm out and waves the dongle attached to Tama's key at the RFID sensor that will open the gate. Thanks to what some might describe as a rather cavalier attitude towards parking, Eloise's hand is a considerable distance from the device and the LED continues to blink red.

'I don't think you've parked close enough,' I say, helpfully.

'I have parked close enough.' Eloise unclips her seatbelt and leans half out of the window, her baggy pants, which to my mind resemble a tie-dye potato sack, snagging on the buckle. Stretching to her full reach, she manages to brush the dongle against the reader and the LED flashes green. With a clunk the gate begins to slide open.

'See,' says Eloise smugly, manoeuvring her torso back into the Tomato.

'Yes, elegantly done. Although if you'd parked closer—'

Eloise puts the Tomato into drive and with a squeal of tyres we lurch through the open gateway.

There are no other vehicles in the eight allocated customer parking spaces, which is fortunate as Eloise manages to abandon the Tomato over two of them; I consider it wise not to mention this. She yanks the handbrake on and slaps me on the leg. 'Time to rock and roll.'

The entry to the warehouse has another RFID scanner which allows us into a security airlock, the doors behind us closing before the ones in front open. Ahead is a long concrete-floored corridor lined with yellow Colorsteel roller-shutter doors with a large black number painted on each. As we step from the airlock sensor, lights flick on one after the other along the corridor's length like a scene from *The X-Files*.

'What's the number on the fob?' I ask, trying to push down a rising fear.

'Thirty-nine,' says Eloise without looking at the keys.

'That's an unlucky number in Afghanistan.'

'Why?'

'I don't know. Something to do with cows, I think.'

'You'd have thought they had bigger things to worry about.'

'Yeah, I suppose.' My uneasiness only increases as we walk. 'Is it just me, or does this remind you of that bit in *The Silence of the Lambs*?'

'Do you really think we're going to find a head in a jar in Tama's lock-up?'

'It just seems a bit odd. Why'd he give us his key? Why didn't he come with us?'

Eloise strides on, activating more sensor lights. 'Perhaps he's busy. He is a DCI.'

'Or perhaps he's involved.' For some reason I check over my shoulder. 'Wouldn't be the first bent copper we've come across.'

'What's brought this on?'

'Those thugs only visited after we'd been to Tama's.' I know I'm probably being unfair, but I'm a naturally suspicious person, a characteristic which was useful in the cops and often a hindrance in civvy street. 'Also, at dinner the other night, he seemed as keen to know what we'd found out as we were keen to pick his brain about the case.'

'So, this is a set-up?'

'I'm just saying if we open the unit and the floor's covered in plastic sheeting we need to run.'

Eloise shakes her head. 'You have an overactive imagination.'

I suppose she's right, although that doesn't stop the prickle at the back of my neck spreading across my shoulders and down my spine as we come to a halt outside unit 39. It's the same feeling I used to get in the police when I had to break into the house of someone who hadn't been seen for some time. If you were lucky, or unlucky depending on how you viewed it, the smell once you'd put in the door would tell you that you had a body to deal with. However, if the occupant was recently deceased, or it was freezing cold and the heating hadn't been on, you'd get no such warning. Then you'd cautiously wander from room to room, expecting to stumble across a corpse but still not be prepared for it when you did.

Eloise unlocks the padlocks either side of the unit and places them on the ground. 'After you.'

'Why do I have to open it?'

'Because you were rude about my driving.'

'I prefer to think of it as factually accurate.' I bend down and grab the rust-flecked handle at the bottom of the roller door, then pause, glancing back at her. 'Ready?'

'I really don't understand what you're expecting to find.'

The door clatters as I heave it up, the harsh rattle of the metal bouncing from the concrete floor and along the corridor. I stare inside.

'Well, not that,' I eventually manage to say.

CHAPTER 27

Eloise: 22 days until Isabella Garrante book launch

I'm standing in front of another entrance to a room long ago and far away. Pinter didn't have a storage unit; he had a locked door in his mother's Victorian house: classic horror-movie stuff.

Mother Pinter is out at Bridge, closely surveilled by a member of our team with enough grey hair to pass as a geriatric player. Pinter himself is at a bar on the other side of town; he's at a writers' meeting, the participants of which we are also closely watching for their own safety.

Paula and I have poked around most of the house. It's old money: large rooms, high ceilings, ancient dusty furniture. A closed door sends the hairs on the back of my neck upright. With expert finesse and a handy bunch of skeleton keys, Paula 'picks' the lock, and the door swings open.

The room is a large library, bookcases on each wall organised alphabetically, by subject. It's beautiful and immaculately clean;

sliding sash windows covered in gauze cast a honeyed flush across a chaise longue upholstered in a glorious amethyst velvet. If I didn't know the room belonged to a psychopathic killer, I would be enamoured enough to linger. The large, leather-topped desk is covered in stacked piles of paper and neatly labelled box files of manuscripts. Closer inspection reveals angry slashes of red over split infinitives and random apostrophes, and frustrated notations of 'No, No, No!'

Then the absolute kicker. A tap on my shoulder from my DS.

'Look.'

I look.

Paula has drawn back a railed tapestry to reveal an incident board not dissimilar to the one back at the nick, and I realise just how good at my job I am. It's an obsessive shrine paying unsolicited homage through a carefully curated dossier on one person. Me. Or the me Pinter believes me to be. I've hooked him. Now to reel him in . . .

'Eloise.' Garth's voice penetrates the fog and I see his hazel eyes puckered in concern.

I'm crouched, hands on knees, breathing raggedly. *Get a grip, woman.* 'Bloody hell.' I straighten up and step inside the unit. 'Quick, get the lights on and shut the door.'

Garth follows me, flicking on the overhead strip light before pulling the roller door nearly to the ground.

'What just happened?' he asks.

'Just felt a bit winded all of a sudden,' I offer, not meeting his eye. 'What the actual fuck is this?'

His attention turns to the scene before us. Fortunately, he's easily distracted.

The whole space is set up like a police incident room. There's a functional desk towards the back wall, with an overhead lamp beside neat piles of papers. The chair is between the back wall and the desk, offering the seated person a view out over the unit. I wander over to the desk, edge myself around to the chair and plonk myself down. The walls to the left and the right are covered in papers, drawings, maps, arrows. I can make out at least three distinct cases on the left-hand wall, but the right-hand wall appears to be dedicated to one, lone mystery. Garth wanders over, and my initial thought is confirmed.

'Tracey.'

I can see why the desk is positioned this way — I wouldn't want my back to the door either. The rear wall has a kitchen bench on which sit a kettle and the makings for hot drinks next to a sink. A mini fridge hums beneath and I can't help but look inside: a couple of beers, a hardened nub of cheese and half a litre of milk, but thankfully no head in a jar. I reach in, unscrew the milk container and sniff. Still fresh. The incident room's usual occupant, presumably Tama, has been here recently.

I look up, nose in plastic, to see Garth staring at me, gob open rather unattractively. He huffs exasperatedly.

'What?'

'We have just discovered something quite shocking, there's all this —' he gestures to the Tracey wall — 'to look at, and you're straight in the fridge sniffing the milk. A bit parched, are you? Getting the kettle on first?'

'Stop being a twat. It's fresh. Tama comes here a lot. Anyway, we're not in any rush.'

I return the milk to its home and move to the centre of the unit. The back wall is also covered in notes, profiles of victims and suspects, crime scenes and investigations. There are four filing cabinets and shelves full of box and lever-arch files above the sink bench.

'This is a lot of stuff. He'd lose his job if anyone found out about this.'

'It's like Trump's classified documents trove at Mar-a-Lago,' breathes Garth.

Not quite, but also not far off. It's a massive no-no for a copper to take stuff out of the nick. It compromises the chain of evidence, risks falling into the wrong hands and is a huge breach of privacy for all involved. Given the risk, why would Tama do this, and why would he trust us with it? I'm starting to feel the weight of responsibility, and try not to give in to panic. Gangsters, rogue coppers, two soft old booksellers out of the job for over a decade. Are we in way over our heads?

'Are we in way over our heads?' gasps Garth, starting to hyperventilate.

I give him a little shove to bring him back from the brink of a full-blown panic attack.

'I think,' I begin slowly, trying to organise my thoughts, 'that we assume only we and Tama know about this place and its contents, and that he really wants our help because something is well off and he can't sort it through official channels.'

'So he comes to a couple of has-beens?' scoffs Garth, breathing more deeply now.

'Speak for yourself. Also, this is clearly bigger than a cold case we can have a bit of nostalgic fun with. I reckon there is danger, yes, but there might be more if we don't investigate.'

Garth nods, parking his bum on the top of a filing cabinet.

'I am actually going to put the kettle on and we can settle in and have a good look through this stuff, then decide what to do next. There's only one mug, so we'll have to share.'

Garth becomes intent upon reading every word on the Tracey wall, so I start on the nearest filing cabinet; it's one of the smaller ones with only one deep drawer, so not too daunting. Alas, it's practically empty, just an old Yellow Pages and some take-away menus. Over to the double-storey monster it is then.

I prise the mug from Garth's fingers, rest it on top of the monster cabinet and open the top drawer. Bingo. The tabs are labelled with names and locations I already recognise from our initial, scant snooping. I'm immediately drawn to *Franklin White*, written in a surprisingly careful, cursive hand. I grab the folder and retreat to the desk, retaining possession of the coffee.

Inside the folder are various photographs, some crystal clear, some blown out or pixelated. The first shows a man in a grey suit, quite tall and slim, head down, briefcase shielding him from rain as he gets into a car — a nice car, too, looks like a Mercedes, although I'm no expert. His back is to the camera and it's impossible to tell his age or race. The next shows the car driving away — it could be in a Havelock North street, but from the Art Deco buildings and amount of traffic I'm picking Napier or Hastings.

The third photo is the most interesting, and very clear. Two massive-looking men have their backs to the camera, power stance, shoulders hunched as if their arms are crossed, heavy leather waistcoats with the Black Dogs patch. I peer at another two men facing them and the camera, and fetch my reading glasses from my trouser pocket. Same grey suit, same build: white guy, quite handsome, face set in a placatory smile, hands palm out. He's younger, slimmer and his suit is cheaper, but I'd know that entitled smirk anywhere. It's Franklin White. The person standing next to him is also white, taller, thin, hair long with a slightly bohemian feel — he has a tee-shirt underneath his jeans jacket, and it's paired with jeans and Chucks. There's an androgynous, almost Bowie-like look to him. I do a quick Google images search and confirm my suspicion: it's Oddbean all right. So, Franklin, and maybe Oddbean were being surveilled, and unless they were doing some kind of community liaison were in with some pretty dodgy characters.

There are some newspaper clippings in the folder, articles and interviews with Franklin about his run for government. There's one headlined 'Local Politician Turns to Poetry', with a grainy image of Franklin with his arm around . . . yes, it's Tracey. I feel a bit nauseous and put the coffee down. The article revolves around Franklin and what a great guy he must be to sponsor the poetry book. It barely mentions Tracey, the actual person who did all the work and made the opportunities for the poets. There's a load of general information, too, on Franklin's now ex-wife Victoria White: background, education, business deals. Who the hell wrote this?

I leave the folder on the desk and go back to the cabinet to look for an Oddbean folder, and there it is. More photos, this time of the art gallery; news clippings, a menu for the coffee shop even. There's a photo in which Oddbean looks happy rather than cool and moody. He's standing next to a man and woman, both in their mid- to late twenties. Hard to tell if they're a couple or not — the body language is friendly but not too close. Oddbean has his skinny, pale arm draped over the guy's shoulders. He's wearing a tee-shirt with the sleeves cut off and some kind of chain on his left wrist. There's a pendant or charm attached to the chain but I can't make it out. The other guy is shorter than Oddbean, bushy eyebrowed and freckled; he's wearing a green shirt and blue cords. The woman, high cheekboned and bubbly, has her head thrown back and is laughing. It's a lovely photo and makes me smile.

By now Garth has retrieved the coffee and is muttering about backwash and dregs as he flicks though the cabinet.

'Trent Meek,' he murmurs.

'The teacher?'

Garth holds up a couple of pages stapled together. 'Uh, yeah. There's a statement here from someone called Darpita Reddy, a classmate of Tracey.'

'Read it out,' I say.

'Okay. Blah blah blah, student at Te Mata High, was in the same English class as Tracey and the teacher was Mr Meek. Aha. Oh, I see—'

'What?'

'Darpita says she actually saw Meek with his arm around Tracey in the corridor after school, and . . . oh . . . She also says she saw Meek kiss Tracey. She went back into the English room after class as she'd forgotten her assignment sheet and . . . and I quote, "Mr Meek was embracing Tracey. As I entered the room, he planted a kiss on her head. As soon as they saw me, they sprang apart and Tracey pretty much just barged out of the room. Mr Meek played it cool and asked if he could help me but I just wanted to get out of there."'

'Shit. I think we need to visit Mr Meek.'

'I think we do. There's a scribbled note saying he's in Taupō. No actual address.'

'Shouldn't be too hard to find. We were detectives.'

'Let's gather as much of the Tracey stuff as we can and get on home. I'm getting claustrophobic.'

'What? Take stuff out of here?' I ask.

'Yes, I think so. It's not a police station, it's not supposed to be here. Tama clearly wants us to have it and it'll be much more convenient if it's at home. I don't think we'll get raided any time soon.'

We methodically begin to pack up the tragic story of Tracey Jervis, then Garth pauses. 'Do you think Tama could have sent us the book in the envelope?'

CHAPTER 28

Garth: 21 days until Isabella Garrante book launch

Eloise pulls the Tomato to a halt just around the corner from Janet Jervis's villa. On my lap is a shoulder bag containing the envelope and book that were so mysteriously dropped at the shop and started this whole investigation — or started it for us at least. I also have a bundle of Janet's witness statements. And yes, there are more than one — three to be precise — although this is not unusual.

First there would have been a missing person's report. If the officer is on to it, a statement may be taken at that point. Usually, this statement is little more than the description of the misper, when they were last seen, and events leading up to the disappearance if they were out of the ordinary, such as an argument. Then, if the person has not materialised after a couple of days, a more detailed statement is taken. This is the CYA statement, because you are starting to have some concern that this is not just a runaway and so you have to Cover Your Arse in case the wheels come off. The third statement is taken by a detective when it appears more than likely that the misper is a victim of crime. Although at this stage the person giving the statement is not officially a suspect, they actually are, because the police are by nature suspicious and everyone involved is a suspect until proven otherwise. The detective will therefore be trying to get as precise details as possible not only about the misper but also about the movements of the person giving the statement in case they conflict with other accounts or evidence gathered.

Shuffling through the statements, I turn to Eloise. 'Are we going to mention the inconsistencies?'

'We're not supposed to have seen the witness statements.'

'We can't just ignore the fact that in Janet's first statement she doesn't mention any altercation, then in her third statement she recalls that Tracey had argued with her father before going out to meet Prudence for the fireworks.'

'Exactly. In her third statement she recalls it. Tracey's been missing for days and Janet's spent every waking moment thinking about it. She's had time to remember.'

'Or time to rehearse her story.'

Eloise pats her tummy. 'My copper's gut says she's being truthful.'

It's a plausible explanation and Eloise is better at judging these things than I am. 'What about the bag?' I say.

In the first two statements Janet doesn't even mention that Tracey had a bag with her when she left home, even though it was later confirmed to be missing from her room. On the surface, this does not seem untoward, because the bag was never found. However, in the third statement Janet says, 'I am one hundred percent certain that when Tracey left she did not have her school backpack with her', which comes across as forced, unnatural even, as we don't tend to be interested in things the victim doesn't have.

'The date of the third statement places it after Tracey's schoolbooks were found in the Redwoods,' says Eloise.

'They didn't find a schoolbag though.'

'No. But if you're a suspicious detective taking the statement, and you know about the items found in the Redwoods, what are you going to be thinking?'

I drum my fingers against the dashboard. 'That I want to tie Tracey to the bag in case it's later found in the murderer's possession.'

'Exactly, so the D taking the statement pressures Janet to *remember* the bag. Janet is firm in her belief that Tracey didn't have the bag and insists that this is documented in her statement. Hence the clunky inclusion.'

'I still think we shouldn't trust Janet. If she wasn't directly involved, her husband could have been.'

'And he's recently died, so don't go making any undiplomatic accusations.'

'Of course not.' I open the car door. 'You know me.'

'And therein lies the problem.'

As we wait at the front door I cast my eye over the garden. It is not overly large but plenty big enough to bury a body. I'm pretty sure the police would have searched it thoroughly; that said, the police still make mistakes. I remember working with a copper called Cuffer Wallace who early one morning stopped a man walking out of the woods with a spade. The man joked that he had just buried his wife, and Cuffer let him on his way. As it turned out, the man had just buried his wife.

Janet invites us in and I take the same seat as before. I keep the envelope and book hidden in a shoulder bag; it's an old interviewing trick of not letting the suspect know what evidence you have until you choose to reveal it. We've told Janet about the strange delivery to our shop, but she doesn't know what the envelope and book look like — unless she's the one who left them for us. I'm hoping her reaction when we reveal them will give us an idea of whether this is the case.

While Janet busies herself making tea, Eloise browses the books in the front room. She glances towards the kitchen, checking that Janet isn't looking, then hurriedly points towards one of the shelves. I squint at the titles, but the spines are too narrow to be able to make them out. Probably poetry.

'What?' I whisper.

In a frantic, exaggerated gesture, Eloise points to the bookcase again, then mouths something I can't entirely make out — *for frog's sake*, possibly — then she pulls a novel from the top shelf and waves it at me. It's an Isabella Garrante. All of the top shelf are Isabella Garrantes and all in pristine condition.

She shoves the novel back and pretends to be interested in a Lloyd Jones that she hastily pulls from the shelf then slides back into position as Janet rejoins us and places a tea tray on the table.

'Thanks for seeing us again.' I reach into the bag but keep my eyes on Janet. 'We've brought the package we were sent.' I pull out the envelope.

There's a slight raise of her eyebrows but no great show of emotion.

I take out the copy of *See You in September*. Again, Janet barely reacts. I flick slowly through the pages with the highlighted words that spell out the message. Still nothing, until I get to the last page, the one with *TRACEY JERVIS* written in Biro. Then Janet's eyes widen, and she sniffs, taking in a sudden breath.

Eloise places a comforting hand on her arm. 'I'm sorry if it's a bit of shock.'

'No. It's all right. You think you've dealt with these things, that it's all over, until you realise that it isn't.'

'I can't even begin to imagine.' Eloise removes her hand so that Janet can drink her tea.

I wish we could have videoed the interview so that later we can rewatch that moment to try to interpret the response. Janet definitely reacted more strongly to the handwritten words than the highlighted text. Could this be the handwriting of Tracey's killer? Is that what Janet has just realised?

Not for the first time I feel guilty about re-investigating the case and opening up old wounds.

Eloise gestures to the envelope and book. 'Does this mean anything to you?'

'She didn't join a cult, if that's what you're implying,' says Janet, clearly familiar with the book's plot.

I take the book back and try a new tack. As I replace the novel, I manoeuvre the envelope so that the writing on the front faces Janet. She catches sight of it — and again her breathing changes. Her response is less marked than before, but it's there, I'm certain of it. I glance at Eloise to see if she noticed, too. It appears not. Her attention is once again focused on the bookshelves.

'Kitty at the shop said that you're a bit of a poet?'

'I dabble. Just for my own enjoyment. I've never been published, not like Tracey.'

'How did you feel about that? The poetry book, I mean?' asks Eloise.

'At first, I was so proud of her.'

'At first?'

'No, I'm still proud. Only if she'd never done the poetry book, Franklin White would never have got his hooks into her.'

'You think Franklin is to blame?' Eloise again places a comforting hand on Janet's arm.

'Him and Tracey's father. Neither could just let her be a schoolgirl.'

Eloise flashes me a look that tells me not to interrupt. I take a sip of my tea instead, letting the pause in conversation lengthen. I become acutely aware of the click, click, click of the second hand of a clock from the kitchen. Eloise must be doing her swede: she hates ticking clocks.

'Tracey's father, he always pushed her too hard — with school-work, with sport, with the poetry book — and in the end he pushed her away from us.'

I ball one hand into a fist, digging my fingernails into my palm to stop me from asking if she thought Tracey's father was more directly responsible. Eloise would never forgive me. Instead, I dwell on Janet's strange phrasing: *Tracey's father.* Not Kelvin, not even *my husband*, but every time *Tracey's father.* Odd.

CHAPTER 29

Eloise: 20 days until Isabella Garrante book launch

It's the last Thursday of the month, so I grab a poetry book from the shop shelf and package it up addressed to 'A brave Uncommon Poet'. We sponsor the monthly open mic, Uncommon Poets, at The Uncommon Room. The bar is a magnet for anyone who needs a safe and welcoming place to hang, and for those who scribble their heart's rages and desires tonight will be a blessed release. Garth is not joining me, claiming to have a lead on Prudence to investigate. He was not forthcoming on the details, so I suspect it was an excuse to avoid the poetry.

The main bar is a long, narrow affair with art painted straight onto the concrete walls, dim lighting, a disco ball and many twinkly lights. There are couches and crazy old brocade chairs, a plethora of living plants hanging from the ceiling despite the lack of sunlight, and a mix of punters young and old, strait-laced and flamboyant, human and canine. The poetry crew is already there, putting poets' names in the hat to be drawn out randomly during the course of the evening to determine the order of performance. One day I will put my own name down, but not yet.

I wander over. Instantly I feel thumbs press deeply into the knot of muscle in my shoulders and a painful but quite amazing sensation takes me over, making my knees buckle a little. It can only be the landlord, Gordon, Garth's Dungeons & Dragons mate.

'Gordon, my friend,' I say.

The kneading turns into a bear hug and Gordon says, 'Have you got a poem tonight?'

'Nah. I'm a listener and a lurker. Hey, that would be a good first line. Maybe I should make a poem out of all the first lines I come up with.'

'Do it. Do you want a drink?'

I order a beer brewed just around the corner. More hugs and smiles from the regular crew gearing up for an evening in which the poetry ranges from hilarious to political, heartwarming to heartbreaking, A for Amazing to E for Effort. It doesn't matter if it's any good. Tonight's MC, Siobhan, sashays up to the stage, a glass of wine in one lace-gloved hand and the hat of names in the other; I manage to plop this month's book into the hat as she passes.

'Say luuurve,' she commands, facing the crowd, arms outstretched. The crowd obeys, gleefully. I don't, because this kind of thing makes me die inside.

Siobhan kicks off with one of her own poems, a new one, uncharacteristically soppy she tells us. It is, as always, moving, raw and deeply honest. The first name out of the hat is Davey, an Uncommon Poets virgin, and up he comes looking nervous as calls of 'Yeah Davey' follow him. He performs hesitantly, stuttering and stumbling, offering a glimpse of his life, the mess inside his head, the light offered by his friends. It's clumsy, but lovely, and when the crowd goes wild he leaves the stage about ten feet taller, and is embraced back at his table by a couple of mates and a lady who has to be his mum. That's why I love this place. We cheer and encourage and gasp and click our fingers (not me; again, no way) as poet after poet takes the stage.

At half time, I seek out Eleanor because, of course, I have an agenda.

Eleanor is in her eighties, about four feet nine, with a mind so sharp it'd cut you soon as look at you. She suffers no fools, but is kind, and I'm confident she'll know about Tracey and the poetry book from back in the day. I eventually spot her talking up at Rima, who must have a foot and a half on her. I walk over and lurk.

'What do you want?' Eleanor turns her head and snaps.

'I want to pick your brains.'

'Not much left but you're welcome to them. Let's go next door. I need to sit down and get away from this bloody racket and I've bored Rima enough.'

We move through to the adjoining room.

'I don't see you for months and now you turn up wanting my brains. Typical.' Eleanor tosses her dark bob, not a streak of grey despite her years.

'I was here last month,' I counter.

'Well, I wasn't,' she replies, and I leave it there. You can't argue with her.

I ask a few questions about Ron, and the children and grand-children, but Eleanor knows I'm after something.

'Stop the small talk, it's really not you. What do you want?'

'Tracey Jervis,' I reply.

'Oh! I wasn't expecting that. What about her?'

'You knew her?'

'Yes, and her mum. Her dad was a complete prick, but Janet is all right. Still see her around. Bloody awful business. You never get over losing a child.'

We let that thought sit for a moment. Eleanor has suffered tragedy in her past, too.

'Soooo . . . you know Garth and I were coppers ages ago?'

'Back when you were young and vivacious? Yes, I know that.'

'Err, yeah. Well, we're kind of looking into Tracey's disappearance, just to see if we can shed any light.'

'Why on earth would you do that?'

'Long story, but someone asked us if we'd lay new eyes on it.'

'Huh. Well, if anyone can find out what happened it will be you and that bloke of yours. Smart people. What shall I tell you?'

'Everything, please.'

'Ha! Well. I mentored Tracey a bit through the local poetry group we had before all these hippy witchy young ones took over the world. And thank god they did. She was a bright thing, Tracey, and not a bad poet. Her themes were very navel gazing, as young people tend to be. She tried a couple of Plathesque daddy poems, confirming my opinion of the prick, and I was a little troubled about one or two of the others, but she definitely had something.'

'Troubled by the daddy poems?'

'Well, yes, but we all knew he was a horror. It was the love poems, if you'd call them that. She'd made them all allegorical — a young sapling swaying in the breeze being overcome by a mature tree, that sort of nonsense — but when you looked at what she was saying, it was young girl falls for older bloke. It was a bit yuck.'

'Did you ask her about them?'

'Yes, of course. She said she was just playing with literary tropes — *Lolita*, the allure of age and power and all that — but it still gave me the willies. I mentioned it to her mother, and when Tracey found that out she cut me off. Ghosted me, in the modern parlance.'

'What did Janet say?'

'She was mortified about the daddy stuff, Tracey airing the dirty family laundry in public, and a bit confused about the older man nonsense. Put it down to adolescent imaginings and the general idiocy of youth. I knew it was a betrayal of Tracey's trust to tell Janet, but I was concerned about it, and you really don't bugger about when a young person might be in danger. For all the good that did us.' Eleanor sighs and looks so sad that for a moment I'm reluctant to continue the questions. Only for a moment though.

'Franklin White?' I say.

'That's what I thought. Creepy bastard. I could tell that Tracey admired him — that was obvious with the poetry book sponsorship and then her going to work for him on his campaign. The allure of power all right. Janet said she'd keep an eye on him, and I backed off. I'd said my piece.'

'Do you have copies of Tracey's poems, by any chance?'

'I do. I'm a bloody hoarder, and I wanted copies in case I got really worried about her. Didn't get a chance though, did I. Will you take them?'

'Yes please.'

Eleanor necks her wine, slams the glass down and forces herself to her feet. 'Oh! Stood up too quickly.' She grips the edge of the table. 'I hope it's my name out of that bloody hat soon. Nearly past my bedtime.' She dismisses me with a flap of the hand and bustles off back into the bar.

I wander after her in time to hear Siobhan introduce part two and shout, 'Eleanor!'

'Thank fuck for that,' comes the reply.

I decide to slip away.

I'm rounding the corner to where I've abandoned the Tomato when my phone trills. As Garth says, I can't walk and chew gum, so I stop to take the call.

'Kia ora, Tama.'

'Oh hey. Sorry to call so late but something was niggling at me about that house in Waipuk, so I hopped onto the database and, well, 32 Pikitea Street was the scene of a sudden death about a year ago.'

'What happened? Who died?'

'The occupant of the house. A . . . Belinda Henare, forty-nine years old, single, lived alone. Unclear as to what happened. It's still Eastern District but I didn't work this one so can't tell you much more at this stage.'

'Okay.' I make a sudden decision. 'I'll go on out to have a look. Thanks for the info.'

'Wait. What? Now?'

'Yeah. I'm in Hastings. Might as well noodle out that way and have a look.'

'There won't be anything to see now, Eloise, you know that.'

'Maybe. But I won't sleep tonight if I don't see the place with my own eyes. Really appreciate your help, mate. I'm sure I'll be grilling you again soon.'

'No, wait, Eloise.'

'What?' I hear a heavy sigh.

'It could be dangerous.'

'Dangerous?'

'I'll see you there in about an hour. Just promise you'll wait for me.'

CHAPTER 30

Garth: 20 days until Isabella Garrante book launch

My knuckles strike the varnished wood with something approaching the force of a 6am arrest warrant execution. This is not the front door of some low-life wanted by the courts; it's the home of Prudence's classmate referred to in the podcast which I managed to blag after a bit of back and forth and a white lie that I would go on the show and talk about the Pinter case. Bloody Pinter. I still can't shake the feeling that he's somehow involved. I've tried to play it down for Eloise's sake, but he's like a devil on my shoulder, always there, always whispering.

The house is a new build on one of the recently developed estates. The painted weatherboard is fresh, the front garden an immaculate arrangement of lawn, gravel and concrete. There is no planting to speak of, no interesting statues or features, no pots of flowers, just a blank canvas that no one has bothered to paint. Incongruously, a rubber doormat says welcome.

I have no authority here, no uniform or warrant card to *encourage* cooperation. To get the information needed I'm going to have to rely on my natural charm and good nature, which for some reason caused Eloise a great deal of concern. She tried to insist on coming with me, and would have done so were it not for her commitment at Uncommon Poets.

Beyond the door's frosted glass a hall light flicks on, showing a figure in silhouette. I take a step back so as not to crowd the doorstep — the opposite of what I would have done in the police, where a size nine hastily forced into a partially open door often saved the need for a sledgehammer.

The door swings inwards and I'm confronted by one of our customers, Beige Dave. The name is somewhat kinder than Amelia's suggestion of Fifty Shades of Beige, a nod to both his clothing and his predilection for the saucier end of the Sci-fi and Fantasy bookshelves. Judging by his tan canvas trousers and camel shirt, it appears that even at home he is committed to his uninspiring dress regime. The only signs of colour are his fluffy slippers which stray dangerously close to peach.

'Mr Sherlock?' His surprise matches my own.

I recover quickly, having over the years become accustomed to a variety of front-door revelations, including some quite literal ones. And I know not to prevaricate. 'Hi, Dave. I need to pop in and have a chat about Tracey Jervis because of some research I'm doing.' My wording is deliberate, *need* implying an immediate pressing requirement, and the addition of a *because* clause scientifically proven to make the request harder to refuse.

Dave has never struck me as having a huge amount of backbone, and I square my shoulders and lift a foot as if about to enter. As I hoped, he capitulates. 'Oh. You'd better come in then.'

The hall corridor is what an interior designer might describe as

Muted Mushroom and what I would describe as beige; the walls in the front room are Tuscan (beige), the carpet Blanched Almond (beige) and the sofa Pale Latte (beige).

'Thanks for taking the time to see me,' I say, as if this was some pre-arranged meeting.

Dave gestures for me to sit on the sofa, and eases into a well-worn La-Z-Boy that has an X-Box controller and TV remote wedged in a side pocket. The room is minimalistic with a large LED TV central on one wall, flanked by two tall speakers that are spaced with an eye to precision and symmetry that I appreciate. Beneath the TV I count three different game consoles and a Sky Box. The dream set-up for a single twenty-something male feels a little sad for a man of forty-plus. The one point of interest is a framed Sisters of Mercy poster on an adjacent wall. It features the cover of the album *Floodland* and adds a splash of colour, if you can count black as a colour.

Making a mental note to ask about the poster later, I launch straight in. 'You were in the same class as Tracey and Prudence, yes?'

'That was all a long time ago.' Dave's fingers tighten over the arm of the La-Z-Boy.

I already know that he was in English and several other classes with the girls, so a simple yes would have sufficed rather than dodging the question.

I put my hands into the pocket of my hoodie, where they connect with my Dictaphone. It's one I proffed from the job back in the day, and which I modified to be totally silent to operate. In the UK Police you had to fill in reams of paperwork and get a magistrate's authority to secretly record someone. As a civilian it's as simple as pressing the record button.

'Probably the sort of thing you remember though?' I encourage.

'Yeah, a girl in your class gets murdered, you don't forget.'

'You think she was murdered?'

'Don't see another explanation.' Dave rubs his nose. Which could signal unease or just be an itch.

I lean forward. 'Who do you think did it?'

Dave shrugs, then lets his shoulders fall. 'That's one for the police, isn't it?'

'You must have some theories.' I point my hand towards him, fingers flat and extended.

'Lots of the kids thought it was Mr Meek. He had to leave in the end.' Dave's avoiding answering again.

'But what do you think?'

'Probably some stranger.'

'Really? I heard you thought it was Prudence.'

Dave squirms in his chair. 'Who told you that? I hardly knew her.'

'She was in your class.'

'With thirty other kids.' Dave folds his arms. I may have pushed him too hard.

'True. I can hardly remember most of the kids I went to school with.'

I lean back, less aggressive, less confronting. He definitely knows more than he's telling.

'Is that it then?' he says. 'Are we done?'

'I think so. Thanks.' I push myself up from the sofa, then gesture to the poster. 'You a Sisters fan?'

'Used to be.'

'What's your favourite track?'

Dave tilts his head, eyeing the poster. '"Lucretia My Reflection".'

'Yeah, the opening riff, classic. "This Corrosion" is mine.' My body moves almost of its own accord in something approaching dancing. 'I got well sweaty at Rock City when they played that one.'

'You saw them live?' For the first time there is a bit of colour to

Beige Dave, as if someone has given him an adrenaline shot. His eyes sparkle.

'A couple of times. What was Prudence's favourite track? "Dominion", I bet?'

'No, she loved "Driven Like the Snow".' A momentary trance of remembrance overcomes Dave, a half-smile on his lips.

'You knew Prudence better than you've let on, didn't you?'

Dave's focus snaps back to the now, aware he's been caught in a lie. He sinks into the La-Z-Boy. 'We had . . .' He thrusts his hands between his thighs. 'I don't know what we had. Something. Nothing. You could never tell with Prudence. There was a maze behind those beautiful blue eyes, one that only Tracey could navigate.'

'Is that why you told the podcast people that you thought she killed Tracey?'

'I never said that.' Dave's fists clench.

'What did you say? I want to know the truth.' An olive branch, an opportunity to set the record straight.

The silence extends, but I'm good at silence.

'Okay. Look. I'll tell you everything, even the stuff I didn't tell them. Only — don't jump to any conclusions.'

CHAPTER 31

Eloise: 20 days until Isabella Garrante book launch

32 Pikitea Street. It's an L-shaped wooden house on the outskirts of the town heading out towards the Pōrangahau Road, a gravel drive snaking through an overgrown lawn, a concrete patio leading to a boarded-up front door. There's a 'For Sale' sign up on the knackered fence.

I put the handbrake on but keep the car engine running. There are lights across a paddock but no close neighbours. I realise I'm glad Tama's coming. What was I thinking, rushing off into the night like this?

There's a ping on my phone.

Garth: What the hell are you up to? Garth.

Oh shit.

> Me: Was just about to text you love. Will be a bit later than I said.

> Garth: Yes. Tama told me where you're going. Bad idea. Come home. Garth.

Tama said? What a snitch. Then I see what I've done. Garth's still shaken by the altercation with the Black Dog dudes and is worried for my safety — no wonder he's so brusque. But I'm here now, so I'll try a bit of reassurance.

> Me: Tama just pulling up now. Won't be long.

It's a lie, but Tama's due any minute so it isn't a big one.

There is stony silence on the end of the text line, and I imagine a middle-aged bookseller in Havelock North, bottom lip out, forehead concertinaed, in a right old sulk. I am in trouble. He can tell me all about his Prudence rabbit hole when I get home, and I will nod encouragingly.

Meantime, I have this spooky house to worry about. I open my phone browser, look up Belinda Henare and scan through the original reports of her death. Neighbours describe her as a quiet woman, a school librarian who lived alone. A later article entitled 'Who was Belinda Henare?' crops up on the *Waipuk Watch*, a blog run by the local Neighbourhood Watch coordinator:

> Ms Henare was a member of Waipukurau Writhe of Writers and had published several short stories and picture books for children which she also illustrated.

I click the link to a webpage about a local makers' market. There's a picture of a smiling woman behind a trestle table covered in books. It's Belinda selling spiral-bound copies of *Kev the Kea Investigates* and

Warwick the Weka Steals a Sandwich. And then the dread creeps in as I make the connection. I imagine a manuscript covered in Pinter's red scrawl, savage comments destroying the dreams and smiles of lovely librarians like Belinda.

Tyres crunch on gravel nearby and I sit up so violently the seatbelt lock engages, pinning me in place. With panicked fingers I battle to release myself, unable to turn. A car door thunks, followed by the scraunch of boots. A familiar face appears at my window.

'What are you doing?'

I release the breath I didn't know I was holding and finally manage to free myself before scrambling out.

'Tama, hi. I was just dicking around on my phone and you startled me.' I try for a laugh but a strangled mewl comes out. 'You didn't have to come out here. I, ah, realise that maybe I could have waited until tomorrow.'

'Ah well, I was out Hastings way. And who doesn't love a spooky house in the wops at dark o'clock, yeah?' He huffs little clouds of warm, condensing breath as he bounces on the balls of his feet. 'Come on then.'

I lock the Tomato in case anyone dives into the back seat only to pop out and murder me on my way home, and Tama turns on a sturdy-looking flashlight. I'm glad one of us is prepared.

There's not much to see at the boarded-up front of the house, so we follow the crazy-paved path around to the back. The windows at the rear are net curtained, presumably for shade rather than privacy, as there's no other house in view. Tama shines the torch through to empty rooms, onto nylon shaggy carpet in an unwise shade of cream. I can almost smell the desolation, as if the house is in mourning.

'Looks like it's been cleared,' says Tama. 'Let's have a look at the garage.'

There's a single garage with a rusty-looking roller door very close to the house. It doesn't appear to be padlocked, so we take an end of the door each and heave.

There are many, many cobwebs and a disgruntled rustling in the far corner. The space has been pretty much cleared out, but a couple of boxes have been dumped as if someone was going to load them up but forgot them at the last minute.

I poke at one of them. It's sealed with packing tape, so I pull my car key out to attack it.

'This is an illegal search,' says Tama.

'Okaaaaay?'

'Just saying it out loud.' He shrugs, so I turn back to my felonious forage and split the tape. I remove a slightly mildewed copy of *Pāora the Pūteketeke Goes Poaching*. Looks like there are about fifty copies in each box.

'What's that all about?' says Tama.

'Belinda wrote books for children, about native birds.'

'Is that relevant to us?'

'Could be.' Although I'm not convinced, seeing as we've found nothing. What are we even doing here in the middle of the night?

'I feel like we're missing something,' I say.

'Letterbox,' says Tama. 'Pinter sent a book, yeah?'

I trail him past our cars to the fence on which sits a box that looks like it was knocked up in a school's hard technology room. I open the back and pick out wads of wrinkled junk mail and a post bag addressed to Belinda Henare. It's from a bookshop in Wellington: Mary's Cat.

'Oh god, Tama, this is it. The book Pinter sent. Why would he send it here after she died?'

'What's the book?' he asks. I rip open the post bag and pull out a copy of *The Cause of Death*. A Mary's Cat business card slips from inside the cover, fluttering to the muddy drive. A message in red

Biro stares up at me from the card's blank back. *Happy Anniversary!*

'Give it here,' says Tama. 'It's been handled by loads of people by now but it's still evidence. We have a locked-up crim in the UK sending a book on New Zealand crime to the house of a dead woman in the next town along from the copper who put him away. It stinks.'

'What the hell is going on?'

'I have no clue. So much for my days off. I'd better get on to the officer that handled Belinda's death and let them know how weird this has got. We'll probably need to speak to your old team leader, too.'

'You won't be asking us back for dinner will you,' I say.

'Hah, don't worry about that. This is the most intriguing thing that's happened to me for a while. It's your husband you want to worry about upsetting.'

'Oh yes. Thanks for dobbing me in.'

'No regrets. You should be more careful with all this crap going on.' His face is stern, and I take the telling off because I know I deserve it.

'Eloise, I need you to back off looking into what this Pinter guy is up to. Just leave it with me for now, eh.'

I nod, relieved that he's taking the load, for now at least.

The cross look on his face turns to a thoughtful one.

'I think we need to confirm Belinda Henare's cause of death.'

CHAPTER 32

Garth: 20 days until Isabella Garrante book launch

Stevie races downstairs, the white tip of his tail swishing from side to side, a metronome of joy. I'm happy to see Eloise home safe, too, but it doesn't stop me from being angry. 'What were you thinking?'

It would be too much to expect Eloise to look contrite, and she doesn't disappoint. 'It was fine, Tama was there.'

'It isn't fine. Tama's a good bloke, but he's still only one copper cruising his last few years until retirement. The last time Pinter was involved we had two surveillance teams, the police helicopter, and the Tactical Support Group watching over you and it still—'

'I know. I was there.'

Knees creaking, I descend the last few stairs, then throw my arms around her, pressing my face into her hair. 'You muppet.'

Stevie presses his own face into the rear of my jeans, cutting the hug short. I push his snoot away. 'Thanks Steve-a-woo.' He looks up at me with eyes that I choose to believe are remorseful, although deep down I suspect he has no shits to give.

Eloise cups a hand to her ear. 'What's that? Do I hear a large glass of syrah calling my name?'

'Yeah, it's probably looking for its three friends that went missing last night.' I give Eloise's hand a squeeze. 'Go cuddle Stevie. I'll get the wine.'

A half bottle and a can of Coke later, I'm caught up on Eloise's adventures both at Uncommon Poets and at the house in Waipuk. We're propped on pillows on the bed in the spare room which is doubling as the incident room. Stevie is cuddled up between us, snoring. His silky head rests on my leg where his dribble is leaving a dark stain on my jeans. I don't mind. I'm just happy to have my family safe and together.

'And you're certain it's Pinter's doing?' I say.

'Nothing's certain where Pinter's involved. That's why I'm going to get Paula to do a prison visit and interview him.'

I stare at the incident board and hesitate before responding. 'Maybe you should hold off on talking to Paula.'

'Why? I need to know what's going on.'

'And talking to Pinter isn't going to help with that. The man lies like a knock-off watch.' Tracey, Pinter, Prudence. There's something important here if only I can grasp it, but the salient detail remains elusive. 'Let's park Pinter for a moment.'

Eloise necks the remains of her third glass. 'I'm not leaving this.'

'Well, let me tell you about my evening, then we'll get back to Pinter.' I pull my Dictaphone from my pocket and fast forward to where the conversation got interesting.

'You know you can get an app that does that?' says Eloise.

I'm sure she's right. Only an app is so difficult to operate without looking at the screen, whereas even hidden in my pocket I can stop and start the tiny device by touch alone. I hit play, and Eloise leans in, concentrating on the muffled conversation in which the weary relief of Dave's voice can be heard:

'Look, Prudence was weird, right. She didn't have many friends. Only Tracey really, and then me as a poor substitute on the occasions she fell out with her.'

'Did they fall out a lot?'

'It had become more frequent. Prudence hated Tracey's dad, said he was too controlling, but things got worse when Tracey got involved with an older man.'

'Franklin White?'

'I'm not saying that, even off the record.'

'What happened then?'

'Prudence got properly upset. I mean she'd always been obsessed with death, had books on serial killers, and kept bleached bird and rat skulls, full on craycray, right. But after Fr—, the man, she started writing these stories.'

'What kind of stories?'

'The first ones were basically all the same with the gothic heroine rescuing her friend from the evil lord. Then they got darker, with the heroine killing the villain, who was either a vampire or a pirate or a criminal mastermind. And then something changed, they became more visceral. The heroine discovered she had been betrayed and so the friend had to die too.'

'Fuck!' Eloise pauses, wine glass midway to her mouth.

I stop the Dictaphone. 'He goes on to say that he thinks Prudence loved Tracey too much to actually kill her but he couldn't rule it out.'

'And he didn't tell the police this. Why?'

'The obvious answer is that he had a thing for Prudence, but I think it's a bit more complicated than that.'

'How so?'

'Prudence told him Tracey was frightened of the police, thought Franklin had someone on the inside.'

'Do we think Prudence might have done it?' Eloise glugs more wine into her glass.

'She has to be more of a suspect now.' I manoeuvre Stevie's head from my leg and shuffle to the end of the bed. From the rack beneath the whiteboard I pick up a red pen and uncap it.

'Give it here.' Eloise shuffles to join me and claims the red pen. I'm not allowed to write on the board because my handwriting is terrible, whereas she has perfect whiteboard technique. In beautiful cursive she writes 'suspect' above Prudence, then adds 'stories of murder' underneath.

'And how does Pinter fit into all this?' Eloise caps the pen and places it back in its one true home on the pen rack.

My thoughts on the matter haven't fully crystallised, being more at the seed-crystal stage. I start to scratch my head, then stop. 'Maybe he doesn't. Maybe he has nothing to do with the envelope and book delivered to the bookshop.'

'Really? That would be a hell of a coincidence.'

'Not necessarily.' More layers solidify around the crystal. 'You only contacted Paula because you jumped to the conclusion that it was Pinter, but—'

'It is him.' Eloise folds her arms. 'We have the phone call from prison and his name given at Mary's Cat bookshop.'

'Yes, that book and the Waipuk thing might be him, only we would never have known about it if we hadn't been delivered the other book and told to investigate.'

'Pinter's not connected to the Tracey Jervis case?'

'I don't think so. Why would he get a book sent to Waipuk by a bookshop if he has someone in Hawke's Bay who can doctor a copy of *See You in September* and hand deliver it to the shop?'

'For that matter, why bother phoning a New Zealand bookshop, why not just use the evil Amazon?' Eloise gives a little laugh that holds no humour. 'I don't see Pinter as the ethically responsible type.'

'Because, ultimately, he wants a trail that leads back to him.'

'Which means Pinter's up to something that's nothing to do with Tracey and we've stumbled across it.' Eloise reaches for the wine bottle, then realises that it's empty.

'And that puts us ahead of the game.'

Eloise lays the bottle on its side and gives it a spin. 'Only we don't know what that game is.'

CHAPTER 33

Eloise: 19 days until Isabella Garrante book launch

I'm feeling more than a little raw this morning. I'm not sure what makes me so convinced that I should rush off and do the things I do. Sometimes it turns out really well, but this time, I don't know. What did I actually achieve by haring off to Waipuk? It's alerted Tama to the fact that something well dodgy probably happened to Belinda, so that's a good thing. It's put Pinter firmly back in my head and turned my life upside down. That's not a good thing.

The shop is all mine this morning. I open up, write a new message on the chalkboard — *New Brando Sando out today!* — and try to find invoices in the emails that distributors have neglected to pop in the box, even though it says 'invoice enclosed'. It all feels so normal, but when I let my thoughts creep from the immediate task, I know that nothing is normal and the life we've created is under threat.

After a rather robust conversation with Garth, I've promised Tama that I'll back off. If Belinda's death is suspicious, Tama, as a DI, may have a crime to investigate and new leads to follow. A case that's been dead for twenty years is one thing, but he can't have a civvy poking around in an active investigation on his watch; he's already having to retrofit our night-time adventures to make them legit, and I can't drop him into an even more unworkable situation by continuing to snoop. It's not my business — though is absolutely my business if Pinter has anything to do with it.

I realise I'm banging around when I slam the door into the stock room and there's a yelp from somewhere at the front of the shop.

'Good morning!' I call, manoeuvring around boxes to come out from behind the counter. 'Sorry about that — the wind must have taken . . . oh, hello, Janet.'

Janet Jervis emerges from behind a card stand.

'Morning. Am I your first customer? I'm out and about early, couldn't sleep, so I'm just looking for cards. You know how you should get them when you see them and . . .' She trails off, arms falling to her sides as a lone tear slides down her cheek.

'Come on up, Janet. The kettle's just boiled.'

I grab the tissue box and set it down on the table, indicating that she should take the comfy chair. She eases herself in, dabs her eyes and crumples. I feel ashamed. I have not lost a child and a husband. I have not been devastated by grief and uncertainty. I'm having my head fucked with by a serial killer, yes, but I know exactly where he is and right this moment I am safe — probably. Still, it feels right that she should have come in this morning. There is some comfort in the two of us, bits of human flotsam, temporarily shored up in a beautiful bookshop haven in Havelock North.

'She was such a bright child. Always asking questions, you know: why is the sky blue today, Mummy? Why do I have to go to bed? Why this, why that. It drives you mad when they're little.' Briefly, she smiles. 'Life could have been so different for Tracey. And for me. If all this hadn't happened.'

'Where did it start to go wrong, do you think?' I ask.

'Early teens, I suppose, when high school starts to get serious. It was just too much. Her father's constant goal-setting and micro-managing. The more she tried to be independent with the poetry book and knocking about with Prudence the more he pulled her back in, squashed any spark of life in her. She was on this Earth to do what he wanted, that's all.' She's pulling bits of tissue apart, creating a tiny snowstorm on her lap.

'What did he do when he suspected her of straying? Did he think she was messing around with Franklin White?'

'He certainly got more controlling, constantly setting curfews and demanding to know where she'd been, who was there, what was said. It was obsessive.'

'Was he like that with you, too?'

She looks up at me, defensive.

'Yes, yes, he was, and I know, I'm weak, I should have done something about it, got help, so he didn't do the same to my daughter.' A sob escapes, a violent rush of emotion. The tissue snowstorm flutters to the floor.

'That's not what I meant, Janet. I can only imagine how hard it was for you to see that behaviour transferring to Tracey.'

Her breath is hitching. She looks me straight in the eye, searching for something.

'I had no one to talk to about it. He isolated us. The men at church group thought he was the most amazing family man, but the women, they sensed it, and instead of rallying round they ignored it, ignored Tracey and me like we were to blame for our own situation. And when Tracey went missing, he got the sympathy and I had failed as a mother.'

'I can't imagine what you went through. It's not fair in so many ways.'

'Thank you for that. I just needed someone to listen. He blamed me for not keeping an eye on her, of course. I told him then, told him it was all his fault, that his behaviour had made her leave.'

'How did he react to that?'

'He barely spoke to me for the remainder of our marriage.' Janet gasps out a contemptuous laugh. 'It was a relief, actually.'

I nod, and brace myself to ask the difficult question.

'Janet, could your husband have hurt Tracey?'

I am surprised by a smile. 'It's not a new theory, Eloise. The police were all over that. No. Even after everything that came afterwards, the questions and insinuations — they always look at the family first, don't they?'

'They do. Quite often it is . . .'

'It wasn't him. He was with me all evening. Clockwatching and ranting that Tracey had broken her curfew.' Janet scrunches the remains of the tissue in her fist. 'Of course, for the police a wife's alibi has little standing.'

'Do you think Franklin White hurt her?'

Janet lets out a little laugh. 'That man. Something happened, and he got away with it, just like he always does.' Her colour is high. 'That's why I'm glad someone's got you on to it. You have the skills without the constraints the police had.'

'Well . . .'

'Maybe we'll finally get some justice.'

I'm saved then by the rumble of a trolley as Meryl shambles up the ramp and round the corner.

'Oh sorry, sorry, didn't realise you were in a meeting. I've come for the Yorkies.' She heads for the counter, neck straining to see if anyone else is around.

'It's just me, Meryl, I won't be a tick.'

Janet stands when I do and surprises me with a quick, tight hug.

'I have faith in you,' she says, and leaves, scattering drifts of tissue.

I remain where I am. My head is full of Pinter, my roiling heart is full of Tracey. I could do with a gin but it's only 8.45am.

'Yorkies please, Eloise. Just that one today. I'll be back next week for at least one of the others.'

'Yes, Meryl, of course.' I ferret around on the Meryl shelf and find the right calendar.

'You all right? Did that woman upset you? I've seen her somewhere before I think . . .'

'I'm fine thanks, Meryl love, just got a lot on my mind.'

'Always something going on in this tiny place,' she says. 'You think it's a sleepy little village but there's drama everywhere.'

Oh, Meryl, you have no idea.

CHAPTER 34

Garth: 14 days until Isabella Garrante book launch

Over the ten years we have been running the bookshop, the local Business Association has gone through numerous iterations. Under some regimes we would meet monthly for a social get-together to chat with other retailers and discuss any problems and possible solutions. Under other steerage we would meet twice a year, once for the AGM and once for the Village awards ceremony, at which I am proud to say our little bookshop consistently won the Village's favourite retailer until they stopped putting it to a public vote, which seemed somewhat counterintuitive.

Currently we are somewhere between the two formats. As well as having the AGM and awards, we meet informally a few times a year at one of the local hostelries. Hence Eloise and I find ourselves mingling in the courtyard to the rear of Piku Chew, a Japanese fusion restaurant which Eloise and I both love. Here a number of eateries cluster around the common courtyard, which has at its centre a circular wooden bench surrounding a budding cherry blossom tree. Adding to the idyllic ambience, deep-green fig vines intertwined with fairy lights run the length of a wide alley to the entrance on Joll Road.

A few association members sit chatting at tables. Others stand about in groups, sharing gossip and making the most of the free drinks and sushi platters. I stick close to Eloise, partly because I'm terrible at small talk and partly because too many loud bangs during my time in the Marines have left me somewhat deaf. In crowds like this it's incredibly difficult to filter out words from the general hubbub, and I often find myself nodding dumbly in what I hope are the appropriate places. Eloise claims it is selective hearing, although the fact that I am totally oblivious to the incessant chirping chorus of cicadas on a warm summer evening adds some credence to my story.

I keep an eye out for the owners of Red Vines. I know IFG insisted on the bookshop as the venue for her launch, but I wonder if she understands how small and unsuitable it really is. I figure if I can get my proposal to use the winery fully fleshed out as an alternative, she may be persuaded to reconsider.

Unfortunately, the vintners have yet to show, so we are currently chatting dogs with the Design and Copy crew who do all of our printing for events. A supremely friendly Labrador often hangs out behind their counter.

'Yes, we tried the Mark Vette method,' says Eloise, gesticulating with the rather colourful strawberry sour cocktail that she clenches in one hand. 'But Stevie was just terrified of the clicker and hid under the bed whenever he heard the click-click, so it was a bit of a bust for us.'

A large black SUV with tinted windows pulls up at the end of the alley. The rear passenger door opens, and a man wearing a light-blue shirt, pale chinos, deck shoes and a straw fedora steps out. I have no doubt who it is. An unsettling feeling creeps over me, like when you're gossiping about someone and they walk into the room.

As the owner of Oddbeans, Franklin has every right to be here, and if the rumours about him wanting to run for council are true, then a meeting like this provides him with an ideal opportunity to press the flesh with an abundance of true-blue voters who may be swayed towards his more right-wing machinations. Well, fair enough, but he won't have counted on me and Eloise. Now he's here, we should take the opportunity to ask him about Tracey, especially as he's been ducking our attempts to contact him.

Snaffling a juice from a passing waiter, I loop my free arm through Eloise's. 'Nice to catch up with you guys,' I say to the Design and Copy crew. 'If you'll excuse us there's someone we need to talk to.'

Eloise flashes me a puzzled look as I guide her away.

'Franklin White,' I whisper. 'Over there.'

'We can't question him here.'

'Why not?' I appreciate that I don't always understand social etiquette, but this seems like an ideal chance.

'He's hardly likely to be forthcoming in such a public venue.'

'He's unlikely to be forthcoming whatever the setting, don't you think?'

Making a face which I've come to associate with conflicted uncertainty, Eloise says, 'I suppose if he's uncomfortable he might let something slip or might finally agree to a meeting with us in private.'

'So, we're doing this?'

Eloise's face hardens, and now it's her dragging me by the arm. 'We're doing this.'

One of the things I've always loved about Eloise is that once she's committed to something there's no stopping her. She's like a bottle-rocket. If you light the blue touch paper, you'd better stand back and enjoy the fireworks.

Franklin has sleazed his way into a group of immaculately groomed women from one of the Village's many beauty salons. They're smiling as he jokes about needing cement rather than Botox for his face. And to be fair to them, they were probably all too young to remember the Tracey Jervis case.

I'm certain he catches sight of us as we approach and angles his body away. Eloise is having none of it, manoeuvring us into the group so that we're standing directly in front of him.

'Franklin.' She holds out a hand in a gesture of civility which I know must be killing her inside. 'We're Eloise and Garth from Sherlock Tomes. We've been trying to get in contact with you.'

'I know who you are.' Franklin looks down at Eloise's hand and ignores it. 'And I know what you want.'

'And what's that?' I push my shoulders back and breathe in, expanding my chest and drawing myself to my full height, matching Franklin.

'Excuse me, ladies,' says Franklin, flashing a brilliant white smile which doesn't manage to cover his annoyance. 'It seems these bookshop people and I have matters to discuss.'

He stalks into a quieter corner, assuming that we will follow, which we do. He lowers his voice. 'You want to drag my name through the mud. You and that bitch Danielle Bright.'

Eloise necks her cocktail and deposits the glass on a table. 'This has nothing to do with Danielle. We're only interested in finding the truth about Tracey Jervis.'

'This has everything to do with Danielle. Do you think I don't know that you're plotting with her?' He shakes his head. 'I can't believe you had the balls to actually hold that meeting in my own coffee shop.'

'We were just talking about the state of local business.' Eloise folds her arms.

'So, the subject of Tracey Jervis never came up?'

Eloise's silence speaks volumes.

'Yeah, I thought as much.' Franklin drains his wine glass and points it at her.

My hands raise instinctively. Not that Eloise can't take care of herself but, gangster or not, if Franklin tries anything I will floor the fucker.

'I'm not having Tracey ruin my chances a second time.' Franklin leans closer and gesticulates with the glass. 'So, you'd better drop all this shit, or it won't go well for you.'

'You're not the first to threaten us, and to be honest the other fellas were scarier,' I say.

'The Black Dogs may seem scarier.' Franklin's smile is mean, confirming that he set the Dogs on us. 'But I am someone that you don't want to mess with.'

I look him up and down. 'I've thrown tougher people than you out of the way just to get to fights.'

'Forget what you think you know. I always get what I want, and I don't care how.' He twists a large gold ring on his finger, and I get the feeling that he's split faces open with it before. 'I'm in negotiation with your landlord to buy the whole block. How do you think that's going to work out for you then?'

It's impossible to know whether Franklin's gaslighting us.

His mean smile widens. 'You think you're special but you're nothing, not to me, not to this Village.'

'Our customers would disagree,' says Eloise.

'Who cares about customers. They're little people, just like you.'

'Well, sometimes little people can do big things.' She pokes

Franklin in the chest — one escalation away from her throwing a right hook.

He's unperturbed. 'You're not old Havelock, you don't have streets named after you. My family's been here for generations and I won't hesitate to force that bookshop you're so pathetically proud of out of business.'

CHAPTER 35

Eloise: 13 days until Isabella Garrante book launch

I am absolutely bloody seething. I knew Franklin White was a piece of work, but I underestimated his arrogance. Still, he's rather underestimated us too — talk about a red rag to a bull. Threaten me or mine and you've had it.

In an attempt to lower my blood pressure, we've decided to defer having to organise the bloody book launch and instead will visit Trent Meek in Taupō. He wasn't too hard to find, being an old-school telephone directory kind of guy. Our first conversation started poorly when he burst into tears at the mention of Tracey's name, but he recovered and suggested it might be best if we drove over to see him.

'What do you make of Franklin's threat?' asks Garth as we set off. We've been going over this a lot.

'He's full of shit. Just an arrogant, puffed-up piece of nothing,' I snarl.

'He's well connected, and there are all those rumours of

underworld shenanigans. What if he could really do us some harm? Oh god. He could ruin the IFG event for us, couldn't he?'

'Any more threats from him and I'll shout it from the rooftops. Who would want to vote in such a corrupt, philandering, cretinous boofhead as councillor?'

'Errr,' says Garth, and we both silently acknowledge that yes, many people worldwide have put corrupt, philandering, cretinous boofheads into positions of power quite recently.

It's one road to Taupō, so we settle into the trip, Garth as usual with pen and paper, eyes glazed. We don't tend to chat much in the car, and I let my brain rest a wee while, patting Stevie's silken noggin every now and again, enjoying the peace. Trent Meek has told us he has an enclosed garden that Stevie can snoof around, and we'll take him for a walk later.

Not far out of Taupō, on the long straight section with forestry either side, I assume the three Harley-style motorbikes that have been cruising a bit behind us for a while will overtake, but they're hanging back, speeding up, then hanging back again, a bunch of middle-aged arseholes gearing up for a weekend on the lake. I roll my eyes and decide to mess with them a bit, taking 20kph off my speed in a few seconds, causing the bikes to blast past. There's a lot of whooping and hollering as they go by, and a couple of hand salutes: that's a bit much for midlife-crisis types. Then I see it — they're patched Black Dogs.

'Garth. Garth!'

'What?'

'Black Dogs. Do you think they've been following us?'

'I didn't notice anything.'

No surprises there. The bikers have taken off now, swerving in and out of each other and gunning their engines, making the most of the straight road. Coincidence? Maybe. But I'm unsettled, and Garth looks so, too, but it could be indigestion seeing as he inhaled the pie we bought at the petrol station faster than Stevie with his dog roll.

'Slow down, Eloise. You're well over the speed limit. Are you trying to catch them up or something?'

'What? In this heap of junk? Not likely.'

He laughs but it's a shaky one. We spend the rest of the trip scanning the road ahead and checking the rear-view and wing mirrors many more times than is natural for jaded, long-term drivers.

The rest of the journey is uneventful and Trent Meek's place is easy enough to find. It's a neat, detached two-bedroomed unit on a quiet street, close enough to the CBD that a reasonably fit old person could walk to the supermarket or the pub. The front garden is neatly planted with perennials and the lavender full of bees. I'm strangely cheered by gentle insects getting on with their busy work, oblivious to the bad guys lurking around the corners. We park up on the street and coax Stevo from his safe place in the rear footwell.

Trent has already started down the drive to meet us in his old-bloke leather slippers. He's slim, wearing what can only be described as 'slacks', mustard in colour, and a flannelette tartan shirt. He's pretty much bald, a few wisps of white combed over his tanned head: the contrasting hair and skin tones make him look like a magician's wand. He seems really pleased to see us.

'Hello, you two and oh my goodness you must be Stevie. So pleased to meet you. Oh dear! Shall we get him in the garden?'

In the grips of a panic attack, Stevie strains against the lead, darting back and forth, choking himself and yanking my arm out of its socket. I wind his lead around my wrist, lock the car and gratefully follow Trent up the driveway and through the high wooden gate. Garth follows, his hand flailing against his chest in what appears to be some weird sort of interpretive dance but is actually an attempt to relieve his clothing of pie crumbs.

Stevie spots the outdoor furniture and makes a dive under the table. He'll settle for a bit now, get his bearings. Trent has the table set for morning tea — plates, cups, sugar bowl, napkins — and is back inside, busying himself with a teapot and a plunger.

'I don't know what you like so I've made both,' he says, bringing a tray. 'But I've got beer and lemonade and probably some other things, too.'

'Oh, coffee please,' says Garth, sounding desperate.

'Me too, thanks.' Our host does one last trip to fetch a plate of what look like homemade Afghan biscuits.

'Mr Meek, this is wonderful. The Afghan is surely the Queen of the biscuit world,' I say.

'And which is the King?'

'Who cares?' I reply, and we both laugh in a manner unbecoming of our age and status. I like him. I really hope he's not a bad guy.

We chat for a bit about the weather, what life is like in Taupō, how he plays bowls and bridge and has made some good friends. He doesn't come back to the Bay unless he really has to.

'Why's that, Mr Meek?' asks Garth, cutting through the small talk.

He sighs. 'Trent, please. When Tracey went missing it was indescribably awful. The rumours, the accusations that were flying around. I was so upset because she was such a lovely girl, and talented, too — I'm sure you've read some of her poems — and I was very fond of her, but in a fatherly way, no funny business at all. Her own father wasn't a very nice man and I never had the opportunity to be a dad, so I suspect I projected my sense of loss at never having had children on to Tracey, if I'm honest.'

He is quiet for a moment, contemplative.

'You would have liked to have had children?' I nudge.

'Yes. It's a regret, but when I was a young man there was no such thing as same-sex marriage or adoption or any of those things that are becoming more common these days. I adored my sister's children, grown up now, of course, but they're in Auckland and I didn't get to see them all that much when they were little.'

'So you kept your sexuality secret up until Tracey disappeared?'

'Well, not secret so much as it wasn't anybody else's business. When the police interrogated me — and it was an interrogation rather than an interview, I can assure you — the gossip at school was unbearable. Staff, students, parents, everyone looked at me differently; there were complaints from parents wanting to pull their children from my classes. I felt awful, ashamed, even though I knew I had done nothing wrong. I "came out", as they say, hoping that would take the spotlight off me as some predatory man who had caused Tracey harm, but all it did was make me the target of a different kind of rumour. Parents still didn't want me teaching their children.'

'People can be such idiots,' says Garth, rather accurately.

Trent nods.

'There was another student who gave a statement that she'd seen you with Tracey, that you'd kissed her,' I say.

'Yes, Darpita. She was jealous of Tracey, I think.'

'Was there any truth to what she said?'

'What? No, no. Well, not really, but Darpita did see something that, taken out of context, could have looked incriminating.' Trent is uneasy now, wringing his hands and looking down at his lap. Guilty as they come.

'Go on.'

'Tracey came to me after class one day. She was very upset. Her father put so much pressure on her to succeed academically. She didn't really get much down time at all. If she wasn't at school or doing after-school work, she was working on projects that would look good on her CV: the poetry book, Franklin White's political campaign. That one I couldn't get my head around.' He sniffs. 'That man and his politics are odious.'

'Yes?' I say, trying not to be too impatient.

'Mr Jervis had locked her in her room the previous evening because she had mentioned she had a terrible headache and didn't want to go to her Scholarship Calculus tuition. No dinner, no toilet facilities, and bruises on her arms in the shape of fingers where her father had grabbed and shoved her. The poor dear girl. I hugged her and, yes, I kissed her on the top of her lovely head. My heart was breaking for her.'

'Did you tell anyone else at school? Take it higher up?' I ask.

'No. Tracey swore me to secrecy. She said she wasn't really in any danger and that her mother was looking out for her. She just needed someone to talk to.'

'What about her friend, Prudence?'

'Indeed. What an unlikely friendship. But when they were together it was the happiest I ever saw either of them. I think Tracey confided in Prudence, but I had noticed some kind of strain on their relationship. As if Tracey was growing up, moving on, with her political interests and whatnot.'

'So what do you think happened to Tracey?' asks Garth.

A deep sigh, right from the depths of old hurts and raw memories.

'I've thought about this a great deal. I like to imagine she ran away with the circus, left her pig of a father behind and started afresh. But I don't think she'd just abandon her mother. She spoke of her with a great deal of affection. I can only draw the conclusion that something awful befell her. Something there was no coming back from.'

A tūī swoops through the garden, landing on a nearby harakeke bush. The black-sheened rascal tips back his head, stretches his pretty throat and announces his chiming news to the world. Stevie looks up, momentarily alarmed, then bends his head to continue his retrieval of abandoned biscuit crumbs. It's so peaceful I'm loath to leave, and I can see Garth is too.

'Come on, old fella,' I say to Garth, rousing myself from my chair and patting his leg. 'We'd better get back on the road and leave Mr Meek here in peace.'

'You will let me know what you find out, won't you?' Trent says. 'I still think of her every day. I'm scared to know what happened, but I think I need to for some kind of closure.'

'I don't know how far we'll get, Trent, but yes, we'll stay in touch.'

Stevie, keeping a keen eye on our movements, senses an imminent trip in the car and pulls hard towards the gate, curtailing any protracted goodbye. That suits Garth right down to the ground.

CHAPTER 36

Garth: 13 days until Isabella Garrante book launch

I've been asleep for most of the drive back, partly because being unconscious is the best way to experience Eloise's driving and partly because when I die I want to die in my sleep. I am, however, rudely awakened as Eloise negotiates the roundabout at the Napier Road and Romanes Drive intersection in some sort of sling-shot manoeuvre. I sit straighter, adjust my seatbelt and grip the edge of the seat.

'Nearly home,' says Eloise cheerily.

'Statistically speaking, seventy-five percent of car accidents happen within three kilometres of home,' I reply.

'Someone's woken up in a grump.'

I don't think I'm being grumpy, not that I can always tell, and am about to point out the unfairness of this accusation when I'm caught by a flash of red and yellow beyond the trees on the Village Green. A hot-air balloon? In Northampton we had a yearly festival when forty-plus balloons would launch in quick succession. It was a spectacular sight and an event I enjoyed policing until the year a propane canister exploded and I was first on the scene of carnage.

The Tomato speeds closer. It's not a balloon, it's something even better: the canvas of a big top being winched up two king poles. The circus is in town.

I'm transported back twenty-plus years to when the circus was here in Tracey's day, tiers of seats thronged with people laughing at the clowns, oblivious to the trauma about to haunt the Village. Before I can fully commit to this image, another thought intrudes. How many people can a big top hold — hundreds? Thousands? However many, it would make a fabulous venue for Isabella Garrante's book launch.

As we pass, I peer back over my shoulder at the caravans, lorries and tents to see if I can spot the name of the circus.

'What is it?' asks Eloise. 'Have you seen those Black Dogs again?'

'Black Dogs?' My train of thought has not just been derailed but is crashing down the embankment and freefalling into a crevasse as I clock the name: *Maloney's*.

'I thought I saw those bikers again on the Napier–Taupō Road. But I couldn't be sure.'

'The same ones?' I grasp my head in a moment of sensory overload.

'They were too far back to tell, but there were three of them and one was a chopper with ape-hangers like before.'

'Ape-hangers?'

'That's what they call those really high curved handlebars.'

Realising that we are too far along this conversational path to backtrack I park the issue of the circus name for now. 'And you know this how?' Even after all these years together, Eloise can still surprise me with the things she knows and the things she doesn't know.

'I used to date a guy who had a chopper.'

The last thing I need now is a stab of unreasonable jealousy. I push it down. We both had lives before we met at Police College and, to be fair, I was no angel either.

'Did you now? Nice. But no, I didn't spot any motorbikes. And this circus here looks like it's the same one in town as when Tracey disappeared.'

'It'll only be the same circus in name. It's not going to have the same people as when Tracey disappeared.'

'Why not? Family tradition and all that.'

'I don't think it works that way anymore. They mostly hire acts in for the season.'

'And how do you know? Were you going to be the amazing tattooed lady or something?'

'How very dare you? No one's ever accused me of being a lady.'

The Tomato judders up the kerb and onto our drive. Eloise jabs at the button for the garage door opener. 'Here we go again,' she says with a degree of resignation as the door steadfastly refuses to open.

'You just have to believe. It can sense your fear.' I take the opener and press the button, holding it down. With a shudder the door begins to lift upwards. 'See?'

My self-satisfaction is premature. I have committed the other cardinal sin of the garage door, which is being too optimistic. It grinds to a halt halfway up. Stevie, who has pushed into the front and is virtually sitting on Eloise's lap, lets out a whine which pretty much matches my own. I get out, re-click the opener and manually assist the door upwards, somewhat negating the whole point of the automatic device.

As soon as I'm back in the house, I charge up the stairs to our impromptu incident room to check the name of the circus associated with Tracey's case. Tama has organised the evidence into sections pertaining to particular lines of enquiry, and I hurriedly sift through the folders: Trent Meek, School, Franklin White, Redwoods, Maloney's Circus.

'Do you want a cup of tea?' Eloise pokes her head through the door.

'It's the same circus.' I wave the folder back at her.

'A curious coincidence?' She comes in, grabs a marker and writes 'Maloney's' on the board.

When we were policing, coincidences were always a paradox. On one hand, if you had two pieces of evidence that seemed to support each other, it would bolster your case. On the other hand, coincidences happen more often than you like to think. I was once surprised in the bookshop when a copper I had known twenty-odd years ago on the other side of the world wandered up to the counter to buy the latest Jack Reacher. It turned out his brother lived just down the road and he was visiting him.

'And what would Gibbs say?' asks Eloise. We were obsessed with *NCIS* for some time until it jumped the shark.

'Rule thirty-nine: There is no such thing as a coincidence.'

CHAPTER 37

Eloise: 12 days until Isabella Garrante book launch

I really need a day off from Tracey; she's doing my head in. As soon as I articulate this thought, I feel guilty — she's vanished without trace and I'm begrudging her a bit of brain space. I should also be grateful that she's taken my mind off Pinter, though less grateful the IFG launch has gone on the back burner again. We really need to get that sorted.

Amelia's chatting with someone in the Young Adult section holding a copy of *Heartstopper* to her chest as if it might actually stop her heart. The words 'delightful' and 'wholesome' hang on the air, and the customer is intrigued.

A gentleman in some kind of uniform of black trousers, black ribbed pullover and work boots arouses suspicion. He's staring at a wall. It takes me a moment to realise he's holding one of those beepy things with a laser that estate agents use to measure rooms, and a clipboard with a pen on a string.

'What are you doing?' I ask.

'Measuring,' he replies, just as bluntly.

'Let's start again. Hello. I'm Eloise and this is my bookshop. Who are you and why are you measuring it?'

He sighs. 'Hello Eloise. I'm Barry from Jones and Brown Hawke's Bay. I'm doing a rent assessment.' He continues past the cookbooks and aims his gadget at the wall behind the counter.

'Watch where you're pointing that thing,' says Amelia, who has just been beeped at.

'What's through here?' he asks, reaching for a door handle.

I hold a hand up. 'Hang on a minute, Barry. We're not due a rent review for at least another year, so I very much doubt that our landlord has sent you.'

'I'm just doing my job,' says Barry, looking at about a 2 out of 10 on the job-satisfaction scale.

'I'm not comfortable with this . . . unannounced inspection or whatever is going on. I'll ring the landlord, and you can come back when it's been sorted out. And after an appointment has been made.' I feel a bit sorry for Barry, but who just wanders into someone's space and starts measuring up?

'Fine,' says Barry, and with a thump of beepy thing onto clipboard, off he stomps down the steps and out of the shop.

I turn to Amelia.

'The cheek!' she says.

'I'll say,' I reply.

'Do you think that's got something to do with Franklin White trying to freak us out?'

Bugger. I'd thought it was just me being paranoid.

'No. Someone will have mixed up the dates of the review, that's all.'

'Okay.' She pats me on the shoulder as she squeezes past to help out a lost soul in the Cookbook section. My attempt at denial and deflection has not fooled her for a second.

Invoices, bills, information sheets for new books, a self-published picture book for my perusal. I flick through the book, and I'm reminded of the late Belinda of Waipukurau and the boxes in her garage — and immediately wish I hadn't been.

'You got the new C.J. Tudor in?' a sombre voice intones behind me.

I spin around to see Dead Girl Deirdre.

'Jesus, Deirdre, you frightened me to death.'

'And yet, there you stand, as alive as ever, unless there's something you're not telling me.'

I don't know how to respond. It's funny, but also not funny.

'C.J. Tudor,' I mutter. 'Yes! Just in and utterly fabulous. I read it overnight.'

'Probably why you're such a zombie today,' comes the dour reply.

'No change there love, eh,' I say, smiling.

I really like Deirdre. She's strange as all hell but drops some interesting comments into the conversation sometimes. Nothing about herself — she keeps the enigma intact — just fun facts about the many types of maggot that can infest dead bodies, and that people smoke embalming fluid to produce a hallucinogenic effect. See, fascinating woman.

'I'll take it. Anything else I should know?'

We wander the shelves together, talking through the books she's recently read and loved, checking out the latest in mortuary non-fiction and medical memoirs: *I. See. You.* gets a yes, *Take a Chill Pill* gets a no. I share her interest in death, which I don't think is as morbid as it sounds. Most people who are drawn to the end of life are really interested in living it to its very fullest and intend to have a wonderful life and an equally wonderful death. Knowledge is power.

Deirdre is looking rather marvellous today. Spiky, aggressively straightened black hair, painted-on eyebrows and eyelashes, a black-and-white stripey tee-shirt tucked into her black jeans. A studded collar graces her pale throat. It's quite a look. I notice a piece of Glad Wrap poking out from her sleeve, a tell-tale sign.

'You've got a new tattoo.'

Deirdre inches her sleeve up and peels the wrap away. It's a small circus tent, red-and-yellow striped, fluttering bunting and all, with the words *the circus never leaves town* dancing beneath in a fine cursive script. It's lovely work, but it gives me an uneasy feeling. Deirdre stares, gauging my reaction.

'Did you get it at Maloney's Circus?'

'Yes. They've had the same tattooist for years. I always get something from her when they come to the Village. She's very good.'

'What's with the text?' I ask.

'You're a clever girl. You can work it out.'

I think about it, but all I can really think about is Tracey and whether she did run away with the circus or if she never left town. It's a circus in my bloody head at the moment, so maybe that's what it means.

We talk tattoos for a bit, what healing cream is best, the pros and cons of colour versus black and white, and head around to the fiction.

'Have you ever read Isabella Garrante?' I ask, wondering how far the elusive novelist's reach goes.

Deirdre stares at me, silent. I stare back for a moment then, taking her silence as a 'No', we move on and she picks out a handful of Deirdre-looking books: *Daisy Darker, Women Talking, Livid*, and, surprisingly, the first in the *Thursday Murder Club* series.

'I like something cosy sometimes. Thought I'd give it a go,' she says.

We share something akin to a smile.

Deirdre pays up, proffering hundred-dollar bills as is her wont, bags up her books and glides off out into the rain. As I'm turning back to the emails, Amelia pops her head out from the stock room.

'Is she gone?' she whispers, gesticulating with a faux-skeletal arm covered in rotting flesh. She's preparing the window display for Halloween, ahead of the game as ever, and in true Amelia style it will be no-holds-barred spectacular. Oh god, that's another thing I have to do. I've been tasked with finding books with mostly orange and/or black covers: we're going full pumpkin, spiders, skeletons, witches and zombies this year. I don't know if Deirdre will love it with all her heart or think it impossibly twee — I've never been able to work her out, which is one of the reasons I like her so much.

'Yes, Amelia. It's safe. I don't know why she gives you the willies so much. One of your favourite books is *A Good Girl's Guide to Murder.* You should be best buds.'

'I know. I find her intriguing but it's the way she just looks at you and doesn't talk. What's she hiding?'

'A rich inner life.'

'Or a regularly re-landscaped back garden,' counters Amelia, eyes narrowing.

'I never thought I'd say this, but you might be reading too many murder books, our Amelia.'

'Never!' Amelia brandishes the arm. 'But it wouldn't surprise me to read in the papers one day that the police have discovered a body farm in her back garden.'

'A body farm?'

'Yes, you know, like they have in the States. The FBI started them. They put a load of bodies in a wood to see how they'd decompose.

I mean it's kind of cool, but surely it's got to be high on the list for ground zero of the zombie apocalypse.' Amelia waves the zombie arm again and retreats back into the stock room.

That was a cool tattoo of Deirdre's; fine, delicate line work and vibrant colour. Lovely, and a bit disturbing, quite like Deirdre. Maybe I could get something done while the circus is still in town? Matching detective tattoos with my clever husband, perhaps? Never. Garth's terrified of needles and is not convinced when I tell him it's not a needle *as such*. Next best thing might be to get to a circus show together. I get my phone out.

> Me: Ayup. Want to go on a date to the circus?

> Garth: To investigate Tracey? Garth.

> Me: Just to have a fun night out really.
> There's popcorn. You love popcorn.

> Garth: K. Garth.

Romance isn't dead then.

It is, of course, another distraction from panicking about the book launch. We've both been waking in the night, worrying. We still don't even have the venue sorted, though Garth reckons it's in hand. And what if we don't have enough stock? What if she cancels and we have way too much stock? What if the mobile Eftpos machine craps out with a 'critical error' like it did at Cristina Sanders' book launch and we had to get everyone's email addresses and invoice them? I should be looking forward to such a dramatic event — embargoes and lawyers and such — but I'll just be glad when it's all over. I try to employ a trick I've used before with a degree of success: borrowing from my future self. Future Eloise and Garth will have had excellent book sales and the kudos of hosting one of the world's most famous authors. It'll be incredible. I hold this thought deep in my heart for a while, and my breathing calms.

Then I start thinking about Tracey, then, worse, Pinter.

CHAPTER 38

Garth: 12 days until Isabella Garrante book launch

Maloney's Circus is as much a travelling fair as a circus. The big top is surrounded by children's carnival rides, food trucks and sideshow games of skill and chance, albeit that chance is greatly stacked against the punters thanks to a surprising insight into the laws of physics and downright trickery.

Eloise is getting some piece of tattoo flash added to the sleeves that are creeping down her arms, so I take in the sights and ponder the logistics of the IFG launch. I have emailed the publisher suggesting the big top for the venue but have yet to hear back and probably won't do until Monday, which will leave us just over a week. In other circumstances this wouldn't be anywhere near long enough, but we are embargoed from promoting the launch until next weekend so maybe still have a bit of wiggle room. To be honest, IFG is such a big name and the mystery around her so intense that we could advertise the event the day before the launch and still expect to sell out. Even so, it would be a massive relief to have the venue confirmed so that we can finalise the other arrangements and put a stop to the incessant angst.

I meander among the stalls, letting the sounds of revelry and the shouts of the hawkers calm my nerves. The flashing lights, the smell of candy floss and diesel-generator fumes send me back nearly a half century to when my Grandad would take my sister and me to Banbury Fair. Dodgems, waltzers and a toffee apple on the way home: it really was the highlight of my year.

The dulled crack of air-rifles firing draws my attention, and despite my better judgement I part with five dollars for ten pellets. It's many years since I've held a firearm of any description, but I ease the stock into my shoulder and adjust my foregrip and sight picture like a pro. Exhaling, I increase the tension on the trigger, releasing the shot as my lungs empty and the foresight and hindsight align. With a satisfying clack, one of the white metal targets on my lane falls. I allow myself a smile.

Nine pellets later, the flat-capped stall holder offers me a large purple teddy bear.

'Have you been here long?' I ask, taking the teddy.

'Couple of days.'

'Sorry, I meant have you been with the circus long?'

'Couple of years.'

Even by my taciturn standards I get the impression the stall holder's not much of a talker. I persist anyway. 'Who do you reckon's been with the circus the longest?'

'Fortune teller.'

'Thanks.' I wave the teddy and wander off in search of Gypsy Rose Charlatan or whatever she's called.

I haven't wandered far when I see one of the shop's good customers trying to reason with a distraught pre-schooler who has simultaneously let go of his helium balloon and then dropped his ice cream while attempting to recapture it. Unlike Eloise, who would immediately know their names, I can't for the life of me remember either, although I can tell you that the pre-schooler loves *Kuwi the Kiwi* books and the mum is a fan of Jenny Pattrick.

Bending down, I make the teddy walk along the ground towards the child. 'Oh, hello,' I say in a silly voice. 'I have lost my balloon, too. Will you look after me?' Tantrum forgotten, the boy opens his arms wide and embraces the toy in a quite literal bear hug.

'Is that okay?' I ask his mum, somewhat belatedly. When we distribute giveaways to kids in the shop, we always like to check with the parents first. In this case, if the answer is no and I have to retrieve the teddy, I will have succeeded only in making matters worse.

'It's great. Are you sure?' She bends down to the toddler. 'What do you say to the nice man?'

'You're old,' says the boy.

'Freddy!'

'It's okay. He means I'm too old for a teddy.' For the sake of my ego, I choose to believe this. 'Anyway, enjoy the rest of the circus.'

I half wave and hastily retreat into the crowd.

At the end of the row of stalls is a caravan fronted with a white picket fence and pot plants of blooming flowers. This is not one of the soulless modern aluminium affairs used by the rest of the circus but has more of a rustic, Romany feel to it. Outside, a chalkboard proclaims the occupant to be Madame Zuiseller, psychic and fortune teller.

I have a low opinion of so-called psychics. Being charitable, I may consider them misguided; at worst, cynical con-artists profiting from people's misery. But this woman might just have the answers I need.

I'm preparing to knock when the small, rounded door opens, reminding me of the old joke: Why do psychics have doorbells?

'Welcome. I sensed your approach,' says a woman who can be none other than Zuiseller. I estimate that she is in her mid-forties to early fifties. Her glossy dark hair is tied back in a ponytail and is mostly concealed by a red-and-white spotted headscarf. Large gold hoop earrings complete an image which is nothing if not traditional.

I don't mention the webcam I spotted amid a floral display hanging alongside the door which I presume will have also sensed my approach.

'I feel that you are hesitant.' Zuiseller ushers me in and onto a cushioned seat at one side of a red velvet-draped table. 'Is this your first time?'

She is either perceptive or has watched me on the webcam while I dithered outside.

'Yes,' I lie, because I don't want to give her any clues.

'Then perhaps the crystal ball may be preferable to tarot,' she suggests, gesturing to a spherical object covered with a black cloth in the centre of the table. Believers say that the purpose of the cloth is to stop the spirits looking back at you. I tend towards a more pragmatic explanation. We once put a crystal ball in our shop window as part of a display and nearly burned the shop down because the glass focused the sun's rays to a precise spot. It was only the smell of burning and the trail of fine smoke drifting up from the window that saved our beloved books.

'Actually, I think I'd like the tarot,' I say, mainly because the crystal ball is just waving your hands about and making shit up while tarot requires finesse, linking the aforementioned shit with the picture on the card.

'As you wish.' She removes the crystal ball and places a

velvet-wrapped package onto the table. Again, a believer would say that the tarot cards should never be touched by anyone but the reader, whereas I would say that traditionally the cards were a most precious item that needed protecting from wear and tear.

Zuiseller gestures to the wrapped cards. 'Please empower the spirits with your offering.'

A nice touch, incorporating the transactional part of the arrangement into the ceremony of the proceedings. I'm tempted to claim that I don't have cash to see if she will produce the Eftpos machine I see lurking in the corner, but I'm not that much of a cock, so I place thirty dollars on the still-wrapped tarot cards.

She takes the money and drops it into what is clearly a cash box despite the mystical symbols painted onto it. Unwrapping the cards, she shuffles them.

With a degree of reverence, Zuiseller places five cards in a cross on the table. It's a simple pattern, being easy and quick to read. My thirty bucks will buy me fifteen minutes of her time, tops.

'The centre card represents what is most important in your life at the moment.' Zuiseller places her black-nailed fingers on the card, pausing for dramatic effect.

I lean forward, genuinely interested; as far as I am aware, dogs don't feature in tarot, so unless this is a rather esoteric deck with the King of Stevies I suspect I am about to be disappointed.

She turns the card. Beneath the picture of a skeleton reaping human-faced flowers is the word 'Death'.

Withdrawing her hand, Zuiseller looks up at me. I guess she's trying to gauge whether I'm freaked out by this and whether she needs to fall back on one of the standard lines: *Of course death does not represent literal death, we all experience death and this is likely referring to a past event . . .*

'You are not surprised.' Zuiseller holds me in her gaze. 'Death is something that you are currently dealing with . . .' Her voice trails off, and I assume she's hoping I will fill in the blanks with details that she can then build on or feed back to me as if she has come up with information herself.

I give her nothing, so she continues and turns the next card. It shows a King upon a throne holding a large gold coin inscribed with a pentacle.

'The King of Pentacles symbolises a wealthy man. I sense that this is not you, so who is this man in your life?'

I ignore the slight; after all, I'm wearing my Sherlock Tomes-branded hoodie, and she'll perhaps understand that bookshop owners are rarely wealthy. I try not to think of who the King of Pentacles might represent. Fortune telling works by throwing out a vague detail and then letting the client fit it to something relevant. But my treacherous brain betrays me, fixating on Franklin White.

Perhaps Zuiseller sees something in my face and is no longer willing to accept my silence. 'He may be a greedy man,' she prompts. 'A Midas figure. The man with the gold makes the rules!'

'Not who makes the rules, breaks the rules,' I say, half to myself, forgetting that I wasn't going to give Zuiseller any clues.

I gaze past her, my head full of Franklin White, and that's when I see the newspaper cutting pressed flat behind glass in a gold frame on the wall.

CHAPTER 39

Eloise: 12 days until Isabella Garrante book launch

I'm finishing up my beer and chips at the hospitality tent, feeling as if the perfectly formed little kōwhai bloom etched into my collarbone has been there forever. I'm in my element here, enjoying the reprieve from all the fretting about book launches and missing girls and the many things I won't let myself think about. I'm taking a swig of the fruity beer when my phone pings. I've conjured him.

Garth: Meet me at charlatan's caravan soon as. Garth

I drain the dregs and, presuming he means the fortune teller, make my way over to the lovely old caravan I've spotted a couple of rows over.

I venture up the wooden steps and knock on Madame Zuiseller's door; it's closed, so I hope it's Garth in there and I'm not disturbing someone's reading.

'Enter,' says a deep, velvety voice that compels me to do as commanded.

I see a fidgety Garth, busting at the seams with information, and a serene, beautifully put-together woman in her sixties, I would guess, possibly of Middle Eastern origin. That, or Middle Earth. She looks the part all right. Bizarrely, the pair of them are drinking tea like old pals having a catch-up.

'Is my husband bothering you, Madame Zuiseller?' I ask.

'Your pronunciation is impressive, dear girl. Not at all. He was drawn here today by the need to unpick a mystery. The spirits moved in ways that brought him to me.'

'Did they now,' I say.

'Sit down, sit down, and look at this.' Garth tugs on my arm.

He shoves a framed newspaper article in front of me. The picture is of a younger but mostly unchanged Madame Zuiseller holding the palm of a rotund white guy with fluffy bits of hair sticking out of the sides of his head like an ungroomed monk. I fish my specs out of my bag and peer more closely. The headline reads, 'The Future Looks Bright for Maloney's', and the caption explains that Madame Zuiseller is reading the palm of the Mayor of Havelock North.

'Lovely,' I say, and look up to find two pairs of brown eyes looking at me, the darker ones with amusement, the lighter, hazel ones with impatience.

'Read the article!' Garth urges. I do so, aloud.

'*In a curious twist of fate, beleaguered circus troupe Maloney's have been saved by a financer none of them saw coming. The Garrante Brothers* — the Garrante Brothers! Bloody hell! — *have bought out the Maloney family, enabling the circus to continue more or less as it has since its inception in 1949.*

'*Maloney's Fortune Teller Madame Ethne Zuiseller is relieved, but not surprised.*

'"I was never too concerned. I couldn't see a big change in our future fortunes or any deviation in the circus's plans, so the fact that we can carry on as we have been makes sense. I am, of course, like the whole circus family, extremely grateful for the Garrante Brothers' faith in our ability to continue. We shall repay their confidence; this I have foreseen."

'Havelock North Mayor Roy Robotham was visiting the circus when Hawke's Bay Today popped in. A long-time fan of Maloney's, he's thrilled that his regular liaisons with his favourite fortune teller will be going ahead as usual. Asked what Mayor Robotham's palm revealed, Madame Zuiseller said she could not reveal her client's reading, but that he should probably cut down on the red meat and the local syrah.'

'Ethne, what a lovely name,' I say, and Madame Zuiseller smiles.

'Roy had a heart attack not long after that photograph was taken. I did warn him,' she says.

'But the Garrante Brothers? Who are they? What are they like?'

'Circus family for generations,' says Madame Zuiseller. 'Their grandfather was a ringmaster for a time, their mother the trapeze artist. The boys worked with the horses when we had them and helped with the fairground side when needed. There is obviously a financial arrangement, and the circus's accountant deals with all that. Apart from an advertising company being brought in to rebrand and raise our profile, and upgrades to our equipment so we could get new, more exciting acts, nothing much has changed.'

I peer more closely at the newspaper clipping. The Garrante Brothers took over the same year Tracey disappeared.

'I'll pop that Derren Brown book in before you leave, Ethne. Just bring it back to the shop next time you're through.'

'Thank you, Garth. It's been a pleasure. Your tea leaves tell me you're making progress in your investigations. Please don't give up.'

Spots dance in front of my eyes as I readjust to the early darkness after the light of the caravan. I suggest we mosey in the direction of the shop, check out Amelia's awesome window display as we go by. It's only about 400 metres down the road, past the library and the back end of the primary school.

'Made a new friend, have you?'

'Ha. An unlikely friendship indeed. You never know when a tarot reader will come in handy.'

'Really?' I'm about to ask when he thinks he'll need a tarot reader again when he changes tack.

'What do you reckon then?'

'Yeah, she seemed genuine enough. You're the one who had the reading. What did she say?'

'No, no, not about Ethne. About the article.'

'Oh. It's a hell of a coincidence that the Garrante Brothers bought the circus and we're about to host Isabella Garrante. I mean, what the fuck? Do you think they're related?'

'Circus brothers and a secretive, enigmatic author? I wouldn't be surprised. What about the takeover happening the year Tracey went missing?' says Garth.

'Yeah, that's a bit sus, too, I reckon.'

'Tracey was flirting with the young Maloney's lad, according to Prudence. She definitely had a link to the circus. What I'm really interested in, though, is where the Garrante Brothers got that amount of cash from. And the circus was failing, so it's a bit of a dramatic comeback.'

'They're still going though, aren't they. Ethne saw it all coming.'

'Hmm. She drew the King of Pentacles as one of my cards. Who do we know who's rich as Croesus and is wrapped up tight in all this?'

'Franklin White? You think he's involved with the circus?'

'I'm not sure but it's an interesting line of enquiry.'

Amelia's spectacularly spooky orange-and-black window display is visible from a fair distance, and even better close up.

'She's surpassed herself,' says Garth.

'Better than the flying Christmas books, you reckon?'

'It's a close-run thing. But hang on — what the hell has happened here?'

The flowers in the trough outside are missing again, stems cropped short rather than roots wrenched. The really weird thing is that new blooms have been planted around the desecrated incumbent ones. They're gaudy, bright orange, matching Amelia's window perfectly.

'Off with their heads,' I murmur.

'Indeed,' says Garth.

CHAPTER 40

Garth: 11 days until Isabella Garrante book launch

I get down to the shop early before Kitty arrives and remove the dead stalks. The bright-orange blooms that replace them coordinate with Amelia's Halloween window and look fantastic. I just hope Kitty will think so, too. There isn't a chance she won't notice; the flower trough is her domain and one over which she rules with a green-fingered iron hand.

The other reason I've come down early is to spruce up the shopfront. There's still no word from the publisher about whether Isabella will agree to our using the circus tent as a venue — assuming, of course, that the circus people are happy for us to use it for a night as well — but whatever happens, Isabella will no doubt visit the shop and it needs to look its very best for her, and for any publicity shots. Now more than ever it's vital that the launch is a success, one that we can capitalise on should Franklin convince our landlord to sell.

Our shopfront has a big window and a small window, which to

avoid confusion we cunningly refer to as the big window and the small window. I've decided to start by sanding and painting the big window, as it's away from the door and easier to cordon off. I'm about to apply the last run of tape along the bottom of the window before getting a first coat on when a certain scent assaults my nostril; *eau de Dafydd* is like being punched in the nose with a turd. He stops behind me, looks at the flowers and tugs on his beard.

'Dead. Nothing I could do,' he mumbles. Then his head snaps around and he stares intently at something only he can see. 'Couldn't stop it.'

'It's a shame about the flowers,' I say. 'But we've replaced them.'

'Irreplaceable.' Dafydd shakes his head and wanders off, still conversing. 'I'd be dead, too, wouldn't I.'

I unroll enough green tape so that it is just past the length of the window, pinch a section between my fingers and rip it free from the roll. Carefully aligning it with the windowsill, I press it firmly against the glass. I stand back and, as if I have executed the last phase of some complex, arcane summoning spell, Eloise appears in the doorway. Dressed in ripped denim dungarees, a paint-spotted shirt and red headscarf, she looks like Rosie the Riveter.

'I thought I'd give you a hand with the fun part.'

Me on a ladder and Eloise doing the lower sections, we work for an hour, although our actual painting time is considerably less, because everyone who comes into the shop engages us in small talk. Thankfully, Eloise does most of the conversational heavy lifting, so I have only to add answers to the odd direct question. As she fends off another enquiry about why we're painting the shop and doesn't it look nice now that it's freshened up, I see Dafydd striding back along the pavement. Neither staring into the ether nor talking to invisible friends, he doesn't even meander but cuts a straight path towards us.

He draws level and turns his attention to the old shelf I'm using to put paintbrushes and other gear. 'Van Gogh, he painted the flowers, he didn't steal them.' He nods to himself and reaches out a hand.

'Thanks, Dafydd. But we're all good with the painting,' I say.

Ignoring me, he picks up a fine-tipped artist's brush. It's my favourite, and one I use for doing the gold detailing on the trim. It's also the only fine brush I have, and it cost a fortune.

I step down from the ladder and hold out my hand like a parent to an errant child. 'Maybe just leave that one, Dafydd, as we need it. Take one of the others if you want.'

Again he ignores me. He dips the tip of the brush into the tin of paint and gets to work on one of the flattened cardboard boxes I've placed on the ground to catch any drips. And I am genuinely amazed. There is no hesitation or dithering; the brush flows across the cardboard with the confident, smooth movements of a true professional.

For the first time ever, I see Dafydd completely focused: he is a changed person, an artist. I'm mesmerised too. Because what he's painting with such deft, delicate brushstrokes is a picture of the shopfront.

'That's fantastic,' I say. 'Can we keep it?'

'Not finished.' Dafydd holds his brush above the paint tin and stares at the picture. 'Flowers.'

I look again at what he's done. The flower trough in his picture is empty.

Dafydd re-dips his brush and works it across the cardboard once more. Only he's not adding flowers; instead, he paints a stooping figure, knife in hand, cutting the blooms from their stems. The figure is not detailed, there is only so much that can be done with emulsion on cardboard, but even so the likeness is unmistakable. Caught red-handed, or more precisely painted red-handed, who needs CCTV when Dafydd can reproduce such a telling image?

CHAPTER 41

Eloise: 11 days until Isabella Garrante book launch

I've finished chatting with an early-morning Jack Russell walker about the merits of compostable poo bags, and turned to see Dafydd wandering away and Garth staring, gobsmacked, at the piece of flattened cardboard box on the footpath.

'What is it?'

I move closer and look down. A detailed rendition of our shopfront features a familiar figure. There they are, snipping the head from one of Kitty's blooms, whilst another four stems rest nearby.

'I told him to leave the brush alone,' says Garth quietly, his expression a mix of wonder, guilt and incredulity.

'Well, you weren't to know. We've only ever seen him as he is now. He was someone's baby once, and a little boy, and to skip forward quite a bit presumably he's had some art training. I mean, look at the detail and the skill. There's no mistaking the culprit.'

Garth, still fixated on the painting, just shakes his head.

'Anyway, I'll put this somewhere safe and think about what I'm going to say to Kitty.' I take the cardboard from him. 'You can get back on with the job. Do you still need my help? I can get the shop set up for the day and join in for a bit if it's quiet . . .'

'No no no,' says Garth. 'It's very kind of you but you'd best man the till and break the news to Kitty when she arrives. I wouldn't mind a coffee, though, if you're making one.'

Of course I'm making one.

I ready the shop for the day, make the coffee, leave Garth in the clutches of an elderly gent who is regaling him with unsolicited painting advice, and await the bloom bandit who will turn up to collect a magazine as usual.

Kitty arrives, slightly late and a little flustered, trailing her morning's haul from the Veggie Shed.

'Kitty. I have something to show you.'

'Oooo, what?'

I pull the cardboard masterpiece from its hiding place and rest it on the bench.

Kitty seems to have no idea what she's looking at. She studies the detail, her eyes flitting over the scene.

'Did Garth do that? It's really good, but why did he do it on a crappy piece of cardboard? Very arty, I must say and—'

And there it is. She's seen it. She looks up.

'What the actual? Why did Garth paint this?'

'It wasn't Garth, it was Dafydd. A dark horse, that boy. I think he saw the theft in progress and he's captured that moment for us.'

'One of those moments at least.'

'The wee bugger will be in this morning,' I say, busying myself with the jug again, and busting out the book club biscuits. This is an emergency after all.

'I'm not sure I should deal with it. I don't know if I can get the words straight.'

'Leave it with me, I'll sort it out. There must be a reason, but it has to stop.'

As expected, a familiar rumbling roll announces the arrival of the flower thief herself. 'What's Garth doing? Is he any good at that sort of thing? Prince Harry's on this week's cover, isn't he. I might have to get a copy for Susan next door.' In she bustles, leg warmers pulled up over leopard-print leggings.

Sensing something off in our unusual silence, Meryl looks up and comes to a halt in front of the counter. She looks from Kitty, seated in the corner but staring right at her, to me, eyeballing her from a mere metre away. I haul out the cardboard once more and slowly place it on the counter, making a deal of facing it towards the perp. Meryl's face goes satisfyingly pale, her cheeks sag and she breathes out slowly.

'Oh. It's not what it looks like.'

'Please explain,' I say.

'I'm so sorry. Well, I'm not really and you won't be when you see. I had no choice. They had to be found, purloined, foraged, and it wouldn't have been authentic if I'd asked you, would it?' She's close to hyperventilating. There's rather a lot of that going on around here these days.

I shove a biscuit into her hand and usher her towards the comfy chair, the one there's not much chance of getting out of unassisted.

Garth's elderly painting expert approaches, eyeing Meryl warily.

'Ah, Garth said the new *Shepherds and Shearers* was in. I'd like two, please, if possible. George's bitch is in it.'

'Yes, of course, just a sec.' Going with the assumption that we're talking sheep dogs, I move towards the magazine wall. My peripheral vision clocks Meryl attempting to heave herself out of the chair.

'Don't move, lady.' It's said sternly enough to ensure the art expert purchases his magazines with impressive speed.

I return to Meryl and take the upright chair to give me the advantage of height and formal posture.

'Start at the beginning please,' I say in the quietly menacing tone that I would use on young offenders.

Meryl nods obediently and clears her throat.

'Pilfered Petals,' she says.

'Go on.'

'It's a guerrilla art project I'm involved in. The theme is flowers, but not as they've been represented before. The subject matter has to have been stolen, and I thought it would be wonderful to include you, make a good story, I know how you love good stories. Obviously, I couldn't tell you. It had to be proper theft. And there's to be an exhibition and I'm going to invite you all and I have something very special for you.' She breathes in deeply, then deflates and stares at her hands in her lap.

I'm trying to remain appropriately cross with her, mainly for Kitty's sake, but really, what an intriguing idea. I glance over at Kitty, whose face has lost its bereft look and is showing something more akin to interest. There's a contemplative silence.

'Where's the exhibition? When?' asks Kitty.

'At the library. I've done something really very beautiful, Kitty, honestly I have, you'll love it. It'll all be worth it, I promise. I'll bring the proper invitations in tomorrow.'

She looks to Kitty again, pleading, then she snaps her focus back to me.

'You're not going to call the cops on me, are you? Eloise, please no, it was for a good thing.'

'No, I'm not calling the cops, Meryl. It was just some bloody flowers.' There's a sharp intake of breath from the corner and I hastily amend. 'Very lovingly planted and nurtured flowers, and you really owe Kitty big time, but we can sort it out between ourselves.'

Her relief is like a ray of sunshine.

Kitty is not to be easily mollified. She ignores Meryl and goes back to riffling through her folder.

'Who created that anyway?' asks Meryl, peering closely at her painted image.

'Dafydd.'

'Oh my goodness. Teddy. Of course he did.'

CHAPTER 42

Garth: 8 days until Isabella Garrante book launch

Today has been a good day, both with sales in the shop and with respect to the launch. Rose from the publishing company has got back to me, IFG is keen to use the big top and, better still, the publishers are going to arrange it; all I have to do is wait for a call from the circus to finalise details.

Relieved as I am that Sherlock Tomes is no longer the location for the actual launch, I've stayed late to finish sprucing up the shopfront. The big window is now all done, and the bright new pōhutukawa and gold looks fantastic. I managed to prep the other little window during the day so am getting stuck into painting it, too. By the time dusk is falling and the moths are pestering the fluorescent tubes outside the shop, I've finished the first coat. I'll get another one done in the morning and then complete the look with the gold detailing tomorrow night.

I tidy my gear and prepare to leave via the back door. Eloise has taken the Tomato, so I've agreed to walk . . . A moment's doubt grabs me: did I lock the front door? Yes, I know I did. But then again maybe I didn't. I'm going to have to go and check. Otherwise, I'll get home and be so anxious I'll have to turn around and come all the way back.

I walk through the darkened shop, grab the front door handle and give it a good shake, ensuring it's locked, and then for good measure say, 'I've rattled the door.' Which is the code Eloise and I shout to each other when we lock up of an evening to prevent us going through this rigmarole.

I exit into the service area where we and the other adjoining shops and businesses have parking and take deliveries. This late at night the car park is mostly empty, with only a few cars parked up near the cinema and a couple of motorbikes occupying a space nearer the shop. One of them has those weird handlebars like Eloise was on about. What were they called again? Monkey bars? No, that's a swingy thing on an assault course . . . Racking my brain, I turn to the back door and fumble the key at the lock. That's it! Not monkey bars, ape-hangers, that's right—

I'm congratulating myself when gravel crunches behind me and a voice says, 'Fuckin' bag him.'

A fist slams into my back and pain explodes through my right kidney. My knees buckle. Only my palms on the flat of the door keep me from falling. I rasp in a shallow breath, struggling for air. What the fuck? Is this Pinter's doing?

Hands like clamps grab my arms, forcing them behind my back. Rough material drags across my face; a thick black sack is thrust over my head. My wrists are pressed together, and plastic cuts into my flesh, zip-ties yanked tight around them.

I should shout to Mei at the dairy next door for help, but I can hardly breathe and with the adrenaline rush chilling my veins it's all

I can do not to puke. I don't know how many assailants there are, but they're dragging me away from the shop now, my feet scuffing over the asphalt, my legs struggling to support my weight. The metallic ring of a van door sliding open bleeds through the bag. My shins collide hard with the vehicle's sill, and I'm bundled inside. My hooded face smacks into floor and I roll onto my side. The door slams shut behind me with a definitive clunk.

The van begins to move, smashing over the pothole near the cinema that no one seems willing to fix. Motorbikes roar to life, their exhausts loud over the rumbling van and my own ragged breathing. Maybe it's the adrenaline kicking in, but I experience a moment of calm, a serene clarity where everything falls into place: this is the Black Dogs, and I'm well and truly screwed.

Sucking in several deep breaths I try to expand the clarity and force away the oncoming panic. I focus on the pain in my kidney, then on the noise and motion of the van. We've turned right out of the car park and gone over two roundabouts; if we hit a third, it means we're going towards Hastings. Yes, a third roundabout and the smell of the McDonald's confirms this.

I'm unsure how this information will help but it makes me feel better that I know where we're heading. I cast my mind back to my escape and evasion training in the Marines. Rule one, don't get caught. Well, that ship has sailed. Rule two, escape at the earliest opportunity. The longer you're captive the harder it gets for you to escape, as the systems for keeping you secure become more robust.

In the police, during riots, we used plasticuffs for securing prisoners. These were like giant zip-ties and had been specifically designed for the task; they were a bugger to escape from. Fortunately, despite what the movies would have you believe, shop-bought zip-ties are easy to snap. Unfortunately, violent action is needed to break them and I'm certain that at least one person is sitting in the van with me.

'Where are we going?' I ask, trying to keep the fear from my voice.

'Fuck up.'

A booted foot hits me in the chest for emphasis. It's not a full-blown kick, but it's going to leave a bruise if I get out of this alive — which is perhaps a rash assumption.

I move my head slightly, trying to peer through the bag. The material is thick and the van's interior is dark; I see nothing.

'Keep still, or I will fuck you up.'

'I can't breathe.' I add extra distress to my voice, hoping that now I'm secure in the van my captors might remove the bag if they think I'm going to die.

'Not my fuckin' problem.'

I cough as if I'm choking. 'It might be if I arrive dead.' Logic suggests that I'm supposed to reach my destination alive or they would have shanked me at the shop.

'You're gonna fuckin' arrive dead if you fuckin' carry on.'

A heavy boot lands on my neck, pushing my face against the van's floor. I don't struggle or complain further. I've broken one of the key teachings of resistance to interrogation training: be the grey man, unimportant, unnoticed, unthreatening. It was worth the gamble; if the bag had been removed, I'd be in a better position to make a run for it. Cuffed and blindfolded as I am, the escape option is rapidly vanishing.

The van slows and turns before coming to a stop. The engine dies and unintelligible shouts sound over the rattle of a roller door closing. A strong hand grabs me and hauls me into a sitting position.

'You fuckin' try anything in front of the boss and you're fuckin' dead.'

My eyebrows raise, although thanks to the bag no one can see.

The thug has let slip some information that may prove useful. I'm going to see the boss. Of course, there are going to be a number of different bosses depending on the thug's status in the organisation, but from the way he said it I get the distinct impression that this boss is important.

The van's door slides open and a second set of hands hauls me out. Not knowing where the ground is, I stumble, like you do when you miss the bottom step of a flight of stairs in the dark. Fortunately, the gangster's grip on my arms stops me from falling. Instead, he and his mates half guide me, half drag me along until I hear the rustle of plastic beneath my feet. Fuck, fuck, fuck, fuck, fuckety fuck. I've watched enough Guy Ritchie movies to know what this means.

I'm never going to see Eloise again. Have I told her enough that I love her? And what about poor Stevie? He's not going to understand where I've gone.

'Ditch the bag and cuffs,' instructs a voice.

The sack is ripped from my head, and I blink instinctively in the fluorescent-tubed light, even though it really isn't that bright. A blade clicks behind me, then the plastic zip-ties digging into my wrists fall away.

I'm in some sort of industrial unit. Chains hang from the iron girders, and on a peg board on one wall hang a variety of power tools, or torture implements: the two are pretty much interchangeable to the enlightened criminal.

Five massive Black Dogs stand in a semi-circle around me. To my front is an older man leaning on a rusted oil drum and smoking a cigarette. He has greying shoulder-length hair and what in other circumstances might be described as a kind face. Like the other Black Dogs, he wears a patched leather waistcoat. Unlike them, he is wiry rather than muscle-bound, not that I take any comfort from this fact; it's a bit like when you see a small bouncer, you know they have to make up for their size with skill or a well-honed violent streak.

The man looks me up and down and takes a long pull on his cigarette before discarding it in the oil drum. He blows a stream of smoke into the air, then says, 'Tracey Jervis. You were told to fucking leave it.'

CHAPTER 43

Eloise: 8 days until Isabella Garrante book launch

I'm home putting the finishing touches to a book review that's due for the local rag tomorrow when my thoughts turn to cooking something decent for dinner given that Garth will have fuelled himself on coffee and biscuits whilst painting.

> Me: Shall I get the tea on?

> Garth: Yeah won't be long. Looking forward to seeing my Tonks x

Huh? What's up with him? How will I know he's the sender if he doesn't sign his name at the end? Odd that he said Tonks and not Stevie, too. Lovely Tonkawoo . . . it's been a while now . . . but odder still that there's a kiss. The paint fumes must have gone to his head.

I chop garlic, onions and ginger, chuck a bit of coconut oil in the pan and soften it all up a wee bit, huffing in that golden smell. In go cauliflower, chickpeas, coconut milk, tomato paste and a big dump of garam masala. Smells amazing. I've tried to resist cracking open a beer but to no avail. There's nothing quite like a cold beer whilst cooking a curry. Or eating it for that matter.

I clean up as I go, and stick the rice on. That bloke of mine better be home soon if he doesn't want soggy cauliflower and a wife two beers in.

Stevie sits right behind me as I stand at the sink rinsing and scrubbing what no longer needs to be used. He helpfully leans against my legs so I know he's there and don't fall over him or boot him one by accident. I can see the driveway from the kitchen and expect to see Garth every time I look up. But nope, just the neighbour's weirdly silent electric car gliding by, like Stevie when he wants to slink off in secret.

I turn the hob off. Soggy cauli and rice and two beers it is then.

Me: Where you at Picasso?

I'm starting to feel uneasy — I hate not knowing where people are — but tell myself to get a grip. He'll be washing his paintbrushes: three million rinses for each brush.

I've just sat down to do some reordering for the shop when Stevie explodes into the room. He's got something in his mouth. It's the courier bag — the one in which the copy of *See You in September* arrived.

'Stevie, come,' I say calmly.

He looks at me, braced in the crouch that tells me he's just about to take off again.

'Stevie, leave,' I say, lowering my voice and attempting to sound stern.

He scampers away, bag in gob, hoofing around the coffee table and hiding behind the old green armchair.

I shall have to resort to bribery if I want the bag back in one piece.

I go into the kitchen for a doggo treat and Stevie bounds after me, empty mouthed and triumphant. He receives his veal jerky or whatever horror Garth has bought for him, and we both go back into the living room and survey the small amount of carnage. Stevie looks pleased with himself — he has, after all, won on two counts — but doesn't go to grab the bag again. He's managed to shred quite a bit of it.

I pick up the first pieces of torn-up, slobbery mush and realise it's too shiny and crinkly to be the usual package stuffing. It actually looks like . . . photo negatives. It is. It's a whole load of strips of chopped-up film, mostly of people by the looks of it. Who the hell would pack a courier bag with that? I pick all the tiny bits of weirdly dismembered arms and legs and face, and put them in an old bread bag, for want of a more suitable receptacle. Garth's brain will explode when he sees this.

Speaking of whom. I dial his number, but it rings out to voicemail.

All motivation to do the reordering has left me. Something's niggling at the back of my memory. I open the file of photos we scanned from the ones in Tama's lock-up, and flick through them, hoping something will ring a bell.

There's Tracey: golden, hopeful. There's Trent Meek: sober, fatherly. And there's Oddbean and his two arty friends. There's something about the three of them, so happy, so loving. I open the browser and google Oddbean.

Mickey 'Oddbean' McCaughey (born Michael Patrick McCaughey, 10 September 1956) was an artist, businessman and entrepreneur, best known for his nudes.

Nudes. Why doesn't that surprise me? I scroll down to the bit that covers 'Disappearance'.

> McCaughey was last seen in October 1999. His final
> piece of work, a sculpture of a coffee bean, is displayed
> outside the café in Havelock North that bears his name.
> No sightings have been reported and police state that he
> remains an active missing person's case. (Citation needed).

I click on images and get a few hits. Lanky, androgynous Oddbean draped around well-dressed, good-looking people, a bit like Bowie but not as handsome. A close-up photo of a probably drunk Oddbean, mouth wide open, pontificating and gesturing, left wrist draped in a chain with a little bear charm on it. Oddbean's café. Oddbean and Franklin announcing a business partnership. And further down, *that* photo. Three happy, possibly drunk friends at an art opening or somesuch. I click on it and see that this image has a caption from a newspaper article:

> Oddbean (left) pictured with friends at the launch of 'Pills
> and Punk: The Lost Years'.

There are examples of the photographs from the exhibition, and Oddbean is clearly trying his damnedest to appear as cool as the photographer's subjects. I get completely sidetracked by photos of The Damned and Ramones until a grumble from Stevie alerts me to the fact that time is passing and our home is still husband/dad-less.

I ring Garth's number and again it goes to voicemail. There's been no reply to my last text. This is really not funny anymore.

I stick my phone in my pocket, chuck on the nearest pair of trainers and head for the stairs. Stevie joins me as soon as he hears signs of an impending trip. We're off to go find his dad.

CHAPTER 44

Garth: 8 days until Isabella Garrante book launch

The semi-circle of Black Dogs surrounding me comes closer. Their heavy boots pound against the stained concrete floor, beating out a rhythm until they are at the edge of the large plastic sheet. I remain silent, trying not to shake. In the military when you were interrogated you were only ever supposed to give your name, rank and number. All other enquiries were to be met with the stock phrase 'I cannot answer that question, Sir.' You weren't even supposed to answer yes or no for fear that saying yes to a question such as 'Would you like a cup of tea?' would be skilfully edited for propaganda purposes as the answer to the question 'Did you burn down that village and kill innocent civilians?'

I doubt the Black Dogs pay heed to the Geneva Convention and I suspect my silence will not be tolerated here. My mind races through myriad possible responses, none of which seem likely to get me out of this unscathed. There isn't really any wiggle room; the thugs who came into the shop couldn't have been any less ambiguous in their demands.

The Black Dogs stand silent, menacing, waiting for some cue from their leader. My heart pounds in my ears, light-headedness making it hard to focus, then a cheerful dinging in my pocket breaks the quiet: it's an incoming text. At this time of day, it will be Eloise.

'You'd better get that,' says the boss. 'Might be important.'

Even under normal circumstances I'm not the best at reading the room. In my current predicament I have no idea whether he's serious. I ease my hand towards my pocket, half expecting to be king-punched from behind.

'And don't say fucking anything that I'm going to have to break your fingers for.'

I craft my response as quickly as I can, praying that Eloise will pick up that something is wrong. I turn the screen towards the boss for him to check. He waves it away, apparently not interested, confident enough in the power of his threat, or savvy enough to know that I really can't divulge anything vital anyway. I press send, and with it offer a little prayer, although I'm not actually religious and expect the chance of the Elder God Cthulhu saving me is as unlikely as any other deity's intervention.

'Now kill it,' instructs the boss.

I hold down the off button. It's not like I have a choice.

'Tracey Jervis. You were told to back off,' he says again. 'Only, that didn't come from me, it was a fuck-up by a couple of Dogs who thought they could make a bit of coin on the side, barking to someone else's tune.'

Behind me there is a disturbance, murmurings and the smack of a fist on leather. I want to turn and look, only I'm like a mouse transfixed by the gaze of a snake. The boss gives a little nod, lifts his chin and points to an oil-stained patch of concrete next to him.

'You're gonna want to get off the plastic for this.'

I hurry to where he's indicated as the thug with slicked-back hair who threatened me in the shop is corralled onto the plastic sheet. I take several deep breaths. I may not be out of the woods yet, but at least the person about to be savaged by wild animals is not me.

The beating is brutal, and all the more so because the victim makes no effort to defend himself. He simply takes blow after blow that would surely kill me. Even when he's floored, no longer able to stand, he doesn't cover up as the kicks fly.

A particularly brutal boot lands between his legs. He makes a cry like a wounded animal, then throws up on the sheet. I turn to look away and feel the boss's hand grip the back of my head, forcing me to watch.

'You like books, right?' says the boss.

I nod, my gaze still fixed on the beating, which appears to be coming to an end.

'Good, because I want to tell you a story.' He lets go of my head. 'Once upon a time there was a king whose wealth came from selling magic beans. All was good in the kingdom until a bunch of bandits started selling their own beans, forcing the price up so the king couldn't afford his next shipment. That was when the king's most trusted warrior told him about a jester who sold beans for the king, a jester that said he knew somewhere else to get magic beans. The king gave the jester a hundred thousand, only the jester disappeared along with all the money.'

I take a moment to decode the allegories. 'And how does Tracey fit into this story?'

The boss takes out a cigarette and places it between his lips. 'That's what I want you to find out.' Flipping open a Zippo in a well-practised move which is actually as cool as the boss thinks it is, he holds the flame under the cigarette's end and inhales.

I'm still uncertain about how his rambling story relates to our investigation and what's expected of me. On the list of things I want in my life right now, working for the Black Dogs is not just at the bottom of the list; it's scribbled out on the other side of the paper with many lines through it.

'There might be no connection,' I suggest hopefully.

The boss points the cigarette at me and flicks away the ash. 'There's already a connection. Franklin fucking White.'

He's right, of course, but I make one last try to get out of this. 'The police found nothing.'

'Cops weren't looking the right way, were they? A schoolgirl goes missing on the same night a drug dealer disappears. Which one gets priority? They didn't fucking care about Oddbean. I don't fucking care about Oddbean. But I do care about who took the hundred grand.'

'Maybe Oddbean is living it up large somewhere with your money?' It's a possibility and surely one he must have considered.

The boss shakes his head. 'A smart person, a careful person, a quiet person might be able to disappear. Oddbean was none of those things. If he'd taken the money, he'd have blown it on sex and drugs, and I'd fucking well know about it.'

'You *talked* to Franklin?' I actually make air quotes with my fingers, a gesture I immediately feel stupid about.

'Franklin was the one with connections. We couldn't touch him then.'

A hundred grand is a lot of money, it was even more so twenty years ago, but something about this still doesn't sit right. The boss must know there's no chance of recovering the cash now, so what is it he really wants?

I square my shoulders and shake my head. 'I don't buy it. The money's gone. Why does it matter?' My tone is firmer than before, not challenging but businesslike. 'I need to understand the truth if I'm to have any chance of success.'

The boss fixes his gaze on me, and I recognise the killer in him. Maybe I've gone too far, been too assertive. The room has gone quiet, the only sound the rustle of plastic and the groans of the pummelled Dog. The silence lengthens and I fight the urge to fill it.

'The truth.' The boss finishes his cigarette, drops the butt on the floor and grinds it beneath his boot. 'The truth is I wasn't the king back then, my papa was. It was me who vouched for Franklin and Oddbean, but it was my papa that paid the price. I owe him justice, and for that I need you to find out what happened.'

I hold my hands out, placating. 'We've not really got any further than the original police investigation with Tracey, and we don't know anything at all about Oddbean.'

The boss's eyes harden. 'You'd better fucking get started then, because next time you won't be walking off that plastic.'

CHAPTER 45

Eloise: 8 days until Isabella Garrante book launch

Stevie and I have just pulled up at the back of the shop when my phone dings:

Garth: At Uncommon Room.

Meet me here.

Please. Garth.

What the hell?

'Stay there, Stevo,' I say as I clamber out of the car. For peace of mind, I need to check Garth's not actually in the shop.

Following instinct, I try the back door. It opens — not locked. He must be in there then.

'Garth? What the fuck is going on?' I yell, wishing he'd just come noodling out, face covered in red paint splats, having made a right mess of the sink behind the counter.

There's no response. I continue down the short corridor and into the shop proper. It's dark but I can already see from the glow of the CCTV screen and the streetlamps out front that there's no one here. I call out again to make sure, then head back the way I came in, locking the door behind me.

I get in the car, and Stevie steps up on the passenger seat. I notice a generous rubbing of his short, silvery grey fur on the side of the seat, and the useless thought that I should really vacuum the car penetrates the worry and confusion. I buckle my belt and dial Garth's number.

'Just come to The Uncommon Room and I'll explain everything,' he says.

I can't remember the last time I felt such relief.

'Okay, love, see you in five.'

In the main bar Garth is sitting at a round table, nursing a whisky. Seated opposite him is Hastings' tiniest poet, Eleanor, looking bewildered. Stevie dives under the table and curls himself up in a safe position. I drop the lead and Garth hugs me around the middle from his seated position, not letting go of that whisky for love nor money.

'It's okay, love, I'm here,' I say.

Gordon brings me a pint and buggers off again.

Eleanor looks at me. 'Not a clue. He hasn't said a word. I'll be in the garden having a smoke if you need me.'

I didn't know she smoked and wonder if she's joking. My mind is already addled, so I sit opposite my husband, take a big swig of beer, and look at him. He's scared and confused and clearly trying to figure out where to begin. His mind moves quickly at the best of times, and I can see he's trying to pull out a swirling thought and articulate it.

'Black Dogs came to the shop. Got me. They want to know where Oddbean is. I was at their pad or somewhere. Then they dropped me here.'

'Okay. Drink your whisky.' So it was the Dogs. I'm momentarily relieved, then angry, then scared.

Garth takes a large gulp as instructed, and winces. 'Oddbean disappeared at the same time as a hundred thousand dollars of Black Dog money. From what I can gather from the head Dog, son of the previous head Dog, Oddbean and Franklin were dealing drugs and Oddbean disappeared at the same time as a wodge of their money. Head Dog Junior wants payback.'

'What's this got to do with us and Tracey?'

'We are now tasked with finding out what happened to Oddbean.'

'Well, aren't we in demand?'

This gets a smile. 'It would appear we have quite a bit of non-book-related work on.'

Gordon appears with another whisky and a sizeable silver bucket of hot chips. He pats Garth on the shoulder and buggers off again.

'Can we move in here?' Garth asks.

'Sure. Are you okay, really?'

'Think so. We need to scour Tama's paperwork for everything we can find on Franklin and Oddbean.'

'We're working for the Black Dogs now, too?'

'I don't see as we have much choice.' Garth adjusts the positioning of the sauce in relation to the chips. 'Besides, I reckon it's all linked in with what happened to Tracey anyway.'

'Okay. I have several things to tell you. Eat some chips whilst I talk. I think we need to tell Tama about what just happened. And Stevie found something odd.'

I fill Garth in about the negatives in the courier bag, and am treated to a front-seat view of a surprised open gob half full of masticated chips.

'Close your mouth, please. Now I reckon we need to talk to Meryl as soon as possible. She told me she's known Dafydd since they were teens. It would be good to find out what happened to him and how much they both know about what Oddbean was up to.'

Garth nods and thinks. I take his hand and he gives mine a squeeze.

'I'm all right. Sorry to have worried you,' he says.

'Yes, well. Next time you go rampaging off to gang pads you could at least let me know. That cauliflower will be inedible by now.'

'That is indeed the nature of cauliflower.'

Eleanor comes back into the bar and takes the empty chair at our table.

'Glad to see beer and chips are still the cure for what ails you.'

'And whisky.' Garth is still clinging to his glass for dear life.

'I have Tracey's poems with me. I've been carrying them around since the other night, moping about Tracey and dwelling on if I did enough to help her.'

Eleanor rummages in her huge red leather bag, pulls out a folder and hands it to me.

'I put the two that I thought most of interest on the top. They're not her best, but I found them rather illuminating. And they're mercifully short.'

I read aloud. Garth doesn't have his glasses on and the light is dim. 'It's called 'Trapped':

'The bear prowls but he's outside the cage,
His demands ever present, ever increasing, ever there.
There's no escape, no rest,
He prowls and growls
Incessant, repressant,

Claws grasping, breath rasping,
Always there, the unbearable bear.
'That's a pretty bad last line,' I say.
'Harsh,' says Garth.
'It's not the worst daddy-issues poem I've ever read,' says Eleanor.
I put the poem aside and read the title of the next: 'Green':
'*He holds me like a precious new leaf,*
My fragility in the palm of his hand.
I am a new thing: green.
Green as his grass,
Fresh and precious but soon,
Inevitably, we fall apart,
And I swap one prowling bear for another.
The green has worn away,
Richness fading to rust.
With green I escape.'
'That's not too shabby. I like the call-back to the bear motif,' says Garth.

'Hmm,' says Eleanor, wrinkling her nose. 'I'll leave them with you. That's enough nauseating juvenilia for me.' She gets up and goes back out into the garden.

'Green as *his* grass. Tracey knew about the drugs,' I say. 'Did she nick off with some of the drug money?'

'That would be a motive for murder,' says Garth.

'What a story. Horrible old bear of a father pressuring her at every twist and turn, and Franklin, a disgusting predatory bear pawing at her too. No wonder she felt trapped.'

We sip our drinks.

'Let's get you home, shall we? You look like you need your bed.'

'Should we call Tama?' Garth says. 'We need to go through things and fit the jigsaw pieces together.'

'Not tonight. Tracey's not going anywhere and we need to process all this new information.' I'm also thinking about how much work I've recently put Tama's way and am a bit embarrassed to call him again so soon.

I put my traumatised family in the Tomato and off we wend.

CHAPTER 46

Garth: 7 days until Isabella Garrante book launch

I've phoned in sick today, which isn't so much phoning in sick as nudging Eloise and asking her if she can get Phyllis to cover. It's one of the perks of owning the business, although the other side of that equation is being first in line when other members of staff are away. Phyllis responds with her stock answer of 'No problem' and a smiley emoji.

I'm not sick as such, more shaken from last night's events, and I feel a new urgency to make some progress on Tracey's case and now Oddbean's, too. I intend to spend the day wading through the files of paperwork, going over them with a fresh eye and a new focus in light of what I've learnt from the Black Dogs.

I fix myself a coffee, instant because I can't be arsed with anything else, then fat-finger my way through a text to Tama:

> Me: Hello M8, There have been some developments.
> Can we meet up to discuss. Garth.

The response is immediate:

Tama: I'm free this evening. What time and where?

Me: 7pm at the storage unit? Garth.

Tama: WHAT STORAGE UNIT?

I guess we're still playing the plausible deniability game.

Me: How about our place? 7pm? Garth.

I don't mention that almost everything from the storage unit pertaining to the case is now in our own incident room, thereby negating any aspects of deniability.

Tama: Kei te pai. See you then.

Meeting arranged, I dive into the paperwork. By lunchtime, I've found nothing on Oddbean but have identified two previously unnoticed anomalies. One is a report that during a police canvass of the Village on the day after Tracey's disappearance a distressed individual was spoken to in Donnelly Street. He seemed to be experiencing some sort of psychotic breakdown and ended up being taken away in an ambulance. His name was Dafydd Edwards — or Teddy, as Meryl informs us he was known as back then.

The second anomaly is in the form of a statement by Victoria White, providing her husband, Franklin, with an alibi on the night of the fifth. There is nothing fundamentally wrong with the statement, no smoking gun that proves it to be untrue, only a gut feeling. To my suspicious copper's mind, it reads like a statement given by someone trying to be deliberately vague so they can't be pinned down later.

In the afternoon I concentrate on the evidence relating to Franklin White. There are two pertinent pieces that catch my attention: a statement and then, a few days later, a voluntarily interview, which tells me he was very much a person of interest but the police didn't have enough evidence to arrest.

The statement is pretty much identical to Victoria's — suspiciously so, in fact — and doesn't go into any detail other than reconfirming his alibi. The interview is more enlightening:

> DS Clark: We know you were involved with Tracey, we just need to know if you saw her the night she went missing?
>
> Franklin White: Tracey worked part time for me and helped with the campaign, it was all strictly professional.
>
> DS Clark: Tracey was seventeen, above the age of consent, so the fact that you were in a relationship is no crime. We're only interested in finding Tracey.
>
> Franklin White: There was no relationship.
>
> (Papers rustle)
>
> DS Clark: We're still canvassing the area and getting witness statements. So, if someone places you with Tracey on the night in question and you haven't told us, that's going to look pretty bad for you. Better to come clean now, eh?
>
> Franklin White: I say again. There was no relationship, and I did not see Tracey on the night that she went missing. I don't think I can be any clearer on those points.

As I replace the interview transcript back on the pile, I can feel my synapses firing, making possible connections. There's something here we might be able to run with. I stare at the incident room's whiteboard with its names, photos and questions for a long time, and a theory forms.

⌒✎⌒

Eloise is stropping with me. I have developed my theory further over the afternoon and feel certain that I'm onto something. My refusal to air my findings during dinner, however, has not gone down well — a similarity it shares with the tofu and kūmara stew that Eloise unceremoniously dumped on my plate.

I really don't understand why she is so upset. I attempt to explain that my behaviour is perfectly reasonable, and that it is quite logical to wait until Tama gets here and I can tell them both at the same time. This serves only to aggravate the situation.

'Do you want me here or shall I go and hide under the bed with Stevie?' she asks as I head downstairs to answer the doorbell.

I ignore her, knowing she won't be able to resist being in on the conversation.

'Welcome, thanks for coming, Tama.'

'Too easy. I'm keen to hear your news.'

'Me too,' shouts Eloise from upstairs. 'Perhaps he'll deem you worthy of telling.'

Tama gives me a quizzical look. I shrug. 'The incident room is upstairs and to the left. Just follow the sound of complaining.'

'I heard that,' shouts Eloise.

'If it's not a good time . . .'

'Oh god, no,' yells Eloise. 'Don't you bloody go, or he'll never tell me.'

Tama finds his way to Eloise's voice and gazes about him. 'Ah, you've relocated the case files from my storage unit, I see.'

'What storage unit?' I reply.

'Touché.'

'It just seemed easier,' says Eloise. 'And we'd already created our own incident room, so we're really just adding to it.'

'And you've discovered something we all missed?' Tama asks.

'I'm not sure. It's more of a theory.' I gesture him to a chair. 'But first we've got to bring you up to speed with a few events.'

'Why do I get from your faces that this isn't good?'

'Because Garth was kidnapped by the Black Dogs,' blurts Eloise.

'What? When?'

'Last night,' I say. 'And I wasn't exactly kidnapped.'

'You were hooded, zip-tied and chucked in a van. What would you call it? Extreme Uber?'

'Yes, that happened. But they mostly just wanted to talk. Or their boss did at least.'

Tama leans forward. 'You met their boss?'

'I think so.'

'Older guy, wiry, smokes all the time and does a thing with his Zippo?' He makes a flicking movement with his wrist in a reasonable imitation.

'Yeah, that's him.'

I outline my encounter with the Black Dogs and Tama's face runs the gamut of surprise, concern, disbelief and astonishment. When I finish, he says, 'I'm so sorry, I didn't mean to put you in danger, but there are certain cases I just can't let go.'

'It's not your fault,' says Eloise. 'We were already investigating and would have continued doing so with or without your encouragement.'

'And if I'm correct' — I tap a red pen on the whiteboard — 'the Black Dogs have opened this investigation right up.'

'How so?' asks Tama.

I uncap the pen and draw a circle around Franklin White's name.

'Franklin was always your prime suspect, am I correct?'

'He was and he still is, although unless he's concreted Tracey's body under his patio I doubt we'd ever be able to prove anything, not after all this time.'

'And why was he your prime suspect?' I ask.

'We believed Tracey was having an affair with him.'

'*He* was having an affair with *her*,' corrects Eloise. 'She was the innocent party in this.'

'Of course.'

Eloise picks up a copy of the poem we got from Eleanor. 'And we can prove it, although maybe only circumstantially.'

'That was the thing with Franklin,' says Tama. 'All we ever had was circumstantial evidence. His alibi for the night of Tracey's disappearance was paper thin. We tried to get his wife Victoria to recant — I mean, who gives their husband an alibi when they're off doing the dirty with a schoolgirl? — but she wouldn't budge.'

'I thought the alibi was odd, too, but we've been looking at this wrong,' I say.

'Stop being bloody mysterious and spill.' Eloise is stern, but it appears I may have been at least temporarily forgiven.

'Victoria's alibi is clearly bogus, but she wasn't alibiing Franklin because he was with Tracey. She was alibiing him because he was with Oddbean.'

'Franklin was cheating on his missus with Oddbean?' Tama rubs the side of his head. 'Oddbean swung both ways but not Franklin. I don't buy it.'

'No.' I point at the board. 'What I'm saying is—'

'Fuckety fuckeroo.' Eloise leaps to her feet and riffles through a stack of papers. She pulls out an envelope and a photo showing Oddbean and a male and female friend at an art opening. 'Look at the photo, I think this is—'

'Meryl Thompson and Dafydd Edwards,' says Tama.

I take the photograph for a closer look. Even knowing who he is, I struggle to see Dafydd in the handsome hippy reveller, but there's no doubt that the pretty woman is Meryl in a pre-dreadlock and legwarmer era. They both seem so young, and beautiful, and successful, and most decidedly mates with Oddbean. 'What does it mean that Meryl and Dafydd knew Oddbean?'

'It means we can question Meryl about it.' Eloise glances at Tama. 'It's got nothing to do with Pinter, so we're okay to be doing that.'

Tama nods. 'What's in the envelope?'

'Photo negatives. All girls, all unsavoury. They were in the padding of the envelope the book came in.' Eloise passes over the envelope and Tama holds one of the acetate strips to the light.

'Sleazy, probably not illegal.' He returns the negative. 'Are any of them Tracey?'

'None of the ones not chewed by Stevie. The others I couldn't tell.'

'It could be Oddbean's work,' says Tama. 'Art, porn, it can be a fine line.'

'Which in a roundabout way brings me back to my original point,' I say. 'Victoria alibied Franklin because he and Oddbean were holding a hundred thousand dollars of the Black Dogs' cash that disappeared.'

'And she was too scared of them to drop him in it in case it blew back on her,' says Eloise.

'Exactly.' I draw three connecting lines on the whiteboard. 'And with the joint disappearances I think we can assume that something went wrong that night between Franklin, Oddbean and Tracey.'

CHAPTER 47

Eloise: 6 days until Isabella Garrante book launch

It's the 'Pilfered Petals' launch and we've all decided to go, more to support Kitty than Meryl. Phyllis, Amelia, Garth and I potter around the shop, waiting for Kitty to be ready. Even with Amelia locking up, me cashing up, Phyllis putting out the final few bits of new stock and Garth getting in the way, we're still running behind schedule because Kitty 'just has to do this one thing'.

At last everyone has had a wee, gathered their keys, phones, lip balm, etcetera and we're out of the front door. I lock it behind me and give it the three-rattle security measure.

As we wander down the road, Phyllis and Kitty are deep in conversation about some murdery book, Garth and Amelia are discussing, quite seriously, the contents of a zombie apocalypse survival kit. I have one of those moments I identify as contentment, its ingredients appreciation, friendship, security, and its measurement 'just enough'. God, I hope I can hang on to this simplicity, this safety.

It's not far. We reach the library and there's a bit of a scuffle as to who should enter first. It's amazing how booksellers talk to people all day long but once you get them out of their natural habitat, they're quite reluctant to socialise. Garth relents and is the first through the automatic doors.

'Team Sherlock!' Lucy, the librarian tasked with the evening's events, hurries over. 'Drinks over there, artists over there, and you know where the loos are.'

Garth and I usually stick together like glue, and there's no change this evening as we head to the drinks table.

'Hello!' An excited figure reaches for my sleeve. It's Meryl. Her cheeks are delightfully rouged, and her pale eyes gleam as though it's Christmas Eve and she's six years old. I've never seen this Meryl. It suits her.

'Congratulations, Meryl. How's it all going?'

'Brilliant. Just brilliant. Please come and see what I created from your beautiful blooms. Where's Kitty? Oh, I see her. Follow me, follow me.' Meryl keeps hold of my sleeve and pulls me around the room, gathering Kitty, Phyllis and Amelia as she goes.

The artworks are set up in a space that's been cleared of book stacks for the purpose, and she leads us to an easel at the very centre.

'Ta-da!'

I look from the easel to Meryl, then back to the easel. My prepared, empty words of benign congratulation die on my lips. It's stunning. The frame of the work must be a metre square, the background painted smooth and black. The creation within is a firework of colour, lacquered petals glowing as they reach from the frame. I glance around. It's easily the most arresting piece in the exhibition; the others may stand up to closer scrutiny, but there's a reason Meryl's piece is front and centre.

There's a sharp intake of breath, and I glance up to see Kitty, hand held to her mouth in astonishment.

'Meryl, it's incredible,' I say. 'I don't know about Kitty, but I would say it's a fine use of our pilfered petals. Thank you for choosing us to steal from.'

Kitty nods. She appears unable to speak.

Tears are running down Meryl's cheeks. 'Oh. My eyes are leaking,' she says.

The team murmur congratulations, offer little pats and smiles, and peel off to investigate the other works.

'When's the last time you exhibited, Meryl?' I ask.

'It's been a while, I'll tell you that. Life took a very odd turn a ways back and I sort of lost my mojo. But there was something about this project that inspired me.'

'Its criminal element?' asks Garth.

'Oh, ha ha, maybe. But I'm not a lawbreaker, not me. I've seen where that leads.'

'Speaking of which, Meryl. I did want to ask you about something I found recently. A photograph of a very beautiful young woman at an art exhibition. She was pictured with friends, I think. Teddy and Oddbean.'

'Friends!' splutters Meryl. 'Teddy was my friend. I hope he still is, somewhere in that fuzzy head of his. Not Oddbean, though. Right nasty git he was. I don't miss him one bit. Oh, my poor, poor boy.' Her eyes leak fresh tears.

Garth and I steer her through to the sofas in the otherwise empty computer area. We sit, and I can see that Meryl is so full of emotion that she keeps scrabbling around, wringing her hands and frantically searching for a hankie in her . . . yes, they actually are sequinned leggings.

'Meryl are you okay to talk now? I don't want to spoil your party,' I say.

Garth frowns at me but keeps his gob shut. He would be quite happy to spoil her party.

Meryl locates her pink-flowered hankie and has a bloody good snort into it. In an ill-advised sequence of events, she wipes her eyes with it, then takes to fiddling with it in her lap. 'I'm fine, I'm fine,' she says. 'This whole thing has brought back memories of the old days anyway. I'd like to get them off my chest.' She smiles and takes a couple of soothing deep breaths.

'Teddy and I were great mates back in the day. He was something of a mentor to me, actually. Thought I had a bit of talent. He'd been to Elam School of Fine Arts and everything. He was always very humble, very quiet about it in his way, but he was one of our generation's most talented artists, I reckon, right up there with the best. He could turn his hand to most things, but his pen-and-ink work was just sublime. I'd watch him work and he was like a whip-crack, so fast and accurate. It was like he could reveal some great deep truth in just a few strokes of his pen. It was unsettling in some ways.'

'And what about Oddbean?'

'Huh. No talent to speak of. A hanger-on and a leech. He knew Teddy was the real deal and that he could cling to his tailcoats and make a killing.'

'Not your favourite bloke then?'

Meryl sniffs with a great deal of disdain. 'I don't know what Teddy saw in him, I really don't. But the one thing I'll say for Oddbean is that I think he truly loved Teddy. The only time the scales fell from his eyes and you could see a decent human being was when he was in Teddy's company.'

'They were in love?'

'Oh yes. Teddy was so happy, so animated when he was with Oddbean. His work reflected it, it really did. Splashes of colour, a new energy to it. It was like he imprinted his love on the page. It was so, so intense that it's understandable what happened when Oddbean disappeared. Shocking, of course, but I totally got it.'

'What do you mean?'

'Well, you don't think Dafydd was always like this, do you? It was pretty sudden. His mind just cracked. I got the news that Oddbean was gone — upped and buggered off, I thought, probably been caught doing something dodgy — and I went to find Dafydd. He wasn't in any of our usual haunts and eventually I saw him in the Village, just walking, hurrying even, as though he had somewhere urgent to be.'

'Did he speak to you?'

'Not really. I tried to get him to hold still, but he wouldn't stop walking. He was muttering phrases on repeat, and I can't remember the guts of it after all this time, but I know he kept saying "Beans, Beans", which I suppose was maybe his pet name for Oddbean.' She sighs. 'That poor boy. I told him about this event, this exhibition, the other day, told him I was exhibiting again, and he just looked at me. I was hoping he might come.'

Meryl hunches, head bowed, as though brought low by this old, deep hurt. Lost friends, lost opportunities. It makes me ashamed at how little I've thought of who she really is, all the experiences that have made her, all the lives she's lived before I ever met her.

'Still, that was then, and this is now.' Meryl gives her face another swish of the soiled hankie, then visibly pulls herself together and stands. 'I'm off to mix with my public. I'm very glad you're here.' And off she goes in search of her wine glass.

'Well,' says Garth, 'I wasn't expecting a love story.'

We stay where we are, away from the general fuss, watching people come and go. It's lovely to see them stop in front of Meryl's work and really look at it, watch their faces react, their wondering smiles.

As we leave, I look more closely at the label on Meryl's frame.

'Oil paint and lacquer, found blooms: A bookshop is a home for more than books.'

CHAPTER 48

Garth: 5 days until Isabella Garrante book launch

'Fuck, fuck, fuck, fuck, fuckety fuck!' I slam the advance reading copy onto the pillow. Stevie looks at me reproachfully, then slinks from the duvet and scrambles under the bed.

It's not even a proper ARC. They normally look like a book, only with myriad promotional quotes and a release date on the back. Sometimes they'll even have a totally different cover which is substantially better than the final cover decided upon by the publishers. However, what I've been reading isn't a book, it's nothing more than a collection of manuscript pages stapled together: the first three chapters of *Dead Girl Gone*, the new Isabella Garrante novel.

Today is my day off, so when Garrante's publishers emailed me an NDA first thing, I signed it and sent it straight back. They then emailed three chapters from *Dead Girl Gone*, informing me that I was extraordinarily lucky to have them, Garrante never sending out advance reading copies or any promotional material until the release date.

Excited by this break from tradition and feeling remarkably privileged, I printed out the pages and stapled them together before jumping onto the bed with Stevie to read them. Three chapters later, my excitement has turned to anxious dread.

My problem isn't with the writing style or authorial voice. As ever, the novel is beautifully written, showing Isabella's unique blend of evocative prose and wonderful dialogue. No, my problem is with the content. From these three chapters it's clear that the story is a thinly veiled retelling of the Tracey Jervis case. Actually, it's not even thinly veiled: it is the Tracey Jervis case. The protagonist, a seventeen-year-old schoolgirl at Te Mata High, is called Tracey, so it couldn't really be clearer.

That's not the worst of it though. In the first three chapters we've met her overbearing father and her best friend Prudence, and — this is the real kicker — seen her have sex on the campaign office desk of Action Now Party candidate Franklin White.

I lean over the side of the bed and look at poor Stevie staring up, his golden eyes wide with concern. 'Oh, Stevie, mate. We are so screwed.'

I fix myself another coffee and go out to the deck to look out over the trees and foliage and rooftops beyond. I love Havelock North; sure, it's not perfect, but where is? And I love our little bookshop. We built it from nothing with hard work, sacrifice and love — ours, our booksellers' and our supporters'. Now the spectre of Franklin White and the misdeeds of his past threaten to destroy it all.

Halfway through the coffee, I give up trying to be calm. This isn't about me and Eloise anymore, it's about Kitty who has a mortgage to pay, and Amelia and Phyllis and all our customers who rely on us. And I really mean who rely on us; when we reopened after the

Covid lockdown, we had customers coming into the shop in tears, grateful that we had weathered the storm and weren't going to close. It made me realise that our little bookshop is so much more than just a retailer; it is a safe, welcoming sanctuary for those who need us, a real community space. And one whose future is now in jeopardy.

It's no good, I've got to go and talk to Eloise right now. We built the bookshop together and we'll save it together.

Eloise and I have had some stellar conversations in our gloomy stock room surrounded by cardboard boxes, bubble wrap and an inordinate amount of junk that Amelia and Kitty refuse to throw away. Today, I deem that it is not discreet enough for the conversation we need to have, so I usher Eloise out of the back door to the car park beyond and do a quick scan for large motorbikes. The area is technically open to the public, but, other than the odd retail assistant going to work and occasional cinema-goer, it's private.

'What is it? What's happened?' We've known each other long enough for her to know that this new venue is significant.

I don't speak, not immediately, trying to fashion my whirlwind thoughts into something that makes sense. 'The Isabella Garrante novel. It's a retelling of the Tracey Jervis disappearance.'

'What? How do you know?'

'The publishers emailed me the first three chapters of the manuscript this morning. I think they wanted to ensure that we could give a proper introduction at the launch.'

'And it's definitely based on the case?'

'It's not based on the case. It is the case. It names Tracey, Prudence, Franklin and a handful of others. It doesn't even try to disguise their identities behind pseudonyms.'

'So, what happened? Who murdered Tracey?'

'I don't know. As I said, it's only the first three chapters.'

'But how can she do that? Isn't it illegal? Do the publishers know?'

'They must do, surely? I appreciate Hawke's Bay isn't Auckland or Wellington, but the case was national news. Someone would remember. Rose would remember — she knows bloody everything.'

'Is that why they sent you the first three chapters? To warn us?'

'They didn't say. It was all official, though. I had to email her a signed NDA this morning.'

'Fuck!' Eloise folds her arms.

'That's what I said.'

'We're the scene of the crime, the scene of the story. That's why Isabella chose us for the launch.'

'It's not a launch, it's a funeral. We'll be ruined. Franklin isn't going to let this slide. He'll do our legs for sure.'

'No. This could work for us.' Eloise tilts her head, playing out some scenario in her mind. 'If he's so discredited by the book, he'll lose any standing he's got. He'll have no power to pressure our landlords into selling, and it might give us the answers we need to get the Black Dogs off our back.'

'Until his lawyers litigate against Isabella and the publishers, and he gets a big fat pay-out and an apology.' I grind the toe of my boot into the gravel. 'He'll be so emboldened he'll come for us next.'

'Isabella must have solid evidence; her publishers would never take the risk otherwise. Maybe she found Prudence, got the truth of what was going on with Tracey and Franklin.'

It's mad, but there's a possibility that fits with the array of facts and rumours we've gathered so far.

'Maybe she *is* Prudence.'

CHAPTER 49

Eloise: 5 days until Isabella Garrante book launch

We've called an emergency staff meeting, which has freaked the team out considerably — a necessary evil seeing as we're not supposed to tell them about the launch. We are, of course, about to tell them about the launch.

'Have you all got a drink, because you're going to need one,' Garth begins.

There's a worried hush.

'So,' he continues. 'If we were to host a world-famous author, who would you want it to be?'

There is full bookseller buy-in; we love playing this game.

'Roddy Doyle,' says Phyllis. 'I have his email if you're interested.' Phyllis knows everyone in Dublin and this is not beyond the realms of possibility. If the stress of hosting IFG wasn't already killing me, I might be tempted.

'Patrick Rothfuss,' says Kitty. 'I have some questions I would like him to answer.' There are muttered agreements and sotto voce threats around the subject of 'book three'.

'Do you mean in actual real life or are we just playing?' says Amelia. 'I've already met Jack Heath and Neal Shusterman, so my life is practically complete.'

'Okay,' says Garth. 'Well, the massive news is that Isabella Garrante is going to launch her new novel *Dead Girl Gone* with us in five days' time. In person. Here in Havelock North.'

There's a brief silence, followed by:

'What?'

'Why?'

'Well, I'm not doing the catering for that.'

'I'll get on to the nuts and bolts in a moment,' says Garth. 'We've signed a non-disclosure agreement because it's such a big deal, had a secret meeting with Rose and everything. All very sneaky beaky.'

'Won't you get into massive trouble if they find out you told us?' asks Amelia.

'I think we're officially allowed to tell you tomorrow, but anyway, you won't snitch and there's a very good reason why you need to know,' I say.

Garth coughs. 'The plot of *Dead Girl Gone* tells the story of Tracey Jervis's disappearance.'

'Well, that's going to create some fireworks.' Amelia makes a 'kaboom my brain just exploded' gesture and falls back in her seat, shaking her head.

'It's worse than you think.' I look to Garth and nod for him to carry on. 'We need to tell you everything.'

Our staff sit in silence as Garth goes on to explain the events of recent days. When he's unloaded, he sits back, lips burbling his relief as if he were a slowly deflating balloon.

'What?' says Kitty.

'Fuck me,' says Phyllis.

'So let me get this straight,' says Amelia. 'Sleazeball Franklin White is one hundred percent dodgy; Tracey Jervis was sleeping with him, which is completely eww and should be illegal by the way even if she was seventeen; and the Black Dogs have threatened you to back off but are now threatening you to investigate? And how the hell does Isabella Garrante fit in? Jesus, you really couldn't make it up.'

'So how far have you read? Why don't you read to the end to find out what happened to Tracey,' says Phyllis, reasonably enough.

'They only sent me the first three chapters. If they release any more, someone will cut their legs off and post them to their grandmothers,' says Garth.

Kitty sighs. 'This is all getting a bit much, Garth. I just want to sell books. I didn't sign up to be threatened by gangs and have my flowers nicked by a local artist.'

'And to make matters worse, sorry, Kitty, Franklin White is threatening us with eviction if we don't back off. Says he has influence with the landlord and will buy the building.'

Phyllis's face hardens. She speaks slowly. 'Well, just let that Franklin White come anywhere near our shop or our flowers and he'll get what's coming to him. I know where he lives.' Her drawl is so menacing that no one questions her assertion. It is followed by a respectful hush.

Amelia breaks the silence. 'It was such a strange time for the Village though. Our Ena was friendly with Victoria White, although goodness knows why, such a stuck-up piece of work, and it all got a bit testy at family gatherings when the Whites came up in conversation. I mean, she was only repeating rumours really, but things went quite sour with cousin Patsy.'

'What was the rumour?' I ask, deciding not to try to untangle the intricacies of Amelia's family tree.

'I can't quite remember. That Franklin and Oddbean were an unlikely pair. That they were mixed up in things way above their criminal capabilities. Hang on . . . I'll just ring Ena and ask her.'

Amelia pulls her phone out and goes onto the landing. Stevie lifts his head for a second, then returns to sniffing and rootling out snack crumbs. There's a hush, and Garth gets up to fetch the usual, comforting dinner. He dumps foil-wrapped garlic bread on the dining table next to a steaming pot of Bolognese, one of penne and one of grated cheese.

'Come on and dig in whilst we think things over and await Ena's report,' I say.

'I don't think I can eat now, I'm too stressed,' says Kitty, getting up. 'Vegan cheese, too, Garth? Are you feeling okay?'

We regroup on the dog-battered sofas, me on the old armchair that's held together by a bit of gaffer tape. Bowls on laps, we resort to the conversation we're most comfortable with.

'She's an extraordinary storyteller. Like Sally Rooney but funny.'

'How old is "YA" anyway? I'm pretty sure I wasn't a young adult when I was twelve.'

'Have you got the reading copy of the Booker? I really ought to give it a go this year.'

Paperbacks are pulled from bags and passed over, compliments made to the chef, particularly around the addition of capers to the recipe, and for a moment this feels like any book team get-together. Then Amelia comes back.

'Oh, start dinner without me, why don't you,' she says, smiling.

'I saved you the best bits of garlic bread,' says Garth. 'The crispy end bits you like.'

'Lovely. You're forgiven then. Anyway, Ena was more than happy to gossip about Traceygate.' She stops and spoons sauce into a bowl before continuing. 'So. Get this for a rumour. Ena says when Tracey disappeared, and then Oddbean, the word on the street in the rotten underbelly of Havelock North was that Franklin had knocked off both of them.'

'He killed Oddbean, too?' says Phyllis. 'What a busy boy.'

'Well, missing people have to end up somewhere, I suppose,' says Amelia.

There's the clanking of forks on bowls and the crunching of garlic bread and the whirring of thoughts as Team Sherlock consider the implications of Ena's juicy gossip.

'This town, huh,' says Phyllis at last. 'Who'd 'a' thought? And I'm from Dublin.'

There's another moment of contemplative chewing, before I address the elephantine unease in the room.

'So, team. Like Kitty says, none of you signed up for this. I don't know how much power Franklin White actually wields, but there is a possibility he could cause us serious problems.'

'Like get us closed down? Do you really think he could?' asks Kitty.

'Maybe,' says Garth, looking focused and solemn. I like him much better when he's away with the story fairies.

'My question is, do you think we should go ahead with the launch?'

'Are you kidding, Eloise?' says Amelia. 'Turn down the chance of launching the biggest book of the year in the whole world?'

'Franklin Shite for Brains is a bully and there's only one way to deal with a bully,' says Phyllis.

'Chop his balls off?' I ask, and the laughter lightens the moment, even if I do get a stern 'Eloise!' from Garth.

'We'll stand up to him,' says Kitty a little shakily. 'He must have something to hide if he's trying to threaten us.'

'Oh my god, I don't know if I'm terrified or thrilled. It's like reading, I dunno, Chris Hammer or something,' says Amelia.

'Or *Hunger Games* maybe?'

'Yeah, or that one where the woman's husband is actually his twin so she's not gaslit so much as they're actually different people.'

But it's Phyllis who gets the conversation back on track. 'We need to act now,' she says. 'The bookshop faithful will be in full support.'

'On it.' Amelia is texting and talking. 'My YA book group can do some great TikToks about the shop, and I've got a million ideas for the best Garrante window display ever.'

'I wonder what flowers she likes. I'll see what's on offer tomorrow,' says Kitty.

'Or we could get Meryl to steal them from Franklin's garden!' adds Phyllis.

I look over to Garth, who is rather overcome.

'You got something in your eye, love?' I ask.

He nods like a small boy who's just been given a puppy.

Amelia gets up and plants herself on the arm of the sofa beside him. 'Don't you worry, boss. We've got your back.'

He bursts into tears.

CHAPTER 50

Garth: 4 days until Isabella Garrante book launch

'Morning, lovely bookshop,' I say as I head through the door painted to look like Doctor Who's Tardis. There is no reply, not as such, although I like to think the shop sighs with a tender warmth. It makes me feel like some kind of traitor for risking everything with the launch.

I count the float into the till, boot up the computers, and open up the POS app and our website. Forgoing the usual vacuuming, I pull up the checklist for the launch. At the top is 'venue', which has now swapped from bookshop to big top. Then there's 'promo', which Eloise is sorting this morning, creating a social media event and walking around the Village with Stevie, putting up posters. The publisher is also going to go hard-out from today with promises of national press and TV. With the change to the bigger venue, I've sorted additional wine from Red Vines and upped the quantities for glass hire. Hungry Havvers Catering are doing platters and have taken our tripled estimate of numbers in their stride. The circus will have its own PA system, but I'll need to check that we are good to use it, and put a question mark next to it. Below this I add 'security?' to the list.

I've never been to a book launch that required security before, but this is Isabella Fucking Garrante. And if the plot of the book leaks beforehand and the press get a hold of it, things could get well out of hand. I take a deep breath to calm myself and cross out the question mark. I suppose the publisher may provide security for Garrante herself — close protection, as we used to call it back in the day. My thoughts of keen-eyed professionals in grey suits with suspicious bulges under their jackets are interrupted by a rapping on the shop door. It's only 8.15am so, yes, the door is still locked and I haven't switched on the main shop lights, but apparently the single fluorescent strip above the computer is enough of an invitation for someone to want me to open up.

I look out. Meryl is peering through the glass, her breath steaming up the window.

I grab my keys from the counter and open up.

'I had to get milk from the dairy,' Meryl explains. 'And I saw that you were open so I thought I might just take a look at my calendars.'

'It was a good exhibition the other day. Were you pleased?' I ask, keeping the thought that we weren't actually open inside my head.

'I sold two pieces.' Meryl pulls her trolley behind her to the counter.

I dutifully haul out her pile, now including 'Namaste Bitches!' and 'Lovecraft of Life — Wit and Wisdom of the Elder Gods', which I've been secretly hoping won't sell so that I can have it.

Meryl sifts through the selection, muttering her proposed calendar recipients. 'I might swap this one.' She passes me the 'Lovecraft' calendar and I take in the picture for September, a swirling mass of many-eyed tentacles in a hypnotic galaxy with the inspiring message from Azathoth: 'In madness we find truth.'

'Yes, I'll get this one instead.' She plucks 'Death a Day — 365 Days of Serial Killers' from the stand.

More than anything, I'd love to meet the intended recipient. 'Shall I add it to your pile?'

'No. I'm going to buy them all today.' Meryl rummages in her trolley. Eventually she pulls out two pristine series five, one-hundred-dollar bills from her purse.

So there's little doubt about who purchased Meryl's artwork.

'Don't forget your keys,' I say, and scoop them from the counter.

Meryl reaches out a hand, then stops, gazing past me, her eyes wide like a cat transfixed by a house ghost.

Scrunching my toes in my shoes, I force away a shiver and turn to see what has bewitched Meryl. The ragged scrap of cardboard with Dafydd's painting of Sherlock Tomes is Blu-tacked to the wall.

'He truly was a genius, had a photographic memory, would paint brilliant scenes from something he'd only ever glimpsed.' Meryl fishes a handkerchief from her sleeve as she makes her way to the door. 'Until he broke.'

I get that itch in my brain where I know I've missed something important. I turn back to Dafydd's painting and examine it afresh. The detail is limited — there's only so much you can do with cardboard and emulsion — but Meryl is correct: Dafydd is a genius, a master at creating an impression with a few brushstrokes.

I open up the shop's Facebook page and scroll back through several posts until I find the image I want. Comparing it to Dafydd's painting, my suspicions are confirmed. I'm not sure what this means for the case, but I can't wait to tell Eloise.

Unfortunately, I have to wait. A text informs me of the following:

Eloise: Going to be late Stevie rolled in something disgusting on his walk. (Poo emoji, Poo emoji)

My thoughts of our wonderful pupperoo joyously squirming on his back while Eloise looks on in horror are interrupted by the tip-tap of the Admiral's cane.

'Heave ho, heave ho, lash up 'n' stow.'

I stand to attention and chuck up a salute. 'Morning, Sir.'

'Any more trouble with those rapscallions?'

There's been plenty more trouble with the Black Dogs, but I'm hardly going to tell the Admiral. 'No. I think they knew they'd met their match.'

'I should cocoa.' The Admiral brandishes his cane. 'Had a signal that my *Wooden Boat* was in port.'

I rummage through the magazines put aside for customers and pull out his order. 'On the house today, Sir, by way of a thank you.'

'Top hole. Jolly decent of you.' He rolls up the magazine and tucks it below one arm like an RSM's pace stick, then saunters from the shop.

The morning continues well: there's a conference on in the Village, and by the number of presents I've wrapped at least three different parties. The back door slams, then in slinks a shiny, clean, shampoo-smelling Stevie. He hrrruffs a complaint at me and settles in the stock room.

'You had a good walk then?'

'One of us did.'

'Well, I've got something to cheer you up.' I point to Dafydd's painting. 'What do you see?'

'The shop?'

'Look at the detail.' I tap a finger against the card.

'I get it. He's a good artist. What I don't get is why you're going off on one.' Eloise folds her arms and looks at me like I'm insane.

'When exactly were we painting the shop?'

'I don't know. A week or so ago?'

'Remember, it was the night after Amelia had put the Halloween window in, because the new orange flowers matched the display.'

'I'm sure there's a point to this.' Eloise picks up the scissors we use for gift wrapping. 'Much like there's a point to these scissors which I'm going to stab you with if you don't tell me in the next five seconds why you're so excited.'

'Look at the books in the shop window. It's not the Halloween window, it's the time before when the flowers were taken.'

'So?' Eloise twirls the scissors with menace.

I pull up the image of the shop window that Amelia took for Facebook. 'The books in the painting are exactly the ones that were in the window at that time. Even their positioning is perfect.'

Eloise's gaze flicks between the two images. 'He's remembered it perfectly,' she says at last. 'You don't think . . .'

'That if Dafydd had witnessed something disturbing on the night of Tracey's disappearance he'd be able to paint it picture perfect.'

CHAPTER 51

Eloise: 4 days until Isabella Garrante book launch

It's stuffy in the shop today, not quite warm enough for the air con but getting there. A glorious morning that holds promise of the summer to come.

The sunlight through the windows gives a great view of the war memorial and the trees across the road. It also gives a great view of the greasy mitts that have pressed against the glass. There are forehead prints, too, at adult height, from where evening Village revellers have peered in, rather myopically if their whole head has been smooshed on the glass. I'll give it a good going over next time we change the display.

I'm peering out of the smudgy glass, taking a pile of books for a wander round the shop, when a couple in their sixties come in. He's Pākehā, very tall and slim, wearing a suit that looks to be worth more than the Tomato. She's petite, really dainty, of Japanese origin I would say. They're first timers, looking up at the chalkboards, taking in the Invisible Dragon's cage on top of the card stand. She's smiling, he's frowning.

'Good morning,' I practically sing. 'Are you happy having a wander, or may I help with anything?'

'For god's sake, we've only just walked in, woman. Save your hard sell for a few minutes at least.'

I've met this guy's type before, and am prepared. 'Certainly, sir. And if you need help finding anything, your manners for instance, do let me know. Enjoy my beautiful bookshop.'

His companion lets out a surprisingly hearty laugh and says, 'Marvellous.' Mr Grey Eyes glares, open mouthed and as unattractive as a bad temper will make you. I smile and slowly continue putting books out, practically marking my territory by keeping in close proximity.

When I feel that the natural order of things has been restored, I sally back up to the counter.

'Exemplary customer service,' says Garth, patting my arm.

'Thank you, love,' I reply.

Garth starts checking the customer orders folder, I begin unpacking a couple of small boxes and loading the stock into the system. The dainty visitor comes up to the counter with a stack of books, including two fairly expensive cookbooks and the latest lush New Zealand interiors tome, *Green is the New Beige*. Mr Grey Eyes is waiting outside, blocking the doorway and staring down the road.

'Don't mind Gavin,' she says. 'He's a bit of a bully but easily faced down, as you demonstrated.'

I can't be bothered to get into a conversation about not enabling such behaviour, especially as she's about to spend about four hundred bucks. We exchange pleasantries: they're staying at the Boutique Hotel and, yes, it's lovely, they have friends who own one of the local wineries, etcetera, etcetera. Off she goes, and Garth tracks her progress until she's well out of the door.

'Gavin,' snorts Garth. 'What a cock.'

'Old Gav.'

We share an age-inappropriate amount of sniggering, then settle back into our tasks. I'm wondering if Franklin White will be so easy to deal with.

It's edging towards lunchtime and I'm starting to think more than is natural about sushi when I spot a familiar figure on the street. I shove a small pile of books at Garth and hare off down the steps and the non-fiction aisle, veering left out of the door and catching up to Dafydd as he's peering into the window of the cashmere shop.

'Hi Dafydd,' I say, too brightly.

Dafydd turns his head slowly and frowns. 'Goats' undercoats,' he replies.

'What? Cashmere? Is it goat wool?' I ask, but I've already lost his attention. He has turned away from the window and is heading off, albeit very slowly, towards Joll Road.

'Dafydd, I wondered if I might ask you a question?' I'm aware I'm already asking a bloody question.

Dafydd behaves as if I don't exist.

'The thing is, Dafydd, I was having a chat with Meryl and she was telling me all about how you and she used to hang out with Oddbean back in the day.'

Dafydd stops so abruptly that I crash into him, grabbing onto his coat. It's quite sticky and smells of wet dog. Does he have a dog somewhere, or does he just smell like one? It's not unpleasant, but

I hold my hands wide open in an effort not to feel it. Dafydd is looking right at me.

'No,' he says firmly, and I see a world of pain pass through those blue eyes which have cleared so that I feel that for once he is seeing me, not just his inner world. Then the moment is lost; his shoulders sag, his eyes cloud and his forehead takes on a vague expression, a confused frown.

'Dafydd? Do you remember Oddbean?' I ask gently.

He doesn't respond, just hums something rhythmic but tuneless, perhaps soothing himself back into his own world. He starts to move on.

'All right, mate. See you soon,' I offer feebly, and watch him wend his way past the bank and out of sight around the corner.

I wend my own way, past the goats' undercoats shop and back to my own.

Hilda from book club is standing outside, staring at the Isabella Garrante poster in the window.

'Eloise! When were you going to tell us about this?' she squeals. She looks equal parts indignant and excited.

'I was just about to email book club, I promise. It's all been very secret and we've only just put the posters up.'

'Why here? Why you? Oh, I know you're a good bookshop and everything, but why is she not doing it in Auckland or Sydney or Paris?'

'She has her reasons and I'm sure we'll find out very soon.' I try to sound enigmatic.

'Well, put me down for the book and a front-row seat at the launch, please. I've been her biggest fan for years.'

I promise I will do just that, although I dread to think how many other requests there'll be from Isabella's 'biggest fans'.

With an order to get the email out to book club, she bids me e noho rā and continues on her way.

'Any luck with Dafydd?' asks Garth, holding his fifth coffee of the morning, watching as I squirt antibacterial soap onto my hands and start giving them a good scrub.

'No. I think there was a reaction to Oddbean's name, but it was gone almost immediately.'

'Bugger.'

'I've been thinking about our staff meeting the other night, though. Amelia's rellie, whatsername, was a friend of Franklin's ex, right?'

'If you say so.'

'I do say so. That's how she got the goss for us. I'll ring her and find out if I can get a number for her — the ex.'

CHAPTER 52

Garth: 3 days until Isabella Garrante book launch

I turn the Tomato from Joll Road into an alley alongside the cinema. Stevie presses his snoot against the windscreen.

'We're going to the shop, Stevie,' I say. 'You like the shop.' This isn't strictly true; he tolerates the shop at best.

We're easing down the inclined car park when I see the motorcycle parked at the shop's rear. It doesn't have ape-hangers, but I have little doubt the owner is a Black Dog. There's no one else about.

I reverse into position alongside the motorcycle. Hastily I slip Stevie's lead over his head. 'Come on, boy, we need to get in.' But before I can get my key into the door, it swings inwards and I'm confronted by a Black Dog.

Stevie takes one look and bolts for the car, dragging my arm painfully behind me.

The Black Dog lifts his chin in a reverse nod. 'The boss wants to know how you're doing.'

'Let me into the shop and I'll tell you,' I reply, eager to get Stevie somewhere safe, or at least confined.

The guy grunts and turns around, not an easy task in the narrow corridor, then he heads through the Tardis door into the shop. I follow him in, dragging Stevie behind me until I can let go of the lead and he dashes into the stock room.

I switch on all the lights, hoping that Meryl might be lurking again, giving me an excuse to open the front door.

'How did you get into my shop?'

He pats one of the pockets on his vest. 'Your locks ain't no good. Easy as with a jiggler key.'

I make a mental note that if I somehow weather my dealings with the Black Dogs, and if Franklin White doesn't make good on his threat to have us thrown out, I should have the landlord upgrade the locks.

'You couldn't have just waited for me to arrive?'

'Wanted to look at the books. My boy needs to big-up his reading else he'll end up like me.'

'Did you find anything?'

For a moment the guy looks sheepish, like he's back at school and been called out by the teacher. 'Nah. Got in here, saw all the books and sort of panicked. Thought you could help me.'

Without thinking, I switch into bookseller mode. 'How old's your boy?'

'He's eleven, but he don't read so good. Maybe the same as my daughter, she's eight. Her mum's real smart.'

'Okay. And what sort of things does your son like?'

'Dragons,' he says. 'He's always had a thing about them.'

The childish glint in his eyes tells me exactly where his son got his thing about dragons. 'Then do I have the perfect book for you . . . and your son.' I pull a copy of James Russell's *The Dragon Defenders* from the shelf. 'He'll love this and it's a series, so once he's read the first one there's another one to go on to.'

'How much is it?'

I check the price label. 'Twenty-two dollars.'

The gangster pulls out a wad of bank notes and slaps a fifty on the counter. 'Give me the second book, too.'

I place the books in a paper bag and hand them over, then realise the till is empty. 'I haven't set up for the day yet, I don't have any change.'

'All good, bro. Chur for the help.' The Black Dog thrusts the paper bag inside his vest. 'Gotta tell the boss summin' about his money. What's it to be?'

That's a tricky one. Far harder than finding the right book for a gangster's son. The puzzle of Oddbean's and Tracey's disappearance is close to fitting together, of that I'm certain, but we need the last few pieces to complete the picture.

'Tell him we've made progress and we'll have an answer for him soon.'

'Yeah-nah.' The Black Dog shakes his head. 'I tell him that, he'll kick seven shades of shit out of me.'

That's a fair one; even to me my answer sounded lame. 'Okay. Tell him, I think I know where the money went and that there's no chance of getting it back but I'm narrowing down on who took it.'

The Black Dog lifts his chin. 'Gonna need to know when you'll be done with your narrowing.'

'Next Wednesday,' I reply with far more confidence than I feel, pinning my hopes on the possibility that Isabella Garrante's novel will provide the missing clues we need.

'Sweet as. See ya next week.' The Black Dog smiles, then swaggers from the shop.

I sag on the counter. And for the first time ever since coming to New Zealand I consider the benefits of returning to Blighty.

I spend the next hour mostly giving further advice on children's books. I've just finished gift-wrapping Leonie Agnew's latest when Tama appears at the counter.

'Ata mārie. Busy morning?'

'It has been. Got my first sale before we even opened.' I don't mention that it was to a Black Dog.

'I thought I'd fill you in on developments if you've got a moment.'

I wait for the customer to depart with her gift. The shop is now empty. 'I'm all ears.'

'Belinda Henare, the death in Waipuk, they're going to take another look at it.'

'That's good, eh?'

Tama screws his mouth up, tilting his head. 'Thing is, she was cremated, so I doubt they'll be able to tell much else.'

'What about the original postmortem?'

'Didn't do one. She'd been to the doctor's a couple of times recently with heart palpitations and was booked in to see a specialist, but you know how long that takes. They just put it down to a dodgy ticker.'

'So, what are they actually investigating?'

'They'll do a bit of digging into her personal life and follow up on the Pinter aspect. But honestly, I don't think they'll uncover any more than you did.'

'Waste of time then?'

'Maybe. You and Eloise still need to keep your beaks out of it.' He rests a hand on the counter and leans a bit closer. 'Right?'

'Sure. Scouts' honour.'

'I was never in the Scouts.'

'Neither,' I say, and wink.

Tama shakes his head. 'I'm beginning to doubt my judgement in involving you two.'

'Involving them in what?' asks Amelia, bustling through the Tardis door.

'My true crime book club.' Tama taps a finger to his nose and strolls out.

'You have a true crime book club?'

'He was joking. It's more like the swapping of war stories. You know, pull up a sandbag . . . Hang on—'

> Unknown: Madame Zuiseller's caravan.
>
> 10am. Much to discuss.

'Something's come up. Amelia, are you good with it being just you and Stevie for an hour or so? He's in the stock room.'

'Of course.' She folds her arms and cocks her head in mock annoyance. 'Go do mysterious things.'

I head straight down to the Village Green where the big top stands. The ticket office is all shut up at this hour of the morning, as are the stalls. In fact, there are no signs of life at all. A rope clatters against a flagpole in the wind; a gust flutters a lone popcorn carton across the well-trodden grass. A passing cloud throws everything into deep shadows. My fists clench. All I need now is the appearance of a couple of creepy clowns and it's going to be brown trouser time.

I've half a mind to retreat to the shop and cower in the stock room with Stevie. Instead, I head for the white picket fence and blooming flowers outside Madame Zuiseller's caravan.

Her door swings open, and the lady herself steps out. She wears a red tasselled skirt, white blouse and sequin-splattered waistcoat. Her long dark hair spills onto her shoulders. She beckons to me with a jewellery-heavy hand.

A surreal sense of providence envelops me.

'Welcome,' Madame Zuiseller says. 'We've been expecting you.' She holds open the caravan door and gestures me inside.

I'm still processing her words, particularly the *we* part, when I'm confronted by two men with the thuggish look of the Mitchells from *EastEnders*. Their thickset frames fill well-worn black leather jackets, and their dark cropped hair shows hints of grey. One has a profusion of gold hoops in his left ear and the other a similar collection in his right.

'Have a seat,' says Left Ear, his voice gruff but not threatening.

I slide into the same spot I took during my tarot reading.

Madame Zuiseller closes the door, leaving me with the Garrante brothers, because that is surely who they are.

'I'm Zac Garrante,' says Left Ear.

'I'm Javier,' says Right. 'You have some things you want to ask us?'

I take a moment to compose myself. 'In a few days' time,' I say, 'my wife and I are launching the new book of an incredibly famous author. You may have heard of her — Isabella Garrante?'

Not a muscle in the brothers' faces moves. I'd hate to play poker against these guys.

'That's already sorted with Ms Garrante,' says Zac. 'Wednesday evening, five until seven thirty, the big top's yours.'

Javier leans forward, fixing me with a gaze that would make a cobra wilt. 'It was something else you wanted to ask us,' he says.

Is he daring or prompting me to ask? I really can't tell. I suppose it doesn't matter; I was always going to ask this question, no matter the circumstance. Now, with the added pressure from the Black Dogs, I have to know.

I deliberately meet Javier's gaze. 'You purchased the circus from the previous owners at the same time as a guy known as Oddbean and a large quantity of cash went missing in Havelock North. How are those things connected?'

CHAPTER 53

Eloise: 3 days until Isabella Garrante book launch

'Mrs White?'

'I don't go by that name anymore.'

Victoria whatever-her-name-is is wearing a lemon linen trouser suit. It's an absolute beauty, as is she, the wide-legged pants and beautifully cut jacket setting off her cropped black hair, surely dyed.

'Sorry, I should have thought.'

'It's perfectly fine. Come on in, Eloise.' She smiles, and I warm to her immediately. I'm easily taken in, though, so make a mental note to stay on my guard.

She leads me through a rimu-floored hallway to a sitting room on the right. I envy it immediately: she has green velvet couches, two of them, and what looks like acres of shiny rimu flooring. The place is spotless. On the bookcase to my left I notice a goodly number of university press titles and a complete set of hardback Isabella Garrantes. Interesting: they're not readily available in New Zealand.

'Oh, you've got *Tarquin*!' I say.

'It's hilarious, isn't it? Lunar is my absolute favourite. She makes me crave sandwiches whenever she steps onto the page.'

'Sandwiches, and a good fight.'

'Yes! Somewhat cathartic, surely.'

'I've been trying to get Gareth Ward to come and do a signing at the shop. I'd love to meet him in real life.'

'Oh, well, do keep me informed. I'd be keen to come along. Now, sit down. Would you like a gin?'

Victoria is not what I was expecting at all.

Gin is poured, we chat about our shared love of green velvet (and gin), make small talk about the delights of our respective houses, then Victoria leans back into her armchair (green, velvet) and falls quiet.

'Go on then,' she says. 'Bring back my trauma by asking all sorts of terrible things about Franklin.' She waves away any chance of apology. 'No, no, I'm joking. Ask away. We've been divorced a good fifteen years and it's water under the bridge.'

'Okay. The night that Tracey Jervis, and Oddbean for that matter, went missing. Where was Franklin?'

Everything I've expected from this woman has been wrong so far, and she continues her run of surprises.

'He was out. I know, I know, I'm changing my tune, but it's been years I've lived with this and I'm quite frankly sick of it, and quite frankly sick of Franklin. I just want everything I have to do with him gone, and this is the last thing.'

She swoops on her gin glass and takes a healthy swig, closes her eyes and lets out a deep sigh.

'He didn't hurt her. Tracey. He doesn't have it in him to hurt a woman — he's old-fashioned like that. He's a con-man and a cheat and a bully, but he's not a wife beater. He came home late that night in quite the tizzy, not able to string a sentence together. He said nothing about Tracey at all.'

'But you knew about their . . . affair,' I hazard, presenting it as fact rather than conjecture.

'Yes. She wasn't the first and she wasn't the last. It was sickening. He kept them just the right side of legal but really, oh god, there's something not quite right about him. It was a few years before I realised, and when I did, I swear a bit of my soul died. I found photos, too.'

'Photos?'

Victoria takes another long gulp of her gin. 'Yes. From the way the girls were posed, I'd say Oddbean was involved, trying to be arty. They were just about decent but, like Franklin, a bit off, if you know what I mean.'

'I'm not sure . . .'

'Scantily clad young women, girls really. Presented as art but, if we're being honest, more like soft porn.'

'Oh.'

'Yup.'

'Forgive me, and I know it's such a cliché, but why did you stay so long? And cover for him?'

'Money and power are absolutely corrupting. You're well read, you must know that. It really is that simple. I needed the stability to get my Interiors business off the ground — Victoria Style in the Village. You know it, don't you?'

I nod. Never heard of it in my life.

'I don't come from money, I'd worked bloody hard and still had to be financed by my moron of a charming, handsome husband. I wasn't going to have it destroyed by dobbing him in for something I'm sure he didn't do. Whatever happened to Tracey, Franklin didn't do it.'

'Do what?'

'Oh, well, I dunno. Whatever was done to her. I mean, there's been no sign for all these years. If she was alive, she would at least have contacted her poor mother, surely?'

Hearing it said so starkly just about breaks my heart. I make a massive effort to gather my thoughts.

'That evening,' I say, 'Franklin came home in a tizzy. Tell me more.' It's a demand, but a polite one.

'Well, it was late, gone midnight, but that wasn't unusual. The door banged and I went into the hall and he was kicking his shoes off, his nice shiny brogues, but they weren't shiny anymore.' I can see Victoria looking at Franklin through her mind's eye. 'They were caked in cement.'

'Cement?'

'Yes. I didn't know it immediately, but he started sort of whisper screeching, as if he was trying to keep his voice down, but he was really quite desperate. "Get it off me, get it off me," he kept saying, and he was scratching at his trousers, practically ripping them off. I rushed over and there were bits of cement splatter all over his clothes. They were ruined, I had to throw his whole ensemble away. I was determined to save the pants, they were Dries Van Noten, but Franklin got quite tetchy about it.'

'What did you do with it all? Clothes, shoes . . . ?'

Victoria flushes. 'Well, it sounds awfully spoilt but I burned them. It would have been over two thousand dollars' worth of stuff. I was faffing about trying to pick and scrub concrete off, and Franklin just ended up yelling at me to get rid of it all. So I burned it, and dug the ashes and bits and bobs into the compost.'

I find that I'm speechless. Victoria composes herself and gathers our glasses. I assume I'm going to be dismissed, but she heads over to the sideboard and pours more gin.

'And you really think, after that performance, he hadn't done anything awful?'

'Oh, I'm not saying that! Just that he wouldn't have hurt Tracey. He cherished her. I saw the way he looked at her, and it made me sick to my bones. He'd clearly been up to no good, but I thought it was to do with the drugs.'

'You knew about that?' I ask, playing as if I know it for sure, too.

'Yes. But I won't admit it to anyone official. I'm not going to suffer any more for that man.'

We sit in silence for a while, sipping gin.

'Tell me what happened that night,' I press.

'I really don't know. And god knows where Oddbean got to, but he must have been spooked, like Franklin clearly was, and done a runner. He had enough underworld contacts that he could easily disappear. He was quite androgynous, you know. I've thought about this a lot. He could have changed his clothes and his identity and just disappeared.'

'How did Franklin react to Oddbean's disappearance? Was he upset?'

'Lord no. He was furious. He took over the running of that dog of a café. It was losing money at quite the clip and I begged Franklin to sell it. But he kept it on, and maybe he was right. It does okay now, by all accounts.'

She seems to relax then.

'I'll tell you if there's anything I think can help you,' she says. 'I just won't put myself in danger for him.'

'Understood.'

'Come on.' She stands. 'Let's sit in the garden. The freesias are just out and the scent is divine.'

Clutching gin number three and an assortment of posh cheeses rustled up from the fridge, we wander out onto the patio and position ourselves to catch the last of the spring sunshine.

I like Victoria, but I don't trust her. She still has a great deal to lose if we find out she helped cover up a murder. I'll say this for her, though: she pours a generous measure of spirits.

CHAPTER 54

Garth: 2 days until Isabella Garrante book launch

I bring a tray with cafetiere, milk, mugs and chocolate Hobnobs into our incident room, and place it on the desk. 'What's your take on Franklin returning home covered in concrete?' I pour the coffee, savouring the aroma. A small part of me hopes Franklin isn't involved: Oddbeans' roast is truly exceptional.

'Not covered. It was more like splashes, from what Victoria said.' Dry erase pen in hand, Eloise updates the incident board now crammed with writing, notes and photographs. Her glittery string is doing a good job of getting completely in the way. On the desk below the board lie open box files of witness statements, police reports and newspaper articles.

'It still doesn't sound good. Do you reckon he's done a bit of a Fred West and put Tracey under the patio?'

'No, I don't think so.' Eloise clicks the lid back on the whiteboard marker. 'Victoria was adamant that Franklin had nothing to do with Tracey's disappearance.'

'It's hardly likely to be something he's going to fess up to. How often do we see the wife protesting her innocence and claiming she knew nothing about her monstrous husband's nocturnal activities?'

'It felt like she was being truthful, I didn't get any red flags.'

'Maybe.' My partner in crime-solving is a good judge of character but it's not like we haven't had the wool pulled over our eyes by crims in the past.

'She was far more forthcoming than I expected,' Eloise continues. 'She revealed much more than she'd told the police. She confirmed that Franklin was into shady dealings with Oddbean and they were definitely well involved with the Black Dogs.'

'That ties in with what I got from the circus. The Garrante brothers admitted that they came into a substantial sum of cash at the time of Tracey's disappearance, allowing them to buy the circus.'

'What did they say about the book launch? Do they know who Isabella Garrante is?'

'They were super-keen on the launch. Anything we need from them we just have to ask, and they'll help with security and corral the masses. They wouldn't be drawn on any possible connection to IFG.'

'Do you think she's family? Their sister? Their mother?'

I shrug. 'Impossible to say.'

'Maybe they're Isabella Garrante.' Eloise writes 'Isabella Garrante' on the whiteboard and draws a question mark next to it. 'Who's to say Isabella is a woman, or even one person. I mean Robert Galbraith is J.K. Rowling and Carmen Mola turned out to be three men.'

'The Garrante brothers didn't strike me as literary types,' I say hesitantly.

'Until Dafydd painted that picture for us you wouldn't have pegged him as a talented artist. We all have secrets.'

Dafydd is an enigma indeed, and I have a feeling that he is

wrapped up in all of this in ways we still don't understand. 'I suppose, although I'm putting my money on Isabella being Prudence.'

'Because?'

'It has to be someone with an intimate knowledge of the case. We know from Beige Dave that she was into writing stories, and she appears to have vanished off the face of the planet. No socials, nothing.'

'You don't have socials.' Eloise dunks a Hobnob in her coffee.

'Yes, but that's because . . .'

'You're weird.' Eloise taps the marker against the whiteboard in a mildly irritating way that I would be chastised for should I have done it. 'Do you think the Garrante brothers nicked the money from Oddbean?'

'Not as such. They claimed they received it as a payment for' — I flash some air quotes — 'services rendered.'

'And naturally you pushed them on what those services were?'

'Again, they refused to venture down that line of enquiry.'

'Sounds like a load of bull.' Eloise folds her arms, which thankfully ends the pen's percussion.

'That's what I thought until Madame Zuiseller whispered in my ear as I was leaving.'

'Did she now?'

'She said that when you run away with the circus, rent and board don't come cheap.'

'Tracey?'

'Or Oddbean.' I take the pen from Eloise and draw a dollar sign next to Oddbean's name. 'He nicks the money and then needs to disappear, so he hides out in the circus. That's why no one could find him. Who knows, maybe he's still travelling with them, pretending to be a clown or something?'

'I suppose that fits.' Eloise sounds less than convinced. 'Is that what you're going to tell the Black Dogs happened?'

'Not yet. I thought I'd wait until after the launch and I've had a chance to read the rest of the story before I jump to any conclusions.'

Eloise snorts in a most unladylike way, not that anyone's ever accused her of being ladylike. 'You think the story is going to be true? It's called fiction for a reason.'

'It might not matter whether it's true or not. Stories have power. We know that as well as anyone. That's why I'm going to have to go and see Franklin White. After the book launches, he stands to be tried by the media all over again.'

'You don't have to warn him. The man's a lecherous toad. He should have been tried in court. He deserves everything that's coming.'

'Probably. Only I'm not doing it for him, I'm doing it to try and save our bookshop.'

Franklin's office — or the one he's agreed to meet me at — is situated at the rear of Oddbeans. I presume this is the one he uses only for the café business and that he has far more salubrious ones at his property development company, because the room and its furniture are dilapidated and musty-smelling, even over the aroma of roasting coffee.

When the door opens and Franklin strides in, I stand, expecting a handshake. He ignores me, continuing behind the cluttered desk where he drops onto a chair which looks only marginally more functional than mine. 'Make this quick,' he says, fiddling with the gold cufflinks on his pale-blue shirt.

'We are hosting a book launch for the writer Isabella Garrante on Wednesday.'

'Never heard of her,' says Franklin. 'I shan't be going.'

'That's probably a wise decision. The local and national press are going to be there. TV, too, I think.'

'What's this got to do with me?'

'Pretty much everything, seeing as the book is about you.'

'What?' He stops toying with his cufflink and places his hands flat on the desk.

'Well, not exactly about you, more the Tracey Jervis case.'

'Are you fucking with me?'

'Not at all. I've only seen the first three chapters but it's clear that the story is about Tracey's disappearance and, given your previous threats, I thought you should know.'

'She can't do this to me. Not again. I had nothing to do with her going missing.'

'And we're not the ones saying you did.' I hold up a placating hand. It doesn't work.

'But you're the ones launching the book. The ones who've been poking their noses into the case, raking up dirt from the past, spying on me.'

'We haven't been spying on you.' My words lack conviction.

'You bloody well have, up at the Redwoods.'

'We weren't spying, we were walking the dog.' This is true, although not entirely. 'What were you doing there, digging with a shovel?'

'I always bury a coin at all of my projects. Not that it's any of your fucking business.'

Franklin launches to his feet, sending his chair crashing backwards. His forehead lowers, his shoulders square back, and for a moment I think he's going to punch me. I'm not scared. Unlike the thugs from the Black Dogs, I reckon I can take Franklin. Given what I know, and the threats that he's made towards my lovely bookshop,

I would gain a good degree of satisfaction from doing so.

'Get out!' he growls. 'You're done for. You and your crappy little bookshop.' He points at the door, his hand trembling.

This time I know his threats are for real.

I hurry from the office. Perhaps Eloise is right, perhaps Franklin does deserve everything that's coming, only he's vindictive enough to take our lovely bookshop down with him. There's nothing more I can do. In two days' time the launch will happen, whatever the consequences.

CHAPTER 55

Eloise: 30 minutes until Isabella Garrante book launch

As if life could get any more surreal, I'm in the green room of a circus. The green tent, I suppose. It's stuffy, smells a bit sweaty and earthy, and I couldn't be more amped. We're about to launch one of the biggest authors in the world.

A scrubbed trestle table stands along one wall, home to a jug of water and some glasses and an assortment of healthy snacks — no blue M&Ms for Ms Garrante then. I zoom in on the drinks table next to it: an array of bottles and even a chiller for the . . . yup . . . that's Veuve Clicquot by the looks. Ancient dining chairs and occasional tables are dotted around, lending a boho chic sort of vibe. I'm fidgety, bordering on panicky.

'Who are we about to meet? I can't wrap my head around it,' I say to Garth.

'Georgia, the publicist, and Isabella Garrante.'

'Yes, yes of course, but who *is* Isabella Garrante?'

'You'll know in a minute,' he says, infuriatingly, saving himself with a delighted grin and 'How cool is this though?'

'Yeah! I can just imagine us in the circus. What's your act going to be tonight, Garth?'

'I am The Great Sherlock Tomes himself, of course,' he says with a deep bow, pretending to suck on a pipe.

He's still bent over, arm outstretched dramatically, when the tent flaps part and in walks Janet Jervis.

'Err, hello,' she says, clearly startled.

'Janet! Why are you here?' I say. Garth rights himself; he's clearly dizzy from standing up too quickly.

'*You're* Isabella Garrante?' Garth asks.

Janet lets out a strange little laugh, a nervous squeak really. 'It's complicated. Shall we sit? It's a bit of a strange tale I have to tell.'

Janet is fizzing, and I'm not sure what with. Nerves? Excitement? We pull chairs around a battered brass table — it has the most intricate engraving of elephants on it — and settle ourselves. Janet, or perhaps Isabella, takes a big breath.

'I hardly know where to start,' she says, and I can't help but imagine a Scooby Doo ending about to unfurl. Are we actually going to get the truth?

'Go on,' we chorus.

'Well . . .'

At the very moment she draws breath to speak, the tent flap flaps and in walks a short, dark, pixie-haired woman, all jingling bangles and Calvin Klein Eternity.

'Well, hello at last!' she trills. 'How wonderful to meet you in person.'

'You're Isabella Garrante?' is my tentative offer.

'Ha, ha, no, I'm Georgia, the publicist. We've been emailing.' She looks to Janet, so we do too. 'Sorry to interrupt. It seems Janet was just about to do the big reveal.' She settles in, clearly enjoying herself.

Janet nods, fizz slightly popped but not entirely flat.

'So . . .'

She begins again and the tent flap emits a furious slap of nylon, and in stalks our very own Phyllis flanked by a truly huge security guard.

I spring to my feet. 'Oh my god, you're not Isabella Fucking Garrante?' I yell.

'What? No, no of course not. This eejit got hold of me as I was coming in to do my job.' She spits the last word at the security guard, who ignores her.

'This lady is in possession of this pole. A clear and present danger to security,' says Mr Jobsworth: massive, softly spoken, completely in control of himself and the situation.

'What? It's a hurley stick. I have a game after work!'

The security guard remains silent, waiting for a decision.

'It's absolutely fine, Mr . . . err. Phyllis works with us and is indeed a keen sportswoman.'

'As you wish, Mrs Sherlock.' The hulk unhands Phyllis, who shakes herself and exits the tent at speed, hurley stick under her arm.

There's a shocked hiatus. Janet brings her hand to her forehead. 'As I was—' Georgia sets out on a mission to the wine chiller.

There's a crunch of baked earth and gravel from just outside the somewhat abused tent flap, and it is gently lifted.

In walks a slender blonde woman, hair pulled into an elegant chignon, expensively draped in a dress of such delicate pale-pink chiffon silk that I immediately worry she's going to get circus dirt on it. She walks over to us and extends a graceful hand.

'Isabella Garrante,' she says with a tinkly laugh and a lovely smile. Her teeth are, of course, white, straight and even.

I'm standing before this vision of perfection with my gob open when Garth says, 'Deirdre?'

It is indeed Dead Girl Deirdre emerging from behind the blonde vision to stand beside her and take her hand. Deirdre has absolutely surpassed herself for the occasion. She's wearing a studded leather choker and an inordinate amount of tattered fishnet. Her hair is wildly crimped. She raises her geometrically painted eyebrows and drops her own bombshell.

'Also Isabella Garrante.' She drops one eyebrow, the other revelling in this strange turn of events and choosing to retain the high ground.

'Your eyes are blue,' I yell at Deirdre. 'Where are your spookily dark eyes?'

'Contacts for the demon peepers.' Her eyebrows are having a wonderful time displaying her amusement.

Blonde Isabella turns her lovely head towards Janet and, continuing this afternoon's game of What the Fuck is Going on Tennis, so do we all.

'Would you mind beginning the story, Mrs Jervis?'

'I was about to and then . . . well, never mind.' Janet gives herself a wee shake, straightens her jacket and draws breath in a fourth-time-lucky manner.

'So you know I'm a writer, and that I go on writing retreats fairly regularly?'

'Yes,' I reply. I glance at Garth, who seems to have lost the power of speech.

'Well, I've actually been visiting my daughter, Tracey.'

Janet pauses and I can tell she's wringing every drop of drama from this revelation. I don't disappoint — I immediately yell 'She's alive!' and clasp my hand to my mouth to stop my fried brains falling out.

Garth, however, keeps his head.

'Go on,' he says.

'When Tracey disappeared, I truly had no clue what was going on. I really thought I'd lost my baby, that something terrible had happened to her. The thoughts that went through my head are things no mother should ever have even to contemplate.' She swallows, takes a moment to compose herself.

Blonde Isabella smiles encouragingly and moves to her side. Garth quietly gets up and pours Janet a glass of water.

'I only had that terror for six days before I knew she was alive — the longest six days of my life.'

Blonde Isabella links arms with Janet, stroking her hand. Their intimacy only adds to my confusion.

'Tracey rang me to say she'd run away but that she would be in real danger, like mortal danger, if anyone found out. I had to keep it from everyone — her father, that poor teacher, everyone. We arranged a time for her to ring me every Sunday when her father was out at a church meeting. If he was home for some reason, I'd pretend it was a wrong number or something and she'd know we'd have to wait until the following week.'

I can't keep my trap shut at this point and have to ask. 'Where was she?'

'She settled down near Raglan. So when I go on my writing retreats up there, it's Tracey I've been visiting. She started to join in some of the writing exercises. Turns out she has quite the talent.' She looks from Blonde Isabella to me.

So does Garth.

'What?' I ask, looking from one to the other.

'Tracey is Isabella Garrante. This lady,' says Garth, gesturing towards the blonde vision, 'is Tracey. Ergo, she is also Isabella Garrante.'

'And so am I,' adds Deirdre.

'Two IFGs?' I say weakly.

There are confused glances and Janet takes the opportunity to conclude her story.

'So when you visited me, and I saw Tracey's handwriting on the envelope, I was flabbergasted. She hadn't said a word! It took me a while to get out of her what she was up to. And here we are.'

'Here we are indeed. Thank you, Mum,' says Blonde Isabella.

'You're . . . Tracey Jervis?' I ask.

'Oh Eloise, do keep up,' says Garth.

'Yes, I am. Or Isabella Garrante, if you like.' Blonde Isabella, Tracey, IFG extends a manicured hand, and I shake its writerly perfection. I study her face and yes, there's teenaged Tracey, just a little more worn. Age suits her.

'Tracey. I'm so very pleased to meet you,' I say, and stand back to let Georgia do the formal introductions as I've suddenly run out of words.

Garth says hello like this is all very normal and she's not the most famous author on the planet *or* a missing girl from twenty-odd years ago. Georgia and Garth pull up more chairs, pour more water, and we all settle again, including Deirdre who is cool as a cucumber. How can she be Isabella Garrante, too? She's not even a fan.

'Sorry for all the drama,' says Tracey.

'I don't think you are, young lady,' says her mum, and they both laugh.

'Why us, Isabella, err Tracey? Why send us that envelope?' I ask.

Tracey crosses her legs and smooths her skirts. There's a lovely ruche around the bottom of the dress and as her calf crosses her knee I notice her shoes, strappy and silver. An exotic creature has joined the circus.

'Mum often mentioned you, the crazy booksellers in the Village. Used to be police officers but now a wannabe author and a woman with pink hair who gets dragged around by a massive dog.'

'He's a rescue, he's . . .'

'Shush,' says Garth.

'I fell in love with the idea of you. You're just perfectly the right people in the right place at the right time. I knew I wanted to come home to launch this book, but I couldn't just ring you up and tell you all about it because of the non-disclosure thing. The book will cause huge ructions and, I have no doubt, a legal battle. There are things in there that are about to cause Franklin White some life-changing problems. I can't prove them on my own and I needed your help.'

Flattery from a lovely lady in a pink ruchy dress works on me, and I am now hanging off her every word. I turn to Garth, who's stroking his beard, eyes narrowed.

'It's taken us to some quite dark places, investigating your disappearance,' he says.

'Yes! I thought you were dead!' I hold my hands to my head.

'We all thought you were dead,' says Garth. 'All of New Zealand thought you were dead.'

'I know. And I am genuinely sorry if I have put you in harm's way. It gets worse, and I can tell you everything now. It's all in the novel but I'd like you to hear it from me. I'm so thankful for what you've done.'

I'm not entirely sure what we have done, to be honest. Perhaps helped the truth to come out, whatever that is.

'So, Franklin,' Tracey continues. 'He was charming, so loving and attentive. I was going mad with all the schoolwork, the constant running from one thing to the next, all of which I had to excel at, according to my father.'

I see Janet wince.

'I fell head over heels. I know now it was a crush, hormones raging and all that, but it felt so real at the time. I can clearly remember how I felt before I saw his true side. My heart still flutters when I think about it.'

Yuck, I think, as Isabella takes a breath and composes herself to continue.

'I was so hothoused that I was stifled — naïve really — and Franklin offered an escape into another world. Ha. I got a lot more than I bargained for, I can tell you.'

'Yes, you can tell us,' says Garth a little sternly, and I throw him a look. I would like this half of Isabella Garrante to stay in love with us, please.

'Well, things progressed as you know and I really thought that Franklin was going to leave his wife, that we would run away together and that I would be free, free to be a poet, or whatever I wanted. I didn't think about the practicalities of it, of course, not until I really had to. Dad was going to move to Wellington when I went to uni to "keep an eye on me" and make sure I continued to excel. I couldn't face it. Franklin was my escape route, not that he ever intended to be, of course.'

Tracey's voice cracks slightly and Janet fishes in her handbag for a tissue. Georgia murmurs comforting words and I get up and head to the drinks chiller. A minute later and my practised hand has opened a bottle of the Veuve Clicquot and handed a flute to Tracey. I offer a glass to each of the assembly; Georgia and Deirdre accept, and Janet and Garth decline. I pour myself a glass just to be friendly.

'Can you continue?' asks Garth, trying to be sympathetic.

Tracey nods. 'Oddbean was around a lot of the time, and Franklin and I used to meet in the garret he had above the art studio. That's what he called it, a "garret". So pretentious now but so romantic I thought then, like something out of a Dickens novel. Oddbean had all his art gear up there, including a small photography studio. Franklin started to take photos of me.'

I inhale sharply. Tracey leans over and pats me on the knee.

'Nothing dodgy . . . at first.' She pauses. She sure knows how to tell a story.

'But before too long he would tease me and joke around and pose me and undress me and, well, the photos became far more risqué. It was so gradual and felt like part of our intimacy. I thought I was enjoying it, but I know now that I was trying so hard to be okay with it, for everything to be perfect. Deep down I was uncomfortable. I think I knew he was taking advantage.

'The only person I ever confided in was Prudence, my dear Prudence.' Tracey laughs her tinkly laugh, glancing at Deirdre. 'She was furious. Said I was being an idiot and that Franklin would have a hold over me forever. At first I put it down to jealousy and ignored her. But she's always been right, haven't you?'

'Yes. I generally am.' Deirdre winks at Tracey, sips her champers and crosses her legs, the leather of her knee-high stilettos squeaking.

'You're Prudence?' I shriek at her.

'Yes. That's one of my names.'

'Blue eyes. Bloody hell.' I'm slowly, slowly catching on. 'But you went to England.'

Deirdre laughs. 'I did. I kept in touch with Tracey after Janet let me know she was alive and well. We've been tinkering about with stories for years as Isabella Garrante. I moved back to the Bay about a year ago, once we hatched the plan to write the novel that would finally give Franklin his come-uppance.'

'And you've been skulking about our bookshelves all this time. Half of Isabella Fucking Garrante.' I shake my head, bewildered and a little bit betrayed.

'Eloise, let Tracey finish, then we can grill Deirdre,' says Garth. 'Franklin had a hold over you, Tracey?' he prods.

'Oh yes. I mean I wanted to belong to Franklin, or so I thought.

But gradually, as things escalated, I started to suspect I'd swapped one repressor for another.'

'Yes. Eleanor kept your poetry and we read it.' I clear my throat. 'My stems, my petals. He caresses—'

Tracey's cool, controlled elegance slips for a moment, and she flushes, interrupting loudly.

'Oh! Oh dear. I must, err, catch up with Eleanor and retrieve those.'

This, I can see, is not the time to tell her we have them filed away in our incident room.

'Anyway, Prudence said we had to get the photos and the negatives of the more incriminating ones. I knew I was heading for trouble and I didn't want to drag Pru into it with me, so when I thought Oddbean was at an arts function I went to the studio, planning to break in.' She stops suddenly and tears prick at her eyes.

Janet shuffles her chair closer and takes Tracey's hand.

'This is the hard bit. There was a set of stairs on the outside of the building leading up to the garret. It was dark and I was being quiet just in case, and as I set foot on the stairs I heard voices. The door to the garret was slightly open and light was spilling out. I recognised the voices: it was Franklin and Oddbean, and they were arguing. I couldn't quite hear the words, so I crept up the steps and looked in the door — it was open just enough so I could peer in.' She pauses again. 'So this is it, Eloise, Garth. This is the crime that happened.'

Janet is looking at the floor; Georgia is fair bursting with excitement, having heard it all already. Garth looks grave, and I suspect I look as sick as I feel. He puts a steadying hand on my shoulder.

'It wasn't me who died that night,' says Tracey. 'As I looked in, I saw Franklin shove Oddbean. He stumbled but didn't fall. He yelled "what the fuck" or something, and made towards Franklin, but

Franklin had picked up a piece of the lighting equipment, a heavy bar from the way he was holding it. He swung it and it hit Oddbean on the side of his head, his temple. Oddbean just crumpled. I can still see it all these years later. He just collapsed in on himself and hit the floor with a thud. He was so still. I was sure he was dead. There was nothing left in him.'

We wait.

'Franklin just kept saying "oh god, oh no". He knelt beside Oddbean and shook him. Nothing. Then he started scrabbling around, I don't know what he was looking for, but it was noisy, so I took the opportunity to creep back down the stairs. Then I ran.'

'Where to?' I ask.

'Quite literally away with the circus. One of the fairground boys I'd been flirting with stowed me away. You couldn't make it up, could you?' she says.

I glance around at the faces: Janet teary, Georgia smiling but pensive, Deirdre deadpan, and Garth frowning.

Something's off. Tracey's a fabulous storyteller, but her acting isn't quite so polished. She's been genuinely reliving trauma in the recounting of Oddbean's death, but this business with the boy feels different. Outside in the big top I hear them sound checking and asking the crowd to take their seats. I park the thought for later.

'When I managed to get in contact with Mum, she helped me to come up with my new identity and Isabella was born. I use the name, and Pru and I write the books together.'

'So why come home now?' asks Garth.

'I never wanted to see my father again. He's dead now. Mum, Pru and I can be ourselves and be happy together at home. It's time to let the sunshine fall on this mess.'

CHAPTER 56

Garth: 5 minutes until Isabella Garrante book launch

I clasp Eloise's hand in mine. Her face is pale, her pupils dark and dilated. We're both struggling to make sense of what's just happened. The sound of excited crowds gathering on the other side of the green room's canvas is a startling reminder that the launch of *Dead Girl Gone* is about to get under way. And I have a feeling that the night has yet to reveal all of its surprises.

Eloise smiles at me, momentarily calming my nerves. I smile back. Whatever happens now, this is going to be one hell of an evening.

Since Tracey's revelations, conversation has been muted. Georgia sips from her glass, her hand tremoring the champagne within. It must have been a difficult decision for them to publish, weighing up the cost of possible legal battles against the potential huge profits from the novel. Tracey is still and quiet, lost in her thoughts. I can't even begin to imagine how she's feeling. She's lived a lie for the last twenty years; now not only is her secret identity as half of a bestselling author about to be revealed but also the fact that the local girl who everyone believed was murdered is well and truly alive. And then there's Prudence, the loyal best friend who suffered poisoned looks and whispered accusations, keeping her friend's secret even when it meant that her family were forced to move to the UK. And then, later, keeping her identity as the other half of Isabella Garrante in the dark rather than revelling in the glory for the same reason.

I glance at my phone: 5.27. 'Three minutes to go. I'll just check everything.'

Tracey doesn't respond. Deirdre, no, Prudence smiles enigmatically while Georgia takes another trembling sip.

Eloise looks at me, and there's a question in her eyes asking me if I'm all right. Surprisingly, I am. My nerves are gone, the pre-launch worries drowned out by adrenaline. I give her hand another squeeze, and stand.

I walk through the door flap into the 'clown alley'. A man in jeans and a casual jacket is standing just outside the green room. He has cropped hair and a rugged face with hard blue eyes that have seen too much of this world's woes. I've met his type before. Despite his relaxed stance I can tell that he is capable of immediate and extreme violence.

'I'm just going to check that we're ready,' I say.

He nods to me but doesn't speak.

I'm assailed by noise as I enter the big top, my appearance creating a wave of excitement. Followed by disappointment. The bleachers are full, as are the additional chairs we have placed in rows on the circus ring itself. These we have reserved for our regulars: the Admiral, Meryl, Bernard, Tama and Chloe, and a host of other Sherlock Tomes stalwarts. Somehow, and much to my annoyance, Franklin White has managed to get a seat amongst them. He has a smile cemented onto his face, one that I expect must be killing him. Or perhaps it's the smile of a shark and he's biding his time before he drags us and our beautiful bookshop below the waters.

To one side of the chairs is the press gallery, thronged with journalists, photographers, and even a TV crew. I raise a hand to Dave Wimply, a journalist who has ruffled more than a few feathers over the years. We've done several events with him, and although I wouldn't class him as a friend I do like him. He smiles mischievously. I have no idea what he's going to make of the next few minutes, but I can guarantee that his report is not going to pull any punches.

Kitty, Amelia and Phyllis stand at velvet-covered tables, Eftpos machines at the ready. There are currently no books on display, the opening of the boxes strictly embargoed until Isabella . . . the Isabellas have given their speech. Overseers from the publishers stand guard near the stacked boxes, ensuring compliance. Loitering near them, perhaps aware that he is a little too ripe to join the seated crowd, is Dafydd.

I move to the podium where the Isabellas are about to speak and check that they have water and that the microphone is switched on. Over by the mixing panel the sound guy gives me the thumbs-up.

Casting one final glance over the gathered crowd I head back past the close protection operator and into the green room. 'We're good to go.'

Eloise looks to Tracey and Prudence. 'Are you ready?'

'I don't think I'll ever be ready,' says Tracey.

'We're ready.' Prudence straightens her leather choker. 'I've waited twenty-three years for this.'

'It'll be great. They're your fans. They're going to be so excited to meet you in person, both of you,' Eloise reassures them. 'I'll introduce you, then it's all yours.'

I wait with Tracey, Prudence, Janet and Georgia as Eloise's voice booms out.

'Welcome, bookshop whānau and friends, to the literary event of the year, possibly the book launch of the century, possibly ever. You are in for the shock of your lives, so I hope you've been to the bar.'

There is an appropriate amount of polite tittering and some uncertain shuffling.

'I'm going to keep this short as I know it's not me you're here to see. So please put your hands together for the two incredible women who make up the whole of . . . Isabella Garrante!'

Wild applause erupts, and my mind buzzes. I seem to disassociate from my body, watching events through someone else's eyes, the world around me slowing and warping as I chaperone Tracey and Prudence to the microphone and stand back to join Eloise.

Tracey flattens her notes on the podium, Prudence a shadow at her shoulder. They wait for the applause to die down. Tracey takes a final glance at the papers, then looks up.

'Thank you for your warm welcome. You know us through our writing as Isabella Garrante, but many of you will know us by different names, our real names, Tracey Jervis and Prudence Ballion.'

A collective gasp escapes as the audience leans forward as one to get a better look. Cameras flash up in the press gallery, and hundreds of smartphones are pulled from pockets and bags, their beeps drowned out by the hubbub. Franklin, his body rigid, stares open mouthed, saliva strands stringing his teeth.

Tracey waits patiently for the noise to subside before continuing. 'We are not here to explain what happened all those years ago.' Prudence holds up a copy of their book. 'For that you will have to read our latest novel. Although *Dead Girl Gone* is indeed sold as a work of fiction, it is the truest story we have ever written.'

Over by the sales stand there is a minor commotion. Dafydd has ripped cardboard from one of the boxes and swiped a marker pen from the table. Shooed away by the publisher's minders, he lopes to a spot alongside the front row of chairs and sits down.

I'm about to head over when Franklin White stands up. 'You let everyone believe that you were dead, that I was a murderer! I had no chance in the elections, my business suffered, my marriage ended, you ruined me.'

'I ruined you?' Tracey meets Franklin's gaze and her face hardens. Georgia signals to the Garrante brothers, who begin to head towards Franklin, but Tracey holds a hand up to stop them. 'I, the seventeen-year-old girl, coerced into a relationship, ruined you?'

Franklin lifts his chin, the hint of a smirk on his face. 'I don't remember it that way.'

'Do you remember pressuring me, a naïve schoolgirl, into sex? Or your attempts to encourage me to get Pru to join us?'

Prudence leans towards the mic, sombre as if she were at a child's funeral. 'I never did.'

'No.' Franklin's voice quavers, making it sound more like regret than denial, then he straightens, forcing his shoulders back. 'Because she's making it all up. More fiction.'

'Am I making it up that you tricked me into being photographed naked?'

'That was—' Franklin blusters, then pauses. A host of cameras from the press gallery click and flash. 'That's a lie. I don't know anything about that.'

'It might be true that you didn't think I knew your true motives, and for a while I didn't. I was suckered in, despite Pru's warnings.' For the first time Tracey's voice trembles, and she clutches the podium for support. Prudence edges nearer and places a hand on hers. 'One of the artists at the gallery told me, tried to warn me off. I had to disappear, I had to make it look like you had murdered me so that you couldn't publish my pictures, so that you would be scared into destroying them. This is all on you and Oddbean.'

Franklin straightens and runs a hand over his coiffed hair. It appears that he is determined to brass neck this one out. 'You truly are a master of fiction. I am the victim here.' He holds up a finger and wags it at Tracey and Prudence. 'You can make up whatever stories you like, but if you put your lies on sale here today, I will see you in court.'

I haven't had a chance to discuss with Eloise what to do about Tracey's revelations. Waiting would be the sensible thing to do, except that seeing Franklin standing there protesting his innocence makes me want to puke.

'Sorry,' I say to Eloise, and take one of the microphones we were going to use for audience questions. I address myself to Franklin. 'And what about Oddbean?'

'What about Oddbean?' He glares at me, but I'm sure I detect a glimmer of fear in his eyes.

'Did you or did you not murder him over a missing hundred grand of Black Dogs' money, then bury his body in concrete?'

There are more gasps, and I feel the weight of hundreds of eyes organic and digital upon me.

Franklin freezes for the briefest of moments, then he's back on the offensive. 'You have no evidence, and you have no body, so in answer to your question, after my lawyers have dealt with this pair's ludicrous fiction' — he waves his arm in the direction of the podium — 'we will take you and your stupid bookshop, and your stupid staff, and your stupid dog to the cleaners.'

CHAPTER 57

Eloise: Isabella Garrante book launch

Garth is fronting up to Franklin when Dafydd presses a piece of cardboard into my hand. This is not how I envisaged the launch going, but what did I expect, really?

Dafydd has made another skilful sketch, and this one reveals a far more serious crime than the theft of flowers. Set outside Oddbean's gallery, it shows Franklin White lifting a long, lean body into what looks like a large plywood mould that stands alongside a pile of gravel and a cement mixer.

I look up at Dafydd whose stricken face glimmers with tears. His blue eyes are blazing, pleading. I nod to him as an idea begins to form. Given the source of the drawing, this evidence is unlikely ever to stand up in court. But it does complete the final piece of the puzzle.

Garth's not going to like my crazy idea one little bit. I'm going to have to do it straight away, too, or what little logical brain I have will take over.

Security is escorting Franklin out of the big top. He's brazening it out, head held high, shaking off the coercive hand on his arm, the picture of a man wronged. Georgia stands beside Tracey and Prudence, and the launch is getting back on a more conventional track, Tracey telling the story of how she began writing and why she has come home, handing over to Prudence at appropriate moments. Tracey's a sensational speaker, even without the sensational story, and Prudence is remarkable for one we've always viewed as taciturn. There's laughter and not a dry eye in the house. I reckon the sales of this one book will match the rest of our year's sales in total. Well done, lassies.

I manoeuvre my way over to the book sales table and grab a piece of paper. I scribble a couple of notes, one to Phyllis and one to Georgia, and head over to the podium where Tracey is in full flow. I hand the note to Georgia, who looks confused again, and grab Garth who is loitering out of the spotlight.

'Come with me,' I whisper.

He looks askance, and I tug his sleeve a little harder.

Back past the green room I keep going.

'What's going on?' Garth's trotting a bit now to keep up.

'I know how we can get Franklin, at least I think I do. You're just going to have to trust me and promise not to be too cross.'

'What?' A note of panic enters his voice.

We hurry through the car park, negotiating straw and mud, Garth trying to ask questions and me shutting him down. I unlock the Tomato and open the driver's door.

'Get in, buckle up and try to relax,' I say.

Garth has gone silent. There's a war going on in his mind, I can tell. He wants to trust me but doesn't trust me at all. He would say he has reason to doubt any plan I've cooked up on the spot, and I don't have time to remind him that the plans he baulks at are the ones he ends up agreeing are my best ones, albeit in retrospect.

I reverse out of the parking space, redistributing the mud and muck. The council's not going to be too happy about the state of the Village Green when the circus has moved on, but I reckon there'll be much bigger news for anyone to truly be bothered about a bit of churned-up grass.

We emerge on to Te Mata Road. I indicate left and pull out, then circle back into the Village, heart thumping. I'm driving slowly and carefully, and it's so unusual as to put Garth on edge.

'Where are we going?' he says.

'Shush.'

As Oddbeans comes into view, my stomach tightens. I really, really hope I'm right about this, or I will look foolish (which doesn't bother me) and Garth will have a mega-sulk for quite some time (which will bother me). On the immediate upside, the car park only has a couple of cars in it and there are no loitering pedestrians.

The coffee-bean statue, surrounded by its white picket fence, is uplit prettily in the cool, clear evening. It's well tended, not a spot of lichen or bird poo to be seen.

'Why . . . ?' says Garth, just as I gun the engine and shove my accelerator foot to the floor, aiming the Tomato squarely at the concrete statue that has stood right there for over twenty years. Our steed emits a sound that I choose to imagine as a war cry.

There's actually no time to panic or to scream. We hurtle through time and space for only a few seconds before there's a massive impact and, thank gods, the airbags deploy. There's an explosive crunch of metal and the shattering of glass. I realise with a sickening jolt that I didn't actually know there were two airbags, and make a mental note not to reveal this to Garth. When I look up, there's a kaleidoscope where the windscreen was; it's really rather lovely how the lights from the car park shine through.

A cold breeze enters the car, along with the smell of dust and petrol. Garth flaps around in the seat next to me, pushing his face out of the airbag.

'What the actual fuck?' he spits, rubbing his nose, which is bleeding just a teensy bit.

'I hope I hit it hard enough,' I reply, unbuckling my seatbelt and attempting to open the driver's door which, for some reason, is sticking. I manage to shove it, and there's a rather nasty metallic screech. I really do hope the bloody thing's a write-off.

'What? What?' It's not just the car making a nasty screech.

I clamber out and can see that Garth is managing to do so on his side. I take a few steps and waft away the smoke emanating from the car's engine. It doesn't seem to be in danger of catching fire.

I walk around to the other side of the statue and — oh my, I was right.

'Look what I found,' I say to Garth.

He staggers to my side.

'Jesus Christ is that . . . is that an arm? Like, a human arm?'

'I hope so.'

'What?' he screeches again.

'Is that the only bloody word you know, man? Why do you think this has been here for twenty-three years, Franklin's never sold the café, and he was covered in concrete after brandishing a lethal weapon at his literal partner in crime?'

'You think that's Oddbean?' Garth's voice is several octaves higher than usual.

'Well, who do you think it is? Look at the chain on his wrist, for a start. It's got a teddy bear charm on it.'

'What?'

I look up at the sound of pounding feet. Tama is barrelling towards us, followed by an assortment of onlookers.

'Are you all right? Do you need an ambula—' he begins, then freezes. He looks to me, to the statue, to Garth, to the statue, then back to me, and eventually adds, 'Ah, excuse me, I need to make a phone call. Several phone calls.'

'You do, Tama. And you need to lock up Franklin White before one of my angels does it for you.'

A cry like that of Lucifer himself shoots across the domain. Franklin is hoofing it across the Green, his scream signalling dismay at the destruction of the sculpture and the uncovering of what it contains. Kitty and Amelia emerge from the big top and attempt to head him off. He has a good twenty metres on them, and he alters his course so they have no chance in their pursuit. He glances back, the hint of a smirk on his face.

From the shadow of a candyfloss stall, Phyllis emerges like the Reaper herself, hurley stick in one hand, sliotar in the other. She tosses the ball up, lets loose with the stick, and the sound of ash hitting leather rips through the air.

Franklin again glances back. The sliotar loops overhead and thwacks square into his face. He goes down like a felled redwood.

'Jesus Christ,' breathes Tama.

I cough, scuff my feet a bit.

'Ah, that's our Phyllis. All-Ireland Camogie championships, winning team 1979.'

CHAPTER 58

Garth: 7 days after Isabella Garrante book launch

I heave open the front door of the shop and a dull pain throbs across my shoulder and chest where the seatbelt bit in. It's a week since the collision; in the police we were never to refer to them as accidents, as the term implies no one is to blame, and in this case there is no doubt about who was to blame.

Otherwise, things have settled down a little from the chaos of that night and some semblance of normality has returned. From the front door of our beautiful shop I gaze across the Village. The early-morning sun gives promise of a spectacular day; its warm rays play across the grass around the war memorial, turning it such a vibrant green you'd think it had been photoshopped. Across the street the woman from Sell your Sole, whose name I still can't remember, is again dressing her window. Business seems to be going well for her, so I'm hoping she'll stay. Meryl bustles up to her, and a conversation ensues; I get the feeling Meryl may have lost her car again.

I take a deep breath, savouring the aroma of roasting coffee that hangs in the air. All seems right with the world, and one might be forgiven for believing that nothing has changed. But it has. The ghost of a probably murdered schoolgirl no longer haunts Havelock North, but it has been replaced by that of Oddbean, whose body has been identified as that inside the now shattered café statue. The police are investigating, and Tama has promised to visit with an update.

I hang out our magazine placards and place our chalkboard sign on the pavement, Eloise's neat handwriting announcing the arrival of the new Catherine Robertson, the Isabella Garrante now requiring no additional publicity of its own.

As I return to the counter, Eloise snaps shut her copy of *Dead Girl Gone*, a minor concussion having slowed her consumption of the story.

'So, what do you think?' I ask.

'Well, it's certainly a work of fiction.' She places the book on the counter.

'How so?'

'It makes no mention of the money.'

'Agreed.' I pick up the copy of *Dead Girl Gone* and riffle through the pages — an action which annoys me immensely when customers do it.

'And it doesn't explain how the contents of her schoolbag ended up in the Redwoods.'

I nod. 'No, it doesn't.'

Neither of these two omissions affects the story. It's only our familiarity with the evidence that makes them stand out, and I have an explanation that accounts for both these facts while making sense of several other aspects of the case.

'A hundred thousand dollars is a considerable sum of money,' I say.

'Yeeessss,' answers Eloise.

'It conjures images of *Breaking Bad* with stacks of bills filling several shrink-wrapped pallets.'

'I was going more with *Ocean's Eleven* because of George Clooney,' says Eloise.

'Whatever.' I shrug. 'The point is that if it's in hundred-dollar bills, it would actually fit into something about the size of, let's say, a schoolbag.'

Eloise opens the till, looking as if she's trying to visualise this, not that our till ever has many notes in it. 'You think Tracey did go to Oddbean's to look for the photos and instead found a stack of money?'

'And she empties her schoolbag, fills it with the money, and then is surprised by Oddbean and Franklin, so has to hide. And that's when she witnesses the murder.'

'What do you reckon they were arguing about?' asks Eloise. 'From what we've read in the files, it seems they were thick as thieves.'

'Could be anything. But let's say Franklin goes to check on the money, finds that it's missing and blames Oddbean. He knows what'll happen when the Black Dogs find out, so either he fights with Oddbean to try to get answers or he decides to kill him as a scapegoat.'

'Oh!' Eloise rests her palms on the counter. 'And Tracey sees all this, realises that it's her fault and thinks she'll be blamed if she goes to the police.'

'She knows Franklin is going to figure out she took the money, and so has no choice but to bribe the circus into hiding her.' I rub my chin. 'It's got legs.'

'Still doesn't explain the stuff in the Redwoods.'

'After Tracey is reported missing, Franklin goes back to Oddbean's to check there's nothing there linking him to Tracey. He needs to get rid of the photos at the very least and he discovers the discarded contents of her schoolbag. In a panic he chucks it in a carrier bag and dumps it at the Redwoods.'

'It's as good a story as any,' I say. 'I guess we'll never know for sure.'

'I guess we won't, although I believe Tracey left us one last clue: the writing on the envelope.'

'Your collar number?'

'No, you dork. The other bit.' Eloise's expression suggests I'm an idiot, and perhaps she's correct. I still don't see what she's getting at.

'She wrote *Please look inside the envelope*. It always struck me as a bit odd, because if you get a mysterious package, of course you're going to look inside.'

'The negatives? You think she actually meant look inside the envelope itself?'

'I do. It was her final mystery, which if we were smart enough to solve it would prove that she was telling the truth — about the photographs at least.'

'But we weren't smart enough to solve it. Stevie was.'

Eloise raises her chin. 'Stevie's a vital part of the team, so I'm claiming it.'

Our wonderful pup pops his head out of the stock room. When it appears that no treats are on offer, he returns to his skulking.

'Mōrena, whānau,' calls Tama, striding up to the counter. 'I was on my way to work and thought I'd catch you up.'

'Thanks. What's the haps?' I ask.

'Franklin's denying everything at the moment. And other than confirming that it's Oddbean, the forensics aren't looking good.'

'He's going to get away scot-free again.' Eloise folds her arms and scowls.

'Not necessarily.' Tama's face stretches into something between a smile and a grimace. 'Now that it appears Oddbean did not run off with the Black Dogs' money, they have come to their own conclusion.'

'And Franklin can expect the meting out of some summary justice.' My mind snaps back to the beating at the Black Dogs' pad, and I'm relieved that my dilemma over what happened to the money has been solved for me.

'Perhaps. Although we're suggesting that if he tells the truth of the matter he can do his time at Christchurch Prison away from the reach of the Black Dogs, so it may end up in front of the court yet.'

'Well, if nothing else, the Tracey Jervis case is closed.' I fossick under the counter for Tama's lock-up keys and pass them over. He makes no move to take them.

'You hang on to those. You've already had more success than me, and you might find another of my troublesome cases you want to dig into.' He winks, and heads out of the shop.

I jangle the keys. 'I'm not sure I want another case, love. Are you?'

'I'm definitely looking forward to going back to just enjoying our quiet little bookshop.'

A faint tip-tapping grows louder, then the Admiral appears in the doorway. 'Permission to come aboard?'

'Granted!'

He makes his way up the ramp. 'Mailies from the motherland.'

'What?' say Eloise and I in unison.

The Admiral waves a padded envelope at us. 'It was on the bookshelf outside.'

Eloise snatches it from him, and I see a flash of the stamps and postmarks, both unmistakably English. She rips the top open, showering the mushed-up padding across the floor. 'It's him.'

'It isn't him.'

Eloise turns the envelope upside down and shakes it. A black book falls onto the counter: *Betrayal* by Harold Pinter.

The End

ACKNOWLEDGEMENTS

This is a work of fiction, but it'll be obvious to anyone who has been near Wardini Books, or us, that there are glaring similarities with certain persons. Garth and Eloise are indeed based on us, but they are funnier, sharper, smarter. Lou's driving is not that bad, and Gareth is much more pompous than Garth.

Our team is the absolute lynchpin of Wardini Books, and our deep and heartfelt thanks go to the Havvers crew of Catt Walsh, Amy Janes and Phill McCaughey for letting us mine your personalities for this book. You have been such good sports and we hope you love the final story. If there's anything you don't like, that bit is absolutely not based on anything you have ever said or done.

Thanks to Brandi Dixon from Charcoal and Brass for her insightful feedback on our early drafts and giving us the encouragement to keep going.

Massive thanks to our publisher Claire Murdoch for taking a punt on the manuscript (and for all the little love heart scribbles), and to our editor Jane Parkin, without whom the book would mainly feature Stevie. The whole team at Penguin Random House New Zealand have been fantastically supportive and we salute you. Special thanks to Cat Taylor for the wonderful cover.

Thank you to everyone in the book industry in Aotearoa — our reps, the publishers, booksellers up and down the country, we love hanging out with you. Never have either of us been in such a supportive and collegial industry. Any teasing in this story is done with a huge amount of affection. Thanks to the loyal customers who support and cherish bookshops across the motu. Thank you to the authors of New Zealand who write so many of the wonderful books that we sell.

Hawke's Bay is a beautiful place to live, vibrant with kindness and creativity, and our intention in placing our story here is to celebrate this awesome community. Apart from the blatantly obvious characters who are inspired by real people, everyone else is a work of fiction or a composite of the bright beings we meet every day. We have never met the bad guys in our lives, our landlords are wonderful, and the local business association is superb.

ABOUT THE AUTHORS

Gareth and Louise Ward are the real-life owners of independent bookshop Wardini Books, with stores in Havelock North and Napier, New Zealand.

Louise is known among the staff as *Fearless Leader* and Gareth as *a bit of a dick*; he is, however, the author of the Tarquin the Honest and The Rise of the Remarkables book series, as well as being the bestselling and award-winning author of *The Traitor and the Thief* and *The Clockill and the Thief*.

Gareth and Louise met at police training college in the UK and are both ex-coppers. Louise has one murder arrest to her name, is an English Literature graduate and as an ex-teacher inflicted Shakespeare on inner-city twelve-year-olds. She regularly reviews books on RNZ.

Both are obsessed with their rescue dog Stevie, avoid housework and gardening, and live in the cultural centre of the universe that is Hawke's Bay, Aotearoa New Zealand.

The Bookshop Detectives is Gareth and Louise's first book together.

For more information about our titles visit
www.penguin.co.nz

CW00696989

Spouted and Spout-Fluid Beds

Fundamentals and Applications

Since the pioneering text by Mathur and Epstein over 35 years ago, much of the work on this subject has been extended or superseded, producing an enormous body of scattered literature. This edited volume unifies the subject, pulling material together and underpinning it with fundamental theory to produce the only complete, up-to-date reference on all major areas of spouted bed research and practice. With contributions from internationally renowned research groups, this book guides the reader through new developments, insights, and models. The hydrodynamic and reactor models of spouted and spout-fluid beds are examined, as well as such topics as particle segregation, heat and mass transfer, mixing, and scale-up. Later chapters focus on drying, particle-coating, and energy-related applications based on spouted and spout-fluid beds. This is a valuable resource for chemical and mechanical engineers in research and industry.

Norman Epstein is Honorary Professor in the Department of Chemical and Biological Engineering at the University of British Columbia. His research areas during the past 60 years have focused on heat, mass, and momentum transfer; on the fluid-particle dynamics of spouted beds and liquid-fluidized beds; and on various aspects of heat exchanger fouling. He is a former Editor of the *Canadian Journal of Chemical Engineering* and has published widely.

John R. Grace is Professor and Canada Research Chair in the Department of Chemical and Biological Engineering at the University of British Columbia. He has more than 40 years' experience working on fluidized and spouted beds, fluid-particle systems, and multiphase flow. His work includes reactor design, hydrodynamics, heat and mass transfer, and applications. Professor Grace has published widely, and has lectured and consulted for industry in these fields.

Both Epstein and Grace are Fellows of the Canadian Academy of Engineering and of the Chemical Institute of Canada, and former Presidents of the Canadian Society for Chemical Engineering.

Spouted and Spout-Fluid Beds

Fundamentals and Applications

Edited by

NORMAN EPSTEIN

University of British Columbia, Vancouver

JOHN R. GRACE

University of British Columbia, Vancouver

CAMBRIDGE UNIVERSITY PRESS
Cambridge, New York, Melbourne, Madrid, Cape Town, Singapore,
São Paulo, Delhi, Dubai, Tokyo, Mexico City

Cambridge University Press
The Edinburgh Building, Cambridge CB2 2RU, UK

Published in the United States of America by Cambridge University Press, New York

www.cambridge.org
Information on this title: www.cambridge.org/9780521517973

© Cambridge University Press 2011

This publication is in copyright. Subject to statutory exception
and to the provisions of relevant collective licensing agreements,
no reproduction of any part may take place without the written
permission of Cambridge University Press.

First published 2011

Printed in the United Kingdom at the University Press, Cambridge

A catalogue record for this publication is available from the British Library.

Library of Congress Cataloguing in Publication Data
Spouted and spout-fluid beds : fundamentals and applications /
[edited by] Norman Epstein, John R. Grace.
   p. cm.
Includes bibliographical references and index.
ISBN 978-0-521-51797-3
1. Spouted bed processes.   I. Epstein, Norman.   II. Grace, John R.   III. Title.
TP156.S57S66   2010
660′.28426 – dc22   2010023741

ISBN 978-0-521-51797-3 hardback

Cambridge University Press has no responsibility for the persistence or
accuracy of URLs for external or third-party Internet websites referred to
in this publication, and does not guarantee that any content on such
websites is, or will remain, accurate or appropriate.

Contents

Contributors

Prof. Xiaojun Bao
Key Laboratory of Catalysis
Faculty of Chemical Science and Engineering
China University of Petroleum
Beijing, China

Prof. Xiaotao Bi
Department of Chemical and Biological Engineering
University of British Columbia
Vancouver, Canada

Prof. Javier Bilbao
University of the Basque Country
Faculty of Science and Technology
Department of Chemical Engineering
Bilbao, Spain

Dr. Esly Ferreira da Costa Jr.
Federal University of Espirito Santo (UFES)
Rural Engineering Department
São Mateus, Brazil

Dr. Wei Du
Key Laboratory of Catalysis
Faculty of Chemical Science and Engineering
China University of Petroleum
Beijing, China

Dr. Eng. Sebastian Englart
Institute of Air-Conditioning and District Heating
Faculty of Environmental Engineering
Wroclaw University of Technology
Wroclaw, Poland

Dr. Norman Epstein
Department of Chemical and Biological Engineering
University of British Columbia
Vancouver, Canada

Prof. J. W. Evans
Department of Materials Science and Engineering
University of California
Berkeley, CA, USA

Dr. Maria do Carmo Ferreira
Chemical Engineering Department
Universidade Federal de São Carlos – UFSCar
São Carlos, Brazil

Dr. Fábio Bentes Freire
Chemical Engineering Department
Universidade Federal de São Carlos
São Carlos, Brazil

Prof. José Teixeira Freire
Chemical Engineering Department
Universidade Federal de São Carlos
São Carlos, Brazil

Prof. John R. Grace
Department of Chemical and Biological Engineering
University of British Columbia
Vancouver, Canada

Prof. Željko B. Grbavčić
Faculty of Technology and Metallurgy
University of Belgrade
Beograd, Serbia

Dr. Andrew Ingram
School of Chemical Engineering
University of Birmingham
Birmingham, UK

Prof. Toshifumi Ishikura
Department of Chemical Engineering
Fukuoka University
Fukuoka, Japan

Prof. Baosheng Jin
Key Laboratory of Clean Power Generation and Combustion Technology of
    Ministry of Education
Thermo-Energy Engineering Research Institute
Southeast University
Nanjing, China

Dr. Vladimír Jiřičný
Institute of Chemical Process Fundamentals
Academy of Sciences of the Czech Republic
Prague, Czech Republic

Prof. Andrzej Kmiec
Institute of Chemical Engineering and Heating Equipment
Technical University of Wroclaw
Wroclaw, Poland

Prof. C. Jim Lim
Department of Chemical and Biological Engineering
University of British Columbia
Vancouver, Canada

Dr. Antonio C. L. Lisboa
Universidade Estadual de Campinas (UNICAMP)
School of Chemical Engineering
Campinas, Brazil

Prof. Emeritus Howard Littman
Department of Chemical and Biological Engineering
Rensselaer Polytechnic Institute
Troy, NY, USA

Prof. Morris H. Morgan III
Department of Chemical Engineering
Hampton University
Hampton, VA, USA

Prof. Arun Sadashiv Mujumdar
National University of Singapore (NUS)
Minerals, Metals and Materials Technology Centre (M3TC)
Faculty of Engineering
Singapore

Dr. Hiroshi Nagashima
Department of Chemical Engineering
Fukuoka University
Fukuoka, Japan

Prof. Martin Olazar
University of the Basque Country
Faculty of Science and Technology
Department of Chemical Engineering
Bilbao, Spain

Dr. John D. Paccione
Department of Environmental Health Sciences
School of Public Health
State University of New York at Albany
Albany, NY, USA

Dr. Elizabeth Pallai
Pannon University, FIT
Research Institute of Chemical and Process Engineering
Veszprém, Hungary

Dr. Sarah Palmer
School of Engineering
University of Warwick
Coventry, UK

Dr. Maria Laura Passos
Laval, QC, Canada

Prof. Norberto Piccinini
Dipartimento di Scienza dei Materiali e Ingegneria Chimica
Politecnico de Torino
Turin, Italy

Prof. Sandra Cristina dos Santos Rocha
Universidade Estadual de Campinas (UNICAMP)
School of Chemical Engineering
Campinas, Brazil

Dr. Giorgio Rovero
Dipartimento di Scienza dei Materiali e Ingegneria Chimica
Politecnico de Torino
Turin, Italy

Prof. Maria J. San José
University of the Basque Country
Faculty of Science and Technology
Department of Chemical Engineering
Bilbao, Spain

Prof. Jonathan Seville
Dean of Engineering
School of Engineering
University of Warwick
Coventry, UK

Dr. Tibor Szentmarjay
Testing Laboratory of Environmental Protection
Veszprém, Hungary

Dr. Osvaldir Pereira Taranto
Universidade Estadual de Campinas (UNICAMP)
School of Chemical Engineering
Campinas, Brazil

Dr. Judith Tóth
Chemical Research Center
Hungarian Academy of Sciences
Institute of Material and Environmental Chemistry
Veszprém, Hungary

Prof. A. Paul Watkinson
Department of Chemical and Biological Engineering
University of British Columbia
Vancouver, Canada

Prof. Rui Xiao
Key Laboratory of Clean Power Generation and Combustion Technology of
    Ministry of Education
Thermo-Energy Engineering Research Institute
Southeast University
Nanjing, China

Dr. Jian Xu
Key Laboratory of Catalysis
Faculty of Chemical Science and Engineering
China University of Petroleum
Beijing, China

Prof. Mingyao Zhang
Key Laboratory of Clean Power Generation and Combustion Technology of
    Ministry of Education
Thermo-Energy Engineering Research Institute
Southeast University
Nanjing, China

Dr. Wenqi Zhong
Key Laboratory of Clean Power Generation and Combustion Technology of
    Ministry of Education
Thermo-Energy Engineering Research Institute
Southeast University
Nanjing, China

Preface

Spouted beds have now been studied and applied for more than 50 years; during this period there has been a continual output of research papers in the engineering literature, considerable efforts to apply spouted beds in agriculture-related and industrial operations, and five international symposia dedicated solely to spouted beds. The book *Spouted Beds* by Kishan Mathur and the first-named editor of this volume summarized the field up to 1974. Since then there have been several reviews,[1–4] but none that have surveyed the entire field comprehensively, including aspects that were barely touched in the earlier book or that were entirely absent. Examples of new areas include mechanically assisted spouting, slot-rectangular spouted beds, spouted and spout-fluid bed gasifiers, spouted bed electrolysis, and application of computational fluid dynamics (CFD) to spouted beds.

Our original intention was to prepare a sequel to the Mathur and Epstein book, but we soon realized that this chore would be too daunting, especially in view of competing time commitments. We therefore adopted the idea of a multiauthored book for which we would provide editing and prepare a subset of the chapters ourselves. Our intent was to choose an international array of authors able to provide a truly comprehensive view of the field, fundamentals as well as applications. Almost all those whom we asked to participate agreed to do so, and they have been remarkably cooperative in submitting material, following instructions, and responding to requests for changes, many of these being editorial in nature.

In addition to acknowledging the authors and the cooperation of Cambridge University Press, we especially acknowledge the secretarial assistance of Helsa Leong, without whom we probably would never have finished. We are also indebted to the Natural Sciences and Engineering Research Council of Canada for continuing financial support. The book is dedicated to Kishan B. Mathur, co-inventor and a pioneer in spouted beds and an inspiration to us both.

References

1. N. Epstein and J. R. Grace. Spouting of particulate solids. In *Handbook of Powder Science and Technology*, ed. M. E. Fayed and L. Otten (New York: van Nostrand Reinhold, 1984), pp. 507–534.

2. A. S. Mujumdar. Spouted bed technology – a brief review. In ***Drying '84***, ed. A. S. Mujumdar (New York: Hemisphere, 1984), pp. 151–157.
3. J. Bridgwater. Spouted beds. In *Fluidization*, 2nd ed., ed. J. F. Davidson, R. Clift, and D. Harrison (London: Academic Press, 1985), pp. 201–224.
4. N. Epstein and J. R. Grace. Spouting of particulate solids. In *Handbook of Powder Science and Technology*, 2nd ed., ed. M. E. Fayed and L. Otten (New York: Chapman and Hall, 1997), pp. 532–567.
5. J. Zhu and J. Hong. Development and current status of research on spouted beds. *Chem. Reaction Engng. & Technol.*, **13** (1997), 207–230 (text in Chinese, references in English).

Common nomenclature

A	cross-sectional area of column, m^2
A_a	cross-sectional area of annulus, m^2
A_i	fluid inlet cross-sectional area, m^2
A_s	cross-sectional area of spout, m^2
Ar	Archimedes number
Bi	Biot number
C_A	concentration of component A in fluid, mol/m^3
C_D	drag coefficient
c_p	heat capacity at constant pressure, $J/(kg \cdot K)$
D	diameter of cylindrical column, m
$\mathcal{D}$	diffusivity or dispersion coefficient, $m^2 s^{-1}$
D_H	diameter of upper surface of bed, m
D_i	diameter of fluid inlet, m
D_o	diameter of cone base, m
D_s	spout diameter, m
d_p	particle diameter or mean diameter, m
d_s	sphere-equivalent diameter of particle based on its surface area, m
d_v	sphere-equivalent diameter of particle based on its volume, m
$F(t)$	output tracer concentration/step input tracer concentration
f	Fanning friction factor
G	superficial mass flux of fluid, $kg/m^2 s$
g	acceleration of gravity, m/s^2
H	bed depth, usually measured as loose-packed static bed depth after spouting, m
H_c	cone height, m
H_f	fountain height, measured from bed surface, m
H_m	maximum spoutable bed depth, m
H_o	static bed depth, m
h	heat transfer coefficient, $W/m^2 K$
i, j	integers
k	chemical reaction rate constant, s^{-1} if first order
L	length, m
M	inventory of particles, kg
m_p	particle mass, kg
Nu	Nusselt number

P	pressure, Pa
Pr	Prandtl number
Q	volumetric flow rate, m^3/s
q	heat transfer rate, W
R	radius of cylindrical column, m
R_g	universal gas constant, 8.315 J/mol · K
Re	Reynolds number
r	radial coordinate, m
S	surface area, m^2
Sc	Schmidt number
Sh	Sherwood number
T	temperature, K
t	time, s
U	superficial velocity of spouting fluid based on D, m/s
U_a	upward superficial velocity in annulus, m/s
U_{aH}	value of U_a at $z = H$, m/s
U_M	superficial velocity corresponding to ΔP_M, m/s
U_m	value of U_{ms} at $H = H_m$, m/s
U_{mf}	superficial velocity at minimum fluidization, m/s
U_{ms}	superficial velocity at minimum spouting, m/s
U_t	free settling terminal velocity, m/s
u	local fluid velocity, m/s
u_i	average fluid velocity at fluid inlet, m/s
u_{msi}	minimum spouting velocity based on D_i, m/s
V_p	particle volume, m^3
v	local particle velocity, m/s
x, y	horizontal Cartesian coordinates, m
z	vertical coordinate measured from fluid inlet, m

Greek letters

α	thermal diffusivity, m^2/s
β	mass transfer coefficient, m/s
ΔP	pressure drop, Pa
ΔP_M	maximum pressure drop across bed, Pa
ΔP_S	spouting pressure drop across bed, Pa
ε	fractional void volume
θ	total included angle of cone
λ	thermal conductivity of fluid, W/(m · K)
λ_p	thermal conductivity of particles, W/(m · K)
μ	absolute viscosity, Pa · s
θ	total included angle of cone
ρ	density of fluid, kg/m^3

ρ_p density of particles, kg/m^3
τ mean residence time, s

Subscripts

A, B component A, B
a annulus, auxiliary
f fountain
ms minimum spouting
p particle
s spout

Abbreviations

CSB   conventional spouted bed
CCSB   conical-cylindrical spouted bed = CSB
CcSB   conical (Coni-cal) spouted bed

1   Introduction

Norman Epstein and John R. Grace

This introductory chapter follows the contours, and in some cases even the exact wording, of Chapter 1 in *Spouted Beds*,[1] the only book prior to the present publication that deals *exclusively* with this subject. Indeed, the current venture was originally to be a revised version of that 1974 book by the present editors. However, after writing the first draft of this chapter for the revision, we realized that the breadth and variety of work on spouted and spout-fluid beds since 1974 required input from a wide range of authors for coverage to be completed in a finite time. Changes in the subsequent draft were mainly with respect to layout of chapter topics (Section 1.6). Despite advances since 1974, the earlier book of that year remains a repository of useful information not available in this volume or elsewhere.

1.1   The spouted bed

Consider a vessel open at the top and filled with relatively coarse particulate solids. Suppose fluid is injected vertically through a centrally located small opening at the base of the vessel. If the fluid injection rate is high enough, the resulting high-velocity jet causes a stream of particles to rise rapidly in a hollowed central core within the bed of solids. These particles, after being carried somewhat beyond the peripheral bed level, rain back onto the annular region between the hollowed core and the column wall, where they slowly travel downward and, to some extent, inward as a loosely packed bed. As the fluid travels upward, it flares out into the annular region. The overall bed thereby becomes a composite of a dilute phase central core with upward-moving solids entrained by a cocurrent flow of fluid, and a dense phase annular region with countercurrent percolation of fluid. A systematic cyclic pattern of solids movement is thus established, giving rise to a unique hydrodynamic system that is more suitable for certain applications than more conventional fluid-solid configurations.

This system is termed a *spouted bed*, the central core a *spout*, the surrounding annular region the *annulus*, and the solids above the bed surface entrained by the spout and then raining down on the annulus are designated as the *fountain*. To eliminate dead spaces at the bottom of the vessel, it is common to use a diverging conical base topped by a

Spouted and Spout-Fluid Beds: Fundamentals and Applications, eds. Norman Epstein and John R. Grace. Published by Cambridge University Press. © Cambridge University Press 2011.

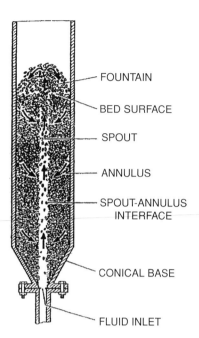

FOUNTAIN

BED SURFACE

SPOUT

ANNULUS

SPOUT-ANNULUS
   INTERFACE

CONICAL BASE

FLUID INLET

Figure 1.1. Schematic diagram of a spouted bed. Arrows indicate direction of solids motion.

cylindrical column, with fluid injection at the truncated apex of the cone (Figure 1.1). The use of an entirely conical vessel is also widely practiced. An example of each is shown in Figure 1.2.

Solids can be added into and withdrawn from spouted beds, so, as for fluidized beds, spouting can be performed both batchwise and continuously with respect to the solids, although batchwise operation is more likely to be adopted in spouting than in fluidization applications. The solids may be fed into the bed at the top near the wall, so they join the downward moving mass of particles in the annulus (Figure 1.3a). Alternatively, the solids may enter by being entrained by the incoming fluid (Figure 1.3b). Because the annular solids are in an aerated state, the solids may be readily discharged through an overflow pipe at the top of the bed, as in Figure 1.3b, or through an outlet at a lower level, such as in the conical base, as in Figure 1.3a. When solids are fed with the inlet fluid and discharged at the top of the bed, as in Figure 1.3b, they are effectively being conveyed vertically, in addition to being contacted with the fluid.

As in fluidization, the fluid in spouting applications, and therefore in research studies, is more likely to be a gas than a liquid. Except where otherwise indicated, most of this book therefore deals with gas spouting, with only one chapter devoted to the mechanics of spouting with a liquid. Although the spouted bed was originally developed as a substitute for a fluidized bed for coarse, uniformly sized particles to overcome the poor quality of gas fluidization obtained with such particles, some of its unique characteristics, including the cyclic recirculation of the solids, have proved valuable, making spouted beds capable of performing certain useful operations more effectively than fluidized beds with their more random solids motion.

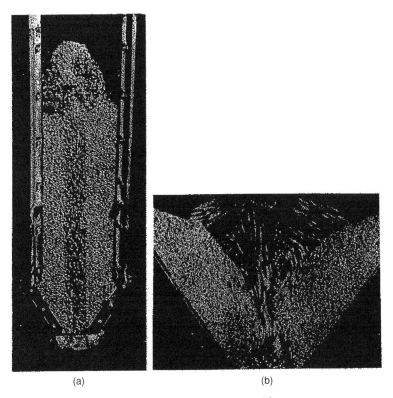

(a)   (b)

Figure 1.2. (a) Spouting in a conical-cylindrical vessel,[1,2] courtesy of National Research Council of Canada. (b) Spouting in a conical vessel.[1,3]

The circular cross-section devices shown in Figure 1.2, now commonly referred to as conventional spouted beds (CSBs), are the principal subject of this book. A wide variety of nonconventional spouting techniques and equipment has also been reported in the literature, and some of these are described in subsequent chapters.

1.2   Brief history

Although the terms *spouting* and *spouted bed* were coined at the National Research Council (NRC) of Canada by Gishler and Mathur (1954)[6] to describe the type of dense-phase solids operation (or CSB) depicted by Figures 1.1 through 1.3, a dilute-phase solids operation activated by an air jet for ore roasting (Robinson, 1879),[7] or coal combustion (Syromyatnikov, 1951)[8] predates the CSB. Such dilute solids spouting, referred to as "air-fountaining"[3] and, more frequently, as "jet spouting,"[9] are alluded to in several succeeding chapters.

The original spouted bed was developed in 1954 as an alternative method of drying to a badly slugging fluidized bed of moist wheat particles.[10] Because of the vigorous particle circulation, much hotter air than in conventional wheat driers could thus be used without damaging the grain.[4] Realizing that the technique could have wider application, the

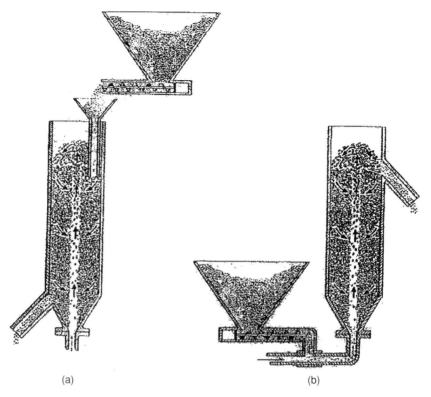

(a)   (b)

Figure 1.3. Continuous spouting operation. (a) Solids fed into annulus from above, after Mathur and Gishler.[4] (b) Solids fed with incoming gas into spout, after Manurung.[5]

NRC group studied the characteristics of spouted beds for a variety of solid materials, with both air and water as spouting media.[2] On the basis of this preliminary study, they asserted that "the mechanism of flow of solids as well as of gas in this technique is different from fluidization, but it appears to achieve the same purpose for coarse particles as fluidization does for fine materials." This assertion is an understatement because, as already noted, spouting has some unique characteristics, different from those of fluidization.

Early research papers continued to originate from Canadian sources – the NRC Laboratories in Ottawa, the Prairie Regional Laboratories of the NRC, and the University of Ottawa. It was only after the publication in 1959 of *Fluidization* by Leva,[11] which summarized the NRC work in a chapter titled "The Spouted Bed," that interest spread to other countries. The translation of Leva's book into Russian in 1961, followed by the publication in 1963 of a book by Zabrodsky (English translation, 1966)[12] appears to have triggered considerable activity on the subject at several research centers in the Soviet Union, with particular emphasis on spouting in conical vessels, rather than in cylindrical columns with conical bases. By the time the book by Mathur and Epstein (1974)[1] was in print, some 250 publications, including patents, on spouted beds had appeared from countries as diverse as Australia, Canada, France, Hungary, India, Italy, Japan, Poland,

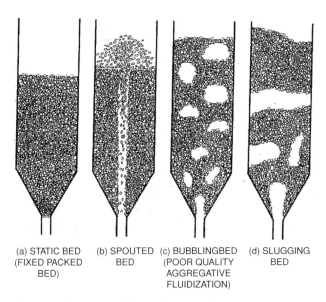

(a) STATIC BED (FIXED PACKED BED) (b) SPOUTED BED (c) BUBBLINGBED (POOR QUALITY AGGREGATIVE FLUIDIZATION) (d) SLUGGING BED

Figure 1.4. Regime transitions with increasing gas flow.

Rumania, the UK, the United States, the USSR (most prolifically), and Yugoslavia. At present, the number of publications on the subject exceeds 1300, and to contributors from the above countries (including mainly Belarus, Russia, Ukraine, and Uzbekistan from the former Soviet Union) should now be added those from Brazil, Chile, China, Mexico, the Netherlands, New Zealand, Spain, and no doubt others.

The first commercial spouted bed units in Canada were installed in 1962 – for the drying of peas, lentils, and flax – that is, drying of the granular particles undergoing spouting. Since than, units have been built in other countries for a variety of other drying duties, including evaporative drying of solutions, suspensions, and pastes in a spouted bed of inert particles, as well as for solids blending, cooling, coating, and granulation. Most commercially successful spouted bed installations have involved such physical operations, but a wide variety of chemical processes have also been subjected to laboratory- and bench-scale spouting investigations; some of these, including electrolysis in a liquid-spouted bed,[13] show considerable promise for further development.

1.3   Flow regime maps encompassing conventional spouting

Spouting, which is visually observable in a transparent column with a fully circular cross-section by virtue of the rapidly reversing motion of particles in the fountain and the relatively slow particle descent at the wall, occurs over a definite range of gas velocity for a given combination of gas, solids, vessel geometry, and configuration. Figure 1.4 illustrates schematically the transition from a quiescent to a spouted bed, and hence often to a bubbling and a slugging bed, as the superficial gas velocity (gas volumetric flow rate/column cross-sectional area) is increased.

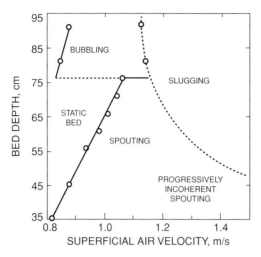

Figure 1.5. Flow regime map for wheat particles (prolate spheroids: 3.2 mm × 6.4 mm, $\rho_p = $ 1376 kg/m^3). $D_c = 152$ mm, $D_i = 12.5$ mm. Fluid is ambient air. After Mathur and Gishler.[2]

Those transitions can be represented quantitatively as plots of bed depth H versus superficial gas velocity U, or regime maps (sometimes referred to as "phase diagrams"), examples of which are given in Figures 1.5 and 1.6. The line representing transition between a static and an agitated (spouted or bubbling-fluidized) bed is more reproducible in the direction of decreasing velocity than vice versa, the resulting static bed then being in the reproducible *random loose packed* condition.[14] Figure 1.5 shows that, for a given solid material contacted by a specific fluid (at a given temperature and pressure) in a vessel of fixed geometry, there exists a maximum spoutable bed depth (or height) H_m, beyond which spouting does not occur, being replaced by poor-quality fluidization. In Figure 1.5, H_m is represented by the horizontal lines at a bed depth of 0.76 m. The minimum spouting velocity, U_{ms}, is represented in the same figure by the inclined line that terminates at H_m, at which U_{ms} can be up to 50 percent greater[15] than the corresponding minimum fluidization velocity, U_{mf}, although less difference between these two critical velocities has usually been found.[16,17] Figure 1.6 shows a gas inlet, particle, and column diameter combination for which spouting does not occur. For the same column and particles, but with a smaller gas inlet ($D_i = 12.5$ mm instead of 15.8 mm), coherent spouting could be obtained.[2]

Becker[16] attempted a more generalized regime diagram by plotting upward drag force (as measured by frictional pressure drop, $-\Delta P_f$) normalized with respect to downward gravitational weight of solids against U/U_m, with H/H_m as a parameter, whereas Pallai and Németh[15] simply plotted $-\Delta P_f$ against U/U_{mf} with H as a parameter. The amount of information provided by these procedures for any given system of fluid, solids, and column geometry is considerable, but the applicability to other systems is quite limited, given the complexity of the regime transitions.

A typical spouted bed in a cylindrical or conical-cylindrical vessel has a depth, measured from the fluid inlet orifice to the surface of the loose-packed static bed or the

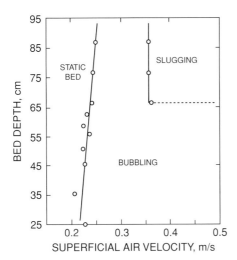

Figure 1.6. Regime map for Ottawa sand ($d_p = 0.589$ mm). $D_c = 152$ mm, $D_i = 15.8$ mm. After Mathur and Gishler.[2]

spouted bed annulus, of at least one-half the cylinder diameter. If the bed is much shallower, the system differs hydrodynamically from true spouting, and any generally formulated principles of spouted bed behavior would not be expected to apply. A minimum spoutable bed depth has, however, not been precisely defined or investigated, except in the case of conical beds,[18] nor have any detailed studies been made about the maximum spouting velocity at which transition from coherent spouting to either bubbling fluidization or slugging occurs. For most practical purposes, however, there is usually sufficient latitude between the minimum and maximum spouting velocity that the fluid flow can be amply increased above the minimum without transition to fluidization.

1.4   Nonaxisymmetric geometries of spouted beds

The photographs of Figure 1.2 and, in most cases, illustrations such as those of Figure 1.4 are obtained from the transparent flat face of semicircular conical or conical-cylindrical vessels, with aligned semicircular gas inlets. Qualitatively, what is seen and what is measured in such half-sectional columns is comparable to what can be detected by various techniques (e.g., piezoelectricity, stop-flow, laser-Doppler anemometry, optical fiber probes) and what is measured in full columns. Quantitatively, however, although some characteristics of spouted beds are well matched in the fully cylindrical and semicylindrical (labeled "full" and "half," respectively) columns, others show significant differences.

Experimental data required to construct a regime map such as Figure 1.5 are, by and large, quite similar when obtained for either a half or a full column. Thus, measured values of U_{ms} from half-columns have been shown to be equal to,[17,19] or at most only 10 percent greater than,[20] U_{ms} for full columns, whereas H_m from half columns has been measured as approximately equal to,[19] and never more than 32 percent smaller than,[20] H_m for full columns. Bed pressure drops and pressure profiles during spouting have also been found to be quite similar for the two-column geometries, as have pitot tube measurements of radial and longitudinal gas velocity profiles,[21] except in the immediate vicinity of the half-column flat wall.

The situation is different for details of particle motion and spout geometry. All walls tend to retard vertical particle motion relative to what occurs a few particle diameters from the wall (typically by about 20 percent or more for smooth walls and smooth spherical particles), whether the motion is downward in the annulus at flat or circular walls[22] or upward in the spout at the flat wall of a half column (measured by laser-Doppler anemometry[23] or by fiber optic probes[24]). Consequently, cinephotographic measurements at the transparent flat face, which are biased toward particles very near the face, tend to underestimate particle velocities in the spout, especially at or near the axis of a full column. Particle velocities in the fountain are, however, well matched between half and full columns.[23] As for the annulus, although the downward particle velocity at the flat wall has sometimes been reported as being equal to that at the corresponding half-round wall, as well as to that at the round wall of a full column,[2,19,20] Rovero et al.,[22] by a carefully monitored stop-flow technique using tracer particles, showed that particle trajectories at the half-column flat face are not representative of full column behavior at the same plane, and that only the middle 60° sector of a half-column is representative of a full column as far as particle velocity is concerned.

Spout geometry is more contentious. Mikhailik,[25] based on a piezoelectric probe for measuring particle velocity in the spout of a fully circular bed, coupled with visual observation of spouting in a larger diameter transparent semicircular column, concluded that the shape and size of the spout were the same in both types of column. However, the longitudinally uniform cylindrical spout shape reported by Mikhailik is at odds with the recorded observations of most other workers, and the criterion used for size equality, given the inequality of vessel diameters and the absence of geometrical similarity between the two systems, was the adherence of measured spout diameters in both cases to the same empirical equation relating average spout diameter to operating system parameters. A more convincing study by He et al.,[26] using optical fiber probes for voidage and particle velocity in geometrically matched semicylindrical and fully cylindrical cone-based columns, showed cross-sectional modification of the full column circular spout to an approximate semiellipse (with the larger axis perpendicular to the flat wall) in the half column. There was longitudinal distortion from monotonic divergence of spout width in the upward direction, both for the full column and for the half-column at 90° to the flat wall, to an S-shape along the flat wall itself. Average spout diameters in the full column were underestimated by about 35 percent if based on measurements along the flat face of the half-column.

The corners of half columns contribute most to distortion of full-column spouted bed behavior.[22] 90°, 60°, and 30° sector columns, which produce ever narrower corners as the sector angle decreases, although they give rise to spouted bed behavior of sorts, do not in most important respects compare well to measurements obtained in full or even half columns, and show increasing instability as the sector angle decreases.[27,28] Unlike half-sectional beds, which retain their value as qualitative and partly quantitative visual simulators of full beds, sector beds are not recommended for these purposes.

As in the case of fluidized bed research, "two-dimensional" beds – that is, beds of particles encased between parallel transparent vertical planes a few millimeters apart with a fluid inlet that spans this thickness – have also been used in spouted bed research to give qualitative insight into three-dimensional behavior. In the case of spouted beds, it has been claimed that such slot-rectangular devices can be scaled up readily – for instance, for grain drying purposes.[29] This claim is discussed in Chapter 17.

1.5   Spouted beds in the gas–solid contacting spectrum

1.5.1   The spectrum

Gas–solid contacting systems may be broadly classified as (1) nonagitated, (2) mechanically agitated, and (3) gas-agitated. Categories (1) and (3), unlike (2), have no moving parts.

Fixed and moving packed beds, which belong to the first category, are applicable to processes that do not call for maintaining high rates of heat and mass transfer between the gas and the coarse solids, and in which uniformity of conditions in different parts of the bed is either not critical or not desirable. In a fixed bed, solids cannot be continuously added or withdrawn, and treatment of the gas is usually the main objective – for example, to recover solvent vapors by gas adsorption, to dry a gas, or to carry out a gas-phase reaction catalyzed by the particles, in which the catalyst has an extended life (limited deactivation). A moving bed provides continuous flow of solids through the reaction zone. Its application therefore extends to chemical and physical treatment of solids in such processes as roasting of ores, calcining of limestone, and drying and cooling pellets and briquettes. In both fixed and moving beds, the gas movement is close to *plug flow*, a feature that is almost always advantageous for chemical reactions, where axial dispersion tends to reduce conversions and yields.

Limited agitation can be imparted to the solids by mechanical means, either by movement of the vessel itself, as in rotary driers and kilns, or by internal impellers. In either case, most of the material remains in a packed-bed condition, but the differential movement of particles improves contacting effectiveness because fresh surface is continually exposed to the gas. Also, the blending of solids by agitation levels out interparticle gradients in composition and temperature. Mechanical systems are used mainly for processes involving solids treatment, such as drying, calcining, and cooling, but are unsuitable for processes that require the gas to be treated uniformly.

In gas-agitated systems, such as fluidized beds or solids transport systems, intense agitation is imparted to each solid particle by the action of the gas stream. In fluidization, whether of the dense, noncirculating (externally), particulate, or bubbling bed variety at one extreme, or dilute, circulating, or fast-fluidization at the other, the large surface area of the fine well-mixed solids gives rise to high particle-to-gas heat and mass transfer rates; coefficients of heat transfer to or from the vessel walls or submerged surfaces (e.g., of heat exchangers) are considerably higher than those at the same superficial gas velocity in the absence of solids or in the presence of a fixed bed of solids. Continuous operation of fluidized beds can be readily accomplished because solids are easily added to, and withdrawn from, such beds. In fluidization, the average residence time of the particles in the bed can be controlled by adjusting the solids feed rate and the holdup of the bed. Because of these basic features, fluidized beds are the preferred contacting method for many processes, including chemical reactions (both catalytic and noncatalytic) involving the gas, as well as physical treatment (e.g., drying) of the solids.

Dilute solids transport (e.g., pneumatic conveying) may be more suitable than fluidization for some gas–solid contacting operations. In such systems the contact time between a given particle and a gas is very short – no more than a few seconds – because of very high gas velocities. Intense turbulence facilitates high coefficients of heat and mass transfer, but the extents of heat and mass transfer to or from the particles is limited by the small residence time of the particles in the reaction zone. Dilute solids transport systems are especially suitable for processes that are surface-rate controlled rather than internal-diffusion controlled with respect to the solid particles. Examples of established applications are combustion of pulverized coal, flash roasting or smelting of metallic sulfides, and flash drying of sensitive materials that can tolerate exposure to heat for only a few seconds.

Because the annular region of a spouted bed, which contains most of the solids, is virtually a moving packed bed, with counterflow of gas, spouted beds have sometimes been categorized as moving-bed systems.[30] However, the dilute solids transport that characterizes the spout region is crucial to overall spouted-bed performance and, inasmuch as bed solids recirculate many times, therefore becoming well mixed, the operation comes closer to conventional fluidization in its attributes. Although the early statement that spouting "appears to achieve the same purpose for coarse particles as fluidization does for fine materials"[2] remains true for certain applications, such as solids drying, the differences in the two operations are important for others. For example, the systematic cyclic movement of particles in a spouted bed, in contrast to more random motion in fluidization, is a feature of critical value for granulation and particle coating processes. In the spectrum of contacting systems, therefore, spouted beds occupy a position that overlaps moving and fluidized beds to some extent, but at the same time they have a place of their own by virtue of certain unique characteristics.

1.5.2   Spouting versus fluidization

In what has become the well-entrenched C-A-B-D classification scheme for distinguishing between various types of fluidization by air at ambient conditions, Geldart[31] proposed the criterion (for air at room temperature and atmospheric pressure as the motive fluid)

$$(\rho_p - \rho)d_p^2 > 10^{-3}\,\text{kg/m}$$

as characterizing particles that "can form stable spouted beds." This criterion was rederived by Molerus[32] as

$$(\rho_p - \rho)gd_p > 15.3\,Pa$$

for particles of diameter d_p and density ρ_p, fluid of density ρ, and gravitational acceleration g. Although both these criteria, which neglect the important role of fluid inlet diameter on spoutability, have been shown experimentally to be strictly invalid,[33] they have the virtue of emphasizing that there is a minimum particle diameter below which spouting becomes impractical. This diameter is about 0.5 to 1.0 mm – that is, within the fluidization transition range of what Squires[34] labeled a relatively flexible "fluid bed" of fine particles and a relatively inflexible "teeter bed" (a term arbitrarily "borrowed from ore dressing technology where it means to fluidize particulately with water") of coarse particles, requiring a wide particle size distribution to avoid channeling. It is possible to operate a miniature spouted bed with considerably finer particles[35] using a very small gas inlet. Indeed, perforated plate distributors for fluidized beds often give rise to formation of small spouts above each hole, with the spouts breaking into bubbles further up the bed.[36] If, however, a single small hole is used to spout fine particles, the allowable holdup and capacity of the bed would also be small, and any attempt at scaleup by enlarging the inlet hole would lead to nonhomogeneous fluidization rather than spouting.[37,38]

The total frictional pressure drop across a fully spouting bed is always lower by at least 20 percent[39] than that required to support the buoyed weight of the bed – in other words, than the frictional pressure drop for particulate fluidization. In this respect, a spouted bed is qualitatively similar to a channeling fluidized bed.[40] Channeling, however, is an undesirable feature of a fluidized bed that involves passage of gas through part of the bed without inducing much movement of, or contact with, the surrounding particles. In spouting, on the other hand, agitation of the entire bed is achieved by the gas jet, and intimate contact between the particles and the gas occurs both in the jet and in the surrounding dense-phase annulus, the latter being fed gas by crossflow from the jet. In a typical spouted bed, well over half the jet gas has already permeated the annulus halfway up the bed. In addition, channeling in fluidized beds is favored by very fine particles,[11,40,41] whereas spouting is normally a coarse particle phenomenon. Thus the similarity between spouting and channeling, stressed by several authors,[11,12,42] can be misleading.[43]

The shape of the longitudinal profile in a spouted bed also distinctly differs from that of a fluidized bed when a cylindrical column, or even a conical-cylindrical column with no bed support, is used in both cases. Thus, for a spouted bed, the longitudinal pressure gradient varies with height, rising to a maximum at the top of the bed. For a fluidized bed, on the other hand, the pressure gradient is nearly constant over the cylindrical portion of the column, despite the fact that for gas fluidization, as for spouting, the usual pattern of solids movement is up at the center and down near the wall.

Apart from achieving favorable gas–solid contact, spouting, more than fluidization, is a means of agitating coarse particles with a gas and of causing solid-solid contacts, the interaction between gas and solid particles being incidental. These additional features of a spouted bed are particularly applicable to mechanical operations such as blending, comminution, and dehusking of solids. The absence of a fluid distributor and its associated problems (e.g., plugging by solids) is another significant aspect of spouting that distinguishes it from fluidization.

Table 1.1, from Cui and Grace,[44] summarizes key differences between gas-fluidized and gas-spouted beds.

1.5.3   Spout-fluid beds

A hybrid reactor that shares some characteristics of both spouting and fluidization, and which is especially useful for coarse, sticky, or agglomerating solids, is commonly referred to as a *spout-fluid bed*. Such a reactor involves a substantial fluid flow through a single central inlet orifice, as in a spouted bed, and an auxiliary fluid flow through a series of holes in a surrounding distributor, as in a fluidized bed. The distributor can be incorporated into either a flat or a conical base of the spout-fluid column, whereas the fluid can be a gas,[45] a liquid,[46] or a gas–liquid mixture.[47]

Often, in spout-fluid beds, and less frequently in spouted beds, a centrally located draft tube is inserted at a small distance above the inlet orifice to decrease crossflow of the spout fluid into the annular region, thus increasing the maximum spoutable bed depth. The draft tube also reduces the intermixing of annular and spout solids, and thus reduces the residence time spread of the solids for solids-continuous processes. A limiting design of a draft-tube spout-fluid bed is the "internally circulating fluidized bed,"[48] in which the draft tube becomes a riser by extending it downward all the way to the fluid inlet orifice, and in which the annular solids are received as spillover from the top of the riser and then returned to the spout via smaller orifices located in the riser wall near its base. By virtue of the net positive pressure difference between the concentrated solids annular region and the dilute solids riser, the riser fluid is prevented from escaping into the annulus, whereas a small fraction of the auxiliary fluid flows through the riser orifices, enhancing the radial influx and hence the circulation of the solids.

1.6   Layout of chapter topics

The three chapters that follow this one, as well as Chapter 8, deal with various aspects of the fluid-particle mechanics of CSBs. Chapter 5 is restricted to conical spouted beds, but covers a broad range of subjects from hydrodynamics to applications. Chapters 6 and 7 again focus mainly on fluid-particle mechanics, but this time respectively for spout-fluid beds without, and for both spouted and spout-fluid beds with, draft tubes.

Table 1.1. Significant differences between gas-spouted beds and gas-fluidized beds.[44]

Aspect	Fluidized Bed	Spouted Bed
Mean particle size	~0.03–3 mm; usually <1 mm	~0.6–6 mm; usually >1 mm
Particle size distribution	Usually broad	Usually narrow
Pressure drop/height within the bed	96–100% of that needed to support the particles, i.e., $\sim(\rho_p - \rho)\,g(1 - \varepsilon)$	Less than ~75% of that needed to support the weight of the particles, i.e., $<0.75 \times (\rho_p - \rho)g(1 - \varepsilon)$
Pressure drop across entry orifices	Usually 30–50% of that across the bed	As small as possible consistent with satisfying the other constraints, e.g., orifice dia. <25 mean particle dia.
Axial gradient of pressure	Virtually independent of height in the column	Varies with height
Temperature gradient	Very uniform temperature over entire fluidized bed region	Significant temperature gradients both axially and radially
Column geometry	Usually cylindrical columns	Usually diverging conical base with or without cylindrical portion above
Orifice diameter	No restriction	Must not exceed 25 mean particle diameters
Orifice number density and configuration	Large number of orifices (typically >100 per square meter); many geometries; no constriction needed at the entrance	Usually a single orifice. For multiple spouting, smaller number density of orifices (typically no more than ~10–50 per square meter); it is helpful to have a constriction at the entrance
Orifice orientation	Most frequently horizontal, downward facing, or oblique with downward component, but may also be upward-facing	Always upward-facing
Orifice feed system	Windbox (sometimes called plenum chamber) feeds all orifices	Separate gas supply and control of each orifice
Gas motion	Less ordered; depends on flow regime and specific geometry	Outward from the spout into the dense phase, except just above inlet
Particle motion	Complex flow regimes and particle motion; region surrounding the gas entry orifices is usually fluidized with few particle-particle contacts	Systematic circulation patterns, up the spout and slowly downward in the annulus. Annulus is in moving packed bed flow with substantial particle–particle contacts
Particle segregation	Very little segregation providing that particles are well fluidized	Significant segregation according to both size and density of particles
Attrition	Normally little except in cyclone or jet regions	Significant in spout region and in fountain above
Bed depth	Broad range of depths, e.g., from 0.1 to 20 m dense bed depth	More limited range of depths, usually between 0.2 and 2.0 m
Superficial gas velocity	Broad range, typically $(U - U_{mf}) = 0.2$ to 10 m/s	More limited range, typically 1.1 to $1.8U_{ms}$
Orifice velocity variation	Some variation with time across each individual orifice as bubbles form and leave the orifice or jet	Essentially steady, as flow is controlled to each hole from an upstream valve
Internals	Common in fluidized bed processes	Rare in spouted bed processes, except for some use of draft tubes and heat transfer coils

Chapter 9 examines various aspects of heat transfer and, to a lesser extent, mass transfer. Chapter 10 reports on a relatively new development known as a powder-particle spouted bed, in which fine particles that serve some useful function (e.g., as an adsorbent) are continuously fed and removed from a spouted bed of coarse particles.

Chapters 11 through 14 describe the four principal physical operations in which spouted or spout-fluid beds have achieved industrial application – drying of particulate solids, evaporative drying of liquids containing dissolved or suspended solids, granulation, and particle-coating. The Wurster process (Chapter 14) is a tablet-coating technique that has achieved much exposure in pharmaceutical journals; it involves a spout-fluid bed with a draft tube. Gasification and combustion of coal and other fuels are dealt with in Chapter 15, whereas catalytic chemical reactor modeling is treated in Chapter 19. Mechanical spouting, in which the solids are elevated mechanically rather than hydro-dynamically, is the subject of Chapter 18. Liquid and liquid–gas spouting are examined in Chapter 20, whereas an important potential application of liquid spouting, its use as an electrochemical reactor, is treated in Chapter 16. Scaleup of spouted beds, either by application of dimensional similitude principles or by alternative designs, is the subject of Chapter 17.

References

1. K. B. Mathur and N. Epstein. *Spouted Beds* (New York: Academic Press, 1974).
2. K. B. Mathur and P. E. Gishler. A technique for contacting gases with coarse particles. *AIChE Journal*, **1** (1955), 157–164.
3. P. G. Romankov and N. B. Rashkovskaya. *Drying in a Suspended State*, 2nd ed. (Leningrad: Chemical Publishing House, 1968), in Russian.
4. K. B. Mathur and P. E. Gishler. A study of the applications of the spouted bed technique to wheat drying. *J. Appl. Chem.*, **5** (1955), 624–636.
5. F. Manurung. Studies in the spouted bed technique with particular reference to low temperature coal carbonization. Ph.D. thesis, University of New South Wales, Kensington, Australia (1964).
6. P. E. Gishler and K. B. Mathur, *Method of contacting solid particles with fluids*, U.S. Patent No. 2,786,280 to National Research Council of Canada, 1957.
7. C. E. Robinson. Improvement in furnaces for roasting ore. U.S. Patent No. 212508 (1879).
8. N. I. Syromyatnikov. Results of tests on furnaces of the fluidized, suspended and spouting types. *Za. Ekonom. Topl.* **2** (1951), 17–21.
9. A. Markowski and W. Kaminski. Hydrodynamic characteristics of jet-spouted beds. *Can. J. Chem. Eng.*, **61** (1983), 377–381.
10. P. E. Gishler. The spouted bed technique – discovery and early studies at N.R.C. *Can. J. Chem. Eng.*, **61** (1983), 267–268.
11. M. Leva. *Fluidization* (New York: McGraw-Hill, 1959).
12. S. S. Zabrodsky. *Hydrodynamics and Heat Transfer in Fluidized Beds* (Cambridge, MA: MIT Press, 1966).
13. S. C. Siu and J. W. Evans. Efficient electrowinning of zinc from alkaline electrolytes. U.S. Patent No. 5958210 (1999).

14. J. Eastwood, E. J. P. Matzen, M. J. Young, and N. Epstein. Random loose porosity of packed beds. *Brit. Chem. Eng.*, **14** (1969), 1542–1545.

15. I. Pallai and J. Németh. Analysis of flow forms in a spouted bed apparatus by the so-called phase diagram. Third International Congress on Chemical Engineering *(CHISA)*, Paper No. C2.4, Czechoslovak Society for Chemical Industry, Prague, 1969.

16. H. A. Becker. An investigation of laws governing the spouting of coarse particles. *Chem. Eng., Sci.*, **13** (1961), 245–262.

17. G. A. Lefroy and J. F. Davidson. The mechanics of spouted beds. *Trans. Instn. Chem. Engrs.*, **47** (1969), T120–T128.

18. M. Olazar, M. J. San José, A. T. Aguayo, J. M. Arandes, and J. Bilbao. Design factors of conical spouted beds and jet spouted beds. *Ind. Eng. Chem. Res.*, **32** (1993), 1245–1250.

19. K. J. Whiting and D. Geldart. A comparison of cylindrical and semi-cylindrical spouted beds of coarse particles. *Chem. Eng. Sci.*, **35** (1980), 1499–1501.

20. D. Geldart, A. Hemsworth, R. Sundavadra, and K. J. Whiting. A comparison of spouting and jetting in round and half-round fluidized beds. *Can. J. Chem. Eng.*, **59** (1981), 638–639.

21. T. Mamuro and H. Hattori. Flow pattern of fluid in spouted beds. *J. Chem. Eng. Japan*, **1** (1968), 1–5.

22. G. Rovero, N. Piccinini, and A. Lupo. Vitesses des particules dans les lits à jet tri-dimensionnels et semi-cylindriques. *Entropie*, **124** (1985), 43–49.

23. M. I. Boulos and B. Waldie. High resolution measurement of particle velocities in a spouted bed using laser-doppler anemometry. *Can. J. Chem. Eng.*, **64** (1986), 939–943.

24. Y. L. He, S. Z. Qin, C. J. Lim, and J. R. Grace. Particle velocity profiles and solid flow patterns in spouted beds. *Can. J. Chem. Eng.*, **72** (1994), 561–568.

25. V. D. Mikhailik. The pattern of change of spout diameter in a spouting bed. In *Collected Works: Research on Heat and Mass Exchanged in Technological Processes* (Minsk, BSSR: Nauka i Tekhnika, 1966), pp. 37–41.

26. Y. L. He, C. J. Lim, S. Qin, and J. R. Grace. Spout diameters in full and half spouted beds. *Can. J. Chem. Eng.*, **76** (1998), 702–706.

27. M. C. Green and J. Bridgwater. The behaviour of sector spouted beds. *Chem. Eng. Sci.*, **38** (1983), 478–481.

28. M. C. Green and J. Bridgwater. An experimental study of spouting in large sector spouted beds. *Can. J. Chem. Eng.*, **61** (1983), 281–288.

29. A. S. Mujumdar. Spouted bed technology – a brief review. In *Drying '84* (New York: Hemisphere/Springer Verlag, 1984), pp. 151–157.

30. J. H. Perry and C. H. Chilton, *Chemical Engineers' Handbook*, 5th ed. (New York: McGraw-Hill, 1973).

31. D. Geldart. Types of gas fluidization. *Powder Technol.*, **7** (1973), 285–292.

32. O. Molerus. Interpretation of Geldart's type A, B, C and D powders by taking into account interparticle cohesion forces. *Powder Technol.*, **33** (1982), 81–87.

33. P. P. Chandnani and N. Epstein. Spoutability and spout destabilization of fine particles with a gas. In *Fluidization V*, ed. K. Østergaard and A. Sorensen (New York: Engineering Foundation, 1986), pp. 233–240.

34. A. M. Squires, Species of fluidization. *Chem. Eng. Progr.*, **58**:4 (1962), 66–73.

35. N. M. Rooney and D. Harrison. Spouted beds of fine particles. *Powder Technol.* **9** (1974), 227–230.

36. S. Fakhimi, S. Sohrabi, and D. Harrison. Entrance effects at a multi-orifice distributor in gas-fluidised beds. *Can. J. Chem. Eng.*, **61** (1983), 364–369.

37. N. I. Gelperin, V. G. Ainshtein, E. N. Gelperin, and S. D. L'vova. Hydrodynamic properties of fluidized granular materials in conical and conical-cylindrical apparatus. *Khimiya i
Tekhonologya Topliv i Mosol*, **5**:8 (1960), 51–57.
38. Yu. P. Vainberg, N. I. Gelperin, and V. G. Ainshtein. On the unique behaviour of granular
substances during fluidization in conical sets. In *Processes and Equipment of Chemical
Technology*, ed. N. I. Gelperin (Moscow: Ministry of Higher Education, 1967), p. 22.
39. J. Németh and I. Pallai. Spouted bed technique and its application. *Magy. Kem. Lapja*, **25**
(1970), 74–82.
40. F. A. Zenz and D. F. Othmer. *Fluidization and Fluid-Particle Systems* (Princeton, NJ: Van
Nostrand-Reinhold, 1960).
41. M. Baerns. Effect of interparticle cohesive forces on fluidization of fine particles. *Ind. Eng.
Chem. Fundam.*, **5** (1966), 508–516.
42. J. F. Davidson and D. Harrison, *Fluidised Particles* (London: Cambridge Univ. Press, 1963).
43. M. Filla, L. Massimilla, and S. Vaccaro. Gas jets in fluidized beds and spouts: a comparison
of experimental behaviour and models. *Can. J. Chem. Eng.*, **61** (1983), 370–376.
44. H. Cui and J. R. Grace. Spouting of biomass particles: a review. *Bioresource Technol.*, **99**
(2008), 4008–4020.
45. A. Chatterjee. Spout-fluid bed technique. *Ind. Eng. Chem. Process Des. Develop.*, **9** (1970),
340–341.
46. H. Littman, D. V. Vuković, F. D. Zdanski, and Z. B. Grbavčić. Basic relations for the liquid
phase spout-fluid bed at the minimum spout fluid flowrate. In *Fluidization Technology*,
vol. 1, ed. D. L. Keairns (Washington, DC: Hemisphere and McGraw-Hill, 1976),
pp. 373–386.
47. H. Kono. A new concept for 3-phase fluidized beds. *Hydrocarbon Processing*, **60** (1980),
123–129.
48. B. J. Milne, F. Berruti, L. A. Behie, and T. J. W. de Bruijn. The internally circulating fluidized
bed (ICFB): a novel solution to gas bypassing in spouted beds. *Can. J. Chem. Eng.*, **70** (1992),
910–915.

2 Initiation of spouting

Xiaotao Bi

2.1 Introduction

In a bed packed with particles, the introduction of an upward-flowing fluid stream into the column through a nozzle or opening in a flat or conical base creates a drag force and a buoyancy force on the particles. A cavity forms when the fluid velocity is high enough to push particles aside from the opening, as illustrated in Figure 2.1(a). A permanent and stable vertical jet is established if the nozzle-to-particle-diameter ratio is less than 25 to 30.[1] Further increase in fluid flow rate expands the jet, and an "internal spout" is established, as in Figure 2.1(b). Eventually, the internal spout breaks through the upper bed surface, leading to the formation of an external spout or fountain, as in Figure 2.1(c). Such an evolution process to a spouted bed, involving cavity formation, internal spout/jet expansion, and formation of an external spout, was well documented in the 1960s.[2]

Figure 2.2 shows the evolution of measured total pressure drop in a half-circular conical bed[3] for 1.16-mm-diameter glass beads and ambient air, starting with a loosely packed bed, Run 1. It is seen that the total pressure drop increases with increasing gas velocity in the gas flow ascending process (shown by closed squares), and reaches a peak value before decreasing to approximately a constant value with a further increase in the gas velocity. When the gas velocity is decreased (closed triangles), after the bed is operated at stable spouting along a gas flow ascending process, the total pressure drop decreases, following a quite different path, with a much lower pressure drop than for the ascending process. Such a pressure-drop-versus-gas-flow hysteresis appears to be a reproducible phenomenon, as shown by repeated runs performed on the same day.[3] For the initially compacted bed, the pressure drop was much higher than for the loosely packed bed in the ascending process, but the results in the descending process were the same as for the other runs. This indicates that the hysteresis is affected by the initial particle packing state, but cannot be eliminated by changing the initial packing state. Such a pressure drop hysteresis is quite different from that observed in a fluidized bed using fine Geldart Group A powders,[4] in which the interparticle forces play the key role and the higher pressure drop in the ascending process is associated with the strength of these forces.

Spouted and Spout-Fluid Beds: Fundamentals and Applications, eds. Norman Epstein and John R. Grace. Published by Cambridge University Press. © Cambridge University Press 2011.

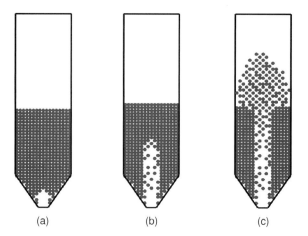

Figure 2.1. Evolution of the spouting process. (a) Formation of small cavity; (b) development of internal spout; and (c) onset of external spout.

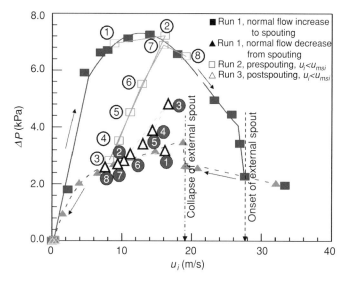

Figure 2.2. Deviation of total pressure drops from the normal ascending or descending process in a semicircular conical spouted bed. Adapted from Wang et al.[3] ($D_i = 0.019$ m, $D_0 = 0.0381$ m, $H_0 = 0.396$ m, $\theta = 45°$, $d_p = 1.16$ mm, $\rho_p = 2490$ kg/m^3.)

The nature of the flow hysteresis phenomenon is further demonstrated in Figure 2.2. In Run 2 (open squares), the gas flowrate first increased to point ①, and then passed the peak pressure drop region to ②, just as in Run 1. Before arriving at external spouting, however, the flow rate was decreased from ② to ③, giving a pressure drop at ③ much lower than in the original ascending process because of the collapse of the internal cavity. When the gas flowrate was increased again from point ③, the pressure drop climbed back to the values achieved in the originally ascending process (points ⑦ and ⑧). Similarly,

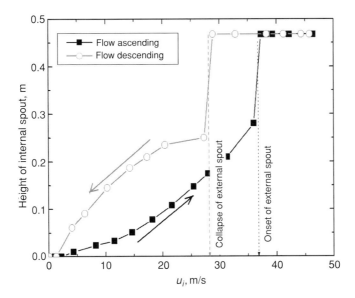

Figure 2.3. Variation of internal spout height with increasing and decreasing gas flowrate in a semicircular conical spouted bed. Closed symbols for increasing u_i; open symbols for decreasing u_i. Adapted from Wang et al.[3] ($D_i = 0.019$ m, $D_0 = 0.0381$ m, $H_0 = 0.468$ m, $\theta = 45°$, $d_p = 1.16$ mm, $\rho_p = 2490$ kg/m^3.)

interrupting the gas flow descending process of Run 3 (open triangles) after the external spout collapsed when the flow rate was decreased from ❶ to ❷, the gas flowrate was increased from ❷ to ❸. The pressure drop then increased to a value much higher than in the normal descending path (closed triangles) because of the compaction created by the collapsed internal spout. The pressure drop returned to the normal values (points ❻ to ❽) when the gas flowrate was decreased again. This confirms that the development of the gas cavity and the internal spout is responsible for the pressure drop versus flow hysteresis in spouted beds.

2.2   Evolution of internal spout

The higher total pressure drop in the ascending process has been explained by the compaction of the curvature region right above the roof of the internal spout,[2] as the region above the jet is in a packed-bed state and particles pushed aside by the gas cavity/jet compact the vicinity around the jet. An additional pressure drop is thus created. Associated with the pressure drop hysteresis, there also exists hysteresis in the development of the internal spout in the ascending and descending processes. As shown in Figure 2.3, the internal spout in the gas ascending process is much shorter than the one in the descending process at the same gas flowrate, as a consequence of the compacted dome region in the ascending process, which imposes an extra stress to suppress the vertical

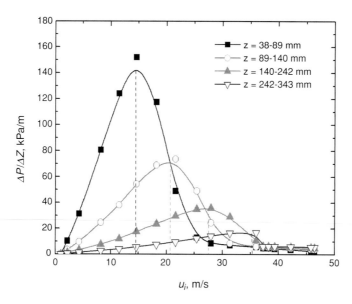

Figure 2.4. Axial pressure gradients measured incrementally at different axial locations of a conical spouted bed for decreasing gas flow. Data from Wang.[27] ($D_i = 0.019$ m, $D_0 = 0.0381$ m, $H_0 = 0.468$ m, $\theta = 45°$, $d_p = 1.16$ mm, $\rho_p = 2490$ kg/m^3.)

penetration of the fluid jet. The difference in pressure drops between the flow ascending and descending processes is thus a combined contribution of the extra resistance created by the particle compaction and the longer packed section above the internal spout in the flow ascending process.

The development of the internal spout is also captured by the evolution of pressure gradients at different levels of the bed. As the gas flowrate increases in the flow ascending process, Figure 2.4 shows that the pressure drop per unit length at the bottom inlet region rises quickly to a peak value several times higher than that required for full suspension of the particles. Such a maximum peak, however, decreases with distance above the inlet, and the peak point at higher elevations is reached at higher gas velocities. The implication is that the "breakup" resistance imposed by the interlocked particles in the compacted zone is weakened as the internal jet or spout develops upward. This "breakup" resistance is thus expected to be smaller in a shallower bed.

The evolution of the axial pressure profiles in the spouted bed is shown in Figure 2.5 (a) and (b) for the flow ascending and descending processes, respectively. It is seen that the pressure drop is much steeper in the lower section at low gas velocities. The high-pressure gradient zone at a given gas velocity shifts upward as the internal spout develops upward with increasing gas flow, and eventually reaches the upper section of the column when the internal spout erupts from the upper bed surface, giving rise to external spouting ($u_{msia} = 37.3$ m/s). In the flow descending process, as shown in Figure 2.5(b), the pressure variation with gas velocity is generally smaller than in the flow ascending process because of the absence of the extra "breakup" resistance.

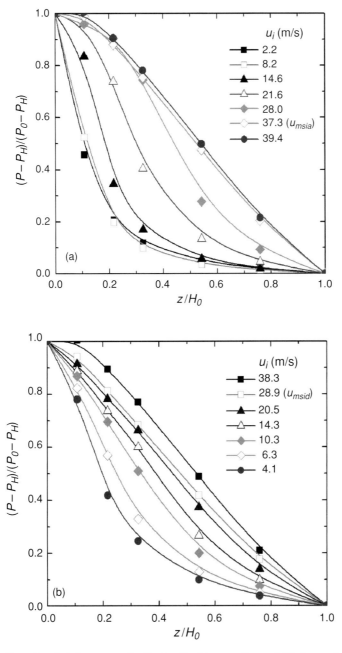

Figure 2.5. Axial pressure distribution for (a) ascending and (b) descending processes in a conical spouted bed. Data from Wang.[27] (Semicircular column, $D_i = 0.019$ m, $D_0 = 0.0381$ m, $H_0 = 0.468$ m, $\theta = 45°$, $d_p = 1.16$ mm, $\rho_p = 2490$ kg/m^3, $u_{msia} = 37.3$ m/s, $u_{msid} = 28.9$ m/s).

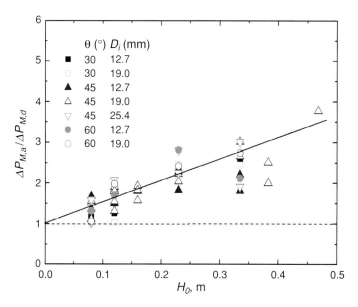

Figure 2.6. $\Delta P_{M,a}/\Delta P_{M,d}$ as a function of the static bed height in conical spouted beds. Adapted from Wang et al.[3] ($D_0 = 0.0381$ m, $H_0 = 0.468$ m, $d_p = 1.16$ mm, $\rho_p = 2490$ kg/m³.)

2.3   Peak pressure drop

As shown in Figure 2.2, there exists a unique peak pressure drop in spouted beds, which is reproducible in a loosely packed bed without precompaction or from repeated spouting runs. Such a peak pressure drop has been measured extensively in spouted bed columns of different geometries (conical and cylindrical, both flat-based and conical-based) with different types of particles and fluids. The peak pressure drop is found to be generally higher than that corresponding to full suspension of bed particles in a cylindrical fluidized bed. The extra pressure drop is attributed to compaction or interlocking of particles above the internal jet, represented by a "breakup" force.[5] As shown in both Figure 2.6 and the correlations of Table 2.1, the peak pressure drop increases with increasing static bed height in conical spouted beds. The Mukhlenov-Gorshtein[6] correlation predicts that peak pressure drop in conical spouted beds increases with increasing cone angle for a given static bed height, whereas the opposite trend is predicted by the correlations of Gelperin et al.[7] and Olazar et al.[8] The recent data of Wang et al.,[3] Figure 2.6, with included cone angles of 30° to 60°, did not show a clear effect of cone angle on the peak pressure drop. The implication is that the cone angle may play only a secondary role, if any. The Manurung[9] correlation predicts that the peak pressure drop increases with decreasing coefficient of internal friction of the particles, *tan γ*, suggesting that the interlocking is likely less severe for particles of poor flowability. This prediction appears to contradict the general interpretation of the particle interlocking phenomenon, and thus requires further investigation. Because the two correlations of Olazar et al.[8,14] were developed from data covering very broad ranges of bed geometry and particle

Table 2.1. Correlations for peak pressure drop in spouted beds.

Authors	Equations	Geometry
Gelperin et al. (1961)[7]	$\dfrac{-\Delta P_M}{\rho_b g H} = 1 + 0.062(D_H/D_i)^{2.54} \times$ $[(D_H/D_i) - 1]\left(\tan\dfrac{\theta}{2}\right)^{-0.18}$	Conical
Manurung (1964)[9]	$\dfrac{-\Delta P_M}{\rho_b g H} = \left[0.8 + \dfrac{6.8}{\tan\gamma}\left(\dfrac{D_i}{D}\right)\right] - 34.4\dfrac{d_p}{H}$	Cylindrical
Mukhlenov and Gorshtein (1965)[6]	$\dfrac{-\Delta P_M}{\Delta P_s} = 1 + 6.65(H/D_i)^{1.2}\left(\tan\dfrac{\theta}{2}\right)^{0.5} Ar^{0.2}$	Conical
Yokogawa and Isaka (1971)[10]	$\dfrac{-\Delta P_M}{(1-\varepsilon)(\rho_p - \rho)gH} = \left[\dfrac{D_i}{D}\right]^{0.14(D-D_i)/H}$	Cylindrical
Asenjo et al. (1977)[11]	$\dfrac{-\Delta P_M}{\rho_b g H} = 1 + 2.8\exp(-0.312H/D)$	Cylindrical
Kmiec (1980)[12]	$\dfrac{-\Delta P_M}{\rho_b g H} = 1 + 0.206\exp(1.24H/D)$	Conical
Ogino et al. (1993)[13]	$\dfrac{-\Delta P_M}{(1-\varepsilon)(\rho_p - \rho)gH} = 1.15(H/D)^{1/2}\left(\dfrac{D_i}{D}\right)^{1/3}$	Cylindrical
Olazar et al. (1993)[8]	$-\dfrac{\Delta P_M}{\Delta P_s} = 1 + 0.116(H/D_i)^{0.5}\left(\tan\dfrac{\theta}{2}\right)^{-0.8} Ar^{0.0125}$	Conical
Olazar et al. (1994)[14]	$-\dfrac{\Delta P_M}{\Delta P_s} = 1 + 0.35(H/D)^{0.1}(D_i/D)^{1.1} Ar^{0.1}$	Cylindrical
Rocha et al. (1995)[23]	$\dfrac{-\Delta P_M}{\rho_b g H} = 1 + 0.0006(D_H/D_i)^{5.04}[d_p/(\phi D_H) - 1]^{-1.92}$ where D and D_i are equivalent diameters	Slot-Rectangular

properties, they are recommended for the estimation of the maximum pressure drop in conical and cylindrical columns, respectively, in combination with measured pressure drop in stable spouting. In the absence of information on stable spouting pressure drops, the correlations of Gelperin et al.[7] (conical column) and Ogino et al.[13] (cylindrical column) can be used.

2.4   Onset of external spouting and minimum spouting velocity

External spouting is reached after the internal spout or jet breaks the packed bed upper surface with increasing gas flowrate. That condition has been called *incipient spouting*.[2] The onset of spouting, on the other hand, has been defined as the neighboring state when the total pressure drop falls to a lower, roughly constant value. External spouting can be maintained at a significantly lower gas velocity when the flow rate is decreased from a stable spouting state, as indicated by Figure 2.2. The gas velocity corresponding to the

Table 2.2. Summary of correlations for minimum spouting velocity in conical spouted beds.

Authors	Correlation
Nikolaev and Golubev (1964)[15]	$(\mathrm{Re}_{msH})_a = 0.051Ar^{0.59}(H/D_H)^{0.25}(D_i/D_H)^{0.1}$
Gorshtein and Mukhlenov (1964)[16]	$(\mathrm{Re}_{msi})_a = 0.174Ar^{0.5}(D_H/D_i)^{0.85}\tan(\theta/2)^{-1.25}$
Mukhlenov and Gorshtein (1965)[6]	$(\mathrm{Re}_{msi})_a = 1.35Ar^{0.45}(H/D_i)^{1.25}\tan(\theta/2)^{0.58}$
Tsvik et al. (1967)[17]	$(\mathrm{Re}_{msi})_a = 0.4Ar^{0.52}(H/D_i)^{1.24}\tan(\theta/2)^{0.42}$
Wan-Fyong et al. (1969)[18]	$(\mathrm{Re}_{msi})_a = 1.24\mathrm{Re}_t(H/D_i)^{0.82}\tan(\theta/2)^{0.92}$ for $16° < \theta < 70°$
	$(\mathrm{Re}_{msi})_a = 0.465\mathrm{Re}_t(H/D_i)^{0.82}\tan(\theta/2)^{0.49}$ for $10° < \theta < 16°$
Kmiec (1977)[19,5]	$(\mathrm{Re}_{ms})_a = 0.0176Ar^{0.714}(H/D)^{1.535}\theta^{0.714}\varepsilon_{ms}^{2.21}$, θ in radians
Markowski and Kaminski (1983)[20]	$(\mathrm{Re}_{msi})_d = 0.028Ar^{0.57}(H/D_i)^{0.48}(D/D_i)^{1.27}$
Kmiec (1983)[5]	$(\mathrm{Re}_{msi})_a^2[1.75 + 150(1-\varepsilon_{ms})/(\mathrm{Re}_{msi})_a] =$
	$\quad 31.3Ar(H/D_i)^{1.757}(D_i/D)^{0.029}\tan(\theta/2)^{2.073}\varepsilon_{ms}^3$
Choi and Meisen (1992)[21]	$(U_{ms})_d/\sqrt{2gH} = 0.147(\frac{\rho_p-\rho}{\rho})^{0.477}(d_p/D)^{0.61}(H/D)^{0.508}(D_i/D)^{0.243}$
Olazar et al. (1992)[22]	$(\mathrm{Re}_{msi})_d = 0.126Ar^{0.5}(D_H/D_i)^{1.68}\tan(\theta/2)^{-0.57}$
Olazar et al. (1996)[24]	$(\mathrm{Re}_{msi})_d = 0.126Ar^{0.39}(D_H/D_i)^{1.68}\tan(\theta/2)^{-0.57}$ for $d_p \leq 1$ mm
Bi et al. (1997)[25]	$(\mathrm{Re}_{msi})_d = [0.30 - 0.27/(D_H/D_i)^2] \times$
	$\quad \left[Ar(D_H/D_i)[(D_H/D_i)^2 + (D_H/D_i) + 1]/3\right]^{0.5}$
	$\quad$ for $D_H/D_i \geq 1.66$
	$(\mathrm{Re}_{msi})_d = 0.202[Ar(D_H/D_i)[(D_H/D_i)^2 + (D_H/D_i) + 1]/3]^{0.5}$
	$\quad$ for $D_H/D_i < 1.66$
Jing et al. (2000)[26]	$A(D_i/D_H)^2(u_{msi})_a + B(D_i/D_H)^4(u_{msi})_a^2 - (1-\varepsilon)(\rho_p - \rho)g = 0$
	$A = 150(1-\varepsilon)^2\mu/[\varepsilon^3(\phi d_p)^2]$ and $B = 1.75(1-\varepsilon)\rho/[\varepsilon^3\phi d_p]$

point at which stable external spouting collapses with decreasing gas flowrate has been defined, especially for cylindrical beds, as the minimum spouting velocity, U_{ms}.

It should be noted, however, that in early studies of shallow conical spouted beds, the minimum spouting velocity was commonly determined following the velocity ascending process, with the reported u_{msi} values thus being generally higher than those from the velocity descending process. To distinguish u_{msi} obtained from ascending and descending processes, the former is subscripted by a and the latter by d in the equations shown in Table 2.2. It should be noted that the use of an upper cylinder diameter D in correlations for conical beds, as with Kmiec[12] in Table 2.1 and with four equations[19,20,5,21] in Table 2.2 (two of which[19,21] also generate U_{ms} based on D rather than U_{msi} based on D_i), limits each of these correlations more than ever to the specific geometries and other conditions on which they are based.

To predict the minimum spouting velocity in conical spouted beds, the Ergun equation[40] has been applied by introducing a "breaking force coefficient"[5] or a data-fitted constant[25] to correct the pressure drop at the onset or collapse, respectively, of the

Table 2.3. List of selected equations for predicting U_{ms} in flat- and cone-based cylindrical spouted beds.

Authors	Correlation
Mathur and Gishler (1955)[28]	$U_{ms} = (d_p/D)(D_i/D)^{1/3}\sqrt{2gH(\rho_p - \rho)/\rho}$
Grbavcic et al. (1976)[41]	$U_{ms}/U_{mf} = 1 - (1 - H/H_m)^3$
Fane and Mitchell (1984)[33]	$U_{ms} = 2.0D^{1-\exp(-7D^2)}(d_p/D)(D_i/D)^{1/3}\sqrt{2gH(\rho_p - \rho)/\rho}$
	for $D > 0.4$ m, with D in meters
Choi and Meisen (1992)[21]	$U_{ms} = 18.5\left(\dfrac{\rho_p - \rho}{\rho}\right)^{0.263}(H/D)^{-0.103}(d_p/D)^{1.19}(D_i/D)^{0.373}\sqrt{2gH}$
Anabtawi et al. (1992)[36]	$U_{ms} = 2.44(d_p/D)^{0.7}(D_0/D)^{0.58}(H/D)^{0.5}[2gH(\rho_p - \rho)/\rho]^{0.28}$
	for square column
Olazar et al. (1994)[14]	$U_{ms} = (d_p/D)(D_i/D)^{0.1}\sqrt{2gH(\rho_p - \rho)/\rho}$
Li et al. (1996)[37]	$U_{ms} = 1.63U_t\left(\dfrac{d_p}{D}\right)^{0.414}\left(\dfrac{D_i}{D}\right)^{0.127}\left(\dfrac{H_m}{D}\right)^{0.452}\left(\dfrac{\rho_p - \rho}{\rho}\right)^{-0.149}$
	based on high temperature data
Du et al. (2009)[39]	$U_{ms} = 0.2^{0.5}U_{mf}\left(\dfrac{H}{0.2H_m}\right)^{1-(2.5H/H_m)}$ assuming $U_{mf} = U_m$
	Applicable range: $0 < (H/H_m) \le 0.2$

external spout. For Geldart[4] Group B and Group D particles, the following relationship was obtained[25]:

$$Re_{msi} = kAr^{0.5}\sqrt{(D_H/D_i)[(D_H/D_i)^2 + (D_H/D_i) + 1]/3}. \qquad (2.1)$$

The relationship $Re_{msi} = \rho u_{msi}d_p/\mu \propto Ar^{0.5}$ and the fact that U_{mf} is approximately proportional to $Ar^{0.5}$ for large Geldart Group D particles implies that u_{msi}/U_{mf} is independent of gas and particle properties, which seems to agree with experimental data.[25] The influence of column geometry includes inlet diameter, bed height, and included cone angle.

Experiments in cylindrical spouted beds have commonly been conducted in columns with a flat base or with a conical base of total included angles ranging from 45° to 90°. A number of correlations have been developed as summarized in Table 2.3, with the Mathur-Gishler[28] correlation being the most widely used.

Some attempts to theoretically[29,31,32] predict U_{ms} have resulted in a net exponent of unity or larger on D_i, but Thorley et al.[30] and Olazar et al.[14] found experimentally that U_{ms} was proportional to $D_i^{0.1-0.33}$. All these equations, however, fail to predict the data obtained from columns of diameter larger than 0.5 m,[33-35] where U_{ms} data were reported to be roughly proportional to H. Fane and Mitchell[33] therefore dimensionally modified the Mathur-Gishler equation for the prediction of U_{ms} in large columns.

Applicability of the correlations relating jet velocity and vertical upward jet penetration length for the prediction of minimum spouting velocity has also been examined.[35,38,42] It was found that commonly used jet penetration correlations, two of which are listed in Table 2.4, gave reasonable agreement with U_{ms} data in spouted beds, especially in shallow beds in which a coherent jet was expected.

Table 2.4. Two empirical equations for predicting vertical upward jet penetration length in gas-solid fluidized beds.

Authors	Correlation
Merry (1975)[43]	$\left[\dfrac{\rho}{\rho_p - \rho} \dfrac{u_j^2}{g D_i} \right]^{1/2} = 0.0084 \left[\dfrac{L_j}{D_i} \left(\dfrac{\rho_p}{\rho} \right)^{0.3} \left(\dfrac{d_p}{D_i} \right)^{0.3} + 5.2 \right]^{2.5} \left(\dfrac{\rho}{\rho_p - \rho} \right)^{1/2}$
Yang and Keairns (1978)[44]	$\left[\dfrac{\rho}{\rho_p - \rho} \dfrac{u_j^2}{g D_i} \right]^{1/2} = 0.154 \left(\dfrac{L_j}{D_i} \right)$

The applicability of the Mathur-Gishler equation to spouted beds of particle mixtures has also been evaluated. It was found[45] that the Mathur-Gishler equation could be used to predict U_{ms} approximately for beds of solids mixtures when a mean particle size and an average particle density were calculated by

$$\bar{d}_p = 1 \bigg/ \sum (x_i/d_{pi}) \tag{2.2}$$

and

$$\bar{\rho}_p = 1 \bigg/ \sum (x_i/\rho_{pi}), \tag{2.3}$$

respectively, with x_i being the mass fraction of species i.

Further discussion of the minimum spouting velocity is given in Chapter 3.

Chapter-specific nomenclature

Ar	Archimedes number $= d_p^3 \rho(\rho_p - \rho)g/\mu^2$
k	dimensionless coefficient in Eq. (2.1), evaluated[25] in Table 2.2
L_j	vertical jet penetration length, m
Re_{ms}	particle Reynolds number in cylindrical section at minimum spouting $= d_p U_{ms} \rho/\mu$
Re_{msH}	particle Reynolds number at upper bed surface at minimum spouting $= d_p U_{msH} \rho/\mu$
Re_{msi}	particle Reynolds number at fluid inlet at minimum spouting $= d_p u_{msi} \rho/\mu$
Re_t	particle Reynolds number based on $U_t = d_p U_t \rho/\mu$
U_{msH}	minimum superficial spouting velocity based on D_H, m/s
U_t	free settling terminal velocity of particles, m/s
u_j	jet velocity based on diameter at jet inlet, m/s
x_i	mass fraction of species i

Greek letters

γ	angle of internal friction, degrees
ε_{ms}	fractional void volume at minimum spouting
ρ_b	bulk density of bed, kg/m^3
ϕ	sphericity of particles

References

1. C. J. Lim and J. R. Grace. Spouted bed hydrodynamics in a 0.91 m diameter vessel. *Can. J. Chem. Eng.*, **65** (1987), 366–372.
2. K. B. Mathur and N. Epstein. *Spouted Beds* (New York: Academic Press, 1974).
3. Z. G. Wang, H. T. Bi, C. J. Lim, and P. C. Su. Determination of minimum spouting velocities in conical spouted beds. *Can. J. Chem. Eng.*, **82** (2004), 12–19.
4. D. Geldart. Types of gas fluidization. *Powder Technol.*, **7** (1973), 285–292.
5. A. Kmiec. The minimum spouting velocity in conical beds. *Can. J. Chem. Eng.*, **61** (1983), 274–280.
6. I. P. Mukhlenov and A. E. Gorshtein. Investigation of a spouted bed. *Khim. Prom.*, **41**:6 (1965), 443–446.
7. N. I. Gelperin, V. G. Ainshtein, and L. P. Timokhova. Hydrodynamic features of fluidization of granular materials in conical sets. *Khim. Mashinostr.*, (Moscow) **4** (1961), 12.
8. M. Olazar, M. J. San José, A. T. Aguayo, J. M. Arandes, and J. Bilbao. Pressure drop in conical spouted beds. *Chem. Eng. J.*, **51**:1 (1993), 53–60.
9. F. Manurung. Studies in the spouted bed technique with particular reference to low temperature coal carbonization. Ph.D. thesis, University of New South Wales, Kensington, Australia (1964).
10. A. Yokogawa and M. Isaka. Pressure drop and distribution of static pressure in the spouted bed. *Hitachi Zosen Giho*, **32**:1 (1971), 47–53.
11. J. K. Asenjo, R. Munoz, and D. L. Pyle. On the transition from a fixed to a spouted bed. *Chem. Eng. Sci.*, **32** (1977), 109–117.
12. A. Kmiec. Hydrodynamics of flows and heat transfer in spouted beds. *Chem. Eng. J.*, **19** (1980), 189–200.
13. F. Ogino, L. Zhang, and Y. Maehashi. Minimum rate of spouting and peak pressure-drop in spouted bed. *Int. Chem. Eng.*, **33**:2 (1993), 265–272.
14. M. Olazar, M. J. San José, A. T. Aguayo, J. M. Arandes, and J. Bilbao. Hydrodynamics of nearly flat base spouted beds. *Chem. Eng. J.*, **55** (1994), 27–37.
15. A. M. Nikolaev and L. G. Golubev. Basic hydrodynamic characteristics of the spouting bed. *Izv. Vyssh. Ucheb. Zaved. Khim. Khim. Tekhnol.*, **7** (1964), 855–867.
16. A. E. Gorshtein and I. P. Mukhlenov. Hydraulic resistance of a fluidized bed in a cyclone without a grate. Critical gas rate corresponding to the beginning of jet formation. *Zh. Prikl. Khim. (Leningrad)*, **37** (1964), 1887–1893.
17. M. Z. Tsvik, M. N. Nabiev, N. U. Rizaev, K. V. Merenkov, and V. S. Vyzgo. The velocity for external spouting in the combined process for production of granulated fertilizer. *Uzb. Khim. Zh.*, **11**:2 (1967), 50–59.
18. F. Wan-Fyong, P. G. Romankov, and N. B. Rashkovskaya. Research on the hydrodynamics of the spouting bed. *Zh. Prikl. Khim. (Leningrad)*, **42** (1969), 609–617.
19. A. Kmiec. Expansion of solid-gas spouted beds. *Chem. Eng. J.*, **13** (1977), 143–147.
20. A. Markowski and W. Kaminski. Hydrodynamic characteristics of jet-spouted beds. *Can. J. Chem. Eng.*, **61** (1983), 377–381.
21. M. Choi and A. Meisen. Hydrodynamics of shallow, conical spouted beds. *Can. J. Chem. Eng.*, **70** (1992), 916–924.
22. M. Olazar, M. J. San Jose, A. T. Aguayo, J. M. Arandes, and J. Bilbao. Stable operation conditions for gas-solid contact regimes in conical spouted beds. *Ind. Eng. Chem. Res.*, **31** (1992), 1784–1792.

23. S. C. S. Rocha, O. P. Taranto, and G. E. Ayub. Aerodynamics and heat transfer during coating of tablets in two-dimensional spouted bed. *Can. J. Chem. Eng.*, **73** (1995), 308–312.

24. M. Olazar, M. J. San Jose, E. Cepeda, R. Oritz de Latierro, and J. Bilbao. Hydrodynamics of fine solids on conical spouted beds. In *Fluidization VIII*, ed. J. F. Large and C. Laguerie (New York: Engineering Foundation, 1996), pp. 197–205.

25. H. T. Bi, A. Macchi, J. Chaouki, and R. Legros. Minimum spouting velocity of conical spouted beds. *Can. J. Chem. Eng.*, **75** (1997), 460–465.

26. S. Jing, Q. Y. Hu, J. F. Wang, and Y. Jin. Fluidization of coarse particles in gas-solid conical beds. *Chem. Eng. & Processing*, **39** (2000), 379–387.

27. Z. G. Wang. Experimental studies and CFD simulations of conical spouted bed hydrodynamics. Ph.D. thesis, University of British Columbia, Vancouver, Canada (2006).

28. K. B. Mathur and P. E. Gishler. A technique for contacting gases with solid particles. *AIChE J.*, **1** (1955), 157–164.

29. L. A. Madonna and R. F. Lama. The derivation of an equation for predicting minimum spouting velocity. *AIChE J.*, **4** (1958), 497.

30. B. Thorley, J. B. Saunby, K. B. Mathur, and G. L. Osberg. An analysis of air and solid flow in a spouted wheat bed. *Can. J. Chem. Eng.*, **37** (1959), 184–192.

31. B. Ghosh. A study of the spouted bed: I. A theoretical analysis. *Indian Chem. Eng.*, **1** (1965), 16–19.

32. J. J. J. Chen and Y. W. Lam. An analogy between the spouted bed phenomena and the bubbling-to-spray transition. *Can. J. Chem. Eng.*, **61** (1983), 759–762.

33. A. G. Fane and R. A. Mitchell. Minimum spouting velocity of scaled-up beds. *Can. J. Chem. Eng.*, **62** (1984), 437–439.

34. J. R. Grace and C. J. Lim. Permanent jet formation in beds of particulate solids. *Can. J Chem. Eng.*, **65** (1987), 160–162.

35. Y. L. He, C. J. Lim, and J. R. Grace. Spouted bed and spout-fluid bed behaviour in a column of diameter 0.91 m. *Can. J. Chem. Eng.*, **70** (1992), 848–857.

36. M. Z. Anabtawi, B. Z. Uysal, and R. Y. Jumah. Flow characteristics in a rectangular spout-fluid bed. *Powder Technology*, **69** (1992), 205–211.

37. Y. Li, C. J. Lim, and N. Epstein. Aerodynamic aspects of spouted beds at temperatures up to 580 °C. *J. Serbian Chem. Soc.*, **61**:4–5 (1996), 253–266.

38. H. T. Bi. A discussion on minimum spouting velocity in spouted beds. *Can. J. Chem. Eng.*, **82** (2004), 4–10.

39. W. Du, H. T. Bi, and N. Epstein. Exploring a non-dimensional varying exponent equation relating minimum spouting velocity to maximum spoutable bed depth. *Can. J. Chem. Eng.*, **87** (2009), 157–162.

40. S. Ergun. Fluid flow through packed columns. *Chem. Eng. Prog.*, **48**:2 (1952), 89–94.

41. Z. B. Grbavcic, D. V. Vukovic, F. K. Zdanski, and H. Littman. Fluid flow pattern, minimum spouting velocity and pressure drop in spouted beds. *Can. J. Chem. Eng.*, **54** (1976), 33–42.

42. M. Filla, L. Massimilla, and S. Vaccaro. Gas jets in fluidized beds and spouts: A comparison of experimental behaviour and models. *Can. J. Chem. Eng.*, **61** (1983), 370–376.

43. J. M. D. Merry. Penetration of vertical jets into fluidized beds. *AIChE J.*, **21** (1975), 507–510.

44. W. C. Yang and D. L. Keairns. Design and operating parameters for a fluidized bed agglomerating combustor/gasifier. In *Fluidization*, ed. J. F. Davidson and D. L. Keairns. (Cambridge: Cambridge Univ. Press, 1978), pp. 208–213.

45. T. Ishikura and H. Shinohara. Minimum spouting velocity for binary mixtures of particles. *Can. J. Chem. Eng.*, **60** (1982), 697–698.

3 Empirical and analytical hydrodynamics

Norman Epstein

This chapter is restricted to conventional cylindrical spouted beds with conical or flat bases. It deals mainly with the dynamics of the fluid flow, with almost total neglect of the solids motion, which in this era is best left to computational fluid dynamics (CFD). The focus is on simple empirical equations or analytical derivations that allow one to determine, at least approximately, initial design parameters such as allowable fluid inlet diameter, minimum spouting velocity, maximum spoutable bed depth, pressure drop, and related quantities.

3.1 Constraints on fluid inlet diameter

Let us start by specifying two geometrical conditions that must be met to effect stable spouting in a conventional cone-base, or even a flat-base, cylindrical column.

The first of these is the ratio of the fluid inlet diameter D_i to the cylinder diameter D. If we assume that for spouting to occur at all, the fluid inlet velocity must equal or exceed the terminal free settling velocity of the particles being spouted, and that termination of spouting at the maximum spoutable bed depth, H_m, occurs when the fluid velocity in the cylinder equals the minimum fluidization velocity, U_{mf}, then at $H = H_m$,

$$\frac{\pi}{4} D^2 U_{mf} \leq \frac{\pi}{4} D_i^2 U_t.$$

(3.1)

Avoidance of this condition requires that[1]

$$\frac{D_i}{D} < \left(\frac{U_{mf}}{U_t}\right)^{1/2}.$$

(3.2)

According to Richardson and Zaki,[2]

$$U_{mf}/U_t \approx \varepsilon_{mf}^n,$$

(3.3)

whence Eq. (3.2) becomes

$$\frac{D_i}{D} \leq \varepsilon_{mf}^{n/2},$$

(3.4)

Spouted and Spout-Fluid Beds: Fundamentals and Applications, eds. Norman Epstein and John R. Grace. Published by Cambridge University Press. © Cambridge University Press 2011.

where the nondimensional Richardson-Zaki index n can be estimated from[3]

$$\frac{4.8 - n}{n - 2.4} = 0.047 Ar^{0.57}.$$ (3.5)

If we take as an example uniformly sized spherical glass beads with $d_p = 5$ mm, $\rho_p = 2500$ kg/m^3 spouted with atmospheric air at $20°$C ($\rho = 1.21$ kg/m^3, $\mu = 0.000018$ Pa · s), then the Archimedes number $Ar = d_p^3 \rho (\rho_p - \rho) g/\mu^2 = 11.44 \times 10^6$, from which $n = 2.405$ by Eq. (3.5). Because for spheres of uniform size,[4] $\varepsilon_{mf} = 0.415$, D_i/D by Eq. (3.4) must not exceed 0.35 for stable spouting, as opposed to bubbling fluidization or slugging, to occur. This value coincides exactly with that proposed by Becker,[5] who found experimentally for wheat spouting that U_m/U_t was equal to 1/8, where U_m is the minimum superficial gas velocity for spouting at $H = H_m$, that is, the maximum possible value of U_{ms} and therefore the "minimum superficial gas velocity causing the onset of... fluidization." The maximum allowable D_i/D by Eq. (3.2) is then $\sqrt{1/8}$, or 0.35. The same value can be applied at $H < H_m$, as the spout-to-annulus crossflow of the gas is then insufficient to fluidize the top of the annulus.

The critical value of D_i/D given by Eq. (3.4) decreases as the Richardson-Zaki index n increases – that is, as Ar in Eq. (3.5) decreases, which occurs when the gas temperature is increased (owing to the resulting decrease of ρ and increase of μ), and/or when the particle density ρ_p and/or particle diameter d_p are decreased. It also decreases if ε_{mf} decreases – for example, when there is a spread, rather than a uniformity, of particle size.[6] Thus, for Ottawa sand having $d_p = 0.42$–0.83 m, it was found experimentally that when D_i/D exceeded 0.10, coherent spouting with ambient air gave way initially to bubbling fluidization and, at higher air velocities, to slugging.[7] The maximum permissible D_i/D for stable spouting thus spans from 0.10 to 0.35.

The second geometric requirement for coherent nonpulsatile spouting, based only on empirical findings, sets an upper limit for D_i when dealing with a fixed particle size, d_p, and a lower limit to d_p for a given value of D_i. That requirement is that the ratio D_i/d_p must not exceed about 25 to 30, irrespective of particle density.[8,9] When one combines this criterion with Eq. (3.4), it follows that to coherently spout particles of diameter d_p in circumstances in which D_i is stretched to the safe limit of $25d_p$, the column diameter D would have to exceed $25d_p/\varepsilon_{mf}^{n/2}$, which, in the previous example of 5-mm glass spheres spouted by ambient air, is 0.36 m. The same criterion of $D_i/d_p \leq 25$ also applies to permanent jet formation in spout-fluidized beds, in which auxiliary gas is introduced into the annulus, and even to multiorifice gas-fluidized beds.[10]

3.2   Minimum spouting velocity

The minimum spouting fluid velocity, U_{ms}, for cone-base (or even flat-base) cylindrical columns, based on the empty cylinder cross-section, is well represented (about $\pm10\%$)[7] in practice for $D_c < 0.5$ m and ambient conditions by the widely used Mathur-Gishler[7] equation, most commonly written as

$$U_{ms} = \left(\frac{d_p}{D}\right) \left(\frac{D_i}{D}\right)^{1/3} \sqrt{\frac{2gH\left(\rho_p - \rho\right)}{\rho}}.$$ (3.6)

U_{ms} is measured at the point at which the pressure drop rises abruptly on decreasing the fluid velocity from the spouting condition. The absence of a coefficient preceding this *empirical* equation – that is, its fortuitous value of unity – is possibly explainable by the fact that adjustment of the exponent on D_i/D_c to best fit all the original data of Mathur and Gishler[7] (with included cone angles varying from 45° to 85°) served as a substitute for an adjustable multiplying coefficient.

The particle diameter d_p in Eq. (3.6) is taken as the arithmetic average of bracketing screen apertures for closely sized near-spherical particles and as the Sauter mean diameter for mixed sizes, using the equivolume sphere diameter for nonspherical but approximately isometric particles. For very nonisometric particles, such as prolate spheroids (e.g., wheat), that align themselves vertically in the spout, Eq. (3.6) works best if d_p is taken as the horizontally projected diameter – that is, the smaller of the two principal dimensions. Although fivefold and sometimes even eightfold particle size spreads have been shown to be tolerable for stable spouting of particles with a maximum d_p of 2 to 5 mm, increasingly incoherent spouting occurs if the size spread exceeds these limits, which are narrower for finer particle mixtures.[11] Furthermore, in the less common case of a spread in particle densities, an average value of ρ_p, weighted according to the solids mass fraction, has been recommended,[7] even though weighting by volume fraction is a measure of the total mass/total volume.

Equation (3.6) may be rewritten as

$$\frac{U_{ms}}{\sqrt{2gH}} = \left(\frac{d_p}{D_i}\right) \left(\frac{D_i}{D}\right)^{4/3} \left(\frac{\rho_p - \rho}{\rho}\right)^{1/2},$$ (3.7)

in which the dimensionless groups D_i/D and D_i/d_p, identified previously as being important in the determination of spouting stability, occur prominently. For the eight variables (seven independent and one dependent) containing three independent dimensions (mass, length, and time) found in Eq. (3.7), the Buckingham pi theorem requires five dimensionless groups, whereas only four appear in that equation. The success of Eq. (3.7), at least for spouting with air at ambient conditions and to a lesser extent with water,[7,11] implies incorporation of additional physics into this empirical equation. The derivation of a mechanistic equation that matches most, though not all, aspects of Eq. (3.7) was effected by Ghosh[9] based on momentum balance considerations. Ghosh argued that, at the minimum spouting condition, a particle from the annulus entering the bottom of the spout is rapidly accelerated by the incoming jet to an upward velocity v, after which it decelerates to a velocity of zero at the top of the bed of height H. By simple Newtonian dynamics, neglecting the upward acceleration distance and the countervailing fluid drag on the particle,

$$v = \sqrt{2gH}.$$ (3.8)

Assume that n particles, which enter the spout from its periphery, occupy the bottom layer of the spout at any instant, the height of the layer being the particle diameter d_p. The time it takes to displace this layer (and thus make room for the next similar layer) is d_p/v. Therefore, the total number of particles accelerated per unit time is nv/d_p. The momentum per unit time gained by the particles, assuming they are spherical, is then

$$M_p = (nv/d_p)(\pi d_p^3/6)(\rho_p - \rho)v, \tag{3.9}$$

where $(\rho_p - \rho)$ is the particle density corrected for buoyancy. The momentum per unit time of the fluid jet at its inlet is

$$M_j = (\pi D_i^2/4)\, u_{msi}\rho \cdot u_{msi}, \tag{3.10}$$

where u_{msi} is the inlet jet velocity at minimum spouting, so

$$u_{msi} = U_{ms}\left(D^2/D_i^2\right). \tag{3.11}$$

Assuming that

$$M_p = KM_j, \tag{3.12}$$

where the proportionality constant K represents the fraction of the inlet jet momentum that is transmitted to the particles, then combination of Eqs. (3.8) through (3.12) leads to

$$\frac{U_{ms}}{\sqrt{2gH}} = \left(\frac{2n}{3K}\right)^{1/2}\left(\frac{d_p}{D_i}\right)\left(\frac{D_i}{D}\right)^2\left(\frac{\rho_p - \rho}{\rho}\right)^{1/2}. \tag{3.13}$$

Aside from the numerical coefficient $(2n/3K)^{1/2}$, the only difference between Eq. (3.13) and Eq. (3.7) is the exponent on (D_i/D). This difference could be due to the likelihood that both n and K are functions of D_i/D.

The Mathur-Gishler equation, aside from its apparent lack of one dimensionless group, as noted previously, ignores any effect of gas viscosity, which increases markedly as gas temperature is increased and decreases even more substantially with increasing temperature if one substitutes a liquid for a gas as the spouting fluid. If we assume that

$$U_{ms} = f\left(D_i, D, H, d_p, \rho_p - \rho, \rho, \mu, g\right) \tag{3.14}$$

then by dimensional analysis,

$$\frac{d_p U_{ms}\rho}{\mu} = \psi\left(\frac{d_p^3(\rho_p - \rho)g}{\mu^2}, \frac{d_p}{D_i}, \frac{D_i}{D}, \frac{H}{D}, \frac{\rho_p - \rho}{\rho}\right), \tag{3.15}$$

that is, $\mathrm{Re}_{ms} = \psi(Ar, d_p/D_i, D_i/D, H/D, (\rho_p - \rho)/\rho)$. $\tag{3.15a}$

Eq. (3.6) or (3.7) is equivalent to

$$\mathrm{Re}_{ms} = \sqrt{2}\,Ar^{1/2}(d_p/D)^{1/2}(D_i/D)^{5/6}(H/D)^{1/2}[(\rho_p - \rho)/\rho]^0, \tag{3.16}$$

in which the neglect of viscosity is manifested by self-cancellation. A comprehensive experimental study by Li et al.[12] of air-spouted beds at temperatures ranging from 20 °C to 580 °C, using a 0.156 m I.D. conical-cylindrical half-column, five narrowly sized fractions of nearly spherical sand $(d_p = 0.915 - 2.025 \text{ mm})$, three orifice sizes, and bed heights up to the maximum spoutable, resulted in the following multiple nonlinear regression equation based on 305 data points for which H exceeded both the cone height (0.12 m) and column diameter:

$$\text{Re}_{ms} = 16.2 \, Ar^{0.506} (d_p/D_i)^{0.630} (D_i/D)^{0.752} (H/D)^{0.467} [(\rho_p - \rho)/\rho]^{-0.272}. \quad (3.17)$$

On determination of goodness of fit, it was found that the average absolute deviation (AAD) of U_{ms} from the 305 experimental points decreased from 14.2 percent by Eq. (3.16) to 6.7 percent by Eq. (3.17), whereas the standard deviation in U_{ms} decreased from 0.147 to 0.067 m/s. From Eq. (3.17),

$$U_{ms} \propto \mu^{-0.012} \rho^{-0.222} \quad (3.18)$$

Raising gas temperature raises gas viscosity and lowers gas density. For small sand particles (e.g., $\ll 1$ mm), in which viscous forces predominate over inertial forces, viscosity is important, and therefore U_{ms} falls as the bed temperature increases.[13] For large particles (e.g., $\gg 1$ mm), in which inertial forces predominate, density is important, and therefore U_{ms} rises as the bed temperature is increased.[12,13] For intermediate sizes, close to 1 mm, U_{ms} remains virtually unaffected by temperature.[12,13] However, Eq. (3.17) is incapable of showing different effects on U_{ms} of either μ or ρ for different particle diameters because it is based on only a 2.2-fold variation in d_p and, more critically, because it is constrained by the assumption of a simple power law relationship involving *all* the dimensionless groups of Eq. (3.15a).

The viscosity effect in Eq. (3.18) is based only on a doubling of air viscosity from 20 °C to 580 °C. Even if the same dependence is assumed for water as for air, despite the 56-fold difference in viscosity at ambient conditions, there would be less than a 5 percent diminution of U_{ms}, probably within the experimental error of its measurement. However, the much larger density effect in Eq. (3.18), based on a tripling of air density from 580 °C to 20 °C, applied to the 826-fold difference in density comparing ambient air with ambient water, yields a 77.5 percent decrease of U_{ms}. The Mathur-Gishler equation (i.e., Eq. 3.6, 3.7, or 3.16) shows an even greater dependence of U_{ms} on ρ, and because it is based on experiments in which the *only* variation in fluid density was between air and water at ambient conditions, it is undoubtedly more reliable for water than is Eq. (3.17), which is based only on experiments with air.

If we adopt a more mechanistic approach than that incorporated in Eq. (3.17) by assuming that fluid viscosity and gravitational acceleration are both accounted for by the terminal free settling velocity, U_t, of the particles, which must be exceeded by the fluid entering the inlet orifice, then

$$U_{ms} = f(U_t, D_i, D, H, d_p, \rho_p - \rho, \rho). \quad (3.19)$$

By dimensional analysis,

$$U_{ms}/U_t = \text{Re}_{ms}/\text{Re}_t = \psi'(d_p/D_i, D_i/D, H/D, (\rho_p - \rho)/\rho), \quad (3.20)$$

where

$$\text{Re}_t = d_p U_t \rho / \mu = \phi(Ar), \tag{3.21}$$

which is most accurately represented by the empirical equation of Clift et al.,[14]

$$\log \text{Re}_t = -1.81391 + 1.34671 \log(4Ar/3) - 0.12427[\log(4Ar/3)]^2$$
$$+ 0.006344[\log(4Ar/3)]^3 \tag{3.22}$$

for $12.2 < \text{Re}_t < 6350$. This range brackets the terminal Reynolds numbers of the particles in the 305-point study discussed previously. On applying multiple nonlinear regression analysis to the same data, the result[12] was

$$U_{ms}/U_t = 1.63(d_p/D_i)^{0.414} (D_i/D)^{0.541} (H/D)^{0.452} [(\rho_p - \rho)/\rho]^{-0.149}, \tag{3.23}$$

with AAD = 5.9 percent and standard deviation = 0.065 m/s. Eq. (3.23) is thus a small improvement on Eq. (3.17) for numerical prediction of U_{ms}, but is theoretically more sound, as it gives *direct* recognition to the role of U_t in the determination of U_{ms}.

Empirical Eq. (3.23) shows an exponent on H of 0.452, rather than 0.5 given by theoretical Eq. (3.13). This smaller dependence of U_{ms} on H can be explained by the fact that the upward acceleration distance of the particles, rather than being negligible, as assumed implicitly by Ghosh,[9] occupies about 25 percent of the bed height at minimum spouting.[11,15] The effective deceleration height is thus smaller than H, and therefore the dependence of U_{ms} on H is decreased: $(H/D)^{0.452}$ approaches $(0.75H/D)^{0.5}$ for H/D between 1.3 and 6.0, as encompassed by the data underlying Eq. (3.23).

All the above equations for U_{ms} break down for shallow beds with $H/H_m \le 0.2$. In such cases, the equation

$$\frac{U_{ms}}{0.2^{0.5} U_m} = \left(\frac{H}{0.2 H_m} \right)^{1-(0.5H/0.2H_m)} \tag{3.24}$$

has received some support.[16] At $H = 0.2H_m$, this equation collapses to

$$\frac{U_{ms}}{U_m} = \left(\frac{H}{H_m} \right)^{0.5}, \tag{3.25}$$

which is equivalent to the result obtained by dividing Eq. (3.6) by Eq. (3.28). As H approaches zero, Eq. (3.24) shows that U_{ms} is directly proportional to H, in agreement with observations on very shallow beds.[16]

Almost every equation for U_{ms} proposed in the literature, including all of the above, apply only for $D < 0.5$ m. The only relationship proposed for $D \ge 0.5$ m, that of Fane and Mitchell,[17] is a crudely empirical modification of Eq. (3.6) that, stripped to its essence, becomes

$$U_{ms} = (RHS \text{ of } Eq. \text{ 3.6}) \times 2D, \tag{3.26}$$

with D in meters. This equation, based primarily on measurements for $D = 1.07$ m and $H/D = 1.0$, reduces to Eq. (3.6) for $D = 0.5$ m. In subsequent measurements for a 0.91-m diameter column,[18] Eq. (3.26) overpredicted U_{ms} when $H/D < 1.0$ and underpredicted when $H/D > 1.0$.

3.3 Maximum spoutable bed depth

The three distinct mechanisms that could conceivably cause conical-cylindrical (or flat-base cylindrical) spouted beds to become unstable beyond a certain bed depth are fluidization of the uppermost annular solids, choking of the spout, and collapse of the spout wall – that is, of the spout-annulus interface.[11] A force balance on the spout wall in which the first and third of these mechanisms act synergistically was the basis of the early derivation by Lefroy and Davidson[19] of an equation approximating the maximum spoutable bed depth, H_m, which neglected entirely the influence of fluid properties and the potent effect of the fluid inlet diameter, D_i, on H_m and failed to show the observable increase[11,12] of H_m with increasing d_p before a subsequent decrease with increasing d_p.

The most successful of several proposed empirical and theoretical equations[11,16] for predicting H_m is the one based explicitly on the first of the above termination mechanisms – that is, on the fact that percolation of fluid from the spout to the annulus causes the upward fluid velocity in the annulus to increase longitudinally, so if the static (loose-packed) bed height is progressively increased, the uppermost layer of solids is eventually fluidized. When this happens, at $H = H_m$, disruption of the smooth downward motion of the annular solids gives way progressively to bubbling or slugging, instead of spouting.

In general,

$$U_m/U_{mf} = b,$$ (3.27)

where U_m is the minimum spouting velocity at the maximum spoutable bed depth, and b usually exceeds unity, but rarely exceeds 1.5.[11,16] A small excess over unity is consistent with the annular fluidization mechanism and explainable by a small excess of velocity in the spout over the annulus, even at minimum spouting, but values of b of the order of 1.5 are not as easy to explain.

To formulate an equation for U_m, we can apply any reliable equation for U_{ms} at $H = H_m$, for which $U_{ms} = U_m$. Because of its simplicity and wide applicability[11] (although, as shown previously, not necessarily its universal superiority), we adopt the Mathur-Gishler relation, Eq. (3.6), in the form

$$U_m = \left(\frac{d_p}{D}\right)\left(\frac{D_i}{D}\right)^{1/3}\sqrt{\frac{2gH_m(\rho_p - \rho)}{\rho}}.$$ (3.28)

To arrive at an equation for U_{mf}, we consider flow through a packed bed at the condition of minimum fluidization, for which the frictional pressure gradient from the Ergun equation[20] is balanced by the buoyed weight of the bed per unit volume. The solution to the resulting quadratic equation in U_{mf} can be expressed as[4]

$$\mathrm{Re}_{mf} = d_v U_{mf}\rho/\mu = \left(C_1^2 + C_2 Ar\right)^{1/2} - C_1,$$ (3.29)

where

$$C_1 = 150(1 - \varepsilon_{mf})/3.50\phi$$ (3.30)

and

$$C_2 = \phi \varepsilon_{mf}^3 / 1.75. \tag{3.31}$$

At least sixteen binary combinations of values or expressions for C_1 and C_2, designed in most cases to eliminate the need for evaluating the sphericity, ϕ, and the voidage at minimum fluidization, ε_{mf}, as separate entities, have been proposed in the literature, some as generalizations for particles of all shapes and others for more specific shapes.[4] Here we adopt the earliest and most common binary pair, namely, $C_1 = 33.7$ and $C_2 = 0.0408$ of Wen and Yu.[21] This choice in Eq. (3.29), with $d_v = d_p$, results in

$$\mathrm{Re}_{mf} = d_p U_{mf} \rho / \mu = 33.7(\sqrt{1 + 35.9 \times 10^{-6} Ar} - 1). \tag{3.32}$$

On combining Eqs. (3.27), (3.28), and (3.32) to eliminate U_m and U_{mf}, we arrive at

$$H_m = \frac{D^2}{d_p} \left(\frac{D}{D_i} \right)^{2/3} \frac{568b^2}{Ar} (\sqrt{1 + 35.9 \times 10^{-6} Ar} - 1)^2. \tag{3.33}$$

McNab and Bridgwater,[22] who first derived Eq. (3.33) following in essence the procedure outlined by Thorley et al.,[15] found that this equation gave the best fit to prior experimental data for H_m in gas-spouted beds at room temperature, with the adjustable parameter $b = 1.11$ (i.e., $568b^2 = 700$), despite considerable data scatter. In the study of Li et al.[12] referred to earlier, seventy-nine measurements of H_m were made for various particle sizes, gas inlet sizes, and bed temperatures. Interestingly, the minimum AAD of 19.6 percent with respect to Eq. (3.33) for these seventy-nine measurements was also achieved with $b = 1.11$, although the minimum standard deviation of 0.111 m occurred at $b = 1.04$.

Measurements of U_m, made in conjunction with each measurement of H_m, were combined with calculations of U_{mf} by Eq. (3.32) to determine b as U_m / U_{mf}. The result for the seventy-nine runs was $(U_m / U_{mf})_{avg} = 1.09$ with a standard deviation of 0.13. A more recent study[16] of thirty-six data sets involving both spherical and nonspherical particles from five reports in the literature for which both U_m and H_m had been measured for spouting with air at ambient conditions again showed a best fit (minimum variance) of Eq. (3.33) with b very close to unity, but U_m / U_{mf} averaged 1.20, with a standard deviation of 0.30 and individual values ranging from as low as 0.55 to as high as 1.77. These values did not correlate at all with Ar.

One conceivable explanation for the large spread in U_m / U_{mf} is the possibility that instability of the spout wall, or, more likely, choking of the spout rather than fluidization of the annulus, determined H_m for the few small particle ($d_p < 1$ mm) runs.[8] A more likely explanation for most of the runs, given the noncorrelation of b with Ar, is the limited accuracy of Eq. (3.32), particularly for very nonspherical particles at $Ar > 223\,000$ (see below). That equation, in the paper by Wen and Yu,[21] is based on 284 data points with an average deviation of ± 25 percent and an overall standard deviation of 34 percent. It is likely that judicious use of other recommended C_1 and C_2 combinations[4] in Eq. (3.29), especially for nonspherical particles, would narrow the spread of U_m / U_{mf}.

That would be even more likely when reliable values of both ϕ and ε_{mf} are available, so C_1 and C_2 can be evaluated directly from Eq. (3.30) and (3.31), respectively (although the Ergun equation also has finite confidence limits). By the same token, equations for U_m and U_{mf} that are better than Eqs. (3.28) and (3.32), respectively, for specific conditions can be used to re-derive an equation for H_m that would give greater quantitative accuracy than Eq. (3.33) for those conditions, although qualitative trends of H_m with process variables would be similar.

From the definition of the Archimedes number, Ar,

$$d_p = [\mu^2 Ar / \rho(\rho_p - \rho)g]^{1/3}. \tag{3.34}$$

Replacing d_p by Eq. (3.34) into Eq. (3.33), differentiating the result by Ar and setting the answer equal to zero generates a critical value of $Ar = 223\,000$, at which H_m is a maximum with respect to d_p, at constant D, D_i, μ, ρ, ρ_p, and g. As $(223\,000)^{1/3} = 60.6$,

$$(d_p)_{crit} = 60.6[\mu^2 / \rho(\rho_p - \rho)g]^{1/3}. \tag{3.35}$$

Thus Eq. (3.33), unlike other empirical or theoretical equations[16] for H_m, shows that if the particles are small enough, H_m increases rather than decreases with increasing particle diameter, in agreement with experimental observations.[11,12,23] If column dimensions and d_p are kept constant and Ar is allowed to vary only by changing μ, ρ, and $\rho_p - \rho$, then Eq. (3.33) can be simplified to

$$H_m = a[(1 + cAr)^{1/2} - 1]^2 / Ar, \tag{3.36}$$

where $a = 568b^2 D^{8/3} / d_p D_i^{2/3}$ and $c = 35.9 \times 10^{-6}$. Differentiation of H_m with respect to Ar results in

$$\frac{d H_m}{d (Ar)} = \frac{a[(2 + cAr) - 2(1 + cAr)^{1/2}]}{Ar^2 (1 + cAr)^{1/2}}. \tag{3.37}$$

Because $(2 + cAr) > 2(1 + cAr)^{1/2}$ for positive c and Ar, $d H_m / d Ar$ is always positive. In the case of gas spouting, for which $\rho_p \gg \rho$ so that $\rho_p - \rho$ is almost invariant with temperature, as the bed temperature rises, μ increases and ρ decreases, and thus Ar decreases. Therefore, H_m decreases with increasing temperature. This trend is illustrated both experimentally and via Eq. (3.33) in Figure 3.1, which, along with its accompanying table, also shows that $(d_p)_{crit}$ increases with temperature as predicted by Eq. (3.35), again because of increasing gas viscosity and decreasing gas density with increasing temperature. Other confirmatory data[24] by spouting with different gases showed H_m increasing as ρ increased at constant μ, and decreasing as μ increased at constant ρ. In the case of gas spouting at elevated pressure, because gas viscosity is only minimally affected by pressure, whereas gas density is nearly proportional to the absolute pressure, one would expect Ar and hence H_m to increase and $(d_p)_{crit}$ to decrease with increasing pressure. The effect of an increase in ρ_p, and hence in Ar for constant d_p and constant gas properties, is to increase H_m and decrease $(d_p)_{crit}$ by Eqs. (3.33) and (3.35), respectively, although the empirical equation of Malek and Lu[25]

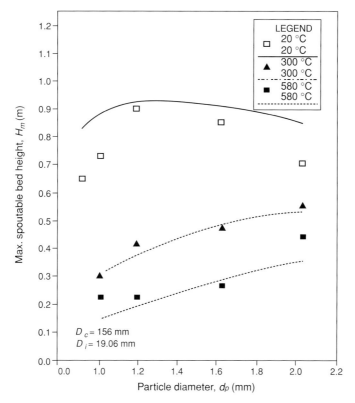

Figure 3.1. Effect of bed temperature and particle diameter on H_m for air-spouting of closely sized, nearly spherical sand particles in a conical-cylindrical column with a cone base diameter = 31 mm and included angle = 55°. Points are experimental; lines are Equation (3.33) with $b = 1.11$. (From Li et al.,[12] courtesy of *Journal of the Serbian Chemical Society*.)

Temperature, °C	20	300	580
ρ, kg/m^3	1.205	0.616	0.414
μ, kg/m · s	1.84×10^{-5}	3.00×10^{-5}	3.79×10^{-5}
$(d_p)_{crit}$, mm, Eq. (3.36)	1.358	2.353	3.139

based on air spouting at ambient conditions shows a small contrary effect of ρ_p on H_m and no critical d_p (with H_m decreasing only with increasing d_p).

There is experimental evidence, backed by confirmatory calculations,[8] that the second spouting instability cited above – choking and consequent slugging of the spout owing to its particle-conveying capacity being exceeded – comes into play for gas spouting of relatively small particles[8] (e.g., $d_p \leq 1.3$ mm[23]), and even for larger particles at elevated temperatures.[24] The critical diameter given by Eq. (3.35) again appears to represent, at least approximately, the transition criterion between the annulus-fluidization and the spout-choking mechanisms.

For liquid spouted beds, H_m is the maximum penetration depth of the spout for a deep bed, as liquid spouting is characterized by the onset of fluidization in the annulus at

$z = H_m$, and by persistence of internal spouting to a depth of H_m, even when $H > H_m$. For such cases, a spouted bed of height H_m is then capped by a particulately fluidized bed of height $H - H_m$.[26] The similarity between spouting and vertical jet penetration in fluidized beds has been otherwise noted, albeit for operation with a gas.[10] Unlike gas spouting, liquid spouting is characterized[23,27] by a decrease of H_m as d_p increases for all d_p.

It should be emphasized that Eq. (3.33) and all other equations for H_m proposed in the literature, are based on data for $D < 0.5$ m. There are no experimental data on H_m, nor are there reliable equations for H_m, when $D > 0.5$ m. An order of magnitude can be estimated by rederiving an equivalent of the McNab-Bridgwater[22] equation, substituting for Eq. (3.28) the Fane-Mitchell[17] modification of the Mathur-Gishler equation applied at $H = H_m$, $U_{ms} = U_m$, namely

$$U_m = (RHS \text{ of Eq. } 3.28) \times 2D. \tag{3.38}$$

Solving Eqs. (3.27), (3.32), and (3.38) for H_m by elimination of U_m and U_{ms}, the result is

$$H_m = (RHS \text{ of Eq. } 3.33) / 4D^2, \tag{3.39}$$

with D in meters. An alternative crude estimate of H_m for $D \geq 0.5$ m can be made using the aforementioned approximate formula of Lefroy and Davidson,[19] which, unlike other equations for H_m in the literature,[16] is not necessarily limited to $D < 0.5$ m – that is,

$$H_m = 0.68 D^{4/3} / d_p^{1/3}. \tag{3.40}$$

Applying those two equations to the example in Section 3.1 of 5-mm glass beads spouted with ambient air, for $D = 1$ m and $D_i = 20 d_p = 0.1$ m, so $D_i/D = 0.1 < 0.35$, Eq. (3.39) with $b = 1$ yields $H_m = 4.29$ m and Eq. (3.41) gives $H_m = 3.98$ m. The close agreement of the two values for this case is probably a sheer coincidence, but 4 m is higher than the highest value of H (2.6 m for $D = 0.91$ m) at which U_{ms} has been reported,[18] and can tentatively be considered an approximate estimate of H_m for $D = 1$ m and the other imposed conditions.

3.4 Annular fluid flow

3.4.1 Mechanistic modeling

Consider the Mamuro-Hattori[28] model of the forces acting in the annulus of a spouted bed, illustrated by Figure 3.2. A vertical force balance on a differential height, dz, of the annulus, neglecting friction at both vertical boundaries of the annulus, gives

$$\sigma_a - (\sigma_a + d\sigma_a) = (\rho_p - \rho)(1 - \varepsilon_a)g dz - [P - (P + dP)]$$

or

$$-d\sigma_a = (\rho_p - \rho)(1 - \varepsilon_a)g dz - (-dP), \tag{3.41}$$

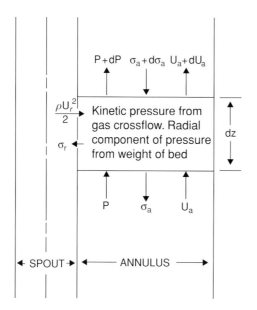

Figure 3.2. Force balance model, after Mamuro and Hattori.[28] (From Epstein and Levine,[32] courtesy of Cambridge University Press.)

where σ_a is the net downward solids force per cross-sectional area of the annulus. Assuming, after Janssen (cited by Brown and Richards[29]), that σ_a, the vertical component of solids pressure, is proportional to the radial component, σ_r, which in turn is in balance with the kinetic pressure owing to crossflow velocity U_r of fluid from the spout into the annulus, then

$$\sigma_a = \kappa \sigma_r = \kappa \rho U_r^2 /2, \tag{3.42}$$

where the constant κ is the reciprocal of the Janssen proportionality ratio. Differentiating with respect to z, we obtain

$$d\sigma_a/dz = \kappa \rho U_r(dU_r/dz). \tag{3.43}$$

Substituting Eq. (3.43) into Eq. (3.41) results in

$$\kappa \rho U_r(dU_r/dz) + (\rho_p - \rho)(1 - \varepsilon_a)g = -dP/dz. \tag{3.44}$$

If we assume invariance of annulus voidage with bed level (an assumption that, as we shall see, is fully justified only at $U \approx U_{ms}$), and neglect the annular solids motion (zero at $U \approx U_{ms}$) relative to that of the fluid, we can write

$$-dP/dz = K_1 U_a + K_2 U_a^2, \tag{3.45}$$

in which, according to Ergun,[20]

$$K_1 = \frac{150\mu (1 - \varepsilon_a)^2}{d_v^2 \phi^2 \varepsilon_a^3} \text{ and } K_2 = \frac{175\rho (1 - \varepsilon_a)}{d_v \phi \varepsilon_a^3} \tag{3.46}$$

Eq. (3.45), the quadratic Forchheimer equation (as cited by Scheidegger[30]), is adopted here rather than the linear viscous flow equation based on Darcy's law,

$$-dp/dz = K_1 U_a \qquad (3.47)$$

adopted by Mamuro and Hattori,[28] because particle Reynolds numbers in the annulus at the midlevel of the bed are typically in the range (e.g., $Re_p = 100$) at which both viscous and inertial effects are significant.

Combination of Eqs. (3.44) and (3.45) leads to

$$\kappa \rho U_r \, (dU_r/dz) + (\rho_p - \rho)(1 - \varepsilon_a)g = K_1 U_a + K_2 U_a^2. \qquad (3.48)$$

Differentiating this equation with respect to z,

$$\kappa \rho d(U_r \cdot dU_r/dz)/dz = K_1 dU_a/dz + K_2 d\left(U_a^2\right)/dz. \qquad (3.49)$$

Assuming that the spout diameter D_s, and hence the annulus cross-sectional area A_a, is independent of z, a fluid balance over height dz yields

$$U_r \cdot \pi D_s dz = A_a dU_a. \qquad (3.50)$$

Substituting U_r from Eq. (3.50) into Eq. (3.49) and rearranging gives

$$\frac{d}{dz}\left(\frac{dU_a}{dz} \cdot \frac{d^2 U_a}{dz}\right) = F_1 \frac{dU_a}{dz} + F_2 \frac{d\left(U_a^2\right)}{dz}, \qquad (3.51)$$

where

$$F_1 = \frac{K_1 \pi^2 D_s^2}{\kappa \rho A_a^2} \quad \text{and} \quad F_2 = \frac{K_2 \pi^2 D_s^2}{\kappa \rho A_a^2}. \qquad (3.52)$$

Eq. (3.51), a third-order nonlinear differential equation, requires three boundary conditions; these are initially taken as

$$\text{B.C.(i): at } z = 0, U_a = 0$$

$$\text{B.C.(ii): at } z = H_m, U_a = U_{aHm} = U_{mf}$$

and

$$\text{B.C.(iii): at } z = H_m, -dP/dz = (\rho_p - \rho)(1 - \varepsilon_a)g = (\rho_p - \rho)(1 - \varepsilon_{mf})g.$$

The first boundary condition states that there is no fluid in the annulus at the bottom of the bed, whereas the second and third signify that the top of the bed is at minimum fluidization for a bed of maximum spoutable depth. From Eq. (3.44), the third condition yields $U_r dU_r/dz = 0$, and hence from Eq. (3.50) either $dU_a/dz = 0$ or $d^2 U_a/dz^2 = 0$ or both are zero at $H = H_m$ [both turn out to be zero for the Mamuro-Hattori solution, Eq. (3.65), based on Darcy's law]. Here, based on abundant experimental data,[11,27,31] we assume simply that $dU_a/dz = 0$ at $z = H_m$, which replaces B.C. (iii), even when[31] experimental estimates of $(-dP/dz)_{H_m}$ fall somewhat short of $(\rho_p - \rho)(1 - \varepsilon_{mf})g$.

Integrating Eq. (3.51) once, we obtain

$$(dU_a/dz)\left(d^2 U_a/dz^2\right) = F_1 U_a + F_2 U_a^2 + C_1. \qquad (3.53)$$

Substituting B.C. (ii) and the above replacement for B.C. (iii) into Eq. (3.53),

$$0 = F_1 U_{mf} + F_2 U_{mf}^2 + C_1. \tag{3.54}$$

Subtracting Eq. (3.54) from Eq. (3.53) gives

$$(dU_a/dz)\left(d^2 U_a/dz^2\right) = F_1\left(U_a - U_{mf}\right) + F_2\left(U_a^2 - U_{mf}^2\right). \tag{3.55}$$

Now let $dU_a/dz = 1/X$, whence $d^2 U_a/dz^2 = -(dX/dU_a)/X^3$, so that Eq. (3.55) becomes

$$-dX/X^4 = F_1(U_a - U_{mf})dU_a + F_2(U_a^2 - U_{mf}^2)dU_a, \tag{3.56}$$

which integrates to

$$1/3 X^3 = F_1 U_a^2/2 - F_1 U_{mf} U_a + F_2 U_a^3/3 - F_2 U_{mf}^2 U_a + C_2. \tag{3.57}$$

Again substituting B.C. (ii) and replacement B.C. (iii) into the above equation,

$$0 = F_1 U_{mf}^2/2 - F_1 U_{mf}^2 + F_2 U_{mf}^3/3 - F_2 U_{mf}^3 + C_2. \tag{3.58}$$

Subtracting Eq. (3.58) from Eq. (3.57) gives

$$1/3 X^3 = F_1(U_a - U_{mf})^2/2 + F_2(U_a^3 - 3U_{mf}^2 U_a + 2U_{mf}^3)/3. \tag{3.59}$$

If the second term on the right-hand side of Eq. (3.59) is neglected relative to the first – that is, we assume Darcy's law, and write $1/X$ again as dU_a/dz, then

$$dU_a/(U_a - U_{mf})^{2/3} = (3F_1/2)^{1/3} dz. \tag{3.60}$$

Integrating leads to

$$3(U_a - U_{mf})^{1/3} = (3F_1/2)^{1/3} z + C. \tag{3.61}$$

Substituting B.C. (ii), we obtain

$$0 = (3F_1/2)^{1/3} H_m + C. \tag{3.62}$$

Subtracting Eq. (3.62) from Eq. (3.61) and cubing the result, we find that

$$U_a - U_{mf} = (F_1/18)(z - H_m)^3. \tag{3.63}$$

Application of B.C. (i) gives

$$0 - U_{mf} = (F_1/18)(0 - H_m)^3. \tag{3.64}$$

Dividing Eq. (3.63) by Eq. (3.64) and rearranging leads to

$$\frac{U_a}{U_{mf}} = 1 - \left(1 - \frac{z}{H_m}\right)^3,$$
(3.65)

which is the well-known Mamuro-Hattori[28] equation.

Now, instead, proceed with Eq. (3.59), rewritten more compactly as

$$(dy/dz)^3 = F_2(y-1)^2(y+\beta),$$
(3.66)

where $y = U_a/U_{mf}$, so that $dy/dz = 1/U_{mf}X$, and

$$\beta = \frac{3}{2} \cdot \frac{F_1}{F_2} \cdot \frac{1}{U_{mf}} + 2 = \frac{3}{2} \cdot \frac{K_1}{K_2} \cdot \frac{1}{U_{mf}} + 2.$$
(3.67)

To evaluate β, the constants K_1 and K_2 at minimum spouting conditions may be estimated from Eq. (3.46) assuming $\varepsilon_a = \varepsilon_{mf}$, or determined experimentally by measuring the axial pressure gradient as a function of superficial fluid velocity for flow through a random loose-packed bed of the given solids. The voidage of such a bed is equal to ε_{mf}, as well as to that of a slowly moving packed bed,[6] and hence equals ε_a, at least at minimum spouting. U_{mf} in Eq. (3.67) may be calculated from Eq. (3.29) or determined experimentally. With the Ergun values of K_1 and K_2, β in Eq. (3.67) then reduces to $[128.6(1 - \varepsilon_a)/\phi \mathrm{Re}_{mf}] + 2$. Thus, when Darcy's law (creeping or viscous flow) holds, $\mathrm{Re}_{mf} \to 0$ and $\beta \to \infty$, whereas when inviscid flow prevails, $\mathrm{Re}_{mf} \to \infty$ and $\beta \to 2$.

Now define a new variable,

$$Y = -\left(\frac{\beta + y}{1 - y}\right)^{1/3}.$$
(3.68)

Eq. (3.66) is then equivalent to

$$dz = \frac{1}{F_2^{1/3}} \cdot \frac{3Y dY}{1 - Y^3},$$
(3.69)

which can be separated into two parts,

$$dz = \frac{1}{F_2^{1/3}} \left(\frac{1}{1 - Y} + \frac{Y - 1}{1 + Y + Y^2}\right) dY,$$
(3.70)

and integrated to give

$$z = C_3 - \frac{1}{F_2^{1/3}} \left[\ln \frac{1 - Y}{(1 + Y + Y^2)} + \sqrt{3} \arctan\left(\frac{1 + 2Y}{\sqrt{3}}\right)\right].$$
(3.71)

Substituting B.C. (ii), according to which $y = 1$, $Y = -\infty$ at $z = H_m$,

$$H_m = C_3 - \frac{1}{F_2^{v_3}}\left[0 + \sqrt{3}\left(-\frac{\pi}{2}\right)\right].$$
(3.72)

Subtracting Eq. (3.72) from Eq. (3.71) gives

$$z - H_m = -\frac{1}{F_2^{1/3}}\left[\ln \frac{1 - Y}{(1 + Y + Y^2)^{1/2}} + \sqrt{3}\left\{\arctan\left(\frac{1 + 2Y}{\sqrt{3}}\right) + \frac{\pi}{2}\right\}\right].$$
(3.73)

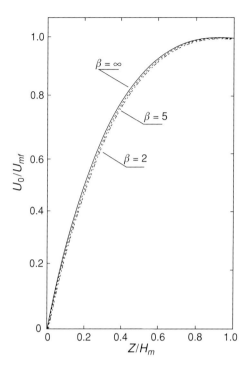

Figure 3.3. The effect of the flow regime parameter β on the normalized fluid velocity profile in the spouted bed annulus as predicted by Eq. (3.75).[31] The curve for $\beta = \infty$ corresponds to Eq. (3.65). (From Epstein et al.,[31] courtesy of *Canadian Journal of Chemical Engineering*.)

Substituting B.C. (i), according to which $y = 0$ and $Y = -\beta^{1/3}$, we obtain

$$-H_m = -\frac{1}{F_2^{1/3}}\left[\ln\frac{1 + \beta^{1/3}}{(1 - \beta^{1/3} + \beta^{2/3})^{1/2}} + \sqrt{3}\left\{\arctan\left(\frac{1 - 2\beta^{1/3}}{\sqrt{3}}\right) + \frac{\pi}{2}\right\}\right].$$

$$(3.74)$$

Dividing Eq. (3.73) by Eq. (3.74) leads to

$$1 - \frac{z}{H_m} = \frac{\left[\ln\dfrac{1 - Y}{(1 + Y + Y^2)^{1/2}} + \sqrt{3}\left\{\arctan\left(\dfrac{1 + 2Y}{\sqrt{3}}\right) + \dfrac{\pi}{2}\right\}\right]}{\left[\ln\dfrac{1 + \beta^{1/3}}{(1 - \beta^{1/3} + \beta^{2/3})^{1/2}} + \sqrt{3}\left\{\arctan\left(\dfrac{1 - 2\beta^{1/3}}{\sqrt{3}}\right) + \dfrac{\pi}{2}\right\}\right]},$$

$$(3.75)$$

which is the Epstein-Levine[32] implicit solution for U_a/U_{mf} as a function of z/H_m under conditions in which both viscous and inertial forces are important.

If one expands the terms in both the numerator and denominator of Eq. (3.75) as power series, and then allows β to approach infinity, it can be shown[31] that this equation collapses to Eq. (3.65) at the viscous flow limit. The other extreme, inviscid flow, is represented by Eq. (3.75) with $\beta = 2$. Values of β for spouted beds are typically in the range of 2.2 to 5. Figure 3.3 plots $y = U_a/U_{mf}$ versus z/H_m for the two extremes and for an intermediate case, $\beta = 5$, which corresponds to $Re_{mf} = 25$ for spherical particles. Surprisingly, the differences between the extremes is such that U_a/U_{mf} with $\beta = \infty$ averages no more than 2 percent above U_a/U_{mf} with $\beta = 2$ from $z/H_m = 0$ to $z/H_m = 1$. These differences are certainly smaller than the experimental error involved in measuring U_a. Apparently it is the use of the same constraining boundary condition $U_a = U_{mf}$ at $z = H_m$, with respect to which both U_a and z are normalized, that attenuates the differences.

Eqs. (3.65) and (3.75) were both derived for $H = H_m$, but to deal with beds for which $H < H_m$, Mamuro and Hattori[28] arbitrarily modified Eq. (3.65) to

$$\frac{U_a}{U_{aH}} = 1 - \left(1 - \frac{z}{H}\right)^3. \tag{3.76}$$

If B.C. (ii) above is simply changed to $U_a = U_{aH}$ at $z = H$ and B.C. (iii) to $\sigma_a = 0$ at $z = H$ (i.e., zero vertical solids pressure at the top of the annulus), so from Eq. (3.42) and (3.50), $dU_a/dz = 0$ at $z = H$, which now replaces B.C. (iii), then following the same derivation sequence as for Eq. (3.65) results in Eq. (3.76). Empirically, however, Eq. (3.76) fails[11] to give good prediction of U_a/U_{aH} as a function of z/H for $H < H_m$. Where this derivation of Eq. (3.76) errs is in the assumption that $\sigma_a = 0$ at $z = H < H_m$. The assumption $\sigma_a = 0$ is reasonable at $z = H = H_m$ because spouting ceases when $H = H_m$, but not when $H < H_m$, at which point spouting results in bombarding the surface of the annulus with particles from the fountain.

There is a broad range of direct and indirect evidence[15,27,31,34] that, for a given column geometry, spouting fluid, and solids material, U_a at any bed level, z, in the cylindrical part of the column is independent of total bed depth, H, provided $U \approx U_{ms}$. Hence Eqs. (3.65) and (3.75) are both applicable to beds for which $H \leq H_m$ and $U \approx U_{ms}$.

Because of its greater simplicity, further discussion is focused on Eq. (3.65). This equation was originally assumed to apply not only at $U = U_{ms}$, but also at $U > U_{ms}$. However, longitudinal pressure gradients measured along the walls of spouting beds[31] indicated an apparent decline in U_a at all bed levels as U was increased and hence an even greater excess of gas flow to the spout than the input excess over minimum spouting. On the assumption that $\varepsilon_a = $ constant $= \varepsilon_{mf}$, this result was first interpreted[31] as owing to the increased circulation, and hence downflow of solids in the annulus, counteracting the upward flow of gas therein. However, subsequent measurements by He et al.[33,34] of annulus voidages using optical fiber probes at $U > U_{ms}$ have indicated, for a given solid material, that for a fixed value of H, ε_a at any bed level increases with increasing U and with increasing radial distance from the spout; that at any H and U/U_{ms}, ε_a increases with increasing z; and that at fixed U/U_{ms}, U_a at any bed level increases as H increases.

Thus the equality of pressure gradients often observed[27,31] at similar bed levels despite large variations in H can no longer be interpreted as signifying equality of U_a, given the significant differences in ε_a at these levels. Similarly, any observed decline in pressure gradients with U can now be better explained as originating from an increase in ε_a rather than from a decrease in U_a. Consequently, Eqs. (3.65) and (3.75), although they remain applicable to $H \leq H_m$, must in all rigor be restricted to $U = U_{ms}$ and should therefore be interpreted as yielding minimum measurable values of U_a – that is, values that will be exceeded in most practical cases. The derivations of these equations also neglect any variations of spout diameter with z, the small radial components of fluid velocity present in the cylindrical part of the column, and the more complex behavior of both fluid and solids in the conical-base region. They are therefore most in line with experimental measurements in the cylindrical part of the column somewhat above the cone (for U close to U_{ms}), particularly[24,34] if U_{mf} is replaced by the measured value of U_{aHm}.

The previous derivations take no account of the vertical shear stresses at the column wall and at the spout–annulus interface. When these are taken into account, additional variables such as the angle of wall friction and the angle of internal friction of the particles are introduced into the problem.[35] The resulting equation for U_a, based on Darcy's law, even when normalized with respect to U_{aHm} measured at $z = H_m$ rather than to U_{mf}, still contains one adjustable parameter,[31] estimation of which requires at least one experimental measurement. Its added complexity thus gives it no advantage over Eq. (3.65), rewritten for $U \geq U_{ms}$ as

$$\frac{U_a}{U_{aHm}} = \frac{U_a}{\alpha U_{mf}} = 1 - \left(1 - \frac{z}{H_m}\right)^3. \tag{3.77}$$

Here α is an adjustable parameter with a value in the order of unity at $U = U_{ms}$. Uncertainty with respect to U_{aHm} can be surmounted, after Grbavčić et al.,[27] by normalization with respect to U_{aH} instead of U_{aHm} – that is, by writing

$$\frac{U_a}{U_{aH}} = \frac{1 - [1 - (z/H_m)]^3}{1 - [1 - (H/H_m)]^3}. \tag{3.78}$$

Eq. (3.78) is more reliably in agreement with experimental results than Eq. (3.65), but unlike Eq. (3.65), use of Eq. (3.78) to predict $U_a(z)$ requires that U_{aH} be measured.

3.4.2   Empirically based modeling

An alternative approach to annulus flow is based on the empirical finding of Lefroy and Davidson[19] that at $U \approx U_{ms}$, the longitudinal pressure distribution of a spouted bed can be represented by

$$P - P_H = -\Delta P_s \cos(\pi z/2H), \tag{3.79}$$

so for the particular case of $H = H_m$,

$$P - P_{Hm} = (-\Delta P_s)_{Hm} \cos(\pi z/2H_m). \tag{3.80}$$

Differentiating Eq. (3.80) with respect to z, one obtains

$$-dP/dz = (\pi/2H_m)(-\Delta P_s)_{Hm} \sin(\pi z/2H_m), \tag{3.81}$$

so at $z = H_m$,

$$(-dP/dz)_{Hm} = (\pi/2H_m)(-\Delta P_s)_{Hm}. \tag{3.82}$$

Dividing Eq. (3.81) by Eq. (3.82) results in

$$\frac{-dP/dz}{(-dP/dz)_{Hm}} = \sin\left(\frac{\pi z}{2H_m}\right). \tag{3.83}$$

Expressing $-dP/dz$ in terms of U_a by means of Eq. (3.45), $(-dP/dz)_{Hm}$ in terms of U_{mf} by means of the same equation with $U_a = U_{mf}$, and expressing the result in terms of $y(= U_a/U_{mf})$ and β, defined by Eq. (3.67), transforms Eq. (3.83) to

$$\frac{2(\beta - 2)y + 3y^2}{2\beta - 1} = \sin\frac{\pi z}{2H_m}. \tag{3.84}$$

If Darcy's law prevails, for example, for small particles ($d_p < 1$ mm), $\beta \to \infty$ and therefore Eq. (3.84) reduces to

$$y = U_a/U_{mf} = \sin(\pi z/2H_m), \tag{3.85}$$

whereas for the opposite extreme of inviscid flow, $\beta = 2$, so Eq. (3.84) becomes

$$y = U_a/U_{mf} = [\sin(\pi z/2H_m)]^{1/2}. \tag{3.86}$$

For coarse particles, Eq. (3.86) gives much better agreement with experimental data than Eq. (3.85), which generally underpredicts for $d_p > 1$ mm, but not quite as good agreement as Eq. (3.84), especially[31] if U_{mf} in the expressions for y and β is replaced by the measured value of U_{aHm}.

Equations (3.65) and (3.85) intersect at $z/H_m = 0.343$, below which values of U_a/U_{mf} from Eq. (3.85) exceed those from Eq. (3.65), and vice versa above $z/H_m = 0.343$.

3.5   Pressure drops, profiles, and gradients

In this section, equations are derived for longitudinal pressure profiles and pressure gradients, as well as total pressure drops, for spouted beds of height H as a function of quantities (e.g., H_m) that depend only on column geometry, fluid properties, and particle properties.

3.5.1   Empirically based modeling

Continuing with the Lefroy-Davidson[19] approach, introduced in the previous section, and assuming that the pressure gradient at the top of a bed of maximum spoutable depth is given by

$$(-dP/dz)_{H_m} = (-dP/dz)_{mf} = (\rho_p - \rho)(1 - \varepsilon_{mf})g, \tag{3.87}$$

substitution of this equation into Eq. (3.83) gives

$$\frac{-dP/dz}{(-dP/dz)_{mf}} = \frac{-dP/dz}{(\rho_p - \rho)(1 - \varepsilon_{mf})g} = \sin\left(\frac{\pi z}{2H_m}\right). \tag{3.88}$$

It is assumed here and elsewhere, after Grbavčić et al.[27] and others,[31,34] that the pressure gradient at level z for a given column geometry and fluid and particle properties, is independent of bed height H, at least when $U \approx U_{ms}$.

If we now substitute Eq. (3.87) into Eq. (3.82), we arrive at

$$(-\Delta P_s)_{Hm} = (\rho_p - \rho)(1 - \varepsilon_{mf})g(2H_m/\pi). \tag{3.89}$$

Eq. (3.89) is generalized to be applicable for all values of H and not just for H_m by writing

$$-\Delta P_s = B(\rho_p - \rho)(1 - \varepsilon_{mf})g(2H/\pi). \tag{3.90}$$

It follows from Eqs. (3.89) and (3.90) that

$$B = \frac{-\Delta P_s/H}{(-\Delta P_s)_{Hm}/H_m}. \tag{3.91}$$

The numerator in this equation is evaluated by differentiating Eq. (3.79) by z, so

$$-dP/dz = (\pi/2H)(-\Delta P_s)\sin(\pi z/2H), \tag{3.92}$$

which at $z = H$ yields

$$-\Delta P_s/H = (2/\pi)(-dP/dz)_H. \tag{3.93}$$

The denominator in Eq. (3.91) is evaluated by putting $z = H$ in Eq. (3.81), so

$$(-\Delta P_s)_{Hm}/H_m = (2/\pi)(-dP/dz)_H/\sin(\pi H/2H_m). \tag{3.94}$$

Combining Eqs. (3.91), (3.93), and (3.94) gives

$$B = \sin(\pi H/2H_m). \tag{3.95}$$

If the entire bed of height H were at minimum fluidization,

$$-\Delta P_f = (dP/dz)_{mf} \cdot H = (\rho_p - \rho)(1 - \varepsilon_{mf})gH. \tag{3.96}$$

Combining Eqs. (3.90), (3.95), and (3.96), we obtain

$$(-\Delta P_s)/(-\Delta P_f) = (2/\pi)\sin(\pi H/2H_m). \tag{3.97}$$

For a bed at its maximum spoutable height, H_m, Eq. (3.97) simplifies to

$$(-\Delta P_s)_{Hm}/(-\Delta P_f)_{Hm} = 2/\pi, \tag{3.98}$$

that is, the pressure drop across a bed of height H_m is 63.7 percent of that required for fluidization.

Pressure gradients determined by Eq. (3.88) and total pressure drops from Eq. (3.97) tend to underpredict the corresponding experimental measurements to varying extents,[31] depending, at least in part, on the magnitude of radial pressure gradients near the fluid inlet nozzle, neglected in the derivation.

Substitution of $(-\Delta P_s)$ by Eq. (3.97) into Eq. (3.79) results in

$$(P - P_H)/(-\Delta P_f) = (2/\pi)\sin(\pi H/2H_m)\cos(\pi z/2H). \tag{3.99}$$

At the inlet, $z = 0$, and therefore $P - P_H = -\Delta P_s$ as given by Eq. (3.97), whereas at the outlet, $z = H$ and therefore $P = P_H$. At $H = H_m$, Eq. (3.99) reduces to Eq. (3.80) with $(-\Delta P_s)_{Hm}$ given by Eq. (3.98).

3.5.2   Mechanistic modeling

Turning now to the force balance model of Figure 3.2, we start by dividing Eq. (3.45) by the same equation applied to minimum fluidization conditions, expressing the result in terms of $y(= U_a/U_{mf})$ and β, and substituting for $(-dP/dz)_{mf}$ according to Eq. (3.87):

$$\frac{-dP/dz}{(-dP/dz)_{mf}} = \frac{-dP/dz}{(\rho_p - \rho)(1 - \varepsilon_{mf})g} = \frac{K_1 U_a + K_2 U_a^2}{K_1 U_{mf} + K_2 U_{mf}^2} = \frac{2(\beta - 2)y + 3y^2}{2\beta - 1}.$$

(3.100)

When Darcy's law prevails, $\beta = \infty$ and the right-hand side (RHS) of Eq. (3.100) reduces to y, whereas for pure inviscid flow, $\beta = 2$ and the RHS equals y^2. For a given value of β between 2 and ∞, Eq. (3.100) can be solved for $-dP/dz$ at specified values of z/H_m by using Eq. (3.75) to generate Y for a given value of z/H_m, and hence the corresponding value of y from Eq. (3.68). Less rigorously, but with little loss of accuracy, answers can be generated with ease by substituting for $y(= U_a/U_{mf})$ in Eq. (3.100) according to Eq. (3.65), so

$$\frac{-dP/dz}{(-dP/dz)_{mf}} = \frac{2\beta(3x - 3x^2 + x^3) - 12x + 39x^2 - 58x^3 + 45x^4 - 18x^5 + 3x^6}{2\beta - 1},$$

(3.101)

where $x = z/H_m$. Eq. (3.101) correctly yields limiting RHS values of $1 - (1 - x^3)$, $[1 - (1 - x^3)]^2, 0$, and 1 for $\beta = \infty, \beta = 2, x = 0$ (all β), and $x = 1$ (all β), respectively. Eq. (3.101) gives[32] $(-dP/dz)$ values over the range $x = 0$ to 1 that typically average only 3 percent above those obtained by the use of Eq. (3.75) with Eq. (3.100). The method of arriving at Eq. (3.101) has been labeled "hybrid" because it combines Eq. (3.100), which is perfectly rigorous, with Eq. (3.65), which nominally applies only to Darcy flow but, as indicated above, is an excellent approximation even for non-Darcy flow. Hybrid methods are similarly applied, as will be shown, to pressure profiles and pressure drops.

To arrive at an equation for the longitudinal pressure profile, Eq. (3.100) is written in integral form with integration limits from z to H and P to P_H:

$$\int_P^{P_H} -dP = (-dP/dz)_{mf} \int_z^H \frac{2(\beta - 2)y + 3y^2}{2\beta - 1} dz.$$

(3.102)

Substituting for $(-dP/dz)_{mf}$ by means of Eq. (3.96), Eq. (3.102) can be transformed to

$$\frac{P - P_H}{-\Delta P_f} = \frac{1}{h(2\beta - 1)} \int_x^h [2(\beta - 2)y + 3y^2] dx,$$

(3.103)

where $h = H/H_m$. Eq. (3.103) is again most rigorously solved numerically by determining y at various values of x from Eq. (3.75) in combination with Eq. (3.68). Adopting the simpler hybrid approach, the term in square brackets within the integral of Eq. (3.103) is equivalent to the numerator on the RHS of Eq. (3.101). The integration then gives

$$\frac{P - P_H}{-\Delta P_f} = \frac{1}{h(2\beta - 1)} \left[2\beta\{1.5(h^2 - x^2) - (h^3 - x^3) + 0.25(h^4 - x^4)\} \right.$$
$$- 6(h^2 - x^2) + 13(h^3 - x^3) - 14.5(h^4 - x^4) + 9(h^5 - x^5)$$
$$\left. - 3(h^6 - x^6) + \frac{3}{7}(h^7 - x^7) \right]. \tag{3.104}$$

At the Darcy's law limit, $\beta = \infty$, this equation reduces to

$$(P - P_H)/(-\Delta P_f) = [1.5(h^2 - x^2) - (h^3 - x^3) + 0.25(h^4 - x^4)]/h. \tag{3.105}$$

The total pressure drop, $-\Delta P_s = P_o - P_H$, is given by substituting $x = 0$ in Eq. (3.104) for the hybrid solution and Eq. (3.105) for the Darcy solution. The hybrid solution is thus

$$\frac{-\Delta P_s}{-\Delta P_f} = \frac{1}{h(2\beta - 1)}[2\beta(1.5h^2 - h^3 + 0.25h^4) - 6h^2 + 13h^3$$
$$- 14.5h^4 + 9h^5 - 3h^6 + 0.429h^7], \tag{3.107}$$

whereas the Darcy ($\beta = \infty$) result is simply

$$(-\Delta P_s)/(-\Delta P_f) = 1.5h - h^2 + 0.25h^3. \tag{3.108}$$

For the opposite extreme of inviscid flow ($\beta = 2$), assuming $H = H_m$ – that is, $h = 1$, Eq. (3.107) reduces to

$$(-\Delta P_s)_{H_m}/(-\Delta P_f)_{H_m} = 0.643, \tag{3.109}$$

which is in excellent agreement with Eq. (3.98). However, the maximum value of the spouted-to-fluidized-bed pressure drop ratio often exceeds 0.64 experimentally,[11,31] probably because of radial pressure gradients and other disturbances near the fluid inlet, and is actually better represented by putting $h = 1$ in Eq. (3.108), so

$$(-\Delta P_s)_{H_m}/(-\Delta P_f)_{H_m} = 0.75. \tag{3.110}$$

Similarly, the Darcy's law-based Eq. (3.108) for pressure drop at any value of h and Eq. (3.105) for pressure profile often fortuitously give better predictions than the corresponding, more rigorous, Forchheimer-based equations containing β defined by Eq. (3.67).[31]

Determination of $-\Delta P_s$ experimentally for comparison with theory is best done either by extrapolation of pressure measurements at different heights to $z = 0$ or by pressure drop measurements across the whole bed, including the inlet during spouting, and for the empty column, using the appropriate procedure to eliminate the effect of the inlet.[11] Unlike annulus voidages and fluid velocities, which increase somewhat with increasing superficial spouting velocity, total pressure drops remain essentially constant.

3.6   Spout diameter

By a force balance on the spout–annulus interface in the cylindrical part of the column in which axial variation of the spout diameter is relatively small, including both hydrodynamic forces and solid stresses based on hopper flow of solids, Bridgwater and Mathur[36] derived

$$\frac{32 f \rho Q_s^2}{\pi^2 (-d\sigma_a/dz)(D - D_s)D_s^4} = 1. \tag{3.111}$$

They then made the following simplifying assumptions:

(1) The volumetric gas flow through the spout, Q_s, above the cone but well below the bed surface, is typically about one-half the total volumetric flow through the bed, that is, $Q_s \simeq 0.5\pi D^2 G/4\rho$.

(2) Flow through the spout is equivalent to flow of a dilute air-solids suspension through a rough pipe with an equivalent sand roughness of $d_p/2D_s$ and a Fanning friction factor $f \approx 0.08$.

(3) From Eq. (3.42), $-d\sigma_a/dz = (\rho_p - \rho)(1 - \varepsilon_a)g - (-dP/dz)$. Assuming again at about the mid-height of the spouted bed that $(-dP/dz)$ is approximately one-half of $(\rho_p - \rho)(1 - \varepsilon_a)g$, and that $\rho \ll \rho_p$, then $(-d\sigma_a/dz) \simeq \rho_p(1 - \varepsilon_a)g/2 = \rho_b g/2$, where $\rho_b = $ bulk density in the annulus.

(4) The analysis is limited to air spouting at ambient conditions, so $\rho = 1.2$ kg/m^3.

(5) $D_s \ll D$, so that $D - D_s \simeq D$.

With these assumptions, Eq. (3.111) reduces to

$$D_s = (\text{constant})G^{1/2}D^{3/4}/(\rho_b g)^{1/4}. \tag{3.112}$$

In parallel with this derivation, McNab[37] developed an empirical equation for the average spout diameter $\bar{D}_s$ by statistically correlating literature data on $\bar{D}_s$ available at that time, all for air spouting at ambient conditions in semicylindrical columns, using the three dependent variables G, D, and ρ_b of Eq. (3.112). The resulting McNab equation, in SI units, is

$$\bar{D}_s = 2.0 G^{0.49} D^{0.68}/\rho_b^{0.41}. \tag{3.113}$$

Eq. (3.113) has served well as a predictor, within about 10 percent of $\bar{D}_s$ observed on the transparent flat face of semicylindrical columns for spouting with air at room temperature, provided that $d_p > 1$ mm. Even for full-column shallow beds (including those with flat bases, in which dead solids at the base form an angle of repose), in which the spout configuration is dominated by gas deceleration and solids acceleration in the cone, and the spout diameter is measured by optical fiber probing, Eq. (3.113) has required[38,39] only minor empirical modifications to account mainly for D_i/D and θ. However, for beds of normal depth in which the dominant contribution to $\bar{D}_s$ comes from the part of the spout well above the cone, distortion of the spout at the flat face of a half-column was found to diminish D_s relative to that in the corresponding full column, so $\bar{D}_s$, via Eq. (3.113), was underpredicted[40] for spouting of 1.44-mm glass beads by as much as 35.5 percent. For particles with $d_p \leq 1.0$ mm, even with D_s measured visually at the flat face of a half-column, Eq. (3.113) underestimated $\bar{D}_s$ by about 25 percent, although it predicted the variation of $\bar{D}_s$ with $G (= U\rho)$ correctly.[41]

For spouting with air at elevated temperatures, or with gases other than air, assumption (4) above is dropped and ρ reinserted as a variable in simplifying Eq. (3.111). We then obtain, instead of Eq. (3.112),

$$D_s = (\text{constant})G^{1/2}D^{3/4}/(\rho_b g)^{1/4}\rho^{1/4}. \tag{3.114}$$

Considering now each variable in Eq. (3.114), as well as gas viscosity μ, which rises with temperature and could affect f and the shear stress at the spout wall, we can write

$$\bar{D}_s = f(D, G, \rho_b g, \rho, \mu). \tag{3.115}$$

By dimensional analysis,

$$\bar{D}_s/D = f(DG/\mu, \rho\rho_b g D^3/\mu^2). \tag{3.116}$$

In the study mentioned previously[12] for sand spouting with air at temperatures from 20 °C to 580 °C, bolstered by an earlier study[24] of spouting similar particles with air up to 420 °C and with both helium and methane at 20 °C, the mean spout diameter was determined based on the longitudinally averaged spout cross-sectional area from visual[24] and photographic[12] measurements of D_s at the transparent flat face of a half-column as

$$\bar{D}_s = \left[\frac{1}{H} \int_o^H \{D_s\,(z)\}^2\, dz \right]^{1/2}. \tag{3.117}$$

A total of 205 runs from the two combined studies[12,24] yielded, as a best fit to a simple power law relationship among the three dimensionless groups in Eq. (3.116),

$$\bar{D}_s/D = 5.59(DG/\mu)^{0.435}(\rho\rho_b g D^3/\mu^2)^{-0.282} \tag{3.118}$$

with an average absolute deviation of approximately 5 percent. By rewriting Eq. (3.118) as

$$\bar{D}_s = 5.59G^{0.435}D^{0.589}\mu^{0.129}/(\rho_b g)^{0.282}\rho^{0.282}, \tag{3.119}$$

we can see that the effect of each of the process variables is qualitatively similar to that displayed by the simplified theory incorporated in Eq. (3.114), with an additional small effect of viscosity. Eq. (3.119), unlike Eq. (3.113), is dimensionally consistent and accounts for variations in gas density and viscosity.

To estimate the final fluid flow split between the spout and the annulus, knowledge of D_{sH}, the spout diameter at the top of the bed where the annulus ends and the fountain begins, is desirable. Zanoelo and Rocha[42] have given detailed plots relating measured spout radius, $D_s/2$, to z/H for five conical-cylindrical spouted beds from three studies in the literature.[24,40,43] They recorded values of $\bar{D}_s$ determined from these experimental data, which were mainly at $U/U_{ms} = 1.1$. From these plots it is possible to obtain the experimental values of D_{sH}. From the five values thus obtained, $D_{sH}/\bar{D}_s = 1.09 \pm 0.04$, and from the corresponding recorded gas inlet diameters, the mean value of D_{sH}/D_i was 1.80 ± 0.3. This value is consistent with the argument of Lefroy and Davidson[19] that to satisfy the conditions of both spout wall stability and gas-jet inlet momentum for spout penetration, $D_{sH} \approx 2D_i$.

3.7   Flow split between spout and annulus

At the common operating velocity of $U = 1.1U_{ms}$, we can determine U_{aH} from Eq. (3.77) applied to $z = H$:

$$\frac{U_{aH}}{\alpha U_{mf}} = 1 - \left(1 - \frac{H}{H_m}\right)^3, \tag{3.120}$$

where U_{mf} is obtained from Eq. (3.32) and H_m from Eq. (3.33). For air spouting at ambient conditions, U_{ms} is given by Eq. (3.6) and $\bar{D}_s$ by either Eq. (3.113) or Eq. (3.119). Taking D_{sH} as $1.09\bar{D}_s$, we can determine the fraction of total airflow through the annulus as $U_{aH}(D^2 - D_{sH}^2)/UD^2$. The superficial gas velocity, U_s, leaving the spout can be determined from the gas flow balance,

$$UD^2 = U_s D_{sH}^2 + U_{aH}\left(D^2 - D_{sH}^2\right). \tag{3.121}$$

Let us apply this procedure to the fluid–solid combination used illustratively in Section 3.1 for a half-column of diameter $D = 0.5$ m, gas inlet diameter $D_i = 0.10$ m, and bed height $H = 0.9H_m$. From Eqs. (3.33) and (3.34), respectively, the latter with b taken as unity, $U_{mf} = 1.934$ m/s and $H_m = 2.70$ m, so $H = 2.43$ m. As $\alpha(= U_{aH_m}/U_{mf})$ at $U/U_{ms} = 1.1$ has been reported[30] for several diverse column dimensions, particle properties, and bed heights as approximately 0.9, this value is adopted here. Then from Eq. (3.120), $U_{aH} = 1.739$ m/s and from Eq. (3.6), for 5-mm spheres of density 2500 kg/m^3 spouted with ambient air ($\rho = 1.21$ kg/m^3), $U_{ms} = 1.817$ m/s. With $G = U\rho = (1.1 \times 1.817)(1.21)$ kg/m^2·s and $\rho_b = \rho_p(1 - \varepsilon_a) = \rho_p(1 - \varepsilon_{mf}) = 2500(1 - 0.415)$ kg/m^3, Eqs. (3.113) and (3.119) yield $\bar{D}_s = 0.0970$ m and 0.0850 m, respectively. Based on the average of those two values, $D_{sH} = 1.09(0.0910) = 0.0992$ m. The airflow fraction through the annulus is then $1.739(0.5^2 - 0.0992^2)/$

$(1.1 \times 1.817)(0.5^2) = 0.836$, and from Eq. (3.121), $U_s = 6.6$ m/s. Hence, the superficial exit spout velocity is about 3.3 times the superficial spouting velocity of 2.0 m/s. In this example, $U_{aH}/U = 0.87$, which compares reasonably[11] with the recorded value of $U_{aH}/U = 0.89$ for ambient air spouting at $U/U_{ms} = 1.1$ in a half-column of comparable dimensions ($D = 0.61$ m, $D_i = 0.102$ m) for particles of comparable size (3.2 mm $\times$ 6.4 mm prolate spheroids) though less dense ($\rho_p = 1380$ kg/m^3), and a somewhat smaller bed height (0.183 m). For a full column, D_{sH} would be larger, and thus both the annulus flow fraction and U_s would be somewhat smaller than calculated above.

Recall that Eq. (3.120) and its antecedents have been derived on the assumption that $\varepsilon_a = $ constant $= \varepsilon_{mf}$ throughout the annulus, which, strictly speaking, applies only at $U = U_{ms}$. The justification for applying it at $U = 1.1U_{ms}$ is that the void fraction increase in most of the annulus[33,34] is then less than 0.02 and that the corresponding small decrease in resistance to fluid flow is counteracted by a voidage decrease near the spout wall, especially in the conical region of the column,[33] and by the downward motion of the annular solids, which is absent at U_{ms} but entrains fluid downward at $1.1U_{ms}$. The use of the adjustable parameter α ($= U_{aHm}/U_{mf}$ theoretically) provides further accommodation of Eq. (3.120) to experimental data. As H is decreased, the value of α apparently decreases.[34] At $U > 1.1U_{ms}$, however, the dependence[33,34] of ε_a on U, H, and z renders Eq. (3.120) increasingly inapplicable, even with adjustments in α. Prediction of the changes in annular voidage and its distribution, a prerequisite for improvements on equations such as Eq. (3.120), is perhaps best pursued by means of computational fluid dynamics (see Chapter 4).

References

1. H. Littman, M. H. Morgan III, D. V. Vuković, F. K. Zdanski, and Z. B. Grbavčić. Prediction of the maximum spoutable height and the average spout to inlet tube diameter ratio in spouted beds of spherical particles. *Can. J. Chem. Eng.*, **57** (1979), 684–687.
2. J. F. Richardson and W. N. Zaki. Sedimentation and fluidization. *Trans. Instn. Chem. Engrs. Part A*, **32** (1954), 35–53.
3. A. R. Khan and J. F. Richardson. Fluid-particle interactions and flow characteristics of fluidized beds and settling suspensions of spherical particles. *Chem. Eng. Commun.*, **78** (1989), 111–130.
4. N. Epstein. Liquid-solids fluidization. In *Handbook of Fluidization and Fluid-Particle Systems*, ed. W.-C. Yang (New York: Marcel Dekker, 2003), pp. 705–764.
5. H. A. Becker. An investigation of laws governing the spouting of coarse particles. *Chem. Eng. Sci.*, **13** (1961), 245–262.
6. J. Eastwood, E. J. P. Matzen, M. J. Young, and N. Epstein. Random loose porosity of packed beds. *Brit. Chem. Eng.*, **14** (1969), 1542–1545.
7. K. B. Mathur and P. E. Gishler. A technique for contacting gases with coarse solid particles, *AIChE J.*, **1** (1955), 157–164.
8. P. P. Chandnani and N. Epstein. Spoutability and spout destabilization of fine particles with a gas. In *Fluidization V*, ed. K. Ostergaard and A. Sorensen (New York: Engineering Foundation, 1986), pp. 233–240.

9. B. Ghosh. A study of the spouted bed, part I – a theoretical analysis. *Indian Chem. Engineer*, **7** (1965), 16–19.

10. J. R. Grace and C. J. Lim. Permanent jet formation in beds of particulate solids. *Can. J. Chem. Eng.*, **65** (1987), 160–162.

11. K. B. Mathur and N. Epstein. *Spouted Beds* (New York: Academic Press, 1974).

12. Y. Li, C. J. Lim, and N. Epstein. Aerodynamic aspects of spouted beds at temperatures up to 580°C. *J. Serbian Chem. Soc.*, **61** (1996), 253–266.

13. E. R. Altwicker and R. K. N. V. Konduri. Hydrodynamic aspects of spouted beds at elevated temperatures. *Combustion Sci. and Tech.*, **87** (1992), 173–197.

14. R. Clift, J. R. Grace, and W. E. Weber. *Bubbles, Drops, and Particles* (New York: Academic Press, 1978), p. 114.

15. B. Thorley, J. B. Saunby, K. B. Mathur, and G. L. Osberg. An analysis of air and solid flow in a spouted wheat bed. *Can. J. Chem. Eng.*, **37** (1959), 184–192.

16. W. Du, X. Bi, and N. Epstein. Exploring a non-dimensional varying exponent equation relating minimum spouting velocity to maximum spoutable bed depth. *Can. J. Chem. Eng.*, **87** (2009), 157–162.

17. A. G. Fane and R. A. Mitchell. Minimum spouting velocity of scaled-up beds. *Can. J. Chem. Eng.*, **62** (1984), 437–439.

18. Y. L. He, C. J. Lim, and J. R. Grace. Spouted bed and spout-fluid bed behaviour in a column of diameter 0.91 m. *Can. J. Chem. Eng.*, **70** (1992), 848–857.

19. G. A. Lefroy and J. F. Davidson. The mechanics of spouted beds. *Trans. Instn Chem. Engrs.*, **47** (1969), T120–T128.

20. S. Ergun. Fluid flow through packed columns. *Chem. Eng. Progr.*, **48**:2 (1952), 89–94.

21. C. Y. Wen and Y. H. Yu. A generalized method of predicting the minimum fluidization velocity. *AIChE J.*, **12** (1966), 610–612.

22. G. S. McNab and J. Bridgwater. Spouted beds – estimation of spouting pressure drop and the particle size for deepest bed. In *Proceedings of the European Congress on Particle Technology* (Nuremberg, Germany, 1977), 17 pages.

23. H. Littman, M. H. Morgan III, D. V. Vuković, F. K. Zdanski, and Z. B. Grbavčić. A theory for predicting the maximum spoutable bed height in a spouted bed. *Can. J. Chem Eng.*, **55** (1977), 497–501.

24. S. W. M. Wu, C. J. Lim, and N. Epstein. Hydrodynamics of spouted beds at elevated temperatures. *Chem. Eng. Commun.*, **62** (1987), 251–268.

25. M. A. Malek and B. C.-Y. Lu. Pressure drop and spoutable bed height in spouted beds. *Ind. Eng. Chem. Process Des. Dev.*, **4** (1965), 123–128.

26. M. H. Morgan III, H. Littman, and B. Sastri. Jet penetration and pressure drops in water spouted beds. *Can. J. Chem. Eng.*, **66** (1988), 735–739.

27. Z. B. Grbavčić, D. V. Vuković, F. K. Zdanski, and H. Littman. Fluid flow pattern, minimum spouting velocity and pressure drop in spouted beds. *Can. J. Chem. Eng.*, **54** (1976), 33–42.

28. T. Mamuro and H. Hattori. Flow pattern of fluid in spouted beds. *J. Chem. Eng. Japan*, **1** (1968), 1–5.

29. R. L. Brown and J. C. Richards. *Principles of Powder Mechanics* (Oxford, UK: Pergamon Press, 1970), p. 70.

30. A. E. Scheidegger. *The Physics of Flow through Porous Media*, 3rd ed. (Toronto: Univ. of Toronto Press, 1974), p. 155.

31. N. Epstein, C. J. Lim, and K. B. Mathur. Data and models for flow distribution and pressure drop in spouted beds. *Can J. Chem. Eng.*, **56** (1978), 436–447.

32. N. Epstein and S. Levine. Non-Darcy flow and pressure distribution in a spouted bed. In *Fluidization*, ed. J. F. Davidson and D. L. Keairns (Cambridge, UK: Cambridge University Press, 1978), pp. 98–103.

33. Y. L. He, C. J. Lim, J. R. Grace, and J. X. Zhu. Measurements of voidage profiles in spouted beds. *Can. J. Chem. Eng.*, **72** (1994), 229–234.

34. Y. L. He, C. J. Lim, and J. R. Grace. Pressure gadients, voidage and gas flow in the annulus of spouted beds. *Can. J. Chem. Eng.*, **78** (2000), 161–167.

35. A. Yokogawa, E. Ogina, and N. Yoshii. *Trans.* The distribution of static pressure and stress in the spouted bed. *Japan Soc. Mech. Engrs.*, **38** (1972), 1081–1086.

36. J. Bridgwater and K. B. Mathur. Prediction of spout diameter in a spouted bed – a theoretical model. *Powder Technol.*, **6** (1972), 183–187.

37. G. S. McNab. Prediction of spout diameter. *Brit. Chem. Eng. & Proc. Technol.*, **17** (1972), 532.

38. M. J. San José, M. Olazar, M. A. Izquierdo, S. Alvarez, and J. Bilbao. Spout geometry in shallow spouted beds. *Ind. Eng. Chem. Res.*, **40** (2001), 420–426.

39. M. J. San José, S. Alvarez, A. O. de Salazar, M. Olazar, and J. Bilbao. Spout geometry in spouted beds with solids of different density and different sphericity. *Ind. Eng. Chem. Res.*, **44** (2005), 8393–8400.

40. Y. L. He, C. J. Lim, S. Qin, and J. R. Grace. Spout diameters in full and half spouted beds. *Can. J. Chem. Eng.*, **76** (1998), 696–701.

41. N. Epstein and P. P. Chandnani. Gas spouting characteristics of fine particles. *Chem. Eng. Sci.*, **42**, (1987), 2977–2981.

42. E. F. Zanoelo and S. C. S. Rocha. Spout shape predictions in spouted beds. *Can. J. Chem. Eng.*, **80** (2002), 967–973.

43. C. J. Lim and K. B. Mathur. Residence time distribution of gas in spouted beds. *Can. J. Chem. Eng.*, **52** (1974), 150–155.

4 Computational fluid dynamic modeling of spouted beds

Xiaojun Bao, Wei Du, and Jian Xu

4.1 Introduction

As reviewed in Chapter 3, numerous theoretical and experimental studies have been carried out in recent decades in an attempt to model the hydrodynamics of spouted beds. Most of the early models are one-dimensional, with spout and annulus considered separately by assuming that some parameters are constant. In addition, these models, though useful as first approximations, are complex, or require parameters to be determined by experiments.

Thanks to the explosion of computational power, the advance of numerical algorithms, and deeper understanding of multiphase flow phenomena, computational fluid dynamics (CFD) modeling has become a powerful tool for understanding dense gas–solid two-phase flows in the recent past. The main advantage of CFD modeling is that a wide range of flow properties of the gas and solids may be predicted simultaneously without disturbing the flows.

Currently, there are two main CFD approaches: the Eulerian-Eulerian approach (two-fluid model, TFM), and the Eulerian-Lagrangian (discrete element method, DEM) approach. In the following two sections, the fundamentals and applications of these two approaches in hydrodynamic modeling of spouted beds are treated separately. In each section, the main aspects of the CFD approach are introduced briefly, followed by application to modeling of spouted bed hydrodynamics. Comparison of the CFD predictions with experimental results is also discussed.

4.2 Eulerian-Eulerian approach

In the Eulerian-Eulerian approach, the fluid and particulate phases are treated mathematically as interpenetrating continua. Several studies (listed in Table 4.1) have shown that this approach is capable of predicting gas-solids behavior in spouted beds. Because the volume of one phase cannot be occupied by the other, the concept of overlapping phases, each with its own volume fraction, is introduced. Volume fractions of the overlapping phases are assumed to be continuous functions of space and time, with their sum always equal to 1. The conservation equations have similar structure for each phase. Owing

Spouted and Spout-Fluid Beds: Fundamentals and Applications, eds. Norman Epstein and John R. Grace. Published by Cambridge University Press. © Cambridge University Press 2011.

Table 4.1. Eulerian simulations of spouted beds.

Investigators	Model closure	Software code	Contribution
Krzywanski et al.[2]		Author-developed code	Developed a multidimensional model to describe gas and particle dynamic behavior in a spouted bed.
Lu et al.[3–6]	Kinetic theory of granular flow; Gidaspow drag model with switch function	K-FIX; M-FIX	Viewed spout and annulus as interconnected regions. Incorporated kinetic-frictional constitutive model: kinetic theory of granular flow; friction stress was calculated by combining normal frictional stress model of Johnson et al.[7] and modified frictional shear viscosity model proposed by Syamlal et al.[8]; behavior of agglomerates of nanoparticles in spouted bed systems was simulated numerically.[6]
Du et al.[9–11]	Kinetic theory of granular flow	FLUENT	Found that the descriptions of interfacial forces and solid stresses play important roles in determining the hydrodynamics for spouting both coarse and fine particles.
Wang et al.[12]	Kinetic theory of granular flow	FLUENT	Found that actual pressure gradient (APG term) in conical spouted beds significantly influences static pressure profiles.
Shirvanian et al.[13]	Kinetic theory of granular flow; Gidaspow drag model	FLUENT	Developed three-dimensional (3D) simulation model to describe isothermal liquid–solid two-phase flow in a rectangular spouted bed; it was able to predict experimentally observed "choking."
Wu and Mujumdar[14]	Kinetic theory of granular flow; Gidaspow drag model with switch function	FLUENT	Described bubble formation and motion inside a 3D spout-fluid bed.
Gryczka et al.[15]	Kinetic theory of granular flow	FLUENT	Compared drag models of Schiller and Naumann,[16] Wen and Yu,[17] Syamlal and O'Brien,[18] Gidaspow et al.,[19] Koch and Hill,[20] van der Hoef et al.,[21] and Beetstra et al.[22] Better agreement with experiments was obtained by applying Schiller and Naumann[16] model.
Gryczka et al.[23]	Kinetic theory of granular flow	FLUENT	Pointed out that an appropriate drag model alone is not sufficient to fit the simulation results to the experimental findings; other contributions such as particle rotation are also important.
Bettega et al.[24–25]	Kinetic theory of granular flow	FLUENT	Obtained experimental data for a semicylindrical spouted bed; compared CFD simulations from a 3D simulation scheme; discussed influence of flat wall on solid behavior in semicylindrical vessel. Presented a numerical scaleup study of spouted beds. Verified that the scale-up relationships of He et al.[26] produced good numerical results.
Santos et al.[27]	Kinetic theory of granular flow	FLUENT	Simulated patterns of solids and gas flows in a spouted bed using 3D Eulerian multiphase model; 3D predictions showed better accuracy than 2D ones.
Duarte et al.[28]	Kinetic theory of granular flow; Gidaspow drag model	FLUENT	Simulated spouted beds of conical and conical-cylindrical geometries. Predicted pressure drops and particle velocities agreed well with experimental values.

to the continuum description of the particle phase, two-fluid models require additional closure laws to describe particle–particle and particle–fluid interactions. The Eulerian-Eulerian approach is often the first choice for simulation because of its lesser use of computational resources.

The full Eulerian-Eulerian approach includes (1) conservation equations of mass and momentum for each phase, with an interphase momentum transfer term; (2) closure of the equations, which requires proper description of interfacial forces, solids stress, and turbulence of the two phases; and (3) meshing of domain, discretization of equations, and solution algorithms.

4.2.1　Conservation equations of mass and momentum

Based on the general Eulerian multiphase model, governing equations of mass and momentum for spouted beds can be derived by assuming that (1) there is no mass transfer between spouting gas and bed particles, (2) the bed pressure gradient for stable spouting is constant, and (3) the densities of both phases are constant.

The partial differential TFM equations for describing particulate and fluid flows in fluidized beds presented by Gidaspow[1] are also commonly adopted for spouted beds. The basic conservation equations are the

volume fraction balance equation ($q = g, s$):

$$\sum_{q=1}^{n} \alpha_q = 1 \tag{4.1}$$

and the

mass conservation equation for phase ($q = g, s$):

$$\frac{\partial \alpha_q}{\partial t} + \nabla \cdot (\alpha_q \vec{v}_q) = 0. \tag{4.2}$$

The momentum conservation equation for phase q ($q = g, s$) is

$$\frac{\partial}{\partial t}(\alpha_q \rho_q \vec{v}_q) + \nabla \cdot (\alpha_q \rho_q \vec{v}_q \vec{v}_q) = -\alpha_q \nabla P + \nabla \cdot \bar{\bar{\tau}}_q$$

$$+ \sum_{p=1}^{n} \vec{R}_{pq} + \alpha_q \rho_q (\vec{F}_q + \vec{F}_{lift,q} + \vec{F}_{vm,q}), \tag{4.3}$$

where $\vec{F}_q$ is the external body force, $\vec{F}_{lift,q}$ the lift force, $\vec{F}_{vm,q}$ the virtual mass force, and $\vec{R}_{pq}$ the interaction force between the two phases. In most investigations, only drag and gravity are considered, with the lift force and virtual mass neglected.

4.2.2　Closure of the equations

4.2.2.1　Drag models

The drag force exerted on particles in fluid–solid systems is usually represented by the product of a momentum transfer coefficient, β, and the relative velocity ($\bar{v} - u$) between the two phases:

$$f_{drag} = \frac{3}{4} C_D \frac{\alpha_s \rho_g}{d_p} |\bar{v} - u| f(\alpha_g)(\bar{v} - u) = \beta(\bar{v} - u). \tag{4.4}$$

Ding and Gidaspow[29] employed the Ergun[30] equation for dense phase calculation and the Wen–Yu[17] equation for dilute phase calculation:

$$\begin{cases} \beta_{Ergun} = 150 \frac{\alpha_s^2 \mu_g}{\alpha_g d_p^2} + 1.75 \frac{\alpha_s \rho_g}{d_p} |\bar{v} - u|, \alpha_g < 0.8 \\ \beta_{Wen-Yu} = \frac{3}{4} C_D \frac{\alpha_s \rho_g}{d_p} |\bar{v} - u| \alpha_g^{-2.65}, \alpha_g \geq 0.8, \end{cases} \tag{4.5}$$

where the drag coefficient is expressed by

$$\begin{cases} C_D = \frac{24}{\alpha_g Re_p} [1 + 0.15(\alpha_g Re_p)^{0.687}], \text{ for } Re_p < 1000 \\ C_D = 0.44, \quad \text{ for } Re_p \geq 1000 \end{cases} \tag{4.6}$$

and

$$Re_p = \frac{\rho_g |\bar{v} - u| d_p}{\mu_g}. \tag{4.7}$$

To avoid discontinuity at the boundary ($\alpha_g = 0.8$, $\alpha_s = 0.2$) between these two equations, Lu et al.[4] introduced a switching function that gives a rapid transition from one to the other:

$$\varphi_{gs} = \frac{\arctan[150 \times 1.75(0.2 - \alpha_s)]}{\pi} + 0.5. \tag{4.8}$$

Thus, the drag model can be expressed as

$$\beta = (1 - \varphi_{gs})\beta_{Ergun} + \varphi_{gs}\beta_{Wen-Yu}. \tag{4.9}$$

4.2.2.2   Kinetic theory of granular flow

Granular flows can be classified into two distinct flow regimes: a rapidly shearing regime, in which stresses arise because of collisional or translational transfer of momentum, and a plastic or slowly shearing regime, in which stresses arise because of friction among particles in contact.[31,32] At high particle concentrations, individual particles interact with multiple neighbors through sustained contacts. Under such conditions, the normal forces and associated tangential frictional forces of sliding contacts are the major contributors to the particle stresses. At low particle concentrations, however, the stresses are caused mainly by particle–particle collisions. The physical basis for such an assumption may capture the two extreme limits of granular flow: a rapidly shearing flow regime in which kinetic contributions dominate, and a quasistatic flow regime in which friction dominates. With the introduction of the concepts of solid "pressure" and "viscosity," the well-known granular kinetic theory[33] is well established and is widely employed to estimate solid stresses.

Closure of the solid phase momentum equation requires a description of the solid phase stress. Analogous to the thermodynamic temperature for gases, a granular temperature Θ_s is introduced as a measure of particle velocity fluctuations:

$$\Theta_s = \frac{1}{3}(v_s'^2).$$

(4.10)

The granular temperature conservation equation is

$$\frac{3}{2}\left[\frac{\partial}{\partial t}(\rho_s\alpha_s\Theta_s) + \nabla\cdot(\rho_s\alpha_s\vec{v}\Theta_s)\right] = (-p_s\overline{\overline{I}} + \overline{\overline{\tau}}_s):\nabla\vec{v}_s - \nabla\cdot(k_{\Theta_s}\nabla\Theta_s) - v\Theta_s + \phi_{gs},$$

(4.11)

where $(-p_s\overline{\overline{I}} + \overline{\overline{\tau}}_s):\nabla\vec{v}_s$ is the generation of energy by the solid stress tensor, $k_{\Theta_s}\nabla\Theta_s$ is the diffusion of energy (k_{Θ_s} is the diffusion coefficient), $\nabla\Theta_s$ is the collisional dissipation of energy, $v\Theta_s = \dfrac{12(1 - e_{ss}^2)g_{0,ss}}{d_p\sqrt{\pi}}\rho_s\alpha_s^2\Theta_s^{3/2}$, and $\phi_{gs} = -3\beta\Theta_s$ is the energy exchange between the fluid and solid phases.

The kinetic solid pressure is given[33] by

$$P_s = \alpha_s\rho_s\Theta_s + 2\rho_s(1 + e_{ss})\alpha_s^2 g_{0,ss}\Theta_s,$$

(4.12)

where $g_{0,ss}$ is the radial distribution function expressed[34] as

$$g_{0,ss} = \left[1 - \left(\frac{\alpha_s}{\alpha_{s,\max}}\right)^{\frac{1}{3}}\right]^{-1}$$

(4.13)

and $\alpha_{s,\max}$ is the maximum particle volume fraction.

The solid bulk viscosity is given[33] by

$$\lambda_s = \frac{4}{3}\alpha_s^2\rho_s d_p g_{0,ss}(1 + e_{ss})\sqrt{\frac{\Theta_s}{\pi}},$$

(4.14)

the solid shear viscosity by[29]

$$\mu_s = \frac{4}{5}\alpha_s^2\rho_s d_p g_{0,ss}(1 + e_{ss})\sqrt{\frac{\Theta_s}{\pi}} + \frac{10\rho_s d_p\sqrt{\pi\Theta_s}}{96(1 + e_{ss})g_{0,ss}}\left[1 + \frac{4}{5}g_{0,ss}\alpha_s(1 + e_{ss})\right]^2,$$

(4.15)

and the dissipation fluctuating energy by[35]

$$\gamma_s = 3\left(1 - e_{ss}^2\right)\alpha_s^2\rho_s g_{0,ss}\Theta_s\left[\frac{4}{d_p}\sqrt{\frac{\Theta_s}{\pi}} - \nabla v\right],$$

(4.16)

where e_{ss} is the interparticle coefficient of restitution, d_p is the particle diameter, and $g_{0,ss}$ is a radial distribution function.

If solid frictional stresses are considered, the solid frictional stress P_f is added to the stress predicted by the kinetic theory of granular flow:

$$\begin{cases} P_s = P_{kinetic} + P_f \\ \mu_s = \mu_{kinetic} + \mu_f. \end{cases} \tag{4.17}$$

The Schaeffer model,[36] developed for very dense gas–solid systems, is used to predict the frictional stress P_f, giving

$$P_f = A(\alpha_s - \alpha_{s,min})^n \tag{4.18}$$

and

$$\mu_f = \frac{P_f \cdot \sin \phi}{\alpha_s \sqrt{\frac{1}{6}\left[\left(\frac{\partial u}{\partial x} - \frac{\partial v}{\partial y}\right)^2 + \left(\frac{\partial v}{\partial y}\right)^2 + \left(\frac{\partial u}{\partial x}\right)^2\right] + \frac{1}{4}\left(\frac{\partial u}{\partial y} + \frac{\partial v}{\partial x}\right)^2}}, \tag{4.19}$$

where ϕ is the internal friction angle of particles. This value can be taken to be 28.5° for glass beads.[7] A and n are constants.

4.2.3 Meshing, discretization, and solving algorithm

Because most spouted bed columns have conical bases, some researchers[12] have meshed the domain with unstructured grids, whereas Lu et al.[4] employed a body-fitted coordinate method and reexpressed the equations of continuity and motion for the gas and solid phases.

Discretization in space produces a system of ordinary differential equations for unsteady problems and algebraic equations for steady problems. Implicit or semi-implicit methods are generally used to integrate the ordinary differential equations, producing a set of (usually) nonlinear algebraic equations. The most common discretization methods are the finite volume method (FVM), finite element method (FEM), finite difference method (FDM), and boundary element method (BEM).[37,38] The FVM is the classical approach, used most often in commercial software and research codes. Through the FVM, the governing equations are solved on discrete control volumes.[39,40]

As seen in Table 4.1, commercial CFD packages such as FLUENT, CFX, and MFIX, which solve sets of complex nonlinear mathematical expressions based on the fundamental equations of fluid flow, heat, and mass transport, are widely adopted for computation. The algebraic equations are solved iteratively using complex computer algorithms embedded within these CFD software packages. The Semi-Implicit Method for Pressure-Linked Equations (SIMPLE) algorithm, developed by the Spalding group, is widely used to solve the momentum equations. Details of this algorithm are discussed in several CFD books, such as that by Patankar.[41]

4.2.4 Comparison with experimental results

Owing to the continuum description of the particle phase, the TFM approach requires additional closure laws to describe particle–particle and particle–wall interactions. In the hydrodynamic modeling of spouted beds by the TFM approach, considerable attention has been paid to closure of the equations, especially to the description of the solid stress. The Lu group[5] viewed the spout and annulus as two interconnected regions, and constitutive equations describing the particulate solids pressure, viscosity, and elasticity moduli were implemented into a hydrodynamic simulation program. They later incorporated a kinetic-frictional constitutive model for dense assemblies of solids[3,4] that treated the kinetic and frictional stresses of particles additively. The kinetic stress was modeled using the kinetic theory of granular flow, whereas the friction stress combines the normal frictional stress model proposed by Johnson et al.[7] and the modified frictional shear viscosity model of Syamlal et al.[8] Interfacial forces other than drag are less significant, and can usually be neglected. Du et al.[9–11] showed that for both coarse and fine particle spouting, the descriptions of interfacial forces and solid stresses play important roles in determining the hydrodynamics. Gryczka et al.[15,23] pointed out that the application of each drag model is limited to a specific range of particle Reynolds numbers. The search for an appropriate drag model alone is not sufficient for an accurate simulation, as other contributions, such as particle rotation, also play a role.[23] Simulation results of Wang et al.[12] showed that the actual pressure gradient (APG) term in conical spouted beds, introduced as the default gravity term, plus an empirical axial solid-phase source term, had the greatest influence on static pressure profiles, and that the introduction of this term can improve the CFD simulation for gas–solid conical spouted beds. On the basis of the foregoing developments, more and more researchers have begun to use this Eulerian-Eulerian model to investigate new structures and scaleup of spouted beds (Chapter 17). These works are listed in Table 4.1.

Although numerical simulation is a useful tool to obtain detailed forecasting of spouting behavior without disturbing the flow, it is important to compare numerical predictions with corresponding experimental results.[42]

4.2.4.1 Particle velocity flow fields

Lu et al.[4] used the Eulerian-Eulerian approach with a kinetic-frictional constitutive model incorporated to simulate spouted beds. The column geometries and particle properties matched those studied experimentally by He et al.[43,44] and San José et al.[45] to facilitate comparison with experimental data.

Figure 4.1 shows the distributions of instantaneous particle concentrations and velocities in a spouted bed for a spouting gas velocity of 12 m/s. The flow patterns in the spouted bed appear to be qualitatively well reproduced: in the spout zone, the particle concentration is low and the particle velocity is high, particles move vertically upward and radially toward the jet axis. Particles are carried by gas to the top of the spout, forming a fountain from which particles cascade downward in the outer region. Particle concentration in the fountain is higher than in the spout, but lower than in the annulus. In the annular zone, particles are predicted to move downward and radially inward with the highest particle concentration and the lowest particle velocity, in agreement with experimental observations.

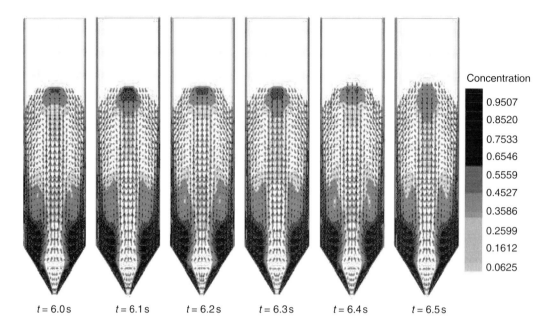

Concentration

0.9507
0.8520
0.7533
0.6546
0.5559
0.4527
0.3586
0.2599
0.1612
0.0625

$t = 6.0\,$s $t = 6.1\,$s $t = 6.2\,$s $t = 6.3\,$s $t = 6.4\,$s $t = 6.5\,$s

Figure 4.1. Instantaneous volumetric concentration and velocity of particles predicted by Lu et al.[4] for an inlet gas jet velocity of 12.0 m/s. ($d_p = 1$ mm, $\rho_p = 1200$ kg/m^3, $\rho_g = 1.2$ kg/m^3, $D_c = 0.19$ m, $D_i = 0.02$ m, $\theta = 60°$.)

4.2.4.2   Particle velocities

Radial profiles of time-average vertical particle velocities simulated by Lu et al.[4] are shown in Figures 4.2 and 4.3, in comparison with experimental results of He et al.[43,44] measured by optical fiber probes. There is reasonable agreement between computational predictions and experimental results. The vertical particle velocity is seen to decrease with height at both superficial gas velocities. In both cases, the vertical particle velocity decreases from the axis in the spout and becomes negative in the annulus.

Figure 4.4 shows simulated[4] and experimental[45] distributions of axial particle velocities in a conical spouted bed for an inlet gas jet velocity of 8.3 m/s. The simulated results are in good agreement with the experimental ones. The particle velocity reaches a minimum somewhere in the annular zone. Figure 4.4 indicates that the magnitude of the axial particle velocity is highest close to the axis, and decreases with distance from the axis.

Time-averaged horizontal particle velocities predicted by Lu et al.[4] are plotted in Figure 4.5. Both the simulated and measured horizontal particle velocities tend to be inward at low heights in the spout zone, but outward at a higher level.

4.2.4.3   Voidage

Figures 4.6 and 4.7 show simulated[4] and experimental[44] profiles of time-averaged voidage for superficial gas velocities of 0.59 and 0.70 m/s, respectively. Comparison

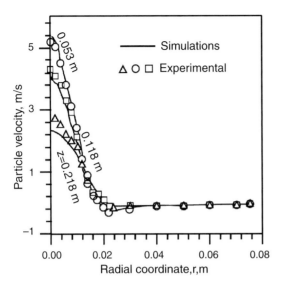

Figure 4.2. Comparison between time-mean vertical particle velocities predicted by Lu et al.[4] with those measured experimentally by He et al.[44] at $U = 0.59$ m/s. ($d_p = 1.41$ mm, $\rho_p = 2503$ kg/m³, $\rho_g = 1.2$ kg/m³, $D_c = 0.152$ m, $D_i = 0.019$ m, $\theta = 60°$.)

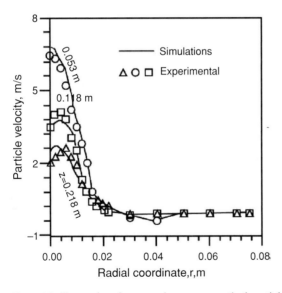

Figure 4.3. Comparison between time-mean vertical particle velocities computed by Lu et al.[4] and experimental measurements by He et al.[44] at $U = 0.70$ m/s. ($d_p = 1.41$ mm, $\rho_p = 2503$ kg/m³, $\rho_g = 1.2$ kg/m³, $D_c = 0.152$ m, $D_i = 0.019$ m, $\theta = 60°$.)

of Figures 4.6 and 4.7 indicates that the local voidage increases slightly with increasing superficial gas velocity throughout the entire spout and annulus zones. The simulation results show that the local voidage decreases with increasing height and with increasing distance from the axis. The time-averaged voidage in the annulus zone is slightly higher than at minimum fluidization.

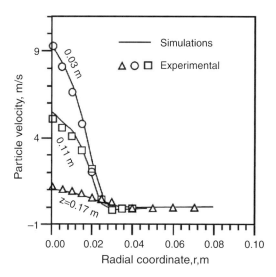

Figure 4.4. Computed time-mean vertical particle velocities in a conical spouted bed[4] compared with San José et al.[45] experimental data for an inlet gas jet velocity of 8.3 m/s. ($d_p = 1.41$ mm, $\rho_p = 2503$ kg/m^3, $\rho_g = 1.2$ kg/m^3, $D_c = 0.152$ m, $D_i = 0.019$ m, $\theta = 60°$.)

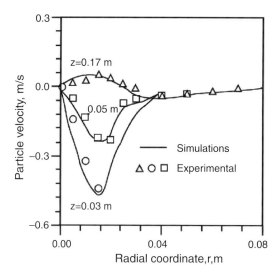

Figure 4.5. Computed time-mean horizontal particle velocities in a conical spouted bed[4] compared with San José et al.[45] experimental data for an inlet gas jet velocity of 8.3 m/s. ($d_p = 1.41$ mm, $\rho_p = 2503$ kg/m^3, $\rho_g = 1.2$ kg/m^3, $D_c = 0.152$ m, $D_i = 0.019$ m, $\theta = 60°$.)

4.2.4.4   Other findings

1. In CFD modeling of gas–solid two-phase flows, the drag force is the most important force acting on particles. Thus it has a critical impact on CFD predictions of dense gas–solid two-phase systems in spouted beds. Du et al.[9] assessed several widely used drag models and incorporated some of them into CFD simulations of spouted beds.

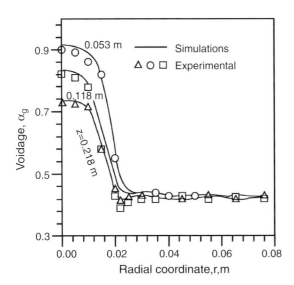

Figure 4.6. Computed voidage distributions in a spouted bed[4] compared with the experimental data of He et al.[43] at $U = 0.59$ m/s. ($d_p = 1.41$ mm, $\rho_p = 2503$ kg/m^3, $\rho_g = 1.2$ kg/m^3, $D_c = 0.152$ m, $D_i = 0.019$ m, $\theta = 60°$.)

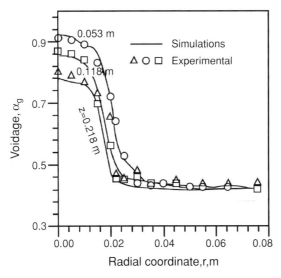

Figure 4.7. Computed voidage distributions in a spouted bed[4] compared with the experimental data of He et al.[43] at $U = 0.70$ m/s. ($d_p = 1.41$ mm, $\rho_p = 2503$ kg/m^3, $\rho_g = 1.2$ kg/m^3, $D_c = 0.152$ m, $D_i = 0.019$ m, $\theta = 60°$.)

It was shown that different drag models led to significant differences in simulations. Among the drag models tested, the Gidaspow model[1] gave the best agreement with experimental observations, both qualitatively and quantitatively. By comparing different drag models, Gryczka et al.[15] found better agreement with experiments based on the Schiller and Naumann model.[16]

Table 4.2. DEM simulations of spouted beds reported in the literature.

Investigators	Model closure	Software code	Contribution
Kawaguchi et al.[50,51]	Newton's 3rd law for coupling between phases	Author-developed	Proposed first Eulerian-Lagrangian approach for spouted beds; obtained typical spouted bed flow patterns.
Takeuchi et al.[49,52,53]		Author-developed	Simulated 3D cylindrical-conical spouted beds. Proposed new method for treating boundary conditions.
Zhong et al.[54]	k-ε turbulent model for gas motion	Author-developed	Simulated turbulent motions of the gas and particles by treating the two phases separately. Particle motion modeled by DEM and gas motion by k-ε model.
Zhao et al.[55,56]	Low Reynolds $k - \varepsilon$ turbulence model for fluid phase	Author-developed	Simulated flow of particles in 2D spouted bed with draft plates with a low Reynolds number k-ε turbulence model for the fluid phase.
Swasdisevi et al.[57]		Author-developed	Simulated aerodynamics of particles and gas flow in slot-rectangular spouted bed with draft plates. Calculated U_{ms} and pressure drop agreed well with correlations of Kalwar et al.[58]
Limtrakul et al.[59]		Author-developed	By combining DEM and mass transfer models, investigated local mass transfer in gas–solid catalytic spouted bed reactor for decomposing ozone; results agreed well with the experimental results of Rovero et al.[60]

2. Particle–particle collisions have been found to have a significant effect on particle motion in the spout zone and almost no effect in the annular zone.[4,10]
3. The computations indicate a major influence of the frictional stress model and parameter selection on modeling dense solids flow.[4,10]

4.3   Eulerian-Lagrangian approach

In the Eulerian-Lagrangian approach, the fluid phase is treated as a continuum by solving the time-averaged Navier-Stokes equations, whereas the dispersed phase is solved by tracking a large number of individual particles through the computed flow field, not requiring additional closure equations.[46] Table 4.2 lists previous computations of this type of model for spouted bed hydrodynamics. The dispersed phase can exchange momentum, mass, and energy with the fluid phase, and the two phases are coupled by interphase forces. The DEM approach offers a more natural way to simulate gas–solid flows, with each individual particle tracked. However, it is much more computationally demanding, especially as the number of particles simulated becomes large.

The framework of the collision model includes hard- and soft-sphere approaches. In hard-sphere models, trajectories of particles are determined by momentum-conserving binary collisions. The interactions between particles are assumed to be pairwise additive and instantaneous. In the simulation the collisions are processed one by one according to the order in which they occur. For a not-too-dense phase, hard-sphere models are considerably faster than soft-sphere models. Hard-sphere models have been used for spout-fluid beds by Link et al.[47,48] For systems of dense phase or inelastic particles, soft-sphere models must be used. In these more complex situations, the particles may interact via short- or long-range forces, and the trajectories are determined by integrating the Newtonian equations of motion. Soft-sphere models use a fixed time step; consequently, the particles are allowed to overlap slightly. The contact forces are subsequently calculated from the deformation history of the contact using a contact force scheme. Soft-sphere models in the literature differ from each other mainly with respect to the contact force schemes used. Most current DEM simulations of spouted beds are based on soft-sphere models.

As pointed out by Takeuchi et al.,[49] there are two problems in DEM simulation of spouted beds. One is that it is extremely difficult to establish stable spouting, regardless of adjustments of related parameters, such as particle diameter, gas velocity, and nozzle-to-bed size ratio. The other is the fact that two-dimensional simulation of spouted beds is more difficult to converge for the fluid phase, which makes it difficult to select a proper turbulence model to describe the central jet.

Kawaguchi et al.[50,51] first proposed an Eulerian-Lagrangian approach to simulate spouted beds, and typical spouted bed flow patterns were obtained. Takeuchi et al.[49,52] further simulated a spouted bed in three dimensions in a cylindrical coordinate system; the predictions showed typical characteristics of spouted beds, in good agreement with experimental results. In later work, Takeuchi et al.[53] proposed a new method for the treatment of the boundary conditions that satisfies both the continuity and momentum-balance requirements for the gas phase in three-dimensional gas flow along the cone surface.

To overcome the problem of turbulence modeling, Zhong et al.[54] simulated the turbulent motion of the gas and particles by treating the two phases separately, with particle motion modeled by DEM and gas motion by the $k - \varepsilon$ turbulent model. Similarly, Zhao et al.[55,56] simulated the motion of particles in a two-dimensional spouted bed with draft plates, using a low Reynolds number $k - \varepsilon$ turbulence model for the fluid phase. Their simulation results were in good agreement with experimental data.

The application of spouted beds as chemical reactors is of increasing interest, both experimentally and for CFD studies. Several authors simulated spouted bed reactors by DEM models coupled with chemical reactions. This work is also summarized in Table 4.2.

4.3.1   Numerical approaches

In the Eulerian-Lagrangian approach, the motion of individual particles is predicted by calculating the contact force on each particle, whereas the gas flow field is based on the continuity and Navier-Stokes equations.

4.3.1.1   Discrete approach for particle motions

In the DEM approach, the translational and rotational motions of particle i are given by

$$m_i \frac{d\vec{v}_i}{dt} = \sum_j \left(\vec{F}_{n,ij} + \vec{F}_{t,ij} \right) + m_i \vec{g} + \vec{F}_{drag,i} \qquad (4.20)$$

and

$$I_i \frac{d\vec{\varpi}_i}{dt} = \sum_j \left(\vec{r}_i \times \vec{F}_{t,ij} - \vec{M}_{ij} \right), \qquad (4.21)$$

where $\vec{v}_i$, $\vec{\varpi}_i$, I_i, and $\vec{F}_{drag,i}$ are the linear velocity vector, angular velocity vector, moment of inertia, and drag force, respectively, of particle i, whereas $\vec{F}_{n,ij}$, $\vec{F}_{t,ij}$, and $\vec{M}_{ij}$ are the normal contact force, tangential contact force, and rolling-resistance torque, respectively, of particle i with neighboring particle j. The normal and tangential contact forces are given, respectively, by

$$\vec{F}_{n,ij} = - \left[k_n \delta_{n,ij} + \eta_n \left(\vec{v}_{ij} \cdot \vec{n}_{ij} \right) \right] \vec{n}_{ij} \qquad (4.22)$$

and

$$\vec{F}_{t,ij} = -\min \left[k_t \delta_{t,ij} + \eta_t \left(\vec{v}_{ij} \cdot \vec{s}_{ij} \right), \mu \left(\vec{F}_{n,ij} \right) \right] \vec{s}_{ij}, \qquad (4.23)$$

where $\vec{n}$ and $\vec{s}$ are normal and tangential unit vectors, and δ_n and δ_t are particle displacements in the normal and tangential directions. Parameters k_n and k_t are the spring stiffness of normal force and tangential forces, respectively; η_n and η_t are the coefficients of dissipation in the normal and tangential directions.

The drag force exerted on particle i can be described by

$$\vec{F}_{f,i} = \left[\frac{\beta}{1 - \varepsilon} \left(\vec{u} - \vec{v}_p \right) - \nabla P \right] V_p. \qquad (4.24)$$

Here $\vec{u}$ is gas velocity, P the gas pressure, $\vec{v}_p$ the particle velocity, V_p the volume of each particle ($= \pi d_p^3 / 6$), and β is the drag coefficient predicted by the Ergun equation[30] for the dense regime and the Wen–Yu equation[17] for more dilute flow, as given by Eqs. (4.5) to (4.7).

The relative rotation between contacting particles or between a particle and a wall in contact produces a rolling resistance because of the elastic hysteresis loss or time-dependent deformation. Because particles circulate internally in spouted beds, they may have a great rolling velocity and, therefore, a significant rolling resistance. The torque resistance expression is given[61] by:

$$M_{ij} = -\mu_r (r_i \vec{\varpi}_i) \left| F_{ij}^n \right|. \qquad (4.25)$$

However, there exists a maximum moment:

$$|M_i| = \left|\sum_j M_{ij}\right| \le I_i \bar{\varpi}_i / \Delta t. \tag{4.26}$$

4.3.1.2   Continuum approach for fluid motion

The locally averaged equation of continuity and equations of motion are used to compute the motion of the gas phase, given, respectively, by

$$\frac{\partial}{\partial t}(\alpha_g \rho_g) + \frac{\partial}{\partial x_i}(\alpha_g \rho_g u_j) = 0 \tag{4.27}$$

and

$$\frac{\partial(\alpha_g \rho_g u_i)}{\partial t} + \frac{\partial}{\partial x_j}(\alpha_g \rho_g u_i u_j) = \frac{\partial}{\partial x_j}\left[\alpha_g(\mu_g + \mu_t)\left(\frac{\partial u_i}{\partial x_j} + \frac{\partial u_j}{\partial x_j}\right)\right]$$
$$- \alpha_g \frac{\partial p}{\partial x_i} - f_d + \rho_g \alpha_g g. \tag{4.28}$$

Here α_g, ρ_g, μ_g, μ_t, and f_{drag} are the local voidage, gas density, gas viscosity, turbulent viscosity, and fluid drag force, respectively. The drag force is again obtained from the Ergun equation[30] and the Wen–Yu equation,[17] depending on the voidage, expressed by Eqs. (4.5) to (4.7).

The solution procedure for the DEM approach differs from that for the TFM approach in the meshing and solving the pressure and velocity fields. Unlike TFM, in DEM computations most researchers – such as Kawaguchi et al.[50] and Zhong et al.[54] – have employed rectangular grids for tapered-wall regions so the grids near the gas entrance are large enough to contain a sufficient number of particles.

Kawaguchi et al.,[50] Takeuchi et al.,[49] and Zhong et al.[54] solved for the fluid phase using the SIMPLE method.[62] Pressure–velocity coupling can be based on the Synthesize Modes and Correlate (SMAC) method, which has been applied successfully in simulating other multiphase turbulent flows.[63]

4.3.2   Comparison with experimental results

4.3.2.1   Flow field

Figure 4.8 shows the distribution of time-averaged particle velocity reported by Kawaguchi et al.[50] for a spouted bed with exactly the same geometry and gas–solid properties as in the experiments of He et al.[43,44] The three characteristic regions – spout, fountain, and annulus – can be clearly observed. Figure 4.9 presents the time-average spout shape and vector field of the solids flow predicted by Takeuchi et al.[49] The spout radius is taken to correspond to the radial distance at which the time-average axial particle velocity is zero. The spout diameter varies from 0.01 m at the nozzle exit to 0.02 m at the bed surface. The predicted spout shape corresponds to one of the possible spout

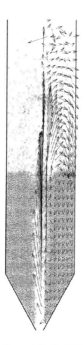

Figure 4.8. Particle velocity vectors predicted by Kawaguchi et al.[50] for a spouted bed at $U/U_{ms} =$ 1.3. ($d_p = 3$ mm, $\rho_p = 2500$ kg/m^3, $\rho_g = 1.2$ kg/m^3, $D_c = 0.152$ m, $D_i = 0.019$ m, $\theta = 60°$, $U_{ms} = 1.46$ m/s.)

shapes identified by Mathur and Epstein.[64] In the region from the nozzle exit to $z = 0.05$ m, particles are entrained strongly toward the spout axis with high velocities in the longitudinal direction, caused by the potential core of gas near the nozzle exit.

Figure 4.10 compares the spout shape computed by Kawaguchi et al.[50] with the experimental measurements of He et al.[43,44] Because the sizes of the particles in the experiments and in the simulation differed, there is some discrepancy. For example, the diameter of the spout in the cylindrical region obtained experimentally[43] is smaller than predicted.[50]

4.3.2.2   Particle velocities in spout

Figure 4.11 shows radial distributions of the vertical component of particle velocity at eight different heights in the spout computed by Kawaguchi et al.[50] Experimental results of He et al.[43] also appear in the figure. With increasing height, the particle velocity decreases along the central axis, but increases at the periphery of the spout. Qualitatively, the experimental results agree well with the simulation results, except for $z > 0.268$ m. The radius of the spout at which the particle velocity becomes zero did not depend much on z in the experiments, whereas it increased with height in the CFD simulations. The quantitative difference in the spout diameter between the simulation and the experimental results arises, at least in part, from different particle sizes.

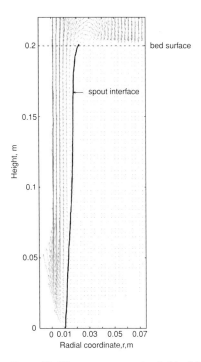

Figure 4.9. Time average vector field of the solids flow and spout shape in a flat-bottomed spouted bed predicted by Takeuchi et al.[49] ($d_p = 2.4$ mm, $\rho_p = 2650$ kg/m^3, $\rho_g = 1.2$ kg/m^3, $D_c = 0.14$ m, $D_i = 0.02$ m, $\theta = 180°$, $U = 1.0$ m/s $= 1.08U_{ms}$.)

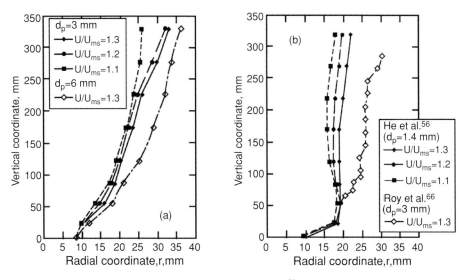

Figure 4.10. Spout shapes: (a) calculated by Kawaguchi et al.[50]; (b) measured experimentally by He et al.[44] and Roy et al.[66] ($\rho_p = 2500$ kg/m^3, $\rho_g = 1.2$ kg/m^3, $D_c = 0.152$ m, $D_i = 0.019$ m, $\theta = 60°$, $U_{ms} = 1.46$ m/s.)

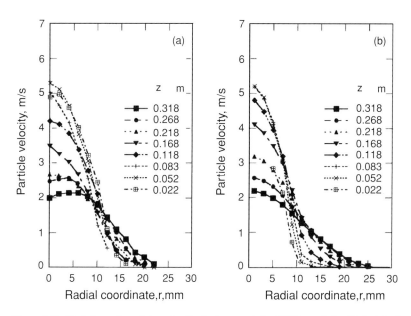

Figure 4.11. Variation of particle velocity in the spout for $U/U_{ms} = 1.1$ with height from the bottom of the vessel: (a) from experimental measurements of He et al.[43] for $d_p = 1.41$ mm, $\rho_p = 2503$ kg/m^3, $\rho_g = 1.2$ kg/m^3, $D_c = 0.152$ m, $D_i = 0.019$ m, $\theta = 60°$; (b) predicted by DEM model of Kawaguchi et al.[50] for $d_p = 3$ mm, $\rho_p = 2500$ kg/m^3, $\rho_g = 1.2$ kg/m^3, $D_c = 0.152$ m, $D_i = 0.019$ m, $\theta = 60°$, $U_{ms} = 1.46$ m/s.

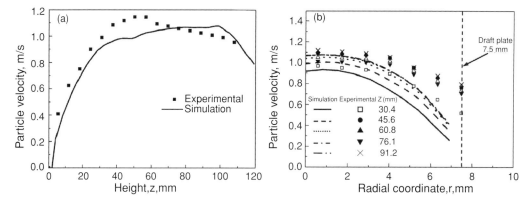

Figure 4.12. Experimental (PIV) measurements compared with simulated (DEM) profiles of particle vertical velocities in the spout[55]: (a) vertical profile along spout axis; (b) lateral profile at various bed heights. ($d_p = 2.03$ mm, $\rho_p = 2380$ kg/m^3, $\rho_g = 1.2$ kg/m^3, $D_c = 0.152$ m, $D_i = 0.009$ m, $U = 1.58$ m/s.)

Zhao et al.[55] simulated the particle motion in a two-dimensional spouted bed (2DSB) with draft plates. Figure 4.12 compares experimental and simulated profiles of vertical particle velocities in the spout. DEM simulation is seen to provide good predictions of the particle vertical velocity profile along the column axis. Particle imaging velocimetry (PIV) measured and DEM-simulated initial particle velocities in the lower part of the

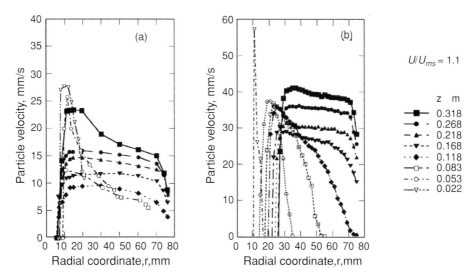

Figure 4.13. Particle velocity profiles in the annulus, where z is the height from the bottom of the vessel: (a) from experimental measurements of He et al.[43] for $d_p = 1.41$ mm, $\rho_p = 2503$ kg/m³, $\rho_g = 1.2$ kg/m³, $D_c = 0.152$ m, $D_i = 0.019$ m, $\theta = 60°$; (b) predicted by the DEM model of Kawaguchi et al.[50] for $d_p = 3$ mm, $\rho_p = 2500$ kg/m³, $\rho_g = 1.2$ kg/m³, $D_c = 0.152$ m, $D_i = 0.019$ m, $\theta = 60°$, $U_{ms} = 1.46$ m/s.

spout agree well. This can be attributed to the application of a turbulence model to describe the jet near the inlet nozzle. The radial profiles from both the DEM and PIV methods indicate that the particle vertical velocities adjacent to the draft plates are lower than the local average value. As the height coordinate, z, increases from 30.4 to 91.2 mm, the particle vertical velocity increases. The difference between the DEM and PIV results near the draft plates may result from overestimation of the wall friction.

4.3.2.3   Particle velocities in annulus

Figure 4.13 shows simulated[50] and experimental[44] radial distributions of the vertical component of particle velocity in the annulus. Note that the downward velocity components are plotted as positive values in this figure, with two different ordinate scales. In the experimental data, the particle velocity profiles are nearly flat in the cylindrical region, but decrease in the neighborhood of the wall and in the near-boundary region of the spout. The reduction of the particle downward velocity near the wall is caused by friction between the particles and the wall. Particle downward velocity increases with height owing to particle entrainment from the annulus to the spout.[44] The predicted particle downward velocity increases with height more than was found experimentally. This can be attributed to the reduction of the cross-sectional area of the annulus with increasing height, because, as shown in Figure 4.10, the spout diameter increases with height.

Radial profiles of axial solids velocities in the annulus predicted by Takeuchi et al.[49] are compared in Figure 4.14 with experimental data of Tsuji et al.,[65] measured in a

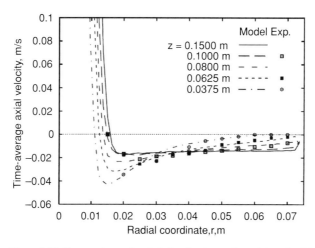

Figure 4.14. Comparison of radial distributions of particle velocities in the annulus at different heights above nozzle exit: CFD predictions are from Takeuchi et al.;[49] experimental results are from Tsuji et al.[65] ($d_p = 2.4$ mm, $\rho_p = 2650$ kg/m³, $\rho_g = 1.2$ kg/m³, $D_c = 0.14$ m, $D_i = 0.02$ m, $\theta = 180°$, $U = 1.0$ m/s $= 1.08 U_{ms}$.)

flat-bottomed vessel of column diameter 0.14 m and nozzle diameter 20 mm. At $z = 0.0375$ and 0.0625 m, the particles near the nozzle exit are strongly entrained to the core of the spout. Particles at $z = 0.10$ and 0.15 m have flat velocity profiles in the annulus. These profiles suggest increased downward particle flow at higher levels in the annulus. The predicted descent velocities are in good agreement with the experimental data.

4.4   Concluding remarks

The characteristic patterns of spouted beds can be well reproduced by both the Eulerian-Eulerian and the Eulerian-Lagrangian approaches. Parameters such as spout diameter, minimum spouting velocity and voidage profile all show reasonably good agreement with experimental data. This indicates that CFD modeling can serve as an important tool for predicting gas and solid behavior in spouted beds.

The Eulerian-Eulerian approach is usually the first choice for simulation because of its lesser use of computational resources. The successful application of this approach depends mainly on closure of the momentum equations, as the simulation is sensitive to the APG, drag coefficient, interparticle coefficient of restitution and solid friction stresses. To describe the solid-phase stresses, the kinetic theory of granular flow has been widely adopted.

Although more computational capacity is required, the Eulerian-Lagrangian approach offers a more physically satisfying way to simulate gas–solid flows, with each individual particle tracked in the simulation. It can be applied readily for particle tracking – for example, for residence time and particle circulation studies.

An important challenge in CFD studies of spouted beds is to describe properly the inherent turbulence for both the solid and gas phases, especially for the spout region.

Further fundamental and experimental studies on the kinematic properties of the two phases are needed to improve the accuracy of the CFD models.

Chapter-specific nomenclature

A	experimental constant in Schaeffer model, N/m^2
D_c	column diameter, m
d_p	particle diameter, m
e_{ss}	coefficient of restitution of particle
F_{drag}	drag force, N
$F_{lift,q}$	lift force, N
$F_{n,ij}$	normal contact force, N
F_q	external body force, N
$F_{t,ij}$	tangential contact force, N
$F_{vm,q}$	virtual mass force, N
$g_{0,ss}$	radial distribution function
I	turbulence intensity
I_i	moment of inertia, kg m/s
k_n	spring stiffness of normal force
k_t	spring stiffness of tangential force
$k_{\Theta s}$	energy diffusion coefficient, J/m^{2}s^2
M_{ij}	rolling resistant torque, N
n	experimental constant in Schaeffer model
P_f	solid pressure predicted by friction model, N/m^2
$P_{kinetic}$	solid pressure predicted by kinetic theory, N/m^2
P_s	solid pressure, N/m^2
R_{pq}	interaction force between phases, N
v	vertical particle velocity, m/s
v_q	phase q velocity, m/s
v'_s	particle velocity fluctuation, m/s

Greek letters

α_g	gas volume fraction
α_q	volume fraction of phase q
α_s	solids volume fraction
$\alpha_{s,max}$	maximum solids volume fraction
β	fluid-particle interaction coefficient, kg/m^{3}s
β_{Ergun}	fluid-particle interaction coefficient in Ergun equation, kg/m^{3}s
β_{Wen-Yu}	fluid-particle interaction coefficient in Wen–Yu equation, kg/m^{3}s
γ_s	dissipation of granular energy, kg/m^{3}s
δ_n	particle displacement in normal direction, m
δ_t	particle displacement in tangential direction, m

η_n	coefficients of dissipation in normal direction, kg/s
η_t	coefficients of dissipation in tangential direction, kg/s
Θ_s	granular temperature, m^2/s^2
λ_s	solid bulk viscosity, Pa s
μ_f	solid viscosity predicted by friction model, Pa s
μ_g	gas viscosity, Pa s
$\mu_{kinetic}$	solid viscosity predicted by kinetic theory, Pa s
μ_s	solid shear viscosity, Pa s
μ_t	turbulent viscosity, Pa s
ρ_g	gas density, kg/m^3
ρ_q	density of phase q, kg/m^3
ρ_s	particle density, kg/m^3
τ_s	solid stress tensor, N/m^2
τ_q	Reynolds stress tensor, N/m^2
ϕ	internal friction angle, degrees
φ_{gs}	switching function in Gidaspow model[1,4]
ω	angular velocity vector
ϕ_{gs}	energy exchange between fluid or solid phase, J/s

Subscripts

g	gas
i, j	individual particle
$kinetic$	kinetic theory
max	maximum
min	minimum
n	normal direction
q	phase (gas or solid)
r	radial direction
s	solid phase
t	tangential direction
z	axial direction
r	radial direction

References

1. D. Gidaspow. *Multiphase Flow and Fluidization: Continuum and Kinetic Theory Descriptions* (London: Academic Press, 1994).
2. R. S. Krzywanski, N. Epstein, and B. D. Bowen. Multi-dimensional model of a spouted bed. *Can. J. Chem. Eng.*, **70** (1992), 858–872.
3. Y. He, G. Zhao, J. Bouillard, and H. Lu. Numerical simulations of the effect of conical dimension on the hydrodynamic behaviour in spouted beds. *Can. J. Chem. Eng.*, **82** (2004), 20–29.

4. H. Lu, Y. He, W. Liu, J. Ding, D. Gidaspow, and J. Bouillard. Computer simulations of gas-solid flow in spouted beds using kinetic-frictional stress model of granular flow. *Chem. Eng. Sci.*, **59** (2004), 865–878.

5. H. Lu, Y. Song, Y. Li, Y. He, and J. Bouillard. Numerical simulations of hydrodynamic behaviour in spouted beds. *Chem. Eng. Res. Des.*, **79** (2001), 593–599.

6. S. Y. Wang, Y. R. He, H. L. Lu, J. X. Zheng, G. D. Liu, and Y. L. Ding. Numerical simulations of flow behaviour of agglomerates of nano-size particles in bubbling and spouted beds with an agglomerate-based approach. *Food and Bioprod. Proc.*, **85** (2007), 231–240.

7. P. C. Johnson, P. Nott, and R. Jackson. Frictional-collisional equations of motion for particulate flows and their application to chutes. *J. Fluid Mech.*, **210** (1990), 501–535.

8. M. Syamlal, W. Rogers, and T. J. O'Brien. MFIX Documentation. US Department of Energy, Federal Energy Technology Center, 1993.

9. W. Du, X. Bao, J. Xu, and W. Wei. Computational fluid dynamics (CFD) modeling of spouted bed: Assessment of drag coefficient correlations. *Chem. Eng. Sci.*, **61** (2006), 1401–1420.

10. W. Du, X. Bao, J. Xu, and W. Wei. Computational fluid dynamics (CFD) modeling of spouted bed: Influence of frictional stress, maximum packing limit and coefficient of restitution of particles. *Chem. Eng. Sci.*, **61** (2006), 4558–4570.

11. W. Du, W. Wei, J. Xu, Y. Fan, and X. Bao. Computational fluid dynamics (CFD) modeling of fine particle spouting. *Int. J. Chem. React. Eng.*, **4** (2006), A21.

12. Z. G. Wang, H. T. Bi, and C. J. Lim. Numerical simulations of hydrodynamic behaviors in conical spouted beds. *China Particuology*, **4** (2006), 194–203.

13. P. A. Shirvanian, J. M. Calo, and G. Hradil. Numerical simulation of fluid-particle hydrody-namics in a rectangular spouted vessel. *Int. J. Multiph. Flow*, **32** (2006), 739–753.

14. Z. H. Wu and A. S. Mujumdar. CFD modeling of the gas-particle flow behavior in spouted beds. *Powder Technol.*, **183** (2008), 260–272.

15. O. Gryczka, S. Heinrich, and J. Tomas. CFD-modelling of the fluid dynamics in spouted beds. In *Micro-Macro-Interactions*, ed, A. Bertram and J. Tomas (Berlin: Springer, 2008), pp. 265–275.

16. L. Schiller and A. Naumann. A drag coefficient correlation. *Verein Deutscher Ingenieure*, **77** (1935), 318–320.

17. C. Y. Wen and Y. H. Yu. Mechanics of fluidization. *Chem. Eng. Progr. Symp. Ser.*, **62** (1966), 100–111.

18. M. Syamlal and T. O'Brien. Computer simulation of bubbles in a fluidized bed. *AIChE Symp. Ser.*, **85** (1989), 22–31.

19. D. Gidaspow, R. Bezburuah, and J. Ding. Hydrodynamics of circulating fluidized beds: Kinetic theory approach. In *Fluidization VII*, ed. O. E. Potter and D. J. Nicklin (New York: Engineering Foundation, 1991), pp. 75–82.

20. D. L. Koch and R. J. Hill. Inertial effects in suspension and porous-media flows. *Ann. Rev. Fluid Mech.*, **33** (2001), 619–647.

21. M. A. Van Der Hoef, R. Beetstra, and J. A. M. Kuipers. Lattice-Boltzmann simulations of low-Reynolds-number flow past mono- and bidisperse arrays of spheres. *J. Fluid Mech.*, **528** (2005), 233–254.

22. R. Beetstra, M. A. Van Der Hoef, and J. A. M. Kuipers. Drag force of intermediate Reynolds number flow past mono- and bidisperse arrays of spheres. *AIChE J.*, **53** (2007), 489–501.

23. O. Gryczka, S. Heinrich, N. G. Deen, M. v. S. Annaland, J. A. M. Kuipers, and L. Mörl. CFD modeling of a prismatic spouted bed with two adjustable gas inlets. *Can. J. Chem. Eng.*, **87** (2009), 318–328.

24. R. Béttega, R. G. Corrêa, and J. T. Freire. Scale-up study of spouted beds using computational fluid dynamics. *Can. J. Chem. Eng.*, **87** (2009), 193–203.

25. R. Béttega, A. R. F. de Almeida, R. G. Corrêa, and J. T. Freire. CFD modelling of a semi-cylindrical spouted bed: Numerical simulation and experimental verification. *Can. J. Chem. Eng.*, **87** (2009), 177–184.

26. Y. L. He, C. J. Lim, and J. R. Grace. Scale-up studies of spouted beds. *Chem. Eng. Sci.*, **52** (1997), 329–339.

27. K. G. Santos, V. V. Murata, and M. A. S. Barrozo. Three-dimensional computational fluid dynamics modelling of spouted bed. *Can. J. Chem. Eng.*, **87** (2009), 211–219.

28. C. R. Duarte, M. Olazar, V. V. Murata, and M. A. S. Barrozo. Numerical simulation and experimental study of fluid-particle flows in a spouted bed. *Powder Technol.*, **188** (2009), 195–205.

29. J. Ding and D. Gidaspow. A bubbling fluidization model using kinetic theory of granular flow. *AIChE J.*, **36** (1990), 523–538.

30. S. Ergun. Fluid flow through packed columns. *Chem. Eng. Progr.*, **48**:2 (1952), 89–94.

31. C. S. Campbell. Granular material flows – an overview. *Powder Technol.*, **162** (2006), 208–229.

32. S. Sundaresan. Some outstanding questions in handling of cohesionless particles. *Powder Technol.*, **115** (2001), 2–7.

33. C. K. K. Lun, S. B. Savage, D. J. Jeffrey, and N. Chepurniy. Kinetic theories for granular flow: Inelastic particles in Couette flow and slightly inelastic particles in a general flow field. *J. Fluid Mech.*, **140** (1984), 223–256.

34. R. A. Bagnold. Experiments on a gravity-free dispersion of large solid spheres in a Newtonian fluid under shear. *Proc. Royal Soc. London Ser. A, Math. and Phys. Sci.*, **A225** (1954), 49–63.

35. J. T. Jenkins and S. B. Savage. A theory for rapid flow of identical, smooth, nearly elastic spherical particles. *J. Fluid Mech.*, **130** (1983), 187–202.

36. D. G. Schaeffer. Instability in the evolution equations describing incompressible granular flow. *J. Diff. Eqns*, **66** (1987), 19–50.

37. J. H. Ferziger and M. Peric. *Computational Methods for Fluid Dynamics*, 3rd ed. (Berlin: Springer, 1999).

38. C. A. J. Fletcher and K. Srinivas. *Computational Techniques for Fluid Dynamics Vol. 1, Fundamental and General Techniques*, 2nd ed. (Berlin: Springer-Verlag, 1991).

39. C. J. Freitas. Perspective: Selected benchmarks from commercial CFD codes. *ASME J. Fluids Eng.*, **117** (1995), 208–218.

40. R. J. LeVeque. Finite Volume Methods for Hyperbolic Problems (Cambridge, UK: Cambridge University Press, 2002).

41. S. V. Patankar. *Numerical Heat Transfer and Fluid Flow* (Washington, DC: Taylor and Francis, 1980).

42. J. R. Grace and F. Taghipour. Verification and validation of CFD models and dynamic similarity for fluidized beds. *Powder Technol.*, **139** (2004), 99–110.

43. Y. L. He, C. J. Lim, J. R. Grace, J. X. Zhu, and S. Z. Qin. Measurements of voidage profiles in spouted beds. *Can. J. Chem. Eng.*, **72** (1994), 229–234.

44. Y. L. He, S. Z. Qin, C. J. Lim, and J. R. Grace. Particle velocity profiles and solid flow patterns in spouted beds. *Can. J. Chem. Eng.*, **72** (1994), 561–568.

45. M. J. San José, M. Olazar, S. Alvarez, M. A. Izquierdo, and J. Bilbao. Solid cross-flow into the spout and particle trajectories in conical spouted beds. *Chem. Eng. Sci.*, **53** (1998), 3561–3570.

46. P. A. Cundall and O. D. L. Strack. A discrete numerical model for granular assemblies. *Geotechnique*, **29** (1979), 47–65.

47. J. Link, C. Zeilstra, N. Deen, and H. Kuipers. Validation of a discrete particle model in a 2D spout-fluid bed using non-intrusive optical measuring techniques. *Can. J. Chem. Eng.*, **82** (2004), 30–36.

48. J. M. Link, L. A. Cuypers, N. G. Deen, and J. A. M. Kuipers. Flow regimes in a spout-fluid bed: A combined experimental and simulation study. *Chem. Eng. Sci.*, **60** (2005), 3425–3442.

49. S. Takeuchi, S. Wang, and M. Rhodes. Discrete element simulation of a flat-bottomed spouted bed in the 3-D cylindrical coordinate system. *Chem. Eng. Sci.*, **59** (2004), 3495–3504.

50. T. Kawaguchi, M. Sakamoto, T. Tanaka, and Y. Tsuji. Quasi-three-dimensional numerical simulation of spouted beds in cylinder. *Powder Technol.*, **109** (2000), 3–12.

51. T. Kawaguchi, T. Tanaka, and Y. Tsuji. Numerical simulation of two-dimensional fluidized beds using the discrete element method. *Powder Technol.*, **96** (1998), 129–138.

52. S. Takeuchi, X. S. Wang, and M. J. Rhodes. Discrete element study of particle circulation in a 3-D spouted bed. *Chem. Eng. Sci.*, **60** (2005), 1267–1276.

53. S. Takeuchi, S. Wang, and M. Rhodes. Discrete element method simulation of three-dimensional conical-base spouted beds. *Powder Technol.*, **184** (2008), 141–150.

54. W. Zhong, Y. Xiong, Z. Yuan, and M. Zhang. DEM simulation of gas-solid flow behaviors in spout-fluid bed. *Chem. Eng. Sci.*, **61** (2006), 1571–1584.

55. X.-L. Zhao, S.-Q. Li, G.-Q. Liu, Q. Song, and Q. Yao. Flow patterns of solids in a two-dimensional spouted bed with draft plates: PIV measurement and DEM simulations. *Powder Technol.*, **183** (2008), 79–87.

56. X.-L. Zhao, S.-Q. Li, G.-Q. Liu, Q. Yao, and J. S. Marshall. DEM simulation of the particle dynamics in two-dimensional spouted beds. *Powder Technol.*, **184** (2008), 205–213.

57. T. Swasdisevi, W. Tanthapanichakoon, T. Charinpanitkul, T. Kawaguchi, T. Tanaka, and Y. Tsuji. Investigation of fluid and coarse-particle dynamics in a two-dimensional spouted bed. *Chem. Eng. Technol.*, **27** (2004), 971–981.

58. M. I. Kalwar, G. S. Raghavan, and A. S. Mujumdar. Circulation of particles in two-dimensional spouted beds with draft plates. *Powder Technol.*, **77** (1993), 233–242.

59. S. Limtrakul, A. Boonsrirat, and T. Vatanatham. DEM modeling and simulation of a catalytic gas-solid fluidized bed reactor: A spouted bed as a case study. *Chem. Eng. Sci.*, **59** (2004), 5225–5231.

60. G. Rovero, N. Epstein, J. R. Grace, N. Piccinini, and C. M. H. Brereton. Gas phase solid-catalysed chemical reaction in spouted beds. *Chem. Eng. Sci.*, **38** (1983), 557–566.

61. N. V. Brilliantov and T. Poeschel. Rolling friction of a viscous sphere on a hard plane. *Europhysics Letters*, **42** (1998), 511–516.

62. T. F. Miller and F. W. Schmidt. Use of a pressure-weighted interpolation method for the solution of the incompressible Navier-Stokes equations on a nonstaggered grid system. *Num. Heat Transf., Part B: Fund.*, **14** (1988), 213–233.

63. A. A. Amsden and F. H. Harlow. A simplified MAC technique for incompressible fluid flow calculations. *J. Comp. Phys.*, **6** (1970), 322–325.

64. K. B. Mathur and N. Epstein. *Spouted Beds* (New York: Academic Press, 1974).

65. T. Tsuji, M. Hirose, T. Shibata, O. Uemaki, and H. Itoh. Particle flow in annular region of a flat-bottomed spouted bed. *Trans. Soc. Chem. Engrs, Japan*, **23** (1997), 604–605.

66. D. Roy, F. Larachi, R. Legros, and J. Chaouki. A study of solid behavior in spouted beds using 3-D particle tracking. *Can. J. Chem. Eng.*, **72**, (1994), 945–952.

5 Conical spouted beds

Martin Olazar, Maria J. San José, and Javier Bilbao

5.1 Introduction

In spite of the versatility of spouted beds of conventional geometry (cylindrical with conical base), there are situations in which the gas–solid contact is not fully satisfactory. In these situations, the process conditioning factors are the physical characteristics of the solid and the residence time of the gas. Thus, conical spouted beds have been used for drying suspensions, solutions, and pasty materials.[1–4] Chemical reaction applications, such as catalytic polymerization,[5] coal gasification,[6] and waste pyrolysis,[7–9] have also been under research and development.

In fast reactions, such as ultrapyrolysis,[10] selectivity is the factor that conditions the design, so the optimum residence time of the gaseous phase can be as short as a few milliseconds. The spouting in conical beds attains these gas residence times, which can be controlled within a narrow range. Nevertheless, until the 1990s, the literature on the principles and hydrodynamics of the flow regimes in conical spouted beds was very scarce, and its diffusion was very limited, partially owing to the scant dissemination in the past of the research on such beds carried out in Eastern Europe.

5.2 Conditions for stable operation and design geometric factors

Operating in conical contactors is sensitive to the geometry of the contactor and to particle diameter, so it is necessary to delimit the operating conditions that strictly correspond to the spouted bed regime and allow for the gas–solid contact to take place stably. The ranges of the geometric factors of the contactor (defined in Figure 5.1) and of the contactor–particle system for stable spouting are as follows[11]:

Inlet diameter/cone bottom diameter ratio, D_i/D_o. This ratio should be between 1/2 and 5/6. The lower limit is imposed by the pressure drop and by the formation of dead zones at the bottom (a serious problem for operating with solids circulation). Exceeding the upper limit gives rise to poor definition of the spout and an increase in instability because of rotational movements.

Spouted and Spout-Fluid Beds: Fundamentals and Applications, eds. Norman Epstein and John R. Grace. Published by Cambridge University Press. © Cambridge University Press 2011.

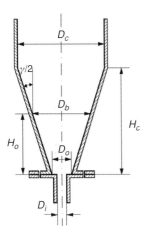

Figure 5.1. Geometry of the conical spouted bed reactor.

Cone angle, γ. The lower limit is 28°, as the bed is unavoidably unstable for lower angles. From a practical point of view, angles >60° are not recommended because the solid circulation rate is then very low, especially for deep beds.

Inlet diameter/particle diameter ratio, D_i/d_p. Whereas for spouting in cylindrical vessels,[12] bed instability occurs at $D_i/d_p \geq 30$, stable operation with conical vessels is obtained for D_i/d_p between 2 and 60.

Maximum spoutable bed height. There is no maximum spoutable bed height in conical spouted beds, at least not in the same sense as is found for $d_p > 1$ mm in cylindrical contactors.[11] Nevertheless, for large particles (glass spheres with diameters > 5 mm) there is a maximum height because of the instability of the spouting regime within the previously described range of the contactor geometric factors.[13] The cause of instability is clearly slugging, which affects the whole section of the bed and whose formation does not bear a direct relation to any individual contactor geometric factor or to particle diameter, but rather is a consequence of all the factors combined. In general, the maximum spoutable bed height increases as the particle diameter decreases, as D_i/D_o decreases, and as the cone included angle increases.

Column diameter. The upper terminal diameter of the contactor, D_c, is a parameter that can be specified at will to treat any volume of solid, as long as the key geometric factors for stability are maintained in the design and the remarks on trajectories of solid particles and bed pressure drop are taken into account. An equation for calculating D_c has been deduced[13] from the relationships between the geometric factors of the contactors, the correlation of minimum spouting velocity, and the correlation for bed expansion:

$$D_c^3 = [D_o + 2H_o \tan(\gamma/2)]^3(1 + \psi) - D_o^3\psi, \qquad (5.1)$$

where

$$\psi = 2.58 \times 10^4 (u/u_{msi})^{3.48} Ar^{-0.52} \left[\frac{D_o + 2H_o \tan(\gamma/2)}{D_i}\right]^{-0.53} [\tan(\gamma/2)]^{-1.84} \gamma^{1.95}$$

$$(5.2)$$

with γ in radians.

Table 5.1. Hydrodynamic correlations for minimum spouting velocity in conical spouted beds.

Authors	Correlation	
Nikolaev and Golubev[16]	$Re_{ms} = 0.051\ Ar^{0.59}(D_i/D_c)^{0.1}(H_o/D_c)^{0.25}$	(5.3)
Gorshtein and Mukhlenov[17]	$Re_{msi} = 0.174\ Ar^{0.5}(D_b/D_i)^{0.85}[\tan(\gamma/2)]^{-1.25}$	(5.4)
Tsvik et al.[18]	$Re_{msi} = 0.4\ Ar^{0.52}(H_o/D_i)^{1.24}[\tan(\gamma/2)]^{0.42}$	(5.5)
Goltsiker[19]	$Re_{msi} = 73\ Ar^{0.14}\ (H_o/D_i)^{0.9}(\rho_p/\rho)^{0.47}$	(5.6)
Wan-Fyong et al.[20]	$Re_{msi} = 1.24\ (Re)_t(H_o/D_i)^{0.82}[\tan(\gamma/2)]^{0.92}$	(5.7)
Markowski and Kaminski[14]	$Re_{msi} = 0.028\ Ar^{0.57}(D_c/D_i)^{1.27}(H_o/D_i)^{0.48}$	(5.8)
Kmiec[21]	$Re_{msi}^2[1.75 + 150(1 - \varepsilon_{ms})/Re_{msi}] =$	
	$31.31\ Ar(H_o/D_i)^{1.757}(D_i/D_c)^{0.029}[\tan(\gamma/2)]^{2.07}(\varepsilon_{ms})^3$	(5.9)
Choi and Meisen[15]	$U_{ms} = 0.147\,(2gH_o)^{0.5}H_o^{0.51}d_p^{0.61}D_i^{0.24}D_c^{-1.36}[(\rho_p - \rho)/\rho]^{0.48}$	(5.10)
Olazar et al.[11]	$Re_{msi} = 0.126\ Ar^{0.5}[D_b/D_i]^{1.68}[\tan(\gamma/2)]^{-0.57}$	(5.11)
Bi et al.[22] $(D_o = D_i)$	for $D_b/D_i > 1.66,$	

$$Re_{msi} = [0.3 - 0.27/(D_b/D_i)^2]\sqrt{Ar(D_b/D_i)[(D_b/D_i)^2 + (D_b/D_i) + 1]/3} \qquad (5.12)$$

$$\text{for } D_b/D_i < 1.66,$$

$$Re_{msi} = 0.202\ \sqrt{Ar(D_b/D_i)[(D_b/D_i)^2 + (D_b/D_i) + 1]/3} \qquad (5.13)$$

5.3   Hydrodynamics

The hydrodynamics of conical spouted beds differ significantly when compared to conventional spouted beds (cylindrical with conical base). Consequently, the values of the hydrodynamic parameters required for stable spouting – minimum spouting velocity, pressure drop, and bed expansion – also differ.[11,14]

5.3.1   Spouted bed

Minimum spouting velocity. Choi and Meisen[15] and Olazar et al.[11] found that the minimum spouting velocity in conical beds is approximately proportional to bed height, whereas it is proportional to the square root of the height in conventional spouted beds.

Correlations developed to predict minimum spouting velocity in conical spouted beds are listed in Table 5.1. The minimum spouting velocity in conical beds has also been modeled based on equations developed from force and momentum balances in the spout region of the bed.[23] However, the applicability of these equations is limited owing to the inclusion of parameters that are not easy to estimate.

The diameter of the cylindrical section of the bed, D_c, should not be used in the correlation for predicting the minimum velocity in conical beds because this velocity will remain unchanged with variations in D_c as long as the bed remains entirely in the conical section (see Figure 5.1). Eqs. (5.3) and (5.8) through (5.10) include D_c as a parameter, which implies that they are valid only for the specific beds tested or for cases in which the static bed upper surface diameter is D_c. Other equations do not include the cone angle, as the authors have not observed any angle influence in the range covered, or

Table 5.2. Correlations for peak pressure drop.

Authors	Correlation	
Gelperin et al.[26]	$-\Delta P_M/H_o\rho_b g = 1 + 0.062\,(D_b/D_i)^{2.54}((D_b/D_i) - 1)(\tan(\gamma/2))^{-0.18}$	(5.14)
Gorshtein and Mukhlenov[17]	$-\Delta P_M/\Delta P_S = 1 + 6.65\,(H_o/D_i)^{1.2}(\tan(\gamma/2))^{0.5}\mathrm{Ar}^{0.2}$	(5.15)
Olazar et al.[27]	$-\Delta P_M/\Delta P_S = 1 + 0.116\,(H_o/D_i)^{0.50}(\tan(\gamma/2))^{-0.80}\,\mathrm{Ar}^{0.0125}$	(5.16)

Table 5.3. Correlations for spouting pressure drop.

Authors	Correlation	
Gorshtein and Mukhlenov[17]	$-\Delta P_S/H_o\rho_p(1 - \varepsilon_0)g = 7.68\,(\tan(\gamma/2))^{0.2}(\mathrm{Re}_{msi})^{-0.2}(H_o/D_i)^{-0.33}$	(5.17)
Markowski and Kaminski[14]	$-\Delta P_S/\rho u_{msi}^2 = 0.19\,(D_c/H_o)^{0.56}\,(D_i/H_o)^{2.39}(H_o/d_p)^{2..35}$	(5.18)
Olazar et al.[27]	$-\Delta P_S/H_o\rho_p(1 - \varepsilon_0)g = 1.20\,(\tan(\gamma/2))^{-0.11}\,(\mathrm{Re}_{msi})^{-0.06}(H_o/D_i)^{0.08}$	(5.19)

only one angle has been studied, as in the case of Eqs. (5.8) and (5.10). All equations in Table 5.1 are empirical except for Eqs. (5.12) and (5.13), which are based on the Ergun equation and literature data. Nevertheless, these equations are deficient in not including bed height or cone angle because there are many combinations of these parameters that provide the same D_b, and u_{msi} is not the same for any combination. In fact, these equations underestimate u_{msi} for small angles. Eq. (5.11) is based on widely varying experimental conditions ($D_i = 0.02$–0.062 m, $D_o = 0.063$ m, $H_o = 0.02$–0.55 m, $D_c = 0.36$ m, $\gamma = 28$–$45°$, $d_p = 0.5$–25 mm, $\rho_p = 14$–2420 kg/m³) and has recorded better results over a wide range of experimental conditions.[24] This correlation is also valid for mixtures of solids of different size,[25] as long as the Sauter mean diameter, d_{sv}, is adopted as the characteristic mean diameter.

Peak pressure drop. As a rough approximation, this pressure drop is 1.5 to 2.5 times higher than the spouting pressure drop. The few correlations for its prediction in conical spouted beds are listed in Table 5.2. Eq. (5.14) does not include particle properties and Eq. (5.16) is a modification of Eq. (5.15) for a wide range of geometric factors and particle properties.

Spouting pressure drop. Correlations for determining the spouting pressure drop are listed in Table 5.3. Eq. (5.18) does not include cone angle because the authors used only a 37° contactor. Eq. (5.19) provides better predictions than Eq. (5.17), mainly because it has been obtained from a wider range of geometry, particle sizes, and particle densities.

A theoretical model has been proposed by Hadzismajlovic et al.[23] for calculating the pressure drop for conical beds. The solution of this model faces an important practical difficulty, as it is necessary to choose an upper boundary that is suitable for integrating the differential pressure gradient.

5.3.2   Dilute spouted bed

A peculiarity of conical spouted bed contactors is that the gas velocity at the inlet can be increased substantially without losing the characteristic cyclic movement of the solids.

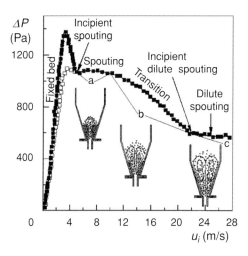

Figure 5.2. Pressure drop evolution with velocity and particle states in the contactor for different flow regimes. $\gamma = 36°$, $D_i = 0.03$ m, $H_o = 0.08$ m, $\rho_p = 2420$ kg/m^3.

Figure 5.2 shows the evolution of bed voidage with gas velocity for a given system. The bed passes through a transition state until it reaches a new regime with different hydrodynamic characteristics, originally termed a jet-spouted bed,[14] but more accurately called a *dilute spouted bed*.[11] Its general characteristics are (1) high gas velocity; (2) bed voidage >0.75, depending on particle size and operating conditions; (3) cyclic movement of the particles if the cone angle is sufficiently high; and (4) minor instability problems that are sensitive to the contactor's geometry.

The velocity required to attain dilute spouting is, according to Markowski and Kaminsky,[14] more than 1.7 times that required for spouting. As shown in Figure 5.2, this number is generally understated; it depends on particle properties and bed geometry. The only correlation in the literature for predicting the minimum velocity for dilute spouting is[11]

$$\mathrm{Re}_{dsi} = 6.9\mathrm{Ar}^{0.35}(D_b/D_i)^{1.48}(\tan(\gamma/2))^{-0.53}. \qquad (5.20)$$

The range of variables encompassed by this correlation is the same as for Eq. (5.11).

Bed expansion is of special interest for the design of conical spouted beds. Several authors[14,28,29] monitored the voidage of conical spouted beds with the ratio of drag forces to gravitational forces, F_D/F_G. Typical expansion curves are shown in Figure 5.3 for two contactors of different cone angles. As observed, there are three zones, although the change from one to the other is not clearly defined. The first one corresponds to bed voidages between a loose-packed bed and the end of the spouting regime, the second from the end of the spouting regime to approximately the beginning of the dilute spouting regime, and the third to velocities higher than those for minimum dilute spouting. Expansion depends greatly on initial bed height and particle size. In fact, a dilute spouted bed is reached for a bed voidage of 0.76 when coarse particles ($d_p > 6$ mm) are spouted, whereas high voidages (>0.99) are required for particles smaller than 1 mm. A few correlations for the prediction of bed voidage variation with gas flowrate

Table 5.4. Correlations for calculating bed expansion in conical spouted beds.

Authors	Correlation	
Gorshtein and Mukhlenov[17]	$\varepsilon = 2.17\,(Re/Ar)^{0.33}(H_o/D_i)^{0.5}(\tan(\gamma/2))^{-0.6}$	(5.21)
Markowski and Kaminski[14]	$(\varepsilon - \varepsilon_0)/(1 - \varepsilon) = 39.7\,(F_D/F_G)^{1.23}(D_c/D_i)^{3.91}(D_i/H_o)^{1.44}$	(5.22)
Olazar et al.[27]	$(\varepsilon - \varepsilon_0)/(1 - \varepsilon) = 215\,(F_D/F_G)^{1.74}(D_b/D_i)^{3.91}\gamma^{1.95}$	(5.23)

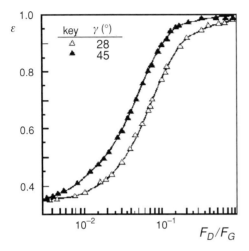

Figure 5.3. Bed expansion for two contactors of different angles. Glass spheres, $H_o = 0.06$ m, $D_i = 0.05$ m, $d_p = 4$ mm, $\rho_p = 2420$ kg/m³.

have been proposed in the literature, as listed in Table 5.4. When the minimum dilute spouting velocity is known from Eq. (5.20), the correlations shown in Table 5.4 can be used to estimate the bed voidage at minimum dilute spouting.

5.4   Gas flow modeling

The models for the prediction of gas flow distribution and tracer dispersion in conical spouted beds are based on the definition of streamtubes according to their geometry and on the knowledge of gas velocity through the spout. Only the dispersion problem is discussed here.

5.4.1   Spouted bed

The geometric model proposed for tracer dispersion in the spouting gas is established in direct relationship with contactor and inlet geometry,[30] Figure 5.4. The conservation equations have been developed from the geometric model by introducing the following assumptions: (1) the gas travels through the spout zone in plug flow; (2) in each volume element of the spout zone, there is mass transfer through the interface toward the annular zone; (3) the gas flowrate is the same in each of the streamtubes of the annular zone;

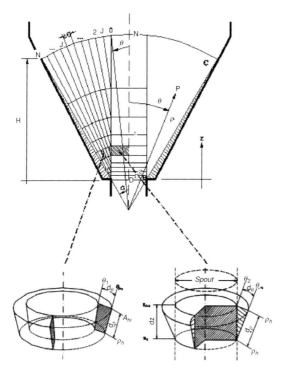

Figure 5.4. Streamtubes and differential volume elements of the gas flow model for the spouting regime.

(4) in each streamtube, the deviation from plug flow is defined by a dispersion coefficient, D, which is the same for all streamtubes; and (5) the concentration gradient obeys Fick's law.

The mass conservation equation for a tracer flowing in unsteady state, for a differential volume element in the annular zone, is

$$\frac{\partial C_a}{\partial t} = D\frac{\partial^2 C_a}{\partial \rho^2} - u_{ij}\frac{\partial C_a}{\partial \rho} + \frac{2D}{\rho}\frac{\partial C_a}{\partial \rho} \qquad (5.24)$$

with the following initial and boundary conditions:

$$\text{for } t \leq 0, C_a = 1 \text{ (negative step function)} \qquad (5.25)$$

and for $t > 0$, at the inlet of the jth streamtube,

$$D\frac{\partial C_a}{\partial \rho} = (C_a - C_s)u_{ij}. \qquad (5.26)$$

At the outlet of the jth streamtube, $\dfrac{\partial C_a}{\partial \rho} = 0.$ $\qquad (5.27)$

In a differential volume element of the spout zone (Figure 5.4),

$$\frac{\partial C_s}{\partial t} + \frac{\partial C_s}{\partial z}\left(u_s + \frac{1}{2}du_s\right) = 0 \qquad (5.28)$$

with the following initial and boundary conditions:

$$\text{for } t \le 0, C_s = 1 \text{ (negative step function)} \tag{5.29}$$

and

$$\text{for } t > 0, \text{ when } z = 0, C_s = C_o \tag{5.30}$$

and

$$\text{when } z = z_N, \frac{\partial C_s}{\partial z} = 0. \tag{5.31}$$

The model requires knowledge of gas velocity along the spout, which has been measured for more than 900 systems.[30] Assuming a flat profile in the spout, axial velocity is given by

$$u_s = 1.6 \times 10^{-2} \left(1 + 300 H_o + 3.8 \frac{H_o}{D_i^2} \right) \gamma^{0.6} (d_p \phi \rho_p)^{0.8} \left(\frac{K}{1+K} \right) \left(\frac{u_i}{u_{msi}} \right), \tag{5.32}$$

where, with all terms in SI units,

$$K = \exp[-C_3(z - C_2)/z], \tag{5.33}$$

$$C_2 = 6.2 D_i - 0.77 \times 10^{-2} (d_p \phi \rho_p)^{0.33} + (0.10 - 1.69 \times 10^{-5} \rho_p), \tag{5.34}$$

and

$$C_3 = 3.68 - 5.24 \times 10^{-4} \rho_p. \tag{5.35}$$

The numerically calculated values of the dispersion coefficient (for glass spheres, rice, and polystyrene) in conical spouted beds are compared,[30] in Figure 5.5, with the values obtained in the literature for other gas–solid contacting methods. The values of U for conical spouted beds in this figure are those at the upper level of the static bed (of diameter D_b). The diverse range of operating conditions studied explains the wide spread of the results for conical spouted beds, with values of D between 2.6×10^{-4} and 6.1×10^{-2} m²/s.

5.4.2 Dilute spouted bed

The geometric model proposed for gas flow is established in direct relationship with contactor and inlet geometry, as in Figure 5.4,[31] but in this case there is no well-defined spout zone, given that voidage is approximately uniform throughout. The gas dispersion coefficients are found by fitting the experimental tracer concentration data to the mass balances for the streamtubes; they are of the same order of magnitude as those for fixed beds (Figure 5.5) and substantially lower than those for fluidized beds.

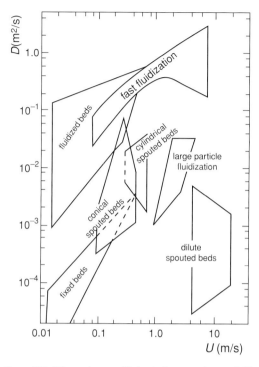

Figure 5.5. Dispersion coefficients for spouting and dilute spouting in conical contactors.

5.5   Particle segregation

Conical spouted beds perform well for the stable treatment of beds formed by particles of different size and density, with low segregation. In fact, the studies carried out indicate that beds of glass beads of significant size distribution[25,32,33] show less segregation for spouting than for fluidization.

   Figure 5.6 shows weight fractions of the particles of greater diameter at different radial and longitudinal positions in a bed for a system with pronounced segregation (50 wt% each of 1- and 7-mm glass spheres).[33] The samples were extracted by a probe connected to a suction pump. As observed in Figure 5.6, the weight fraction of larger particles, X_B, passes through a minimum that corresponds approximately to the interface between the spout and annular zones. For the higher bed levels, the mass fraction of the larger particles, X_B, passes through a maximum, corresponding to an intermediate position in the annular zone.

   In addition to less segregation, the inversion of segregation is an important difference from fluidized beds. In conical spouted beds, the component of greater size is in greater proportion at the top of the bed. This can be explained by the fact that the larger particles (theoretically jetsam) falling back from the fountain into the annulus tend to follow radial positions near the annulus–spout interface, and so describe shorter trajectories than smaller ones. The segregation produced in the fountain is important in this situation, in which the heavier components (by size or density) describe shorter trajectories than

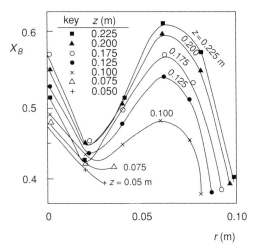

Figure 5.6. Weight fraction of particles of greater diameter at different radial and longitudinal positions. Binary mixture of glass spheres: 50% each of 1- and 7-mm particles. $\gamma = 33°$, $D_i = 0.03$ m, $H_o = 0.18$ m, $u_i/u_{msi} = 1.05$.

lighter ones. This has also been observed for segregation by both size and density by Piccinini et al.[34] through the transparent wall of a conical-cylindrical spouted bed.

Bed segregation in binary mixtures has been characterized by a mixing index that is analogous to that proposed by Rowe et al.[35] for fluidized beds:

$$M_b = (\overline{X_B})_u/\overline{X_B}, \tag{5.36}$$

where $(\overline{X_B})_u$ is the weight fraction of the particles of greater diameter in the upper half of the bed volume and $\overline{X_B}$ is the weight fraction of the same particles in the whole bed. The ternary mixing index has been calculated using a distribution function[33]:

$$M_t = f(d_{sv})_u/f(d_{sv}), \tag{5.37}$$

where $f(d_{sv})_u$ is the average value of the particle size distribution function in the upper half of the bed volume and $f(d_{sv})$ in the whole bed, defined by

$$f(d_{sv})_u = (d_{svu} - d_{pS})/(d_{pB} - d_{pS}) \tag{5.38}$$

and

$$f(d_{sv}) = (d_{sv} - d_{pS})/(d_{pB} - d_{pS}). \tag{5.39}$$

Segregation attenuates as D_i/D_o and u_i increase, and is more pronounced as static bed height increases. On changing the proportion of the solid components, segregation reaches a peak for mixtures with the same weight fraction of each component and is more pronounced as the ratio between the particle diameters deviates further from 1.

The stability of spouting regimes in conical spouted beds with inert particle mixtures has been studied by Bacelos and Freire[32] using the statistical analysis of pressure fluctuations. These authors used glass spheres with a size range from 0.78 to 4.38 mm and binary, flat, or Gaussian distributions. They applied the same analysis as San José et al.[33]

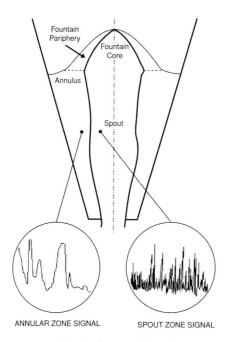

Figure 5.7. Signals from optical probe in annulus and spout. From: San José et al.[36]

to quantify segregation. Their main conclusion is that their conical spouted beds produce more particle segregation than those of San José et al. for particle size mixtures. Given that cone angle is the main difference between the beds used by both research teams – 60° in the study of Bacelos and Freire[32] and 36° in the case of San José et al.[33] – the smaller angle used by San José et al. must be responsible for the lower segregation. In fact, particle circulation rate is much higher with the smaller angle, which enhances particle mixing and reduces segregation.

5.6   Local properties

Knowledge of local properties in a conical spouted bed is essential for developing models of gas and solid flow. The properties of interest are (1) spout and fountain geometry; (2) local bed voidage in the annulus, spout, and fountain; and (3) velocity and trajectory of particles.

Experimental studies have been carried out at pilot plant scale using glass spheres and plastics (d_p = 1–6 mm) in conical contactors of different geometry (γ = 28–45°, D_i = 0.03–0.05 m, D_o = 0.062 m) and under different operating conditions (H_o = 0.05–0.30 m and U/U_{ms} from 1 to 2).

5.6.1   Spout and fountain geometry

The interface between the spout and the annulus has been detected by the differences in the signals from an optical probe[36] (Figure 5.7). When the tip of the probe is in the annulus, the corresponding signal is formed by wide peaks. Likewise, the two zones of

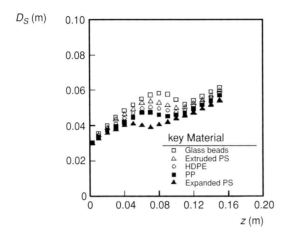

Figure 5.8. Evolution of spout diameter at minimum spouting with bed level for different materials. $\gamma = 33°$, $D_i = 0.03$ m, $H_o = 0.16$ m. Particle densities: glass beads 2420 kg/m³; extruded PS 1030 kg/m³; HDPE 940 kg/m³; PP 890 kg/m³; expanded PS 65 kg/m³. From San José et al.[36]

the fountain, the core or particle ascending zone and the periphery or particle descending zone, may be delimited based on the signals from the optical probe. When the probe is in the core, the delay times indicate that particles are ascending. Qualitatively, the shape of the spout zone is similar in all conical spouted beds and has a pronounced expansion near the inlet of the contactor, followed by a neck, and then a further expansion toward the fountain.

The geometry of the contactor and the operating conditions (including particle density) greatly influence the geometry of the spout. Figure 5.8 shows that as the solid density is increased, the spout diameter significantly increases, the neck is more pronounced, and its position reaches higher levels in the bed.

The average diameter of the spout is much higher than the inlet diameter. A correlation has been developed for its estimation, based on statistical analysis[36]:

$$\overline{D_S} = 0.52 G^{0.16} D_i^{0.41} \gamma^{-0.19} D_b^{0.80} (u_i/u_{msi})^{0.80}, \tag{5.40}$$

with γ in radians and other terms in SI units (kg, m, s).

Fountain height increases as air velocity is increased and particle size and shape factor are decreased. A correlation proposed for its calculation is[36]

$$H_f = 1.01 \times 10^{-2} \gamma^{-0.14} (D_o/D_i)^{1.14} (D_i/d_p)^{0.83}$$
$$\times (H_o/D_o)^{-0.52} (u_i/u_{msi})^{4.80} \rho_p^{-0.12} \phi^{-1.45}, \tag{5.41}$$

with γ in radians and ρ_p in kg/m³.

5.6.2   Bed voidage

In conical spouted beds and on the basis of experimental observations, bed voidage in the spout decreases with increasing height.[12] More recently, bed voidage has been measured using an optical fiber probe in the three zones of conical spouted beds: spout,

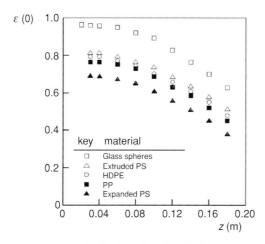

Figure 5.9. Longitudinal profile of bed voidage at spout axis for different materials at minimum spouting: $\gamma = 33°$, $D_i = 0.03$ m, $H_o = 0.18$ m, glass spheres of $d_p = 3.5$ mm. Particle densities as in Figure 5.8.

annulus, and fountain.[37] Figure 5.9 shows the results for different materials under given operating conditions. As observed, bed voidage has a maximum value at the central point of the gas inlet, where it is almost unity for solids with a density similar to glass. This maximum voidage decreases as solid density is decreased.

Bed voidage in the fountain has a similar profile for all the systems studied.[37] First, it decreases radially from the axis to the core–periphery interface, then increases sharply in the periphery, and, finally, decreases slightly near the external surface of the fountain. It has also been observed that particle shape factor does not significantly affect the voidage in the two regions of the fountain, which shows that a greater fountain volume caused by a decrease in sphericity leads to an increase in the amount of solids in the fountain.

5.6.3   Particle velocity and trajectory

According to studies on conventional spouted beds, the solids flow rate in the lower conical section is much greater than in the upper cylindrical section.[38] The few papers dealing with particle velocities in conical spouted beds reveal the peculiar characteristics of particle velocity in the spout.[39–41] Thus, the maximum velocities in the spout of conical spouted beds are higher than those corresponding to cylindrical spouted beds and are reached closer to the base. Furthermore, annulus particles near the spout–annulus interface descend relatively quickly just before entering the spout.[41,42]

The vertical component in the spout (Figure 5.10a) reaches a maximum at the axis, which differs from what was observed by He at al.[43] for conventional spouted beds. These authors observed that the maximum particle velocity in the spout is displaced slightly from the axis in the upper section of the bed. This displacement of maximum velocity was theoretically predicted by Krzywanski et al.,[44] who attributed it to the radial movement of the particles and interparticle collisions in the spout.

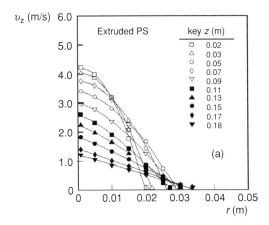

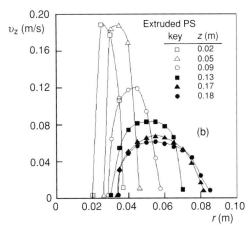

Figure 5.10. Radial profiles of vertical component of particle velocity in (a) spout and (b) annulus. $\gamma = 33°$, $D_i = 0.03$ m, $H_o = 0.18$ m, extruded polystyrene of $d_p = 3.5$ mm. From San José et al.[47]

An equation similar to that proposed by Epstein and Grace[45] is valid for predicting the radial profile at any level in the spout:

$$v_z = v_z(0)\left[1 - \left(\frac{r}{r_s}\right)^m\right].$$

(5.42)

The exponent m decreases from a value of 3 at the bottom of the contactor to a value of 1 at the top of the bed. Epstein and Grace[45] reported that $1.3 \leq m \leq 2$ for conventional spouted beds, but these values provide suitable profiles only at the intermediate section of the bed. Although Olazar et al.[39] developed a procedure for accurate estimation of this parameter, a linear decrease from the bottom to the surface provides acceptable results.

The vertical component of downward particle velocity in the annulus (Figure 5.10b) reaches a maximum at an intermediate position between the spout and the wall. Comparison of these velocities with those for conventional spouted beds in both spout and annulus shows that they are greater in conical spouted beds, especially for steeper contactor angles.[46]

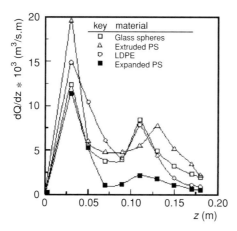

Figure 5.11. Effect of solid density and shape on solids cross-flow from annulus to spout. $\gamma = 33°$, $D_i = 0.03$ m, $H_o = 0.18$ m, $d_p = 3.5$ mm. Particle densities: LDPE 923 kg/m³, other particle densities as in Figure 5.8. From San José et al.[47]

When spout shape, local voidage, and vertical components are known, the horizontal components (and, therefore, velocity vectors and particle trajectories) can be determined by solving the mass conservation equations for differential volume elements in the spout and annulus with the corresponding boundary conditions[47]:

$$\frac{\partial}{\partial z}\left[(1 - \varepsilon)\,\rho_s\,v_z\right] + \frac{1}{r}\frac{\partial}{\partial r}\left[r\,(1 - \varepsilon)\,\rho_s\,v_r\right] = 0. \tag{5.43}$$

This procedure also allows calculation of the solids crossing from the annulus into the spout, although this may also be determined by an optical probe to count the particles ascending in the spout.[47] Figure 5.11 shows the crossflow profile as a function of bed height. The most important solids crossflow is seen to occur near the contactor bottom, and the other zone of preferential solids crossflow is at an intermediate longitudinal position in the spout, located approximately at the spout neck. Solids crossflow at the neck is very low for the lighter solid (expanded polystyrene) where this neck is barely discernible.

The cycle times in conical spouted beds are significantly shorter than those in cylindrical ones, especially for steep contactor angles. This is because of the higher particle velocities and, hence, higher solid flow rates. For example, for a conical bed of $H_o = 0.25$ m, the average cycle time ranges from 2.5 to 3.5 s.

5.7   Numerical simulation

Compared with other multiphase systems, numerical simulations of spouted beds, especially conical ones, have received less attention, and simulated results are limited and disputed. Lu et al.[48,49] simulated conical spouted beds operated by San José et al.[37] by taking the kinetic theory approach for granular flow. They investigated the effect of the restitution coefficient and frictional viscosity and showed that both affect especially the radial voidage distribution. Wang et al.[50] simulated the axial and radial distributions of static pressures and vertical particle velocities of conical spouted beds. Simulation results show that the axial solid phase source term has the most significant influence on static pressure profiles, followed by the restitution coefficient and shear viscosity. These authors prove that the introduction of a source term to modify the gravity term in the annulus is essential to obtain reasonable agreement with experimental static pressure profile and particle velocity data.

Diaz et al.[51] simulated the hydrodynamic behavior of uniform glass beads and sand of wider size distribution, based on an Eulerian-Eulerian approach. This approach is able to predict the experimental results for glass beads, but the predictions for sand were unsatisfactory. Key issues need to be addressed to improve computational fluid dynamics (CFD) predictions, such as the inclusion of shape factor, definition of slip boundary condition at the walls, inclusion of granulometric distribution, and turbulence model improvement. This approach is not able to suitably predict peak pressure drop. Duarte et al.[52] modeled fluid-particle flows in spouted beds and, specifically, the evolution of pressure drop with air velocity in conical beds, but their model also underestimates peak pressure drop.

More recently, Barrozo et al.[53] carried out an experimental study and CFD simulation based on an Eulerian-Eulerian granular multiphase model. They found that CFD is a useful technique for predicting the hydrodynamic behavior of all three regimes in conical beds, namely, spouting, transition, and dilute spouting.

5.8   Applications

Conical spouted beds are especially suitable for operations such as drying, coating, and granulation, and for others with promising future potential, such as catalytic polymerization,[5] treatment of wastes (biomass, plastics, and tires),[7–9] and selectivity-conditioned catalytic reactions.[10,54]

5.8.1   Minimum spouting under vacuum and high temperatures

Eq. (5.11), formulated at ambient conditions, overestimates the minimum spouting velocity for the intermediate or high temperatures used in many chemical processes. Olazar et al.[55] studied the effect of pressure and temperature on minimum spouting velocity using beds of sand of 0.65 and 1.4 mm particle diameter, which are those of practical interest in these processes. The temperatures ranged from ambient to 600 °C, and the pressure from 0.25 to 1 atm (the aim was vacuum pyrolysis). The authors observed that as temperature and pressure increased in these ranges, there was a significant decrease in the minimum spouting velocity, owing mainly to the increase in gas viscosity with temperature and gas density with pressure, and therefore to the increase in the momentum transfer from the gas to the solids. Accordingly, a new equation was proposed by changing only the coefficient and the Archimedes exponent in Eq. (5.11) to give

$$\mathrm{Re}_{msi} = 0.0028 \mathrm{Ar}^{0.822} \left(\frac{D_b}{D_i}\right)^{1.68} \left[\tan\left(\frac{\gamma}{2}\right)\right]^{-0.57}. \tag{5.44}$$

Subsequently, this equation was found to be valid for temperatures up to 900 °C.

5.8.2   Catalytic polymerization

Catalytic polymerization has peculiar characteristics that condition the design of the reactor: high exothermicity, fusion of particles that are growing by coating with polymer, wide particle size distribution, and the need for continuous catalyst circulation (imposed by production requirements). Accordingly, one of the first chemical applications of the dilute spouted bed was catalytic polymerization,[5] with gaseous benzyl alcohol polymerization carried out in the range of 250 °C to 310 °C on silica alumina and Y-zeolite acid catalysts to obtain stable polybenzyls.

A model has been proposed to predict the production of stable polybenzyls based on the definition of streamtubes described in Section 5.4.1. The gas (benzyl alcohol) flow rate along each streamtube at steady state is given by

$$u_{ij}\frac{\partial P_A}{\partial \rho} - D\frac{\partial^2 P_A}{\partial \rho^2} - \frac{2D}{\rho}\frac{\partial P_A}{\partial \rho} + \frac{\rho_c RT(1-\varepsilon)}{M_p \varepsilon}\dot{r}_p = 0, \tag{5.45}$$

where the polymerization rate is given by a Langmuir-Hinshelwood-type expression,[56] and the boundary conditions are:
    at the inlet of the jth streamtube (reactor inlet):

$$P_A = P_{Ao} \tag{5.46}$$

and

$$D\frac{\partial P_A}{\partial \rho} = u_i(P_{Ao} - P_A), \tag{5.47}$$

and at the outlet of the jth streamtube (bed surface):

$$\frac{\partial P_A}{\partial \rho} = 0. \tag{5.48}$$

5.8.3   Waste treatment

5.8.3.1   Biomass drying and pyrolysis

Conical spouted beds have proven to be suitable for the drying of wood and agro-forest residues of wide particle size distribution and irregular texture, without the need for inert solids to promote solids circulation.[57] Eq. (5.11), developed for granular materials, is valid for calculating the minimum gas velocity for biomass beds (sawdust and wood residues) at ambient or low-temperature conditions.

Conical spouted beds have also proven to be especially suitable for biomass pyrolysis with a small amount of sand in the bed (<50% by volume).[7] Figure 5.12 shows a

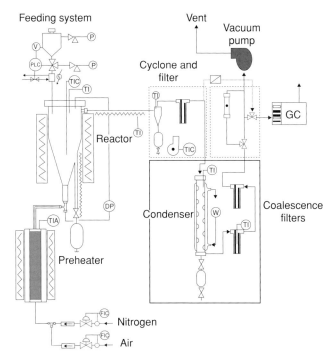

Figure 5.12. Conical spouted bed pyrolysis reactor.

pyrolysis unit designed for a biomass flow rate of 10 g/min. The total height of the reactor is 0.34 m (H_c = 0.205 m, γ = 28°, D_c = 0.123 m, D_o = 0.02 m, and D_i = 0.01 m). The short gas residence time (milliseconds) and the good gas–solid contact allow operation at moderate pyrolysis temperatures (<500 °C) and at both atmospheric pressure and vacuum conditions.[7,55] The maximum liquid yield is similar to that in fluidized beds, close to 70 percent, but at a lower temperature, 450 °C.[7] Furthermore, segregation in the fountain allows extracting the spent char through a lateral outlet at the bed surface.

5.8.3.2 Waste plastic pyrolysis

Thermal decomposition, or pyrolysis, is one of the methods with the best perspective for upgrading plastic wastes to obtain feedstock and fuel. Operating in a fluidized bed presents problems because of particle agglomeration caused by fusion of inert particles coated with plastic.[58] The good behavior of the conical spouted bed reactor is quantified on the basis of the critical thickness of the fused plastic that may be handled. The critical thickness is the value above which the particles fuse when they collide and is a function of the plastic's viscosity and the size and momentum of the colliding particles:[58]

$$\delta_{crit} = r_p \left[\exp\left(\frac{\sqrt{2} m_p v}{\mu \pi r_p^2} - 1 \right) \right]. \tag{5.49}$$

Consequently, an increase in particle velocity, v, and voidage by increasing the air velocity leads to a higher processing capacity. In fact, operating in the transition regime between dense and dilute spouting in the experimental unit shown in Figure 5.12 (30–100 g of sand, $d_p = 0.6$–1.2 mm, 500 °C), the average velocity of the particles in the annular (limiting) zone may be controlled above 0.25 m/s, and the critical thickness predicted by Eq. (5.49) is 250 μm.[59] The critical thickness of the fused plastic in bubbling fluidized beds is between 4 and 7 μm.[58] Aguado et al.[59] were able to feed 4 g/min of plastic, an order of magnitude greater than that in a fluidized bed, with the same amount of sand.

5.8.3.3   Scrap tire pyrolysis

Recovering value from scrap tires has received considerable attention in developed countries, where an average of 6 kg of used tires per person per year is generated. The unit shown in Figure 5.12, in which particles are sticky, large, irregular, and with a wide size distribution, has been applied successfully to the pyrolysis of scrap tires.[9] The good performance is a result of (1) high heat and mass transfer rates between phases, favored by the countercurrent gas–solid contact, and (2) short gas residence time, which minimizes the secondary reactions of devolatilization products.

High yields of primary products are obtained at lower temperatures than in fluidized beds. Furthermore, a very high yield of d-limonene, 23.4 percent, was obtained with this reactor at a temperature of 450 °C.[9] Limonene, the dimer of natural rubber, has extensive industrial applications, and its production is increasing at a steady pace. This product is very sensitive to temperature, and the features of the conical spouted bed reactor generate a high yield.

Chapter-specific nomenclature

C_a, C_o, C_s	dimensionless tracer concentration in the annulus, inlet and spout
C_D	drag coefficient, $(24/Re)(1 + 0.15\,Re^{0.687})$
D	dispersion coefficient, m^2/s
D_b	upper diameter of static bed, m
D_c	cylindrical column diameter marking termination of cone, m
d_{pB}	diameter of larger particles, m
d_{pS}	diameter of smaller particles, m
d_{sv}	Sauter mean diameter in the whole bed, m
d_{svu}	Sauter mean diameter in upper half of bed, m
F_D/F_G	ratio between drag and gravitational forces, $\frac{3}{4}\,C_D\,Re^2/Ar$
$f(d_{sv})$	average value of particle size distribution function in the bed
$f(d_{sv})_u$	average value of particle size distribution function in upper half of the bed
M_b	mixing index for binary mixtures
M_p	average molecular weight of polymer, g/mol
M_t	mixing index for ternary mixtures
m_p	mass of the particle coated with plastic, g

P_A	partial pressure of benzyl alcohol at any point, Pa
P_{Ao}	partial pressure of benzyl alcohol at the inlet, Pa
Re_{msi}	Reynolds number for minimum spouting velocity based on D_i
Re_{dsi}	Reynolds number for minimum dilute spouting velocity based on D_i
Re_t	terminal particle Reynolds number
r_p	radius of the particle coated with plastic, m
$\dot{r}_p$	polymerization rate, (mass polymer)/(mass catalyst)·(time), s^{-1}
u_{ij}	gas velocity at the ith volume element in the jth streamtube, m/s
u_s	average air interstitial velocity in the spout at a given level, m/s
v_z	vertical component of local particle velocity, m/s
$v_z(0)$	vertical component of local particle velocity at axis of contactor, m/s
X_B	weight fraction of bigger particles
$\overline{X_B}$	weight fraction of bigger particles in whole bed
$(\overline{X_B})_u$	weight fraction of bigger particles in upper half of bed volume

Greek letters

γ	included angle of cone, degrees or radians
δ_{crit}	critical thickness of plastic layer, m
ε_o	fractional void volume of static bed
μ	viscosity of material coating the particle, kg/m·s
ρ	spherical coordinate defined in Figure 5.4, m (where not used as fluid density)
ρ_c	density of catalyst, kg/m^3
ϕ	particle sphericity
ψ	parameter in Eq. (5.1)

References

1. Q. T. Pham. Behavior of a conical spouted spouted-bed dryer for animal blood. *Can. J. Chem. Eng.*, **61** (1983), 426–434.
2. A. S. Markowski. Drying characteristics in a jet-spouted bed dryer. *Can. J. Chem. Eng.*, **70** (1992), 938–944.
3. M. L. Passos, G. Massarani, J. T. Freire, and A. S. Mujumdar. Drying of pastes in spouted beds of inert particles: design criteria and modelling. *Drying Technol.*, **15** (1997), 605–624.
4. M. L. Passos, L. S. Oliveira, A. S. Franca, and J. Massarani. Bixin powder production in conical spouted bed units. *Drying Technol.*, **16** (1998), 1855–1879.
5. J. Bilbao, M. Olazar, A. Romero, and J. M. Arandes. Design and operation of a jet spouted bed reactor with continuous catalyst feed in the benzyl alcohol polymerization. *Ind. Eng. Chem. Res.*, **26** (1987), 1297–1304.
6. O. Uemaki and T. Tsuji. Gasification of a sub-bituminous coal in a two-stage jet spouted bed reactor. In *Fluidization V*, ed. K. Ostergaard and A. Sorensen (New York: Engineering Foundation, 1986), pp. 497–504.
7. M. Olazar, M. J. San José, G. Aguirre, and J. Bilbao. Pyrolysis of sawdust in a conical spouted bed reactor. Yields and product composition. *Ind. Eng. Chem. Res.*, **39** (2000), 1925–1933.

8. R. Aguado, M. Olazar, M. J. San José, B. Gaisán, and J. Bilbao. Wax formation in the pyrolysis of polyolefins in a conical spouted bed reactor. *Energy and Fuels*, **16** (2002), 1429–1437.

9. M. Arabiourrutia, G. Lopez, G. Elordi, M. Olazar, R. Aguado, and J. Bilbao. Product distribution obtained in the pyrolysis of tyres in a conical spouted bed reactor. *Chem. Eng. Sci.*, **62** (2007), 5271–5275.

10. R. K. Stocker, J. H. Eng, W. Y. Svrcek, and L. A. Behie. Ultrapyrolysis of propane in a spouted-bed rector with a draft tube. *AIChE J.*, **35** (1989), 1617–1624.

11. M. Olazar, M. J. San José, A. T. Aguayo, J. M. Arandes, and J. Bilbao. Stable operation conditions for gas-solid contact regimes in conical spouted beds. *Ind. Eng. Chem. Res.*, **31** (1992), 1784–1791.

12. K. B. Mathur and N. Epstein. *Spouted Beds* (New York: Academic Press, 1974).

13. M. Olazar, M. J. San José, A. T. Aguayo, J. M. Arandes, and J. Bilbao. Design factors of conical spouted beds and jet spouted beds. *Ind. Eng. Chem. Res.*, **32** (1993), 1245–1250.

14. A. Markowski and W. Kaminski. Hydrodynamic characteristics of jet spouted beds. *Can. J. Chem. Eng.*, **61** (1983), 377–381.

15. M. Choi and A. Meisen. Hydrodynamics of shallow, conical spouted beds. *Can. J. Chem. Eng.*, **70** (1992), 916–924.

16. A. M. Nikolaev and L. G. Golubev. Basic hydrodynamic characteristics of a spouting bed. *Izv. Vyssh. Ucheb. Zaved. Khim. Tekhnol.*, **7** (1964), 855–857.

17. A. E. Gorshtein and I. P. Mukhlenov. Hydraulic resistance of a fluidized bed in a cyclone without a grate. ii. Critical gas rate corresponding to the beginning of jet formation. *Zh. Prikl. Khim.*, **37** (1964), 1887–1893.

18. M. Z. Tsvik, M. N. Nabiev, N. U. Rizaev, K. V. Merenkov, and V. S. Vyzgo. External flow rates in composite production of granulated fertilizers. *Uzb. Khim. Zh.*, **11** (1967), 50–51.

19. A. D. Goltsiker. Doctoral dissertation. Lensovet Technology Inst., Leningrad (1967). Quoted by Mathur and Epstein[12] and cited (in Russian) on p. 42 of Romankov and Rashkovskaya, ref. 3 in Chapter 1.

20. F. Wan-Fyong, P. G. Romankov, and N. B. Rashkovskaya. Hydrodynamics of spouting bed. *Zh. Prikl. Khim.*, **42** (1969) 609–617.

21. A. Kmiec. The minimum spouting velocity. *Can. J. Chem. Eng.*, **61** (1983), 274–280.

22. H. T. Bi, A. Macchi, J. Chaouki, and R. Legros. Minimum spouting velocity of conical spouted beds. *Can. J. Chem. Eng.*, **75** (1997), 460–465.

23. Dz. E. Hadzismajlovic, Z. B. Grbavcic, D. V. Vucovic, D. S. Povrenovic, and H. Littman. A model for calculating the minimum fluid flowrate and pressure drop in a conical spouted. In *Fluidization V*, ed. K. Ostergaard and A. Sorensen (New York: Engineering Foundation, 1986), pp. 241–248.

24. M. Al-Jabari, T. G. M. van de Ven, and M. E. Weber. Liquid spouting of pulp fibers in a conical vessel. *Can. J. Chem. Eng.*, **74** (1996), 867–875.

25. M. Olazar, M. J. San José, F. J. Peñas, A. T. Aguayo, and J. Bilbao. Stability and hydrodynamics of conical spouted beds with binary mixtures. *Ind. Eng. Chem. Res.*, **32** (1993), 2826–2834.

26. N. I. Gelperin, V. G. Aynshteyn, E. N. Gelperin, and S. D. Lvova. Hydrodynamic characteristics of pseudo-liquefaction of granular materials in conical and conico-cylindrical equipment. *Khim. Tekhnol. Topliv Masel*, **5** (1960), 51–57.

27. M. Olazar, M. J. San José, A. T. Aguayo, J. M. Arandes, and J. Bilbao. Pressure drop in conical spouted beds. *Chem. Eng. J.*, **51** (1993), 53–60.

28. A. Kmiec. Expansion of solid-gas spouted beds. *Chem. Eng. J.*, **13** (1977), 143–147.

29. M. J. San José, M. Olazar, A. T. Aguayo, J. M. Arandes, and J. Bilbao. Expansion of spouted beds in conical contactors. *Chem. Eng. J.*, **51** (1993), 45–52.

30. M. J. San José, M. Olazar, F. J. Peñas, J. M. Arandes, and J. Bilbao. Correlation for calculation of the gas dispersion coefficient in conical spouted bed. *Chem. Eng. Sci.*, **50** (1995), 2161–2172.

31. M. Olazar, M. J. San José, F. J. Peñas, J. M. Arandes, and J. Bilbao. Gas flow dispersion in jet spouted beds. Effect of geometric factors and operating conditions. *Ind. Eng. Chem. Res.*, **33** (1994), 3267–3273.

32. M. S. Bacelos and J. T. Freire. Flow regimes in wet conical spouted beds using glass bead mixtures. *Particuology*, **6** (2008), 72–80.

33. M. J. San José, M. Olazar, F. J. Peñas, and J. Bilbao. Segregation in conical spouted beds with binary and tertiary mixtures of equidensity spherical particles. *Ind. Eng. Chem. Res.*, **33** (1994), 1838–1844.

34. N. Piccinini, A. Bernhard, P. Campagna, and F. Vallana. Segregation phenomenon in spouted beds. *Powder Technol.*, **18** (1977), 171–178.

35. P. N. Rowe, A. W. Nienow, and A. J. Agbim. The mechanics by which particles segregate in gas fluidized beds–binary systems of near-spherical particles. *Trans. Instn. Chem. Engrs.*, **50** (1972), 310–323.

36. M. J. San José, M. Olazar, S. Alvarez, A. Morales, and J. Bilbao. Spout and fountain geometry in conical spouted beds consisting of solids of varying density. *Ind. Eng. Chem. Res.*, **44** (2005), 193–200.

37. M. J. San José, M. Olazar, S. Alvarez, A. Morales, and J. Bilbao. Local porosity in conical spouted beds consisting of solids of varying density. *Chem. Eng. Sci.*, **60** (2005), 2017–2025.

38. G. Rovero, C. M. H. Brereton, N. Epstein, J. R. Grace, L. Casalegno, and N. Piccinini. Gas flow distribution in conical-base spouted beds. *Can. J. Chem. Eng.*, **61** (1983), 289–296.

39. M. Olazar, M. J. San José, S. Alvarez, A. Morales, and J. Bilbao. Measurement of particle velocities in conical spouted beds using an optical fiber probe. *Ind. Eng. Chem. Res.*, **37** (1998), 4520–4527.

40. A. Kmiec. Hydrodynamics of flow and heat transfer in spouted beds. *Chem. Eng. J.*, **19** (1980), 189–200.

41. M. I. Boulos and B. Waldie. High-resolution measurement of particles velocities in a spouted bed using laser-Doppler anemometry. *Can. J. Chem. Eng.*, **64** (1986), 939–943.

42. T. Robinson and B. Waldie. Particle cycle times in a spouted bed of polydisperse particles. *Can. J. Chem. Eng.*, **56** (1978), 632–635.

43. Y. L. He, S. Z. Qin, C. J. Lim, and J. R. Grace. Particle velocity profiles and solid flow patterns in spouted beds. *Can. J. Chem. Eng.*, **72** (1994), 561–568.

44. R. S. Krzywanski, N. Epstein, and B. D. Bowen. Multi-dimensional model of a spouted bed. *Can. J. Chem. Eng.*, **70** (1992), 858–872.

45. N. Epstein and J. R. Grace. Spouting of particulate solids. In *Handbook of Powder Science and Technology*, ed. M. E. Fayed and L. Otten (New York: Van Nostrand Reinhold, 1984), pp. 507–536.

46. M. Olazar, M. J. San José, M. A. Izquierdo, A. Ortiz de Salazar, and J. Bilbao. Effect of operating conditions on the solid velocity in spout, annulus and fountain of spouted beds. *Chem Eng. Sci.*, **56** (2001), 3585–3594.

47. M. J. San José, M. Olazar, S. Alvarez, M. A. Izquierdo, and J. Bilbao. Solid cross-flow into the spout and particle trajectories in conical spouted beds consisting of solids of different density and shape. *Chem. Eng. Res. Des.*, **84** (2006), 487–494.

48. H. Lu, Y. Song, Y. Li, Y. He, and J. Bouillard. Numerical simulations of hydrodynamic behaviour in spouted beds. *Chem. Eng. Res. Des.*, **79** (2001), 593–599.

49. H. Lu, Y. He, L. Wentie, J. Ding, D. Gidaspow, and J. Bouillard. Computer simulations of gas–solid flow in spouted beds using kinetic–frictional stress model of granular flow. *Chem. Eng. Sci.*, **59** (2004), 865–878.

50. Z. G. Wang, H. T. Bi, and C. J. Lim. Numerical simulations of hydrodynamic behaviors in conical spouted beds. *China Particuology*, **4** (2006), 194–203.

51. L. Diaz, I. Alava, J. Makibar, R. Fernandez, F. Cueva, R. Aguado, and M. Olazar. A first approach to CFD simulation of hydrodynamic behaviour in a conical spouted bed reactor. *Int. J. Chem. Reactor Eng.*, **6** (2008), A31.

52. C. R. Duarte, M. Olazar, V. V. Murata, and M. A. S. Barrozo. Numerical simulation and experimental study of fluid–particle flows in a spouted bed. *Powder Technol.*, **188** (2009), 195–205.

53. M. A. S. Barrozo, C. R. Duarte, N. Epstein, J. R. Grace, and C. J. Lim. Experimental and computational fluid dynamics study of dense-phase, transition region, and dilute-phase spouting. *Ind. Eng. Chem. Res.*, **49** (2010), 5102–5109.

54. K. G. Marnasidou, S. S. Voutetakis, G. J. Tjatjopoulos, and I. A. Vasalos. Catalytic partial oxidation of methane to synthetic gas in a pilot-plant-scale spouted-bed rector. *Chem. Eng. Sci.*, **54** (1999), 3691–3699.

55. M. Olazar, G. Lopez, H. Altzibar, R. Aguado, and J. Bilbao. Minimum spouting velocity under vacuum and high temperature in conical spouted beds. *Can. J. Chem. Eng.*, **87** (2009), 541–546.

56. M. Olazar, G. Zabala, J. M. Arandes, A. Gayubo, and J. Bilbao. Deactivation kinetic model in catalytic polymerizations – taking into account the initiation step. *Ind. Eng. Chem. Res.*, **35** (1996), 62–69.

57. M. Olazar, M. J. San José, R. Llamosas, and J. Bilbao. Hydrodynamics of sawdust and mixtures of wood residues in conical spouted beds. *Ind. Eng. Chem. Res.*, **33** (1994), 993–1000.

58. M. L. Mastellone and U. Arena. Fluidized-bed pyrolysis of polyolefin wastes: predictive defluidization model. *AIChE J.*, **48** (2002), 1439–1447.

59. R. Aguado, R. Prieto, M. J. San José, S. Alvarez, M. Olazar, and J. Bilbao. Defluidization modelling of pyrolyis of plastics in a conical spouted bed reactor. *Chem. Eng. Proc.*, **44** (2005), 231–235.

6 Hydrodynamics of spout-fluid beds

Wenqi Zhong, Baosheng Jin, Mingyao Zhang, and Rui Xiao

The spout-fluid bed is a very successful modification to the conventional spouted bed. It reduces some limitations of spouting and fluidization by combining features of spouted and fluidized beds. In spout-fluid beds, in addition to supplying spouting fluid through the central nozzle, auxiliary fluid is introduced through a porous or perforated distributor surrounding the central orifice. Compared with spouted beds, spout-fluid beds obtain better gas–solid contact and mixing in the annular dense region and reduce the likelihood of particle agglomeration, dead zones, and sticking to the wall or base of the column. However, the hydrodynamics of spout-fluid beds are more complex than those of conventional spouted beds. This chapter briefly presents up-to-date information on the fundamentals and applications of spout-fluid beds without draft tubes, based on the limited reported work.

6.1 Hydrodynamic characteristics

6.1.1 Flow regimes and flow regime map

Different flow regimes occur in a spout-fluid bed when the central spouting gas flowrate and the auxiliary gas flowrate are adjusted.[1-6] A schematic representation of familiar flow regimes is presented in Figure 6.1. These are the fixed bed (FB), internal jet (IJ), spouting with aeration (SA), jet in fluidized bed with bubbling (JFB), jet in fluidized bed with slugging (JFS), and spout-fluidizing (SF) regimes. The criteria for the description of these flow regimes are as follows:

- *Fixed bed*: A fixed bed (immobile particles) is formed if the total flow of the central spouting gas and the annular auxiliary gas is less than the minimum fluidizing or minimum spouting velocity, whichever is lower for the particular geometry and flow configuration.
- *Internal jet*: A submerged cavity or jet forms at the air inlet orifice, whereas the rest of the bed remains a fixed bed. When increasing the spouting gas flowrate, the jet height increases until it reaches a maximum.

Spouted and Spout-Fluid Beds: Fundamentals and Applications, eds. Norman Epstein and John R. Grace.
Published by Cambridge University Press. © Cambridge University Press 2011.

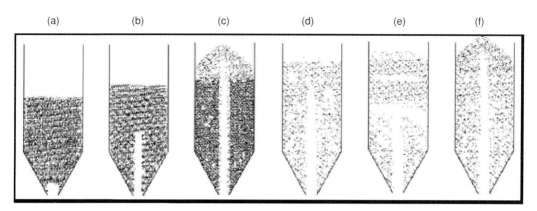

Figure 6.1. Schematic representation of flow regimes[5]: (a) FB; (b) IJ; (c) SA; (d) JFB; (e) JFS; (f) SF.

- *Spouting with aeration*: The bed has the appearance of a conventional spouted bed in this flow regime. However, it is less stable than conventional spouted beds, owing to the larger porosity of the annular region and large bubbles at the bed surface.
- *Jet in fluidized bed with bubbling*: Bubbles lift off from the top of the jet, causing bubbling in the upper part of the bed. However, a distinct jet is also observed.
- *Jet in fluidized bed with slugging*: Large bubbles form in the middle and upper parts of the bed and periodic slugging occurs in these regions. The behavior is similar to conventional fluidized beds operated in the slug flow regime.
- *Spout-fluidization*: In this regime, stable spouting is difficult to achieve. Instead, particles in the upper section are fluidized, while the spout below exhibits instability, periodically discharging bubbles near the bed surface.

Other flow regimes are also possible. For example, local fluidization can be observed if the spouting gas flowrate is very small while the fluidizing gas flowrate is large.[3,6] Unfortunately, there is no uniformity in the literature in designating some flow regimes. For example, the regime of jet, slug, and bubble in fluidized bed (JSBF), defined by He et al.,[3] is said to include four different states, in which the flow regimes of IJ, JFB, and JFS are involved.

The transitions of flow regime with spouting and fluidizing gas flowrates can be represented clearly in flow regime maps. Figures 6.2 and 6.3 present typical flow regime maps for a small spout-fluid bed[2] and a relatively large spout-fluid bed,[3] respectively. These two flow regime maps have many similarities. However, the transition from FB to SA in a larger column is direct, differing from observations in a small column,[1–6] in which a JFB regime separates the FB and SA regimes. Preliminary investigations show that the flow pattern and transitions in a spout-fluid bed can be distinguished by analysis of pressure fluctuation signals, such as by power spectrum analysis[7] or Shannnon entropy analysis.[8]

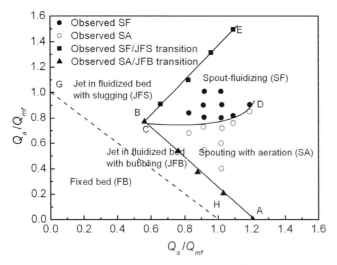

Figure 6.2. Regime map of a small spout-fluid bed[2] ($D = 152$ mm, $D_i = 19.1$ mm, $H = 0.6$ m, $\theta = 60°$, $d_p = 2.9$ mm, $\rho_p = 1040$ kg/m³, air at $20\,°C$ and 1.03 bar, G–fluidization at minimum condition, A–spouting at minimum condition, C–spout-fluidization at minimum condition).

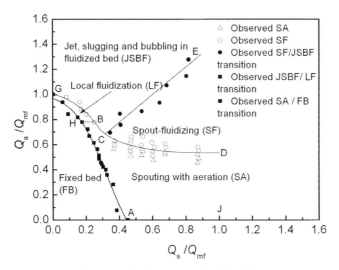

Figure 6.3. Regime map of a large spout-fluid bed[3] ($D = 0.91$ m, $D_i = 88.9$ mm, $\theta = 60°$, $H_0 = 1.5$ m, $d_p = 3.25$ mm, polystyrene particles, air at $20\,°C$ and 1.03 bar, G–minimum fluidization, A–minimum spouting, C–spout-fluidization at minimum condition).

6.1.2 Pressure drop and pressure distribution

The bed pressure drops in spout-fluid beds depend on the flows of both spouting gas and fluidizing gas. As shown in Figure 6.4, the pressure drop of a spout-fluid bed shares the characteristics of a conventional spouted bed when the spouting gas velocity is increased at a constant auxiliary gas velocity,[9–12] whereas the pressure drop across a spout-fluid bed varies in a manner similar to that of a fluidized bed when increasing the auxiliary

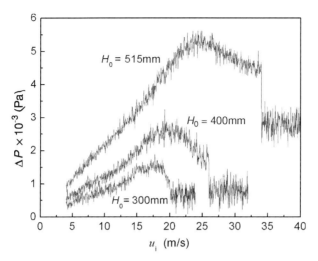

Figure 6.4. Pressure drop versus spouting gas velocity[12] ($A = 0.3$ m $\times$ 0.03 m, $A_i = 0.03$ m $\times$ 0.03 m, $\theta = 60°$, $U_a/U_{mf} = 0.39$, $d_p = 3.2$ mm, $\rho_p = 1640$ kg/m³).

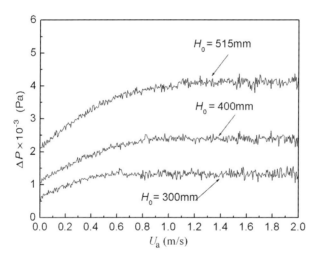

Figure 6.5. Pressure drop versus auxiliary ("fluidizing") gas velocity[12] ($A = 0.3$ m $\times$ 0.03 m, $A_i = 0.03$ m $\times$ 0.03 m, $\theta = 60°$, $u_i = 10$ m/s, $d_p = 3.2$ mm, and $\rho_p = 1640$ kg/m³).

gas velocity while maintaining the spouting gas velocity constant.[11,12] As illustrated in Figure 6.5, the pressure drop increases gradually with increasing fluidizing gas velocity and then approaches a constant level.

In a spout-fluid bed, the maximum pressure drop required to initiate spouting increases with increasing static bed height, spout nozzle diameter, and particle density, but decreases with increasing particle diameter. These tendencies are similar to those of conventional spouted beds. Furthermore, the maximum pressure drop across a spout-fluid bed decreases with increasing fluidizing gas velocity.[12]

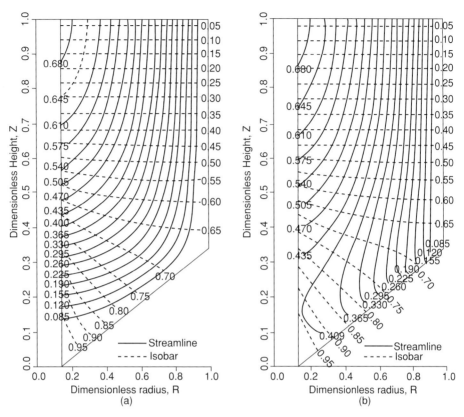

Figure 6.6. Comparison of fluid flow and pressure distribution of a conventional spouted bed and a spout-fluid bed[3] ($D = 0.91$ m, $D_i = 88.9$ mm, $\theta = 60°$, $H_0 = 2$ m, polystyrene, $d_p = 3.25$ mm): (a) $Q_a = 0$; (b) $Q_a = 0.2$ m³/s.

Addition of auxiliary gas causes the pressure distribution to be more uniform in the radial direction, even in the conical lower part of the column. The pressure gradient in the vertical direction is substantially higher with auxiliary flow present because of increased interstitial flow through the annulus.[3,11] The Epstein-Levine[13] and Lefroy-Davidson[14] equations have been found to be in reasonable agreement with experimental pressure profiles in the annulus.

A computer model that involves finite difference solutions of the vector form of the Ergun[15] equation gives useful qualitative predictions of the fluid flow distribution and good predictions of the pressure profiles in the annulus. A typical comparison of fluid flow and pressure distribution of a spouted bed with a spout-fluid bed based on the vector form[3] of the Ergun equation is shown in Figure 6.6. Solid curves represent streamlines, whereas dashed lines represent predicted isobars in the annulus. The distribution of flow leaving the bed through the top of the annulus is virtually the same for the conventional spouted bed and the spout-fluid bed. However, more gas enters the annulus from the spout near the central inlet for the spouted bed. As the auxiliary flow rate increases, some gas even enters the spout from the annulus.

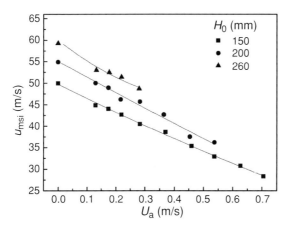

Figure 6.7. Variation of minimum spouting velocity with fluidizing gas velocity[17] ($D = 0.125$ m, $D_i = 18$ mm, $\theta = 60°$, $d_p = 1.62$ mm, $\rho_p = 2490$ kg/m³).

6.1.3   Minimum spouting velocity and minimum spout-fluidizing velocity

The minimum spouting velocity of a spout-fluid bed can be defined as the spout nozzle-based spouting gas velocity, u_{msi},[12] or as the column-based superficial spouting gas velocity, U_{ms},[16,17] when spouting is initiated in the central spout region at a certain auxiliary gas velocity. Both definitions share the characteristics of a conventional spouted bed[18,19] in that both u_{msi} and U_{ms} increase with increasing static bed height, particle density, particle diameter, and spout nozzle diameter. However, they also decrease with increasing fluidizing gas velocity, as indicated in Figure 6.7.

The minimum spout-fluidizing velocity, U_{msf}, of a spout-fluid bed, defined as the minimum total superficial gas velocity when spouting is initiated in the central spout region and the annulus is aerated, also increases with increasing static bed height, particle density, particle diameter, and spout nozzle diameter.[12,16,17] An increase in auxiliary gas velocity also leads to increasing U_{msf},[12] as plotted in Figure 6.8. The bed diameter and perforated distributor configuration (e.g., cone angle, gas distribution geometry, and hole orientation angle) all affect U_{msf}. By comparing U_{msf} for a small column[2] with a large column,[3] it is found that U_{msf} decreases with increasing column diameter. Moreover, U_{msf} decreases with increasing included cone angle, but increases with increasing hole orientation angle (angle from the horizontal).[17]

The correlation of Tang and Zhang[17] based on 590 groups of experimental data,

$$\frac{1}{1-\varepsilon_{mf}}\frac{d_p U_{ms}\rho}{\mu} = \cos(\theta/6)\sin(\theta/2)\tan(\varphi)f(D/D_{cref})$$
$$\times \left(\frac{H_o}{D}\right)^{0.43}\left(\frac{d_p}{D}\right)^{1.90}\left(\frac{D_i}{D}\right)^{0.33}\left(\frac{\rho(\rho_p-\rho)gD^3}{\mu^2}\right)^{0.65}$$
$$\times \left(0.051 - 0.00046\left(\frac{d_p U_{mf}\rho}{\mu}\right)^{0.83}\right), \qquad (6.1)$$

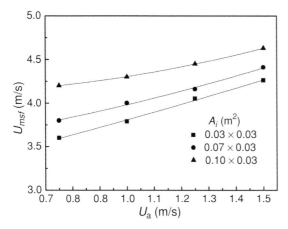

Figure 6.8. Variation of minimum spout-fluidizing velocity with fluidizing gas velocity[12] ($A = 0.3$ m × 0.03 m, $\theta = 60°$, $H_0/D = 1.72$, $d_p = 2.8$ mm, $\rho_p = 1018$ kg/m³).

can predict reasonable trends for U_{ms} in terms of cone angle, θ, gas distribution geometry, hole orientation angle, φ (angle between fluidizing gas inlet line and distributor plane), bed diameter, D, and reference diameter,[18] D_{ref}, by using modified functions of $\cos(\theta/6)$, $\sin(\theta/2)$, $\tan(\varphi)$, and $f(D/D_{ref})$.

The spout-nozzle-based u_{msi} correlation of Zhong et al.,[12] based on 314 groups of experimental data, can also be used. This correlation has a similar form to that of Choi and Meisen,[19] but adds the term $(1 + U_a/U_{mf})$ to cover the effect of fluidizing gas, giving

$$u_{msi} = 24.5\,(2gH_o)^{0.5} \left(\frac{d_p}{D}\right)^{0.472} \left(\frac{D_i}{D}\right)^{0.183} \left(\frac{H_o}{D}\right)^{0.208} \left(1 + \frac{U_a}{U_{mf}}\right)^{-0.284}$$

$$\times \left(\frac{\rho_p - \rho}{\rho}\right)^{0.225} \quad U_a \geq 0. \tag{6.2}$$

To determine the minimum spout-fluidizing velocity, U_{msf}, the correlations of Nagarkatti and Chatterjee[9] and Zhong et al.[12] predict the right trends. However, these correlations still need to be further tested and improved based on additional experimental data.

6.1.4   Voidage and particle velocity

Typical radial profiles of local voidage measured by an optical probe[20] are presented in Figure 6.9. Spout voidage decreases with increasing auxiliary airflow; this finding is nearly independent of particle size. The local voidage in the annulus increases with increasing height, whereas there is no consistent trend with increasing auxiliary airflow. Spout shapes, determined from voidage profiles and plotted in Figure 6.10, are similar to those in conventional spouted beds.[21] The spout diameter increases with increasing particle size. The proportion of auxiliary air has remarkably little influence on the spout diameter.[20,22]

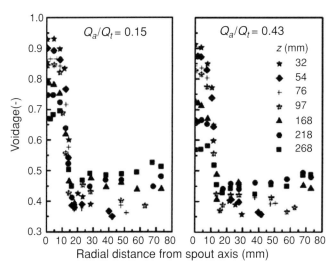

Figure 6.9. Radial profiles of local voidage at different heights[20] ($D = 0.152$ m, $D_i = 19.1$ mm, $\theta = 60°$, $H_0 = 0.28$ m, $d_p = 1.33$ mm, $\rho_p = 2493$ kg/m^3, $U_{ms} = 0.672$ m/s, $Q_t = Q_s + Q_a = 1.2Q_{ms}$).

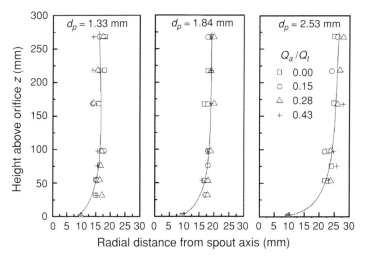

Figure 6.10. Vertical profiles of spout radii for three particle sizes[20] ($D = 0.152$ m, $D_i = 19.1$ mm, $\theta = 60°$, $H_0 = 0.28$ m, glass beads, $Q_t = Q_s + Q_a = 1.2Q_{ms}$).

The particle velocity profiles in the spout are of similar shape to those in conventional spouted beds,[23] as shown in Figure 6.11. A maximum velocity is reached at some distance above the orifice, above which the particle velocity generally decreases with increasing height. Increasing the proportion of auxiliary gas, Q_a/Q_t, may reduce the local particle velocity in the spout and reduce the difference in local particle velocity between the bottom and top of the bed. Velocity profiles in the annulus for a spout-fluid bed resemble those reported by He et al.[21] for a conventional spouted bed. The vertical

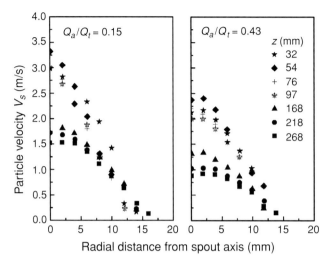

Figure 6.11. Radial profiles of particle velocities in the spout[20] ($D = 0.152$ m, $D_i = 19.1$ mm, $\theta = 60°$, $H_0 = 0.28$ m, $d_p = 1.84$ mm, $\rho_p = 2485$ kg/m^3, $U_{ms} = 0.795$ m/s, $Q_t = Q_s + Q_a = 1.2Q_{ms}$).

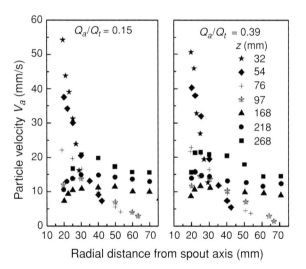

Figure 6.12. Radial profiles of particle velocities in the annulus[20] ($D = 0.152$ m, $D_i = 19.1$ mm, $\theta = 60°$, $H_0 = 0.28$ m, $d_p = 1.84$ mm, $\rho_p = 2485$ kg/m^3, $U_{ms} = 0.795$ m/s, $Q_t = Q_s + Q_a = 1.2Q_{ms}$).

particle velocities decrease with decreasing height. Particles also travel more slowly near the outer wall of the column and there is limited influence of the proportion of gas entering as auxiliary gas, as portrayed in Figure 6.12.

Time-average solids mass flowrates in the spout and annulus of spout-fluid beds can be calculated by integrating the voidage and particle velocity profiles, based on the steady state requirement that the upward-moving solids mass flow in the spout should equal the downward-moving solids mass flow in the annulus (see He et al.[23]). As for conventional

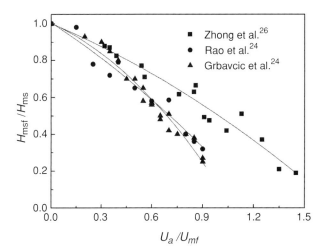

Figure 6.13. Effect of auxiliary gas flowrate on H_{msf}/H_{ms} ($D = 90$ mm, $D_i = 10.3$ mm, $d_p = 1.84$–2.42 mm, $\rho_p = 2600$ kg/m³)[24]; ($D = 144$ mm, $D_i = 25$ mm, $d_p = 2.03$–4.12 mm, $\rho_p = 2511$–2573 kg/m³)[25]; ($A = 0.3$ m $\times$ 0.03 m, $A_i = 0.03$ m $\times$ 0.03 m, $d_p = 1.3$–3.2 mm, $\rho_p = 1018$–2600 kg/m³).[26]

spouted beds, the solids mass flowrates in the spout and annulus increase with increasing height, with particles entering the spout over its entire height. As reported by Pianarosa et al.,[20] with increasing auxiliary gas flow there is some decrease in net solids circulation owing to less entrainment of particles by the centrally injected spouting gas.

6.1.5   Spoutable bed height

The maximum spoutable bed height, H_m, is an important characteristic of both conventional spouted beds and spout-fluid beds, because it is directly related to the amount of material that can be processed by spouting. In spout-fluid beds, H_m can be determined by adding particles stepwise until periodic and incoherent spouting can no longer be achieved for any spouting gas velocity at a given auxiliary gas flowrate.

H_m for a spout-fluid bed decreases with increasing particle size and increasing spout orifice diameter.[24–27] Increasing the fluidizing gas flowrate leads to a sharp decrease in H_m, as presented in Figure 6.13, where H_{msf} and H_{ms} are the maximum spoutable bed heights with and without fluidizing gas, respectively. Existing H_m correlations for conventional spouted beds[24,25,27] are subject to large discrepancies when used to predict H_m for spout-fluid beds, because they neglect the effect of the auxiliary gas.[26]

When bed materials are tested with bed depth exceeding the maximum spoutable bed height, the region of stable flow pattern is narrow, and a stable coherent spout or fountain cannot be obtained. Instead, periodic and incoherent spouting and spout-fluidizing occur.[26] A stable flow pattern of JFB may form; this is of special interest for some applications, such as coal gasification.[27] In this case, the spout-fluid bed resembles a jetting fluidized bed, as described by Yang.[28,29]

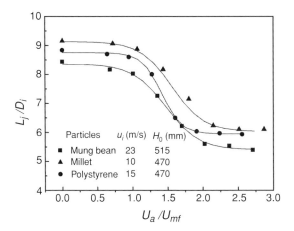

Figure 6.14. Effect of fluidizing gas flowrate on jet penetration depth L_j[35] ($A = 0.3$ m $\times$ 0.03 m, $A_i = 0.03$ m $\times$ 0.03 m, $\theta = 60°$).

6.1.6   Jet penetration depth

One of the features of gas injection into a spout-fluid bed is the distance to which fluid dynamic disturbances associated with the injection extend, known as the *jet penetration depth*. The jet penetration depth of spout-fluid beds operated in the flow regime of JFB is similar to that in a jetting fluidized bed.[29–34] The jet penetration depth increases with increasing spouting gas velocity and with increasing spout orifice diameter, whereas it decreases with increasing particle density, particle diameter, static bed height, and auxiliary gas flowrate.[35] Figure 6.14 shows the typical variation of jet penetration depth with auxiliary gas flowrate.

6.1.7   Gas mixing

Mixing of spouting gas and auxiliary gas of spout-fluid beds has been investigated by tracer techniques. Experiments found that transfer of spouting gas into the annulus and of auxiliary gas into the spout take place simultaneously,[29,36–41] leading to mixing of spouting and auxiliary gases. Increasing the spouting gas velocity and fluidizing gas flowrate can promote both axial and radial gas mixing in spout-fluid beds,[38–40] but increasing the auxiliary gas flowrate is more effective.[40,41] The axial and radial gas mixing become poor when the flow pattern undergoes a transition from stable to unstable flow, and it is difficult to obtain effective mixing in the wall layers.[41]

The mechanism of gas mixing in spout-fluid beds is complex, according to the findings in the literature on diffusive mixing, on convective transport[29,37,38] owing to pressure gradient, and on combined convection and diffusion[39–41] because of pressure and concentration gradients. Based on different gas mixing mechanisms, different models have been proposed.[37,39,41] The probabilistic model of Freychet et al.[39] indicates that the gas exchange rate between the spout jet and annulus increases rapidly with increasing auxiliary gas velocity. Similar results have been predicted by a three-region mixing model.[41]

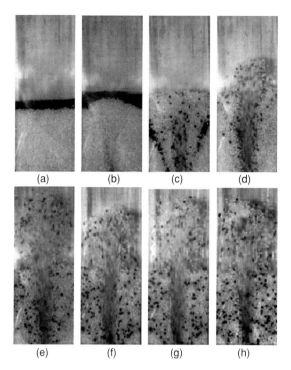

Figure 6.15. Sequential stages of particle mixing[44] ($A = 0.1$ m $\times$ 0.03 m, $A_i = 0.01$ m $\times$ 0.03 m, flat-bottom spout-fluid bed, $d_p = 0.5$ mm, $\rho_p = 2650$ kg/m^3, $u_i/u_{msi} = 1.4$, $U_a/U_{mf} \geq 0$): (a) $t = 0$ s; (b) $t = 2$ s; (c) $t = 4$ s; (d) $t = 6$ s; (e) $t = 10$ s; (f) $t = 15$ s; (g) $t = 20$ s; (h) $t = 30$ s.

6.1.8   Particle mixing

Particle tracer and digital image processing have been used to investigate particle mixing in spout-fluid beds. Increasing both the spouting velocity and the auxiliary gas velocity can promote mixing.[42,43] Axial mixing varies more than radial mixing with increasing spouting gas velocity, whereas this is reversed when increasing the auxiliary gas velocity.[43] The initial tracer location affects the rate of mixing. For example, in one study,[44] mixing was much faster for middle loading than for top, side, and bottom loading, but the final degree of mixing was independent of the initial tracer location.

The particle mixing process can be divided into three sequential stages: a macromixing stage, a micromixing stage, and a stable mixing stage.[43] In the macromixing stage (Figures 6.15a–c), the mixing speed is high, but the degree of mixing is low; in the micromixing stage (Figures 6.15d,e), tracer particles mix with the bed material at the individual particle level; in the stable mixing stage (Figures 6.15f–h), a dynamic equilibrium is achieved. Particle mixing in spout-fluid beds is caused by diffusion, transportation, circulation, and the action of bubbles.[43,44] Diffusion, transportation, and circulation dominate solids mixing at high spouting gas flowrates, whereas bubble action becomes dominant at large auxiliary gas flowrates.[44]

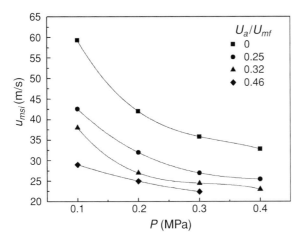

Figure 6.16. Effect of pressure on minimum spouting velocity[45] ($D = 0.1$ m, $D_i = 0.01$ m, $\theta = 60°$, $d_p = 2.3$ mm, $\rho_p = 1330$ kg/m³, $H_0/D = 1.5$).

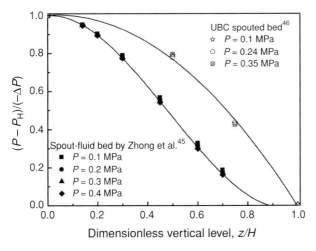

Figure 6.17. Effect of pressure on axial dimensionless pressure drop[45,46] ($D = 100$ mm, $D_i = 10$ mm, $\theta = 60°$, $d_p = 2.3$ mm, $\rho_p = 1330$ kg/m³, $H_0/D_0 = 3.0$, $U_s/U_{ms} = 1.35$, $U_a/U_{mf} = 0.6$)[45]; ($D_0 = 76.2$ mm, $D_i = 9.5$ mm, $\theta = 60°$, $d_p = 1.09$ mm, $\rho_p = 2445$ kg/m³, $H_0/D = 1.78$, $U_s/U_{ms} = 1.2$).[46]

6.1.9 Hydrodynamics at elevated pressures and temperatures

Increasing the pressure leads to decreases in both minimum spouting velocity (Figure 6.16) and spout-fluidizing velocity.[45] Pressure increases also cause an increase in fountain height. As for the conventional spouted bed tested by He et al.,[46] the axial pressure profile in a spout-fluid bed is insensitive to changes in mean pressure[45] (see Figure 6.17), whereas the amplitude of pressure fluctuations is reduced at elevated pressures. As shown in Figure 6.18, the overall extent of the stable flow

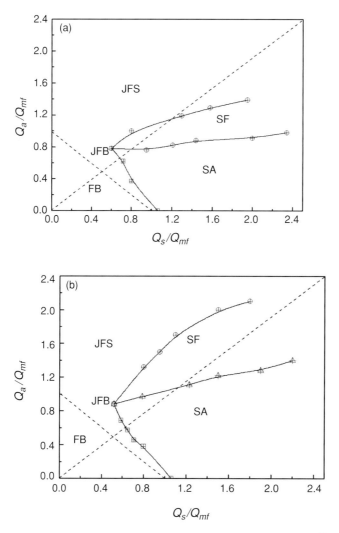

Figure 6.18. Typical flow pattern map at various operating pressures[47] ($D = 0.1$ m, $D_i = 0.01$ m, $\theta = 60°$, $d_p = 2.3$ mm, $\rho_p = 1330$ kg/m^3, $H_0/D = 2.0$): (a) 0.1 MPa; (b) 0.3 MPa.

regions – that is, JFB, SA, and SF ranges – becomes larger when the bed pressure is increased.[47]

For large particles, the minimum spouting velocity generally increases with increasing temperature, whereas for small particles it decreases. Auxiliary air has more influence on the minimum spouting velocity at elevated temperature than at room temperature.[48] Each of the flow regimes observed at low temperatures can also occur at high temperatures. However, high temperatures tend to shift the behavior to less stable flow regimes – pulsatory spouting, submerged jets, and slugging are more likely to occur at high temperatures than at room temperature.[49]

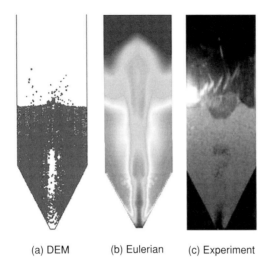

(a) DEM   (b) Eulerian   (c) Experiment

Figure 6.19. Typical simulated flow patterns compared with experiment[53] ($A = 0.3$ m $\times$ 0.03 m, $A_i = 0.03$ m $\times$ 0.03 m, $\theta = 60°$, $H_0 = 500$ mm, $d_p = 2.8$ mm, $\rho_p = 1020$ kg/m^3, $U_s/U_{ms} = 0.76$, $U_a/U_{mf} = 0.78$).

6.1.10   Numerical simulation of hydrodynamics

Two kinds of CFD models – Eulerian-Lagrangian[50–54] and Eulerian-Eulerian[55,56] – have been developed to predict the hydrodynamics of spout-fluid beds (see Chapter 4). These models can be used to predict the gas-solid flow regimes (see Figure 6.19). They may also provide information that is very difficult to obtain experimentally. For example, DEM simulation shows that the drag force dominates the particle motion in the jet region, whereas interparticle contact forces dominate the particle motion in the dense annular region, especially near the wall.[54] Eulerian simulation shows that particle velocities and concentrations at high temperature and pressure behave in similar manners to those at ambient pressure and temperature.[56] Eulerian simulations are useful to predict the hydrodynamics of large-scale spout-fluid beds because of limited computational requirements (CPU and memory).

In addition to the simulation of hydrodynamics, the kinetic theory of granular flow, based on the Eulerian method and involving mass transfer, momentum transfer, heat transfer, and chemical reaction, has been demonstrated to be effective in analyzing and optimizing energy-conversion processes in spout-fluid beds, such as for pressurized coal gasification.[57,58]

6.2   Typical applications

6.2.1   Combustion

Researchers at the University of British Columbia have investigated the combustion of low-grade solid fuels in spout-fluid beds[49,59,60] in a 0.15-m diameter half-column

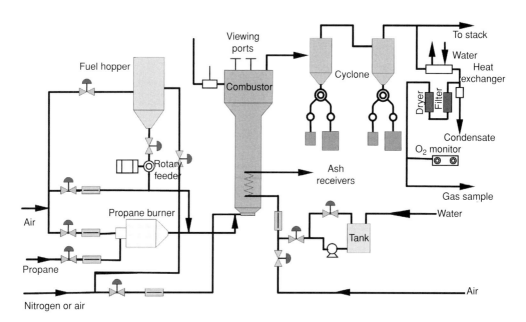

Figure 6.20. Schematic of spout-fluid bed combustion system at University of British Columbia.[60]

and a 0.3-m-diameter cylindrical spout-fluid bed combustor. Three bituminous coals or coal rejects of differing ash contents were burned in the spout-fluid bed to compare the relative throughput capacity and combustion efficiency of spouted and fluidized beds. A schematic of the 0.3-m-diameter spout-fluid bed combustion system is shown in Figure 6.20. Experimental results indicate that the spout-fluid bed gave somewhat higher combustion efficiencies at low temperatures, greater temperature uniformity, and improved bed-to-surface heat transfer compared with the other modes of operation.[60]

The Asian Institute of Technology in Thailand has also carried out combustion of coal and carbon in spouted and spout-fluid beds to test the use of Thai lignite and pyrolyzed electrode carbon as fuels.[61] Mindanao Polytechnic State College of the Philippines applied different configurations of "spout-fluidized" beds, namely, a multiple-spouted and a spout-fluid bed, to combustion of rice husk fuel.[62] The spout-fluidized bed combustor body was made of 3.4-mm-thick mild steel with a cross-sectional area of 0.7 m × 0.7 m. The emission of pollutants and the feasibility of burning rice husk in these different configurations at different excess airflow rates, primary-to-secondary air ratios, and method of feeding fuel were tested. The work showed that spout-fluid bed combustion could be a suitable technology for converting a wide range of agricultural residues into energy because of its fuel flexibility, low emission of pollutants, low operating temperature, and isothermal operating conditions.

6.2.2   Gasification

The British Coal Corporation developed a spout-fluid bed gasification process at its Coal Research Establishment for the production of low-calorific-value fuel gas.[63] The work

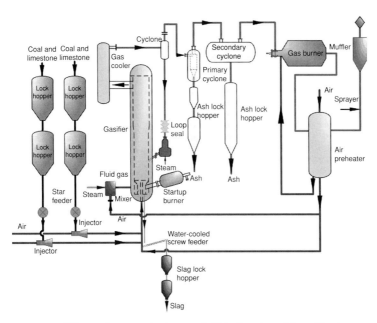

Figure 6.21. Pilot-scale pressurized spout-fluid bed coal partial gasification system operated by the Southeast University of China.[65]

provided a flexible low-cost process for onsite production of industrial fuel gas (gross calorific value $\sim$4 MJ/m^3) as an integral component of a high-efficiency (conversion efficiency up to 95%), low-cost electric power generation system, known as the British Coal topping cycle.

Southeast University of China constructed spout-fluid bed pressurized coal partial gasification-based advanced pressurized fluidized bed combustion-combined cycle systems for low rank coals. They built 0.08-m-, 0.1-m-, and 0.45-m-diameter cylindrical pressurized spout-fluid bed gasifiers.[64–66] A schematic of the pilot scale spout-fluid bed coal partial gasification system is shown in Figure 6.21. For a deep-bed gasification process (H_0/D up to 9), the temperature in the dense bed was uniform (variation along the bed height $<30\,°C$), and the gas generated had a heating value up to 4.8 MJ/Nm^3. The product gas could burn steadily in the combustor at a temperature of 1100 °C to 1150 °C, allowing a gas turbine inlet temperature range of 1100 °C to 1300 °C without adding auxiliary fuels.

The Asian Institute of Technology of Thailand presented a feasible option for converting municipal solid waste (MSW) to useful energy based on spout-fluid bed gasification.[67] The gasifier was 0.45 m square in cross-section with a height of 3 m from the distributor plate to the top of the enlargement zone. The producer gas higher heating value (HHV) was in a narrow range of 4.4 to 4.6 MJ/Nm^3. The gasification efficiency and carbon conversion efficiency were raised, respectively, from 35.8 percent and 55.3 percent (25% of stoichiometric air at base case) to 39.0 percent and 65.3 percent (25% of stoichiometric air without secondary air supply). The range of compositions were CO 14.8%$\sim$18.5%, H$_2$ 7.1%$\sim$9.7%, CH$_4$ 2.8%$\sim$3.1%, and CO$_2$ 16.6%$\sim$18.5%.

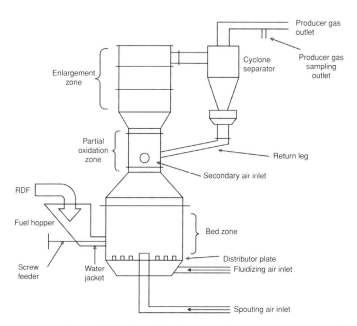

Figure 6.22. Spout-fluid bed gasification setup for municipal solid waste.[67]

The producer gas could be used for direct heat application or industrial steam production (Figure 6.22).

6.2.3   Other applications

Other applications, such as biomass gasification,[68] drying,[69] and production of granules or particles through granulation,[70] are under development. In addition, there are successful applications of spout-fluid beds with draft tube, such as for dry premixing of cementitious materials and sand[71,72] and for drying of agricultural products,[73] as covered in other chapters.

6.3   Closing remarks

As a modified gas-solid contacting technique, the spout-fluid bed reduces some of the limitations of both conventional spouting and gas-fluidization. However, the hydrodynamics of spout-fluid beds are more complex than those for conventional spouted beds. Hydrodynamic properties and scaleup cannot, at this stage, be predicted with confidence. This chapter summarizes information on the fundamentals and applications of spout-fluid beds without a draft tube, based on the limited work reported this far. More experimental and theoretical work is required to more fully understand and apply spout-fluid beds.

Chapter-specific nomenclature

D_{ref} reference diameter[18] of column, m
H_{msf} maximum spoutable height of spout-fluid bed, m
H_{ms} maximum spoutable height of spouted bed, m
L_{j} jet penetration depth, m
Q_s volumetric flow rate of entering spouting gas, m^3/s
Q_t total gas volumetric flow rate, m^3/s
U_a superficial velocity of entering auxiliary gas, based on D, m/s
U_{msf} superficial gas velocity at minimum spout-fluidizing, m/s
U_s superficial velocity of entering spouting gas, based on D, m/s

Greek letters

φ hole orientation angle

References

1. D. V. Vuković, Dž. E. Hadžismajlović, Ž. B. Grbavčić, R. V. Garić, and H. Littman. Flow regimes for spout-fluid beds. *Can. J. Chem. Eng.*, **62** (1984), 825–829.
2. W. Sutanto, N. Epstein, and J. R. Grace. Hydrodynamics of spout-fluid beds. *Powder Technol.*, **44** (1985), 205–212.
3. Y. L. He, C. J. Lim, and J. R. Grace, Spouted bed and spout-fluid bed behaviors in a column of diameter 0.91 m. *Can. J. Chem. Eng.*, **70** (1992), 848–857.
4. T. Ishikura. Regime map of binary particle mixture in a spout-fluid bed. *Kagaku Kōgaku Ronbunshū*, **19** (1993), 1189–1192.
5. W. Q. Zhong, M. Y. Zhang, B. S. Jin, and X. P. Chen. Flow pattern and transition of rectangular spout-fluid bed. *Chem. Eng. Proc.* **45** (2006), 734–746.
6. J. Y. Zhang and F. X. Tang. Prediction of flow regimes in spout-fluidized beds. *China Particuology*, **4** (2006), 189–193.
7. W. Q. Zhong and M. Y. Zhang. Pressure fluctuation frequency characteristics in a spout-fluid bed by modern ARM power spectrum analysis. *Powder Technol.*, **152** (2005), 52–61.
8. W. Q. Zhong and M. Y. Zhang. Characterization of dynamic behavior of a spout-fluid bed with Shannon entropy analysis. *Powder Technol.*, **159** (2005), 121–126.
9. A. Nagarkatti and A. Chatterjee. Pressure and flow characteristics of a gas phase spout-fluid condition. *Can. J. Chem. Eng.*, **52** (1974), 185–195.
10. H. Littman, D. V. Vukovic, F. K. Zdanski, and Z. B. Grbavcic. Pressure drop and flowrate characteristics of a liquid phase spout-fluid bed at the minimum spout-fluid flow rate. *Can. J. Chem. Eng.*, **52** (1974), 174–179.
11. C. Heil and M. Tels. Pressure distribution in spout-fluid bed reactors. *Can. J. Chem. Eng.*, **61** (1983), 331–342.
12. W. Q. Zhong, X. P. Chen, and M. Y. Zhang. Hydrodynamic characteristics of spout-fluid bed: pressure drop and minimum spouting/spout-fluidizing velocity. *Chem. Eng. J.*, **118** (2006), 37–46.

13. N. Epstein and S. Levine. Non-Darcy flow and pressure distribution in a spouted bed. In *Fluidization*, ed. J. F. Davidson and D. L. Keairns (Cambridge, UK: Cambridge University Press, 1978), pp. 98–103.

14. G. A. Lefroy and J. F. Davidson. The mechanics of spouted beds. *Trans. Instn Chem. Engrs.*, **47** (1969), 120–128.

15. S. Ergun. Fluid flow through packed columns. *Chem. Eng. Progr*, **48**:2 (1952), 89–94.

16. Z. Mohammed and Z. Anabtawi. Minumum spouting velocity, minimum spout-fluidized velocity and maximum spoutable bed height in a gas-solid bidimensional spout-fluid bed. *J. Chem. Eng. Japan*, **26** (1993), 728–732.

17. F. X. Tang and J. Y. Zhang. Multi-factor effects on and correlation of minimum spout-fluidizing velocity in spout-fluid beds. *Chem. Industry & Engng. (China)*, **55** (2004), 1083–1091.

18. A. G. Fane and R. A. Mitchell. Minimum spouting velocity of scaled-up beds. *Can. J. Chem. Eng.*, **62** (1984), 437–439.

19. M. Choi and A. Meisen. Hydrodynamics of shallow, conical spouted beds. *Can. J. Chem. Eng.*, **70** (1992), 916–924.

20. D. L. Pianarosa, L. P. Freitas, C. J. Lim, J. R. Grace, and O. M. Dogan. Voidage and particle velocity profiles in a spout-fluid bed. *Can. J. Chem. Eng.*, **78** (2000), 132–142.

21. Y. L. He, C. J. Lim, J. R. Grace, J. X. Zhu, and S. Z. Qin. Measurement of voidage profiles in spouted beds. *Can. J. Chem. Eng.*, **72** (1994), 229–234.

22. W. Sutanto. Hydrodynamics of spout-fluid beds. MASc. thesis, Univ. of British Columbia, Vancouver, Canada (1983).

23. Y. L. He, S. Z. Qin, C. J. Lim, and J. R. Grace. Particle velocity profiles and solids flow patterns in spouted beds. *Can. J. Chem. Eng.*, **72** (1994), 561–568.

24. K. B. Rao, A. Husain, and C. D. Rao. Prediction of the maximum spoutable height in spout-fluid beds. *Can. J. Chem. Eng.*, **63** (1985), 690–692.

25. Ž. B. Grbavčić, D. V. Vuković, Dž. E. Hadžismajlović, R. V. Garić, and H. Littman. Prediction of the maximum spoutable bed height in spout-fluid beds. *Can. J. Chem. Eng.*, **69** (1991), 386–389.

26. W. Q. Zhong, M. Y. Zhang, and B. S. Jin. Maximum spoutable bed height of spout-fluid bed. *Can. J. Chem. Eng.*, **124** (2006), 55–62.

27. H. Littman and M. H. Morgan. New spouting regime in beds of coarse particles deeper than the maximum spoutable height. *Can. J. Chem. Eng.*, **64** (1986), 505–508.

28. W. C. Yang and D. L. Keairns. Design and operating parameters for a fluidized bed agglomerating combustor/gasifier. In *Fluidization*, ed. J. F. Davidson and D. L. Keairns. (Cambridge, UK: Cambridge University Press, 1978), pp. 208–213.

29. W. C. Yang. Comparison of the jet phenomena in 30-cm and 3-m diameter semicircular fluidized beds. *Powder Technol.*, **100** (1998), 147–160.

30. T. M. Knowlton and I. Hirsan. The effect of pressure on jet penetration in semi-cylindrical gas-fluidized bed. In *Fluidization*, ed. J. R. Grace and J. M. Matsen (New York: Plenum, 1980), pp. 315–324.

31. T. R. Blake, H. Webb, and P. B. Sunderland. The nondimensionalization of equations describing fluidization with application to the correlation of jet penetration depth. *Chem. Eng. Sci.*, **45** (1990), 365–371.

32. T. Kimura, K. Horiuchi, T. Watanabe, M. Matsukata, and T. Kojima. Experimental study of gas and particle behavior in the grid zone of a jetting fluidized bed cold model. *Powder Technol.*, **82** (1995), 135–143.

33. R. Y. Hong, H. Z. Li, M. Y. Cheng, and J. Y. Zhang. Numerical simulation and verification of a gas–solid jet fluidized bed. *Powder Technol.*, **87** (1996), 73–81.

34. Q. J. Guo, G. X. Yue, and J. Y. Zhang. Hydrodynamic behavior of a two-dimension jetting fluidized bed with binary mixtures. *Chem. Eng. Sci.*, **56** (2001), 4685–4694.

35. W. Q. Zhong and M. Y. Zhang. Jet penetration depth in a two-dimensional spout-fluid bed. *Chem. Eng. Sci*, **60** (2005), 315–327.

36. M. Filla, L. Massimilla, and S. Vaccaro. Gas jets in fluidized beds and spouts: a comparison for experimental behavior and models. *Can. J. Chem. Eng.*, **61** (1982), 370–376.

37. W. C. Yang, D. L. Keairns, and D. K. McLain. Gas mixing in a jetting fluidized bed. *AIChE Symp. Ser.*, **80** (1984), 32–41.

38. E. A. M. Gbordzoe, N. Freychet, and M. A. Bergougnou. Gas transfer between a central jet and a large two-dimensional gas-fluidized bed. *Powder Technol.*, **55** (1988), 207–222.

39. N. Freychet, C. L. Briens, M. A. Bergougnou, and J. F. Large. A new approach to jet phenomena gas entrainment and recirculation in a bidimensional spouted fluidized bed. *Can. J. Chem. Eng.*, **67** (1989), 191–199.

40. W. Q. Zhong, R. Xiao, and M. Y. Zhang. Experimental study of gas mixing in a spout-fluid bed. *AIChE J.*, **52** (2006), 924–930.

41. W. Q. Zhong, M. Y. Zhang, B. S. Jin, and R. Xiao. Experimental and model investigations on gas mixing behaviors of spout-fluid beds. *Int. Chem. Reactor Eng.*, **5** (2007), A32.

42. W. Q. Zhong, M. Y. Zhang, B. S. Jin, Y. Zhang, R. Xiao, and Y. J. Huang. Experimental investigation of particle mixing behavior in a large spout-fluid bed. *Chem. Eng. Process: Process Intensification*, **46** (2007), 990–995.

43. Y. Zhang, B. S. Jin, and W. Q. Zhong. Experimental investigations on the effect of the tracer location on mixing in a spout-fluid bed. *Int. Chem. Reactor Engng.*, **6** (2008), 44.

44. Y. Zhang, B. S. Jin, and W. Q. Zhong. Experiment on particle mixing in flat-bottom spout–fluid bed. *Chem. Eng. Process: Process Intensification*, **48** (2009), 745–754.

45. W. Q. Zhong, Q. J. Li, M. Y. Zhang, B. S. Jin, R. Xiao, Y. J. Huang, and A. Y. Shi. Spout characteristics of a cylindrical spout-fluid bed with elevated pressure. *Chem. Eng. J.* **139** (2008), 42–47.

46. Y. L. He, C. J. Lim, and J. R. Grace. Hydrodynamics of pressurized spouted beds. *Can. J. Chem. Eng.*, **76** (1998), 696–701.

47. W. Q. Zhong, X. F. Wang, Q. J. Li, B. S. Jin, M. Y. Zhang, R. Xiao, and Y. J. Huang. Analysis on chaotic nature of a pressurized spout-fluid bed by information theory based Shannon entropy. *Can. J. Chem. Eng.*, **87** (2009), 220–227.

48. B. Ye, C. J. Lim, and J. R. Grace. Hydrodynamics of spouted and spout-fluidized beds at high temperature. *Can. J. Chem. Eng.*, **70** (1992), 840–847.

49. J. Zhao, C. J. Lim, and J. R. Grace. Flow regimes and combustion behaviour in coal-burning spouted and spout-fluid beds. *Chem. Eng. Sci.*, **42** (1987), 2865–2875.

50. J. Link, C. Zeilstra, N. Deen, and J. A. M. Kuipers. Validation of a discrete particle model in a 2D spout-fluid bed using non-intrusive optical measuring techniques. *Can. J. Chem. Eng.*, **82** (2004), 30–36.

51. J. M. Link, L. A. Cuypers, N. G. Deen, and J. A. M. Kuipers. Flow regimes in a spout-fluid bed: A combined experimental and simulation study. *Chem. Eng. Sci.*, **60** (2005), 3425–3442.

52. J. M. Link, W. Godlieb, N. G. Deen, and J. A. M. Kuipers. Discrete element study of granulation in a spout-fluidized bed. *Chem. Eng. Sci.*, **62** (2007), 195–207.

53. W. Q. Zhong. Investigations on flow characteristics and scaling relationships of spout-fluid beds. Ph.D. thesis, Southeast University (China), 2007.

54. W. Q. Zhong, Y. Q. Xiong, Z. L. Yuan, and M. Y. Zhang. DEM simulation of gas-solid flow behaviors in spout-fluid bed. *Chem. Eng. Sci.*, **61** (2006), 1571–1584.

55. W. Q. Zhong, M. Y. Zhang, B. S. Jin, and Z. L. Yuan. Three-dimensional simulation of gas/solid flow in spout-fluid beds with kinetic theory of granular flow. *Chin. J. Chem. Eng.*, **14** (2006), 611–617.

56. W. Q. Zhong, M. Y. Zhang, B. S. Jin, and Z. L. Yuan. Flow behaviors of a large spout-fluid bed at high pressure and temperature by 3D simulation with kinetic theory of granular flow. *Powder Technol.*, **175** (2007), 90–103.

57. Z. Y. Deng, R. Xiao, B. S. Jin, H. Huang, L. H. Shen, Q. E. Song, and Q. J. Li. Computational fluid dynamics modeling of coal gasification in a pressurized spout-fluid bed. *Energy Fuels*, **22** (2007), 1560–1569.

58. Q. J. Li, M. Y. Zhang, W. Q. Zhong, X. F. Wang, R. Xiao, and B. S. Jin. Simulation of coal gasification in a pressurized spout-fluid bed gasifier. *Can. J. Chem. Eng.*, **87** (2009), 169–176.

59. J. Zhao, C. J. Lim, and J. R. Grace. Coal burnout times in spouted and spout-fluid beds. *Chem. Eng. Res. Des.*, **65** (1987), 426–430.

60. C. J. Lim, A. P. Watkinson, G. K. Khoe, S. Low, N. Epstein, and J. R. Grace. Spouted, fluidized and spout-fluid bed combustion of bituminous coals. *Fuel*, **67** (1988), 1211–1217.

61. S. Tia, S. C. Bhattacharya, and P. Wibulswas. Combustion behaviour of coal and carbon in spouted and spout-fluid beds. *Int. J. Eng. Res.*, **15** (1991), 249–255.

62. D. O. Albina. Emissions from multiple-spouted and spout-fluid fluidized beds using rice husks as fuel. *Renewable Energy*, **31** (2006), 2152–2163.

63. M. S. J. Arnold, J. J. Gale, and M. K. Laughlin. The British Coal spouted fluidised bed gasification process. *Can. J. Chem. Eng.*, **70** (1992), 991–997.

64. R. Xiao, M. Y. Zhang, B. S. Jin, Y. J. Huang, and H. C. Zhou. High-temperature air/steam-blown gasification of coal in a pressurized spout-fluid bed. *Energy and Fuels*, **20** (2006), 715–720.

65. R. Xiao, M. Y. Zhang, B. S. Jin, Y. Q. Xiong, H. C. Zhou, Y. F. Duan, Z. P. Zhong, X. P. Chen, L. H. Shen, and Y. J. Huang. Air blown partial gasification of coal in a pilot plant pressurized spout-fluid bed reactor. *Fuel*, **86** (2007), 1631–1640.

66. R. Xiao, L. H. Shen, M. Y. Zhang, B. S. Jin, Y. Q. Xiong, Y. F. Duan, Z. P. Zhong, H. C. Zhou, X. P. Chen, and Y. J. Huang. Partial gasification of coal in a fluidized bed reactor: Comparison of a laboratory and pilot scale reactors. *Korean Chem. Eng.*, **24** (2007), 175–180.

67. T. Maitri and D. Animesh. An investigation of MSW gasification in a spout-fluid bed reactor. *Fuel Proc.* **89** (2008), 949–957.

68. P. Suwannakuta. A study on biomass gasification in spout-fluid bed. Master's thesis, AIT (Thailand), 2002.

69. I. Białobrzewski, M. Zielińska, A. S. Mujumdar, and M. Markowski. Heat and mass transfer during drying of a bed of shrinking particles – simulation for carrot cubes dried in a spout-fluidized-bed drier. *Int. J. Heat Mass Transfer*, **51** (2008), 4704–4716.

70. J. M. Link, W. Godlieb, P. Tripp, N. G. Deen, S. Heinrich, J. A. M. Kuipers, M. Schönherr, and M. Peglow. Comparison of fibre optical measurements and discrete element simulations for the study of granulation in a spout fluidized bed. *Powder Technol.*, **189** (2009), 202–217.

71. J. L. Plawsky, S. Jovanovic, H. Littman, K. C. Hover, S. Gerolimatos, and K. Douglas. Exploring the effect of dry premixing of sand and cement on the mechanical properties of mortar. *Cem. Conc. Res.* **33** (2003), 255–264.

72. K. B. Park, J. L. Plawsky, H. Littman, and J. D. Paccione. Mortar properties obtained by dry premixing of cementitious materials and sand in a spout-fluid bed mixer. *Cem. Concr. Res.*, **36** (2006), 728–734.

73. S. Rakic, D. Povrenovic, V. Tesevic, M. Simic, and R. Maletic. Oak acorn, polyphenols and antioxidant activity in functional food. *J. Food Eng.*, **74** (2006), 416–423.

7 Spouted and spout-fluid beds with draft tubes

Željko B. Grbavčić, Howard Littman, Morris H. Morgan III, and
John D. Paccione

The draft tube spout-fluid bed (DTSFB) is an extremely versatile fluid–particle system
that can be widely applied industrially. This configuration aids performance because
control of the fluid residence time and solid cycle time distributions can be accomplished
easily. Thus understanding the solid and fluid phase hydrodynamics is essential to
optimizing DTSFB operation.

A typical DTSFB system consists of four interconnected zones, as shown in Figure 7.1:
a spout-fluid bed feeder, a moving bed annulus, a draft tube (pneumatic conveyor), and a
freeboard fountain. For a given geometry and particles, five control quantities determine
the bed hydrodynamics: the inlet jet fluid mass flowrate, F_{j0}; the inlet auxiliary fluid mass
flowrate, F_{ax0}; the internal annulus fluid mass flowrate, F_a; the inlet section length, L_i;
and the annulus height, H_a. The draft tube inlet length, L_i, controls both the fluid leakage
and solids crossflow. The auxiliary fluid mass flow, F_{ax0}, controls the pressure drop across
the bed and alters the internal solids flow. To describe the overall and local dynamics of
such systems, appropriate fluid and particle models must be devised for each separate
region of the DTSFB. The discussion in this chapter addresses operating characteristics,
applications, and design concepts. Initially we focus on the basic hydrodynamic features
of these systems, and then we provide an overview of applications involving the basic
DTSFB and novel hybrid configurations.

7.1 Operation of draft tube spout-fluid beds

Grbavčić et al.[1] provided one of the first comprehensive examinations of the basic
properties – minimum fluid flow rate, pressure drop and solids circulation rate – of a
DTSFB. Figure 7.2 summarizes some of their initial findings. One might expect that
all the quantities plotted in that figure should approach their spouted bed values as
$U_{a0} \rightarrow 0$ and $L_i/H \rightarrow 1$. For a given bed, however, two lower limits of L_i/H are encountered: (1) a minimum inlet section length below which no particle circulation occurs,
and (2) a maximum value, less than bed height H, at which vertical pneumatic transport
cannot be achieved in the draft tube because air short-circuits through the annulus.

Grbavčić et al.[2] also examined the fluid flow pattern and solids circulation rate of
liquid–solid spout-fluid beds equipped with draft tubes. They employed a 196-mm

Spouted and Spout-Fluid Beds: Fundamentals and Applications, eds. Norman Epstein and John R. Grace.
Published by Cambridge University Press. © Cambridge University Press 2011.

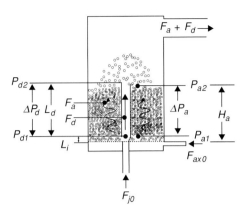

Figure 7.1. Schematic of draft tube spout-fluid bed.

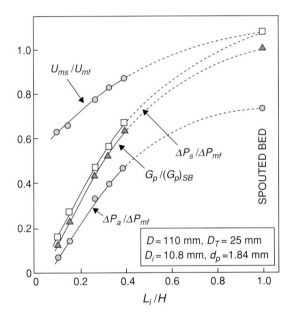

Figure 7.2. Variation of basic spouting parameters with inlet section length ($H = 0.23$ m, $U_{mf} = 0.95$ m/s, $\Delta P_{mf} = 3.47$ kPa, $(G_p)_{SB} = 562$ kg/h). Adapted from Grbavčić et al.[1]

diameter semicircular column equipped with a semicircular draft tube of diameter 34.5 mm. Spherical glass particles of 1.20, 1.94, and 2.98 mm diameter were spouted with water. For a fixed annulus inlet volumetric flowrate, V_{a0}, the transition to stable particle circulation exhibited several key features with increasing spouting flowrate, V_{n0}. At low spouting flowrates, a cavity formed just above the spout inlet nozzle, and there were no particles in the draft tube. Further increases of V_{n0} caused particles to be entrained from the annulus, and at a certain value of V_{n0}, particulate fluidization of the solids occurred in the draft tube. With an additional increase in V_{n0}, the fluidized medium in the draft tube expanded, but the voidage there remained nearly constant

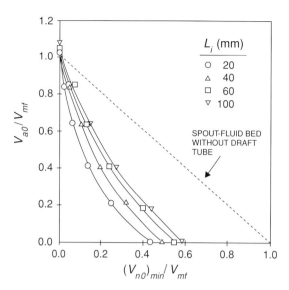

Figure 7.3. Minimum spouting flowrates required to initiate draft tube particle circulation ($d_p =$ 1.94 mm, $V_{mf} = 5.17$ cm^3/s, $H = 585$ mm). Adapted from Grbavčić et al.[2]

because particles were continually entrained from the annulus into the draft tube. At a critical value of V_{n0}, called the *minimum turnover flowrate*, the expanded fluidized bed reached the top of the draft tube, and particles began to leave the top of the draft tube. The draft tube voidage at this point, estimated from the pressure gradient there, slightly exceeded the minimum fluidization voidage. The minimum flow rate necessary to produce particle flow through the draft tube increased as L_i increased, as shown in Figure 7.3. V_{n0} for minimum turnover decreased with increasing V_{a0} and the Littman et al.[3] spout-fluid line, shown by a dashed line, provides an upper bound for this quantity.

Figure 7.3 shows that the solids mass flux in the draft tube increases rapidly with L_i for fixed V_{a0} and V_{n0}. The solid circulation in a DTSFB can be established without spouting if V_{a0} is sufficiently large, as shown in Figure 7.4. In addition, if the annulus height is slightly below the top of the draft tube, the annulus region cannot be fluidized. When increasing V_{a0} ($V_{n0} = 0$), it was found that close to the minimum fluidization velocity of the annulus, the bed expanded. When V_{a0} slightly exceeded V_{mf}, hydraulic transport in the draft tube began, and the annulus remained un-fluidized. With a further increase in V_{a0}, the solids flow rate in the draft tube also increased, but without fluidization of the annulus solids. In addition to the spouting and annular flow rates, the most important factors affecting the fluid flow distribution between the annulus and draft tube sections include the entrance region (including the inlet nozzle), the length of the inlet section, cone angle, draft tube diameter, and particle size.

Hadžismajlović et al.[4] and Povrenović[5] investigated the hydrodynamic behavior of a 0.95-m-diameter spout-fluid bed equipped with a 0.25-m-diameter draft tube. Polyethylene particles 3.6 mm in diameter were spouted by water. Experiments were conducted over a wide range of inlet nozzle sizes, annulus air flowrates, and inlet section lengths. Their results extended the Grabavcić et al.[2] observations. A value of 66.7 was obtained

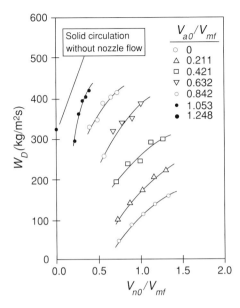

Figure 7.4. Effect of the spouting flow rate on solids mass flux in a draft tube system ($d_p = 1.94$ mm, $V_{mf} = 5.17$ cm³/s, $H = 585$ mm). Adapted from Grbavčić et al.[2]

for the critical D_i/d_p ratio for stability, substantially higher than the value of 25 reported by Chandnani and Epstein[6] for stable spouting of fine particles in a gas-spouted bed without a draft tube.

Hadžismajlović et al.[4] proposed a movable nozzle (Figure 7.5). To initiate particle flow in the draft tube, the nozzle tube was retracted to the desired inlet section length. At the completion of a run, the inlet nozzle tube was reinserted into the draft tube to prevent particle backflow from the annulus.

Cecen-Erbil[7] used pulse injection of a tracer to define fluid streamlines and to determine the liquid flow distribution between the draft tube and annulus in a semicircular flat-bottomed spouted bed, 80 mm in diameter, with an inlet tube of diameter 10 mm. A semicircular draft tube of 20 mm internal diameter and 800 mm length was located 32 mm above the distributor. The particles were glass spheres of diameter 3 mm, and the spouting fluid was water. The superficial liquid velocity through the draft tube was found to vary linearly with the total flow rate through the bed. Under certain conditions, it was found that liquid could leak from the annulus inlet flow into the draft tube. An empirical correlation was proposed to predict this leakage fraction.

Ijichi et al.[8-10] investigated the effects of gas flowrate, inlet section length, conical base angle, particle diameter, and bed weight on the solids circulation rate and annular gas velocity. Both semicircular and circular draft tube columns were studied. The annular gas velocity was found to increase with increasing inlet section length (L_i), angle of conical base, and mean particle diameter, but decreased with increasing bed mass. The particle circulation rate increased with increasing tube cone clearance, mean particle diameter, and bed mass.

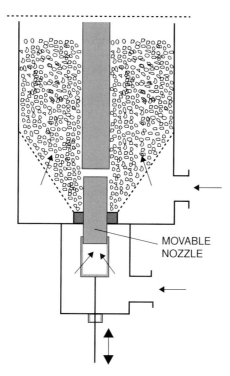

Figure 7.5. Draft tube spout-fluid bed with movable nozzle.[4]

A similar study by Zhao et al.[11] investigated the vertical particle velocity profiles and solids circulation rate in a cylindrical-conical spouted bed, with and without a draft tube. They devised a kinematic model to simulate the granular flow in the annulus. Experiments were conducted in a column of 0.196 m diameter and 1.2 m height, with a 60° conical base, 0.0257 m inlet diameter, 0.42 m static bed depth of millet particles of 1.34 mm mean diameter and 1430 kg/m^3 density, at ambient temperature and pressure. Draft tubes of diameter 30 and 40 mm were tested. The particle velocity in the annulus of such beds (DTSFB) increased slightly with increasing radial position, contrary to the trend for conventional spouted beds (CSBs). Average particle velocities in the DTSFB were much lower than in the CSB, but essentially equivalent to those of the draft-tube spouted bed (DTSB).

Nagashima et al.[12] compared results for binary mixtures of glass beads in a draft tube system with those for a bed of similar size containing coarser particles. Both the minimum spouting velocity and gas velocity in the annulus decreased with increasing mass fraction of finer particles, and decreased with decreasing L_i.

A three-phase investigation by Cecen-Erbil and Turan[13] focused on developing a model for the energy dissipation inside the draft tube of spout-fluid beds. Their goal was to calculate the shear stress, velocity gradient, and turbulence fluctuation parameters inside the draft tube to assess the performance of a novel backwashing filter process. Gas spouting inlet flow and liquid annulus flow were introduced through two independent lines. Air was also introduced with the liquid into the annulus through the same distributor. The proposed model suggested that a desired shear stress/velocity gradient could be achieved by judicious selection/combination of draft tube size, particle size, and flow rates.

7.2   Novel applications and experimental studies

7.2.1   Cylindrical and rectangular designs

Zhao et al.[14] studied the particle motion in a two-dimensional thin slot-rectangular spouted bed (2DSB) with draft plates using particle image velocimetry (PIV). A discrete element method (DEM) (see Chapter 4), in conjunction with computational fluid dynamics (DEM-CFD), was used to examine gas turbulence effects. The experiments were conducted in a rectangular column, 152 mm wide and 15 mm thick, equipped with a 60°-angle conical-base section. The two draft plates were 15 mm apart. The static bed depth was 100 mm, and the inlet length ranged from 10 to 40 mm. The particles were glass spheres of diameter 2 mm. The PIV results indicated that the inlet section length had little influence on the vertical particle velocity, but a greater effect on the particle circulation rate. DEM-CFD simulations did a good job of predicting the longitudinal particle velocity profile along the center line and showed that particles travel upward individually, without clustering.

CFD simulations for grains of 0.22, 2.0, 3.7, and 1.0 mm diameter, by Szafran and Kmiec,[15] confirmed that fluctuations are caused by particle clusters originating at the bottom of the column. Solids were observed to cross into the jet, cover the column inlet, and be transported periodically through the draft tube, contrary to the finding of Zhao et al.[14] The fluctuating solids inflow produces slugs and explains variations in fountain height and porosity. Modified and extended scaling relationships were proposed by Shirvanian and Calo[16] for conical-based rectangular spouted vessels with draft tubes. A CFD model was devised to investigate the hydrodynamics and to predict the solid volume fraction, solid and liquid velocities in the draft tube, and fluid volume-average fraction in the draft tube as a function of height. The CFD model predicted the solids circulation rate to within 17 percent.

Another multizone spouting model was developed by Eng et al.[17] for nonisothermal dynamic simulation of a DTSB for ultrapyrolysis of hydrocarbons. This model focused on the nonisothermal dynamic response of the spout gas to disturbances and investigated the effect of hydrodynamic behavior on unsteady heat transfer. The simulations predicted that the spout gas responded in two different time scales: an initial pseudo-steady state was established within 30 ms, followed by a long-time response after 15 min.

Takeuchi et al.[18] applied a DEM to a cylindrical system with a conical base. The authors devised a new method for treating the boundary condition for the three-dimensional gas flow along the conical surface, based on a technique developed originally for particle-induced turbulent flows. The simulated particle circulation and velocity profiles in the spout and annulus agreed well with experimental observations. In the cylindrical region, the axial particle velocity profiles were self-similar, of Gaussian shape. A small reverse gas flow was observed near the bottom of the conical base, decreasing

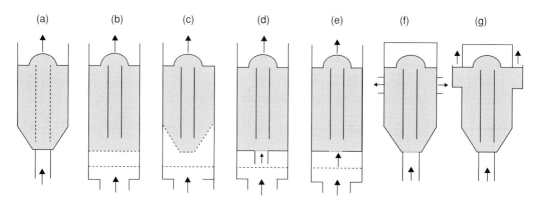

Figure 7.6. Draft tube spouted/spout-fluid bed designs: (a) porous draft tube spouted bed, adapted from Claflin and Fane[23] and Ishikura et al.[24]; (b) flat screen gas inlet; (c) conical screen gas inlet; (d) nozzle gas inlet; (e) orifice gas inlet. Subfigures b, c, d, and e are adapted from Hattori et al.[27–29]; f and g are adapted from Hattori et al.[30,31]

with increasing cone angle. Kmiec and Ludwig[19,20] proposed a simple one-dimensional model for the axial profiles of particle velocity, gas velocity, and voidage along the draft tube of such systems.

7.2.2   Conical and other design modifications

Altzibar et al.[21] pointed out that conical spouted beds have low particle segregation, making them excellent for treating particles of wide size distribution. They investigated experimentally the hydrodynamics of draft-tube conical-spouted beds. Correlations were proposed for the minimum spouting velocity, pressure drop, and peak pressure drop as functions of bed and column characteristics. Altzibar et al. also found that the minimum spouting velocity decreased with a reduction in fluid inlet diameter and that the spouting pressure drop increased with increasing inlet section length. A very pronounced hysteresis in the pressure drop versus air velocity occurs in conical DTSB units, much larger than in conventional conical spouted beds.

San José et al.[22] studied the effect of draft tube diameter and inlet length on stability of a conical contactor with the top of the central draft tube at the same level as the upper bed surface. Bed stability was enhanced when $D_T/D_i \geq 1$, providing that $5 \leq D_T/d_p \leq 50$ and $L_i/d_p > 10$. They provided a correlation for the minimum spouting velocity for conical spouted beds with and without draft tubes.

Several variants of porous draft tube systems (see Figure 7.6a) were studied by Claflin and Fane[23] and Ishikura et al.,[24] with an emphasis on the effect of design changes on annular fluid flow. In the Ishikura et al.[24–26] investigation, the porous draft tubes were 0.30 m in length and varied from 0.012 to 0.018 m in diameter. The inlet section length, L_i, was restricted to between 0.02 and 0.04 m. Their porous-wall draft tube was made of sintered stainless steel containing pores 120 μm in diameter, with a void fraction of ~40 percent. Binary mixtures of glass beads ($d_p = 1.35$ mm and 0.477 mm) were the spouting solids. In most experiments a small fraction of fine particles was added to

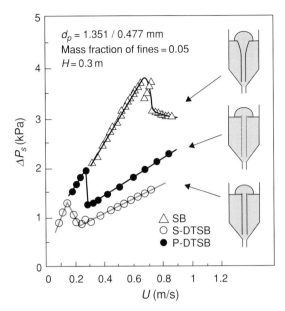

Figure 7.7. Typical pressure drop–superficial gas velocity curves for a binary mixture spouted in systems without and with a draft tube (SB; conventional spouted bed, S-DTSB; spouted bed with nonporous draft tube, P-DTSB; spouted bed with porous draft tube). Adapted from Ishikura et al.[24]

the coarser particles. As anticipated, the porous draft tube led to a higher annular gas through-flow than a nonporous one. Figure 7.7 shows the dependence of the spouting pressure drop on the gas superficial velocity for a conventional spouted bed (SB), a spouted bed with a nonporous draft tube (S-DTSB), and a spouted bed with a porous draft tube (P-DTSB).

For both the porous and the nonporous draft tube systems, ΔP_s and solids circulation increased with increasing gas superficial velocity. In addition, ΔP_s and U_{ms} for the spouted bed with nonporous draft tube was always lower than ΔP_s and U_{ms} for the spouted bed with a porous draft tube of the same size. The addition of even a small fraction of fine particles was found to reduce the minimum spouting gas velocity.

Hattori et al.[27-29] investigated four modifications of the conventional draft tube spouted bed design, as shown in Figure 7.6: (b) a flat screen gas inlet, (c) a conical screen gas inlet, (d) a nozzle gas inlet, and (e) an orifice gas inlet. Configurations (b) and (c) (screen bottoms) required much higher gas velocities to initiate minimum spouting (0.55 and 0.61 m/s, respectively) than configurations (d) and (e) (0.35 and 0.36 m/s, respectively), for similar particles and bed dimensions. The solids circulation rate of the screen-bottomed spouted beds was considerably larger than the rate for the nozzle or orifice designs (Figure 7.8a). In addition, the gas velocity in the annulus of screen bottom units was almost three times higher than that for the nozzle and orifice configurations (Figure 7.8b).

Hattori et al.[30-32] also developed a side-outlet draft tube spouted bed (Figure 7.6f). Particles as small as 0.27 mm could be effectively spouted in air without instabilities

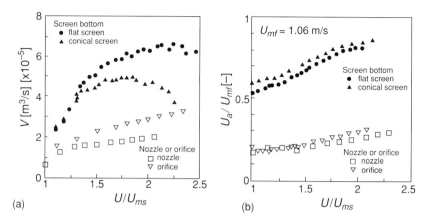

Figure 7.8. Solids circulation rate (a) and gas velocity in the annulus (b) versus superficial gas velocity in a modified draft tube spouted bed. Adapted from Hattori et al.[28]

in the draft tube. It was later shown[44] that, for any given geometrical configuration of column and draft tube, there is an optimum vertical location of the side outlet that produces a maximum conversion for a catalytic reaction. To avoid screen plugging by fine particles, Hattori et al. also proposed the configuration shown in Figure 7.6(g). Kim[33] reported that proper selection of the ratio of upper column diameter to lower column diameter was crucial for stability. Ijichi et al.[34] demonstrated that very fine particles (Group C in the Geldart[35] classification), could be processed effectively in a draft tube spouted bed if it was equipped with a converging nozzle inlet.

Ar and Uysal[36] studied the potential application of liquid spouting with multiple draft tubes for nonfouling heat exchangers. Liquid was introduced through the center multitubular zone. A conical barrier just below the return pipe diverted the liquid flow toward the draft tube entrances around a return pipe. Both entrained solid particles coming from the return pipe and liquid rose in the draft tubes. Predictive models for the solids circulation rates proposed by Grbavčić et al.[2] and Nitta and Morgan[37] met with limited success.

Follansbee et al.[38] proposed a continuous photocatalytic reactor design for removal of organic compounds from wastewater. Their reactor (Figure 7.9) contains an annular moving packed bed of TiO_2-activated carbon catalyst supported on large silica particles ($d_p = 1.94$ mm). The contaminated water stream is in continuous countercurrent contact with a photocatalytic adsorbent catalyst. Treated water leaves the column at the top of the annulus, whereas spent adsorbent is transported through the draft tube into the UV exposure chamber. Regenerated particles fall onto the annulus top for another adsorption cycle. The UV chamber serves two functions: (1) activation of the photocatalytic component to promote surface oxidation and (2) regeneration of the sorbent. The authors achieved 90 percent removal of the organic contaminant from the wastewater.

Arsenijevic et al.[39] developed a combined system for ethylene oxide (EtO) removal based on a draft tube spouted bed (DTSB) loaded with Pt/Al_2O_3 catalyst. The annular region was partitioned into a "hot" zone (desorber and catalytic incinerator) containing

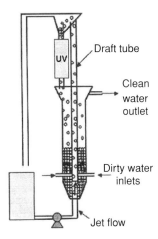

Figure 7.9. Schematic diagram of draft tube spouted bed adsorber/photocatalytic reactor. After Follansbee et al.[38]

about 7 percent of catalyst, and a "cold" zone (sorber), containing the rest of the catalyst. To obtain sufficient catalyst residence time in the reaction section, the draft tube riser had to operate in a pulsating mode. This DTSB reactor achieved the same efficiency as a fixed bed reactor, and it was particularly suitable for low EtO concentrations. In fixed bed reactors the combustion heat released by low levels of EtO was insufficient to preheat the reaction mixture to the ignition point. On the other hand, with a DTSB reactor, sufficient reaction heat was available to raise the EtO adsorption temperature above the ignition point.

Hattori et al.[40] studied ozone decomposition over an iron oxide catalyst in four spouted bed systems: a top-sealed side-outlet DTSB, a screen-bottomed DTSB, and a top-outlet spouted bed with and without a draft tube. The top-sealed DTSB and the screen-bottomed DTSB gave the highest conversions. The gas–solid contacting efficiency of these spouted beds was comparable to that of an isothermal fixed bed. The top-outlet spouted bed with a draft tube produced the poorest contacting. Both the top-sealed spouted bed and the screen-bottomed spouted bed could be operated at lower gas flowrates, making them particularly useful for slow reactions. The top-outlet spouted bed with a draft tube did not provide good gas–solid contacting efficiency, because the draft tube prevented gas exchange between the spout and annulus.

Horio et al.[41] tested a spouted bed equipped with a special draft tube for partial combustion of acetylene in a circulating fluidized bed (CFB) to develop a continuous diamond powder production process. They investigated deposition kinetics, observed the flame structure, and conducted emission spectroscopy on a laboratory-scale CFB reactor. They found that diamond particles could be deposited evenly on ordinary carbon and/or alumina substrates. Diamonds with 100 facets were obtained over a narrow range of acetylene/oxygen ratio. For carbon particle deposition, the optimum acetylene/oxygen ratio was found to be slightly below stoichiometric, indicating gasification of carbon substrate. This CFB design with a riser (dilute flow) and downcomer (rapid dense phase flow) appears to be promising for large-scale diamond coating or powder generation.

Hatate et al.[42] demonstrated the effectiveness of a DTSB as a coal gasifier. Ceramic particles acted as the thermal carrier, providing sufficient heat for the production of a hydrogen-rich gas from sub-bituminous coal loaded with potassium carbonate. Investigations were carried out for a coal feed of 1 kg/h at 1 atm pressure and a temperature of ~800 °C. In a follow-up study, Hatate et al.[43] showed that this reactor had the following virtues: (1) there is plug flow in the gasification zone; (2) classification of the feed coal particles is unnecessary; and (3) air can be used instead of oxygen.

Chapter-specific nomenclature

D_T	diameter of draft tube, m
F_a	annulus fluid mass flowrate, kg/s
F_{ax0}	auxiliary inlet fluid mass flowrate, kg/s
F_{n0}	spouting inlet fluid mass flowrate, kg/s
H_a	annulus height, m
G_p	solids circulation rate, kg/s
L_D	length of draft tube, m
L_i	length of inlet section, m
U_{a0}	superficial fluid velocity at inlet to annulus, m/s
U_D	superficial velocity in draft tube, m/s
V_{a0}	inlet annulus flowrate, m^3/s
V_{n0}	fluid flowrate in spout inlet tube, m^3/s
V_{mf}	minimum fluidizing volumetric flowrate, m^3/s
W_D	solids mass flux in draft tube, kg/m^{2}s
ΔP_{mf}	pressure drop across bed at minimum fluidization, Pa

References

1. Ž. B. Grbavčić, D. V. Vuković, Dž. E. Hadžismajlovic, R. V. Garić, and H. Littman. Fluid mechanical behaviour of a spouted bed with a draft tube and external annular flow. Presented at the 2nd International Symposium on Spouted Beds, 32nd Can. Chem. Engng. Conference (Vancouver, BC, Canada, 1982).
2. Ž. B. Grbavčić, D. V. Vuković, S. Dj. Jovanović, R. V. Garić, Dž. E. Hadžismajlovic, H. Littman, and M. H. Morgan. III. Fluid flow pattern and solids circulation rate in a liquid phase spout-fluid bed with draft tube. *Can. J. Chem. Eng.*, **70** (1992), 895–904.
3. H. Littman, D. V. Vuković, F. K. Zdanski, and Ž. B. Grbavčić. Pressure drop and flowrate characteristics of liquid phase spout-fluid bed at the minimum spout-fluid flowrate. *Can. J. Chem. Eng.*, **52** (1974), 174–179.
4. Dž. E. Hadžismajlović, Ž. B. Grbavčić, D. S. Povrenović, D. V. Vuković, R. V. Garić, and H. Littman. The hydrodynamic behavior of a 0.95 m diameter spout-fluid bed with a draft tube. In *Fluidization VII*, ed. O. E. Potter and D. J. Nicklin (New York: Engineering Foundation, 1992), pp. 337–344.

5. D. S. Povrenović. Fluid mechanical characteristics and stability of a large diameter spout-fluid bed with a draft tube. *J. Serbian Chem. Soc.*, **61** (1996), 355–365.

6. P. P. Chandnani and N. Epstein. Spoutability and spout destabilization of fine particles with a gas. In *Fluidization V*, ed. K. Ostergaard and A. Sorensen (New York: Engineering Foundation, 1986), pp. 233–240.

7. A. Cecen-Erbil. Annulus leakage and distribution of the fluid flow in a liquid spout-fluid bed with a draft tube. *Chem. Eng. Sci.*, **58** (2003), 4739–4745.

8. K. Ijichi, M. Miyauchi, Y. Uemura, and Y. Hatate. Characteristics of flow behavior in semi-cylindrical spouted bed with draft tube. *J. Chem. Eng. Japan*, **31** (1998), 677–682.

9. K. Ijichi, Y. Tanaka, Y. Uemura, Y. Hatate, and K. Yoshida. Solids circulation rate and holdup within the draft tube of a spouted bed. *Kagaku Kogaku Ronbunshu*, **16**, 924–930 (1990).

10. K. Ijichi and Y. Tanaka. Hydrodynamics of a spouted bed with a draft tube. *Kagaku Kogaku Ronbunshu*, **14** (1988), 566–570.

11. X.-L. Zhao, Q. Yao, and S.-Q. Li. Effects of draft tubes on particle velocity profiles in spouted beds. *Chem. Eng. & Technol.*, **29** (2006), 875–881.

12. H. Nagashima, T. Ishikura, and M. Ide. Hydrodynamics of a spouted bed with an impermeable draft tube for binary particle systems. *Korean J. Chem. Eng.*, **16** (1999), 688–693.

13. A. Cecen-Erbil and M. Turan. Assessment of the energy dissipation parameters inside the draft tube of a liquid spout-fluid bed. *Envir. Sci. & Technol.*, **39** (2005), 2898–2905.

14. X.-L. Zhao, S.-Q. Li, G.-Q. Liu, Q. Song, and Q. Yao. Flow patterns of solids in a two-dimensional spouted bed with draft plates: PIV measurement and DEM simulations. *Powder Technol.*, **183** (2008), 79–87.

15. R. G. Szafran and A. Kmiec. Periodic fluctuations of flow and porosity in spouted beds. *Transport in Porous Media*, **66** (2007), 187–200.

16. P. A. Shirvanian and J. M. Calo. Hydrodynamic scaling of a rectangular spouted vessel with a draft duct. *Chem. Eng. J.*, **103** (2004), 29–34.

17. J. H. Eng, W. Y. Svrcek, and L. A. Behie. Dynamic modeling of a spouted bed reactor with a draft tube. *Ind. Eng. Chem. Res.*, **28** (1989), 1778–1785.

18. S. Takeuchi, S. Wang, and M. Rhodes. Discrete element method simulation of three-dimensional conical-base spouted beds. *Powder Technol.*, **184** (2008), 141–150.

19. A. Kmiec and W. Ludwig. A model of the two-phase gas-solids flow in fluidizing apparatus with the draft tube. I. Model development. *Inz. Chem. Proc.*, **19** (1998), 557–573.

20. A. Kmiec and W. Ludwig. A model of the two-phase gas-solids flow in fluidizing apparatus with the draft tube. II. Model solution. *Inz. Chem. Proc.*, **19** (1998), 575–589.

21. H. S. Altzibar, S. Alvarez, M. J. San José, R. Aguado, J. Bilbao, and M. Olazar. Hydrodynamic aspects and correlations for the design of draft-tube conical spouted beds. In *Fluidization XII*, ed. X. T. Bi, F. Berruti, and T. Pugsley (Brooklyn, NY: Engineering Foundation, 2007), pp. 561–568.

22. M. J. San José, S. Alvarez, A. O. De Salazar, M. Olazar, and J. Bilbao. Operating conditions of conical spouted beds with a draft tube. Effect of the diameter of the draft tube and of the height of entrainment zone. *Ind. Eng. Chem. Res.*, **46** (2007), 2877–2884.

23. J. K. Claflin and A. G. Fane. Spouting with a porous draft-tube. *Can. J. Chem. Eng.*, **61** (1983), 356–363.

24. T. Ishikura, H. Nagashima, and M. Ide. Hydrodynamics of a spouted bed with a porous draft tube containing a small amount of finer particles. *Powder Technol.*, **131** (2003), 56–65.

25. T. Ishikura, H. Nagashima, and I. Mitsuharu. Hydrodynamics of a spouted bed with a porous draft tube. *Kagaku Kogaku Ronbunshu*, **22** (1996), 615–621.

26. T. Ishikura, H. Nagashima, and M. Ide. Minimum spouting velocity of binary particle systems in a spouted bed with a draft tube. *Kagaku Kogaku Ronbunshu*, **24** (1998), 346–348.

27. H. Hattori, S. Ito, T. Onezawa, K. Yamada, and S. Yanai. Fluid and solids flow affecting the solids circulation rate in spouted beds with a draft-tube. *J. Chem. Eng. Japan*, **37** (2004), 1085–1091.

28. H. Hattori, T. Nagai, Y. Ohshima, M. Yoshida, and A. Nagata. Solids circulation rate in screen bottomed spouted bed with draft-tube. *J. Chem. Eng. Japan*, **31** (1998), 633–635.

29. H. Hattori, and T. Nagai. Spouted bed with a draft-tube without gas inlet nozzle or orifice. *J. Chem. Eng. Japan*, **29** (1996), 484–487.

30. H. Hattori, K. Tanaka, and K. Takeda. Minimum spoutable gas flow rate in side-outlet spouted bed with inner draft-tube. *J. Chem. Eng. Japan*, **14** (1981), 462–466.

31. H. Hattori and K. Takeda. Side-outlet spouted bed with inner draft-tube for small-sized solid particles. *J. Chem. Eng. Japan*, **11** (1978), 125–129.

32. H. Hattori, A. Kobayashi, I. Aiba, and T. Koda. Modification of the gas outlet structure on the spouted bed with inner draft-tube. *J. Chem. Eng. Japan*, **17** (1984), 102–103.

33. S. J. Kim. Fluid and particle flow characteristics in a draft tube spouted bed with modified fluid outlet. *Korean J. Chem. Eng.*, **7** (1990), 74–80.

34. K. Ijichi, Y. Uemura, Y. Yoshizawa, Y. Hatate, and K. Yoshida. Conveying characteristics of fine particles using converging nozzle. *Kagaku Kogaku Ronbunshu*, **24** (1998), 365–369.

35. D. Geldart. Estimation of basic particle properties for use in fluid-particle process calculations. *Powder Technol.*, **60** (1990), 1–13.

36. F. F. Ar and B. Z. Uysal. Solid circulation in a liquid spout-fluid ded with multi-draft tubes. *J. Chem. Technol. Biotech.*, **72** (1998), 143–148.

37. B. V. Nitta and M. H. Morgan III. Particle circulation and liquid bypassing in three phase draft tube spouted beds. *Chem Eng. Sci.*, **47** (1992), 3459–3466.

38. D. M. Follansbee, J. D. Paccione, and L. L. Martin. Globally optimal design and operation of a continuous photo-catalytic advanced oxidation process featuring moving bed adsorption and draft-tube transport. *Ind. Eng. Chem. Res.*, **47** (2008), 3591–3600.

39. Z. Lj. Arsenijević, B. V. Grbić, Z. B. Grbavčić, N. D. Radić, and A. V. Terlecki-Baricević. Ethylene oxide removal in combined sorbent catalyst system. *Chem. Eng. Sci.*, **54** (1999), 1519–1524.

40. H. Hattori, E. Hata, and T. Uchino. Ozone decomposition in four types of spouted beds, with or without a draft-tube. *J. Chem. Eng. Japan*, **40** (2007), 761–764.

41. M. Horio, A. Saito, K. Unou, H. Nakazono, N. Shibuya, S. Shrma, and A. Kosaka. Synthesis of diamond particles with an acetylene fired circulating fluidized bed. *Chem. Eng. Sci.*, **51** (1966), 3033–3038.

42. Y. Hatate, H. Mihara, K. Ijichi, T. Yoshimi, S. Arimizu, Y. Uemura, and D. F. King. Catalytic coal gasification using a draft tube spouted bed gasifier. *Kagaku Kogaku Ronbunshu*, **22** (1996), 1180–1184.

43. Y. Hatate, Y. Uemura, S. Tanaka. Y. Tokumasu, Y. Tanaka, and D. F. King. Development of a spouted bed-type coal gasifier with cycling thermal medium particles. *Kagaku Kogaku Ronbunshu*, **20** (1994), 758–765.

44. C. M. H. Brereton, N. Epstein, and J. R. Grace. Side-outlet spouted bed with draft tube: effect of varying the position of the outlet. *Can. J. Chem. Eng.*, **74** (1996), 542–546.

8   Particle mixing and segregation

Giorgio Rovero and Norberto Piccinini

This chapter starts from the state of the art on particle mixing in spouted beds, as presented in the classical book by Mathur and Epstein.[1] In subsequent years, segregation has been considered in fundamental studies aimed at describing real systems of various bed compositions.

8.1   Gross solids mixing behavior

The mixing properties of spouted beds result from interaction among the spout, fountain, and annulus. In a continuously operated unit, the positioning of the solids inlet port with respect to the discharge opening is of fundamental importance to prevent bypassing. Dead zones could arise from problematic solids circulation – for example, because of an incorrect base design. To prevent segregation, the simplest conceivable operating condition corresponds to a mono-sized particulate material and a single unit in which each particle undergoes many cycles before being discharged. In such cases and for continuous operation, the internal circulation far exceeds the net in-and-out flow of solids in all cases studied. The very different particle residence times in the spout (progressively loaded with solids along its height), in the fountain (where the particles have both axial and radial velocity components), and in the annulus (where particles travel downward in nearly plug flow) generate nearly well-mixed overall solids residence time distributions (RTDs).

Stimulus-response techniques have been applied to determine the RTD of particles.[1] A typical downstream normalized tracer concentration at the discharge, called the *F curve*, generated in response to an upstream step input of colored particles, is given in Figure 8.1. A more comprehensive summary of experimental data also appears in the literature.[1] More than 90 percent of the spouted bed volume appears to operate as a perfectly mixed system. The ratio of the solids tracer concentration in the bed to the initial concentration immediately after a tracer pulse injection is given by

$$I(\theta) = C_b(\theta)/C_{b0} = e^{-a(\theta-b)}, \tag{8.1}$$

where θ is the dimensionless time since the pulse injection – that is, the elapsed time divided by the mean residence time. Note that $a = 1$ and $b = 0$ for perfect mixing,

Spouted and Spout-Fluid Beds: Fundamentals and Applications, eds. Norman Epstein and John R. Grace. Published by Cambridge University Press. © Cambridge University Press 2011.

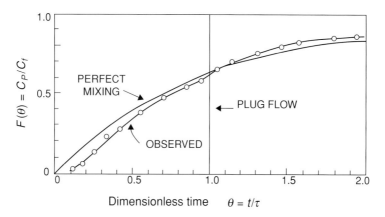

Figure 8.1. Typical output response to step change in solids input.[1] $D = 0.15$ m, $H_0 = 0.08$–0.12 m, $D_i = 6$–17 mm, $\tau = 25$–40 min, $\theta = 82°$.

whereas fitted values were $a \approx 1.09$ and $b \approx 0.10$. It is clear that a single-stage spouted bed approaches perfect mixing as far as the solids are concerned.

Mathur and Epstein[1] refer to a model for a unit operating with a continuous feed rate F: the annulus was represented by a plug flow volume V_p, with no short-circuiting from the annulus to the spout. This model contained a recycle ratio R_{cfr} (ratio of internal circulation to feed rate), representing the solids circulation rate in the spout. By smoothing the response to a step input, it was demonstrated that a small value of R_{cfr} generates an output approaching plug flow, whereas rapid mixing in the system is obtained for $R_{cfr} > 5$. The cycle time in the model is represented by

$$t_c = V_{PF}/(R_{cfr} + 1)F, \tag{8.2}$$

which, when combined with the mean solids residence time, $\tau = V_{PF}/F$, gives

$$\tau = t_c(R_{cfr} + 1). \tag{8.3}$$

For good mixing in the spouted bed, one should have $\tau \geq 6\,t_c$.

Experimental results in the literature[1] demonstrate that, by measuring the maximum mass circulation of solids at the top of the bed, $z = H$, the cycle time increases sharply with increasing column diameter at constant H/D. The minimum residence time for good mixing then increases in proportion. These considerations also suggest that to minimize the spread of the overall RTD of the solids in a continuous process, a cascade of small units is far better than a limited number of larger-diameter spouted beds, with good mixing in each unit to minimize bypassing.

Based on phenomenological observations, a realistic description was proposed in the literature,[1] based on the approach described earlier. Tracer particles filled the upper third of the annulus volume. The batch unit was idealized as combining a well-mixed region composed of combined spout and fountain containing 15 percent of the particles, and n perfectly stirred tanks in series, representing the annulus, each contributing to

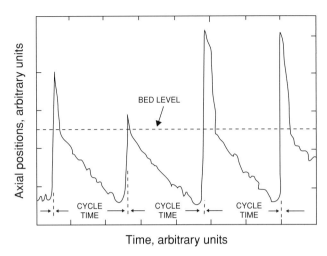

Figure 8.2. Characteristic axial particle position vs. time in spouted beds.[2] $D = 0.075$ m, $\theta = 40°$. Reprinted with permission of John Wiley & Sons, Inc.

solids recirculation by crossflow. To study the mixing dynamics, concentration-versus-time profiles were given in the upper and lower portions of the bed. Equilibrium was achieved, with n as the model parameter. Near-homogeneity was attained in a time less than $2t_c$ for a relevant number of stirred units.

To extend the previous description, in view of the actual motion of particles in a spouted bed, sensible modeling is given by plug flow in the annulus, continuous crossflow into the spout, and perfect mixing in the spout and fountain lumped together, where a solids holdup ranging between 2 percent and 6 percent of the total bed volume is suggested.[1]

A different approach, aimed at measuring the solids cycle time, was carried out[1] to study the solids circulation in a two-dimensional 40°-cone-based spouted bed of silica gel particles of diameter 2.5 and 4.3 mm. Two tracer particles opaque to X-rays were introduced and motion-picture sequences taken. The sequences were then analyzed to compute turbulence parameters such as correlation times and mixing lengths. Effective particle diffusion coefficients were also evaluated as a function of spouting velocity, reaching a maximum at $U_s \sim 2U_{ms}$, with the bed operating in a state of maximum mixing effectiveness.

A noninvasive method for determining the flow patterns of solids in spouted beds was developed,[2] based on a single radioactive particle whose axial location was monitored with a scintillation counter. The particle cycle time distribution (CTD) and the circulation rate in the bed were determined from a large number of passages through the top of the bed, as shown in Figure 8.2. However, owing to limited instrumentation, only qualitative results were reported.[2] A simpler method was developed[3] based on the electromagnetic signal generated by a single tracked particle passing through a coil. The authors investigated a spouted bed column equipped with a draft tube. Application of this technique to standard systems could, however, cause several problems associated with uncertainty regarding the location of the spout and interference of the sensor with the spout itself.

Takeda and Yamamoto[4] carried out an interesting study of the interaction between modeling and experimentation. A two-region model was conceived in which the spout and fountain together represent a perfectly mixed volume whereas the annulus moves in plug flow, with a minor portion acting as a well-mixed zone. The spout diameter was based on the McNab equation.[5] A second model parameter is the active height for particle migration from the annulus to the spout. The solids holdup in the spout and fountain and the circulation flow rate were determined in two vessels of 0.06 and 0.09 m ID with 45° included angle and spherical alumina particles of $d_p = 1$ mm, based on a go-and-stop procedure after dropping a few grams of marked particles into the mixed region. By progressively analyzing the tracer concentration in the annulus along the bed depth, both parameters were obtained. It was concluded that (1) particle mixing can be interpreted according to the model, (2) ingress of particles from the annulus into the spout is limited to the cone region (in agreement with most observations in half-sectional columns), and (3) a portion of the annulus, less than 10 percent of its total volume, contributes to the perfectly mixed volume. It seems likely that a minor mixing role in the annulus is played by gradual migration of particles from the vessel wall toward the center, whereas shear along the entire spout-to-annulus boundary makes a more major contribution.

Roy et al.[6] applied a computer-automated radioactive particle tracking (CARPT) technique, adapted from flow field measurements in gas–solid fluidized beds, bubble columns, and three-phase fluidized systems, to spouted beds. The apparatus consisted of a 152-mm-ID column with a 60° angle base and $D_i = 19$ mm. Glass beads of $d_p = 3$ mm were tested. The single tracer particle was prepared by mixing soda lime and scandium oxide, activated by neutron bombardment. The motion of the single radioactive particle was then monitored at 30-ms intervals and count rates were determined by several detectors at different levels and angular positions. This noninvasive technique allowed a number of hydrodynamic parameters, not otherwise quantifiable, to be evaluated. Several hundred thousand measurements allowed determination of the velocity field, cycle time distribution, spout profile, and solids exchange distribution at the annulus–spout interface. Figure 8.3 illustrates radial profiles of the mean vertical (v_z) and radial (v_r) particle velocities at three levels: $z = 375$ mm in the fountain, $z = 235$ mm in the cylindrical region of the bed, and $z = 55$ mm in the conical base. Particles in the fountain rise near the axis and fall closer to the wall, whereas the mean radial solid velocities increase as particles approach the wall and then begin to decelerate. In the annulus region, the solids move downward in near-plug flow, with an upward velocity adjacent to the spout and a minimal radial component. In the conical region, the solid flow is characterized mainly by inward radial acceleration from the annulus toward the spout.

These noninvasive measurements were extended in a later paper.[7] With the aid of many trajectories, the three-dimensional spouted bed reactor was depicted by an axisymmetric vector plot. Contour fields were provided for particle residence time and axial and radial velocity in each volume cell. A flow reversal line demarcated the ascent and descent

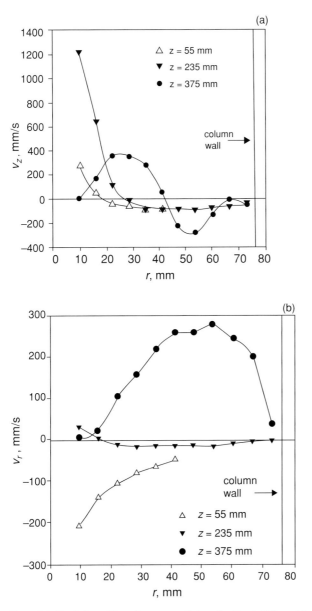

Figure 8.3. Radial profiles of mean particle velocity at different levels in the spouted bed.[6] $U/U_{ms} = 1.3$; $H = 314$ mm: (a) vertical; (b) radial. Reprinted with permission of John Wiley & Sons, Inc.

regions. If the boundary layer between this line and the spout–annulus interface is included with the spout, a higher solids holdup can be attributed to the spout itself, contributing to the gross mixing of solids. The mean circulation time was caused by abrupt upward acceleration in the spout, reversal in the fountain, deposition on the annulus top, and slow downward motion in the annulus. The mixing dynamics were

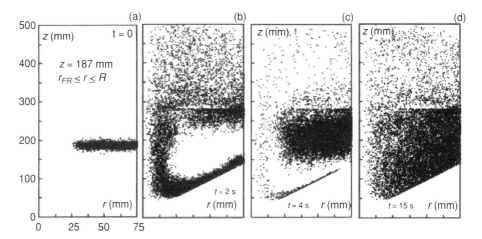

Figure 8.4. Snapshots[7] showing evolution of a clump of 15,385 particles injected simultaneously in the cylindrical annulus at $z = 187$ mm between $r_{FR} < r < R$: (a) $t = 0$, (b) $t = 2$ s, (c) $t = 4$ s, (d) $t = 15$ s.

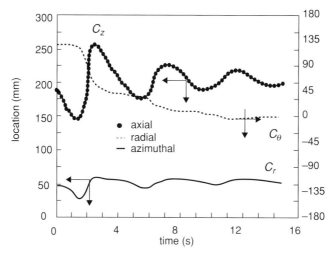

Figure 8.5. Mixing in axial, radial, and azimuthal directions, demarcated by centroid location versus time of a clump of tracer particles, each injected[7] at time 0 into the annulus at $z = 187$ mm.

evaluated by an ergodic approach, simulating the introduction of a clump of particles, each following independent trajectories. Figure 8.4 shows the locations of particles at subsequent times after being marked in a thin slice in the annulus at $t = 0$. It is seen that (1) some vertical mixing occurs in the annulus; (2) the spout–annulus interface is not impervious to mass exchange; (3) radial and circumferential mixing is chiefly caused by the fountain; and (4) mixing also occurs in the bottom cone owing to shear. The last of these factors requires more attention.

The axial, radial, and circumferential mixing response curves plotted in Figure 8.5 suggest that axial mixing needs more than four cycle times to reasonably damp

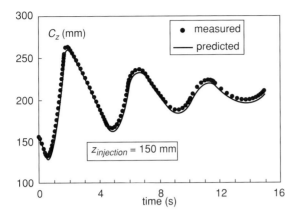

Figure 8.6. Axial mixing time for three different heights of release. Measured versus simulated mixing curves.[7]

fluctuations, whereas radial mixing requires less than a single cycle time, and circumferential uniformity is achieved in about two cycles. An idealized spouted bed model was proposed with a descriptive parameter-free four-region (cylindrical and conical annulus, spout, and fountain) two-dimensional axisymmetric stochastic model to simulate the tracer trajectories. This model can be used predictively after defining the jump probabilities at the spout/annulus interface and within the annulus, the fountain height, relative maximum residence time of particles, and the flow reversal radius. Model validation was carried out by comparing the controlling mixing components with experimental results from γ-ray particle tracking. Figure 8.6 demonstrates this method.

Original correlations have been proposed[8] for calculating the average cycle time in a 0.152-m unit from the geometric factors, θ and D_i, and experimental conditions, H_0, d_p, and U. The distribution of cycle times was determined experimentally by monitoring a colored particle trajectory with an image analysis system. Particle trajectories in the annulus and spout were calculated by dividing each zone into streamtubes having the same particle mass flow, and their Stokes stream functions were solved in cylindrical coordinates based on the experimental values of v_z; v_r was derived by solving local mass balances. Particle flow patterns were indicated by local velocity vectors. By comparing these maps for different geometries and operating conditions, the effect of each parameter was clarified. Cycle times and frequencies were then calculated and compared with the experimental results. In Figure 8.7 the effect of the base angle is evident from a comparison of the results in (a) and (b). The average cycle time doubled and a wider distribution was obtained as the included cone angle increased.

Gross mixing of sawdust was evaluated[9] in a continuously operating spouted bed drier in terms of the RTD. A tracer was introduced as a pulse and sampled after entrainment. The drying reactor ($D = 0.3$ m, height $= 1.9$ m) behaved as an almost perfectly mixed unit: it was modeled first as a continuous stirred-tank reactor (CSTR) connected to a plug flow reactor and later as a dispersed plug flow system, with a Peclet number, Pe, as the fitting parameter. Both descriptions were demonstrated to be in excellent agreement,

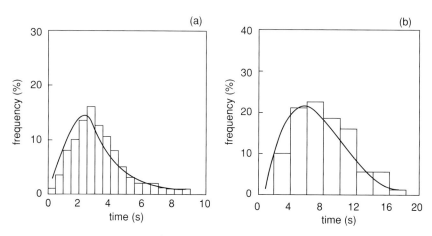

Figure 8.7. Cycle time frequency.[8] Histograms: experimental results. Lines: calculated from the trajectories. Experimental conditions: $D = 0.152$ m, $D_i = 0.03$ m, $H_0 = 0.20$ m, $d_p = 4$ mm, $U = 1.02\ U_{ms}$: (a) $\theta = 45°$ (b) $\theta = 120°$. Reprinted with permission of American Chemical Society, by Copyright Clearance Center.

with $Pe < 1$, indicating that the material in the drying chamber is well mixed, regardless of the discharge mode. Another mixing model, which considers elutriation of fines from a continuous spouted bed, is also available[10]; the authors claim good agreement between experimental data and fitted model predictions.

Spouted beds as well-mixed reactors for coating applications were reviewed by Piccinini[11] for batch pyrolytic carbon deposition. The deposition reaction, homogeneous on the nuclear fuel particles circulating in the system, maintained excellent performance throughout the many hours required for multilayer coating with simple adjustment of gas flowrate and gas composition. Continuous processes may be conceived for coating operations, but variation of particle diameter and density with time and the extent of coating may be challenging issues.

8.2   Mixing in a pulsed spouted bed

Spouting mechanism, mixing properties, maximum spoutable bed depth, and solids circulation rates were studied in a pulsed spouted bed.[12] The pulsing is intended to reduce energy consumption and to be applied where mass transfer controls the process. The authors operated a cylindrical column of 0.17 m ID, $D_i = 10$ and 20 mm, with $3.1 < d_p < 6.7$ mm, $0.61 <$ particle sphericity < 0.85, and $930 < \rho_p < 1280$ kg/m³. Air pulsations at frequencies from 0.2 to 2 Hz were induced through a solenoid valve, with the low frequency being the minimum required by the inertial time of particles to start their circulation. Colored particles permitted determination of the stagnant zone height at the column base. Flow regime diagrams (spouting/transition/slugging) were traced as a function of frequency for different bed depths.

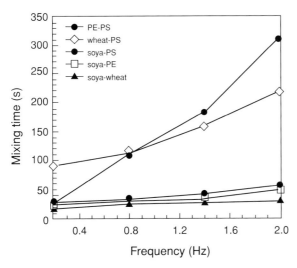

Figure 8.8. Time to obtain well-mixed state for different particulate mixtures.[12] $D = 0.7$ m, $D_i = 10$ mm, $U = 0.21$ m/s, $H_0 = 0.2$ m (equal height layers).

The mixing effectiveness was determined by spouting 50 percent v/v binary mixtures and sampling at different times to detect concentration differences less than 5 percent, defined as the mixing time criterion; this procedure was repeated at various bed locations. An example of the influence of the frequency of pulsations on mixing is plotted in Figure 8.8: the mixing time increased with frequency for all the binary mixtures tested, whereas solids circulation at the top of the annulus reached a maximum at a frequency of 1.2 Hz. This apparent inconsistency might be caused by local nonhomogeneity (i.e., segregation) or zones characterized by a lower circulation (e.g., next to the bottom stagnant zone).

8.3   Origin of segregation studies

Most studies on granular materials mixing have been carried out with particle tracers that satisfy the requirement of being typical of the bulk in terms of size, shape, and density. In most practical cases, however, there is a distribution of properties. In addition, these properties may vary with time, for instance, because of drying, coating, or gas–solid chemical reactions. In such cases, segregation or demixing can take place because of the hydrodynamics of the spout and fountain, percolation of fines in the interstices of coarse particles, and buoyancy differences between light and dense components.

Understanding and being able to control segregation phenomena leads to improved process control. Another important consideration is whether the process is batch or continuous. In the former case, segregation mainly gives rise to zones of different concentration, whereas in the latter, after attaining steady state, the bed composition eventually differs from that of the incoming mixture. If virtually well mixed, the outlet composition is very similar to the bed composition.

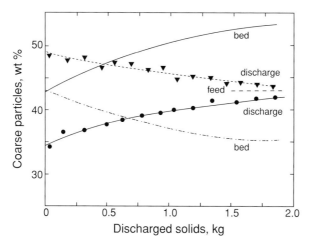

Figure 8.9. Composition in bed and in discharge stream[14]: $D = 80$ mm, $D_i = 6$ mm, $m_p =$ 0.67 kg, $Q_s = 1.64 \times 10^{-5}$ kg/s, $U = 0.66$ m/s, $\theta = 40°$, $H_0 = 130$ mm, $\rho_p = 2,650$ kg/m³, $N_{si} = 1.58$, coarse material: glass, $d_p = 1.24$ mm; fine material: glass, $d_p = 0.78$ mm.
—— and —•— submerged discharge $D_p = 7$ mm, $N_{sf} = 1.72$;
—·—·— and —·—▼—·— overflow discharge $D_p = 14$ mm, $N_{sf} = 1.44$.

Spouted beds often generate an inverted segregation with respect to fluidized beds. Because of entrainment in the spout, jetsam material is raised into the upper portion of the bed. Then the fountain separates the components differing in mass according to stochastic trajectories, whereas the annulus keeps circulating the particulate solids along well-defined streamlines.

8.4   Segregation in continuously operated spouted beds

A particular application of spouted beds that motivated an early study[13] was the coating of prosthetic devices with pyrolytic carbon. In this process, characterized by a slow deposition of material on the circulating solids, few particles represent the product, whereas the bulk acts as a buffer. Spouting features must be maintained over time. Control is provided by selectively discharging some of the ever-growing coarse particles. The spouting vessel had $D = 0.08$ m, $\theta = 40°$, and $D_i = 6$ mm. A 14-mm ID overflow pipe was positioned 130 mm above the base to control the bed depth and to sample the solids. A binary mixture of glass ballotini was used, with solids fed independently to prevent upstream segregation. Figure 8.9 depicts the system dynamics from an initial bed composition matching the feed solids concentration to a stationary discharge identical to the feed. The solids feed rate did not appreciably affect the concentration profiles.

An equilibrium condition, displayed in Figure 8.10, was demonstrated to exist between the internal (averaged over the entire bed) and the outgoing solids. It was expressed by

$$Y = X^n, \tag{8.4}$$

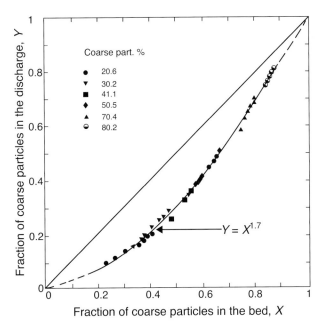

Figure 8.10. Relationship between bed and discharge mass fraction of coarse component for feed compositions shown in the legend[13]; $H_0 = 130$ mm, $D = 80$ mm, $D_i = 6$ mm, $\theta = 40°$, $\rho_p = 2,650$ kg/m³, $N_s = 1.7 \pm 0.1$, d_p fine material $= 0.55$ mm, d_p coarse material $= 0.92$ mm. Reprinted with permission of John Wiley & Sons, Inc.

where n depends on the gas flowrate in the vessel and the particle mixture according to the relationship

$$n = c - d \log_{10}(U/U_{ms} - 1),\qquad(8.5)$$

where c and d depend on the particle mixture. If we consider a different situation with a higher gas flowrate (a more developed fountain and more vigorous mixing), the equilibrium curve approaches the diagonal, signifying less segregation. The controlling mechanism is then due primarily to trajectories and collisions in the fountain, rather than to fine particle buoyancy at the bed surface. Different segregation may be obtained in deeper beds, owing to higher gas velocity in the annulus.

An additional contribution and quantification of segregation phenomena, as well as of the dynamics to reach steady state, was presented[14] to study the effect of the height of the discharge port on the side and in the freeboard, with overflow, submerged, and bottom openings. The composition of the stream collected directly from the fountain was typically richer in fines, except for a fully overdeveloped and particle-crowded fountain that generated local chaotic mixing (with U/U_{ms} approaching 2). An overflow opening receives the solids according to fountain trajectories, bouncing on the bed surface or entrainment, so discharge of fines is more probable. A submerged opening can release a stream either richer or leaner in coarse material, depending on the gas flowrate, with the U/U_{ms} ratio affecting the composition of the discharge stream. Segregation owing to strain-induced interparticle percolation generates some voidage increase and preferential rolling out of the coarser particles. Depending on the operating conditions and the geometry, a spouted bed of identical binary mixtures can evolve toward different steady state composition distributions. In summary, the dynamics of a continuously operating spouted bed can be shortened by using two different openings with their total surface area chosen to obtain adequate solid material discharge.

During continuous operation, segregation induces substantial modifications in the bed that can cause the system to change its behavior – for example, with the fountain undergoing a transition to an underdeveloped state[15] and even with spouting collapse. Contours of the particle velocity vectors were defined in the three zones of a spouting unit with $D = 0.19$ m, for both shallow and deep beds, based on stereophotogrammetric measurements. The fountain height was shown to be linearly related to the gas mass flux, by having as a parameter the bed depth. Comparing these vectors clearly demonstrates particle recirculation. Given the major role of fountain trajectories, particle demixing is expected to play a significant role in large-scale units.

A case in which steady state segregation of coarse particles occurred in a continuous coating process was reported[16] for a thermochemical reactor in which large bodies (heart valves or bone prostheses) were circulated in a spouting unit. When all surfaces in direct contact with a reacting hydrocarbon (or silane) underwent coatings as thick as 500 μm, the increase of bed volume could be controlled by continuously feeding fine particles and removing the grown ones.

Segregation was compared in half and full beds by Cook and Bridgwater[17]: the qualitative particle concentration profiles demonstrated that angular and radial segregation occurred, indicating that half-bed experiments are questionable for particle mixing measurements. Batch experiments in a 0.193-m ID unit, with glass beads dispersed in mustard seeds, allowed relative concentration profiles to be traced. By comparing the results of tests carried out at different gas flowrates, an overdeveloped fountain caused the glass beads to land closer to the outer wall; however, the concentration profile was reversed by percolation along the annulus, favored by appreciable entrainment of the lighter particles.

Experiments were carried out by Kutluoglu et al.[18] in a 0.152-m ID half-column with $D_i = 12.7$ mm, $\theta = 60°$, and four types of spherical particles ($980 < \rho_p < 2890$ kg/m^3, $1.1 < d_p < 2.2$ mm). The trajectories of colored particles were film-recorded at high frequencies and analyzed frame by frame. The mixing properties of the fountain were evaluated by relating the landing radial position of particles to the radial profile of axial velocity component at the top of the spout exit, which is well described by a parabolic distribution. Figure 8.11 accounts for this effect. Light particles were deflected more than heavier particles because of collisions at the top of the fountain, whereas collisions of particles against the column wall caused counteracting motion. The sloping profile of the annulus-top free surface also provided some redistribution. Binary systems were tested to evaluate the cumulative distributions at the annulus–spout–fountain boundaries for segregating conditions. An effective representation was provided by triangular diagrams depicting the three regions: whereas segregation/demixing was generated in the fountain, the annulus and particularly the spout promoted remixing

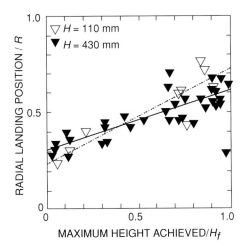

Figure 8.11. Radial landing position of polystyrene particles on the annulus surface as a function of the maximum height achieved by the particle.[18] Reprinted with permission of John Wiley & Sons, Inc.

and desegregation. An important conclusion was reached by operating with a mixture formed by the same binary components of different particle densities and diameters, but virtually identical particle masses: in this case no segregation occurred.

Bed depth affects the fountain solids load: the deeper the bed, the more pronounced the component separation becomes. Shallow beds counteract segregation owing to an inward sloping top bed surface, which generates a preferential inward rolling of light particles, counteracting the greater outward motion of the light particles because of collisions in the fountain. Surface bouncing, on the contrary, has a random effect, with the heavier component having a tendency to be embedded and follow the particle streamlines. Fine particles, depending on their mass and local gas velocity, may percolate or be entrained: both mechanisms act in favor of generating concentration profiles in the axial and radial directions. Installing conical deflectors in the fountain region was shown[18] to reduce segregation.

Uemaki et al.[19] studied segregation of silica sand in a 0.20-m ID spouted bed by means of batch tests with d_p ratios from 1.47 to 3.40. In addition to generating a correlation for the minimum spouting velocity of particle mixtures, the experimental program led to detailed mapping of the coarse component concentration in the annulus without interrupting the spouting. The particle size ratio and gas flowrate were the test variables. It was demonstrated that the degree of segregation increased with increasing particle size ratio. With the solids tested and $U = 1.20\ U_{ms}$, homogeneity was not achieved in the bed for the mixtures tested.

8.5   Top surface segregation

Local segregation at the free surface of a spouted bed was demonstrated by Rovero.[20] Any particle characterized by a minimum fluidization velocity (owing to its density or size) lower than that typical of the solids bulk has a tendency to separate, provided that the local gas velocity is sufficient to promote fluidization. Fines or fragments of the material constituting the bed of particles could frequently be observed to concentrate at the vessel wall, particularly when the fountain mixing properties were hindered, owing to moderate spouting with a narrow fountain, or by insertion of a horizontal baffle. Baffle segregation could be induced by having $U_{aH} > U_{mf}$ of the flotsam particle, locally at a given vertical coordinate z. With this local segregation near the exit port, a highly concentrated stream of flotsam particles could be discharged, while maintaining well-mixed conditions in the annulus.

Baffle-induced segregation can be relevant to continuous processes in which a reacting solid phase undergoes a thermochemical reaction and the product particles differ in size or density from the reactant particles. This baffle segregation phenomenon was proven to be useful in an autothermal pyrolysis-gasification process under controlled devolatilization conditions.[21]

A possibly similar mechanism, in which the discharge pipe itself offers some cover from fountain pouring, was mentioned[22] for the continuous release of light char dropping from the freeboard and preferentially segregated to the region near the vessel wall.

8.6   Mixing and segregation in conical spouted beds

The success of conical spouted beds (CcSBs) for drying/granulation of pasty material has been replicated in other applications with solids of irregular shapes. Fast reactions, such as combustion, gasification, and pyrolysis, do not need deep beds. Spout stability, linked to solids circulation and homogeneity, has been demonstrated to benefit from a decrease in the diameter ratio of binary mixtures.[23] In the same paper, the mixing index, M_b, between 0.95 and 1.05 corresponded to negligible segregation. The mixing index was found to be a function of the geometry of the bed and the air velocity.

The same authors[24] performed tests in a conical column unit with binary and tertiary mixtures of glass beads ($1 < d_p < 8$ mm). By optimizing the sampling conditions, detailed radial and vertical profiles of the coarse fraction were obtained. Two empirical correlations were proposed for the two phases, each giving good fit to the experimental results. The highest M_b was obtained for 50 percent by mass of the coarser solid. Figure 8.12 plots the relationship between M_b and U/U_{ms}, showing increasing homogeneity with increasing U/U_{ms}. A similar mixing index was also evaluated for tertiary solids mixtures (M_t), with a maximum for similar proportions by mass of all three components (see Figure 8.13).

The mixing characteristics of conical spouted beds were evaluated indirectly in terms of the solids circulation patterns.[25] D, d_p, ρ_p, Φ, θ, solids loading, and U were varied in the tests. The mean radial and vertical particle velocities v_r and v_z were detected by an optical probe and the streamtube mapping traced. The volumetric solids circulation was then computed by cross-sectional integration of the particle flux. The circulation rate increased as the particle sphericity, Φ, decreased, and as the particle density increased. The spout-to-annulus volume ratio was much higher in the conical configuration, with

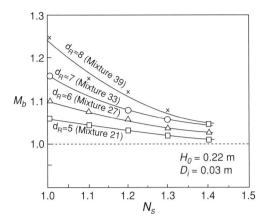

Figure 8.12. Effect of relative air velocity, $u_R = u_c/u_{msi}$, on mixing index for binary mixtures,[24] M_b. $\theta = 36°$, $H_0 = 0.22$ m, $D_i = 0.03$ m. Reprinted with permission of American Chemical Society via Copyright Clearance Center.

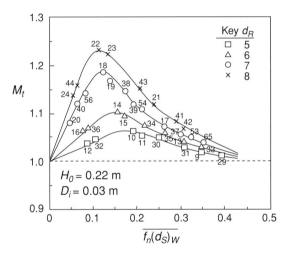

Figure 8.13. Values of the mixing index for ternary mixtures, M_t, versus bed average value of Sauter mean diameter distribution function, $f_n(d_S)_W$, for different particle diameter ratio,[24] d_R, $\theta = 36°$, $H_0 = 0.32$ m, $D_i = 0.03$ m. Reprinted with permission of American Chemical Society via Copyright Clearance Center.

the result that the radial component of particle velocity was more effective in causing mixing, thus countering segregation. The non-monotonic radial concentration profiles of coarse particles provide a qualitative indication of the improved mixing effectiveness.

Bacelos and Freire[26] demonstrated that spouting stability and particle segregation are related. Spouting stability was evaluated by calculating the standard deviation of pressure fluctuations in the bed. Some particle mixtures generated unstable spouting, in particular for fine materials and mixtures of high particle diameter ratio. It seems that decreased bed permeability, which is likely to cause incipient instability, also resulted in increased segregation. Percolation of a coarser fraction and/or entrainment of a finer fraction was enhanced by moderate system pulsation. For the range of experimental conditions tested, a deeper bed improved spouting stability while decreasing segregation.

8.7   Mixing and segregation in a multispouting vessel

A novel fluid–solids contactor featuring an annular geometry was studied by Huang and Hu.[27] The degree of mixing was investigated in both the axial and the circumferential directions. To compensate for peripheral elongation, an alternative axisymmetric circular feeding device was also proposed. Both the axial and the lateral mixing rates were demonstrated to increase as the spouting airflow rate increased. The static bed depth had a noticeable effect on the final degree of mixing, first increasing and then decreasing with height, although the degree of lateral mixing showed a monotonic decrease with height. It is likely that this contradictory result is caused by interference of the experimental method, with some segregation occurring in the vertical direction for the coarser tracer particles used, especially for deeper beds. In a second study,[28] the authors used inclined conical nozzles to enhance the peripheral circulation of the granular solids. They observed minor dead zones on the sides of their V-shaped deflectors. This unforeseen finding is believed to be caused by the nature of the material used.

Taha and Koniuta[29] reported work on the Cerchar fluidization distributor, which has all the characteristics of 2×2 and 3×3 modules in a multiple spouting unit (see Chapter 17). The mixing obtained with this grid was compared to that resulting from a conventional fluidized bed distributor. By operating over a range of particle size and at density ratios between 1 and 7, it was demonstrated that adequate homogeneity was obtained at a superficial velocity exceeding 50 percent of the minimum operating conditions, whereas an excess of 150 percent was unable to disperse the jetsam in standard fluidization.

Stimulus–response experiments were conducted[30] in four different rectangular columns containing two and three spout cells. Each cell had a square cross-section with 0.075, 0.10, or 0.15 m sides and a $60°$ included angle at the bottom. The fluid inlet to each cell was 12 mm in diameter, independent of the side dimension. This geometry caused different spouting conditions. Polymeric cylindrical chips ($d_p = 1.8$ mm and $l = 3.4$ mm, $\rho_b = 556$ kg/m^3) constituted the bed material. After achieving steady state by carefully adjusting the air supply to individual cells and continuous feeding through a screw feeder, colored tracer was added as a pulse. Samples at the outlet were collected at regular time intervals over two to five mean residence times. A plug flow compartment in series with mixed flow was used to fit the experimental data, giving an internal age distribution of

$$I(\theta) = \exp[-(V/V_m)(\theta - V_{PF}/V)]. \tag{8.6}$$

The solids flow rate and superficial gas velocity were recognized as important operating parameters affecting the mixing properties of a multiple spouted bed. A dimensionless "spout mixing number,"

$$\alpha = (N\,L\,H_0\,U)/(F_s/\rho_b), \tag{8.7}$$

which accounts for mixing, was proposed. An excessively high fountain height, as well as fountain wandering, was found to increase the volume fraction of the mixed region in their system.

A recent paper[31] examined the hydrodynamics of a multiple square-based reactor for solid state polymerization. There was difficulty in controlling the levels in the stages. This negative feature did not affect the chemical performance. The difficulty was ascribable to a very high solids throughput, related to the mixing and solids circulation of each cell. The findings suggest that it may be important to consider changes in the angle of repose, at least in instances in which the solids properties vary during the process.

8.8   Mixing and segregation in a modified spouted bed

Modification of the inlet geometry from a plain circular orifice to an annular one, in which a dead inner zone communicates with a bottom dead collector,[32] indicates that it may be possible to segregate and selectively discharge particles (or aggregates) that are much bigger than the average bed particles. The overall mechanism, although not fully investigated, is likely to involve (1) gas percolation in the annulus maintaining the solids circulation, together with entrainment by the central spout, and (2) congregation of the coarser component within inner circulation loops, triggering particle transfer probability between annulus and spout (defined as "jump probability" by Larachi et al.[7]), dropping the heavy body into the dead zone. It was demonstrated that a smaller dead zone diameter (corresponding to a broader annular area and a reduced gas flow at the inlet) assisted the separation/discharge effectiveness. This phenomenon, interesting for some applications (such as ash agglomerate removal and nonhomogeneous granulation), requires corroboration with materials of lesser density difference.

Waldie[33] simulated the discharge of large particle agglomerates from the central orifice of a spout-fluid bed by controlling both the central and auxiliary gas flowrates. A relatively small column ($D = 0.1$ m) was provided with an external porous conical distributor for fluidization air. A phase diagram was traced to select possible operating conditions for spout-fluidization of glass ballotini ($d_p = 380$ μm). The dilute coarse fraction was characterized by a particle size ratio between 5 and 16. Tests confirmed that once the coarser material entered the upper inner zone of the bed, it tended to cycle repeatedly there, with a small possibility of dropping out from the central orifice.

Acknowledgment

The authors thank Ms. Marta Barberis Pinlung for her effective collaboration in editing.

Chapter-specific nomenclature

C_b	concentration of solids tracer in bed, mol/m^3
C_{b0}	C_b at $t = 0$, mol/m^3
C_f	fractional concentration of solids tracer in feed after step change
C_p	fractional concentration of solids tracer in product after step change
C_r	radial coordinate, mm
C_z	axial coordinate, mm
C_θ	azimuthal coordinate, deg
d_R	particle diameter ratio, larger to smaller, in binary mixtures
D_{disp}	axial dispersion coefficient of solids, m^2/s
D_p	pipe diameter, mm
$f_n(d_S)_W$	average value of Sauter mean diameter for the whole bed
F	feed rate of solids, m^3/s
F_s	solids flow rate, g/s
H_d	height of drying chamber, m
$I(\theta)$	internal age distribution function
l	length, m
L	cell size, m
M_b	mixing index for binary solids mixtures
M_t	mixing index for tertiary solids mixtures
N	number of spout cells in the volume
N_s	spouting number $= U/U_{ms}$
Pe	Peclet number, $= v_z H_d / D_{disp}$
Q_s	mass flow rate, kg/s
r_{FR}	flow reversal radius, mm
R_{cfr}	internal circulation to feed rate ratio
t_c	cycle time, s
V	total bed volume, m^3
V_m	mixed flow volume, m^3
V_{PF}	plug flow volume, m^3
v_r	mean radial particle velocity, m/s
v_z	mean vertical particle velocity, m/s
W	circulation rate of solids in annulus and spout, m^3/s
X	mass fraction of coarse component in bed
Y	mass fraction of coarse component in discharge stream

Greek letters

ρ_b	bulk density of solids, kg/m^3
Φ	particle sphericity

Subscripts

i	initial conditions
f	final conditions

References

1. K. B. Mathur and N. Epstein. *Spouted Beds* (New York: Academic Press, 1974).
2. D. Van Velzen, H. J. Flamm, H. Langenkamp, and A. Casile. Motion of solids in spouted beds. *Can. J. Chem. Eng.*, **52** (1974), 156–161.
3. U. Mann and E. J. Crosby. Cycle time distribution measurements in spouted beds. *Can. J. Chem. Eng.*, **53** (1975), 579–581.
4. H. Takeda and Y. Yamamoto. Mixing of particles in a spouted bed. *J. Nucl. Sci. Technol.*, **13** (1976), 372–381.
5. G. S. McNab. Prediction of spout diameter. *Brit. Chem. Eng. Proc. Tech.*, **17** (1972), 532.
6. D. Roy, F. Larachi, R. Legros, and J. Chaouki. A study of solid behavior in spouted beds using 3-D particle tracking. *Can. J. Chem. Eng.*, **72** (1994), 945–952.
7. F. Larachi, B. P. A. Grandjean, and J. Chaouki. Mixing and circulation of solids in spouted beds: particle tracking and Monte Carlo emulation of the gross flow pattern. *Chem. Eng. Sci.*, **58** (2003), 1497–1507.
8. M. J. San José, M. Olazar, M. A. Izquierdo, S. Alvarez, and J. Bilbao. Solid trajectories and cycle times in spouted beds. *Ind. Eng. Chem. Res.*, **43** (2004), 3433–3438.
9. J. Berghel, L. Nilsson, and R. Renstrom. Particle mixing and residence time when drying sawdust in a continuous spouted bed. *Chem. Eng. Proc.*, **47** (2008), 1246–1251.
10. T. Ishikura, I. Tanaka, and H. Shinohara. Residence time distribution of particles in the continuous spouted bed of solid-gas system with elutriation of fines. *J. Soc. Powder Tech. Japan*, **15** (1978), 453–457.
11. N. Piccinini. Coated nuclear fuel particles. In *Advances in Nuclear Science and Technology*, Volume 8, ed. E. J. Henley and J. Lewins (New York: Academic Press, 1975), pp. 304–341.
12. S. Devahastin and A. S. Mujumdar. Some hydrodynamic and mixing characteristics of a pulsed spouted bed dryer. *Powder Technol.*, **117** (2001), 189–197.
13. N. Piccinini, A. Bernhard, P. Campagna, and F. Vallana. Segregation phenomenon in spouted beds. *Can. J. Chem. Eng.*, **55** (1977), 122–125.
14. N. Piccinini. Particle segregation in continuously operating spouted beds. In *Fluidization III*, ed. J. R. Grace and J. M. Matsen (New York: Plenum Press, 1980), pp. 279–285.
15. G. S. McNab and J. Bridgwater. Solids mixing and segregation in spouted beds. In *Third European Conference on Mixing* (York, UK: BHRA, 1979), pp. 125–140.
16. N. Piccinini and G. Rovero. Thick coatings by thermo-chemical deposition in spouted beds. *Can. J. Chem. Eng.*, **61** (1983), 448–453.
17. H. H. Cook and J. Bridgwater. Segregation in spouted beds. *Can. J. Chem. Eng.*, **56** (1978), 636–638.
18. E. Kutluoglu, J. R. Grace, K. W. Murchie, and P. H. Cavanagh. Particle segregation in spouted beds. *Can. J. Chem. Eng.*, **61** (1983), 308–316.
19. O. Uemaki, R. Yamada, and M. Kugo. Particle segregation in a spouted bed of binary mixtures of particles. *Can. J. Chem. Eng.*, **61** (1983), 303–307.
20. G. Rovero. Baffle-induced segregation in spouted beds. *Can. J. Chem. Eng.*, **61** (1983), 325–330.
21. G. Rovero and A. P. Watkinson. A two stage spouted bed process for autothermal pyrolysis or retorting. *Fuel Process. Technol.*, **26** (1990), 221–238.
22. R. Aguado, M. Olazar, M. J. San José, G. Aguirre, and J. Bilbao. Pyrolysis of sawdust in a conical spouted bed reactor. Yields and product composition. *Ind. Eng. Chem. Res.*, **39** (2000), 1925–1933.

23. M. Olazar, M. J. San José, F. J. Penas, A. T. Aguayo, and J. Bilbao. Stability and hydrodynamics of conical spouted beds with binary mixtures. *Ind. Eng. Chem. Res.*, **32** (1993), 2826–2834.

24. M. J. San José, M. Olazar, F. J. Penas, and J. Bilbao. Segregation in conical spouted beds with binary and ternary mixtures of equidensity spherical particles. *Ind. Eng. Chem. Res.*, **33** (1994), 1838–1844.

25. M. J. San José, S. Alvarez, A. Morales, M. Olazar, and J. Bilbao. Solid cross-flow into the spout and particle trajectories in conical spouted beds consisting of solids of different density and shape. *Chem. Eng. Res. Des.*, **84** (2006), 487–494.

26. M. S. Bacelos and J. T. Freire. Stability of spouting regimes in conical spouted beds with inert particle mixtures. *Ind. Eng. Chem. Res.*, **45** (2006), 808–817.

27. H. Huang and G. Hu. Mixing characteristics of a novel annular spouted bed with several angled air nozzles. *Ind. Eng. Chem. Res.*, **46** (2007), 8248–8254.

28. H. Huang, G. Hu, and F. Wang. Experimental study on particles mixing in an annular spouted bed. *Energy Convers. Mgmt*, **49** (2008), 257–266.

29. B. Taha and A. Koniuta. Hydrodynamics and segregation from the Cerchar FBC fluidization grid. In Poster Session, Fluidization VI Conference (Banff, Canada, 1989).

30. M. B. Saidutta and D. V. R. Murthy. Mixing behavior of solids in multiple spouted beds. *Can. J. Chem. Eng.*, **78** (2000), 382–385.

31. C. Beltramo, G. Rovero, and G. Cavaglià. Hydrodynamics and thermal experimentation on square-based spouted bed for polymer upgrading and unit scale-up. *Can. J. Chem. Eng.*, **87** (2009), 394–402.

32. T.-C. Chou and Y.-M. Uang. Separation of particles in a modified fluidized bed by a distributor with dead-zone collector. *Ind. Eng. Chem. Process Des. Dev.*, **24** (1985), 683–686.

33. B. Waldie. Separation and residence times of larger particles in a spout-fluid bed. *Can. J. Chem. Eng.*, **70** (1992), 873–879.

9 Heat and mass transfer

Andrzej Kmiec and Sebastian Englart

9.1 Introduction

A great number of processes carried out in spouted beds require the application of different modes of heat and/or mass transfer. We may distinguish among the following modes[1,2]:

- Heat transfer, mass transfer, simultaneous heat and mass transfer – between fluid and particles,
- Heat transfer between wall and bed, and
- Heat transfer between submerged object and bed.

For each mode, transfer mechanisms are examined; then experimental findings and, in some cases, theoretical studies are discussed.

9.2 Between fluid and particles

9.2.1 Transfer mechanisms and models

Quite often, the basic assumption for analysis of heat or mass exchanged between fluid and particles is that heat is transferred to the particles under conditions of external control, neglecting heat transmission within the particles. For heat transfer in the absence of mass transfer, this is justified when the particle heat transfer Biot number is sufficiently small (e.g., <0.1) and the corresponding Fourier number exceeds 0.2.[2] For simultaneous heat and mass transfer, such as when the particles are well wetted at the surface, the average temperature at the particle surfaces is substantially uniform, and external control again prevails.

Assuming plug flow conditions through the bed, the axial fluid temperature distribution can be described by a dimensionless function.[2] Because the spouted bed consists of two distinct regions, with the average gas velocity in the spout being one or two orders of

Spouted and Spout-Fluid Beds: Fundamentals and Applications, eds. Norman Epstein and John R. Grace. Published by Cambridge University Press. © Cambridge University Press 2011.

magnitude greater than that in the annulus, the decline of gas temperature in these two zones is quite different; it is slight in the spout and considerable in the annular zone. In fact, the annulus gas attains thermal equilibrium with the bed solids within a few centimeters of its entry into the bed.[2,3]

Mass transfer of a vapor from particles to the surrounding gas is under external control conditions if the drying rate is constant. It can usually be assumed that the particles under these conditions remain at a constant uniform temperature – namely, the adiabatic saturation temperature of the inlet gas. Although the vapor transfer mechanism from an individual particle is analogous to that of heat transfer, an analogy is not fulfilled for the bed as a whole, as pointed out by Mathur and Epstein,[2] Kmiec,[4–6] Oliveira et al.,[7] and Kmiec et al.[8]

In some processes – for example, solids drying during the falling rate period – considerable temperature gradients in some parts of the bed can occur. For unsteady state heating or cooling of a particle, the resulting intraparticle temperature differences relative to the differences between the particle surface and fluid are solely related to the Biot number, $Bi_H = h_p r_p / \lambda_p$, provided that the Fourier number, $Fo_H = \alpha t / r_p^2$, exceeds a minimum value of 0.2.[9] A number of mathematical models have been developed for heat transfer in spouted bed drying,[10–14] but they require sophisticated mathematical or numerical methods to solve a system of differential equations. Devahastin et al.[10] assumed no conduction of heat and moisture between particles, no heat losses, and no effects of particle shrinkage. Markowski[11] developed a model in which he introduced the additional heat flux connected with the wet film evaporation from the surface of an inert particle. Another heat- and mass-transfer model was developed by Feng et al.[12] to simulate combined microwave and spouted-bed drying of diced apples, a hygroscopic porous material. In the solutions of both these models, the surface heat transfer coefficient, h_p, used for the boundary condition, was calculated from Kmiec's second correlation.[6] On the other hand, Jumah and Raghavan,[13] in their numerical solution of the differential equation for heat transfer in spouted bed microwave-assisted drying, used Kmiec's first correlation[4] to calculate the convective heat transfer coefficient in the boundary condition.

Ando et al.[15] developed a so-called cell model, which was defined to include average air volume associated with a single seed particle. On the other hand, Niamnuy et al.[16] analyzed coupled transport phenomena and mechanical deformation of shrimp during drying in a jet spouted bed dryer. The model consisted of coupled heat conduction and mass diffusion equations coupled with static solid mechanics equations. The simulated results, in terms of the shrimp moisture content, mid-layer temperature, and shrinkage, were compared with the experimental results, and good agreement was generally observed.

Currently, CFD modeling is used more and more often to describe the heat and mass transfer during the drying of grain in spouted bed dryers.[17,18] The Eulerian-Eulerian multifluid modeling approach has been applied in those studies to predict gas–solid flow behavior.

Table 9.1. Correlations of fluid-to-particle heat transfer in spouted beds.

Author	Correlation	
Uemaki and Kugo[19]	$Nu = 0.0005 \left(\frac{d_p U_{ms} \rho_g}{\mu}\right)^{1.46} \left(\frac{U_s}{U_{ms}}\right)^{1.30}$	(9.1)
Reger et al.[22]	$Nu = 0.0597\, Re_i^{2.0}\, Ar^{-0.438}\, Gu^{0.61} (H_o/d_p)^{-1.0}$	(9.2)
Kmiec[4,5]	$Nu = 0.897\, Re^{0.464}\, Pr^{0.333}\, Ar^{0.116} \left(\tan\frac{\theta}{2}\right)^{-0.813} \left(\frac{H_o}{d_p}\right)^{-1.19} \phi^{2.261}$	(9.3)
Kmiec[6]	$Nu = 0.0451\, Re^{0.644}\, Pr^{0.333}\, Ar^{0.226} \left(\tan\frac{\theta}{2}\right)^{-0.852} \left(\frac{H_o}{d_p}\right)^{-1.47} \left(\frac{D_i}{d_p}\right)^{0.947} \phi^{2.304}$	(9.4)
Kmiec and Kucharski[26]	$Nu = 9.4723\, Re^{0.6128}\, Pr^{0.333}\, Ar^{0.2302} \left(\frac{H_o}{d_p}\right)^{-1.031} \left(\frac{\dot{m}_s}{\dot{m}_g}\right)^{0.8135} (1 - C_s)^{0.795}\, \phi^{0.8326}$	(9.5)
Kmiec and Jabarin[27]	$Nu = 2.673\, Re^{0.516}\, Pr^{0.333}\, Ar^{0.033} \left(\tan\frac{\theta}{2}\right)^{-2.331} \left(\frac{H_o}{d_p}\right)^{-1.334} \left(\frac{D_i}{d_p}\right)^{0.602} \phi^{2.102}$	(9.6)
Englart et al.[29]	$Nu = 0.0030\, Re^{0.836}\, Pr^{0.333}\, Ar^{0.236}\, Gu^{-2.527} \left(\frac{D_i}{d_p}\right)^{3.356} \left(\frac{D_H}{d_p}\right)^{-4.121} \left(\frac{\dot{m}_w}{\dot{m}_g}\right)^{0.600} \phi^{-0.918}$	(9.7)
Kudra et al.[45]	$Nu = 1.975\, Re^{0.64} \left(\frac{H_o}{d_p}\right)^{-1.20} \left(\frac{H_o}{w}\right)^{0.45} \left(\frac{s}{d_p}\right)^{0.26}$	(9.8)
Rocha et al.[47]	$Nu = 0.9892\, Re^{1.6421}\, Pr^{1/3} \left(\frac{H_o}{\phi d_p}\right)^{-1.3363} \left(\frac{\dot{m}_s}{\dot{m}_g}\right)^{0.71} \left(\tan\frac{\theta}{2}\right)^{0.1806}$	(9.9)

9.2.2 Experimental findings

The mechanism of the fluid-to-particle heat transfer process outlined theoretically by Mathur and Epstein[1,2] has been confirmed to some extent by a number of experimental studies. Table 9.1 shows a series of empirical correlations. A pioneering investigation was carried out by Uemaki and Kugo,[19] who developed an empirical correlation for air $(Pr = 0.7)$ – Eq. (9.1) in Table 9.1. The values of h_p obtained are rather low as a result of overestimation of the temperature driving force, which was attributed to the spout gas alone.

A number of investigations of particle-to-fluid mass transfer in spouted beds have also been reported. Table 9.2 shows a series of equations. The first work was again by Uemaki and Kugo,[20] whose correlation was Eq. (9.10). Numerical values of the Sherwood number for their range of conditions were found to be at least an order of magnitude smaller than calculated values for comparable fixed and fluidized beds.[2] El-Naas et al.[21] found that the Uemaki-Kugo correlation underestimated the convective mass transfer coefficient by an average factor of 3.

Another early study, on heat transfer during drying of organic dyes on glass beads, was carried out by Reger et al.[22] A correlation, Eq. (9.2) in Table 9.1, was developed on the assumption that the overall process is controlled by the rate of drying of the surface film rather than by the rate of its attrition. A recent analysis of heat and mass transfer of a liquid film at the surface of a single inert particle was given by Leontieva et al.[23] Further research on the drying process for various kinds of particles was carried out

Table 9.2. Correlations of particle-to-fluid mass transfer in spouted beds.

Author	Correlation	
Uemaki and Kugo[20]	$Sh = 0.00022 \cdot Re^{1.45} \cdot \left(\frac{D}{H_o}\right)$	(9.10)
Kmiec[4,5]	$Sh = 0.829 \cdot Re^{0.687} \cdot Sc^{0.333} \cdot Ar^{0.031} \cdot (\tan\frac{\theta}{2})^{-0.915} \cdot \left(\frac{H_o}{d_p}\right)^{-1.227} \cdot \phi^{1.754}$	(9.11)
Kmiec[6]	$Sh = 0.01173 \cdot Re^{0.8} \cdot Sc^{0.333} \cdot Ar^{0.229} \cdot (\tan\frac{\theta}{2})^{-0.961} \cdot \left(\frac{H_o}{d_p}\right)^{-1.446} \cdot \left(\frac{D_i}{d_p}\right)^{1.036} \cdot \phi^{1.922}$	(9.12)
Kmiec and Kucharski[26]	$Sh = 5.314 \cdot Re^{1.072} \cdot Sc^{0.333} \cdot \left(\frac{H_o}{d_p}\right)^{-0.901} \cdot \left(\frac{\dot{m}_s}{\dot{m}_g}\right)^{0.687} \cdot (1 - C_s)^{0.533} \cdot \phi^{0.164}$	(9.13)
Kmiec and Jabarin[27]	$Sh = 1.371 Re^{0.567} Sc^{0.333} Ar^{0.044} \left(\tan\frac{\theta}{2}\right)^{-2.442} \left(\frac{H_o}{d_p}\right)^{-1.353} \left(\frac{D_i}{d_p}\right)^{0.735} \phi^{2.252}$	(9.14)
Kmiec et al.[8]	$Sh = 0.0095 Re^{0.843} Sc^{0.333} Ar^{0.172} Gu^{-2.586} \left(\frac{D_i}{d_p}\right)^{3.124} \left(\frac{D_H}{d_p}\right)^{-4.078} \left(\frac{\dot{m}_w}{\dot{m}_g}\right)^{0.605} \phi^{-1.310}$	(9.15)
El-Naas et al.[21]	$Sh = 0.000258 Re^{1.66}$	(9.16)

by Kmiec.[4-6] Measurements of the constant-rate drying rate of solids yielded heat and mass transfer coefficients. The experimental data were correlated by Eq. (9.3). Then correlations listed in Table 9.1 by Kmiec and colleagues were developed to describe heat transfer in coating processes,[24-27] coal drying,[28] or air humidification.[8,29] Kmiec and Jabarin[27] were able to describe the heat transfer coefficient h_p in the coating of shaped rings by Eq. (9.6). In all studies, an analogy between heat and mass transfer was not fulfilled, as discussed by Kmiec et al.[8] in detail.

These correlations and the same body of experimental data were used for analysis in the development of a new system, a spouted bed with a side swirling stream,[5,30] which appeared to induce a considerable increase in the heat transfer coefficient, h_p, especially at higher airflow rates.

Extensive investigations of gas-to-particle heat transfer were also carried out by Kilkis and Kakac,[31] Dolidovich and Efremtsev,[32,33] and Freitas and Freire.[34] No correlations were developed, however. Heat transfer in various new types of spouted beds have been investigated.[35-37] Khoe and Van Brakel[35] showed that there was a linear relationship between the quantity $h_p(1 - \varepsilon)$ and the drying efficiency η of a spouted bed dryer with a draft tube. Nemeth et al.[38] reported experimental studies on heat transfer in their "mechanical" spouted bed, in which solids are conveyed mechanically in the spout region.

Chatterjee and Diwekar[39] developed a model to estimate the gas-to-particle heat transfer coefficient using the bubbling bed concept for both spout-fluid and spouted beds. The heat transfer coefficients h_p for spouted beds were found to be comparable to the data calculated from Kmiec's first correlation.[4] Dolidovich[40] investigated interphase heat transfer in a "swirled" spouted bed system. It was shown that pressure drop was 20 to 30 percent lower and the incipient spouting velocity 40 to 50 percent lower, whereas interphase heat transfer rate was 15 to 25 percent higher, than their respective values in a classical spouted bed. Also, Akulich et al.[41] showed that peripheral gas jets could intensify gas-to-particle heat transfer in spouted beds.

Many papers have been concerned with heat transfer in drying of liquid solutions on inert particles.[8,29,42–44] Oliveira and Freire[43] developed a three-region model for analysis of evaporation rate in a spouted bed sprayed with liquids. Littman et al.[44] modeled water evaporation in a pneumatic transport system of glass beads, which is mechanistically similar to the spout in a spouted bed. Kmiec et al.[8,29] carried out both experimental and modeling studies of heat transfer in sprayed spouted beds. Their experimental data could be correlated by Eq. (9.7) in Table 9.1.

Investigations of heat transfer in two-dimensional spouted beds were carried out by Kudra et al.,[45] Swasdisevi et al.,[46] and Rocha et al.[47] Kudra et al.[45] studied convective heat transfer to particulate material during drying. The experimental data were correlated by Eq. (9.8). Swasdisevi et al.[46] developed a model for both gas-particle dynamics and heat transfer. Rocha et al.[47] correlated heat transfer coefficients during coating of tablets with solutes of solutions sprayed on them in two-dimensional spouted beds, by Eq. (9.9). Their Reynolds number exponent was more than twice as high as that in Kudra's equation.

9.2.3 Recommended design equations

As mentioned earlier and as shown by Mathur and Epstein,[2] gas in the annulus would achieve thermal equilibrium with bed solids even in the shallowest of beds. For sufficiently deep beds, as would be usual on an industrial scale, the spout gas would also attain equilibrium with the surface of the particles, allowing the development of design formulas for gas cooling and solids heating. In the case of batch heating of cold solids, the heat balance takes the form:

$$W_b c_{ps} dT_b = U A \rho_g c_{pg}(T_{gi} - T_b)dt, \qquad (9.17)$$

which, for initial conditions $t = 0$, $T_b = T_{b0}$, is integrated to

$$t = \frac{W_b c_{ps}}{U A \rho_g c_{pg}} \ln \frac{T_{gi} - T_{b0}}{T_{gi} - T_b(t)}. \qquad (9.18)$$

For the case in which thermal equilibrium between exit gas and bed solids is not achieved, it is recommended that a gas-to-particle heat transfer coefficient h_p for the bed as a whole be defined by the equation[2]

$$q = \rho_g U A c_{pg}(T_{gi} - T_{ge}) = h_p S_p \Delta T_{Lm}, \qquad (9.19)$$

which is equivalent to

$$\ln \frac{T_{gi} - T_b}{T_{ge} - T_b} = St \frac{S_p}{A}, \qquad (9.20)$$

where the Stanton number, St, is given by $h_p/(c_{pg} U \rho_g)$. The term x, which is the fractional temperature approach to equilibrium, $(T_{gi} - T_{ge})/(T_{gi} - T_b)$, can be seen to depend only on St (Re, Pr) and S_p/A, as $x = 1 - (T_{ge} - T_b)/(T_{gi} - T_b)$. Thus, in the absence of thermal equilibrium between exit gas and bed solids, Eqs. (9.17) and (9.18) can be generalized, respectively, to

$$W_s c_{ps}(T_b - T_{si}) = U A \rho_g c_{pg}(T_{gi} - T_b)x \tag{9.21}$$

and

$$t = \frac{W_b c_{ps}}{x U A \rho_g c_{pg}} \ln \frac{T_{gi} - T_{b0}}{T_{gi} - T_b(t)} = \frac{W_b c_{ps}}{x \dot{m}_g c_{pg}} \ln \frac{T_{gi} - T_{b0}}{T_{gi} - T_b(t)}. \tag{9.22}$$

Similar formulas were developed by Claflin and Fane,[36] but they also introduced other parameters, such as drying efficiency and heat transfer losses. Their equation has the form

$$t = \frac{W_b c_{ps}}{\left(\dot{m}_g c_{pg} \eta + K\right)}$$
$$\times \ln \left(\left(\dot{m}_g c_{pg} \eta \left(T_{gi} - T_{b0}\right) + K \left(T_a - T_{b0}\right)\right) / \left(\dot{m}_g c_{pg} \eta \left(T_{gi} - T_b\right) + K \left(T_a - T_b\right)\right)\right), \tag{9.23}$$

where T_a is ambient air temperature, K denotes heat losses, and contacting efficiency η is defined by

$$\eta = \frac{K}{\dot{m}_g c_{pg}} \frac{T_b - T_a}{T_{gi} - T_b}. \tag{9.24}$$

Assuming no heat losses, $K = 0$ J/s·K, and with contacting efficiency η equal to unity, Eqs. (9.23) and (9.18) are identical.

9.3 Between wall and bed

A number of processes carried out in spouted beds require either supplying supplementary heat to the bed or removing heat from the bed. We therefore address the problem of heat transfer between column wall and bed.

9.3.1 Transfer mechanisms

Heat transfer from (or to) the wall takes place through transverse conduction in conjunction with convective transport by the particles moving downward in the annulus, whereas inside the spout, the governing mechanism is more or less the same as in dilute fluidized beds.[48] For spouting with gas (air), a characteristic thermal boundary layer about 1 cm in thickness is developed along the wall vertically downward.[1,2]

9.3.2 Experimental findings

Numerous studies on heat transfer between column wall and bed have been carried out.[19,49–52] A number of different empirical equations for gas spouting, based on dimensional analysis, have been developed. First, Malek and Lu,[49] working with their data and those of Klassen and Gishler,[50] obtained Eq. (9.25), Table 9.3, whereas Uemaki

Table 9.3. Correlations of heat transfer from wall or submerged vertical tube to spouted beds.

Author	Correlation	
Malek and Lu[49]	$\frac{h_w d_p}{\lambda} = 0.54 \left(\frac{g d_p^3 \rho_g^2}{\mu^2}\right)^{0.52} \left(\frac{\rho_b c_{ps}}{\rho_g c_{pg}}\right)^{0.45} \left(\frac{\rho_g}{\rho_b}\right)^{0.08} \left(\frac{d_p}{H_o}\right)^{0.17}$	(9.25)
Uemaki and Kugo[19]	$\frac{h_w d_p}{\lambda} = 13.0 \left(\frac{U d_p \rho_g}{\mu}\right)^{0.10} \left(\frac{g d_p^3 \rho_g^2}{\mu^2}\right)^{0.46} \left(\frac{\rho_s c_{ps}}{\rho_g c_{pg}}\right)^{-0.42} \left(\frac{D_i}{d_p}\right)^{0.2} (1-\varepsilon)$	(9.26)
Chatterjee et al.[51]	$\frac{h_w d_p}{\lambda} = 0.42 \left(\frac{U d_p \rho_g}{\mu}\right)^{1.16} \left(\frac{c_{pg} \mu}{\lambda}\right)^{0.89} \left(\frac{\rho_b c_{ps}}{\rho_g c_{pg}}\right)^{0.24} \left(\frac{d_p}{H_o}\right)^{0.08}$ for $U d_p \rho/\mu < 4.0$	(9.27)
Chatterjee et al.[51]	$\frac{h_w d_p}{\lambda} = 0.6 \left(\frac{U d_p \rho_g}{\mu}\right)^{0.39} \left(\frac{c_{pg} \mu}{\lambda}\right)^{0.72} \left(\frac{\rho_b c_{ps}}{\rho_g c_{pg}}\right)^{0.12}$ for $U d_p \rho/\mu > 4.0$	(9.28)
Macchi et al.[57]	$\frac{h_{ws} d_p}{\lambda} = 0.0196 A r^{0.36} \left(\frac{\rho_p (1-\varepsilon) c_{ps}}{\rho_g c_{pg}}\right)^{0.28}$ in the spout at $r/R = 0$	(9.29)
Macchi et al.[57]	$\frac{h_{ws} d_p}{\lambda} = 0.009 A r^{0.35} \left(\frac{\rho_p (1-\varepsilon) c_{ps}}{\rho_g c_{pg}}\right)^{0.38}$ in the annulus at $r/R = 0.59$	(9.30)

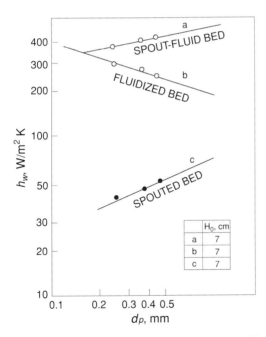

Figure 9.1. Effect of particle diameter on wall-to-bed heat transfer coefficient for three possible modes of contact in the same setup.[51] *Can. J. Chem. Eng.*, **61** (1983), 390–397. Copyright © 2009 by Can. Soc. Chem, Eng. Reprinted with permission of John Wiley & Sons, Inc.

and Kugo[19] proposed a somewhat different correlation, Eq. (9.26). The term ε in the latter equation is an overall spouted bed voidage, calculated from the total volume of the spouted bed.

For spout-fluid beds, Chatterjee et al.[51] developed Eqs. (9.27) and (9.28). Comparison of their results for three gas-solids contacting modes is shown in Figure 9.1.

9.3.3   Theoretical model

Epstein and Mathur[1,2] developed a theoretical model based on the analysis of heat transfer from a cylindrical wall to a moving bed of sand by Brinn et al.[53] For solids in the annulus of a spouted bed, they adopted a two-dimensional penetration model after Higbie.[54] Neglecting axial conduction relative to transverse conduction, the solution in terms of the surface-mean coefficient h_w over heated length Z was

$$h_w = 1.129(v_z \rho_b c_{ps} \lambda_b / Z)^{1/2}. \tag{9.31}$$

The proposed model was found to be in qualitative agreement with experiment by Epstein and Mathur,[1,2] and later by Freitas and Freire.[37] Its accuracy depends to a large extent on correct evaluation of the annulus parameters in Eq. (9.31).

9.4   Between submerged object and bed

The next mode of heat transfer can be realized by the use of heating or cooling elements submerged in the bed. This method of heat transmission is especially useful for chemical reactors.

9.4.1   Transfer mechanisms

As for moving beds, there are two parallel heat transfer mechanisms involved: (1) forced gas convection past the submerged object (a pipe or a coil), and (2) particle convective heat transferred through unsteady state conduction to the particles in contact with the surface of a heater, followed by absorption of that heat by the bulk of the bed. The contact time of particles with the heating surface is one of the main governing factors. The gas convective heat transfer coefficient, h_{gc}, is based on the heat exchanged with the gas percolating along the surface in the interstitial voids between the particles.[53]

9.4.2   Experimental findings

Extensive research work in this area was carried out by Zabrodsky and Mikhalik[55] and Klimenko et al.[56] toward the end of the 1960s, and more recently by Macchi et al.[57]

Investigations by Macchi et al.[57] of heat transfer from a vertical tube submerged in a spouted bed showed that h_{ws} reaches a maximum at the spout axis and monotonically decreases toward the column wall, as illustrated in Figure 9.2. The decrease was largest at the spout–annulus boundary. Most of the effects of different parameters could be explained by the flow patterns of the gas, although particle convection still contributed, to some extent, to the heat transfer. The radial profile of vertical gas velocity flattens out progressively with elevation, as more and more gas moves from the spout into the annulus.[2,3,37] Local heat transfer coefficients obtained by Klimenko et al.,[56] as well as by Macchi et al.,[57] are consistent with this gas velocity trend. Separate correlations

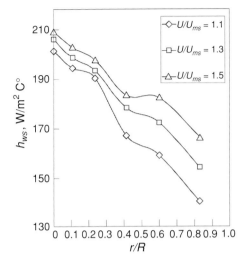

Figure 9.2. Effect of superficial gas velocity on radial profiles of h_{ws} for spouting of glass particles ($d_p = 1.6$ mm, $H = 0.27$ m, $z = 0.21$ m, $D_i = 0.019$ m, $D = 0.0127$ m).[57] *Can. J. Chem. Eng.*, **77** (1999), 45–53. Copyright © 2009 by Can. Soc. Chem. Eng. Reprinted with permission of John Wiley & Sons, Inc.

were developed by Macchi et al.[57] for heat transfer coefficients in the spout and in the annulus, assuming that gas convection is the predominant mode of heat transfer, but without neglecting particle convection. By least squares fitting of their data, they generated Eqs. (9.29) and (9.30) in Table 9.3.

9.5   Temperature uniformity

Temperature distribution within the spouted bed is of great importance in some processes, such as coffee or barley roasting.[14,58] To control the product quality, it is desirable to model the temperature and moisture profiles of the grain during roasting.

9.5.1   Within individual particles

A number of models are available in the literature for the drying of cereal grains, according to Robbins and Fryer,[58] who considered two alternatives:

- Model 1 – lumped temperature, where the temperature of the grain, T, is assumed uniform, so the heat balance becomes

$$\rho_s c_{ps} \frac{dT}{dt} = h_p a (T_g - T), \tag{9.32}$$

where $T = T_0$ at $t = 0$.

- Model 2 – distributed temperature, where the temperature is a function of position within the grain:

$$\rho_s c_{ps} \frac{\partial T}{\partial t} = \nabla(\lambda_p \nabla T) \tag{9.33}$$

with the boundary condition

$$\lambda_p \frac{\partial T}{\partial r} = h_p(T_g - T_s) \tag{9.34}$$

and initial condition $T = T_0$ at $t = 0$.

Robbins and Fryer[58] analyzed both temperature and moisture distributions in the grain numerically, where Eq. (9.3) was used to calculate h_p in the boundary condition.

9.5.2   Between spout and annulus

Kmiec[3] and Englart et al.[29] analyzed heat transfer between spout and annulus by writing separate differential equations for the hot spout and the cold annular regions and solving them numerically. The difference at each level between the axially falling bulk temperature of the spout and the axially-rising bulk temperature of the annulus is the driving force for heat transfer between the two zones, exclusive of particle convection.

Chapter-specific nomenclature

a	specific surface area of grain, m^2/m^3
C_s	mass ratio of solute to solution, kg/kg
Gu	Gukhman number, $(T_g - T_{gw})/T_g$
h_p	fluid-to-particle heat transfer coefficient, W/m^{2}K
h_w	wall-to-bed heat transfer coefficient, W/m^{2}K
h_{ws}	surface-to-bed heat transfer coefficient, W/m^{2}K
$\dot{m}_g$	gas mass flow rate, kg/s
$\dot{m}_w$	mass flow rate of the liquid, kg/s
$\dot{m}_s$	mass flow rate of the solution, kg/s
Re	Reynolds number, $d_p U \rho / \mu$
Re$_i$	Reynolds number, $d_p u_i \rho / \mu$
r_p	particle radius, m
T_0	uniform bed temperature outside thermal boundary layer at wall, K
T_b	bulk bed solids temperature, K
T_{b0}	T_b at $t = 0$, K
T_{ge}	exit gas temperature, K
T_{gi}	inlet gas temperature, K
T_{gw}	wet bulb temperature, K
T_w	wall temperature, K
W_b	mass of bed, kg

W_s mass flow rate of solids, kg/s
w bed width, m
s slot width, m

Greek letters

ΔT_{Lm} logarithmic mean temperature driving force, K
ϕ particle shape factor (reciprocal of sphericity), $\phi \geq 1$

Subscripts

b bulk
g gas
s solids, surface

References

1. N. Epstein and K. B. Mathur. Heat and mass transfer in spouted beds – a review. *Can. J. Chem. Eng.*, **49** (1971), 467–476.
2. K. B. Mathur and N. Epstein. *Spouted Beds* (New York: Academic Press, 1974).
3. A. Kmiec. Hydrodynamics of flows and heat transfer in spouted beds. *Chem. Eng. J.*, **19** (1980), 189–200.
4. A. Kmiec. Simultaneous heat and mass transfer in spouted beds. *Can. J. Chem. Eng.*, **53** (1975), 18–24.
5. A. Kmiec. Rownoczesna wymiana ciepla i masy w ukladach fluidalnych fontannowych. *Inz. Chem.* (in Polish), **6** (1976), 497–516.
6. A. Kmiec. Bed expansion and heat and mass transfer in fluidized beds. *Scientific Papers of Inst. of Chemical Engineering and Heating Equipment of Wroclaw Technical University, No. 36, Monographs No. 19* (Wroclaw, Poland: Publishing House of Wroclaw University of Technology, 1980).
7. W. P. Oliveira, J. T. Freire, and G. Masarani. Analogy between heat and mass transfer in three spouted bed zones during the drying of liquid materials. *Drying Technol.*, **16** (1998), 1939–1955.
8. A. Kmiec, S. Englart, and A. Ludwinska. Mass transfer during air humidification in spouted beds. *Can. J. Chem. Eng.*, **87** (2009), 163–168.
9. M. Jacob. *Heat Transfer* (New York: Wiley, 1949), vol. 1, chapters 13, 20.
10. S. Devahastin, A. S. Mujumdar, and G. S. V. Raghavan. Diffusion-controlled batch drying of particles in a novel rotating jet annular spouted bed. *Drying Technol.*, **16** (1998), 525–543.
11. A. S. Markowski. Drying in a jet-spouted bed dryer. *Can. J. Chem. Eng.*, **70** (1992), 938–944.
12. H. Feng, J. Tang, R. P. Cavalieri, and O. A. Plumb. Heat and mass transport in microwave drying of porous materials in a spouted bed. *AIChE J.*, **47** (2001), 1499–1512.
13. R. Y. Jumah and G. S. V. Raghavan. Analysis of heat and mass transfer during combined microwave-convective spouted-bed drying. *Drying Technol.*, **19** (2001), 485–506.
14. B. Heyd, B. Broyart, J. A. Valdovinos-Tijerino, and G. Trystran. Physical model of heat and mass transfer in a spouted bed coffee roaster. *Drying Technol.*, **25** (2007), 1243–1248.

15. S. Ando, T. Maki, Y. Nakagawa, N. Namiki, H. Emi, and Y. Otani. Analysis of the drying process of seed particles in a spouted bed with a draft tube. *Adv. Powder Technol.*, **13** (2002), 73–91.

16. C. Niamnuy, S. Devahastin, S. Soponronnarit, and G. S. V. Raghavan. Modeling coupled transport phenomena and mechanical deformation of shrimp during drying in a jet spouted bed dryer. *Chem. Eng. Sci.*, **63** (2008), 5503–5512.

17. R. G. Szafran and A. Kmiec. CFD modeling of heat and mass transfer in a spouted bed dryer. *Ind. Eng. Chem. Res.*, **43** (2004), 1113–1124.

18. R. G. Szafran and A. Kmiec. Point-by-point solution procedure for the computational fluid dynamics modeling of long-time batch drying. *Ind. Eng. Chem. Res.*, **44** (2005), 7892–7898.

19. O. Uemaki and M. Kugo. Heat transfer in spouted beds. *Kagaku Kogaku*, **31** (1967), 348–353.

20. O. Uemaki and M. Kugo. Mass transfer in spouted beds. *Kagaku Kogaku*, **32** (1968), 895–901.

21. M. H. El-Naas, S. Rognon, R. Legros, and R. C. Meyer. Hydrodynamics and mass transfer in a spouted bed dryer. *Drying Technol.*, **18** (2000), 323–340.

22. O. Reger, P. G. Romankov, and N. B. Rashkovskaya. Drying of paste-like materials on inert bodies in a spouting bed. *Zhurnal Prikladnoj Khimii (Leningrad)*, **40** (1967), 2276–2280.

23. A. I. Leontieva, K. V. Bryankin, V. I. Konovelov, and N. P. Utrobin. Heat and mass transfer during drying of a liquid film from the surface of a single inert particle. *Drying Technol.*, **20** (2008), 729–747.

24. J. Kucharski and A. Kmiec. Hydrodynamics, heat and mass transfer during coating of tablets in a spouted bed. *Can. J. Chem. Eng.*, **61** (1983), 435–439.

25. J. Kucharski. Heat transfer in a spouted bed granulator. *Hung. J. Ind. Chem.*, **17** (1989), 437–448.

26. A. Kmiec and J. Kucharski. Heat and mass transfer during coating of tablets in a spouted bed. *Inz. Chem. i Procesowa*, **1** (1993), 47–58.

27. A. Kmiec and N. A. Jabarin. Hydrodynamics, heat and mass transfer during coating of rings in a spouted bed. In *Proceedings of the 12th International Drying Symposium (IDS)*, ed. P. J. A. M. Kerkhof, W. J. Coumans, and G. D. Mooiweer. (Noordwijkerhout, Netherlands: Elsevier, 2000), CD-ROM, Paper No. 19, pp. 1–13.

28. A. Kmiec, J. Kucharski, and S. Mielczarski. Hydrodynamics and kinetics during drying of coal in a spouted bed dryer. *Proceedings of the 3rd International Drying Symposium*, ed. J. C. Ashworth (Wolverhampton, UK: Drying Research Ltd., 1982), Vol. 2, pp. 184–190.

29. S. Englart, A. Kmiec, and A. Ludwinska. Heat transfer in sprayed spouted beds. *Can. J. Chem. Eng.*, **87** (2009), 185–192.

30. A. Kmiec and G. Kmiec. Kinetics of drying of microspherical particles in circulating fluidized beds. In *Proceedings of the 6th International Conference on Circulating Fluidized Beds*, ed. J. Werther (Frankfurt: DECHEMA, 1999), pp. 367–371.

31. B. Kilkis and S. Kakac. Heat and mass transfer in spouted beds. *NATO Advanced Study Institute on Convective Heat and Mass Transfer in Porous Media* (Izmir, Turkey, 1990), pp. 835–862.

32. A. F. Dolidovich and V. S. Efremtsev. Hydrodynamics and heat transfer of spouting beds with a two-component (gas-solid) dispersing medium. *Can. J. Chem. Eng.*, **61** (1983), 398–405.

33. A. F. Dolidovich and V. S. Efremtsev. Studies of spouted beds with small outlet-inlet cross-section ratios. *Can. J. Chem. Eng.*, **61** (1983), 382–389.

34. L. A. P. Freitas and J. T. Freire. Heat transfer in spouted beds. *Drying Technol.*, **11** (1993), 303–317.

35. G. K. Khoe and J. Van Brakel. Drying characteristics of a draft tube spouted bed. *Can. J. Chem. Eng.*, **61** (1983), 411–418.

36. J. K. Claflin and A. G. Fane. Fluid mechanics, heat transfer and drying in spouted beds with draft tubes. In *Drying '84*, ed. A. S. Mujumdar (New York: Hemisphere, 1984), pp. 137–141.

37. L. A. P. Freitas and J. T. Freire. Gas-to-particle heat transfer in the draft tube of a spouted bed. *Drying Technol.*, **19** (2001), 1065–1082.

38. J. Nemeth, E. Pallai, M. Peter, and R. Toros. Heat transfer in a novel type spouted bed. *Can. J. Chem. Eng.*, **61** (1983), 406–410.

39. A. Chatterjee and U. Diwekar. Spout-fluid bed and spouted bed heat transfer model. In *Drying '84*, ed. A. S. Mujumdar (New York: Hemisphere, 1984), pp. 142–150.

40. A. F. Dolidovich. Hydrodynamics and interphase heat transfer in a swirled spouted bed. *Can. J. Chem. Eng.*, **70** (1992), 930–937.

41. P. Akulich, A. Reyes, and V. Bubnovich. Effect of peripheral gas jets on hydrodynamics and transfer phenomena of spouting beds. *Powder Technol.*, **167** (2006), 141–148.

42. L. A. O. Martinez, J. G. Brennan, and K. Niranjan. Drying of liquids in a spouted bed of inert particles: Heat transfer studies. *J. Food Eng.*, **20** (1993), 135–148.

43. W. P. Oliveira and J. T. Freire. Analysis of evaporation rate in the spouted bed zones during drying of liquid materials using a three-region model. In *Drying '96*, ed. C. Strumillo and Z. Pakowski, series ed. A. S. Mujumdar (Lodz, Poland: Drukarnia Papaj, 1996), vol. A, pp. 504–512.

44. H. Littman, J. Y. Day, and M. H. Morgan III. A model for the evaporation of water from large glass particles in pneumatic transport. *Can. J. Chem. Eng.*, **78** (2000), 124–131.

45. T. Kudra, A. S. Mujumdar, and G. S. V. Raghavan. Gas-to-particle heat transfer in two-dimensional spouted beds. *Int. Comm. Heat and Mass Transfer*, **16** (1989), 731–741.

46. T. Swasdisevi, W. Tanthapanichakoon, T. Charinpanitkul, T. Kawaguchi, T. Tanaka, and Y. Tsuji. Prediction of gas-particle dynamics and heat transfer in a two-dimensional spouted bed. *Adv. Powder Technol.*, **16** (2005), 275–293.

47. S. C. S. Rocha, O. P. Taranto, and G. E. Ayub. Aerodynamics and heat transfer during coating of tablets in two-dimensional spouted bed. *Can. J. Chem. Eng.*, **73** (1995), 308–312.

48. H. S. Mickley and D. F. Fairbanks. Mechanism of heat transfer to fluidized beds. *AIChE J.*, **1** (1955), 374–384.

49. M. A. Malek and B. C. Y. Lu. Heat transfer in spouted beds. *Can. J. Chem. Eng.*, **42** (1964), 14–20.

50. J. Klassen and P. E. Gishler. Heat transfer from column wall to bed in spouted, fluidized and packed systems. *Can. J. Chem. Eng.*, **36** (1958), 12–18.

51. A. Chatterjee, R. R. S. Adusumilli, and A. V. Deshmukh. Wall-to-bed heat transfer characteristics of spouted-fluid beds. *Can. J. Chem. Eng.*, **61** (1983), 390–397.

52. B. Ghosh and G. L. Osberg. Heat transfer in water spouted beds. *Can. J. Chem. Eng.*, **37** (1959), 205–207.

53. M. S. Brinn, S. J. Friedman, F. A. Gluckert, and R. L. Pigford. Heat transfer to granular materials. *Ind. Eng. Chem.* **40** (1948), 1050–1061.

54. R. Higbie. The rate of absorption of a pure gas into a still liquid during short periods of exposure. *Trans. AIChE*, **31** (1935), 365–389.

55. S. S. Zabrodsky and V. D. Mikhalik. The heat exchange of the spouting bed with a submerged heating surface. In *Intensification of Transfer of Heat and Mass in Drying and Thermal Processes* (Minsk, BSSR: Nauka i Technika, 1967), pp. 130–137.

56. Yu. G. Klimenko, V. G. Karpenko, and M. I. Rabinovich. Heat exchange between the spouting bed and the surface of a spherical probe element. In *Heat Physics and Technology* (Kiev: Ukr. SSR Acad. of Sci., 1969), No. 15, pp. 81–84.

57. A. Macchi, H. T. Bi, R. Legros, and J. Chaouki. An investigation of heat transfer from a vertical tube in a spouted bed. *Can. J. Chem. Eng.*, **77** (1999), 45–53.

58. P. T. Robbins and P. J. Fryer. The spouted-bed roasting of barley: development of a predictive model for moisture and temperature. *J. Food Eng.*, **59** (2003), 199–208.

10 Powder–particle spouted beds

Toshifumi Ishikura and Hiroshi Nagashima

This chapter is a systematic summary of the characteristics and applications of spouted beds, called powder–particle spouted beds (PPSBs), consisting of fine powders contacted with coarse particles. The main aspect of conventional spouting that is relevant to PPSBs is the final elutriation of the dried or partially dried fines, often produced by attrition, from a coarse particle bed.

Figure 10.1 shows the operating conditions of several kinds of fluidization for particles of density 2500 kg/m^3, according to Geldart's classification,[1] indicating also the fine particle size and gas velocity ranges in four reported studies of PPSBs. The two solid lines show the superficial gas velocity at minimum fluidization (U_{mf}) and the terminal velocity of a single particle (U_t). In a PPSB, as one of the operating conditions, the gas velocity is determined by the diameter and density of the coarse particles and is usually greater than U_t of the fine powders, so the fines are elutriated from the coarse particle bed.

10.1 Description of powder–particle spouted beds

Conceptual illustrations of a PPSB are shown in Figure 10.2. Group D particles in Geldart's classification usually act as the coarse particles and Group A, B, or C particles as the fine powders. As shown in Figure 10.2a, for a Group C–D particle system, the coarse particles in the bed are first spouted and raw powders (fine particles) in a dry or partially dried state are then continuously fed to the bottom of the spouted bed with spouting gas. Because the coarse particle movement is very vigorous in the bed, agglomerates of fines can be readily broken up. The fine powders, which adhere to the surface of the coarse particles, are eventually elutriated from the bed based on the difference in the terminal velocity of the fine and coarse particles, and are collected by bag filters. For the Group C–D particle system, agglomerating powders should be pneumatically conveyed into the column by the spouting gas. Freitas and Freire[2] pointed out that one advantage of bottom feeding over top or side feeding is its axial symmetry, helping to maintain spouting stability, which is useful for scaleup, especially if thermal or concentration gradients are present. However, particle attrition is greater with bottom feeding than with top or side feeding.

Spouted and Spout-Fluid Beds: Fundamentals and Applications, eds. Norman Epstein and John R. Grace. Published by Cambridge University Press. © Cambridge University Press 2011.

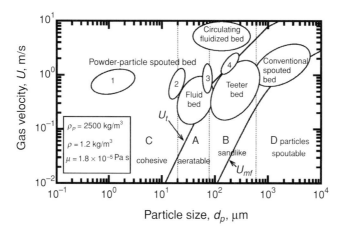

Figure 10.1. Operating conditions for spouting and several kinds of fluidization: 1: Xu et al.,[4] bottom feeding of fines; 2: Ishikura et al.,[5] top feeding; 3: Zhu et al.,[19] bottom feeding; 4: Ishikura et al.,[16] top feeding.

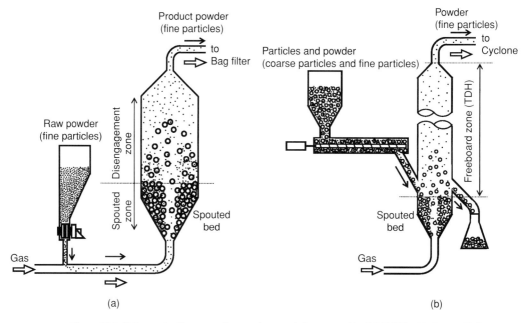

Figure 10.2. Schematic diagram of a powder–particle spouted bed (PPSB). (a) Group C–D particle system, bottom feeding of fines; (b) Group B–D particle system, top feeding of solids.

On the other hand, as shown in Figure 10.2b, for a Group B–D particle system, the mixture of fine and coarse particles, introduced at the top of the bed through the screw feeder, is blown up to the freeboard above the top of the spout by the spouting gas. Some fines are elutriated out of the column and collected by a cyclone, whereas others fall back either into the discharge pipe or onto the surface of the spouted bed annulus. The discharge pipe should be on the opposite side from the feeding pipe to prevent short-circuiting of fresh particles. The position of the discharge pipe strongly affects the composition of the steady bed, and this must be taken into consideration. Also, for a Group B–D particle system, the freeboard height at which the elutriation rate becomes constant, often called the transport disengaging height (TDH), is usually achieved within the PPSB.[3] The effects of the apparatus structure on the elutriation rate have been confirmed.[3]

For the application of a conventional spouted bed, as in combustion and gasification, attrition is caused by particle collisions, especially in the spout, so coarse particles become smaller and fines tend to be elutriated from the spouted bed. The elutriation of fines creates problems of decreasing thermal efficiency and increasing air pollution. Moreover, when the spouted bed is used as a reactor, the freeboard above the bed provides space not only for the disengagement of particles but also for additional reaction between the ejected particles and the gas.

10.2   Fundamentals

To design and operate a PPSB stably for chemical or physical processes, it is important to understand how fine powders behave in a PPSB.

10.2.1   Elutriation phenomena

If the gas velocity exceeds the terminal velocity of a fine powder, then the fines are completely carried out of the bed. This phenomenon is called *elutriation*. Estimation of the elutriation rate of fines from a PPSB is crucial to determining the operating gas flowrate, to estimating the reaction yield, and to recovering valuable materials such as reactants or catalysts.

For a Group C–D particle system, Xu et al.,[4] who investigated the effects of operating parameters on the holdup of fine powders, interpreted their results from the viewpoint of the cohesive force of the fines. The holdup of fines in the bed (X) was defined as the mass fraction of the fines in the mixture of fine and coarse particles. This was found to increase with increasing feed rate of the fines and their cohesive force, and with decreasing gas velocity and particle diameter of the fines. Similar results were reported by Ishikura et al.[5] Taking these factors into account, it was considered that the holdup of fines within a PPSB is controlled by a balance between the adhesion rate of the fines to the surface of the coarse particles in the annulus and fountain, and the separation rate of the fines in the spout and fountain.

An elutriation rate constant, K (units: kg/m^2s), for a PPSB has been proposed based on the mass balance of the fine and coarse particles and a first-order model for a batch system,[3,6,7] such that the elutriation rate is

$$V = K \cdot A \cdot X/(1 - X), \qquad (10.1)$$

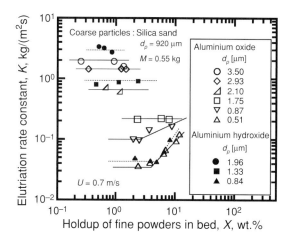

Figure 10.3. Relationship between elutriation rate constant and holdup of fines in bed with diameter of fines varied for Group C–D particle system and bottom feeding of fines; data from Xu.[8]

where A is the cross-sectional area of the column and X is the holdup of fines in the bed. Eq. (10.1) has also been applied to a continuous system using the holdup of fines at the discharge pipe.[3,6,7] For $X \ll 0.1$, Eq. (10.1) can be approximated[5,8] by

$$V = K \cdot A \cdot X. \tag{10.2}$$

In an operation such as the one shown in Figure 10.2a, the steady-state elutriation rate of fines (V) is equal to the feed rate of the fines. Eq. (10.2) implies that V is proportional to X. The elutriation rate constant (K) at a steady state was calculated from Eq. (10.1) or (10.2) by measuring both X and V.

From Figure 10.3, for a Group C–D particle system,[8] K is hardly affected by X as long as the superficial gas velocity (U) is kept constant, if the diameter of the fines is larger than 1 μm. This finding is consistent with results[3,6,7] using fine powders of diameter greater than 100 μm, as shown in Figure 10.4. Figure 10.5 shows the effect of the diameter of fines on the elutriation rate constant (K) for several kinds of fine powders. K decreases with decreasing diameter of fines for the Group C–D particle system, because the adhesive force of the fines increases, so the fines adhere to the surface of the coarse particles more readily and do not easily separate from them. This behavior is completely contrary to the elutriation phenomenon using fines of size greater than 100 μm,[3,6,7] as also shown in Figure 10.5. Thus, for the Group B–D particle system, K increases with decreasing diameter of the fines because the driving force for elutriation increases owing to a decrease in the terminal velocity of the particles. Wang et al.[9] investigated the effect of hydrodynamic factors on the elutriation rate of wet calcium carbonate powder from a coarse particle bed with aeration of the annulus.

For a liquid–solid system, Ishikura et al.[10,11] investigated the effects of the operating conditions on the elutriation rate coefficient based on a first-order model, and correlated the elutriation rate coefficient for a column height above the TDH with the modified

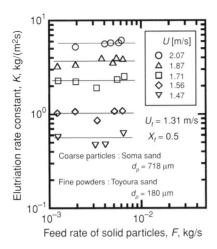

Figure 10.4. Relationship between elutriation rate constant and feed rate of solid particles with gas velocity varied for Group B–D particle system and top feeding of fine component, above TDH. Data from Ishikura et al.[3]

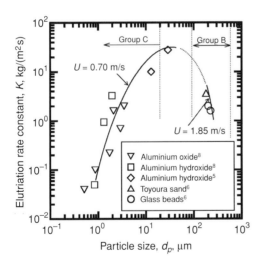

Figure 10.5. Effect of diameter of fines on elutriation rate constant with several kinds of fines. (□,▽: data from Xu[8]; ◇,△, ○: data from Ishikura et al.[3,5])

Froude number of the fine particles, defined as $(U - U_t)^2 \rho / g \cdot d_p (\rho_p - \rho)$. The elutriation of fines was closely related to the stratified length of the particle transport bed for the Group B–D particle system. Al-Jabari et al.[12,13] described the experimental aspects of the elutriation process from a conical spouted bed and used an existing first-order model to determine the elutriation rate coefficient of fines from a pulp fiber suspension.

For a Group B–D particle system, the particle entrainment rate from the top of the spout in a PPSB provides a basis for estimating the elutriation rate of the finer component from the column. Therefore, Ishikura et al.[14,15] attempted to estimate the entrainment rate of a binary particle mixture from the top of the spout, using the mass and momentum balance for the gas and particles within the spout. To interpret the decrease in elutriation rate of fines along the freeboard in Figure 10.2b, the holdup of fines, their local velocity, and the fluctuating gas velocity at an arbitrary height of the freeboard were examined by using a shutter plate, a fiber optic probe, and a hot-wire anemometer, respectively.[16,17] The exponential decrease of the elutriation rate of the fines along the freeboard was verified.

From those experimental results, Ishikura et al.[14–16] suggested the following three elutriation mechanisms in the freeboard:

(1) This process occurs in the fountain region. Sufficient column height is required for the formation of a spouted bed with ample freeboard for particle transport disengagement. The velocity distribution of the gas jet leaving the top of the spout is spread out radially, imparting a relatively large radial velocity to both the fine and coarse particles. Hence, the axial component of the particle velocity decreases sharply.
(2) There are no coarse particles present in the freeboard, and the elutriation rate of the fines decreases exponentially with increasing freeboard height. This decrease is presumably caused by the exponential dissipation of the effective gas velocity in the freeboard. It is considered that turbulent radial migration of fines occurs.
(3) The elutriation rate becomes constant above the TDH.

Based on this model, the elutriation height coefficients for each process were determined, and the values could be used to estimate the elutriation rate of fines for any column height.[7,18]

The residence time of fines to be treated is an important factor in a PPSB. For example, the conversion of reactants is determined by the residence time of the reactant, and the residence time of the solid materials affects their treatment efficiency. Xu[8] showed that the residence time of fines increases with decreasing diameter of fines and decreasing gas velocity, and with increasing static bed depth and diameter of the coarse particles in the bed. Similar results were obtained by Ishikura et al.[5] Xu[8] found that the mean residence time of fines in the bed is 20 to 1200 times longer than that of the spouting gas for a Group C–D particle system.

10.2.2   Other hydrodynamic characteristics

The minimum spouting velocity with fine powders entrained in spouting gas (U_{msF}) is an important parameter in the design and operation of a PPSB because it signifies the minimum velocity that can be steadily processed in the bed.

For a PPSB of the type shown in Figure 10.2a, U_{msF} was measured by Zhu et al.[19] in the same way as the minimum spouting velocity (U_{ms}) for an ordinary spouted bed is reproducibly determined (see Chapter 2). First they spouted the bed steadily with

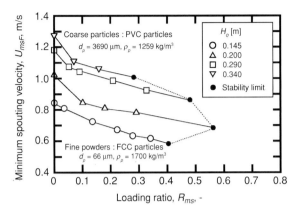

Figure 10.6. Effect of loading ratio (based on minimum spouting velocity of coarse particles alone) on minimum spouting velocity with fine powder entrainment for different values of bed depth ($D = 144$ mm, $D_i = 19.1$ mm); data from Zhu et al.[19]

coarse particles alone at a constant gas velocity, then introduced the fines steadily, and finally decreased the gas flow slowly until the bed collapsed. The velocity at which the bed collapsed was then taken as U_{msF}. For convenience, they defined a loading ratio based on the minimum spouting condition with coarse particles alone as $R_{ms} = F/(\rho \cdot A \cdot U_{ms})$. Figure 10.6 shows that as the loading of the fine powders increases, U_{msF} decreases and becomes progressively smaller than U_{ms} for spouting with the coarse particles alone. This trend resembles the behavior observed for continuous feeding of the coarse particles alone to the bottom of the bed.[20] Finally, the increase in loading leads to unstable spouting or slugging, and the critical points are joined by stability limit lines, as shown in Figure 10.6.

Zhu et al.[19] investigated the change of spouting pressure drop with the feeding of powders in a PPSB. At any gas velocity and bed depth, the pressure drop increased with time during powder feeding, then the pressure drop stabilized. The stable pressure drop increased as the feed rate of the powders, bed depth, and gas flowrate increased. However, pressure drop stabilization ceased when the feed rate became so high that slugging occurred instead of spouting, behavior that was accompanied by large pressure drop fluctuations. In the future, the effect of fines holdup on the pressure drop of the bed should be investigated in detail.

Maximum spoutable bed depth (H_m) is an important parameter in the design and operation of a PPSB because it is directly related to the amount of material that can be processed batchwise in a bed. Above this particular bed depth, bubbling and slugging begin in a PPSB. The maximum spoutable bed depth was examined by Zhu et al.[19] in the same way as H_m for an ordinary spouted bed is determined reproducibly. They indicated that H_m decreases with an increase in the loading of powders fed to the bed bottom with spouting gas. In contrast, Fane et al.[20] reported that H_m increases with an increase in loading of the coarse particles fed to the bottom of the column where coarse particles are spouted alone.

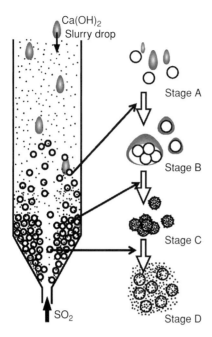

Figure 10.7. Mechanisms at work in a PPSB desulfurizer. Stage A: slurry dropping; Stage B: reaction and drying; Stage C: diffusion controlling; Stage D: entraining. Model of Guo et al.[21]

10.3   Applications

A PPSB can be applied to such chemical processes as desulfurization and the development of particulate products, and to such physical processes as the separation of fines.

10.3.1   Semidry flue gas desulfurization

The desulfurization efficiency of the semidry flue gas desulfurization (FGD) process has not reached the level of wet scrubbers. The major reason is that the residence time of the SO_2 sorbent is very short in existing processes such as spray drying. Accordingly, the development of low-cost high-efficiency FGD technologies is significant.

Guo et al.[21] developed a new type of semidry FGD process using a PPSB as a main reactor. In this process, droplets of fine SO_2 sorbent slurry were fed continuously into a spouted bed, in which coarse inert particles were spouted with hot gas containing SO_2. This process enabled the long time reaction of sorbent powders with SO_2 in the liquid and gas phases, as well as in drying the spent sorbent powders, because they adhered strongly to the surface of the coarse particles. Finally, the dried spent sorbent was elutriated from the spouted bed and collected by a bag filter, and effective SO_2 removal was thus achieved.

As shown in Figure 10.7, a mechanism of spouted bed desulfurization was indicated by Guo et al.,[21] who suggested the following four stages related to SO_2 removal in a

PPSB. Stage A: Slurry drops collide with coarse particles, and a film of sorbent solution begins to react with the flue gas. Stage B: Slurry on the surface of the coarse particles begins to evaporate and the sorbent powders adhering to the coarse particles react with SO_2 in a humidified flue gas. Stage C: Water moves to the outside surface of the sorbent and SO_2 diffuses from the outside to the inside of the sorbent. New surface of the sorbent is exposed owing to collision and separation of particles. Stage D: Reacted and dried sorbent particles are entrained.

From this description, the authors pointed out that using a PPSB in the semidry FGD process offers the following advantages:

(1) The properties of the coarse particles allow the system to operate at a high gas velocity, as shown in Figure 10.1.
(2) As the coarse particles are spouted, the fine SO_2 sorbent is well dispersed.
(3) The mean residence time of the sorbent in the reactor is much longer.
(4) The drying of the slurry, as well as the reaction between SO_2 and the sorbent, occur simultaneously in the reactor.

For suitable operation, design, and scaleup of a PPSB, it is important to understand the hydrodynamics and the chemical reaction phenomena in terms of the main operating variables. Many researchers[21–27] have examined the effect of such operating parameters as types of SO_2 sorbent, particle diameter of SO_2 sorbent, apparent mean residence time of gas in the bed, sorbent-to-SO_2 stoichiometric ratio, approach to saturation temperature, static bed depth, and gas velocity on the SO_2 removal efficiency – that is, the removal limit of SO_2 in the flue gas.

Ma et al.[24] tried to use limestone to remove SO_2 from the flue gas in the semidry FGD process with a PPSB. Reactivity of SO_2 was compared with limestone and hydrated lime based on their structural properties. Limestone was indicated as an attractive SO_2 sorbent by choosing the appropriate conditions in terms of removal efficiency, price, and availability of sorbent. Nakazato et al.[26] investigated semidry FGD in a PPSB with several kinds of SO_2 sorbents, including slaked lime, limestone, magnesium hydroxide, and industrial alkaline waste. They pointed out that an increase in the apparent mean residence time of the gas in the bed improves SO_2 removal efficiency. However, the apparent mean residence time of gas is a function of bed depth and gas velocity. There is a minimum spouting velocity (U_{msF}) and a maximum spoutable bed depth (H_m) for any specific PPSB, as mentioned previously. This implies that there is a limited operating range of possible contacting times for a specific PPSB. Moeini and Hatamipour[27] examined two models for SO_2 removal from flue gas in a PPSB with hydrated lime as the SO_2 sorbent. Their analysis was based on one-dimensional[28] and streamtube models[29] proposed previously for a conventional spouted bed. Predictions from these two models were compared with published experimental data.[25] It was found that the two models are both valid, as they are indeed equivalent.[30] For practical applications, Xu et al.[25] proposed a novel design of a multiple large-scale PPSB suitable for commercial utilization, as a small PPSB is limited in throughput. In the future, it will be important to examine the applicability of such a design.

10.3.2   Other applications

Nakazato et al.[31] developed a new simple process for semidry production of very fine calcium carbonate powder using a PPSB. The PPSB provided a multitask reactor in which the dispersion of the hydrated lime slurry, the reaction of the hydrated lime with carbon dioxide, the drying of the produced calcium carbonate, and its pulverization occurred simultaneously in the bed. This semidry PPSB process produced calcium carbonate powders with a mean particle diameter of ~1 μm and hydrated lime conversion of about 90 percent. Similar research was reported by Lin et al.[32]

In a liquid–solid system, Al-Jabari et al.[12,13] developed a simple new technique for separating fine powders from pulp fiber suspension, using a conical spouted bed, in a process called elutriation spouting. At suitable operating conditions, the fibers remained in the circulating zone, whereas fine powders moved upward with the liquid and were elutriated efficiently.

PPSBs show various flow patterns depending on the properties of particles, such as the diameters of the coarse and the fine particles. Therefore, PPSBs are likely to be used for a wide variety of chemical and physical processes in the future.

Chapter-specific nomenclature

F	feed rate of solid particles, kg/s
FGD	flue gas desulfurization
K	elutriation rate constant of fine powders, kg/(m^2·s)
R_{ms}	loading ratio based on minimum spouting of coarse particles alone
TDH	transport disengagement height, m
U_{msF}	minimum spouting velocity with fine powders entrainment, m/s
U_t	terminal velocity of a particle, m/s
V	elutriation rate of fine powders, kg/s
X	holdup of fine powders in bed
X_f	holdup of fine powders in feed

References

1. D. Geldart. Types of gas fluidization. *Powder Technol.*, **7** (1973), 285–292.
2. L. A. P. Freitas and J. T. Freire. Analysis of fluid dynamics in a spouted bed with continuous solids feeding. *Drying Technol.*, **16** (1998), 1903–1921.
3. T. Ishikura, I. Tanaka, and H. Shinohara. Elutriation of fines from spouted bed: effects of apparatus structure, *J. Soc. Powder Technol. Japan*, **13** (1976), 535–540.
4. J. Xu, Y. Washizu, N. Nakagawa, and K. Kato. Hold-up of fine particles in a powder-particle spouted bed. *J. Chem. Eng. Japan*, **31** (1998), 61–66.
5. T. Ishikura, H. Nagashima, and M. Ide. Behaviour of cohesive powders in a powder-particle spouted bed. *Can. J. Chem. Eng.*, **82** (2004), 102–109.

6. T. Ishikura, S. Suizu, I. Tanaka, and H. Shinohara. Elutriation of fines from a small spouted bed in solid-gas system. *Kagaku Kogaku Ronbunshu*, **5** (1979), 149–154.

7. T. Ishikura and H. Shinohara. Estimation of elutriation rate of fine particles from a continuous spouted bed in solid-gas system. *Fukuoka Daigaku Kogaku Shuho*, **40** (1988), 245–252.

8. J. Xu. Investigation on the powder-particle spouted bed. Ph.D thesis, Gunma University, Japan (1998).

9. G. Wang, L. Ding, and W. Guo. Drying and elutriation of wet powder particle in spouted bed with aeration. *J. Shenyang Inst. Chem. Technol.*, **15** (2001), 8–12.

10. T. Ishikura, I. Tanaka, and H. Shinohara. Elutriation of particles from a batch spouted bed in solid-liquid system. *J. Chem. Eng. Japan*, **12** (1979), 148–151.

11. T. Ishikura and I. Tanaka. Behavior and removal of fine particles in a liquid-solid spouted bed consisting of binary mixtures. *Can. J. Chem. Eng.*, **70** (1992), 880–886.

12. M. Al-Jabari, M. E. Weber, and T. G. M. Van de Ven. Particle elutriation from a spouted bed of recycled pulp fibres. *J. Pulp and Paper Sci.*, **22** (1996), J231–J236.

13. M. Al-Jabari, M. E. Weber, and T. G. M. Van de Ven. Modeling fines elutriation from a spouted bed of pulp fibers. *Chem. Eng. Comm.*, **148–150** (1996), 456–476.

14. T. Ishikura, I. Tanaka, and H. Shinohara. Elutriation of fines from a continuous spouted bed in solid-gas system: Effects of column height on elutriation rate of fines. *Kagaku Kogaku Ronbunshu.*, **6** (1980), 448–454.

15. T. Ishikura, H. Shinohara, and I. Tanaka. Elutriation of fines from a continuous spouted bed containing a solid-gas system: Effect of column height on the fines elutriation rate. *Internat. Chem. Eng.*, **22** (1982), 346–354.

16. T. Ishikura, H. Shinohara, and I. Tanaka. Behavior of fine particles in a spouted bed consisting of fine and coarse particles. *Can. J. Chem. Eng.*, **61** (1983), 317–324.

17. T. Ishikura and K. Funatsu. Behavior of fine particles and gas in freeboard of a gas-solid spouted bed consisting of fine and coarse particles. *Fukuoka Daigaku Kogaku Shuho*, **35** (1985), 103–115.

18. T. Ishikura and H. Shinohara. Estimation of elutriation rate of fine particles from a continuous spouted bed in solid-gas system: Based on particle transport mechanism in the freeboard region. *Micromeritics*, **32** (1988), 42–48.

19. Q. Zhu, C. J. Lim, N. Epstein, and H. T. Bi. Hydrodynamic characteristics of a powder-particle spouted bed with powder entrained in spouting gas. *Can. J. Chem. Eng.*, **83** (2005), 644–651.

20. A. G. Fane, A. E. Firek, and C. W. P. Wong. Spouting with a solids-laden gas stream. *CHEMECA*, **85** (1985), 465–469.

21. Q. Guo, N. Iwata, and K. Kato. Process development of effective semidry flue gas desulfurization by powder-particle spouted bed, *Kagaku Kogaku Ronbunshu*, **22** (1996), 1400–1407.

22. Q. Guo and K. Kato. The effect of operating condition on SO_2 removal in semidry desulfurization process by powder-particle spouted bed. *Kagaku Kogaku Ronbunshu*, **24** (1998), 279–284.

23. X. Ma, T. Kaneko, Q. Guo, G. Xu, and K. Kato. Removal of SO_2 from flue gas using a new semidry flue gas desulfurization process with a powder-particle spouted bed, *Can. J. Chem. Eng.*, **77** (1999), 356–362.

24. X. Ma, T. Kaneko, T. Tashimo, T. Yoshida, and K. Kato. Use of limestone for SO_2 removal from flue gas in the semidry FGD process with a powder-particle spouted bed. *Chem. Eng. Sci.*, **55** (2000), 4643–4652.

25. G. Xu, Q. Guo, T. Kaneko, and K. Kato. A new semidry desulfurization process using a powder-particle spouted bed. *Adv. Environ. Res.*, **4** (2000), 9–18.

26. T. Nakazato, Y. Liu, and K. Kato. Removal of SO_2 in semidry flue gas desulfurization process with a powder-particle spouted bed. *Can. J. Chem. Eng.*, **82** (2004), 110–115.

27. M. Moeini and M. S. Hatamipour. Flue gas desulfurization by a powder-particle spouted bed. *Chem. Eng. Technol.*, **31** (2008), 71–82.

28. K. B. Mathur and C. J. Lim. Vapour phase chemical reaction in spouted bed: a theoretical model, *Chem. Eng. Sci.*, **29** (1974), 789–797.

29. C. J. Lim and K. B. Mathur. A flow model for gas movement in spouted beds. *AIChE J.*, **22** (1976), 674–680.

30. C. M. H. Brereton and J. R. Grace. A note on comparison of spouted bed reactor models, *Chem. Eng. Sci.*, **39** (1984), 1315–1317.

31. T. Nakazato, Y. Liu, K. Sato, and K. Kato. Semi-dry process for production of very fine calcium carbonate powder by a powder-particle spouted bed. *J. Chem. Eng. Japan*, **35** (2002), 409–414.

32. C. Lin, T. Zhu, Y. Zhu, and J. Zhang. Experiments and modeling of the preparation of ultrafine calcium carbonate in spouted beds with inert particles. *Chinese J. Chem. Eng.*, **11** (2003), 726–730.

11 Drying of particulate solids

Maria Laura Passos, Esly Ferreira da Costa Jr., and Arun Sadashiv Mujumdar

This chapter focuses on analyzing the design of spouted bed dryers for particulate solids whose drying curve is characterized by the falling rate period only (Figure 11.1a), as well as those displaying both constant and falling-rate drying periods (Figure 11.1.b).

Because compromise among costs, efficiency, product quality, and a clean environment is required in the design and operation of any process equipment, simulation and optimization of the drying process are the best ways to obtain the appropriate dimensions and operating conditions for a dryer and its ancillary equipment. This chapter starts with a brief review of recent developments in the drying of particulate solids in spouted beds (SBs). A concise analysis of various possible dryer design models follows. Three different model levels, which have been used for modeling SB drying of particulate solids, are considered.

11.1 Various spouted bed dryers for particulate solids

The SB technique, originally developed by Mathur and Gishler[12] for drying wheat, has found numerous applications, not only for drying of particulate solids, but also in combined operations, such as drying–powdering, drying–granulation, drying–coating, and drying–extraction. Therefore this chapter also provides information for the design of such combined operations, which are considered elsewhere in this book.

The conventional spouted bed (CSB), characterized by a conical-cylindrical column geometry, has its use for drying essentially limited to pilot-scale operation because of two serious disadvantages, which restrict its application on a large scale:

1. The CSB dryer capacity is limited by the bed depth (H) and the column diameter (D), as H must be less than H_m to ensure stable spouting and $D \lesssim 1$ m to avoid dead zones inside the bed of particles.
2. The CSB dryer efficiency is restricted by the technique itself, as the gas flowrate is limited by the requirements of the spouting regime rather than those of heat and mass transfer.

These limitations are confirmed by simulated data for drying wheat in optimized CSB dryers, shown in Figure 11.2. The feed rate of wheat is up to 1000 kg/h for an acceptable dryer efficiency.

Spouted and Spout-Fluid Beds: Fundamentals and Applications, eds. Norman Epstein and John R. Grace.
Published by Cambridge University Press. © Cambridge University Press 2011.

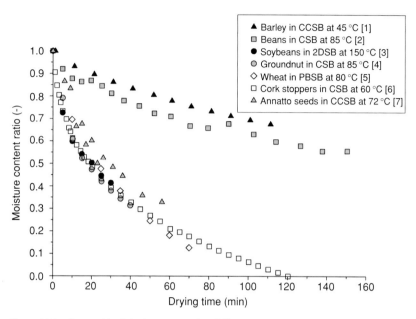

Figure 11.1a. Spouted bed drying curves for different particulate solids with low initial moisture content (in falling-rate drying period). Moisture content ratio $= Y_p/Y_{p0}$ (ratio of the solids moisture content at specific drying time to initial solids moisture content); temperature displayed $= T_{g|in}$ (inlet air temperature).

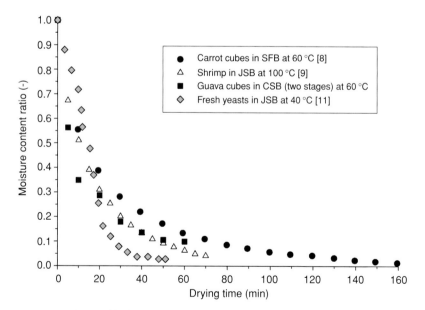

Figure 11.1b. Spouted bed drying curves for shrinkable solids with high initial moisture content (in constant-rate and falling-rate drying periods). Moisture content ratio $= Y_p/Y_{p0}$ (ratio of solids moisture content at specific drying time to initial solids moisture content); temperature displayed $= T_{g|in}$ (inlet air temperature).

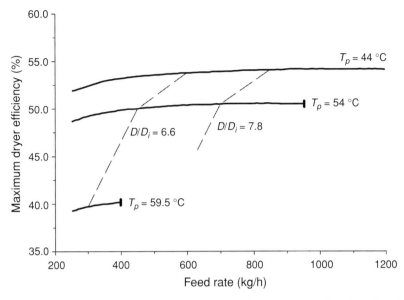

Figure 11.2. Simulated dryer efficiency curves vs. wheat feed rate as function of particle temperature, T_p, in an optimized CSB unit. Drying conditions: $Y_{p|in} = 0.25$ and $Y_{p|out} = 0.15$; ambient air temperature $= 32\,°C$; relative humidity $= 51\%$. Dashed curves: locus of constant D/D_i with dryer efficiency defined as amount of energy required to heat solids and evaporate water per total energy to heat and pump air (after Passos et al.[13]).

To overcome the dryer capacity limitation of CSBs, numerous alternative SB configurations have been proposed in the literature.[13–17] The most practical and useful configurations for drying particulate solids are summarized in Table 11.1.

Mathur and Epstein[14] were the pioneers in organizing all information on the SB technique available by the early 1970s. They analyzed the fluid flow and solids motion in the spout, annulus, and fountain regions, as well as the basic problems associated with spout stability in the CSB geometry. Using this analysis and updating information from the literature, Passos et al.[13,16] presented, proposed, and discussed the basic principles and criteria for design of SB grain dryers, based on the CSB and the two-dimensional spouted bed (2DSB) configurations, and the simplified diffusion drying model proposed by Becker and Sallans.[18] Their conclusions show that the maximum dryer capacity and efficiency depend not only on the type of grain and column geometry, but also on the particle properties such as size, shape, porosity, and density.

Based on the Becker and Sallans[18] model for drying of wheat in a SB and the Zahed and Epstein[19] review of mathematical models, Freitas[7] simulated the drying of annatto seeds in a batch conical spouted bed (CcSB) to subsequently help apply this technology to extraction of bixin powder from these seeds.[20,21] Kmieć and Szafran[22] presented a good review of CcSB applications, emphasizing the use of an internal draft tube to stabilize the spouting regime for small particles ($d_p < 1$ mm). These authors combined the constant drying rate model with the diffusion model to simulate the drying of microspherical particles ($d_p = 0.22$ mm) produced from the dust emitted by an electrical power station

Table 11.1. Some spouted bed configurations applied to drying of particulate solids.

Configuration	Main characteristics	Solids dried (typical cases)
CSB	• Easy to process coarse particles • High inlet gas temperature without thermal damage of product • Low investment cost • Limitation of the bed depth and the column diameter (without draft tube) • Gas flowrate dictated by spouting	• Seeds and grains[1,2,4,12−19,21,34] • Seeds and grains[38,47,49,58] • Shrinkable foodstuffs[10,11,17] • Cork stoppers[6] • Polyvinyl choride[17]
CcSB	• No limitation of bed depth • Easy to handle equidensity particles with wide size distribution • Low minimum pressure drop • Gas flowrate dictated by spouting	• Seeds and grains[7,16,20] • Coal microspheres[22] • Fine sand particles[23,24]
2DSB	• Increase in capacity by adding extended units • High gas flowrate and low pressure drop at minimum spouting (*ms*) • Draft plates: no limitation of bed depth, controlled solids motion, decrease in gas flowrate at *ms* and in downcomer	• Seeds and grains[3,13,25−30,49] • Spice capsules[45] • Grain popping[42]
TSB	• Increase in capacity by inserting units in a hexagonal configuration with a gas injector at the hexagon center • Insertion of draft plate is required for stable spouting	• Seeds and grains[30−32]
PBSB	• More stable spouting regime • Lack of data and information	• Seeds and grains[5]
SFB	• Greater operating flexibility • High annular gas flowrate • *ms* condition dependent on the inlet annular gas flowrate • More complex grid design	• Seeds and grains[2,34] • Shrinkable foodstuffs[8]
RJSB	• Greater operating flexibility • Different intermittancy of spouting to attend to drying needs • Low thermal and mechanical damage • High costs (nozzle: construction and maintenance)	• Seeds and grains[41−43] • Heat-sensitive materials[42]
JSB	• Similar to CSB or CcSB but with larger D_i	• Foodstuffs[9,35−37] • Sawdust[39]

fired by coal. Even with a draft tube (or plates, in the case of 2DSBs), which can improve spouting stability and solids circulation, as well as decrease the pressure drop and gas flowrate at minimum spouting, caution is needed to design such a modified bed, as the amount of gas flowing into the annular or downcomer region is always reduced by such internal elements. Moreover, particle abrasion can be enhanced by impacts on the walls of the draft tube or plates, causing mechanical damage of fragile particles. On the other hand, wall–particle collisions can improve powder extraction from particles, as shown by Cunha et al.[21] for the case of bixin production. Because of low particle size segregation in CcSBs,[23] Altzibar et al.[24] have proposed insertion of a porous or open-sided draft tube in a CcSB dryer for sand with a wide size distribution. Their results confirm that improvement of annulus aeration reduces the drying time for sand when using an open-sided draft tube instead of a nonporous one.

Two-dimensional spouted beds, as well as triangular spouted beds (TSBs), work better with draft plates to ensure stable spouting. Because of the severe bed depth limitation in a 2DSB geometry,[13] Kalwar et al.[25] proposed and developed a pilot scale 2DSB ($L_1 = 0.75$ m, $L_2 = 0.06$ m, $L_i = 0.05$ m, $30° \leq \theta \leq 180°$, and 1.35 m depth) with adjustable draft plates to dry grains, such as shelled corn, soybeans, and wheat. Their results confirmed the high quality of dried grains. An empirical model described the grain-drying kinetics as a function of various geometrical and operating parameters. Dias et al.[26] demonstrated that black beans dried in a 2DSB ($L_1 = 0.40$ m, $L_2 = L_i = 0.10$ m, $\theta = 60°$, and 1 m depth) at 50 °C were of high quality without damage in their physical and cooking properties. Wiriyaumpaiwong et al.[3,27] analyzed the drying of soybeans in a pilot-scale 2DSB with draft plates ($L_1 = 0.60$ m, $L_2 = 0.15$ m, $L_i = 0.04$ m, $\theta = 60°$ and 2 m depth) for posterior use in the food industry. They considered the quality of the dried grain (percentage of cracking and breakage, as well as urease enzyme activity) and recycled part of the exit air to improve the dryer efficiency. They concluded that the best conditions for drying soybeans and for inactivating the urease enzyme, thus preserving the protein content, were inlet air temperature not lower than 140 °C with 80 percent to 90 percent of outlet air recycled. These conditions ensure energy consumption of 30 to 50 MJ/kg water evaporated. Earlier works[28,29] had already confirmed the technical and economic feasibility of the 2DSB for drying of rice paddy at 150 °C, with recycling of 70 percent of the outlet air. In their pilot-scale study, the volumetric capacity of the 2DSB dryer was easily improved by connecting several units together, thereby simplifying scaleup.[15] In Thailand, the capacity of these dryers has been increased up to 3500 kg/h of grains (soybean, corn, and rice paddy) with energy consumption comparable to that of other commercial dryers.[28]

The triangular spouted bed (TSB) with draft plate was first implemented in Australia for drying rice paddy from 25 percent to 15 percent wet basis (w.b.) as part of a project with Thailand, China, and Vietnam.[30] With favorable results obtained on the laboratory scale,[31] a pilot-scale unit was built to dry 85 kg of rice paddy[32] ($L_1 = 0.314$ m, $\theta = 60°$, 2.4 m depth, 1.2 m of draft plate inserted at 0.0025 m from the column base). To avoid mechanical and thermal damage of the grains, this unit was operated using two successive inlet air temperatures: 150 °C during the first 2 hours and then 80 °C until the end of drying. The main characteristic of this geometry, as noted in Table 11.1, is the possibility of increasing the volumetric dryer capacity by inserting similar units in a novel hexagonal design. The insertion of six units to form a hexagon yields a batch processing capacity of 510 kg of rice paddy.

Another SB configuration proposed more recently is the parabolic-cylindrical spouted bed (PBSB),[5] whose shape mimics the particle trajectory at the base of the annulus region. Because this configuration stabilizes spouting, reducing the minimum spouting pressure drop and airflow rate, this should ensure an increase in dryer capacity. However, its impact on drying particulate solids is not as expected intuitively when compared to a 2DSB and a TSB; hence the complexity of constructing a parabolic-cylindrical column does not appear to be justified.

The insertion of mechanical stirrers in a bed of cohesive particles can ensure good air–particle mixing and spout stability.[17,33] Modifications of the CSB to improve dryer performance for high-moisture-content particles (Figure 11.1b) include combinations of two or more techniques of fluid–solid contact, such as spout-fluid beds,[2,8,34] fixed-spouted-fluidized bed combinations,[10,11] and jet-spouted beds.[9,35,36] Passos et al.[34] demonstrated by computer simulation the potential for using a spout-fluid bed (SFB) dryer to control the airflow rate required to dry different grains. Lima and Rocha[2] found that a SFB can dry black beans; however, a fixed-bed dryer was shown to dry batches of these grains more efficiently.

With the aid of a simulation model for the drying kinetics of carrot cubes in a SFB, Białobrzewski et al.[8] demonstrated that SFBs can effectively dry foodstuffs of high moisture content, maintaining their quality; this is attributed to the additional aeration of the annular region. Grabowski et al.[11] showed the advantages of SBs for predrying fresh yeast particles of high moisture content (70% w.b.). Almeida et al.[10] proposed different airflow regimes (fixed bed, fluidization, spouting, and slugging) to dry guava cubes, as this material is very cohesive and shrinks greatly during drying. For drying cohesive particles of high moisture content, Kudra and Mujumdar[35] suggested jet-spouted-beds (JSBs), because their diluted annular region contributes to reducing particle contacts and, consequently, the potential for particle agglomeration. This type of SB has an inlet nozzle diameter, D_i, larger than that in CSBs. Wachiraphansakul and Devahastin[36] used a JSB ($D/D_i = 2$, $D = 0.20$ m, $\theta = 40°$, and 0.192 m depth) for drying of okara (a fibrous and insoluble by-product of soy milk left after the soy milk has been extracted from the ground soybean purée) from 75 percent to 80 percent to 9 percent w.b. Adsorbing particles (silica gel) were added to the JSB to improve the drying operation, lowering the drying temperature and improving the product quality (reduced oxidation level, faster rehydration, and greater protein solubility). Niamnuy et al.[9] dried shrimp in a JSB and developed a model to describe the shrimp temperature, moisture content, internal stress, and shrinkage during drying to optimize the JSB for product quality.

For preservation of food quality, Feng et al.[37] proposed to combine, in the same equipment, microwave and spout-bed techniques for drying diced apples and showed that these combined techniques can accelerate drying when optimized for quality (color and texture, in the case of apples). Jumah and Raghavan[38] modeled the drying kinetics of wheat in a microwave-spouted bed, assuming that the heat generated by microwaves is homogeneously distributed in the spouted bed of particles, making the drying operation more uniform and favoring its application to dry heat-sensitive solids. Working in a pilot-scale unit, Berghel[39] demonstrated the feasibility of drying sawdust in a superheated steam-spouted bed for producing granulated fuel. The advantages of superheated steam drying are well known.[40]

Parallel to these modified SBs, an important innovation that effectively improves the SB dryer efficiency is intermittency of the spouting flow regime. Jumah and Mujumdar[41] proposed and successfully developed a rotating jet-spouted bed (RJSB), whose inlet fluid nozzle consisted of two injectors: a central one, which produced a conventional spout in the central zone of the bed, and a rotating one, which produced a single spout in the annulus region of the bed as it rotated slowly (Table 11.1). Thus, in RJSBs, the entire annulus is not spouted continuously. Periodic spouting of the annular region reduces the net consumption of air and power required for spouting. This device thus spouts part of the bed locally in an intermittent fashion, providing flexibility to match the drying requirements of any particulate material. RJSBs can be operated in different modes, such as with two spouts (one central and another rotating radially at an angular velocity as required by the drying objectives), with only one central and intermittent spout, or with only one lateral and rotating spout. Jumah[42] confirmed the technical and economic feasibility of this RJSB for drying grains, with energy savings up to 40 percent and a higher quality of dried grains (reduction in grain fissures and breakage induced by thermal-mechanical damage). Jumah[42] and Jumah and Mujumdar[41] developed a diffusion-based model to describe grain drying in a batch RJSB under different operating conditions (continuous spouting and heating, continuous spouting and sinusoidal heating, intermittent spouting and heating, continuous spouting and intermittent heating, continuous spouting and sawtooth heating, etc.).

Although the investment and maintenance costs of RJSBs should be higher than those of CSBs, the results confirm the wide and flexible conditions under which this type of dryer can work, especially for heat-sensitive solids.[41–42] RJSBs improve the dryer performance and product quality, reducing the operating cost by saving energy. Devahastin et al.[43] simplified the RJSB design to obtain only an annular periodic spout for drying of wheat. Devahastin and Mujumdar[44] demonstrated that a pulsed spouted bed, operated at a specific pulse frequency range, could dry heat-sensitive grains in a manner similar to that of the RJSB, but with lower construction and operating costs.

The concept of spout intermittency has also been applied in SB dryers. A batch 2DSB with intermittent spout was used for drying cardamom[45] (an aromatic Indian spice), saving 25 percent of thermal energy and improving product quality with respect to color and texture, as well as oleoresin extraction. A CcSB with inert particles and intermittent feed of the liquid suspension improved the drying–powdering process when the control of the intermittent feed intervals was linked to changes in outlet air temperature.[46] Two different types of intermittency were used in a batch CSB dryer of black beans.[47] One involved a periodic reduction in the airflow rate for a cyclic change in flow regimes (spouting to a fixed bed and vice versa), and the other periodic injection (on/off) of airflow. The latter mode resulted in the best dryer efficiency (more than twice as high as the efficiency achieved in a continuous air injection CSB).

11.2   Dryer design models

Published models for drying particulate solids in a SB can be divided into three levels, according to the complexity of the model equations. Based on Oakley,[48] *zero-level* models are composed of simple mass and energy balances for gas and solid phases, at the entrance and exit of the dryer. They result in simple algebraic equations, which are easy to solve. Knowing the inlet conditions of both phases and the outlet (or final) conditions of the solid phase, the outlet air conditions are immediately determined. *One-level* models involve overall mass and energy balances for the gas and solid phases, at the entrance and exit of the dryer, as well as the sorption curve for the particulate solid. Besides the outlet air conditions, these models can also provide quickly the outlet or final solid moisture content in the continuous or batch SB dryer. These two classes of models are unable to provide data or information for scaleup, design, or control of SB dryers.

Two-level models, subdivided into types A and B, consider that the gas mixture (air and water vapor) behaves as a continuous medium, described by the Eulerian approach, whereas the particulate solids behave as a discrete phase, described by the Lagrangian approach. Consequently, these models are more complex and require numerical solutions of the governing equations. The 2A models simplify the gas and particle motion inside the SB dryer by assuming the statistical mean particle path to be the standard for all particles and by incorporating all significant changes into the main gas flow direction. Because of these simplifications, the time for solving their equation system is compatible with one required for a drying control application. The 2B models are significantly more complex, as they incorporate the CFD package into their solution program for describing the gas flow in three directions and for tracking large numbers of individual particles. These models require many hours of advanced computer time for solving the equations. They can be used to explore a new SB design, and for generating data to validate criteria for spout stability and scaleup.

The schematic flowchart in Figure 11.3 represents a generic model used to determine the best SB dryer dimensions for continuously drying a specific particulate solid. The discrete motion of the solid phase is considered in the residence time distribution (RTD) of the particles, which is incorporated into the drying kinetics model. Souza[49] developed a similar model for defining optimal design of CSB and 2DSB units for drying grains.

11.3   Drying model formulation

11.3.1   Mass and energy balances

A generic formulation of the 2A models is based on the assumption that the gas flow and solid circulation are predominantly longitudinal,[29,50,51] so the annular and spout regions can be divided into n-infinitesimal segments of depth H/n and unit cross-sectional area. Mass and energy balances can be written for each segment, considering that the solid and gas properties vary from one segment to the next, as shown in Table 11.2. These properties are, in principle, independent of the two other spatial coordinates; their values

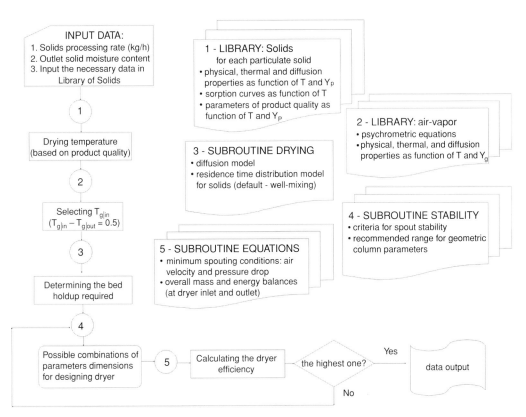

Figure 11.3. Computer program flowchart for optimizing SB dryer based on its efficiency and on the quality of solids (after Souza[49]).

in each infinitesimal segment represent averages along these two coordinates. This approach has been used to model the fluid flow behavior in a CcSB,[52] the solid-stress distribution in CSBs,[53] and bed failure mechanisms in CcSBs.[54]

In the mass and energy balances (Table 11.2), the superficial mass flux of fluid, G, and the mass flow rate of particles, W_p, are expressed in terms of the dry gas and dry solids, whereas the gas humidity, Y_g, and solids moisture content, Y_p, are in d.b. (dry basis).

The continuous gas phase, composed of air and water vapor, moves in plug flow in the SB dryer. Hot air is injected continuously into the bed of particles at a known mass flow rate, $G_{s|in} A_i$, temperature, $T_{g|in}$, and humidity, $Y_{g|in}$. If the annulus is aerated from below with a volumetric flow rate, Q_{a0}, and at the same temperature and humidity as the inlet spouting air, then the only change that enters the present analysis is that $Q_a(z)$ at $z = 0$ becomes Q_{a0} instead of zero. The discrete phase, formed by wet particles, has its properties (ρ_p, d_p, sphericity, ε_{mf}, $c_{p\text{-}p}$, λ_p) known as a function of temperature, moisture content, and, for the case of sorption $Y_p{}^{eq}$ curves, the air relative humidity. The spouting regime is stable ($U > U_{ms}$) and particles move cyclically, entering the spout at the base of the column and the annulus (or downcomer) at the top of the bed. Bypassing or short-circuiting of particles is neglected. Therefore, the mass flow rate of particles,

Table 11.2. Mass and energy balance equations in annulus, spout and fountain regions.

ANNULUS REGION

$$G_a(i)A_a(i)Y_{g|a}(i) + W_p Y_{p|a}(i-1)$$
$$= W_p Y_{p|a}(i) + G_a(i-1)A_a(i-1)Y_{g|a}(i-1)$$
$$\quad + G_{it}(i)A_{it}(i)Y_{g|it} \tag{11.1}$$

$$G_a(i)A_a(i)c_{p-g|a}(i)\{T_{g|a}(i) - T_R\}$$
$$\quad + W_p c_{p-p|a}(i-1)\{T_{p|a}(i-1) - T_R\} + \Delta H_v W_p$$
$$\quad \times \{Y_{p|a}(i) - Y_{p|a}(i-1)\}$$
$$= q_i + W_p c_{p-p|a}(i)\{T_{p|a}(i) - T_R\}$$
$$\quad + G_a(i-1)A_a(i-1)c_{p-g|a}(i-1)$$
$$\quad \times \{T_{g|a}(i-1) - T_R\}$$
$$\quad + G_{it}(i)A_{it}(i)c_{p-g|it}(i)\{T_{g|it}(i) - T_R\} - q_{lost} \tag{11.2}$$

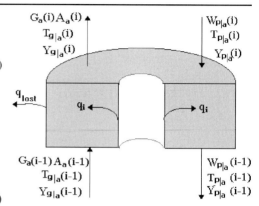

SPOUT REGION

$$G_s(i)A_s(i)Y_{g|s}(i) + W_p Y_{p|s}(i)$$
$$= W_p Y_{p|s}(i-1) + G_s(i-1)A_s(i-1)Y_{g|s}(i-1)$$
$$\quad - G_{it}(i)A_{it}(i)Y_{g|it} \tag{11.3}$$

$$G_s(i)A_s(i)c_{p-g|s}(i)\{T_{g|s}(i) - T_R\}$$
$$\quad + W_p c_{p-p|s}(i)\{T_{p|s}(i) - T_R\}$$
$$\quad + \Delta H_v W_p \{Y_{p|s}(i-1) - Y_{p|s}(i)\}$$
$$= W_p c_{p-p|s}(i-1)\{T_{p|s}(i-1) - T_R\}$$
$$\quad + G_s(i-1)A_s(i-1)c_{p-g|s}(i-1)$$
$$\quad \times \{T_{g|s}(i-1) - T_R\} - G_{it}(i)A_{it}(i)c_{p-g|it}(i)$$
$$\quad \times \{T_{g|it}(i) - T_R\} - q_i \tag{11.4}$$

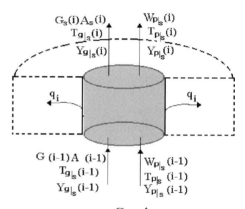

FOUNTAIN REGION

$$W_p\{Y_{p|s}(N) - Y_{p|a}(N)\} = G_{s|in}A_i(Y_{g|out} - Y_{g|f}) \tag{11.5}$$

$$G_{s|in}A_i c_{p-g|out}(T_{g|out} - T_R)$$
$$\quad + W_p c_{p-p|a}(N)\{T_{p|a}(N) - T_R\}$$
$$\quad + \Delta H_v W_p \{Y_{p|s}(N) - Y_{p|a}(N)\}$$
$$= G_{s|in}A_i c_{p-g|f}(T_{g|f} - T_R)$$
$$\quad + W_p c_{p-p|s}(N)\{T_{p|s}(N) - T_R\} \tag{11.6}$$

with

$$U_{g|f} = \frac{G_a(N)A_a(N)Y_{g|a}(N) + G_s(N)A_s(N)Y_{g|s}(N)}{G_{s|in}A_i}$$

$$T_{g|f}$$
$$= \frac{G_a(N)A_a(N)c_{p-g|a}(N)\{T_{g|a}(N) - T_R\} + G_s(N)A_s(N)c_{p-g|s}(N)\{T_{g|s}(N) - T_R\}}{G_{s|in}A_i c_{p-g|f}}$$
$$\quad + T_R$$

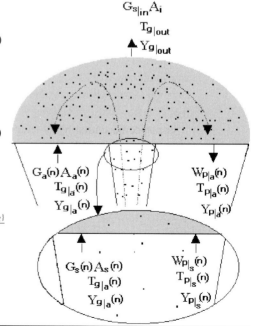

W_p, is constant in all bed segments. The upward gas superficial velocity in each annular segment, $U_a(i) = G_a(i)/\rho$, must be determined by an appropriate gas–solid flow model (discussed in Chapter 3), as must also the minimum spouting conditions (U_{ms} and ΔP_{ms}), the spout diameter or width along the axial coordinate, $D_s(z)$ or $L_s(z)$, the fractional void volume in the three regions, ε_a (generally close to ε_{mf}), ε_s, and ε_f, the fountain height, H_f, and finally the particle circulation rate, W_p.

The interaction between the annulus and spout regions occurs at the interface in two different ways: air crosses this interface from the spout to the annulus, or possibly vice versa when there is annulus aeration, and heat transfers between the spout air and particles that descend at this spout–annulus interface. The airflow rate passing through this interface is calculated by a mass balance for each segment: $G_{it}(i)A_{it}(i) = G_a(i)A_a(i) - G_a(i-1)A(i-1)$. When $G_{it}(i)$ is positive, air flows through this interface toward the annular region, then $Y_{g|it}(i) = Y_{g|s}(i)$ in Eqs. (11.1) and (11.3). Conversely, when $G_{it}(i)$ is negative, air flows through this interface toward the spout region; then $Y_{g|it}(i) = Y_{g|a}(i)$ in Eqs. (11.1) and (11.3). The heat transfer rate across the interface, q_i, for each segment can be described by a convective heat transfer coefficient between descending particles and ascending air, an effective contact area between them, and a temperature difference between the spout air and particles in the annular segment.[51] If the dryer is not thermally insulated, a significant amount of heat is lost to the surroundings through the column wall. This rate, q_{lost}, can also be specified for each segment by a convective heat transfer coefficient between the bed of particles and ambient air, an effective contact wall area, and the temperature difference. Most 2A models in the literature neglect these heat losses.[29,31,49] However, as pointed out by Freitas,[7] heat losses can be higher than those estimated by the convective heat transfer coefficient formulation, because of flanges, screws, connections, and metallic supports attached to the column acting as extended surfaces, and also because of radiant heat transfer. Hence, it is better to consider this heat transfer coefficient as an adjustable parameter to be determined experimentally for each SB column.

Because particles also undergo drying in the fountain region (depending on their moisture content), the fountain region can be represented by an additional finite segment with a paraboloidal shape and height H_f, as shown in Table 11.2. The overall mass and energy balances in this segment can be formulated by the equations in this table.[51]

The specific enthalpy for evaporating water, ΔH_v, is determined at the reference temperature ($T_R = 273$ K), comprising the latent heat of water vaporization added to the heat of water desorption from the solids. This heat of desorption, obtained from the sorption curves,[7,18] is taken into account only in the falling-rate drying period.

To solve these mass and energy balance equations in each segment, the following complementary equations are needed to couple gas and particle temperatures in the annulus, spout, and fountain regions, respectively:

$$\pm W_p c_{p-p|j}(i-1)\{T_{p|j}(i-1) - T_R\} \pm \Delta H_v W_p\{Y_{p|j}(i) - Y_{p|j}(i-1)\}$$
$$= \pm W_p c_{p-p|j}(i)\{T_{p|j}(i) - T_R\} + h_{p|j}(i)A_{p|j}(i)$$
$$\times \frac{[T_{g|j}(i) - T_{p|j}(i)] + [T_{g|j}(i-1) - T_{p|j}(i-1)]}{2} \tag{11.7}$$

and

$$W_p c_{p-p|a}(N)\{T_{p|a}(N) - T_R\} + \Delta H_v W_p\{Y_{p|s}(N) - Y_{p|a}(N)\}$$

$$= W_p c_{p-p|s}(N)\{T_{p|s}(N) - T_R\} + h_{p|f} A_{p|f}$$

$$\times \frac{\left[T_{g|out} - \dfrac{T_{p|s}(N) + T_{p|a}(N)}{2}\right] - \left[T_{g|f} - \dfrac{T_{p|s}(N) + T_{p|a}(N)}{2}\right]}{\ln\left\{\dfrac{T_{g|out} - \dfrac{T_{p|s}(N) + T_{p|a}(N)}{2}}{T_{g|f} - \dfrac{T_{p|s}(N) + T_{p|a}(N)}{2}}\right\}}. \qquad (11.8)$$

In Eq. (11.7), the positive sign of "±" represents the annulus segment with $j = a$, whereas the negative sign represents the spout segment with $j = s$. In Eqs. (11.7) and (11.8), the convective heat transfer coefficients, $h_{p|j}$, in the annulus ($j = a$), spout ($j = s$), and fountain ($j = f$) regions are calculated using empirical equations presented elsewhere.[14] The effective area for heat transfer is expressed as $A_{p|j}(i) = \dfrac{S_p[1 - \varepsilon_j(i)]A_j(H/n)}{V_p}$, with $j = a, s, f$ for the annulus, spout, and fountain regions, respectively.

11.3.2 Drying kinetics models

To solve this set of equations (from 11.1 to 11.8), the rate of evaporation must be determined, knowing that the evaporated water transfers from the particle surface to the bulk of the gas. There are, generally, two periods of drying: the constant- and falling-rate drying periods (Figure 11.1b). The first, or constant-rate, period is characterized by evaporation of free or unbound water that covers the particle surface, owing to the heat supplied by hot air. During this period, the thin air layer surrounding the particle surface becomes saturated with water vapor, the particle temperature equals the wet-bulb temperature, and the drying rate is constant. Consequently, if drying of particulate solids occurs in this period, the decrease of the solids moisture content in the i-segment of the bed can be described by the convective vapor transfer from the thin saturated gas layer surrounding the particle to the bulk of the gas:

$$\pm W_p\{Y_{p|j}(i) - Y_{p|j}(i-1)\} = \beta_{p|j}(i)A_{p|j}(i)[\Delta Y_{g|j}(i)]_M \qquad (11.9)$$

with

$$[\Delta Y_{g|j}(i)]_M = \frac{\{Y_{g|j}^{sat}(i) - Y_{g|j}(i)\} - \{Y_{g|j}^{sat}(i-1) - Y_{g|j}(i-1)\}}{\ln\left\{\dfrac{Y_{g|j}^{sat}(i) - Y_{g|j}(i)}{Y_{g|j}^{sat}(i-1) - Y_{g|j}(i-1)}\right\}}. \qquad (11.9a)$$

In Eq. (11.9), $j = a$ for the annular segment with the first term of this equation (on the left side) being positive; $j = s$ for the spout segment with the first term of this equation (on the left side) being negative. The convective mass transfer coefficient, $\beta_{p|j}$, can be estimated by empirical correlations discussed elsewhere.[14] A similar formulation can be developed for the fountain segment.[51]

In the course of this first drying period, particulate solids can shrink, decreasing their volume and, sometimes, changing their shape. The volume reduction, when considerable, must be correlated to the amount of evaporated water and incorporated into the model. In the specific case of isotropic particle shrinkage with unchanging density, the decrease in the mean volumetric sphere-equivalent diameter of a particle, d_v, can be formulated as

$$d_v = d_{v0} \left(1 - \frac{(Y_{p0} - Y_p)\rho_{p0}}{(1 + Y_{p0})\rho_w} \right)^{1/3}, \tag{11.10}$$

with the subscript 0 denoting the initial drying time. Eq. (11.10) or a similar equation must be added to the set of model equations for determining changes in the particle properties and their effect on the SB operation in each segment of the bed during this initial drying period.

The constant drying rate period lasts until the appearance of the first nonsaturated zones on the particle surface, signifying that the particle moisture content has attained its critical value, Y_p^{cr}. From this point on, the water to be evaporated is adsorbed on or below the particle surface, and there is therefore an additional mass transfer resistance to removal of this bound water. Consequently, the drying rate starts to decrease, and the particle temperature begins to increase, as the heat supplied by the hot air no longer dictates the amount of water evaporated. The drying kinetics of nonporous or partially porous solids in this falling rate period can be formulated adequately by liquid diffusion theory.[7,18,49] According to this theory, water moves from the particle interior to the particle surface owing to a concentration gradient. Water evaporates at the particle surface only, following the liquid–vapor thermodynamic equilibrium. The resistance offered by the particle to this water diffusion is expressed by an effective diffusion coefficient, D, a property of the particulate solid. In this theory, other factors that can affect the water movement inside the solid structure, such as the capillarity, temperature, or pressure gradient, are neglected.[55] Even though this liquid-diffusion theory is a simplified formulation of the actual drying kinetics in the falling-rate period, errors are minimized by the experimental determination of D in a given application. This coefficient should be evaluated using a corrected procedure to represent the SB drying operation.[7,18,49] The theory has been commonly applied for drying particulate solids in SB dryers during the falling-rate period.[6,7,13–19,22,27–29,31,34,41–42,49–50]

The three-dimensional Fick diffusion model[56] of moisture transfer can be written as:

$$\frac{\partial Y_p}{\partial t} = \nabla \cdot (D\nabla Y_p). \tag{11.11}$$

Eq. (11.9) must be linked to Eq. (11.11) to complete the simulation of the drying operation for all types of particulate solids (shrinkable or not). At $Y_p = Y_p^{cr}$, Eq. (11.9) is replaced by Eq. (11.11). When Y_p^{cr} is unknown as a function of temperature, its value can be estimated by the sorption curve of the material at the given particle temperature and an air relative humidity of 95 percent. This estimate is verified if the drying rate in the falling-rate period equals that in the constant-rate drying period at $Y_p = Y_p{}^{cr}$. Eq. (11.11) must be solved numerically to describe the falling-rate drying period, with appropriate boundary and initial conditions for particles in each segment.

Niamnuy et al.[9] successfully used Eq. (11.11) together with the energy equation to describe the drying of shrimp, a case in which there is considerable volume shrinkage. Białobrzewski et al.[8] used the same approach to simulate the drying of carrot cubes in a SFB.

Improvements in the simulation of particle drying by using computer tools favor the analysis of the product quality, supplying information to define criteria for preserving the particle quality during drying.[8,9] This is an open area to be pursued in future years.

11.3.3   Additional considerations

Additional information about the drying operation mode must be incorporated in the model equations. For batch drying of particulate solids, the number of cycles particles require to reach their final moisture content establishes their mean residence time in the dryer. Therefore, this number specifies the final drying time. Initial conditions of the particulate solids, such as Y_{p0}, T_{p0}, and M, need to be added to the input data.

Extension of the model formulation given previously to continuous drying of particulate solids requires knowledge of the RTD for the specific SB configuration. An RTD relationship must be incorporated in the model to provide the age of each particle in the i-segments of the bed and, consequently, its actual moisture content, as well as other properties that depend on its age (actual time in the dryer). As particles form the discrete phase, their overall properties in each i-segment of bed are calculated as the sum of their individual values. In CSB dryers, perfect mixing of particles is commonly assumed.[13,16–18,57] Zahed and Epstein[19] assumed good, but not perfect, mixing, coupled with the assumption of isothermal solids to provide a better description of the continuous drying of wheat in CSB dryers. Madhiyanon et al.[29] showed that the RTD function for continuously drying rice in a 2DSB with draft plates follows the well-known tanks-in-series model. Therefore, the specific SB column design determines the best RTD function to be incorporated in the model formulation.

Input and output streams must be added to the mass and energy balance equations at the specific segment of the bed. The first relates to the feed of solids, with the known variables inlet solids flow rate, $Y_{p|in}$ and $T_{p|in}$. The second represents the product discharge with the unknown variables $T_{p|out}$ and/or $Y_{p|out}$. Typically, the feed of solids is at the top of the vessel column, and solids are discharged near the bottom. However, for modified SB configurations, these input/output streams may be located at other positions. To extend this model formulation to an intermittent spouting operation, it is necessary to define the temporal functions for injecting air and/or for varying the inlet air temperature, to complete the set of model equations. Jumah[42] and Bon and Kudra[58] give the details necessary to define these functions.

Finally, the incorporation of the quality of the particulate solids should be in the form of quantitative inequalities (for severe restrictions) and empirical correlations that can form an objective function for controlling or optimizing the process.

Table 11.3. Assumptions and main results of CFD models in spouted bed drying of particulate solids.

Assumptions: gas-particle flow[59]	Assumptions: drying model	Results and applications
• Gas-particle: Eulerian-Eulerian two-fluid model • Interphase momentum exchange: Gidaspow drag model[60] • Kinetic-frictional solid stress: granular kinetic theory (derived by Lun et al.)[59,60] • Turbulence: standard $k - \varepsilon$ turbulence model • 2D axial symmetry • Grid: triangular (conical base) and quadrilateral (cylindrical region) • Code: FLUENT® (Fluent Inc., Lebanon, NH): 6.1[61] and 6.2[62] • Same considerations as those in the preceding row • Code: COMSOL Multiphysic® (Comsol AB, Sweden) – 3a with chemical engineering and heat transfer modules[8]	• Isotropic spherical particles with volumetric shrinkage and negligible internal temperature gradients • Neglected: heat and mass transfer between particles; heat losses • Drying kinetics: constant-rate period coupled with falling-rate period (diffusion) • Transition between these periods (drying rate in second period equals that in first period) • Drying model incorporated into CFD code by user-defined function • Regular cubic particles (three-dimensional) • Negligible effect of water evaporation on air properties • Linked: heat, mass transfer, and shrinkage of particle • Empirical model of changes in particle volume coupled with particle moving boundary model	• Grain drying[61,62] • Validation based on experimental data of gas–solid flow • Drying of microspherical porous particles in a CSB with draft-tube: computer simulations predict well the mass transfer rates, underpredict heat-transfer rates[61] • Drying simulations for a CSB: considering decrease in particle density along drying and its effects on the gas flow[62] • Drying of carrot cubes in a SFB[8] • Computer simulations underpredict heat transfer rates (need to double the convective heat transfer coefficient predicted by SB correlation to achieve highest accuracy)[8] • Product quality: particle deformation vs. changes in drying temperature[8]

11.4   Computational fluid dynamic models

Focusing on the 2B-level models, various commercial CFD computer packages have been used recently to describe and analyze the drying of particulate solids. Wojciech[59] critically reviewed the key aspects of developing a CFD simulation model of a spouted-bed grain dryer. Table 11.3 summarizes some of the more important assumptions and results obtained in the SB dryer of particulate solids.

Chapter-specific nomenclature

W_p solids circulation rate, kg of dry solids/s
Y_g gas humidity, kg water vapor/kg dry air
Y_p particle or solids moisture content, kg water/kg dry solids

Subscripts

g gas
in inlet

it	spout–annulus interface
lost	losses
mf	minimum fluidization
out	outlet
R	reference
w	water
0	initial

Superscripts

cr	critical
eq	equilibrium
sat	saturated

References

1. M. Markowski, W. Sobieski, I. Konopka, M. Tańska, and I. Białobrzewski. Drying characteristics of barley grain dried in a spouted-bed and combined IR-convection dryers. *Drying Technol.*, **25** (2007), 1621–1632.

2. A. C. C. Lima and S. C. S. Rocha. Bean drying in fixed, spouted and spout-fluid beds: a comparison and empirical modeling. *Drying Technol.*, **16** (1998), 1881–1901.

3. S. Wiriyaumpaiwong, S. Soponronnarit, and S. Prachayawarakorn. Soybean drying by two-dimensional spouted bed. *Drying Technol.*, **21** (2003), 1735–1757.

4. K. M. Kundu, A. B. Datta, and P. K. Chatterjee. Drying of oilseeds. *Drying Technol.*, **19** (2001), 343–358.

5. D. Evin, H. Gül, and V. Tanyldz. Grain drying in a paraboloid-based spouted bed with and without draft tube. *Drying Technol.*, **26** (2008), 1577–1583.

6. A. Magalhães and C. Pinho. Spouted bed drying of cork stoppers. *Chem. Eng. Process.*, **47** (2008), 2395–2401.

7. M. E. A. Freitas. Modeling the transient drying of grains in conical spouted beds. M.Sc. dissertation, Federal University of Minas Gerais (1996) (in Portuguese).

8. I. Białobrzewski, M. Zielińska, A. S. Mujumdar, and M. Markowski. Heat and mass transfer during drying of a bed of shrinking particles – simulation for carrot cubes dried in a spout-fluidized-bed drier. *Int. J. Heat Mass Transfer*, **51** (2008), 4704–4716.

9. C. Niamnuy, S. Devahastin, S. Soponronnarit, and G. S. V. Raghavan. Modeling coupled transport phenomena and mechanical deformation of shrimp during drying in a jet spouted bed dryer. *Chem. Eng. Sci.*, **63** (2008), 5503–5512.

10. M. M. Almeida, O. S. Silva, and O. L. S. Alsina. Fluid-dynamic study of deformable materials in spouted-bed dryer. *Drying Technol.*, **24** (2006), 499–508.

11. S. Grabowski, A. S. Mujumdar, H. S. Ramaswamy, and C. Strumillo. Evaluation of fluidized versus spouted bed drying of baker's yeast. *Drying Technol.*, **15** (1997), 625–634.

12. K. B. Mathur and P. E. Gishler. A technique for contacting gases with coarse solid particles. *AIChE J.*, **1** (1955), 157–164.

13. M. L. Passos, A. S. Mujumdar, and G. Massarani. Scale-up of spouted bed dryers: criteria and applications. *Drying Technol.*, **12** (1994), 351–391.

14. K. B. Mathur and N. Epstein. *Spouted Beds* (New York: Academic Press, 1974).

15. A. S. Mujumdar. Spouted bed technology – a brief review. In *Drying '84*, ed. A. S. Mujumdar (New York: Hemisphere McGraw-Hill, 1984), pp. 151–157.

16. M. L. Passos, A. S. Mujumdar, and V. G. S. Raghavan. Spouted beds for drying: principles and design considerations. In *Advances in Drying*, vol. 4, ed. A. S. Mujumdar (New York: Hemisphere, 1987), pp. 359–397.

17. E. Pallai, T. Szentmarjay, and A. S. Mujumdar. Spouted bed drying. In *Handbook of Industrial Drying*, 3rd ed., ed. A. S. Mujumdar (Boca Raton, FL: CRC Press, 2006), pp. 363–384.

18. H. A. Becker and H. R. Sallans. Drying wheat in spouted bed: on continuous moisture diffusion controlled drying of solid particles in a well-mixed isothermal bed. *Chem. Eng. Sci.*, **13** (1961), 97–112.

19. A. H. Zahed and N. Epstein. Batch and continuous spouted bed drying of cereal grains: the thermal equilibrium model. *Can J. Chem. Eng.*, **70** (1992), 945–953.

20. M. L. Passos, L. S. Oliveira, A. S. Franca, and G. Massarani. Bixin powder production in conical spouted bed units. *Drying Technol.*, **16** (1998), 1855–1879.

21. F. G. Cunha, K. G. Santos, C. H. Ataíde, N. Epstein, and M. A. S. Barrozo. Annatto powder production in a spouted bed: an experimental and CFD study. *Ind. Eng. Chem. Res.*, **48** (2009), 976–982.

22. A. Kmieć and R. G. Szafran. Kinetics of drying of microspherical particles in a spouted bed dryer with a draft tube. In *Proceedings of the 12th International Drying Symposium, IDS2000*, ed. P. J. A. M. Kerkhof, W. J. Coumans, and G. D. Mooiweer (Amsterdam: Elsevier Science, 2000), paper 15 (CD-ROM).

23. M. Olazar, M. J. San José, F. J. Peñas, and J. Bilbao. Segregation in conical spouted beds with binary and tertiary mixtures of equidensity spherical particles. *Ind. Eng. Chem. Res.*, **33** (1994), 1838–1844.

24. H. Altzibar, G. Lopez, S. Alvarez, M. J. San José, A. Barona, and M. Olazar. A draft-tube conical spouted bed for drying fine particles. *Drying Technol.*, **26** (2008), 308–314.

25. M. I. Kalwar, T. Kudra, G. S. V. Raghavan, and A. S. Mujumdar. Drying of grains in a drafted two-dimensional spouted bed. *J. Food Proc. Eng.*, **13** (1991), 321–332.

26. M. C. Dias, W. M. Marques, S. V. Borges, and M. C. Mancini. The effect of drying in a two-dimensional spouted bed black beans (*Phaseolus vulgaris*, L.) on their physical and technological properties. *Ciênc. Tecnol. Aliment.*, **20** (2000), 339–354 (in Portuguese).

27. S. Wiriyaumpaiwong, S. Soponronnarit, and S. Prachayawarakorn. Drying and urease inactivation models of soybean using two-dimensional spouted bed technology. *Drying Technol.*, **24** (2006), 1673–1681.

28. T. Madhiyanon, S. Soponronnarit, and W. Tia. Industrial-scale prototype of continuous spouted bed paddy dryer. *Drying Technol.*, **19** (2001), 207–216.

29. T. Madhiyanon, S. Soponronnarit, and W. Tia. A mathematical model for continuous drying of grains in a spouted bed dryer. *Drying Technol.*, **20** (2002), 587–614.

30. G. Srzednicki and R. H. Driscoll. Implementation of a two-stage drying system for grains in Asia. In *Using Food Science and Technology to Improve Nutrition and Promote National Development*, ed. G. L. Robertson and J. R. Lupien (Oakville, Canada: Internat. Union Food Sci. and Technol., 2009), Chapter 7, www.iufost.org/publications/books/IUFoSTFoodScienceandTechnologyHandbook.cfm (accessed March 2, 2009).

31. L. Hung-Nguyen, R. H. Driscoll, and G. Srzednicki. Modeling the drying process of paddy in a triangular spouted bed. In *Proceedings of the 12th International Drying Symposium,*

IDS2000, ed. P. J. A. M. Kerkhof, W. J. Coumans, and G. D. Mooiweer (Amesterdam: Elsevier Science Ltd., 2000), paper 269 (CD-ROM).

32. L. Hung-Nguyen, R. H. Driscoll, and G. Srzednicki. Drying of high moisture content paddy in a pilot scale triangular spouted bed dryer. *Drying Technol.*, **19** (2001), 375–387.

33. A. Reyes and I. Vidal. Experimental analysis of a mechanically stirred spouted bed dryer. *Drying Technol.*, **18** (2000), 341–359.

34. M. L. Passos, A. S. Mujumdar, and V. G. S. Raghavan. Spouted and spout-fluidized beds for grain drying. *Drying Technol.*, **7** (1989), 663–696.

35. T. Kudra and A. S. Mujumdar. *Advanced Drying Technologies*. (New York: Marcel Dekker, 2002).

36. S. Wachiraphansakul and S. Devahastin. Drying kinetics and quality of okara dried in a jet spouted bed of sorbent particles. *LWT Food Sci. Technol.*, **40** (2007), 207–219.

37. H. Feng, J. Tang, and R. P. Cavalieri. Combined microwave and spouted bed drying of diced apples: effect of drying conditions on drying kinetics and product temperature. *Drying Technol.*, **17** (1999), 1981–1998.

38. R. Y. Jumah and G. S. V. Raghavan. Analysis of heat and mass transfer during combined microwave convective spouted-bed drying. *Drying Technol.*, **19** (2001), 485–506.

39. J. Berghel. The gas-to-particle heat transfer and hydrodynamics in spouted bed drying of sawdust. *Drying Technol.*, **23** (2005), 1027–1041.

40. A. S. Mujumdar. Superheated steam drying. In *Handbook of Industrial Drying*, 3rd ed., ed. A. S. Mujumdar (Boca Raton, FL: CRC Press, 2006), pp. 439–452.

41. R. Y. Jumah and A. S. Mujumdar. A mathematical model for constant and intermittent batch drying of grains in a novel rotating jet spouted bed. *Drying Technol.*, **14** (1996), 765–803.

42. R. Y. Jumah. Flow and drying characteristics of a rotating jet spouted bed. Ph.D. thesis, McGill University (1995).

43. S. Devahastin, A. S. Mujumdar, and G. S. V. Raghavan. Hydrodynamic characteristics of a rotating jet annular spouted bed. *Powder Technol.*, **103** (1999), 169–174.

44. S. Devahastin and A. S. Mujumdar. Some hydrodynamic and mixing characteristics of a pulsed spouted bed dryer. *Powder Technol.*, **117** (2001), 189–197.

45. M. Balakrisnan, V. V. Sreenarayanan, and G. S. V. Raghavan. Batch drying kinetics of cardamom in a two-dimensional spouted bed. In *Proceedings of the 13th International Drying Symposium, IDS2002*, ed. C. W. Cao, Y. K. Pan, X. D. Liu, and Y. X. Qu (Beijing: Beijing Univ. of Chemical Technology, 2002), vol. B, pp. 767–781.

46. M. L. Passos, A. L. G. Trindade, J. V. H. d'Angelo, and M. Cardoso. Drying of black liquor in spouted bed of inert particles. *Drying Technol.*, **22** (2004), 1041–1067.

47. C. A. Oliveira and S. C. S. Rocha. Intermittent drying of beans in a spouted bed. *Braz. J. Chem. Eng.*, **24** (2007), 571–585.

48. D. E. Oakley. Spray dryer modeling in theory and practice. *Drying Technol.*, **22** (2004), 1371–1402.

49. C. C. Souza. Computer simulator for the best design of spout-bed dryers of grains. M.Sc. dissertation, Federal University of Minas Gerais (1993) (in Portuguese).

50. T. Madhiyanon, S. Soponronnarit, and W. Tia. Two-region mathematical model for batch drying of grains in a two-dimensional spouted bed dryer. *Drying Technol.*, **19** (2001), 1045–1064.

51. E. F. Costa, Jr., M. Cardoso, and M. L. Passos. Simulation of drying suspensions in spout-fluid beds of inert particles. *Drying Technol.*, **19** (2001), 1975–2001.

52. D. S. Povrenovic, Dz. E. Hadismajlovic, Z. B. Grbavčić, D. V. Vukovic, and H. Littman. Minimum fluid flowrate, pressure drop and stability of a conical spouted bed. *Can. J. Chem. Eng.*, **70** (1992), 216–222.

53. G. S. McNab and J. Bridgwater. The theory for effective solid stresses in the annulus of a spouted bed. *Can. J. Chem. Eng.*, **57** (1979), 274–279.

54. E. F. Costa, Jr., M. L. Passos, E. C. Biscaia, Jr., and M. Massarani. New approach to solve a model for the effective solid stress distribution in conical spouted beds. *Can. J. Chem. Eng.*, **82** (2004), 539–554.

55. M. Fortes and M. R. Okos. Drying theories: their bases and limitations as applied to food and grains. In *Advances in Drying*, vol. 1, ed. A. S. Mujumdar (Washington, DC: Hemisphere, 1982), pp. 110–154.

56. J. Crank. *The Mathematics of Diffusion*, 2nd ed. (New York: Oxford Univ. Press, 1975).

57. K. Viswanathan. Model for continuous drying solids in fluidized/spouted beds. *Can J. Chem. Eng.*, **64** (1986), 87–95.

58. J. Bon and T. Kudra. Enthalpy-driven optimization of intermittent drying. *Drying Technol.*, **25** (2007), 523–532.

59. S. Wojciech. Selected aspects of developing a simulation model of a spouted-bed grain dryer based on the Eulerian multiphase model *Drying Technol.*, in press.

60. H. Lu, Y. He, W. Liu, J. Ding, D. Gidaspow, and J. Bouillard. Computer simulations of gas-solid flow in spouted beds using kinetic-frictional stress model of granular flow. *Chem. Eng. Sci.*, **59** (2004), 865–878.

61. R. G. Szafran and A. Kmiec. CFD Modeling of heat and mass transfer in a spouted bed dryer. *Ind. Eng. Chem. Res.*, **43** (2004), 1113–1124.

62. W. Zhonghua and A. S. Mujumdar. Simulation of the hydrodynamics and drying in a spouted bed dryer. *Drying Technol.*, **25** (2007), 549–574.

12 Drying of solutions, slurries, and pastes

José Teixeira Freire, Maria do Carmo Ferreira, and Fábio Bentes Freire

12.1 Introduction

In a system consisting of a liquid and solids dispersed within it, such as slurries and pasty materials, the structure and characteristic properties are defined by the solids concentration, shape, and size distribution. A variety of solid–liquid mixtures, such as suspensions, dispersions, sludges, and pulps, is included in these categories.[1] Solutions with a solute that crystallizes out on evaporation are also included. The drying of solutions in beds of inert particles of spoutable size was developed in the late 1960s at the Lenigrad Institute of Technology[2] for applications in which the dried solids are ultimately required in the form of a fine powder. Spouting with inert particles was applied successfully by the Leningrad group to dry organic dyes and dye intermediates, lacquers, salt and sugar solutions, and various chemical reagents.[2] Since then, a large number of materials have been successfully dried, demonstrating the applicability and versatility of this method. A partial list of dried materials is given in Table 12.1.

12.2 Drying process

12.2.1 Description

The drying of pastes (or slurries or solutions, all referred to henceforth in this chapter generically as *pastes*) is performed in the presence of inert particles, which are both a support for the paste and a source of heat for drying. The paste may be atomized or dropped into the bed by a nozzle or dropping device. An example of an experimental facility for research in paste drying is shown in Figure 12.1. Usually, the paste is introduced at the bed's top surface, as there is evidence that feeding at this position leads to stable operation with a low accumulation of the product in the bed.[3] However, reports of feeding at the entrance region are also available.[4–6]

As the bed becomes wet, the paste coats the inert particle surfaces, forming a thin layer of slurry material. The sources of heat for drying the layered material are conduction from the particles and convection from the hot air. The drying process is well understood: The coating layer gradually dries and becomes fragile and friable. As moisture is reduced,

Spouted and Spout-Fluid Beds: Fundamentals and Applications, eds. Norman Epstein and John R. Grace. Published by Cambridge University Press. © Cambridge University Press 2011.

Table 12.1. Solutions, slurries, and pastes dried in spouted beds with inerts.

Material	Spouted bed configuration	Inerts
Animal blood[8]	CcSB; $D = 1.04$ m	Polypropylene beads, $d_p = 3{-}4$ mm; $\varphi = 0.80$
Solutions of cobalt carbonate and zinc carbonate[5]	MSB; $D = 0.14$ m	Glass spheres, $d_p = 6.00$ mm
Animal blood, hydroalcoholic vegetable solutions[9]	CcSB; $D = 0.14$ m	Polypropylene beads, $d_p = 3.9$ mm
Low-fat milk; corn flour suspensions and starch factory effluents[10]	CCSB; $D = 0.30$ m	Celcon beads, $d_p = 2.5$ mm
Solutions of antibiotics; baker's yeast[7]	JSB; $D = 0.48$ m	PFTE cubes; $d_p = 4$ mm
Sodium chloride solutions and alumina suspensions[4]	CCSB; $D = 0.15$ m	Glass and plastic beads, $d_p = 2{-}5$ mm
Ferric hydroxide–zinc hydroxide sludge[11]	HCCSB; $D = 0.154$ m	Sand, $d_p = 2.36$ mm
Microparticle slurry and salt-water solution[12]	CCSB; $D = 0.104$ m	Silica sand; alumina, $d_p = 460{-}1000\ \mu$m
Suspensions of maltodextrins; starch; aqueous carbohydrate solutions[6]	CCSB; $D = 0.60$ m	Polypropylene chips, $d_p = 3.4$ mm; $\varphi = 0.9$
Microparticle slurries[13]	CCSB; $D = 0.104$ m	Silica sand, $d_p = 650\ \mu$m
Xanthan gum dispersions[14]	2DSB; 0.05×0.3 m^2	Glass spheres, $d_p = 3.8$ mm
Modified pulps of tropical fruits[15]	CcSB; $D = 0.18$ m	Polyethylene particles, $d_p = 3.0$ mm; $\varphi = 0.76$
Homogenized egg paste; animal blood; xanthan gum solutions[16]	CcSB; $D = 0.30$ m	Glass spheres, $d_p = 2.6$ mm
Black liquor[17]	CcSB; $D = 0.15$ m and 0.30 m	Glass spheres, $d_p = 3$ mm Polypropylene beads, $d_p = 4.22$ mm; $\varphi = 0.86$
Extract of *Maytenus ilicifolia* leaves[18]	JSB; $D = 0.34$ m	Teflon beads, $d_p = 5.45$ mm; $\varphi = 0.96$
Homogenized egg paste[19]	CcSB; $D = 0.30$ m	Glass spheres, $d_p = 2.8$ mm
Vegetable starch solutions[20]	JSB; $V = 0.035$ m^3 (lab.) and $V = 0.660$ m^3 (pilot)	Teflon cubes, $L = 5$ mm
AlO(OH) suspensions, tomato concentrates, bovine serum albumin[21]	MSB; $D = 0.145$ m	PFTE particles, Size n.i.
Soy residue[22]	JSB; $D = 0.20$ m	Silica gel particles, $d_p = 3.33$ mm
Carbonate solutions; low fat milk; sewage sludge[23]	CcSB; $D = 0.30$ m	Glass spheres, $d_p = 2.2$ mm

JSB (jet spouted bed); CcSB (conical s.b.); CCSB (conical-cylindrical s.b.); MSB (mechanical s.b.); HCCSB (half-conical-cylindrical s.b.).

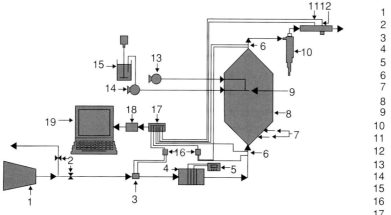

1	blower
2	valves
3	flow meter
4	air heater
5	temperature controller
6	thermocouples
7	samplers
8	spouted bed
9	paste feeding
10	cyclone
11	wet bulb thermocouple
12	dry bulb thermocouple
13	air compressor
14	peristaltic pump
15	paste tank
16	pressure transducers
17	signal conditioner
18	data acquisition board
19	PC computer

Figure 12.1. Experimental setup in paste drying experiments.[23]

the coating reaches a critical level that allows it to be removed as a powder by the successive collisions to which the particles are subjected. The powder is elutriated and collected by a separation device, such as a cyclone. As the paste is fed continuously, the stages of spouting, layer formation, drying, film fracture, and powder elutriation occur simultaneously. The time required for a complete cycle depends on the paste rheological characteristics, adhesion features, attrition rates, and other factors. The drying and layer removal rates must be high enough to avoid agglomeration from accumulation of paste in the bed.

12.2.2   Analysis

For pastes of high moisture content, water evaporation is the limiting stage of drying, which occurs at a constant rate. For the stages involving layer adhesion and subsequent breaking, the frequency of collisions and the drying rate are the major factors influencing the process.[7] The energy of collisions is affected by a number of variables, including the solid circulation rate, the mass ratio of paste to inert particles, and the drying rate itself. The inert solids circulation rate governs the time required for a complete cycle of coating–drying–removal of film from a particle. An increase in the drying rate favors an increase of film friability, enhancing the process. Solids circulation rates, mass of inert particles, and drying rates are parameters related to spouting operating conditions, so it might be useful to analyze the paste drying process from different perspectives.

   The interaction between the fluid and a particle moving through the bed differs with the distinct regions of a spouted bed – spout, annulus, and fountain – each of which has a very different distribution of air and particles and a different velocity profile. Typically, a particle leaves the annular region and enters the spout. Its velocity, initially close to zero, rapidly increases as it is entrained by the air rising through the spout. The gas inlet region is characterized by intense momentum transfer, similar to the solids accelerating region in a pneumatic riser. As the spout is very dilute, possible interactions among particles may be neglected and a particle may be analyzed as a single element in contact with the fluid, subject to weight, buoyancy, and drag forces. Adhesion forces, typically of a physical–chemical nature and acting on a molecular scale, keep a film of paste bound to the particle surface. The particle and its coating layer experience strong shear from the airflow. The conditions at the interface of a coated particle and fluid are established by the rheological characteristics of the paste and by the complex interactions at the boundary layers around the particles. Even in a simplified analysis, considering a single particle in the flow, the magnitude of the shear stress depends on many factors, including the air velocity at the entrance of the spouted bed and the paste rheological properties. The rheological properties, in turn, are likely to be time-dependent, changing as the drying proceeds. After short periods, as the material dries, the film properties and rheological characteristics change considerably. Evidence from experimental data suggests that, in steady-state operation, the moisture content of the film coating the particles is only slightly higher than the moisture content of powder collected at the cyclone exit.[16,19,23] A rigorous analysis of this situation is extremely complex and has not been satisfactorily addressed.

As the particle moves up the spout, it decelerates toward and within the fountain. Eventually, as the gravitational force predominates, the particle falls back onto the surface of the annulus. In this region, the structure is similar to that of a packed bed, and the particle is in direct contact with others. In the early stages of drying, liquid bridges may form because of paste surface tension, contributing to enhanced particle–particle interactions. The whole bed of wet particles descends toward the conical base, from which the particles are again propelled into the spout, and a new cycle starts. As the drying proceeds and the moisture content on the film coating decreases, the liquid bridges are likely to be replaced by other interaction forces.

An aspect that deserves closer inspection relates to the adhesion forces at the interface between the coating and inert particles. From theoretical work on adhesion, it is known that the magnitude of adhesion forces, resulting from chemical, mechanical, or molecular interactions, depends crucially on the substrate properties.[24] Although these interactions are extremely complex and will not be approached in depth here (see references elsewhere[24,25]), it is interesting to consider a few points. The substrate for adhesion is provided by the spouting particles and the interaction at this level is expected to affect the processes of coating and removal of layered material. As an example, it is known that solid surfaces – even the glass beads commonly used in spouting and often referred to as smooth – usually display some degree of surface roughness. The surface roughness contributes to increased contact area, which may enhance significantly the strength of the interface for a specific substrate–coating pair. Chemical composition, viscosity, surface tension, and other rheological properties of the coating material also play a role. However, as the rheological behavior changes with the drying, a given paste may become sticky or friable, or present other features that affect the interaction forces. As a result, the film removal process might differ for each coating–substrate pair. Detachment of layers of food pastes dried over glass substrates, for instance, was reported to depend on the glass transition temperature of the paste.[26] Even this superficial analysis indicates that the term *inert* may not always be accurate when applied to the substrates. The complex interactions involved in the interfaces of different substrates and coatings have not yet been investigated in depth.

For effective drying of a given paste on inert particles, the rate at which the film is coated and removed must be higher, or at least equal to, the rate at which the paste is fed into the bed.[10] To reach steady-state operation, the rates of film coating and removal must be equal. The film layer over a particle is expected to be thin enough to allow operation at a constant drying rate, with no significant moisture diffusion resistance through it. As a particle moves along the distinct regions of the spouted bed, the coating dries and is removed, and the resulting powder is elutriated. The film removal depends on the magnitude of the adhesion force. Powder removal efficiency is associated with friability, which depends on the frequency of collisions and on the properties of boundary layers around the particles. In addition, it is affected by the paste moisture content, temperature, and chemical composition. The shear stress acting on coated particle surfaces is affected by the paste composition and properties, air temperature, and particle slip velocity. The number of effective collisions is controlled by such variables as the solid circulation rate, mass of coated material on each particle, and drying rate.

12.2.3 Drying rate

The key response variables of a drying process – air outlet relative humidity and temperature, and powder moisture content – are closely related to the drying rate, which depends on previously mentioned characteristics associated with the internal bed structure. The steady-state evaporation rate (W) is a function not only of the paste characteristics but also of spouted bed geometry and configuration, quantity and properties of inert particles, and all other independent variables of the process. Research efforts have focused on obtaining the maximum evaporation rate for a specific set of independent variables (Q_{air}, T_i, H_o, P) and a combination of feed material/dryer/inert particles. Water is commonly adopted as feed in preliminary experiments to allow the maximum evaporation capacity of a system to be estimated. When tested under similar conditions, every other feed material yields evaporation rates that are lower than, or equal to, those obtained using water.[6,23] By drying different materials in a conical spouted bed at $T_i = 100\ °C$ and $U = 1.30U_{ms}$, Almeida[23] obtained similar values of W_{max} and air outlet relative humidity for water, sewage sludge suspension, low-fat milk, and 3 percent calcium carbonate solution. When drying homogenized whole egg paste at similar conditions, bed collapse was observed at values of W_{max} 25 percent lower and air outlet relative humidity 70 percent lower than their respective values for water.

Experimental investigations[6,23] showed that W_{max} is increased significantly by increasing U and T_i and increased only slightly by increasing H_o. Pham[8] proposed a simplified model that allows W_{max} to be estimated as a function of air outlet temperature and humidity. In this model, the maximum evaporation rates depend linearly on the air outlet temperature.

In conical spouted beds operated at constant H_o, it was verified[27] that the use of a 60° cone angle resulted in higher W_{max} compared with beds with 45° and 30° angles. Results are deceptive, however, as the authors observed more intense solid circulation rates in the beds with smaller cone angles, probably a result of the simultaneous variation of cone angle and quantity of inert particles required to maintain the same H_0 for different beds, so the quantity of inerts varied in the experiments. Laboratory assays with equal quantities of particles yielded no conclusive results about the effect of cone angle on solid circulation rates and W_{max}.

There is insufficient information in the current literature to provide a full understanding of how all such variables affect W_{max}.

12.3   Influence of paste on the fluid dynamic parameters

Pham[8] was one of the first authors to report clear evidence on changes in dynamic behavior of spouted beds operating with pastes. In the drying of animal blood, he observed the formation of dead zones that had not appeared in the operation of dry beds. Since then, several studies have been carried out to identify the effects of the presence of a liquid or slurry on spouted bed dynamics. These experiments have been conducted either in batch mode or continuous operation. Changes in rheological, physical, and chemical properties commonly observed during drying often led to unstable spouting, so experimental data could be obtained for only a narrow range of experimental conditions. This problem has been overcome by employing pure liquids, such as water or glycerol, to keep the beds wet, thus simulating to some degree the presence of a paste. Significant contributions reporting fluid dynamic behavior of wet beds are listed in Table 12.2. These references provide important evidence that the presence of a liquid or paste does indeed alter the fluid dynamic parameters, as it engenders interparticle cohesive forces that may change the solid and fluid circulation patterns. The effects of paste on fluid dynamic parameters are discussed in the following sections.

12.3.1   Pressure drop for stable spouting

Most researchers listed in Table 12.2 found that the minimum spouting pressure drop in wet beds is less than that in dry beds (ΔP_{ms0}), regardless of whether the feeding is in the batch or continuous mode. The reduction of ΔP_{ms} is attributed to the decrease in airflow rate through the annulus[4,28] because the liquid or pasty material contributes to particle agglomeration and to increased resistance to flow in this region, forcing more air toward the spout region. The stronger interaction forces in the annulus also contribute to reducing the number of particles leaving this region toward the spout, thus reducing solid circulation rates, a feature that also contributes to lower pressure drop.

Passos and Mujumdar[29] investigated the effects of cohesive forces on the spouting of wet particles in a two-dimensional column (see Table 12.2) and evaluated the dynamic parameters for different liquid contents by changing the amount of glycerol injected into the bed. They observed that, as the bed was operated at a low liquid content, ΔP_{ms} of the wet bed was initially greater than for the dry bed. As the liquid content increased, ΔP_{ms} dropped to values as low as 50 percent of the dry bed value (see Figure 12.2).

Table 12.2. Studies investigating the effect of paste on spouted bed dynamics.

Paste or liquid	Bed dimensions	Inert materials	Variables investigated
Glycerol, distilled water (BF)[28]	CCSB; $\theta = 60°$ $D = 0.15$ m $D_i = 0.02$ m	Glass spheres Acrylic resin spheres PVC cylinders Irregular particles	$\Delta P^{ms} = f(V^l)$ $H_f = f(U_{ms})$ $U_{ms} = f(V_l, T)$
Glycerol, water (BF)[4]	CCSB; $\theta = 65°$ $D = 0.15$ m $D_i = 0.02$ m	Glass spheres PVC cylinders Acrylic resin spheres	$\Delta P_{ms}/\Delta P_{ms0} = f(V_l/V_t, \mu)$ $H_f = f(V_l/V_t, t)$ $U_{ms}/U_{ms0} = f(V_l/V_t)$ $U_{ms} = f(t)$
Animal blood; homogenized chicken egg; water (CF)[16]	CcSB; $\theta = 60°$ $D = 0.3$ m $D_i = 0.05$ m	Glass spheres	$\Delta P_{ms}/\Delta P^{ms0} = f(Q_p)$ $U_{ms}/U_{ms0} = f(Q_p)$
Glycerol (BF)[29]	2DSB $L_1 = 0.2$ m $L_2 = 0.015$ m $L_N = 0.015$ m	Plastic pellets	$\Delta P_{ms}/\Delta P_{ms0} = f(V_l/V_p)$ $U_{ms}/U_{ms0} = f(V_l/V_p)$
Glycerol; homogenized egg paste (CF, BF)[16,19]	CcSB; $\theta = 60°$ $D = 0.3$ m $D_i = 0.05$ m	Glass spheres	$\Delta P_{ms}/\Delta P_{ms0} = f(s)$ $U_{ms}/U_{ms0} = f(s)$
Modified and in-nature mango pulps (BF)[15]	CCSB; $\theta = 60°$ $D = 0.13$ m $D_i = 0.03$ m	Polyethylene particles	$\Delta P_{ms}/\Delta P_{ms0} = f(t)$ $H_f/H_f0 = f(t)$ $U_{ms}/U_{ms0} = f(V_l/V_p)$
Sewage sludge, egg paste, carbonate solutions (BF)[23]	CcSB; $\theta = 60°$ $D = 0.47$ m $D_i = 0.05$ m	Glass spheres	$\Delta P_{ms}/\Delta P_{ms0} = f(s, t)$ $H_f/H_{f0} = f(s, t)$ $U_{ms}/U_{ms0} = f(s, t)$

(BF) batch feeding of paste; (CF) continuous feeding; 2DSB two-dimensional spouted bed

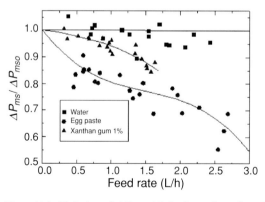

Figure 12.2. Variation of ΔP_{ms} with feed rate (based on data from Spitzner Neto et al.[16]).

This behavior agrees with data from other authors[30,31] and is attributed to differences in the nature of interaction forces developed by the liquid bridges as the liquid content increases.

At low liquid content, weak liquid bridges are formed and the liquid acts as a lubricant, increasing the solid circulation rate and the pressure drop at minimum spouting. As the liquid content increases and approaches a critical value (which is a function of inert material and liquid characteristics), the thickness of the coating layer formed over the particles grows, and stronger liquid bridges are formed. The mean voidage of the annulus is reduced, as well as the solids circulation rate, causing a decrease in pressures drop. Bacelos et al.[19] measured a small increase in ΔP_{ms} at low liquid contents in batch feeding experiments (with glycerol) and continuous feeding experiments (with homogenized egg paste). As the variation was within the range of experimental accuracy, however, the authors assumed that ΔP_{ms} was not significantly affected by the paste. Physical and rheological characteristics of the paste also affect ΔP_{ms}, as illustrated in Figure 12.2, which shows experimental data obtained for water, homogenized egg paste, and xanthan gum solutions.[16] Almeida[23] observed that the ΔP_{ms} behavior may change as a result of varying the concentration of a given paste. By operating a spouted bed with carbonate solutions of different concentrations, the author showed that the pressure drop decreased for solutions with concentration close to 3 percent, but increased for 9 percent concentrated solutions. At intermediate carbonate concentrations of 5 percent, both types of behavior were observed, depending on the feed rate. Higher feed rates usually led to a decrease in pressure drop, behavior attributed to spouting instabilities generated by liquid accumulation in the bed.

12.3.2   Minimum spouting velocity

Results obtained for minimum spouting velocity of wet beds are contradictory, particularly for beds containing glycerol. Schneider and Bridgwater[4] identified an initial increase in U_{ms} at low glycerol contents and a decrease after spouting with a maximum glycerol content. Some researchers[16,19,28] measured a reduction in U_{ms} as the glycerol content increased, as a result of the lower solids circulation rates observed in wet beds, as discussed previously. With lower solids circulation rates, a smaller air velocity is required to maintain spouting. However, in a "two-dimensional spouted bed" (see Chapter 17) operating with glass beads and polypropylene particles, Passos and Mujumdar[29] reported an increase of U_{ms} with glycerol content. A similar result was reported by Santana et al.,[31] who operated a half-column conical spouted bed. The different bed geometries employed by those authors may be partly responsible for these apparently contradictory results; additional research is needed for a conclusive analysis.

For liquids and pastes other than glycerol, several authors reported a decrease in U_{ms} as the paste content increased.[16,19] These authors mentioned that the dynamic behavior of conventional pastes is very different from that in beds wetted by water or even glycerol (see Figure 12.3). The distinct behavior may be attributed to differences in interaction forces on the particles: whereas only liquid bridges are formed with glycerol, conventional pastes generate different kinds of bridges, associated with powder formation as the coating material dries.[18] As already mentioned, experimental results indicate that the moisture content in the film of paste coating the spouted particles is very similar to the moisture content of the collected powder,[16,19,23] thus corroborating that the particles at that stage are not linked by liquid bridges.

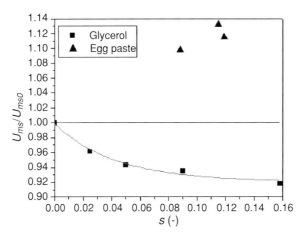

Figure 12.3. Variation of U_{ms} with saturation degree (based on data from Spitzner Neto et al.[16]).

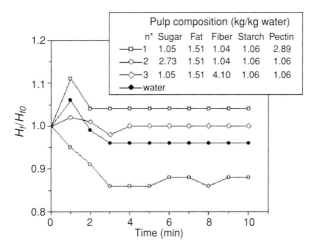

Figure 12.4. Effect of paste composition on fountain height (based on data reported by Medeiros[33]).

12.3.3   Fountain height

In dry beds, the fountain height increases as the airflow rate is raised. In wet beds, stable spouting is not achieved at short fountain heights owing to the stronger interparticle forces, which require greater airflow rates to maintain spouting.[4,28] In tests with glycerol, Spitzner Neto[32] verified experimentally that the fountain height increased as the amount of liquid fed to the bed increased, maintaining a spheroidal contour and linear dependence on the airflow rate. Medeiros et al.[15] carried out drying experiments for pulps of different tropical fruits, in batch operation, a condition for which both the paste rheology and the bed saturation changed with time. They compared fountain heights measured with time for dry and wet beds and observed a marked dependence of fountain height on pulp composition (see Figure 12.4).

From the previous discussion, it is clear that the presence of paste influences such hydrodynamic parameters as ΔP_{ms}, U_{ms}, and H_f. Paste also affects bed voidage, permeability, solid circulation rate, and other fluid dynamic parameters. Despite the evidence from many experimental studies, however, it is still not possible to predict reliably the effect of the liquid on the fluid dynamics for a given paste. A severe shortcoming is that the modeling of the fluid dynamics of wet spouted beds has so far not been successful in effectively incorporating the paste characteristics into the description of the spouting dynamics. Advances in modeling of the drying process on inert particles are considered next.

12.4 Modeling of drying

Modeling of flow in a spouted bed commonly considers the three different regions (spout, annulus, and fountain) separately, to take into account their distinct structures. It is difficult to describe the complex circulation dynamics and particle–paste–air interactions. Modeling attempts have relied on three main approaches: (1) totally empirical, (2) based on differential or integral balances applied over each bed region, and (3) based on analysis of interparticle forces.

Models based on dimensionless groups arranged empirically, aided by physical or statistical procedures, may be useful for preliminary investigations and to enhance physical understanding of the phenomenon under study. They have not been consistently applied to model the drying of pastes in spouted beds and are not treated here. An example of such an application may be found elsewhere.[34]

12.4.1 Models derived from heat and mass transfer balances

Models based on differential or integral balances are listed in Table 12.3. The assumptions adopted are not always physically consistent, but some authors have shown that by arbitrarily fitting thermal and mass parameters, it is possible to obtain good predictions for drying rates, outlet air humidity, and outlet air temperature.

The models originally proposed by Kmiec[35] and Pham[8] were implemented by Oliveira[37] to describe water evaporation and drying of animal blood in a conical bed of $D = 300$ mm. Modified versions of the original models were also proposed, including an additional term to take into account thermal losses through the column walls. In two of these models it was assumed that evaporation occurs mainly in the annulus,[8] a hypothesis contradicted by experimental data, as, according to Oliveira, only about 40 percent of evaporation occurred in this region.[37] Nonetheless, good predictions of evaporation rates and humidity at the bed exit were obtained with both Pham's original model and the modified version, with deviations within ± 10 percent. The model of Kmiec[35] yielded larger deviations. Only the modified version of Pham's model provided good estimates of gas outlet temperature, with deviations in the range of ± 10 percent.[37] The mass and thermal parameters in the model were fitted from experimental data obtained in the same equipment. Thermal parameters were fitted from experiments on heat transfer in

Table 12.3. Models describing paste drying in spouting with inert particles.

Model	Model characteristics	Assumptions and shortcomings
Kmiec[35]	Global model (based on drying of particulate solids)	– Every particle is coated with an identical mass of paste – Heat exchange only between the gas and moist coating – Negligible thermal losses
Pham[8]	Based on application of enthalpy balances for gas and particles	– Drying occurs only in the annulus – Paste does not affect bed dynamic patterns – Negligible thermal losses
Barrett and Fane[10]	Qualitative model	– Paste does not affect bed dynamics – Requires a very complex mathematical analysis
Oliveira and Passos[36]	Bed is divided into n segments, and mass and energy balances are applied to each	– Evaporation and convective heat transfer occur only in the annulus – Bed dynamics are not affected by the paste – Inert particles have no film coating as they enter the spout – Spout air has constant humidity, which is equal to that at the entrance
Almeida[23]	Model applies global mass and energy balances with a lumped approach	– Bed is modeled as a well-mixed vessel – Each paste requires a fitted equation to describe drying kinetics

the dry bed. Mass transfer parameters were obtained from experiments involving water evaporation and drying of animal blood and 10 percent concentrated $Al(OH)_3$ suspensions. The Lewis analogy for heat and mass transfer was verified for the experimental conditions investigated. Because the model has not been confirmed using parameters estimated from literature correlations, there is insufficient evidence that Pham's model can be generalized to other experimental conditions.

Almeida[23] applied lumped heat and mass transfer balances to predict gas outlet temperatures and air humidities with time in transient drying of pastes in a spouted bed of inert particles. The fitted kinetic equations varied according to both the type of paste and its feed rate. This lumped approach provided very good predictions for these variables, but it also depended on a fitting procedure for the drying rate, which must be performed individually for each paste.

12.4.2   Models derived from analysis of interparticle forces

Interparticle forces are extremely important in the analysis of dynamic behavior of inert particles in spouted beds containing pastes. In a review of these forces in wet fluidized beds, Seville et al.[38] have mentioned the presence of Van der Waals forces, as well as forces created by liquid bridges and sintering. The size of spouted bed particles is usually in the range of 1 to 6 mm. For such large particles, Van der Waals forces are not expected to be significant, as compared with the other two. Liquid bridges exhibit both dynamic and static forces and are dissipative of energy. The static liquid bridge force results from the sum of the surface tension force and the force arising from the pressure deficit in the liquid bridge.[38] The viscous force (dynamic) is caused by the resistance offered to liquid flow in the radial direction of a liquid bridge, and, unlike the static force, always opposes relative motion.

The magnitude of the interaction forces owing to the presence of a liquid depends on the liquid saturation level, given by the ratio of liquid and particle volumes. The interaction force is a function of a number of variables, such as the amount of liquid, the surface tension, contact angle between liquid and particle, distance between the particles, and particle geometry.[39,40] If a small amount of liquid is added to a system, enough only to form a thin film coating the particles, cohesiveness increases because the liquid smoothes the particle surface roughness by filling irregularities and decreasing the specific surface area. The liquid will also reduce the separation distances among particles, allowing electrostatic forces to become more significant. When the amount of liquid is sufficient to fill all the interparticle voids, the system is in the capillary state, in which particles are bonded by the capillary suction forces acting at the air–liquid interfaces on the particle surfaces. When the particles are completely immersed in the liquid, the system is in an overcapillary state, and the adhesion is caused by surface tension on the liquid convex surfaces.

Solid bridges are stronger than liquid ones and may be generated by sintering, chemical reaction, particle fusion, recrystallization, and evaporation.[39–41] Only those formed by evaporation occur in the drying of pastes on inert particles.

Passos and Mujumdar[29] identified the types of interaction forces developed in wet spouted and fluidized beds by adding metered amounts of glycerol. They pointed out that these forces can affect gas and solid flows, leading to uncontrollable particle agglomeration and poor gas–solid contact. They also showed that spout formation and bed collapse in wet beds differ for spherical and nonspherical particles. They proposed an empirical model for predicting ΔP_{ms} and U_{ms} in wet beds of nonspherical particles and the minimum conditions for the internal spouting regime in wet two-dimensional beds of spherical particles. The models yielded good predictions of U_{ms} and ΔP_{ms} in beds with glycerol, but observed that the predicted trends contradict some literature data obtained with conventional pastes.

To predict the minimum spouting velocity in wet beds, Spitzner Neto et al.[16] developed a model based on the analysis of interaction forces in the annulus. They applied the model to the drying of animal blood and homogenized egg paste. Their model assumes that the particles in the annulus form a huge particle-agglomerate that offers the major resistance to fluid dynamic circulation. It also considers that the air velocity at minimum spouting is the minimum value required to break particle bonds. At this condition, the force of the airflow on the particle-agglomerate would represent the maximum resistance offered by the agglomerate. This force has been estimated from the interparticle forces and liquid saturation in the bed. Another simplifying assumption is that the drag force required for spouting the wet particles is given by the drag force in the dry bed plus the cohesive forces acting on the wet particles. The pressure drop over the particle-agglomerate has been estimated from the Ergun[42] equation, and only liquid bridges were considered. The theory of Schubert et al.[39] was employed to estimate the magnitude of the liquid bridge interaction forces.

This modeling led to an equation for estimating U_{ms} in wet beds for a given saturation rate, given the liquid saturation and U_{ms0} (minimum spouting velocity for the dry bed). U_{ms} in the final equation is also a function of a number of other variables, such as the bed height, bed surface diameter, air inlet diameter, resistive tension between two particles, and total number of particles. The authors compared the model predictions with experimental values obtained from drying egg paste at 60 °C and reported poor agreement, with estimates always higher than experimental values. This poor performance was attributed to overestimation of the magnitude of interaction forces by the model, consistent with the conclusion that particle cohesion is associated mainly with interaction forces among particles coated by a low-moisture powder, rather than by liquid.

The discrepancies in the trends predicted by the model of Passos and Mujumdar[29] and those verified experimentally in beds operating with real pastes indicate that glycerol should not be used as a standard paste to simulate a wet bed. A real paste shows a very different wetting pattern and suffers significant changes in rheological properties during the process. It is added into the bed either as a liquid or as a high-moisture-content slurry, but its compositon changes dramatically during drying, with the liquid or paste turning into a low-moisture-content powder. These changes are not accounted for in the model. The same shortcomings apply to the model of Sptizner Neto et al.,[16] which considered neither the paste composition changes nor the existence of dynamic forces linking the particles.

Employing interparticle forces to model the drying of pastes in beds of inert particles is appealing, but considerable further investigation is required to achieve consistent modeling and reasonable results. Microscopic measurements of interaction forces, such as those reported by Pagliai et al.[43] for wet fluidized beds, are still lacking for wet spouted beds. The evidence obtained so far is all based on macroscopic measurements of bed dynamic parameters, such as ΔP_s and U_{ms}. The evidence that in steady-state operation the particles are coated by a low-moisture powder, rather than by a liquid, must also be incorporated into the modeling.

12.5   Final remarks

In this chapter, a review of the published developments in paste drying on inert particles since 1974 has been presented. An extensive list of materials that have been dried successfully has been found, which is encouraging, but it is obvious that considerable further work is required to investigate paste drying and design of efficient dryers. An analysis on drying of sludge from metals finishing wastewater treatment plants showed that a spouted bed is cost-competitive with conventional technology.[11] The main focus of recent research is to study how paste composition affects drying behavior, and a few contributions on this topic have already been published.[15,23] Another aspect demanding attention is scaleup: most studies have been conducted in small dryers, with diameters from 0.15 to 0.5 m, and very few investigators have operated dryers of diameter greater than 0.5 m. Scaleup, however, is challenging.

As far as transport parameters are concerned, it is clear that the paste affects not only the dynamic behavior of the bed, but also heat and mass transfer phenomena. Most experimental investigations, however, still focus on fluid dynamic parameters (ΔP_s, U_{ms}, particle circulation, etc.). Thermal and mass transfer parameters need further investigation.

The modeling of drying on inert particles has not yet been successful in faithfully describing the process. Simulations are far from providing good predictions of process variables, and no model may be safely recommended. No model has succeeded in incorporating the effects of the presence of a paste on the bed dynamics or in describing the complex changes observed as the liquid becomes a powder during the drying. Models based on interparticle forces are promising, but require more realistic assumptions. Finally, there is some evidence that the particles used as a support for drying do not really constitute an inert material. This is another aspect that demands further investigation.

Chapter-specific nomenclature

Q_a	Volumetric airflow rate, m^3/s
Q_p	Volumetric paste or solution feed rate, m^3/s
s	Saturation degree, defined as $(1 - \varepsilon)V_l/(\varepsilon V_p)$
V	Bed volume, m^3
V_l	Solution or paste volume, m^3
V_p	Volume of particles in the bed, m^3
V_t	Volume of the static bed of particles, m^3
φ	Particle sphericity

Subscripts

0	Property of dry bed
i	Inlet conditions
N	Nozzle
o	Outlet conditions

References

1. C. Strumillo, A. Markowiski, and W. Kaminski. Modern developments in drying of pastelike materials. In *Advances in Drying*, vol. 2, ed. A. S. Mujumdar (Washington, DC: McGraw-Hill, 1983), pp. 193–231.
2. K. B. Mathur and N. Epstein. *Spouted Beds* (New York: Academic Press, 1974).
3. C. R. F. Souza and W. P. Oliveira. Spouted bed drying of *Bauhinia forticata* link extract: the effects of feed atomizer position and operating conditions on equipment performance and product properties. *Braz. J. Chem. Eng.*, **22** (2005), 239–247.
4. T. Schneider and J. Bridgwater. The stability of wet spouted beds. *Drying Technol.*, **11** (1993), 277–301.

5. T. Szentmarjay and E. Pallai. Drying of suspensions in a modified spouted bed dryer with an inert packing. *Drying Technol.*, **7** (1989), 523–536.

6. A. Reyes, G. Díaz, and R. Blasco. Slurry drying in gas-particle contactors: fluid-dynamics and capacity analysis. *Drying Technol.*, **16** (1998), 217–233.

7. A. S. Markowski. Quality interaction in a jet spouted bed dryer for bio-products. *Drying Technol.*, **11** (1993), 369–387.

8. Q. T. Pham. Behavior of a conical spouted-bed dryer for animal blood. *Can. J. Chem. Eng.*, **61** (1983), 426–434.

9. M. I. Ré and J. T. Freire. Drying of pastelike materials in spouted beds. In *Drying '89*, ed. A. S. Mujumdar and M. A. Roques (New York: Hemisphere, 1989), pp. 426–432.

10. H. Barrett and A. Fane. Drying of liquid materials in a spouted bed. In *Drying '89*, ed. A. S. Mujumdar and M. A. Roques (New York: Hemisphere, 1990), pp. 415–420.

11. C. Brereton and C. J. Lim. Spouted bed drying of sludge from metals processing industry wastewater treatment plants. *Drying Technol.*, **11** (1993), 389–399.

12. Q. Guo, S. Hikida, Y. Takahashi, N. Nakagawa, and K. Kato. Drying of microparticle slurry and salt-water solution by a powder-particle spouted bed. *J. Chem. Eng. of Japan*, **29** (1996), 152–158.

13. J. Xu, S. Osada, and K. Kato. Limiting efficiency for continuous drying of micro-particle slurries in a powder-particle spouted bed. *J. Chem. Eng. of Japan*, **31** (1998), 35–40.

14. R. L. Cunha, K. G. Maialle, and F. C. Menegalli. Evaluation of drying process in spouted bed and spout fluidized bed of xanthan gum: focus on product quality. *Powder Technol.*, **107** (2000), 234–242.

15. M. F. D. Medeiros, S. C. S. Rocha, O. L. S. Alsina, C. E. M. Jerônimo, U. K. L. Medeiros, and A. L. M. L. da Mata. Drying of pulps of tropical fruits in spouted bed: effect of composition on drying performance. *Drying Technol.*, **20** (2002), 855–881.

16. P. I. Spitzner Neto, F. O. Cunha, and J. T. Freire. Effect of the presence of paste in a conical spouted bed dryer with continuous feeding. *Drying Technol.*, **20** (2002), 789–811.

17. M. L. Passos, A. L. G. Trindade, J. V. H. d'Angelo, and M. Cardoso. Drying of black liquor in spouted bed of inert particles. *Drying Technol.*, **22** (2004), 1041–1067.

18. D. S. Cordeiro and W. P. Oliveira. Technical aspects of the production of dried extract of *Maytenus ilicifolia* leaves by jet spouted bed drying. *Int. J. Pharmac.*, **299** (2005), 115–126.

19. M. S. Bacelos, P. I. Spitzner Neto, A. M. Silveira, and J. T. Freire. Analysis of fluid dynamics behavior of conical spouted beds. *Drying Technol.*, **23** (2005), 427–453.

20. M. Benali and M. Amazou. Drying of vegetable starch solutions on inert particles: quality and energy aspects. *J. Food Eng.*, **74** (2006), 484–489.

21. E. Pallai-Varsányi, J. Tóth, and J. Gyenis. Dying of suspensions and solutions on inert particle surface in mechanically spouted bed dryer. *China Particuology*, **5** (2007), 337–344.

22. S. Wachiraphansakul and S. Devahastin. Drying kinetics and quality of okara dried in a jet spouted bed. *LW*, **40** (2007), 207–219.

23. A. R. F. Almeida. Analysis of paste drying in a spouted bed. PhD thesis, Federal Univ. of São Carlos, Brazil (in Portuguese) (2009).

24. K. W. Allen. "At forty comes understanding" – a review of some basics of adhesion over the past four decades. *Int. J. Adhesion & Adhesive*, **23** (2003), 87–93.

25. C. Gay. Stickiness – some fundamentals of adhesion. *Integr. Comp. Biol.*, **42** (2002), 1123–1126.

26. F. P. Collares, J. R. D. Finzer, and T. G. Kieckbush. Glass transition control of the detachment of food pastes dried over glass plates. *J. Food Eng.*, **61** (2004), 261–267.

27. C. C. Rodrigues. Analysis of the drying of suspensions in spouted bed with inert particles. M.Sc. dissertation, Federal Univ. of São Carlos, Brazil (in Portuguese) (1993).

28. K. Patel, J. Bridgwater, C. G. J. Baker, and T. Schneider. Spouting behavior of wet solids. In *Drying '86*, ed. A. S. Mujumdar and M. A. Roques (New York: Hemisphere, 1986), pp. 183–189.

29. M. L. Passos and A. S. Mujumdar. Effect of cohesive forces on fluidized and spouted beds on wet particles. *Powder Technol.*, **110** (2000), 222–238.

30. M. L. Passos, A. S. Mujumdar, and G. S. V. Raghavan. Spouting and spout-fluidization of dry-wet particles in a two-dimensional bed. In *Drying of Solids*, ed. A. S. Mujumdar (New Delhi: Sarita, Prakaschan, 1990), pp. 211–220.

31. J. D. A. Santana, A. L. T. Charbel, M. L. Passos, and G. Massarani. Effect of interparticle forces on the spouted bed flow behavior. In *Proceedings of IADC '97* (Itu, SP, Brazil: Univ. of Campinas Press, 1997), vol. A, pp. 135–142.

32. P. I. Spitzner Neto. Study of paste drying and fluid dynamics of spouted beds in the presence of pastes and liquids. Ph.D. thesis, Federal Univ. of São Carlos, Brazil (in Portuguese) (2001).

33. M. F. D. Medeiros. Influence of the material properties on the drying of pulp fruit in spouted beds. Ph.D. thesis, Univ. of Campinas, Brazil (in Portuguese) (2001).

34. I. Taruna and V. K. Jindal. Drying of soy pulp (okara) in a bed of inert particles. *Drying Technol.*, **20** (2002), 1035–1051.

35. A. Kmiec. Simultaneous heat and mass transfer in spouted beds. *Can. J. Chem. Eng.*, **53** (1975), 18–24.

36. I. M. Oliveira and M. L. Passos. Simulation of drying suspension in a conical spouted bed. *Drying Technol.*, **15** (1997), 593–604.

37. W. P. Oliveira. Study of paste drying in conical spouted bed. Ph.D. thesis, Federal Univ. of São Carlos, Brazil (in Portuguese) (1996).

38. J. P. K. Seville, C. D. Willet, and P. C. Knight. Interparticle forces in fluidization: a review. *Powder Technol.*, **113** (2000), 261–268.

39. H. Schubert, W. Herrmann, and H. Rumpf. Deformation behaviour of agglomerates under tensile stress. *Powder Technol.*, **11** (1975), 121–131.

40. H. Schubert. Principles of agglomeration. *Int. Chem. Engng.*, **21** (1981), 363–377.

41. P. J. Sherrington and R. Oliver. *Granulation* (London: Heyden and Sons, 1981).

42. S. Ergun. Fluid flow through packed columns. *Chem. Eng. Progr.*, **48**:2 (1952), 89–94.

43. P. Pagliai, S. J. R. Simons, and D. Kudra. Towards a fundamental understanding of deflu-idisation at high temperatures: a micro-mechanistic approach. *Powder Technol.*, **148** (2004), 106–112.

13 Granulation and particle coating

Sandra Cristina dos Santos Rocha and Osvaldir Pereira Taranto

13.1   Introduction

Particle coating and granulation have attracted increasing attention in the past decade, with the objective of modifying particle physical and physicochemical properties. The increasing interest has appeared in several industrial sectors, such as the chemical, food, pharmaceutical, iron ore, agricultural, and nuclear industries. Cosmetics, flavorings, essences, enzymes, proteins, vegetables, seeds, fertilizers, sweets and candies, drugs, pigments, and nuclear fuel microspheres are examples of products that have been modified by coating or granulation processes.[1-4]

Until the 1950s, rotary panels or drums were the predominant types of equipment for particle coating and granulation. Since then, new equipment and processes have been implemented by the pharmaceutical industry, owing to the replacement of tablets coated with sugar solutions by those coated with polymer films. In this new equipment, a suspension or solution is atomized on particles suspended by hot air. A thin film is deposited on the particle surfaces and dried by the hot air as the particles circulate through the chamber. Among the equipment, spouted beds, including Wurster coaters (Chapter 14) and other designs, are intended to improve the process performance and fluid dynamics – for example, by applying vibration and adding draft tubes.[5-12]

The choice of the most adequate equipment depends on the physical properties of the particles to be coated, as well as on the coating material. The process conditions are also critical to obtain a good-quality coated product. Fluidized and spouted beds[1,13] have been extensively used recently, mainly for the film coating of particles.[14-21] This application of spouted beds is justified by its fluid dynamic characteristics, such as good particle circulation, guaranteeing product homogeneity and effective solid–fluid contact, as well as high rates of heat and mass transfer. Spouted beds also offer the possibility of process automation and use of the same equipment for other applications such as granulation, drying, and coating of other products.

In the coating and granulation processes, the properties of the final product are determined by the equipment geometry, operating conditions, coating material formulation, and characteristics of the material to be coated.[22-25] The gas distributor and the column geometry determine the particle dynamics in the bed, thereby influencing the process

Spouted and Spout-Fluid Beds: Fundamentals and Applications, eds. Norman Epstein and John R. Grace.
Published by Cambridge University Press. © Cambridge University Press 2011.

performance. The type and position of the spray nozzle are also important, as they govern droplet formation and drying of agglomerates, consequently affecting process efficiency.

Operating variables such as particle loading and spouting airflow rate also have a direct impact on the formation of agglomerates and on film drying because of their influence on bed fluid flow, particle dynamics, and regime stability. Another key process parameter is the air temperature, which affects the drying, and hence agglomerate formation. Atomization conditions, such as air and coating material, must be chosen to avoid the formation of large droplets, which are difficult to dry and favor the formation of unwanted agglomerates. At the same time, it is important to avoid the formation of very small droplets, which dry too quickly, even before reaching the particles. The coating material flowrate must also be balanced with the solvent evaporation capacity, controlling formation of agglomerates and premature drying of suspended droplets.

The film-forming material is usually a polymer for film-type coating processes and therefore a factor limiting the process thermal conditions. The choice of polymer depends on the specific coating objectives; its concentration affects the processing time and coating quality; its temperature influences the viscosity, and consequently droplet formation and particle agglomeration; its surface tension and contact angle, responsible for adhesion of droplets to the solid surface, directly affect the process performance. The solvent determines the thermal conditions and the requirement for safety.

Physical properties of the particulate material to be coated, such as shape, size, and cohesiveness, directly affect the fluid dynamics and, as a consequence, help to govern the drying and coating distribution, thus influencing the process and the final product quality. It is also known that the success of the coating depends on the wettability of the solution, suspension, or hot melt on the particle surface. The wettability (characterized by the contact angle) depends on the solid surface characteristics and the liquid surface tension.

13.2   Granulating and coating mechanisms

Because the "industrial art" of coating and granulation originated in several relatively independent industries, terminology tends to be confusing. The term *coating* is sometimes applied indiscriminately to all processes in which material is added to a solid surface. For instance, extruded pellets, containing several particles, may be called coated particles. The terms *coating*, *granulation*, *balling*, *pelletization*, and *agglomeration* are sometimes used interchangeably, and the particles resulting from those processes may be called *granules*, *balls*, *pellets*, or *agglomerates*.[22] However, the terms more commonly used are *agglomeration* or *granulation*, *coating* (or *film coating*), and *hot melt coating*, depending on the definitions and mechanisms described in the following subsections.[22,26]

13.2.1   Granulation or agglomeration

In granulation or agglomeration, granules are formed by atomization, followed by drying of a bonding liquid on their surface. This bonding solution or suspension (e.g., of sugar or starch) spreads over the particles and builds liquid bridges between the original

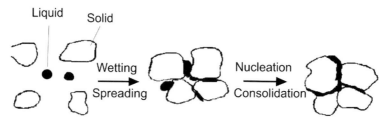

Figure 13.1. Formation of agglomerates.

particles, as shown in Figure 13.1. The liquid bridges are then dried by hot air, resulting in agglomerates. When the liquid is atomized continuously, the particles continue to agglomerate, causing growth of the granule. During the growth process, smaller particles may also be produced because of attrition among particles, or even among the agglomerates themselves.

Granulation or agglomeration is carried out to achieve one or several of the following objectives: improved flowability, better handling and compression, desired particle size distribution, preferred shape, modified particle density, improved appearance, better dissolution time, or simply elimination of fine particles. The desirable characteristics of an agglomerated product are dust-free granules of optimum size distribution depending on the application, low rigidity, low apparent density, porous structure, good dispersibility, and excellent solubility.

13.2.2   Film coating

Fluidized and spouted beds with top, bottom, or tangential atomization can be used to perform film coating on the surface of particles of a wide range of diameters. Objectives are to improve the particle appearance; mask unpleasant taste and/or odor; improve flow properties; reduce the tendency to agglomerate; prevent formation of cakes or lumps; improve product dispersion in solvents; avoid generation of dust or powder; reduce losses and handling hazards; protect the product from atmospheric humidity, light, or heat; isolate incompatible substances (by keeping one in the particle nucleus and the other in the coating); control the release of active components; and diminish side effects, especially for pharmaceutical agents.

The coating material can be a solution, suspension, emulsion, latex, or hot melt (as described below), resulting in a film. The key components of a film-coating formulation are a polymer, a plasticizer, pigments, and a solvent. The most common polymers are cellulose and acrylic derivatives, usually dissolved in water or organic solvents. Polymers that are insoluble in water, such as methylcellulose, can still be used as aqueous dispersions.[27] The desired characteristics of film coatings are small variation of the product weight (usually from 2% to 8%), size, and shape; short processing times; high process efficiency; flexibility in coating formulation; and good resistance of the film to attrition conditions or exposure to light and humidity.

Film coating is a complex dynamic process that involves formation of coating material droplets, contact and spreading of droplets on the particle surface (providing that the

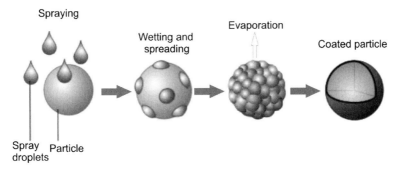

Figure 13.2. Film coating mechanism. Adapted from Glatt.[30]

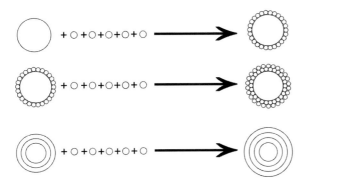

Figure 13.3. Coating by layer formation.

solid surface is wetted by the liquid), and evaporation of the solvent (Figure 13.2). In addition to interfacial properties, the spreading of the liquid on the solid surface is facilitated by low liquid viscosity and by small droplets.

The final product is obtained by deposition of several layers on each particle, as shown schematically in Figure 13.3.

Coated materials are expected to exhibit good stability, good flowability, smooth surfaces, prescribed colors, and other specific properties, defined for each case.

13.2.3 Hot melt coating

When coating with hot melt material, the coating agent is applied in its molten state, and solidifies on the surface of the particles. This type of process produces a desirable coverage, eliminating the solvent. The process mechanism is similar to film coating, except that solvent evaporation is replaced by cooling solidification of the coating material on the particle surface.

13.3 Advances in spouted bed granulation/coating

Granulation/coating in spouted beds is regarded in the literature as a single process consisting of injecting a liquid phase into a bed of particles or seeds to be granulated or coated, together with hot air to promote spouting. A thin layer of the liquid deposits on the particle surfaces as they pass through the atomization zone; this layer is then dried by hot air, while the particles travel up the central spout and then descend through the annulus.[1]

If liquid bridges form and then dry, leading to bonding of particles and growth by agglomeration, the product will be either a granule or an agglomerate. By controlling the process conditions, the process may result in layer-by-layer growth, leading to a coated product. The first patents covering this type of spouted bed application were obtained by Berquin[28] and Nichols.[29]

Spouted bed granulation/coating may be carried out in batches or continuously. Atomization of the suspension or solution can be performed at the top, at the bottom, or tangential to the bed. One coating/granulation equipment manufacturer[30] lists the following capacities for film coating:

Batch systems:

- From 2 g to 1,500 kg/batch (top spray coating)
- From 50 g to 700 kg/batch (bottom spray coating)
- From 500 g to 250 kg/batch (tangential coating)

Continuous spouted bed coating: bottom spray – from 2 g to 3 metric tonnes per hour.

Brazilian Petrol S.A. described the operation of the first commercial urea granulation plant in Brazil, based on a multistage spout-fluid granulator.[31] This process is owned by Toyo Engineering Corporation (TOYO). This spout-fluid bed granulation process is applied in 17 urea plants worldwide, varying from 50 to 3250 tonnes/day production capacities.

The existence of a region of high porosity, high gas velocity, and high gas temperature at the bottom of the spouted bed makes it ideal for spraying liquids in continuous coating or granulation processes. The rapid evaporation in this zone causes the temperature of the gas to drop before the gas contacts the particles, making it possible to operate at high gas temperatures without thermal damage, but promoting high evaporation rates. The most important advantage of spouted beds for this type of operation is the cyclic and systematic particle movement, which results in a homogeneously coated product.

Figure 13.4 shows a schematic of a spouted bed batch granulation or coating system[72] with atomization at the bottom of the bed. Although this is the most popular configuration, top spray is also common, especially in laboratory-scale units.[32,17]

Experimental studies on spouted bed coating processes often analyze the influence of the operating conditions on the efficiency of film adhesion to the particle surface, to find appropriate conditions for a final product of good quality.

The efficiency of adhesion in a spouted bed coating process, defined as the ratio of the mass of solids adhering to the particles to the mass of solids supplied to the bed,[33] is given by

$$\eta = \frac{M_t - M_0}{Q_{sp}\rho_{sp}C\,t}. \qquad (13.1)$$

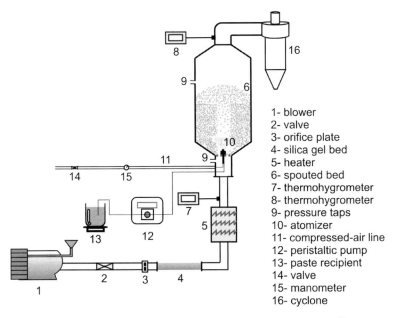

Figure 13.4. Experimental setup for spouted bed coating or granulation.[72]

This measure has been used by several researchers.[16,34–38] Several authors have verified that particles grow linearly with time. A growth constant is then represented by

$$K = \frac{m_{pt} - m_{p0}}{t}.$$ (13.2)

Empirical correlations for η and K, obtained by data fitting or from statistical analysis of factorial experimental design, are available in the literature for spouted bed coating of several products. For example, Kucharski and Kmiec[33] analyzed the coating of tablets with sucrose solution and obtained:

$$\frac{\eta}{\eta_{in}} = 0.3253 \mathrm{Re}_p^{1.089} \left(\frac{H_0}{d_p}\right)^{-0.0646} \left(\frac{W_{sp}}{W_{air}}\right)^{0.0393} (1 - C)^{1.0074} \phi^{-5.53},$$ (13.3)

where η_{in} is the efficiency of inertial fixation of the atomized droplets, given by

$$\eta_{in} = Stk^2/(Stk + 0.25)^{1.012}.$$ (13.4)

Here the Stokes number is defined as

$$Stk = \frac{d_p^{s\,2} \rho_{sp} u_{H=0.002m}}{36 \mu d_p}.$$ (13.5)

The Sauter mean diameter of the atomized droplets, d_p^s, can be estimated from the correlation of Nukiyama and Tanasawa,[39] whereas gas velocity at the central (spout) zone, $u_{H=0.002m}$, is estimated from the equation proposed by Kmiec,[40] or it can be simply taken as the orifice velocity.

In an investigation of coating alumina with aqueous solutions of sucrose and talc, Oliveira et al.[34] developed correlations for the growth coefficient and efficiency as a function of operating conditions:

$$K = 0.143 \left(\frac{W_{sp}}{W_{air}} \right)^{0.440} \left(\frac{Q_{air}}{Q_{ms}} \right)^{0.225} - 0.00817, \tag{13.6}$$

$$\eta = 6.05 \left(\frac{Q_{air}}{Q_{ms}} \right) - 1.944 \left(\frac{Q_{air}}{Q_{ms}} \right)^2 + 174.2 \left(\frac{W_{sp}}{W_{air}} \right) - 17980 \left(\frac{W_{sp}}{W_{air}} \right)^2 - 4.204. \tag{13.7}$$

Other authors have also found that the atomization pressure and air temperature influence process efficiency and particle growth kinetics. One correlation for process efficiency, working with independent encoded variables X_1 to X_4 (each within the -1 to $+1$ range), corresponding to spouting gas mass flowrate, spouting gas temperature, atomization pressure, and coating suspension mass flowrate, respectively, is[37]:

$$\eta = 67.80 - 6.15X_2 + 2.22X_3 + 2.72X_4 - 2.84X_1X_4 + 5.83X_2X_3$$
$$- 2.56X_2X_4 + 4.57X_3X_4 + 2.12X_1X_2X_3 - 3.29X_2X_3X_4. \tag{13.8}$$

This equation is based on a 2^4 factorial experimental design with four central points. Statistical analysis was applied to quantify and correlate the effects of operating independent variables on the process efficiency of urea coating with aqueous polymer suspension. The ranges of the independent variables included when developing this correlation were $1.33 \times 10^{-2} \leq W_{air} \leq 1.66 \times 10^{-2}$ kg/s; $50 \leq T_{air} \leq 70 \,°C$; $1.38 \times 10^2 \leq P_{at} \leq 2.07 \times 10^2$ kPa; and $1.077 \times 10^{-2} \leq W_{sp} \leq 1.425 \times 10^{-2}$ kg/s.

Empirical analyses of spouted bed coating operations for different products and a large range of experimental conditions are available in the literature. Some studies have also evaluated product quality and have provided results concerning such properties as uniformity, particle protection, and controlled release. Table 13.1 summarizes the main publications from which data are available.

High efficiencies are reported in all papers cited in Table 13.1, sometimes surpassing 95 percent, showing the viability of spouted beds for coating of particles. Some authors[16,47,49–52] have also confirmed the ability of this technology to provide a product of high quality.

Spouted bed coating of spherical submillimeter nuclear fuel kernels of uranium oxide or uranium carbide with pyrolytic carbon (pyC) and/or pyrolytic silicon carbide (SiC), to contain fission products generated in a high-temperature gas-cooled nuclear reactor, has been studied intensively.[53,75,58] The pyrocarbon can be generated[75] by thermal decomposition of methane[1] or of other hydrocarbons,[75] whereas the SiC is produced[76] by pyrolysis of methylsilane, various methylchlorosilanes, or mixtures of a hydrocarbon with either SiH_4 (silane) or $SiCl_4$. The coating process has typically been carried out in a conical-cylindrical spouted bed furnace of 55 to 130 mm ID at temperatures of 1450 °C for porous pyC coatings to 2150 °C for high-density isotropic pyC, and kernel charges of around 1 kg for each coating.[53] An earlier bistructural isotropic (BISO) fuel consisted

Table 13.1. Empirical analysis of granulation/coating in spouted beds.

Reference	Column geometry	Particle/process	Results
Weiss and Meisen[41]	Cone-cylindrical	Urea/coating with hot-melt sulfur	Process efficiency and product quality
Kucharski and Kmiec[42]	Cone-cylindrical	Tablets/coating with sucrose aqueous solution	Process efficiency and mass distribution on particles
Kucharski and Kmiec[33]	Cone-cylindrical	Tablets/coating with sucrose aqueous solution	Particle growth kinetics
Oliveira et al.[34]	Cone-cylindrical	Alumina/coating with sucrose and talc aqueous solution	Process efficiency and particle growth kinetics
Taranto et al.[15]	Cone-cylindrical	Tablets/film coating with aqueous polymeric suspension	Fluid dynamics and heat transfer
Barrozo et al.[36]	Cone-cylindrical	Soybean seed/coating with fertilizers	Particle growth
Oliveira et al.[35]	Cone-cylindrical	Tablets/film coating with aqueous polymeric suspension	Fluid dynamics and particle growth kinetics
Ayub et al.[43]	Two-dimensional	Urea/coating with hot-melt sulfur	Growth kinetics and process efficiency
Donida and Rocha[44]	Two-dimensional	Urea/film coating with aqueous polymeric suspension	Growth kinetics and process efficiency
Silva et al.[45]	Cone-cylindrical	Tablets/film coating with aqueous polymeric suspension	Process efficiency
Donida and Rocha[37]	Two-dimensional	Urea/film coating with aqueous polymeric suspension	Process efficiency and coating quality
Almeida[46]	Cone-cylindrical spouted and fluidized beds	Broccoli seeds/film coating with aqueous polymeric suspension	Process efficiency and coating quality
Pissinati and Oliveira[16]	Cone-cylindrical	Gelatinous capsules/film coating with aqueous polymeric suspension	Process efficiency and coating quality
Publio and Oliveira[47]	Cone-cylindrical	Tablets/film coating with aqueous polymeric suspension	Process efficiency and coating quality
Kfuri and Freitas[38]	Spout-fluid bed	Tablets/film coating with aqueous polymeric suspension	Process efficiency
Oliveira et al.[48]	Cone-cylindrical	Gelatinous capsules/film coating with aqueous polymeric suspension	Process efficiency
Martins et al.[49]	Cone-cylindrical	Gelatinous capsules/film coating with aqueous polymeric suspension	Process efficiency and coating quality
Borini et al.[50]	Cone-cylindrical	Excipient and dosage with acetaminophen/hot melt granulation with polyethylene glycol (MW 4000)	Particle growth and product quality

of ~0.8 mm kernels, each coated with an inner buffer layer of porous pyC under an outer layer of high-density pyC, to a final diameter of ~1 mm. Later, operation at higher temperature resulted in a tristructural isotropic (TRISO) fuel consisting of 0.5-mm or smaller kernels, each uniformly coated first by a thin layer of gas, then a porous buffer layer of low-density pyC, followed by a sealing layer of graphite powder treated with thermosetting resins, an inner isotropic SiC interlayer, and finally an outer envelope of high-density isotropic pyC, with the overall diameter approaching 1 mm.[53,58] More recent efforts[77] are exploring fuel designs that incorporate zirconium carbide, either as a supplementary layer or to replace the SiC.

The choice of spouting over fluidization for this coating process is dictated partly by its more systematic particle cycling, but mainly by the absence of a distributor plate, on which deposition of pyrolysis products could cause blockage.[1] Essentially the same technique has been used in pyrolytic coating of prosthetic devices, such as aortic heart valves and hip joints, with a biocompatible silicon–pyrocarbon alloy.[76] These devices are much larger and more complex in shape than nuclear fuel particles. They are distributed in a spouted bed of smaller inert particles, and their coatings are much thicker than for nuclear fuel particles. This bioengineering process, even more than nuclear fuel coating, thus gives rise to considerable particle segregation (Chapter 8), and has generated study of segregation,[54] as well as an account of the differences between thermochemical coating in the nuclear and bioengineering areas.[55]

Simulation and modeling have also been applied to spouted bed coating and granulation. Models have been based both on basic conservation equations[56–59] and on population balances.[2,32,60,61] For example, Piña et al.[62] proposed a model to describe a silicon chemical vapor deposition (CVD) spouted-bed reactor. A phenomenological model including hydrodynamics, interphase mass exchange between the different regions of the bed, and kinetic rates for heterogeneous and homogeneous reactions was implemented, together with a population balance accounting for growth and agglomeration of silicon particles. Such models contribute to understanding the complex simultaneous phenomena involved in particle granulation/coating in a spouted bed. They may also assist in achieving reliable scaleup from pilot to industrial units.

13.4   Surface properties influencing granulation/coating processes

Recent studies on granulation in fluidized beds and particle coating in spouted beds have evaluated the influence of particle and suspension properties on adhesion and, therefore, on the characteristics of the final product and process efficiency. In addition to liquid viscosity, density, and surface tension, which directly influence the coating by affecting atomization, the suspension-particle wettability is an important factor in determining process performance.[20,63–68]

For liquids, surface tension plays a crucial role with respect to adhesion. If the liquid wets the surface, it spreads on the solid surface. An adhesive of low energy levels or low surface tension is readily adsorbed by high-energy-level solids; the contact angle decreases and the wetting is effective. If the solid surface has a lower energy, the contact angle is high and wetting is poor.[69] Wettability, the ability of a drop to wet and spread on the surface of a particle, governs the adhesion and growth rate of particles in coating processes.[66,70–72] It can be quantified by the contact angle formed by the three phases: solid, liquid, and gas. The contact angle is a property of the solid–liquid–gas system,

Table 13.2. Suspension compositions (% by mass) in coating study of Rocha et al.[68]

Suspension composition (mass %)	HEC	Polyethylene glycol (PEG)	Magnesium stearate	Titanium dioxide	Tween 80®	Colorant	Talc	Water
1	5.5	0.75	1.0	1.25	–	1.0	3.5	87.0
2	3.5	0.75	–	1.25	1.0	1.0	3.5	89.0
3	3.5	0.75	1.0	1.25	–	1.0	3.5	89.0

HEC = Hydroxyethylcellulose

Table 13.3. Contact angles of particle-suspensions in coating study of Rocha et al.[68]

	Contact angle (degrees)			
Material	Glass	ABS®	PS*	PP*
Suspension 1	37.8 ± 1.4	70.4 ± 1.4	76.7 ± 2.4	79.0 ± 2.3
Suspension 2	34.9 ± 2.4	54.3 ± 3.5	57.5 ± 3.3	70.9 ± 2.4
Suspension 3	37.9 ± 2.3	70.0 ± 1.5	79.5 ± 1.6	80.9 ± 1.2

*PS = polystyrene; PP = polypropylene

depending on characteristics of both the liquid (e.g., surface tension) and the solid (e.g., hygroscopicity, roughness, and surface tension).

In the study of Rocha and Donida,[68] glass beads, ABS®, polypropylene (PP), and polystyrene (PS) of different sizes, shapes, densities, and surface tensions, as well as three suspensions of different formulations, were used to analyze the influence of particle-suspension wettability when atomizing suspensions over beds of spouted particles. The suspension compositions are shown in Table 13.2, and the system contact angles are presented in Table 13.3.

For each type of particle, suspensions 1 and 3 supplied similar contact angles, owing to their similar surface tensions. On the other hand, for suspension 2, the contact angles were smaller because of its lower surface tension. The variability in glass wettability (or contact angles) for the three suspensions was small. The effect of the high glass surface energy (85×10^{-3} N/m) is predominant when seeking good wettability (low contact angles), which was found to be nearly independent of the liquid surface tension in the range analyzed (from 46.3 to 67.5×10^{-3} N/m).

For ABS and PS, which have intermediate surface energies (34×10^{-3} and 32×10^{-3} N/m, respectively), the variability of contact angles was great, showing the strong influence of the liquid surface tension in this range of solid surface energies. PP has the lowest surface energy (30×10^{-3} N/m) and, as in the case of the glass, the wettability variation was small for the three suspensions. In this case of low solid surface energy, contrary to the glass results, wettability was poor for all three cases with high contact angles for the three suspensions.

Tests were carried out in a typical spouted bed coating system shown in Figure 13.4, including an acrylic cone-cylindrical column.[72] The following conditions were maintained constant in each run: fixed bed height 155 mm; ratio of air velocity to minimum spouting velocity 1.15; spouting air temperature 60 °C; suspension flow rate 6.0 mL/min; atomization pressure 239 kPa; processing time 30 min.

By analysis of the process behavior, it was possible to sort the particles into two groups: the first group included glass particles and ABS, which, because of their wetting characteristics (contact angle $\leq 70°$), were coated by the suspensions; the second group included PS and PP particles, which, also because of their superficial characteristics (contact angle $> 76°$), promoted drying of the suspension, resulting in a powdery product collected in the cyclone. High contact angles indicate poor wettability and weak adhesion; the interparticle friction inside the bed tends to strip off any dry film adhering weakly to the particle surface, resulting in suspension drying.

These results are in agreement with those of Vieira et al.,[66] who investigated the adhesion of an aqueous polymeric suspension to several types of inert particles (glass, ABS, placebo, PP, PS, and low-density polyethylene [LDPE]) in a spouted bed with top atomization of the suspension.

The process performance was evaluated by particle relative growth, coating efficiency, and solids loss from elutriation, which was found to be also related to the wetting and adhesion characteristics:

- The smallest growth was obtained with a suspension of glass and ABS particles, associated with a glass-only suspension and for the suspension with the greatest polymer (HEC) concentration.
- The glass coating efficiencies for all three suspensions were high and very similar. In these cases, the high glass surface energy led to strong adhesion of the film formed on the particle, regardless of the suspension surface tension, for the range analyzed.
- For ABS particles, the efficiency was of the same order as for the glass-only suspension, which presented better wettability and therefore greater adhesion. All efficiencies were in the range considered satisfactory for pharmaceutical industry processes, $\eta > 65\%$.
- As for the coating process of glass and ABS, aside from material adhering to the solids surface and the powder collected by the cyclone, another part of the suspension remained in the bed. The loss by elutriation was smaller, but the process efficiency also diminished. For conditions that result in poor wettability and, consequently, weak adhesion, the film tended to detach from the particles and form small dry plates that remained in the bed. This can cause instabilities in the bed fluid dynamics, interfering with the solids circulation and also with the pressure drop,[68] in the same way as reported for drying of pastes in spouted beds[73,74] (see Chapter 12).

To summarize, adhesion characteristics (solid surface energy and liquid–solid wettability) significantly influence particle coating in spouted beds. Particles of high surface energy and suspensions giving low contact angles favor the process, resulting in high particle growth, high efficiency, and steady spouting.

13.5 Concluding remarks

Particle granulation and coating in spouted beds have aroused industrial and research interest since their development in the 1960s. A considerable number of studies have been reported in the literature. The results of these studies indicate that it is possible to obtain high process efficiencies by controlling the variables that influence spouting dynamics and the granulation or coating mechanisms. Conditions that provide strong adhesion of the liquid to the particle surface (low contact angle) and choosing adequate operating conditions can lead to products of superior quality compared with competing equipment, in some cases with lower process times. Modeling of particle coating and granulation has contributed to understanding process mechanisms, as well as in predicting important process and equipment parameters, assisting scaleup.

   This evolution in the development of spouted bed particle granulation and coating has resulted in medium- and large-scale units, mainly in the chemical and pharmaceutical sectors. Equipment is available to produce up to 3 tonnes/h of coated particles continuously. For granulation, TOYO's spout-fluid bed urea granulation technology has been applied to plants in different countries with production capacities between 50 and 3250 tonnes/day. Spouted beds have been proven to provide reliable granulation and coating processes, resulting in round uniform products with high drying and adhesion efficiencies. This field is open to investigation to enhance the process fundamentals and to provide new products.

Chapter-specific nomenclature

C solids concentration, kg of solids/kg of suspension
K growth coefficient, kg/s
W mass flow rate, kg/s

Greek letters

η adhesion efficiency
η_{in} efficiency of inertial fixation of atomized droplets
ϕ sphericity

Subscripts

0 initial
air air
at atomization
sp suspension
t at time t

References

1. K. B. Mathur and N. Epstein. *Spouted Beds* (New York: Academic Press, 1974).
2. L. X. Liu and J. D. Litster. Coating mass distribution from a spouted bed seed coater: Experimental and modeling studies. *Powder Technol.*, **74** (1993), 259–270.
3. A. G. Taylor, P. S. Allen, J. S. Bennett, and M. K. Misra. Seed enhancements. *Seed Science Res.*, **8** (1998), 245–256.
4. E. Tenou and D. Poncelet. Batch and continuous fluid bed coating – review and state of the art. *J. Food Engng.*, **53** (2002), 325–340.
5. S. C. S. Rocha. Tablets coating. In *Special Topics in Drying*, ed. J. T. Freire and D. J. Sartori (São Carlos, Brazil: Federal University of São Carlos Press, 1992), pp. 297–330 (in Portuguese).
6. D. E. Wurster. Method of applying coatings to tablets or the like. U. S. Patent 2,648,609. 1953.
7. R. E. Singiser, A. L. Heiser, and E. B. Prillig. Air-suspension tablet coating. *Chem. Eng. Progr.*, **62**:4 (1966), 107–111.
8. R. Gupta and A. S. Mujumdar. Aerodynamics of vibrated fluid beds. *Can. J. Chem. Eng.*, **58** (1980), 332–338.
9. V. A. S. Moris and S. C. S. Rocha. Vibrofluidized bed drying of adipic acid. *Drying Technol.*, **24** (2006), 303–313.
10. F. Berruti, J. R. Muir, and L. A. Behie. Solids circulation in a spouted-fluid bed with draft tube. *Can. J. Chem. Eng.* **66** (1988), 919–923.
11. Y. T. Kim, B. H. Song, and S. D. Kim. Entrainment of solids in an internally circulating fluidized bed with draft tube. *Chem. Eng. J.*, **66** (1997), 105–110.
12. H. B. Song, Y. T. Kim, and S. D. Kim. Circulation of solids and gas bypassing in an internally circulating fluidized bed with a draft tube. *Chem. Eng. J.*, **68** (1997), 115–122.
13. D. Kunii and O. Levenspiel. *Fluidization Engineering*, 2nd ed. (New York: John Wiley and Sons, 1991).
14. A. Meisen and K. B. Mathur. Production of sulphur coated urea by the spouted bed process. In *Proceedings of the 2nd International Conference on Fertilizers*, British Sulphur Corp., **I** (1978), pp. 2–18.
15. O. P. Taranto, S. C. S. Rocha, G. S. V. Raghavan, and G. E. Ayub. Coating of tablets with polymeric suspension in two-dimensional spouted beds with and without draft plates. In *Proceedings of the 1st Inter-American Drying Conference (IADC)*, ed. M. A. Silva and S. C. S. Rocha (Itu, Brazil: Gráfica Paes, 1997), pp. 272–279.
16. R. Pissinati and W. P. Oliveira. Enteric coating of soft gelatin capsules by spouted bed: Effect of operating conditions on coating efficiency and on product quality. *European J. Pharmaceutics & Biopharmaceutics*, **55** (2003), 313–321.
17. M. W. Donida, S. C. S. Rocha, and F. Bartholomeu. Influence of aqueous polymeric coating suspension characteristics on the particle coating in a spouted bed. In *Proceedings of the 14th International Drying Symposium – IDS 2004*, ed. M. A. Silva and S. C. S. Rocha (São Paulo, Brazil: Ourograf Gráfica e Editora, 2004) **A**, pp. 217–224.
18. K. G. H. Desai and H. J. Park. Recent developments in microencapsulation of food ingredients. *Drying Technol.*, **23** (2005), 1361–1394.
19. C. Almeida, S. C. S. Rocha, and L. F. Razera. Polymer coating, germination and vigor of broccoli seeds. *Sci. Agricola*, **62**:3, 221–226.

20. M. W. Donida, S. C. S. Rocha, B. D. Castro, and A. M. M. Marques. Coating and drying in spouted bed: influence of the liquid-particle work of adhesion. *Drying Technol.*, **25** (2007), 319–326.

21. M. W. Bacelos, M. L. Passos, and J. T. Freire. Effect of interparticle forces on the conical spouted bed behavior of wet particles with size distribution. *Powder Technol.*, **174** (2007), 114–126.

22. L. K. Kadam. *Granulation Technology for Bioproducts* (Boston: CRC Press, 1991).

23. E. Kleinbach and T. Riede. Coating of solids. *Chem. Eng. Proc.*, **34** (1995), 329–337.

24. K. Dewettinck and A. Huyghebaert. Fluidized bed coating in food technology. *Trends in Food Sci. & Technol.*, **10** (1999), 163–168.

25. S. Shelukar, J. Ho, J. Zega, E. Roland, N. Yeh, D. Quiram, A. Nole, A. Katdare, and S. Reynolds. Identification and characterization of factors controlling tablet coating uniformity in a Wurster coating process. *Powder Technol.*, **110** (2000), 29–36.

26. R. Dreu, J. Sirca, K. Pintye-Hodi, T. Burjan, O. Planinsek, and S. Srcic. Physicochemical properties of granulating liquids and their influence on microcrystalline cellulose pellets obtained by extrusion-spheronisation technology. *Intern. J. Pharmaceutics*, **291** (2005), 99–111.

27. J. T. Freire and W. P. Oliveira. Technological aspects of particles coating processes. In *Special Topics in Drying*, ed. J. T. Freire and D. J. Sartori (São Carlos, Brazil: Federal University of São Carlos Press, 1992), pp. 253–293 (in Portuguese).

28. Y. F. Berquin. Method and apparatus for granulating melted solid and hardenable fluid products. U. S. Patent 3,231,413 (1966). Equivalent Brit. Patent 962,265 (1964).

29. F. P. Nichols. Improvements in and relating to the production of granular compositions such as fertilizers. Brit. Patent 1,039,177 (1966).

30. Glatt group of companies, http://www.glatt.com, accessed December 21, 2009.

31. R. P. da Silva and E. Sakata. First urea granulation plant in Brazil. In *Proceedings of the IFA (International Fertilizer Industry Association) Technical Symposium* (São Paulo, Brazil: 2008), http://toyo-eng.co.jp, accessed May 25, 2009.

32. C. R. Duarte, J. L. V. Lisboa, R. C. Santana, M. A. S. Barrozo, and V. V. Murata. Experimental study and simulation of mass distribution of the covering layer of soybean seeds coated in a spouted bed. *Brazilian J. Chem. Eng.*, **21** (2004) 59–67.

33. J. Kucharski and A. Kmiec. Kinetics of granulation process during coating of tablets in a spouted bed. *Chem. Eng. Sci.*, **44** (1989), 1627–1636.

34. W. P. Oliveira, J. T. Freire, and J. R. Coury. Analysis of particle coating by spouted bed process. *Intern. J. Pharmaceutics*, **158** (1997), 1–9.

35. W. P. Oliveira, M. C. P. Publio, and G. D. Silva. Effect of tablet mass increase and feed of atomizing air on fluid dynamic parameters of a spouted bed coater. In *Proceedings of the VII Latin-American Congress on Heat Mass Transfer – LATCYM* (Salta, Argentina: 1998), **1**, 276–280.

36. M. A. S. Barrozo, J. R. Limaverde, and C. H. Ataíde. The use of a spouted bed in the fertilizer coating of soybean seeds. *Drying Technol.*, **16** (1998), 2049–2064.

37. M. W. Donida and S. C. S. Rocha. Coating of urea with an aqueous polymeric suspension in a two-dimensional spouted bed. *Drying Technol.*, **20** (2002), 789–811.

38. C. R. Kfuri and L. A. P. Freitas. Comparative study of spouted and spout-fluid beds for tablet coating. *Drying Technol.*, **23** (2005), 2369–2387.

39. R. H. Perry and C. H. Chilton. *Chemical Engineers' Handbook*, 5th ed. (New York: McGraw Hill, 1973), p. **18**–64.

40. A. Kmiec. Hydrodynamics of flows and heat transfer in spouted beds. *Chem. Eng. J.*, **19** (1980), 189–200.

41. P. J. Weiss and A. Meisen. Laboratory studies on sulphur-coating urea by the spouted bed process. *Can. J. Chem. Eng.*, **61** (1983), 440–447.

42. J. Kucharski and J. A. Kmiec. The effect of process parameters on mass distributions and the efficiency of tablets coating in a spouted bed. In *Drying '88*, ed. M. A. Rogues and A. S. Mujumdar (Versailles, France: Hemisphere, 1988), **II**, pp. 27–31.

43. G. E. S. Ayub, S. C. S. Rocha, and A. L. I. Perrucci. Experimental study of coating of urea with sulphur in a two-dimensional spouted bed. In *Proceedings of the XXVI Brazilian Congress on Particulate Systems* (Teresópolis, Brazil: 1999), **I**, pp. 283–290 (in Portuguese).

44. M. W. Donida and S. C. S. Rocha. Analysis of efficiency and of growth kinetics for the process of coating of urea particles in a two-dimensional spouted bed. In *Proceedings of the 2nd Inter-American Drying Conference*, ed. K. W. Waliszewski (Veracruz, Mexico: Editorial Ducere SA de CV, 2001), pp. 463–472.

45. G. D. Silva, M. C. P. Publio, and W. P. Oliviera. Evaluation of the tablet coating by the conventional spouted bed process. *Drug Dev. Ind. Pharmacy*, **27** (2001), 213–219.

46. C. Almeida. Coating of broccoli seeds in spouted and fluidized beds. Ph.D. thesis, Univ. of Campinas, Brazil (2002) (in Portuguese).

47. M. C. Publio and W. P. Oliveira. Effect of the equipment configuration and operating conditions on process performance and on physical characteristics of the product during coating in spouted bed. *Can. J. Chem. Eng.*, **82** (2004), 122–133.

48. H. V. A. Oliveira, M. P. G. Peixoto, and L. A. P. Freitas. Study on the efficiency of hard gelatin capsules coating in spouted bed. *Drying Technol.*, **23** (2005), 2039–2053.

49. G. Z. Martins, C. R. F. Souza, T. M. Shankar, and W. P. Oliveira. Effect of process variables on fluid dynamics and adhesion efficiency during spouted bed coating of hard gelatin capsules. *Chem. Eng. Proc.*, **47** (2008), 2238–2246.

50. G. B. Borini, T. C. Andrade, and L. A. P. Freitas. Hot melt granulation of coarse pharmaceutical powders in a spouted bed. *Powder Technol.*, **189** (2009), 520–527.

51. H. Ichikawa, M. Arimoto, and Y. Fukumoria. Design of microcapsules with hydrogel as a membrane component and their preparation by a spouted bed. *Powder Technol.*, **130** (2003), 189–192.

52. N. Laohakunjit and O. Kerdchoechuen. Aroma enrichment and the change during storage of non-aromatic milled rice coated with extracted natural flavor. *Food Chem.*, **101** (2007), 339–344.

53. N. Piccinini. Coated nuclear fuels particles. *Adv. Nucl. Sci. Technol.*, **8** (1975), 255–341.

54. N. Piccinini, A. Bernhard, P. Campagna, and F. Vallana. Segregation phenomenon in spouted beds. *Can. J. Chem. Eng.*, **55** (1977), 122–125.

55. N. Piccinini and G. Rovero. Thick coatings by thermo-chemical deposition in spouted beds. *Can. J. Chem. Eng.*, **61** (1983), 448–451.

56. J. Kucharski and A. Kmiec. Analysis of simultaneous drying and coating of tablets in a spouted bed. In *Proceedings of the 5th International Drying Symposium*, ed. A. S. Mujumdar (Washington, DC: Hemisphere, 1986), pp. 204–217.

57. K. KuShaari, P. Pandey, and R. Turton. Monte Carlo simulations to determine coating uniformity in a Wurster fluidized bed coating process. *Powder Technol*, **166** (2006), 81–90.

58. S. Pannala, C. S. Daw, C. E. A. Finney, D. Boyalakuntla, M. Syamlal, and T. J. O'Brien. Simulating the dynamics of spouted-bed nuclear fuel coaters. *Chem. Vapor Deposition*, **13** (2007), 481–490.

59. J. M. Link, W. Godlieb, N. G. Deen, and J. A. M. Kuipers. Discrete element study of granulation in spouted-fluidized bed. *Chem. Eng. Sci.*, **62** (2007), 195–207.

60. C. R. Duarte, V. V. Murata, and M. A. S. Barrozo. The use of a population balance model in the study of inoculation of soybean seeds in a spouted bed. *Can. J. Chem. Eng.*, **82** (2004), 116–121.

61. M. Paulo Filho, S. C. S. Rocha, and A. C. L. Lisboa. Modeling and experimental analysis of polydisperse particles coating in spouted bed. *Chem. Eng. Proc.*, **45** (2006), 965–972.

62. J. Piña, V. Bucalá, N. S. Schbib, P. Ege, and H. I. de Lasa. Modeling a silicon CVD spouted bed pilot plant reactor. *Intern. J. Chem. Reactor Eng.*, **4** (2006), 1–19.

63. V. Pont, K. Saleh, D. Steinmetz, and M. Hemati. Influence of the physicochemical properties on the growth of solids particles by granulation in fluidized bed. *Powder Technol.*, **120** (2001), 97–104.

64. B. Guignon, E. Regalado, A. Duquenoy, and E. Dumoulin. Helping to choose operating parameters for a coating fluid bed process. *Powder Technol.*, **130** (2003), 193–198.

65. K. Saleh, D. Steinmetz, and M. Hemati. Experimental study and modeling of fluidized bed coating and agglomeration. *Powder Technol.*, **130** (2003), 116–123.

66. M. G. A. Vieira, M. W. Donida, and S. C. S. Rocha. Adhesion of an aqueous polymeric suspension to inert particles in a spouted bed. *Drying Technol.*, **22** (2004), 1069–1085.

67. M. W. Donida, S. C. S. Rocha, and F. Bartholomeu. Influence of polymeric suspension characteristics on the particle coating in a spouted bed. *Drying Technol.*, **23** (2005), 1–13.

68. S. C. S. Rocha, M. W. Donida, and A. M. M. Marques. Liquid-particle surface properties on spouted bed coating and drying performance. *Can. J. Chem. Eng.*, **87** (2009), 695–703.

69. B. Bhandari and T. Howes. Relating the stickiness property of foods undergoing drying and dried products to their surface energetics. *Drying Technol.*, **23** (2005), 781–797.

70. K. C. Link and E. U. Schlünder. Fluidized bed spray granulation and film coating. A new method for the investigation of the coating process on a single sphere. *Drying Technol.*, **15** (1997), 1827–1843.

71. S. M. Iveson, J. D. Litster, K. Hapgood, and B. J. Ennis. Nucleation, growth and breakage phenomena in agitated wet granulation process: a review. *Powder Technol.*, **117** (2001), 3–39.

72. A. M. M. Marques. Influence of particle-suspension adhesion during spouted bed coating with bottom atomization. M.Sc. dissertation. Univ. of Campinas, Brazil (2007) (in Portuguese).

73. P. I. Spitzner Neto and J. T. Freire. Study of pastes drying in spouted bed: influence of the paste presence on the process. In *Proceedings of the XXV Brazilian Congress on Particulate Systems*, ed. J. T. Freire (São Carlos, Brazil: Federal Univ. of São Carlos Press, 1997), **2**, pp. 520–525 (in Portuguese).

74. M. F. D. Medeiros, S. C. S. Rocha, O. L. S. Alsina, C. E. M. Jerônimo, U. K. L. Medeiros, and A. L. M. L. da Mata. Drying of pulps of tropical fruits in spouted bed: effect of the composition on dryer performance. *Drying Technol.*, **20** (2002), 855–881.

75. R. L. R. Lefevre and M. S. T. Price, Coated nuclear fuel particles: the coating process and its model. *Nuclear Technol.*, **35** (1977), 227–237,

76. E. H. Voice. Coatings of pyrocarbon and silicon carbide by chemical vapour deposition. *Chem. Engr.* (Dec. 1974), 785–792.

77. D. W. Marshall, Idaho National Laboratory. Private communication to J. R. Grace (2009).

14 The Wurster coater

Sarah Palmer, Andrew Ingram, and Jonathan Seville

14.1 Introduction: particle coating techniques

The Wurster coater is a special variant of a fluidized or spouted bed (Figure 14.1) that resembles a spouted bed in being of conical-cylindrical construction, but normally has a gas distributor at its base, through which an upfacing spray nozzle projects. This nozzle is usually of the two-fluid type and is used to introduce a coating material – usually a solution, but sometimes a suspension or melt. It is customary to install a draft tube into the column, so particles are constrained to circulate upward inside the draft tube and downward in the annulus surrounding the draft tube. In this respect, Wurster coaters have similarities to spout-fluid beds containing draft tubes. Their main use is for coating pharmaceutical tablets and pellets, for which this is one of the most common methods.

Within the pharmaceutical industry, particulate materials are coated for a number of reasons[1,2]: to produce controlled release dosage forms, to mask unpleasant tastes, to protect ingredients within the tablet/pellet from the environment (light, moisture, air, or undesirable pH), for aesthetic appeal, and to protect the consumer from toxic compounds that may cause gastric distress or nausea.

In industrial practice, particle coating is accomplished using several types of equipment, most notably rotating drum (or perforated pan) and fluidized bed coaters. (Fluidized beds are also used to agglomerate particles, but agglomeration is undesirable in coaters, which are therefore designed to minimize it.) Rotating drums are used primarily to coat tablets (usually having a particle diameter $\gtrsim 6.0$ mm). Although rotating drums provide a low-mechanical-stress environment for tablet coating, their use can result in high tablet-to-tablet coating variability and/or long batch processing times because of poor heat and mass transfer compared with fluidized beds.[3,4] To minimize variability in coating thickness, as required for precision coating of the active ingredient onto tablets, bottom-spray (Wurster) type beds are advantageous.[4–6] Wurster coaters are sometimes considered to be fluidized beds, rather than spouted beds, but they meet the spouting conditions outlined in Chapter 1.

The Wurster coater is used extensively in the pharmaceutical industry for film coating of pellets, tablets, and other particulate dosage forms; in the food industry for coating

Spouted and Spout-Fluid Beds: Fundamentals and Applications, eds. Norman Epstein and John R. Grace. Published by Cambridge University Press. © Cambridge University Press 2011.

(a)

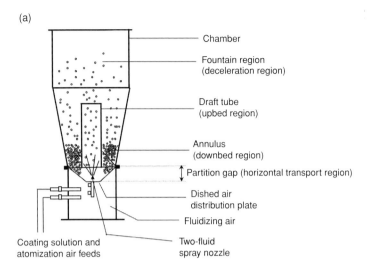

Chamber

Fountain region
(deceleration region)

Draft tube
(upbed region)

Annulus
(downbed region)

Partition gap (horizontal transport region)

Dished air
distribution plate

Fluidizing air

Coating solution and
atomization air feeds

Two-fluid
spray nozzle

(b)

(c)

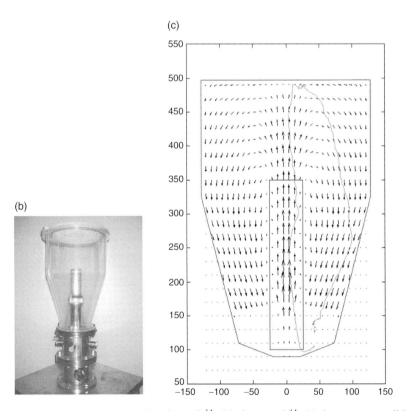

Figure 14.1. Wurster coater: (a) schematic[14]; (b) photograph[14]; (c) time-average solids motion (black arrows) and a single particle trajectory (line).

food ingredients; and in the agricultural industry for production of controlled-release fertilizers.

14.2   Features of the Wurster coater

The Wurster coater was invented and developed by Dale E. Wurster in the early 1950s at the University of Wisconsin.[7] In 1954, Abbott Laboratories produced the first commercially available film-coated tablet using this device.[1] Although originally designed to coat tablets, the process is now widely used to coat smaller particles, such as the pellets used to fill pharmaceutical capsules.[6,8,9]

As indicated earlier, the key feature of the Wurster-type coater is the draft tube (or "partition"), which is separated by a gap from the gas distributor plate. Compared with conventional spouted beds, the more complex gas distribution arrangement yields some of the properties of both spouted and fluidized beds, enabling the operating range to be extended downward in particle size from Geldart Group D particles,[10] which are easily spouted, to Geldart Groups A and B.[11]

The fluidization airflow serves several functions; aerating the annulus, enabling pneumatic transport of particles up through the draft tube, and providing drying capacity. Typically, the distributor plate possesses larger holes in the central region (beneath the draft tube) and smaller holes in the outer region (beneath the annulus), favoring gas flow in the former.

Christensen and Bertelsen[12] identified four different regions in the Wurster coater according to particle motion: upbed (draft tube), deceleration (fountain), downbed (annulus), and horizontal transport regions. These are characterized as follows:

- *Upbed region*. Particles pass through the gap between the distributor and the draft tube and are pneumatically transported upward while receiving coating from the spray nozzle located at the center of the distribution plate. Spray droplets strike the particle surfaces and may then spread, coalesce, and dry to form a film. The air and particle velocities are not uniform across the draft tube; velocities at the center significantly exceed those at the wall. Particles close to the wall rise more slowly or may even move downward along the inside of the draft tube. In unfavorable circumstances, internal circulation may occur within the draft tube.
- *Deceleration region*. After leaving the draft tube, the particles enter the fountain region, where they decelerate, continue drying, and fall downward onto the top of the downbed (annulus) region.
- *Downbed region*. Particles within the annulus are in close contact with one another and move slowly downward as a moving packed bed. It is in this region that sticking and agglomeration are most likely to occur if the particles are not sufficiently dry; this is undesirable in terms of coating quality. Air volume in the downbed depends on the size and number of holes in the outer region of the distributor plate. According to Jones,[6] the airflow in the annulus should be at or close to that necessary for incipient fluidization, to ensure continuous downward movement toward the partition gap.

- *Horizontal transport region.* This name is given to the region below the draft tube, in which particles pass horizontally through the partition gap. From this region, particles reenter the upbed region. The partition gap controls the flow of particles into the upbed region, and thus the solids circulation rate.

This cyclic pattern of solids motion is repeated until the desired thickness of coating is deposited on the particles.

In addition to better coating performance than with the top-spray methods,[5] advantages of the Wurster coating process include excellent heat and mass transfer within the bed, leading to short batch processing times, ability to handle particles as small as 100 μm, and mechanical simplicity, with no moving parts. A disadvantage is that the process is mechanically harsh (compared with that of rotating drums); particle attrition can become an issue with increasing particle size because of increased momentum of collisions at the higher air velocities needed for circulation.[13] Spray nozzle blockage is also an issue because, should it occur, the problem cannot be easily resolved, as nozzle removal during operation is impossible.[6,13] For tablet coating, dead zones can exist within the annulus near the inner chamber wall; this is undesirable because dead zones contribute significantly to tablet-to-tablet coating variability. A further limitation of the process is that fine (<100 μm) particles tend to agglomerate rather than coat (unless special enhancements are used) and may adhere to chamber walls.[8]

In industrial practice, optimum operating conditions are based largely on past experience and experimentation via trial and error; the results from such methods are therefore system-specific. Despite the widespread industrial use of Wurster coaters, the fundamental mechanisms controlling the process are not well understood.

14.3   Uniformity and quality of coating

Depending on the application, the performance of coated particles in their end use may depend crucially on the uniformity and quality of the coating. Uniformity can vary from particle to particle and also from point to point on the surface of each particle. Most studies have concentrated on the former, although both can be important. Methods for measuring both are reviewed by Palmer.[14]

Cheng and Turton[9] list the variables that affect coating uniformity and quality, as summarized in Table 14.1. Coating occurs only within the spray region. It is then reasonable to assume, as suggested by Mann et al.[15] and Cheng and Turton,[9] that the particle-to-particle variability in coating arises from a combination of (1) variation in the number of passes made by particles through the spray region and (2) variation in the amount of coating per pass (Figure 14.2).

The total mass of coating, M_{total}, on a given particle is given by

$$M_{total} = \sum_{i=1}^{N} x_i,$$

(14.1)

Table 14.1. Variables affecting coating uniformity and quality.[9] The factors in bold are most significant.

Design variable	Process variable	Product variable
Type of equipment	Temperature of fluidizing air	Solvent (water or organic)
Type of nozzle	Humidity of fluidizing air	Coating material
Type of distributor plate	Spray rate (liquid and air)	Coating solution composition
Diameter of draft tube	Atomization pressure	Particle properties
Spacing of draft tube to	**Batch size**	
base (partition gap)	**Velocity of air (inner and**	
Length of draft tube	**outer regions)**	

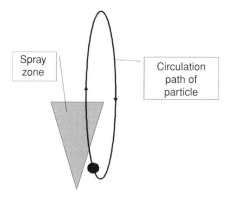

Figure 14.2. Circulation of a particle through the spray zone (after Cheng and Turton[9]).

where N is the number of passes through the spray zone and x_i is the amount of coating applied during the ith pass. Mann et al.[15] showed that the coefficient of variation (CV) for coating mass per particle can be expressed as:

$$CV = \frac{\sigma_{total}}{\mu_{total}} = \sqrt{\left(\frac{\sigma_x}{\mu_x}\right)^2 \frac{1}{\mu_n} + \left(\frac{\sigma_n}{\mu_n}\right)^2},$$

(14.2)

where the two terms on the right-hand side refer to the variation in mass deposited per pass and the variation in the number of passes, respectively. Mann[16] showed that CV could be represented more usefully in terms of the circulation time distribution:

$$CV = \frac{\sigma_{total}}{\mu_{total}} = \sqrt{\left(\frac{\sigma_x}{\mu_x}\right)^2 \frac{\mu_{ct}}{t_{coat}} + \left(\frac{\sigma_{ct}}{\mu_{ct}}\right)^2 \frac{\mu_{ct}}{t_{coat}}},$$

(14.3)

where t_{coat} is the total coating time. The coefficient of variation is therefore proportional to $\sqrt{1/t_{coat}}$, implying that any desired CV can be obtained by extending the run time appropriately.

Cheng and Turton[17] and Shelukar et al.[18] demonstrated the usefulness of this approach experimentally and have shown that in most cases it is the variation in coating per pass through the spray zone that dominates the overall particle-to-particle coating variability. This has important consequences for the design of Wurster coaters, as discussed later.

14.4   Particle motion studies

Mann and Crosby[19] investigated particle cycle times in a spouted/fluidized bed with a draft tube in which the air supplies to the spout and annulus were independently controlled. They used a magnetically labeled particle and a detecting coil around the top of the draft tube to record each pass of the particle. With increasing air supply to the annulus, the cycle time decreased and became less variable. It was concluded that the increased airflow slightly expanded the bed, reducing the friction between particles and the adjacent walls and allowing higher and more uniform particle flow toward the gap.

Wesdyk et al.[20] investigated the effect of bead size in the range 850 to 1400 μm on film thickness in a Wurster coating unit. Results from dissolution testing and scanning electron microscopy (SEM) analysis indicated that larger beads received a thicker coating than smaller ones. This effect was said to be caused by differences in particle trajectories: smaller beads projected further into the expansion chamber of the coater and therefore cycled fewer times through the coating zone. It was also argued that lighter beads may accelerate more rapidly through the coating zone, therefore receiving less film coating.

Cheng and Turton[17] carried out extensive batch coating on 1-mm spherical particles in which the cycle time of a magnetically labeled particle and the final spread in coating within the batch were measured. They investigated the effect of partition gap, gas flowrate, partition diameter, and partition height on particle motion and coating uniformity. For the range of parameters studied, the partition gap exerted the strongest influence on the rate of particle circulation. Cheng and Turton also found that the mean and standard deviation of the particle cycle time distribution were approximately proportional over a wide range of operating conditions. By assuming that the time-averaged behavior of the labeled particle was representative of the ensemble behavior of the bed, they were able to correlate coating uniformity with operating conditions, using the approach described in Section 14.3. The authors argued that nonuniformity in coating per pass derives from variation in trajectories through the draft tube: particles passing close to the spray source pick up more coating and shelter those farthest away. This important observation will be considered further in relation to modeling.

By using both a magnetic tracer particle and dye pulse injection in a bed with a draft tube, Shelukar et al.[18] were able to measure both the cycle time variability and the variation in coating per pass and to relate these to coating distribution as in Eq. (14.3).

The effects of partition gap and auxiliary fluidization airflow rate on solids circulation rate, airflow distribution between annulus and draft tube, and pressure drop were studied in Wurster coaters of different sizes by Choi,[21] with solids circulation rate estimated visually through a sight glass at the wall. This work again identified the partition gap as being critical in determining the overall circulation rate of solids.

Fitzpatrick et al.[22] examined the effects of operating conditions (airflow rate and particle loading) and coater configuration (partition gap) on solids motion using positron emission particle tracking (PEPT) to follow the trajectory of a single tracer particle in the absence of coating liquid spray. Mean particle cycle time was found to increase with

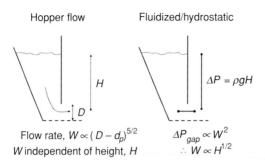

Figure 14.3. Two alternative analyses for solids discharge through partition gap.

increasing batch and tablet size and with decreasing airflow rate and partition gap. The variability (relative standard deviation) in particle cycle time increased with decreasing airflow rate and batch size. This was attributed primarily to the formation of dead zones in the lower portion of the annulus, associated with ordered packing at the wall.

Palmer[14] studied the coating of 710–1000-μm spherical microcrystalline cellulose pellets, using PEPT to correlate particle motion with coating uniformity over a range of operating conditions (partition height, batch size, and gas flowrate). Coating was most variable at the high and low extremes of batch size and partition gap. Variability tended to correlate with irregularity in the flow and trajectories of the particles. In particular, certain conditions gave rise to recirculation of particles within the draft tube, with particles then passing several times through the spray zone before exiting.

An important question in understanding Wurster coater operation is: What controls the flow through the partition gap? There are two possibilities, according to whether or not the annulus is fluidized (Figure 14.3). If the annulus is not fluidized, solids flow from the annulus is hopperlike,[23] and obeys a Beverloo-type equation:

$$W = C\rho g^{0.5}(D_0 - kd_p)^{5/2}, \tag{14.4}$$

where W is the mass discharge rate through the orifice, D_0 is the hydraulic diameter of the discharge orifice (equal to $4 \times$ (cross-sectional area)/(outlet perimeter)); d_p is the particle diameter; C and k are empirical discharge and shape coefficients, respectively; ρ is the flowing bulk density; and g is the acceleration from gravity. Given that, as in hopper flow, the weight of the solids is supported mostly by friction at the walls, the solids circulation rate is little affected by the head of solids in the annulus and might therefore be relatively independent of batch size. On the other hand, if the annulus is fluidized, the fluidized solids behave as a liquid and their flow through the partition gap is then governed by a Bernoulli expression (taking pressure as constant):

$$1/2\rho v^2 + \rho g H = \text{constant}, \tag{14.5}$$

where ρ is the solids bulk density, v the solids discharge velocity, and H the height of material in the annulus, so that $W \propto H^{1/2}$ – that is, the mass flow rate is proportional to the square root of the solids head. The complicating factor is that the division of gas flow between the draft tube and the annulus is itself affected by the head of solids in

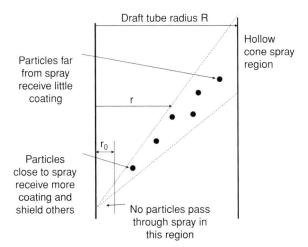

Figure 14.4. Effect of sheltering in the spray region (Cheng and Turton[17]). Note that the spray is of the hollow cone type.

the annulus, and therefore by the batch size, and by the solids entrainment rate into the draft tube. Experimental results from the literature suggest that different combinations of design and operating variables have resulted in operation in both these modes. No comprehensive hydrodynamic model yet exists.

14.5   Modeling of coating thickness variation

Turton[24] summarized the modeling approaches taken by different investigators:

- Classical chemical engineering compartment models, typified by the two-compartment model of Sherony[25] and further developed, for example, by Crites and Turton[11]; this category of model sometimes includes population balances and size-dependent growth.[26]
- Monte Carlo methods, in which particle movement is a random walk, sometimes related to experimentally observed particle motion. The amount of coating depends on time and location within the spray zone.[27]
- Fully computational methods such as computational fluid dynamics (CFD), including discrete element methods (DEM).

A conceptual model developed by Cheng and Turton[17] is interesting from the point of view of equipment design; it focuses on the coating received per pass. Within the spray region, the concentration of particles is sufficiently high that particles shield each other from the spray – a "sheltering" effect. The simplest model assumption was a binary one, in which particles receive either a "standard" coating amount or none. However, this resulted in predictions that were in poor agreement with experimental results. In a more sophisticated approach (Figure 14.4), the amount of coating material received per pass was assumed to be proportional to the particle projected area ($\propto d_p^2$), to decrease with distance from the spray nozzle, and to depend on the void fraction within the draft tube (spray region). Because of the sheltering effect, models of this kind predict an increase in the coefficient of variation as the void fraction in the spray region decreases. Moreover, as the radius of the draft tube increases – for instance, because of equipment scaleup – increased sheltering again causes an increase in the coefficient of variation.

Palmer[14] adopted a similar approach, previously developed by Seiler et al.[28] for conventional spouted bed coating, to predict the evolution of coating mass distributions in a Wurster coater using particle cycle time distributions and time-averaged spray region void fraction data obtained from PEPT experiments. Probability parameters were used to determine the entry height of particles from the annulus to the spout and spray-to-particle contact at each height interval within the spray zone. To determine the extent of coating, a statistical collection factor was calculated, which included the spray density effect. The predicted coating mass distributions compared well with experimental distributions.

As Turton[24] noted, none of the existing models offers a priori prediction of coating behavior, but DEM may make this possible in the near future.

14.6   Developments in design

Several researchers and industrial manufacturers of Wurster-type coaters have investigated improvements to the basic design, as indicated in Figure 14.5. Identifying the transition between the cone and distributor as a cause of "dead" zones or regions of little particle motion, Shelukar et al.[18] used an additional cone of shallower angle to prevent this problem. Subramanian et al.[4] reduced the variation in coating per pass by adding a profiled "tablet deflector" around the spray nozzle, the major effect being to increase the void fraction near the spray zone, hence reducing problematic local wetting and enhancing coating uniformity.

GEA Pharma Systems, a pharmaceutical equipment manufacturer, introduced a variant on the bottom-spray coater in which some of the inlet air is introduced with significant swirl around the spray nozzle to create a high-velocity low-pressure spray zone, thereby enhancing particle movement into the zone and accelerating subsequent drying of coated particles. This design demonstrated improved coating relative to the conventional Wurster design, including reduced particle agglomeration and fewer coating defects.[29]

Acknowledgments

The authors gratefully acknowledge financial assistance from the UK Engineering & Physical Sciences Research Council and Merck Sharp & Dohme Ltd, and loan of equipment from GEA Pharma Systems.

(a)

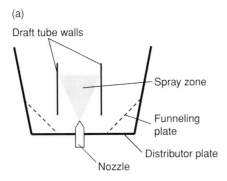

(b)

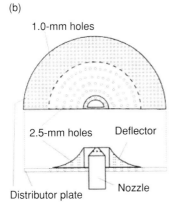

Figure 14.5. Schematic diagrams of (a) funneling plate used by Shelukar et al.[18]; and (b) tablet deflectors used by Subramanian et al.[4]

Chapter-specific nomenclature

N	number of passes through spray zone
t_{coat}	total coating time, s
x_i	mass of coating added in ith pass through spray zone, kg
μ	mean value
σ	standard deviation

Subscripts

ct	coating time
n	number of passes
x	per pass

References

1. G. Cole. Tackling the tablet. *Chem. Engr.*, **618** (1996), 22–31.
2. J. Hogan. Coating of tablets and multiparticulates. In *Pharmaceutics: The Science of Dosage Form Design*, ed. M. E. Aulton (London: Churchill Livingstone, 2002), pp. 441–448.
3. M. Tzika, S. Alexandridou, and C. Kiparissides. Evaluation of the morphological and release characteristics of coated fertilizer granules produced in a Wurster fluidized bed. *Powder Technol.*, **132** (2003), 16–24.
4. G. Subramanian, R. Turton, S. Shelukar, and L. Flemmer. Effect of tablet deflectors in the draft tube of fluidized/spouted bed coaters. *Ind. Eng. Chem. Res.*, **42** (2003), 2470–2478.
5. E. Teunou and D. Poncelet. Batch and continuous fluid bed coating – review and state of the art. *J. Food Eng.*, **53** (2002), 325–340.
6. D. Jones. Air suspension coating. In *Encyclopedia of Pharmaceutical Technology*, ed. J. Swarbrick and J. Boylan (New York: Dekker, 1988), pp. 189–216.
7. D. E. Wurster. Means for applying coatings to tablets or like. *J. Amer. Pharmaceutical Assoc.*, **48** (1950), 451.
8. K. Jono, H. Ichikawa, M. Miyamoto, and Y. Fukumori. A review of particulate design for pharmaceutical powders and their production by spouted bed coating. *Powder Technol.*, **113** (2000), 269–277.
9. X. X. Cheng and R. Turton. The prediction of variability occurring in fluidized bed coating equipment. I. The measurement of particle circulation rates in a bottom-spray fluidized bed coater. *Pharmac. Dev. & Technol.*, **5** (2000), 311–322.
10. D. Geldart. Types of gas fluidization. *Powder Technol.*, **7** (1973), 285–292.
11. T. Crites and R. Turton. Mathematical model for the prediction of cycle-time distributions for the Wurster column-coating process. *Ind. Eng. Chem. Res.*, **44** (2005), 5397–5402.
12. F. N. Christensen and P. Bertelsen. Qualitative description of the Wurster based fluid bed coating process. *Drug Develop. & Ind. Pharm.*, **23** (1997), 451–463.
13. R. Turton and X. X. Cheng. The scale-up of spray coating processes for granular solids and tablets. *Powder Technol.*, **150** (2005), 78–85.
14. S. E. Palmer. Understanding and optimisation of pharmaceutical film coating using the Wurster coater. Ph.D. thesis, Univ. of Birmingham, UK (2007).
15. U. Mann, M. Rubinovitch, and E. J. Crosby. Characterization and analysis of continuous recycle systems, *AIChE J.* **25** (1979), 873–882.
16. U. Mann. Analysis of spouted-bed coating and granulation. 1. Batch operation. *Ind. Eng. Chem. Proc. Des.Dev.*, **22** (1983), 288–292.
17. X. X. Cheng and R. Turton. The prediction of variability occurring in fluidized bed coating equipment. II. The role of nonuniform particle coverage as particles pass through the spray zone. *Pharm. Dev. & Technol.*, **5** (2000), 323–332.
18. S. Shelukar, J. Ho, J. Zega, E. Roland, N. Yeh, D. Quiram, A. Nole, A. Katdare, and S. Reynolds. Identification and characterization of factors controlling tablet coating uniformity in a Wurster coating process. *Powder Technol.*, **110** (2000), 29–36.
19. U. Mann and E. J. Crosby. Cycle time distribution measurements in spouted beds. *Can. J. Chem. Eng.*, **53** (1975), 579–581.
20. R. Wesdyk, Y. M. Joshi, N. B. Jain, K. Morris, and A. Newman. The effect of size and mass on the film thickness of beads coated in fluidized bed equipment. *Int. J. Pharmaceutics*, **65** (1990), 69–76.

21. M. Choi. Hydrodynamics of commercial-scale Wurster coaters. Presented at annual AIChE meeting (1998).

22. S. Fitzpatrick, Y. Ding, C. Seiler, C. Lovegrove, S. Booth, R. Forster, D. J. Parker, and J. P. K. Seville. Positron emission particle tracking studies of a wurster process for coating applications. *Pharmaceutical Technol.*, **27** (2003), 70–78.

23. J. P. K. Seville, U. Tüzün, and R. Clift. *Processing of Particulate Solids* (Glasgow: Chapman and Hall/Blackie, 1997).

24. R. Turton. Challenges in the modelling and prediction of coating of pharmaceutical dosage forms. *Powder Technol.*, **181** (2008), 186–194.

25. D. F. Sherony. A model of surface renewal with application to fluid bed coating of particles. *Chem. Eng. Sci.*, **36** (1981), 845–848.

26. L. X. Liu and J. D. Litster. Coating mass distribution from a spouted bed seed coater: experimental and modelling studies. *Powder Technol.*, **74** (1993), 259–270.

27. K. KuShaari, P. Pandey, Y. Song, and R. Turton. Monte Carlo simulations to determine coating uniformity in a Wurster fluidized bed coating process. *Powder Technol.*, **166** (2006), 81–90.

28. C. Seiler, P. J. Fryer, and J. P. K. Seville. Statistical modelling of the spouted bed coating process using positron emission particle tracking (PEPT) data. *Can. J. Chem. Eng.*, **86** (2008), 571–581.

29. P. W. S. Heng, L. W. Chan, and E. S. K. Tang. Use of swirling airflow to enhance coating performance of bottom spray fluid bed coaters. *Int. J. Pharmaceutics*, **327** (2006), 26–35.

15 Gasification, pyrolysis, and combustion

A. Paul Watkinson and Antonio C. L. Lisboa

A common set of reactions, given in Table 15.1, occurs when carbonaceous solids undergo thermal processing. Whether the aim is pyrolysis, gasification, or combustion, each of these reactions occurs in some parts of the reactor because of gas–solids contacting. In this chapter, we consider, in order, gasification as an endothermic process to generate H_2 and CO mixtures for fuel or synthesis gas, pyrolysis as a process to generate useful tars (or liquids), and combustion as a process to produce heat.

15.1   Gasification background

Most commercial gasifiers use coal as feed, and may be classified by the type of solids–gas contacting (moving, entrained, fluidized, or spouted bed), by the state of the ash (dry, agglomerated, or molten), and by the oxidant (air, air–steam, or oxygen–steam). A low-calorific-value gas results from air–steam gasification, and a medium-calorific-value gas from using steam or steam–oxygen mixtures. The carbonaceous feedstock may be fed as a dry solid, a sludge, or a slurry.

Performance measures can be identified for comparing gasifiers of different designs and operating conditions. For production of fuel gases, the heating value of the produced gas is important and is usually reported on a dry gas basis. For synthesis gas or pure hydrogen production, the molar ratio of H_2/CO leaving the gasifier is critical. Low tar yields are usually beneficial, unless a raw fuel gas is desired. For sizing scaled-up gasification processes, throughput of solids feed per unit cross-section of reactor (kg/m^2s) is of major importance. A high gas velocity in the gasifier is beneficial, as it usually corresponds to a high solids throughput. A high carbon conversion into reducing gases – excluding CO_2 – by the reactions of Table 15.1 is of greatest importance in single-stage gasification. When gasification is followed by a second stage of char combustion (for example, to produce electrical power), high carbon conversion in the gasification reactor is of less importance. In such cases, mild partial gasification or devolatilization of the feed with low conversion of carbon may be desired.

Spouted and Spout-Fluid Beds: Fundamentals and Applications, eds. Norman Epstein and John R. Grace.
Published by Cambridge University Press. © Cambridge University Press 2011.

Table 15.1. Subset of simplified reactions in gasification or combustion systems.[*]

Pyrolysis	Carbonaceous solid $\rightarrow$ char + tar + gases	Neutral
	(H_2, CO, CO_2, H_2O, CH_4, C_nH_m)	
Gasification	C (char) + H_2O $\rightarrow$ CO + H_2	Endothermic
	C (char) + CO_2 $\rightarrow$ 2CO	Endothermic
	C (char)+ $2H_2$ $\rightarrow$ CH_4	Endothermic
Combustion	C (char) + O_2 $\rightarrow$ CO_2	Exothermic
	C (char) + $\frac{1}{2}O_2$ $\rightarrow$ CO	Exothermic
Gas phase	CO + H_2O $\rightarrow$ CO_2 + H_2	Exothermic
	CH_4 + H_2O $\rightarrow$ CO + $3H_2$	Exothermic
	CO + $\frac{1}{2}O_2$ $\rightarrow$ CO_2	Exothermic

[*] Ignores tar cracking, gas phase combustion, reforming of C_nH_m and tars, reactions of N, S, minerals in feed solid.

15.2   Spouted bed gasification of coal and coke

Spouted beds have been used to gasify coal, coke, carbonaceous sludges, biomass, and municipal solid waste. In most cases the feed material has been coal, and the spouted bed gasifier has been operated at atmospheric pressure in dry ash mode with an air–steam mixture as the gasifying agent. Some authors have reported studies at elevated pressures, with oxygen–steam mixtures, or in the ash-agglomerating mode. For small-scale (<0.25-m diameter) units, electrical furnaces can provide heat for the gasification through the reactor walls; otherwise, operation can be autothermal, with the heat generated in situ by combustion reactions driving the endothermic char–steam or char–CO_2 reactions. A variety of feeding arrangements have been used. Coal particles, typically a few millimeters in diameter, can be added on top of the spouted bed, through the side of the reactor, at the apex (bottom) with the entering oxidant gas flow, or in other ways, as shown in Figure 15.1. In attempts to develop spouted bed gasification technology, various configurations such as normal spouting, spout fluidization, and spouting with draft tubes have been explored.

From the early 1980s, publications appeared on spouted bed gasification of coal mainly from Canada, the United Kingdom, Japan, and the United States. Recent work has come from China, where most of the world's coal gasification systems are found.[1] Table 15.2 summarizes equipment and operating conditions, together with some key results.

After reporting initial results from a 0.15-m diameter reactor,[2] Foong et al.[3] and Watkinson et al.[4,5] carried out most of their subsequent work in a 0.31-m diameter, autothermal atmospheric pressure spouted bed gasifier, with coal feed rates up to 60 kg/h. Although top feeding was tested, in most work coal of size 0.7 to 3.5 mm was conveyed into the bottom of the reactor (Figure 15.1a) with the spouting air–steam mixture. Ash was removed from the produced gas and recovered by cyclone. The inert bed was composed of crushed gravel of 1 to 3.4 mm diameter. The bed reached a steady-state carbon content and temperature for autothermal operation, depending on coal feed rate and reactivity. The spouted bed gasifier was shown to be operable with coals of all ranks, including caking coal, as well as with delayed coke.[6] With caking coal, top-feeding

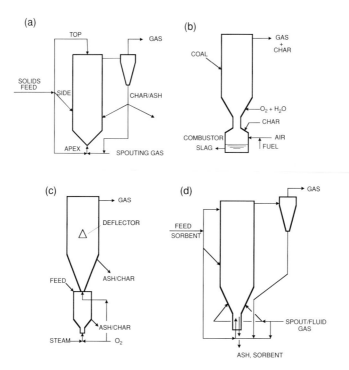

Figure 15.1. Solids and gas feeding arrangements for different gasifier configurations: (a) spouted bed, adapted from Watkinson et al.[3-7]; (b) agglomerating ash gasifier, adapted from Kikuchi et al.[8]; (c) jet-spouted bed, adapted from Tsuji et al.[9-11]; (d) spout-fluid bed, adapted from Arnold et al.[13]

should be avoided. Throughputs and carbon conversion were both higher for more reactive, lower-rank, noncaking coals. Outlet gas quality and yield were reported as functions of such properties as coal feed rate, particle size, bed temperature, and oxidant-to-coal ratio. Results were obtained for single pass versus char recycle,[3] with oxygen–steam versus air–steam blowing in agglomerating versus dry-ash operation, with addition of catalyst,[5] and with addition of limestone and dolomite for sulfur capture.[6] In cases in which an inert bed was not used, the resulting char bed was less stable, with the bed depth undergoing significant changes over time. In-bed temperature and composition profiles were measured.[7] Figure 15.2 shows that oxygen is limited to the lower regions of the spout; higher up, the spout is under reducing conditions. Oxygen is virtually absent from the annulus, which is largely a reducing zone, with highest concentrations of CO and H_2 at the top of the bed. The temperatures reflect the gas analyses, with the oxidation in the spout resulting in temperatures at the top that exceed those in the annulus. Such data provided inputs for modeling studies.

Kikuchi et al.[8] developed an agglomerating ash gasifier system using the configuration shown in Figure 15.1b, with an upper spouted gasifier of $D = 0.4$ m, operated with oxygen–steam mixtures injected both below the conical section and two-thirds of the way up the cone height. Up to 100 kg/h coal was fed through the side of the reactor into

Table 15.2. Summary of spouted bed gasification studies by reactor size and throughput.*

Feed	Reactor type	D (m)	Feed rate (kg/h)	Oxidant	P_{max} (MPa)	T (°C)	Max. solids flux (kg/m²-s)	Reference No.
coal	S	0.028	0.16	O_2-N_2	1.3	850—900	0.07	21
coal	S	0.076	–	N_2 + St	2	900	–	23
coal	SF	0.08	5—12	A + St	0.5	870—1030	0.66	17
biomass	S, F	0.09	4.2	A	0.1	607—842	0.18	28
coal, an	S	0.10	5	St, O, A	1.8	550—865	0.18	14—15
c.coal	S	0.13	10—16	A	0.1	980—1185	0.33	27
coal	S	0.15	2.5—12	A + St	0.1	750—930	0.20	2
coal	S, J	0.21	4—8	A + St	0.1	727—1027	0.06	9
coal	J	0.20	7—10	O + St	0.1	1007—1120	0.09	11
biomass	SF	0.26	80	A	0.1	700—765	0.42	24
coal	S, F	0.305	60	A + St	0.1	805—985	0.23	3, 4
coal	S	0.305	28—42	O + St	0.1	710—1120	0.16	5
coke	S	0.305	16—41	O + St	0.1	900—970	0.16	6
coal	S	0.4	50—100	O + St	0.1	1050—1170	0.17	8
coal	SF	0.4	360—490	A + St	1.8	970—1020	0.90	13
coal	SF	0.45	317—330	A + St	0.5	940—980	0.60	18
msw	SF	0.45 × 0.45	~70	A	0.1	662—777	0.10	26
msw	S	1.0	700	O + St	0.1	540—870	0.25	25
coal	SF	1.2	500	A + St	0.1	950—1020	0.12	12, 13
coal	S	1.0	2490	A + St	1.2	980	0.90	19

* Feed: an = anthracite, c.coal = charcoal, msw = municipal solid waste
Reactor type: S = spouted, SF = spout-fluid, F = fluidized, J = jet spouted
Oxidant: A = air, St = steam, O = oxygen

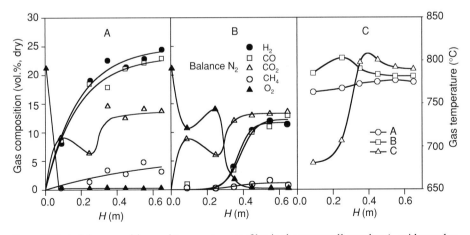

Figure 15.2. Axial composition and temperature profiles in the near-wall annulus A, mid-annulus B, and spout C, adapted from Haji-Sulaiman et al.[7]

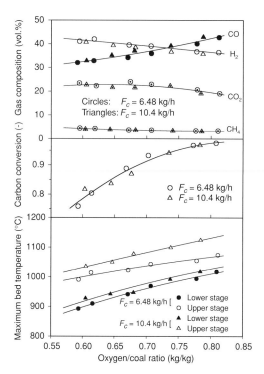

Figure 15.3. Effects of oxygen/coal mass ratio on outlet gas composition, carbon conversion, and gasifier bed temperatures in a jet-spouted bed, adapted from Tsuji and Uemaki[11]. F_c = coal feed rate.

a relatively shallow bed. Temperatures were 1050 °C to 1170 °C, at which 2- to 10-mm-diameter ash agglomerates of low (<4%) carbon content formed, and fell through the throat into a pool of slag, into which cyclone char was injected. The effects of key process variables were presented. Uemaki and Tsuji[9–11] describe a dry-ash, jet-spouted bed (Figure 15.1c) oxygen–steam-fed gasifier system of $D = 0.2$ m with a coal feed rate of ~10 kg/h. In this case, a sharper cone angle ($\theta = 40°$) and a shallow bed system ($H/D \sim 2$) were used at velocities of 0.8 to 1.8 m/s. This resulted in a high bed voidage ($\varepsilon \sim 0.9$), which permitted operation up to 1150 °C without ash agglomeration. Relatively uniform axial temperature profiles were found. Effects of key process variables on gas quality, gas yield, and carbon conversion were explored. Figure 15.3 shows the interplay of oxygen–coal ratio, temperature, carbon conversion, and gas quality typical of gasification processes. As the O/C ratio is raised with a fixed flow of coal, temperatures and carbon conversion values rise, and the H_2/CO ratio in the produced gas declines. Because the heats of combustion per mole of hydrogen and carbon monoxide are very similar, the gas heating value increases only weakly with increasing O/C ratio.

British Coal developed an atmospheric pressure spout-fluid bed gasifier for low-calorific-value gas[12,13] in which most of the air–steam mixture is introduced at the apex of the conical section, and the remainder along the cone (Figure 15.1d). For a bed deeper than H_m, the upper portion behaves as a slugging fluidized bed. Units have been operated at up to 500 kg/h with different coals, feed sizes up to 25 mm, different bed materials and bed depths, with air enrichment by oxygen, and with limestone injection. The benefits of operating with a dense, inert bed of solids (bauxite), rather than a char bed, were demonstrated. With some coals, unwanted agglomeration occurred at bed temperatures above 1000 °C in silica sand beds. Carbon conversion up to 94 percent was possible with char recycle. Gas heating values were about 3.9 MJ/m³. Eighty-five percent desulfurization of the gas was achieved. Scaleup issues for the atmospheric pressure unit to a 0.5-m diameter gasifier have also been discussed.[13] A pressurized spout-fluid gasifier unit, capable of throughputs of 490 kg/h, at pressures to 1.8 MPa with a 0.32-m-diameter × 10-m tall pressure vessel, had been fabricated and commissioned by 1992.

Pressurized spouted bed gasification in a 0.1-m-diameter, 2–5 kg-coal/h gasifier blown with steam or steam–oxygen mixtures, and able to operate at pressures to 1.8 MPa, was described by Sue-A-Quan et al.[14,15] When firing with steam alone, pressure effects on gas composition were minimal, and carbon conversion was shown to increase linearly with pressure up to ~1.5 MPa before leveling out. Oxygen addition was necessary when using anthracite because of its low reactivity. Catalysts were shown to be effective in increasing carbon conversion at a given temperature. A gasifier based on a draft tube spouted bed (Chapter 7) was described in a series of papers by Hatate and co-workers.[16]

Recent work from China by Xiao et al.[17] featured an 0.08-m diameter spout-fluid unit operated at a pressure of 0.5 MPa with a high-temperature (700 °C) inlet air–steam mixture to gasify up to 12 kg/h of high-ash coal at 870–1030 °C. Pressure and temperature effects are delineated, with carbon conversion in the absence of char recycle reaching about 86 percent at the highest temperature. The dense bed was essentially isothermal. Spout temperatures were 20–30 °C higher than in the annulus, in rough agreement with previous work.[7] In subsequent research, Xiao et al.[18] developed a spout-fluid bed pilot plant that is said to be insensitive to the high ash levels in their low rank coals. This 0.45-m diameter × 10.5-m-high air–steam blown gasifier was designed for operation at 0.5 MPa and 950–980 °C. Bed inert material is 1.85-mm-diameter boiler ash, which provides a deep bed (3.6 m depth), in a manner similar to the British Coal process. Coal fed at 330 kg/h is gasified using preheated air–steam mixtures at a superficial velocity of 1.3 m/s. Carbon conversion efficiencies up to 69.4 percent are reported, with produced gas heating values of 4.5 MJ/m³. In a combustor unit, bottom ash containing up to 39 percent carbon is to be burned with 52 percent carbon content fly ash from the cyclones.

In the United States, the Power Systems Development Facility (PSDF) circulating fluid bed system under development in the early 1990s included a pressurized spouted bed "carbonizer" or mild gasifier.[19] Here a 1-m-diameter × 18-m-high spouted bed treated 2490 kg/h of <3.2 mm coal mixed with 475 kg/h sorbent at a temperature of 980 °C and a pressure of 1.3 MPa, to produce a fuel gas of heating value 4.9 MJ/m³ and a char product for subsequent combustion.

Sulfur capture from troublesome gases such as H_2S and COS is mentioned above. Ammonia formation during coal gasification has been investigated[20,21] in a very-small-diameter ($D = 28$ mm) spouted bed able to operate up to high (20 bar) pressures at a coal feed rate of about 0.2 kg/h. NH_3 levels of up to 2750 ppmv were reported. The same system was used to gasify dried sewage sludge of 36 percent ash[22] at 770°C to 790°C and pressures of 0.2 to 0.4 MPa with air. The gas produced had heating values of 1.6 to 5.1 MJ/m^3, and, as well as considerable H_2S, contained up to 8000 ppm NH_3 arising from the 4.5 percent by weight N in the feed. High temperatures led to reduced ammonia concentrations.

Effects of coal particle size on both pyrolysis and steam gasification at 900°C in deep beds of small (76 mm) diameter have been investigated.[23] Coal particle size effects are also mentioned in other work.[3,12]

15.3   Spouted bed gasification of biomass and wastes

The extensive increase in gasification research over the past decade or so, focused mostly on biomass feedstocks, has yielded relatively little recent work on spouted beds. Early spout-fluid bed gasification of biomass wastes was reported by Zak and Nutcher.[24] By 1993, the spouted bed reactor was described as an "emerging technology" for recycling waste,[25] with solid wastes gasified at temperatures of 538–870°C by highly super-heated steam to produce a syngas product and an inert granular solid. Carbonaceous feedstocks with heating values of 7 to 28 MJ/kg, including coal-tar-contaminated soils, petroleum refinery wastes, and municipal solid wastes, could be treated. A unit of approximately 1 m diameter, with bed material of 1.6 to 6.4 mm silica sand, treated up to 680 kg wastes/h and produced a gas of 12 to 18 MJ/m^3 and an ash containing 1 percent to 2 percent carbon. Auxiliary fuel and oxygen were fed at the bottom; char was oxidized in the cyclone to produce a molten inert ash. Gasification of simulated municipal solid waste in a spout-fluid bed of square cross-section was described by Thamavithya and Dutta[26]; feed rates and temperatures were not given. Salam and Bhattacharya[27] reported on spouted bed gasification of wood charcoal with both a normal circular gas inlet orifice and a novel circular slit orifice. Hoque and Bhattacharya[28] compared fluidized and spouted bed gasification of coconut shells.

15.4   Throughput and scale of spouted bed gasification

The scale to which spouted bed gasification has been demonstrated is of key interest in assessing the potential for industrial implementation. The previous survey covered results from spouted bed units processing from less than 5 kg coal/h to 2490 kg/h, a scale factor of more than 500 in terms of feed rate. Table 15.2 indicates that the increased throughput has been achieved by expanding reactor diameters from 0.15 m to 1.2 m, a scaleup in cross-sectional area of about 60. By operating at 1.0 MPa rather than atmospheric pressure, a further capacity increase of roughly a factor of ten occurs. It is not surprising that variations in solids throughput are significant, given the variations in reactivity that arise from coal rank, and the fact that feed rates have not all been converted to a moisture- and ash-free basis, as well as differences in such factors as feed location and particle size. Nevertheless, the data summarized in Table 15.2 suggest that at atmospheric pressure, with coal feed, units operate at solid feed mass fluxes of about 0.1 to 0.2 kg/m^{2}s, which can be raised to 0.3 to 0.6 kg/m^{2}s at $P = 0.5$ MPa, and to 0.9 kg/m^{2}s at $P = 1.2$–1.8 MPa. Wood charcoal[27] throughput appears to be higher.

Variations from normal spouting have been adopted in many cases. Either bed depths were reduced, as in high velocity "jet-spouting," or deep spout-fluid beds were adopted with some gas fed through the cone walls. Spouting must also occur in some commercial fluid bed units such as the high-temperature Winkler and Kellogg-Rust-Westinghouse[1] gasifiers, both of which operate with gases entering at the apex of a conical section in vessels that have no grid or distributor.

Direct comparisons of the effects of different reactor configuration for the same feedstocks have been reported. The capability of the spouted bed to better accommodate agglomerating feedstocks, such as caking coals, has often been cited. Watkinson et al.[4] compared a spouted bed directly with a bubbling fluidized bed. The performances of the two types of reactor were very similar, although optimal conditions for each may not have been achieved. Normal spouting versus "jet spouting" gasification can be compared,[9–11] although temperature and other conditions were not quite identical. For charcoal gasification, two variants of spouting have been compared.[27] With coconut shells, a fluid bed gave slightly better quality gas than a flat-bottomed bed spouted via a single central orifice.[28]

Although the spout-fluid gasifier appears to be the most successful type of spouted bed for coal as scale has increased to ~1 m in diameter, for much larger integrated power plant processes, higher temperature entrained-bed slagging gasifiers appear to be favored over dry-ash units such as the spouted bed.[1] For municipal solid waste, spouted beds have been investigated[25] at a substantial demonstration scale of 680 kg/h.

15.5   Modeling of spouted bed gasification

Numerous efforts have been made to model spouted bed gasification. These range from simple mass-balance equilibrium models, which do not consider solids or gas motion,[2,15] through streamtube models that treat only the gas phase reactions.[29] The pyrolysis step is usually treated separately as an instantaneous reaction with or without an equilibrium stage. Jet-spouting (i.e., dilute spouting) models have been developed[10] using simplified kinetics. Both isothermal and nonisothermal two-region models are available that treat the spout and the annulus as plug flow sections.[30] Conversion of char in the gasifier is most readily handled with backmix flow models and simplified kinetics for the gas–solid reactions listed in Table 15.1.[31] Li et al.[32] recently outlined a three-dimensional kinetic and computational fluid dynamic model for a pressurized spout-fluid bed and provided verification based on experimental studies.

15.6   Spouted bed pyrolysis of coal, shale, biomass, and solid wastes

Pyrolysis is of considerable importance on its own as a process for producing liquid products from solids such as coal, shale, heavy oil, biomass, and waste plastics. It is also a step preceding gas–char reactions in gasification or combustion processes. Key features of pyrolysis not evident in the single equation of Table 15.1 are reflected in a two-stage reaction, which allows for tar cracking:

$$Carbonaceous\ Solid \longrightarrow Char_1 + Tar + Gas_1 \qquad (R1)$$

$$Tar \longrightarrow Char_2 + Gas_2 \qquad (R2)$$

The main heat requirement in pyrolysis is to raise the solids to the devolatilization temperature, at which reactions R1 and R2 proceed with small endothermic or exothermic heat effects. For processes whose purpose is to produce liquids, tar destruction reactions such as R2 should be minimized. Liquid yields go through a maximum with increasing temperature, as high temperatures promote reaction R2. In biomass gasification, by contrast, a tar-free gas is desired, and conditions that favor reactions such as R2 should be promoted. Char is a by-product of pyrolysis. Because of its low market value, coal char is usually either gasified or combusted in a separate unit. However, production of biochar from biomass feedstocks is an active area of research and development.

Pyrolysis of coals and oil shales has been investigated in spouted bed systems for liquid production, as well as for its effect on subsequent char gasification. Results are summarized in Table 15.3. Most lab-scale investigations have been aimed primarily at determining tar, char, and gas yields and compositions as functions of feedstock and spouted bed operating conditions (e.g., temperature, solid and gas feed rates, particle size, bed materials).

Pioneering work on coal carbonization in Australia[33] was intended to produce a smokeless char rather than to recover liquids. This work showed that a spouted bed could accommodate caking (agglomerating) coals. Pyrolysis or retorting of shale to produce oil has been pursued since the 1960s and 1970s.[34,35] Beginning in the 1980s, Petrobras evaluated spouted bed pyrolysis for oil shale material too small to be used as feed in its moving bed retort. Leite et al.[36] initially used a 0.08-m-diameter spouted bed for retorting oil shale of 1.11 mm size. Subsequent work[37] was performed in a 0.3-m-diameter unit that processed 110 to 240 kg/h of oil shale as a demonstration of the technology, using a nonideal feed containing about 45 percent of particles smaller than 0.84 mm.

A miniature spouted bed with a continuous feed of 0.002 to 0.05 kg/h was used by Teo and Watkinson[38] to prepare coal pyrolysis liquids for subsequent detailed chemical characterization. On a larger scale, studies of both coal pyrolysis[39] and oil shale retorting[40] were carried out in 0.15-m-diameter beds at 1 to 8 kg/h solid feed rate to establish temperature, feed rate, bed composition, and particle size for maximum liquid yields. Maximum liquid yields from coals of the order of 25 percent were observed at bed temperatures of about 525 °C to 600 °C, depending on the rank of the coal and other factors. For low-rank coals in particular, the liquid contains an aqueous fraction that can

Table 15.3. Spouted bed pyrolysis studies of coal, oil shale, and biomass.*

Feed	Reactor type	D (m)	Spout gas	Feed rate (kg/h)	Mass flux (kg/m²s)	Max. liq. yield %	T (°C)	Bed material	Bed. mat. dia (mm)	Ref.
coal, lignite	S	0.03	N_2	<0.05	0.028	30	440–740	silica	0.43	38
coal	S	0.13	$N_2 + CO_2$	0.6–6	0.13	20	480–650	sand	0.8–1.4	39
coal	S	0.15	air-N_2	6–18.5	0.29	–	490–635	char	2.5	33
shale	S	0.08	N_2, St							36
shale	S	0.13	$N_2 + CO_2$	1–4.5	0.097	7.4	454–555	sand/shale	0.8–1.2	40
shale coal	S	0.15	flue gas	1.6–3.5	0.055	11 shale 15 coal	475–650	char, sand shale	1.3–1.5	41
shale	CS	0.17	air-pyr. gas	9.5	0.12		510–730	shale	<6.4	34
shale	S	0.30	air	150	0.59	~4	430–600	shale	0.8–6.4	37
biomass	CS	0.12	N_2	0.1–0.6	0.015	72	350–700	silica	0.7–1.4	42
biomass	SD	0.15	N_2	<4	0.063	73	440–520	–		44
wood	S	0.19	N_2, N_2–St	1.5	0.015	14	500–700		<6.4	43

* Spout gas: St = steam; pyr. gas = pyrolysis gas
Reactor type: S = spouted, SD = spouted with draft tube, CS = conical spouted

inflate liquid yield data. For oil shales, the corresponding oil yield maxima are about 10 percent, depending on the Fischer assay of the shale. Several studies, such as that by Jarallah and Watkinson,[39] have shown that the prominence of secondary reactions (R2) increases with particle size. Therefore, smaller particles are preferred.

In a commercial process, the sensible heat needed for pyrolysis must be provided somehow. Injection of a small amount of air, with coal[33] or shale,[37] results in lowering of tar yield, although this permits much larger solids throughputs. Tamm and Kuehler[35] described a second spent shale combustion reactor, with recirculation of heat transfer solids to the retort. Rovero and Watkinson[41] developed a vertical two-stage autothermal unit with coal or shale pyrolysis in an upper spouted bed in which the heat for the pyrolysis came from the gases exiting the lower reactor, in which combustion or gasification of the spent char or shale took place. Liquid yield reaching a maximum with increasing temperature is shown in Figure 15.4.

The use of a large spouted bed "mild-gasifier," carbonizer, or pyrolyzer in the PSDF power plant system[19] was included under gasification in Table 15.2. The very high temperature of 980 °C would minimize production of liquids.

Pioneering work on the conical spouted bed reactor, including its use for pyrolysis of wood waste, cork waste, postconsumer plastics, and tire material, is covered in Chapter 5. As an example, sawdust is fed at up to 0.6 kg/h together with 0.7- to 1.3-mm sand, to a 0.12-m-diameter pyrolyzer. Data on effects of temperature on yields and compositions of gas, liquid, and char are presented by Aguado et al.[42] Table 15.3 summarizes other spouted bed biomass and waste pyrolysis studies. Janarthanan and Clements[43] operated a 0.2-m-diameter gasifier, primarily in the pyrolysis mode, and at

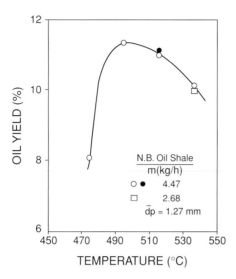

Figure 15.4. Oil yield from New Brunswick shale versus spouted bed pyrolyzer temperature.[41]

low throughput. Fast pyrolysis of biomass in a spout-fluidized bed reactor equipped with a draft tube (Chapter 7) was reported by Chen et al.[44] Maximum liquid yield of about 72 percent occurred at about 450 °C,[42,44] which is typical for wood pyrolysis. Throughput of the draft-tube spout-fluid bed seems to have been substantially higher than for the conical spouted bed for the single case reported for each.

Pyrolysis of dry sewage sludge over short periods of time to determine gas yield and composition has been mentioned previously.[22] The use of a plasma jet to provide heat within a spouted bed has been investigated to provide reducing gases for a solid oxide fuel cell[45] using biomass feed. No liquid production was reported in either of these studies.

15.7   Combustion of solid fuels

Combustion of solids may be carried out using a number of diverse contacting techniques, including bubbling fluidized beds, circulating fluidized beds, entrained beds, and spouted beds. Whereas coal is often burned as a powder in power plants, in developing countries the most common way to produce steam or hot gases has been by feeding larger particles onto a vibrating grate, which moves the particles horizontally while air rises across the bed. The vibration avoids sintering (agglomeration) of particles, a problem always present in moving or fixed beds. The burning rate is usually limited by the resistance to diffusion of oxygen along the particle pores, rather than by the intrinsic kinetics or external transport resistance. Therefore, to increase the combustion rate, actions need to be taken to reduce the internal resistance posed by the diffusion of oxygen within the pores. As little can be done to increase the effective diffusivity of oxygen within the pores, higher coal combustion rates can be accommodated by reducing the particle size and selecting an adequate gas–solid contacting technique to handle it.

Each of the aforementioned gas–solid contacting techniques is suitable for a specific particle size range. From large to small size, the choices would be: vibrating moving bed, spouted bed, bubbling fluidized bed, circulating fluidized bed, and entrained bed. Each technique must impose brisk agitation to prevent sintering, an ever-present threat to smooth operation.

The spouted bed technique is most suited to particles in the diameter range of 1 to 20 mm. When the feedstock to be burned is within this size range, a spouted bed may be a viable option. As in gasifiers, spouting can be maintained using an inert material of convenient size distribution, with a solid fuel stream of different size fed to the bed. Typical size distributions for spouted bed combustors and other operational features are discussed in the next section.

15.8   Spouted bed combustion of coal and other solids

The most common feedstock in investigations of spouted bed combustion has been coal[46–54] of various qualities, including sub-bituminous, bituminous, coal rejects of differing ash contents, low-rank coals, lignite, highly caking coals, and anthracite. Usually the bed includes an inert material such as sand or gravel, which dictates the hydrodynamics of the bed. The fuel is fed either on top or with the spouting gas.

Many other materials have also been used for spouted bed combustion: sawdust[55] peat,[46,56] low-heating-value fuels and wastes,[46,57,58] rice husks,[59,60] and sewage sludge.[61] Efficiencies of three different designs of spouted beds have been determined in combustion of wood charcoal.[62] Oil shale has also been partially combusted in a spouted bed[37] as part of the retorting process. Continuous and batch operations have been carried out with extensive operating time, demonstrating that the spouted bed can operate steadily at high temperature. Figure 15.5 shows a photo of batch combustion of coal in a half-cylindrical column in which the bed material was 1.8-mm sand and the fuel was 0.55- to 2.2-mm coal particles.[47–48]

Investigations on batch and pilot scales indicate that the spouted bed technique is mature enough to be applied at larger scales. A significant characteristic of a spouted-bed combustor, first demonstrated with liquid fuels,[63] is to lower the effective lean flammability limit – that is, to be able to burn fuels with low heating value. Another advantage is the ability to use bed materials, such as alumina or bauxite, that can withstand high temperatures.

Table 15.4 summarizes some details of spouted bed solids combustion studies. In a typical operation burning bituminous coal in a 0.30-m diameter vessel[49] (Figure 15.6) at temperatures of 740 °C to 980 °C, and coal feed rates of 6 to 22 kg/h, efficiencies were above 90 percent at an excess airflow of 15 percent to 20 percent. This investigation compared the spouted bed with fluidized and spout-fluid bed operation and concluded that "the spout-fluid bed tended to give somewhat higher combustion efficiencies at the lower temperatures, greater temperature uniformity and improved bed-to-immersed-surface heat transfer than the other two modes of operation."

Table 15.4. Summary of studies on spouted and spout-fluid bed combustion of solid fuels.[*]

Feed	Reactor type	Dia. (m)	Feed size (mm)	Feed rate (kg/h)	Inert bed	Inert size (mm)	Temp. (°C)	Efficiency %	XS air (%)	Ref.
coal	S	0.077	1−3.4	0.5	sand	0.8−1	700−850			51, 52
coal	S	0.15	0.4−2.4	batch	sand	1−2.4	590−810			47, 48
coal	SF	0.28	6.3−19	45	lstone	3−12	880	94	20	50
coal	S, SF, F	0.30	0.1−5	6−22	grav., sand	1.2−2.8 0.5−2.0	740−980	<90	15−20	49
coal, wastes	S, SF, F	0.30	1−3	8−23	grav	1−3	700−950	83−99	70−140	46
rice husk	MSF	0.7 × 0.7		~20	sand	0.3−1	400−900	85−91	0−30	59
ag. waste	MHS	2 × 2		1725	sand	1.6−4		97		58
sew. sludge	S	0.18	1.2	~6	none	−		99	25	61
wood char.	S	0.15	0−5	1	sand	0.3−0.6	860	<97	<31	62
shale	S	0.30	<6.4	110−240	none		430−600		<0	37

[*] MHS = multiple horizontal spout, MSF = multiple spout-fluid, lstone = limestone, grav. = gravel, Ref. = reference.

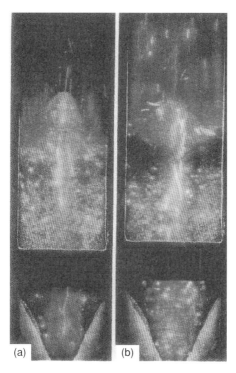

(a)   (b)

Figure 15.5. Coal burning in a half-column combustor under (a) stable, and (b) pulsatory spouting.[48]

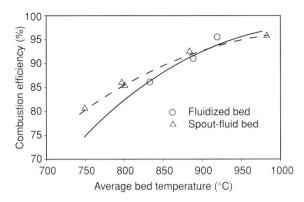

Figure 15.6. Combustion efficiency versus bed temperature in spout-fluid and fluidized bed reactors, adapted from Lim et al.[49]

The Battelle spout-fluid combustor[50] burned 45 kg/h coal in a 0.28-m-diameter unit equipped with a unique design of wall cooling and bayonet cooler. At a velocity of about 2 m/s, throughput was markedly higher than in the study of Lim et al.[49] Spout air was 25 percent to 40 percent of the total. A direct comparison was made of the spout-fluid bed and the fluidized bed with limestone injection, which showed lowering of NO_x and better sulfur capture in the spout-fluid bed.

The largest spouted bed combustion system found in this review,[58] a 7-MW combustor of 4 m^2 bed area, was developed by 1980, prior to most other solids combustion research in spouted beds. In this design, a multiplicity of individual spouts (Chapter 17), created by horizontally directed air jets, promoted the circulation of the 1.6- to 4-mm sand bed material. Although not strictly a spouted bed, this combustor possessed similar characteristics of solid circulation promoted by gas jetting. Operating characteristics of two commercial units were discussed. Units had been sold for incineration of solid agricultural materials, such as grain milling wastes, and industrial liquid wastes. A bench-scale unit of 0.055 m^2 with a single spout had been in operation for more than 5000 hours to test feedstocks, bed materials, and a proprietary distributor.

The 0.30-m-diameter spouted bed reactor of Lisboa and Watkinson,[37] mentioned previously, employed air as the spouting gas to promote in situ combustion during retorting of oil shales. The reactor temperature was maintained at a level sufficient for pyrolysis without air preheating. Some runs were carried out just to burn shale and a mixture of shale and shale oil sludge. The spouted-bed pilot plant is shown in Figure 15.7.

Vuthaluru et al.[51–54] investigated several methods to reduce agglomeration during coal burning in a spouted bed: (1) mineral additive, (2) alternative bed inert solids, and (3) pretreatment of coal. Coal blends were also used with the same purpose; the authors observed that "no particle agglomeration and bed de-fluidization were evident after 15 h of operation with the blends at 800 °C."

Table 15.4 shows that most studies of spouted-bed combustion have used the classical spouted bed geometry – a cylindrical column with a conical bottom. A large range of internal angles, defined as the angle between the central axis and the wall, have been

Figure 15.7. Photograph of five-story spouted bed pilot plant for oxidative pyrolysis of oil shale.[37]

used, from 90° (flat bottom) to the sharp angles of a patented[64] conical spouted bed combustor (Chapter 5). The largest column diameter reported for classical spouting seems to be 0.30 m. Larger vessels not based on the classical geometry were mentioned by Albina,[59,60] in particular a 0.7 m × 0.7-m square cross-section vessel with four air supply nozzles, undoubtedly a solution for scaling up, and by Baker and Wilkinson,[58] described earlier, with multiple spouts created by horizontally directed air jets. Other ways to inject air, which could also be used on a larger scale, were developed by Rasul,[62] with the introduction of air into a cylindrical column through a circular slit and into a square-duct column through a rectangular slit spanning the whole cross-section. Particles can be fed either on top of the bed or pneumatically with the spouting air, as shown in Figure 15.1a.

15.9   Concluding remarks

This chapter highlights the wide spectrum of spouted bed applications in gasification, pyrolysis, and combustion, in which many feedstocks have been examined under various operating conditions. The scale of normal spouted beds or spout-fluid beds also covers a wide range, with diameters of single vessels up to about 1 m. As is evident elsewhere in this book, challenges for spouting processes occur at large scale. As diameters approach ~1 m and greater, spout-fluid contacting appears to be more advantageous for thermal processing. For gasification processes, pressurized operation is advantageous, and high-capacity units are appearing for limited reactor diameters. For combustors, particularly for biomass and wastes, multiple spout units in square vessels operated at atmospheric pressure have been developed.

References

1. R. Fernando. *Coal Gasification*. International Energy Agency Clean Coal Centre Report CCC/140, Oct. 2008.
2. S. K. Foong, C. J. Lim, and A. P. Watkinson. Coal gasification in a spouted bed. *Can. J. Chem. Eng.*, **58** (1980), 84–91.
3. S. K. Foong, G. Cheng, and A. P. Watkinson. Spouted bed gasification of Western Canadian coals. *Can. J. Chem. Eng.*, **59** (1981), 625–630.
4. A. P. Watkinson, G. Cheng, and C. B. Prakash. Comparison of coal gasification in fluidized and spouted beds. *Can. J. Chem. Eng.*, **61** (1983), 468–473.
5. A. P. Watkinson, G. Cheng, and C. J. Lim. Oxygen-steam gasification of coals in a spouted bed. *Can. J. Chem. Eng.*, **65** (1987), 791–798.
6. A. P. Watkinson, G. Cheng, and D. P. C. Fung. Gasification of oil sand coke. *Fuel*, **68** (1989), 4–10.
7. Z. Haji-Sulaiman, C. J. Lim, and A. P. Watkinson. Gas composition and temperature profiles in a spouted bed coal gasifier. *Can. J. Chem. Eng.*, **64** (1986), 125–132.
8. K. Kikuchi, A. Suzuki, T. Mochizuki, S. Endo, E. Imai, and Y. Tanji. Ash-agglomerating gasification of coal in a spouted bed reactor. *Fuel*, **64** (1985), 368–372.
9. O. Uemaki and T. Tsuji. Gasification of a sub-bituminous coal in a two-stage jet-spouted bed reactor. In *Fluidization V*, ed. K. Ostergaard and A. Sorensen (New York: Engineering Foundation, 1986), pp. 497–504.
10. T. Tsuji, T. Shibata, K. Yamaguchi, and O. Uemaki. Mathematical modeling of spouted bed coal gasification. In *Proceedings of the International Conference on Coal Science* (Tokyo: New Energy Development Organization, 1989), pp. 457–460.
11. T. Tsuji and O. Uemaki. Coal gasification in a jet-spouted bed. *Can. J. Chem. Eng.*, **72** (1994), 504–510.
12. J. Gale and C. J. Bower. Development of the British Coal gasification process for the manufacture of low calorific value gas. Presented at Applied Energy Conference, Swansea, September 1989.
13. M. St. J. Arnold, J. J. Gale, and M. K. Laughlin. The British Coal spouted fluidised bed gasification process. *Can. J. Chem. Eng.*, **70** (1992), 991–997.
14. T. Sue-A-Quan, A. P. Watkinson, R. P. Gaikwad, C. J. Lim, and B. R. Ferris. Steam gasification in a pressurized spouted bed reactor. *Fuel Proc. Technol.*, **27** (1991), 67–81.
15. T. Sue-A-Quan, G. Cheng, and A. P. Watkinson. Coal gasification in a pressurized spouted bed. *Fuel*, **74** (1995), 159–164.
16. Y. Hatate, Y. Uemura, S. Tanaka, Y. Tokumasu, Y. Tanaka, D. F. King, and K. Ijichi. Development of a spouted bed-type coal gasifier with cycling thermal medium particles. *Soc. Chem. Engrs, Japan*, **20** (1994), 758–764.
17. R. Xiao, M. Zhang, B. Jin, and Y. Huang. High-temperature air/steam-blown gasification of coal in a pressurized spout-fluid bed. *Energy & Fuels*, **20** (2006), 715–720.

18. R. Xiao, M. Zhang, B. Jin, Y. Xiaong, H. Zhou, Y. Duan, Z. Zhong, X. Chen, L. Shen, and Y Huang. Air blown partial gasification of coal in a pilot plant pressurized spout-fluid bed reactor. *Fuel*, **86** (2007), 1631–1640.

19. D. L. Moore, Z. Haq, T. E. Pinkston, R. E. Rush, P. Vimalchaud, J. D. McClung, and M. T. Quandt. Status of the advanced PFBC at the Power Systems Development Facility. Report DOE/MC/25140–94/C0353 (1994), pp. 127–137.

20. N. Paterson, Y. Zhuo, D. R. Dugwell, and R. Kandiyoti. Investigation of ammonia formation during gasification in an air-blown spouted bed: reactor design and initial tests. *Energy & Fuels*, **16** (2002), 127–135.

21. Y. Zhuo, N. Paterson, B. Avid, D. R. Dugwell, and R. Kandyoti. Investigation of ammonia formation during gasification in an air blown spouted bed: the effect of the operating conditions on ammonia formation and the identification of ways of minimizing its formation. *Energy & Fuels*, **16** (2002), 742–751.

22. N. Paterson, Y. Zhuo, G. P. Reed, D. R. Dugwell, and R. Kandiyoti. Pyrolysis and gasification of sewage sludge in a spouted-bed reactor. *Water & Envir. J.*, **18** (2004), 90–94.

23. S. Hanson, J. W. Patrick, and A. Walker. The effect of coal particle size on pyrolysis and steam gasification. *Fuel*, **81** (2002), 531–547.

24. C. Zak and P. B. Nutcher. Spouted fluid-bed gasification of biomass and chemical wastes-some pilot plant results. In *Energy from Biomass and Wastes X*, ed. D. K. Klass (London: Elsevier and Chicago: Institute of Gas Technology, 1987), pp. 643–653.

25. U.S. Environmental Protection Agency Report EPA/540/F-93/XXX. "Energy Technology Bulletin – Spouted Bed Reactor," Energy and Environmental Research Corporation (Irvine, CA, 1993).

26. M. Thamavithya and A. Dutta. An investigation of MSW gasification in a spout-fluid bed reactor. *Fuel Proc. Technol.*, **89** (2008), 949–957.

27. P. A. Salam and S. C. Bhattacharya. A comparative study of charcoal gasification in two types of spouted bed reactors. *Energy*, **31** (2006), 228–243.

28. M. M. Hoque and S. C. Bhattacharya. Fuel characteristics of gasified coconut shell in a fluidized and a spouted bed reactor. *Energy*, **26** (2001), 101–110.

29. C. J. Lim, J. P. Lucas, M. Haji-Sulaiman, and A. P. Watkinson. A mathematical model of a spouted bed gasifier. *Can. J. Chem. Eng.*, **69** (1991), 596–606.

30. J. P. Lucas, C. J. Lim, and A. P. Watkinson. A non-isothermal model of a spouted bed coal gasifier. *Fuel*, **77** (1998), 683–694.

31. B. H. Song and A. P. Watkinson. Three-stage well-mixed reactor model for a pressurized coal gasifier. *Can. J. Chem. Eng.*, **78** (2000), 143–155.

32. Q. Li, M. Zhang, W. Zhong, X. Wang, R. Xiao, and B. Jin. Simulation of coal gasification in a pressurized spout-fluid bed gasifier. *Can. J. Chem. Eng.*, **87** (2009), 169–176.

33. R. K. Barton, G. R. Rigby, and J. S. Ratcliffe. The use of a spouted bed for the low temperature carbonization of coal. *Mech. Chem. Eng. Trans.*, **4** (1968), 105–112.

34. L. P. Berti and J. H. Gary. Spouted bed oil shale retort. *Colorado School of Mines Quart.*, **61** (1966), 553–560.

35. P. W. Tamm and C. W. Kuehler, Spouted-bed shale retorting process. U.S. Patent 4,125,453 (1978).

36. A. C. B. Leite, R. M. P. Wodtke, A. C. L. Lisboa, and F. Restini. Pyrolysis of oil shale fines in a spouted bed reactor. XVI Congresso Latino Americano de Quimica, Rio de Janeiro, October 1984.

37. A. C. L. Lisboa and A. P. Watkinson. Pyrolysis with partial combustion of oil shale fines in a spouted bed. *Can. J. Chem. Eng.*, **70** (1992), 983–990.

38. K. C. Teo and A. P. Watkinson. Rapid pyrolysis of Canadian coals in a miniature spouted bed reactor. *Fuel*, **65** (1986), 949–959.

39. A. Jarallah and A. P. Watkinson. Pyrolysis of Western Canadian coals in a spouted bed. *Can. J. Chem. Eng.*, **63** (1985), 227–236.

40. T. Tam. Pyrolysis of oil shale in a spouted bed pyrolyser. M.A.Sc. thesis, University of British Columbia (1987).

41. G. Rovero and A. P. Watkinson. A two-stage spouted bed process for auto-thermal pyrolysis or retorting. *Fuel Proc. Technol.*, **26** (1990), 221–238.

42. R. Aguado, M. Olazar, M. San José, G. Aguirre, and J. Bilbao. Pyrolysis of sawdust in a conical spouted bed reactor. Yields and product composition, *Ind. Eng. Chem. Res.*, **39** (2000), 1925–1933.

43. A. K. Janarthanan and L. D. Clements. Gasification of wood in a pilot scale spouted bed gasifier. In *Dev. Thermochem. Biomass Conversion*, vol. 2, ed. A. V. Bridgwater and D. G. B. Boocock (Amsterdam: Kluwer Academic, 1997), pp. 945–959.

44. M. Chen, J. Wang, X. Wang, X. Zhang, S. Zhang, Z. Ren, and Y. Yan. Fast pyrolysis of biomass in a spout-fluidized bed reactor–analysis of composition and combustion characteristics of liquid product from biomass. *Chin. J. Proc. Eng.*, **6** (2006), 192–96.

45. J. Jurewicz and A. Lemoine. Solid oxide fuel cell combustible by plasma spouted bed gasification of granulated biomass. *Prep. Pap. Amer. Chem. Soc. Div. Fuel Chem.*, **49** (2004), 916–917.

46. C. J. Lim, S. K. Barua, N. Epstein, J. R. Grace, and A. P. Watkinson. Spouted bed and spout-fluid bed combustion of solid fuels. In *Fluidised Combustion: Is It Achieving Its Promise?* Third International Fluidised Bed Combustion Conference, Institute of Energy, London (1984).

47. J. C. Zhao, C. J. Lim, and J. R. Grace. Coal burnout times in spouted and spouted-fluid beds. *Chem. Eng. Res. Dev.*, **65** (1987), 426–429.

48. J. C. Zhao, C. J. Lim, and J. R. Grace. Flow regimes and combustion behavior in coal-burning spouted and spout-fluid beds. *Chem. Eng. Sci.*, **42** (1987), 2865–2875.

49. C. J. Lim, A. P. Watkinson, G. K. Khoe, S. Low, N. Epstein, and J. R. Grace. Spouted, fluidized and spout-fluid bed combustion of bituminous coals. *Fuel*, **67** (1988), 1211–1217.

50. F. W. Shirley and R. D. Litt. Advanced atmospheric fluidized-bed combustion design-spouted bed. Final Report to U.S. Department of Energy from Battelle Columbus Laboratories, February 1988.

51. H. B. Vuthaluru, T. M. Linjewille, D. Zhang, and A. R. Manzoori. Investigations into the control of agglomeration and defluidisation during fluidised-bed combustion of low-rank coals. *Fuel*, **78** (1999), 419–425.

52. H. B. Vuthaluru and D. Zhang. Control methods for remediation of ash-related problems in fluidised-bed combustors. *Fuel Proc. Technol.*, **60** (1999), 145–156.

53. H. B. Vuthaluru, D. Zhang, and T. M. Linjewile. Behaviour of inorganic constituents and ash characteristics during fluidised-bed combustion of several Australian low-rank coals. *Fuel Proc. Technol.*, **67** (2000), 165–176.

54. H. B. Vuthaluru and D. Zhang. Effect of coal blending on particle agglomeration and defluidisation during spouted-bed combustion of low-rank coals. *Fuel Proc. Technol.*, **70** (2001), 41–51.

55. M. J. San José, M. J. Aguado, S. Alvarez, and J. Bilbao. Combustion of sawdust and forestry waste in conical spouted beds. *Rev. de Inform. Tecnol.* **13** (2002), 133–137.

56. M. Khoshnoodi and R. Z. Abidin. Utilization of Malaysian peat in spouted bed burner. In *Proceedings of the 10th Malaysian Chemical Engineering Symposium* (Penang: Institute of Chemical Engineers, Malaysia, 1994).

57. E. R. Altwicker, R. K. N. Konduri, and M. S. Milligan. Spouted bed combustor for the study of heterogeneous hazardous waste incineration. AIChE Meeting, Philadelphia, Paper 82c (1989).

58. R. S. Baker and R. C. Wilkinson. The commercial development of spouted/fluidised bed combustion in Australia. In *Fluidised Combustion: Systems and Applications.* Institute of Energy Symposium Series, Vol. 1, No. 4 (1980), pp. 1–11.

59. D. O. Albina. Combustion of rice husk in a multiple-spouted fluidized bed. *Energy Sources,* **25** (2003), 893–904.

60. D. O. Albina, Emissions from multiple-spouted and spout-fluid beds using rice husks as fuel. *Renew. Energy,* **31** (2006), 2152–2163.

61. M. Barz. Sewage sludge combustion in a spouted bed cascade system. *China Particuology,* **1** (2003), 223–228.

62. M. G. Rasul. Spouted bed combustion of wood charcoal: performance comparison of three different designs. *Fuel,* **80** (2001), 2189–2191.

63. H. A. Arbib and A. Levy. Combustion of low heating value fuels and wastes in the spouted bed. *Can. J. Chem. Eng.,* **60** (1982), 528–531.

64. J. Bilbao, M. Olazar, and M. J. San José. Dispositivo para la combustion en continuo de residuos solidos, Oficina Espanola de Patentes y Marcas, 2,148,026 (2001), 9 pages.

16 Spouted bed electrochemical reactors

J. W. Evans and Vladimír Jiřičný

16.1 Introduction

Electrochemical reactions are used in the chemical, metallurgical, pharmaceutical, and other industries, as such reactions typically allow precise control of reactions by adjustment of voltage. Such reactions usually carry a high capital and energy cost, however, and there has been much investigation to improve space-time yield, current efficiency, and electric power consumption.

Figure 16.1 shows schematically the geometric arrangement of several electrochemical reactors. Broadly, these designs have two electrodes separated by a liquid electrolyte, and in some instances a separator capable of ion transport. Electrochemical reactions are inherently heterogeneous, occurring at the interface between an electronic and an ionic conductor; mass transport of ions to and from such interfaces therefore plays an important role. Unlike other heterogeneous reactions, such as reaction of a gas on a solid catalytic surface, transport on the other side of the interface (of charge, i.e., electrical current) is also significant. The need for this latter conduction motivates many aspects of design in Figure 16.1, as discussed in this chapter. An important parameter of the designs in Figure 16.1 is the electrode surface area per unit of reactor volume; the higher this value, the higher the space-time yield, other things being equal. Moving along the top row and down to the bottom row should provide designs in which space-time yields are high and perhaps designs in which high mass transfer rates can be exploited as well.

Another design consideration arises from the nature of the reaction products: solid, gas, or solution. If no additional phases are formed, such as in an organic synthesis in which reaction products at both electrodes could remain in solution, then no issue arises. If a solid is formed, as in the electrodeposition of metals from solution, then designs such as the narrow gap cell or the Swiss-roll cell are unsuitable, because their flow paths are rapidly blocked by deposits. This is true of the extreme form of the narrow gap cell, the electrochemical microreactor in which the interelectrode gap is typically of the order of 100 μm. In the case of gas evolution at an electrode, the possible interference of gas bubbles with either electrolyte flow or conduction in the electrolyte must be considered.

From the considerations of the last paragraph, it is clear that reactors in which the electrodes are particulate, and there is relative motion between particles and electrolyte,

Spouted and Spout-Fluid Beds: Fundamentals and Applications, eds. Norman Epstein and John R. Grace.
Published by Cambridge University Press. © Cambridge University Press 2011.

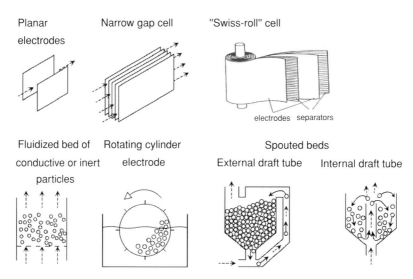

Figure 16.1. Electrochemical cell principles.

might be especially beneficial. For reactions in which neither gases nor solids form, a packed bed of particles could be expected to function well.[1] (Electrodes that are porous are similar.) If solids or gases form, an electrode in which the particles are in motion would seem preferable – that is, a fluidized or spouted bed, or a bed in which particles are mechanically agitated, as in rotating cylinder electrodes. In all these cases the electrodes become, in a sense, three-dimensional; when operating properly, electrochemistry occurs throughout the whole volume of the bed of particles.

16.2   Spouted bed electrodes

The sketches of particulate electrodes in Figure 16.1 are incomplete in that they do not show how electrical connection is made to the particles, nor do they show the counter-electrode that completes the cell design. More detailed designs appear in Figure 16.2. Simplest in concept is the spouted bed electrode (SBE) of A, in which a central jet of electrolyte in a cylindrical-conical bed of particles sweeps a flow of particles upward. At the top of the bed the jet (spout) expands, and the upswept particles fall back onto the top of the bed. The particles then move slowly downward in an annular region, dense with particles, in a manner characteristic of spouted beds, as described throughout this volume. Just visible in the sketch is a "current feeder" (or "current collector," depending on whether the bed acts as an anode or cathode) in the form of a conducting material placed outside the bed. This is electrically connected to one side of the DC power supply. Above the bed is a counterelectrode, such as a disk of conducting material, connected to the other side of the power supply. From the previous section, it will be clear that only particles that are in electrical connection with the power supply will function electro-chemically. Therefore particles in the annular region will be active, but those in the spout

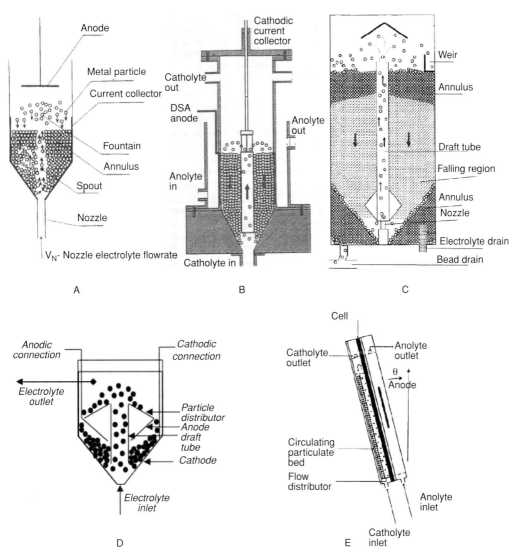

Figure 16.2. Geometrical arrangements of SBEs: (A) conventional conical-cylindrical spouted bed without draft tube or separator[1]; (B) conical-cylindrical spouted bed with draft tube and separator[2]; (C) rectangular spouted bed with draft tube and separator[11,12]; (D) conical-cylindrical SBE with draft tube and without separator[3,4,34]; (E) circulating rectangular SBE with separator and without draft tube.[35]

will not. (Less facile electrical contact of the particles is one disadvantage of fluidized bed electrodes compared with SBEs.)

Design A suffers from the spreading of the upflowing jet of electrolyte and particles higher in the bed, so that above one to a few bed diameters the cross-section is mostly fluidized, with poor electrical contact of the particles. Design B, an SBE with a central draft tube, is intended to allow vertical scaleup, while maintaining the slowly moving downward bed in the annular region. In this design the draft tube also functions as a current collector, and the periphery of the bed is contained within a separator, outside of which sits the cylindrical counterelectrode. The remaining designs in Figure 16.2 are similar in concept to the second, but intended to facilitate aspects of cell operation, such as the addition and removal of particles. In design C the geometry is no longer cylindrical; the flat current feeder sits in front of the plane of the figure, whereas the flat counterelectrode sits behind that plane, with a separator between it and the bed so there is no direct electrical contact between counterelectrode and bed. If the counterelectrode is a mesh, then the separator is conveniently supported by the counterelectrode. The bed in C has a weir, which is intended to limit vertical growth of the bed in the case of particle growth by deposition (not shown is a discharge of particles from the volume to the right of the weir). Much of the rest of this chapter is devoted to SBEs of a design similar to C, particularly their application to the electrodeposition of metals.

SBEs with draft tubes have been extensively studied for use in metal electrodeposition from aqueous solutions in which the bed is connected to the negative side of the power supply (via the current collector) and the particles grow as metal deposits on them because of cathodic reaction. Typically the reaction at the counterelectrode (an anode) evolves oxygen.

In metal electrodeposition, particle movement must be sufficient that particles are not joined by electrodeposited metal, lest the bed stop moving and become a rigid mass. Consequently, care must be taken to avoid "dead regions" in the SBE in which particles are stationary, or at least these regions must be electrochemically inactive. The jet of electrolyte entering through a nozzle at the bottom of the bed typically moves mostly upward through the draft tube and annular region (although at high particle circulation rates the motion of electrolyte in the annular region can be partly or wholly downward). Particles from the bed fall though the gap between the bottom of the draft tube and the (inclined) sidewall of the bed and are then swept up the draft tube. At the top of the draft tube the particles fall out of the spout of electrolyte and land on top of the bed to again undergo a slow descent, during which they are in electrical contact with the current collector (mostly via their fellow particles) and undergo electrochemical reaction.

Particle circulation, electrolyte flow, and electrochemical reactions are affected by features of the cell design, notably:

- Shape of the reactor body
- Draft tube(s) position and shape
- Annular regions – shape, dimensions, wall at bottom
- Electrolyte nozzle
- Electric current and liquid flow arrangements
- Separator(s)

16.2.1   Shape of the reactor body

Early versions of SBEs were mostly cylindrical.[1–5] This geometry is particularly convenient if design A of Figure 16.2 is used, in which the macroscopic flow of electrolyte and electric current are both vertical; a separator is then unnecessary. However, the design is not efficient in its use of either (floor) space or energy. There are limitations on scaleup in the direction of current flow, because the bed of particles is fairly conductive and, therefore, the path of least resistance within the bed itself is particle to particle, rather than through the electrolyte. It is therefore the particles closest to the counterelectrode that are most electrochemically active, whereas those close to the bottom of the bed are essentially inert, particularly for tall beds. Consequently, an SBE of this design usually leads to a reactor of large horizontal dimensions if significant productivity is to be achieved. Energy consumption per unit of production is largely a matter of cell voltage, and design A is likely to have a high voltage owing to the need to conduct electricity through a few centimeters of electrolyte between the top of the bed and the counterelectrode. This might also be true for design D.

A more extensively studied reactor shape is that of design C. This design has been used for both laboratory-scale studies,[2,6–10] and pilot-scale investigations[11,12] of electro-deposition of metals, including zinc (from both acid and alkaline electrolytes) and copper. It has also been used to study scaleup, from the viewpoint of ensuring proper particle motion, including beds with multiple draft tubes.[13] The design has the disadvantage of needing a separator, but the proximity of the counterelectrode and bed, separated by only a few millimeters of separator, yields reasonable cell voltages, even at high current density (current per unit of separator area).

16.2.2   Draft tube

The draft tube of design C in Figure 16.2 is internal to the bed of particles; this is the common arrangement. However, external draft tubes have also been used (see Figure 16.1) and might then better be called hydraulic lifts.

Work at Berkeley[13] determined that the particle circulation rate increases as the position of the bottom of an internal draft tube is raised. If the draft tube is too high, however, it becomes difficult to start (restart) particle motion as there is initially a tall packed bed immediately above the nozzle, restricting its flow. The work at Berkeley has also determined the effect of such design parameters as draft tube width and length and the slope of the inclined surfaces bounding the bottom of the bed. The last were designed to eliminate "dead zones" in the corners, in which particles were stationary.

SBEs with external draft tubes have worked well, as particle motion is easy to start. The draft tube is longer than an internal one, however, and particle residence time in the draft tube might be greater. This can be an issue if undesired side reactions occur in the draft tube – for instance, in the chemical dissolution of zinc in acidic electrolytes when the intention is to electrodeposit zinc in the annular region.

16.2.3   Annular regions

The regions on either side of the draft tube are referred to as "annular," even though they are not truly annular in shape in some of the designs of Figure 16.2. These are the asdf

regions in which electrochemistry takes place and in which, in the case of deposition of solids, sustained gentle downward motion of the particles is necessary. Such motion is encouraged by smooth walls and by eliminating horizontal surfaces or corners in which particles are likely to rest. For example, at a transition from a vertical to an inclined surface, it is best to have a curve with a radius much larger than that of the largest particles.

An alternative to inclined walls at the bottom of the annular region is to allow corners, such as those in design C, but to arrange the current collector and counterelectrode so that they are not near the regions of stationary particles.

16.2.4 Nozzle

Some investigation of nozzle design was reported by Verma et al.[13] Robinson et al.[11,12] developed a nozzle relying on a Venturi effect for sweeping the particles into a draft tube.

16.2.5 Electric current and liquid flow arrangements

Several aspects of current and liquid flow have been discussed already. An additional point can be seen in design C (Figure 16.2), in which a flow diverter in the shape of an inverted V is placed above the draft tube to encourage disengagement of particles from the spout.[11,12] In this way, carryover of particles via the electrolyte exit is minimized, even for a small headspace above the bed.

16.2.6 Separators

The separator has the purpose of preventing electrical contact between the particles in the annular regions and the counterelectrode in designs B, C, and E of Figure 16.2. It is of a material that is not an electronic conductor, but allows the passage of at least some of the ions in solution (conduction of current is otherwise impossible). Porous plastics[7,10,14] or plastic meshes have been the most common separators, although ion exchange membranes are another possibility. It is essential that the particles not stick to the separator. A particle stuck in this position, when the bed is electrochemically active, forms a growing deposit that is likely to extend through the separator and short the cell. Smoothness is therefore an important characteristic of a suitable membrane, as are toughness, to resist the abrasion by particles, and low resistance to ionic conduction. If the separator has limited permeability to electrolyte flow, it becomes possible to operate the cell with somewhat different electrolytes on the two sides of the cell. For example, in electrowinning zinc, one might use a highly acidic (highly conducting) electrolyte on the anode side (to minimize cell voltage) with a less acidic electrolyte on the cathode side (which has the effect of increasing current efficiency). The authors of this chapter believe that identifying a suitable separator material is usually the most difficult task in developing the SBE for applications entailing solid deposition, such as metal electrowinning.

16.3   Applications of SBEs

As with all electrodes, the SBE obeys Faraday's law so that the productivity (say, in kg/s) is proportional to the product of current and current efficiency. There is, therefore, incentive to increase the current. Ultimately there is a limit, imposed by mass transfer from electrolyte to electrode surface, on the current achievable in a cell, but it is usual to operate cells well below this limiting current. Increase in current typically results in an increase in cell voltage and sometimes in a decrease in current efficiency. The consequence is that the electrical energy expenditure per unit of product is proportional to cell voltage over current efficiency and increases with current. A compromise between lower capital cost per unit of product and higher energy cost per unit of product is therefore a feature of all cell development, including in application of SBEs. The SBE usually has an advantage over more conventional designs in that it can be operated at greater current density (current per unit area of separator or, equivalently, space-time yield) for the same voltage.

The driving force for electrochemical reactions is the *overpotential* at the electrode in question. This is the difference between the electrode potential at which it is in equilibrium with the adjacent electrolyte and the actual electrode potential. The rate of the electrochemical reaction (say in moles/m^{2}s) is a complicated function of overpotential, mass transfer, electrolyte composition and temperature. The reader is referred to standard texts on electrochemistry for details.[15] In the case of SBEs it is usual for the overpotential to vary across the electrode. Potential gradients are necessary, both in the electrolyte and from particle to particle, to drive current; it is uncommon for these two gradients to match, as particle-to-particle conduction in the SBE is better than conduction in the electrolyte. Hence the overpotential, reaction rate, and local space-time yield are typically highest at positions closest to the counterelectrode and small deeper into the bed. Consequently the overall space time yield of the SBE increases only marginally beyond a certain bed thickness (direction of macroscopic current flow), and most applications have employed beds only a centimeter or two in thickness. Scaleup is then in the two dimensions parallel to the separator or counterelectrode, coupled with stacking of cells next to each other. Figure 16.3 illustrates (left side) laboratory scale cells (one disassembled) used at UC Berkeley and (right side) the scaleup of a cell to a final pilot-scale cell with dual draft tubes. Models based on the porous-electrode theory of Newman and Tobias[16] have been advanced to guide in the selection of a suitable bed thickness or other dimensions.[4,17] Models aiding in prediction of particle and electrolyte hydrodynamics have also been published.[17]

16.3.1   Metal electrowinning

Most of the world's zinc and much of its copper are produced by technology that entails the electrodeposition of metals from aqueous solutions generated by leaching ores or processed concentrates. Similar technology is seen in the production of lead, nickel, cobalt, and other metals. This production is almost entirely in cells with designs that date back well over a century. The cells contain numerous parallel slablike electrodes

Figure 16.3. Scaleup of SBE developed at UC Berkeley. The two devices in the left-hand photograph (one shown disassembled) have beds approximately 100 mm in width. One of these also appears in the right photograph (far right), in which the largest SBE is 270 mm wide.

Table 16.1. Comparison of conventional and spouted bed electrowinning.

Technology	Current density (A/m^2)	Voltage (V)	DC electrical energy consumption (kWh/kg metal)
Copper: conventional	200–300	2	2
Copper: SBE	1200–4500	1.6–2.5	1.3–3
Copper: SBE – matte leaching	1100–3300	0.9–2.2	0.8–1.9
Zinc: conventional	300	3.5	3.3
Zinc: SBE – acid electrolyte	1000–5000	2.7–3.7	2.8–3.4
Zinc: SBE – alkaline electrolyte	2500–4400	3.0–3.2	2.5

(about a meter in size) that are alternating cathodes and anodes. In these conventional cells, the cathodes grow from thin "starter sheets" of the same metal or are deposits forming on "cathode blanks" of some inert metal. The anodes are "inert" in a sense that they are intended not to pass into solution, but rather to be the site of another reaction, such as the generation of oxygen. Electrodes are spaced a few centimeters apart. An important parameter indicative of the space-time yield is the current density (current per unit area of slab surface), whereas cell voltage is indicative of energy consumption per kilogram of metal. Both these economic parameters are adversely affected by lower current efficiency. Table 16.1 gives representative values for commercial electrowinning of copper and zinc,[18,19] as well as typical results from laboratory and pilot-scale SBEs.

Electrowinning of metals in SBEs is well illustrated by the case of copper and zinc. The standard electrode potential for copper is greater than that of hydrogen, which means that, even in acidic copper salt electrolytes, copper, instead of hydrogen, deposits onto a cathode (by reduction of hydrogen ions). Hence copper electrowinning from copper sulfate electrolytes typically proceeds at high current efficiency in either conventional

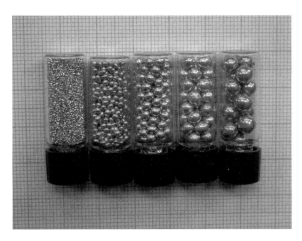

Figure 16.4. Copper particles grown from 0.4 mm to 5 mm; seed particles were cut copper wire.

cells or ones with SBEs. In contrast, the standard electrode potential of zinc is less than that of hydrogen, implying that thermodynamically zinc should not deposit on a cathode from aqueous solutions, but rather hydrogen should be generated. The fact that zinc can be electrowon is due to the slow kinetics of hydrogen deposition on a zinc surface; nevertheless, current efficiency is a major concern in zinc electrowinning, and care must be taken to minimize hydrogen evolution (e.g., by using highly purified electrolytes to avoid impurities that would otherwise catalyze hydrogen evolution).

As Table 16.1 shows, the electrowinning of copper at an SBE has been quite practical on a laboratory scale.[3,6–8,12,14,20–23] Experiments at Berkeley and in Prague have shown current efficiencies comparable with those of conventional cells, at current densities (and therefore space-time yields) an order of magnitude greater than in conventional cells. This has been achieved with specific energy consumptions comparable with those of conventional cells. In electrowinning using an SBE, "seed particles" are fed to the cell and grown to some final size. This is vividly shown in Figure 16.4, in which are seen 0.4-mm seeds (commercially available cut wire particles) grown to 5 mm, an increase in mass by a factor of about 2400. The copper deposits were dense and shiny. Scaleup of copper electrowinning to a large pilot reactor has been described by Robinson et al.[11,12]

Electrolytes used in conventional copper electrowinning are generated by leaching of ores, followed by concentration and purification of the solution by solvent extraction. An alternative technology using copper matte (a solid copper–iron sulfide produced in the alternative pyrometallurgical route to copper) as the starting point was explored by Jiricny and coworkers.[7,8] In one part of that study, the matte was leached by a ferric-ion-containing solution produced on the anode side of a cell. The resulting solution (containing copper and ferrous ions) then passed through the spouted bed cathode of the same cell to deposit copper. The ferrous-ion-containing solution then flowed into the anode side for oxidation of the ferrous ions to ferric ions. Low energy consumptions at high current densities were reported.

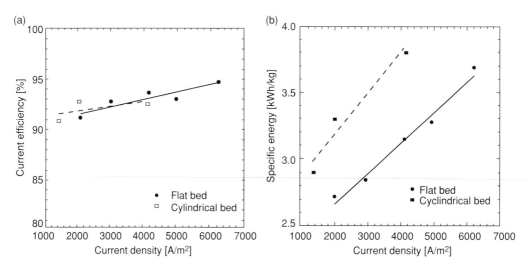

Figure 16.5. (a) Current efficiency in electrowinning of zinc. Zinc concentration reduced by 50 g/L, with neutral initial catholytes; (b) Specific electric energy consumption of SBEs for same zinc concentration reduction.[2] With permission of Springer Science and Business Media.

The use of SBEs to electrowin zinc has proven to be more challenging. In conventional electrowinning, the whole of the zinc electrode is electrically connected to the power supply and zinc deposition effectively competes with hydrogen generation. In the case of the SBE, many particles, such as those in the draft tube or spout, are electrically isolated and subject to dissolution if the electrolyte is acidic. (Many readers will recall chemistry experiments in which hydrogen is generated by adding zinc particles to dilute sulfuric acid.) Figure 16.5a, from Salas-Morales and colleagues,[2] illustrates the consequence. Current efficiency is seen to drop in these batch experiments as zinc is stripped from solution and acid is generated (by reaction at the anode) as the amount of charge passed increases with time. Figure 16.5b from this same investigation illustrates the consequence for specific electrical energy consumption.

As the current density is raised, the current efficiency increases because there is more metal deposition to compete with the (current-insensitive) metal dissolution. This increase is overwhelmed by an increase in cell voltage, however, so the specific energy consumption exceeds conventional values at a few thousand amps/m^2. These current densities are much higher than those of the conventional cell (Table 16.1), implying a much higher space-time yield.

Although the use of the SBE for electrowinning zinc from the usual acid electrolytes[9,13,24] appears to be problematic, its use for electrodeposition from alkaline electrolytes[5,10,25–28] seems more promising, because the near absence of hydrogen ions in the electrolyte makes hydrogen deposition or chemical dissolution of zinc less of an issue and high current efficiencies can be expected. Alkaline electrolytes are not encountered in the present production of zinc from ores, but technology for recycling zinc from galvanized steel[25] (sodium hydroxide leaching) or spent electrolyte from zinc-air batteries (potassium zincate solutions) entail such solutions. Figure 16.6 shows particles

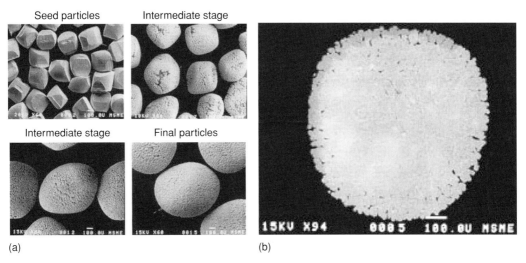

Seed particles   Intermediate stage

Intermediate stage   Final particles

(a)   (b)

Figure 16.6. (a) Zinc particles grown from 0.5 mm diameter to 1 mm from alkaline electrolyte; (b) SEM micrograph of cross-section of zinc final size particle.[27] With permission of Springer Science and Business Media.

electrowon from alkaline electrolyte in an SBE. The morphology of the deposit is not as smooth or as dense as that of the copper in Figure 16.4, but this might be acceptable for some applications. As detailed in Table 16.1, the cell voltage and specific energy consumption for this use of the SBE are low.

In the majority of metal electrowinning experiments using SBEs, the anode has differed from the lead alloy anodes of conventional electrowinning. A typical anode is DSA®, a titanium mesh anode with a proprietary coating that is catalytic for oxygen evolution. The higher cost of such an anode might be justified by the high current density typical of a cell with an SBE.

16.3.2   Wastewater treatment

Waste solutions containing ionic species are common in semiconductor processing, electroplating, and photofinishing. Although chemical precipitation may be used to precipitate ions from solution, this typically introduces other species into solution, so that disposing or recycling of the water from the wastestream is inhibited. Electrolytic deposition of ions may overcome this difficulty. Because ion concentrations are typically low, mass transfer rates to electrode surfaces are low and large electrode surface areas are necessary if equipment is to remain compact. This suggests a three-dimensional electrode of the sort seen in the lower half of Figure 16.1.[29–31] Scott[32] has examined various three-dimensional electrodes for this application, including the SBE. One difficulty is that the electrolyte flow rate needed for particle circulation results in a low fraction of ions extracted from solution per pass. Hence batch operation, a number of units in series, or incorporation of additional steps, such as ion exchange, are necessary.[29,32]

Use of the SBE for treatment of organic pollutants has been suggested by Spiegel et al.[33]

16.4   Concluding remarks

The SBE appears to be a promising tool for electrochemical production, particularly of metals that can be deposited from aqueous solutions. The electrode results in cells that can be operated at much higher space-time yields than conventional cells with planar electrodes and, thereby, a plant with a much smaller "footprint." This should be achievable while maintaining specific energy consumptions comparable to those of conventional cells. The electrowinning of metals in conventional cells requires that the cell remain open because starter sheets/cathode blanks are inserted, and finished cathodes removed, through the top of the cell. Seed introduction and particle removal from a cell with an SBE occurs as a suspension in electrolyte flowing into or out of the cell. The cell can therefore be closed, which presents the opportunity for control or capture of cell emissions, such as oxygen generated at anodes.

The particulate nature of the metal product from an SBE is both an advantage (ease of material handling compared with meter-square slabs of metal) and a disadvantage (current metal processing technology is designed for handling slabs, e.g., in melting furnaces, rather than particles). However, the principal impediments to commercial implementation of the SBE appear to be the high capital cost of the sophisticated cell (compared with the simple tanks of conventional cells), the lack of engineering know-how necessary for plant construction, and the longevity of the separators in the cells that employ them.

It seems likely that the SBE will see its first commercial application in removal of metal ions from wastewater streams. Because of low concentrations in solution, simple batch operation becomes possible with the bed of particles being replaced en masse only at long intervals. In such application, the large surface area per unit volume offered by a three-dimensional electrode is particularly advantageous.

References

1. D. E. Hadzismajlovic, M. G. Pavlovic, and K. I. Popov. The annulus of a spouted bed as a 3-dimensional electrode. *Hydrometallurgy*, **22** (1989), 393–401.
2. J. C. Salas-Morales, J. W. Evans, O. M. G. Newman, and P. A. Adcock. Spouted bed electrowinning of zinc. 1. Laboratory-scale electrowinning experiments. *Metal. & Mat. Trans. B—Proc. Metal. & Mat. Proc. Sci.*, **28** (1997), 59–68.
3. P. A. Shirvanian and J. M. Calo. Copper recovery in a spouted vessel electrolytic reactor (SBER). *J. Appl. Electrochem.*, **35** (2005), 101–111.
4. P. A. Shirvanian, J. M. Calo, and G. Hradil. Numerical simulation of fluid-particle hydrodynamics in a rectangular spouted vessel. *Internat. J. Multiph. Flow*, **32** (2006), 739–753.
5. Eveready Battery Company, Inc., Alkaline electrochemical cell with reduced gassing, J. L. Stimits (Inventor), U.S. Patent 0226976 (A1) (2008).

6. V. Jiricny, A. Roy, and J. W. Evans. A study of the spouted-bed electrowinning of copper. In *Proceedings of the 4th International Conference COPPER 99/COBRE 99* (Warrendale, PA: TMS, 1999), pp. 629–642.

7. V. Jiricny, A. Roy, and J. W. Evans. Copper electrowinning using spouted-bed electrodes: Part I. Experiments with oxygen evolution or matte oxidation. *Metal. & Mat. Trans. B—Proc. Metal. & Mat. Proc. Sci.*, **33** (2002), 669–676.

8. V. Jiricny, A. Roy, and J. W. Evans. Copper electrowinning using spouted-bed electrodes: Part II. Copper electrowinning with ferrous ion oxidation as the anodic reaction. *Metal. Mat. Trans. B—Proc. Metal. Mat. Proc. Sci.*, **33** (2002), 677–683.

9. O. M. G. Newman, P. A. Adcock, M. J. Meere, P. Freeman, J. W. Evans, and S. Siu. Investigations of spouted bed electrowinning for the zinc industry. Presented at 5th International Symposium on Hydrometallurgy in honour of Ian M. Ritchie (Vancouver, BC, Canada, 2003).

10. A. Roy, S. Siu, V. Jiricny, J. W. Evans, and O. M. G. Newman. Electrowinning of zinc from acid and alkaline electrolytes using a spouted bed electrode. Presented at International Symposium on Zinc and Lead Processing (Calgary, Alberta, Canada, 1998).

11. De Nora Elettrodi S. P. A., Spouted bed electrode cell for metal electrowinning, D. J. Robinson, S. A. MacDonald, V. Jiricny, D. Oldani, F. Todaro, L. Carrettin, G. N. Martelli, and D. Scotti (Inventors), WO Patent 007805 (A2) (2004).

12. D. Robinson, S. MacDonald, and F. Todaro. Commercial development of a descending packed bed electrowinning cell, part 2: Cell operation. Presented at 5th International Symposium on Hydrometallurgy in honour of Ian M. Ritchie (Vancouver, BC, Canada, 2003).

13. A. Verma, J. C. Salas-Morales, and J. W. Evans. Spouted bed electrowinning of zinc. 2. Investigations of the dynamics of particles in large thin spouted beds. *Metal. Mat. Trans. B—Proc. Metal. Mat. Proc. Sci.*, **28** (1997), 69–79.

14. De Nora Elettrodi S. P. A., Method for copper electrowinning in hydrochloric solution, D. J. Robinson, S. A. MacDonald and V. Jiricny (Inventors), U.S. Patent 163082 (A1) (2006).

15. J. S. Newman and K. E. Thomas-Alyea. *Electrochemical Systems*, 3rd ed. (Hoboken, NJ: John Wiley and Sons, 2004).

16. J. S. Newman and C. W. Tobias. Theoretical analysis of current distribution in porous electrodes. *J. Electrochem. Soc.*, **109** (1962), 1183–1191.

17. P. A. Shirvanian and J. M. Calo. Hydrodynamic scaling of a rectangular spouted vessel with a draft duct. *Chem. Eng. J.*, **103** (2004), 29–34.

18. F. M. Doyle. Teaching and learning environmental hydrometallurgy. *Hydrometallurgy*, **79** (2005), 1–14.

19. F. Habashi. *Principles of Extractive Metallurgy, Volume 4: Amalgam and Electrometallurgy* (Sainte-Foy, Québec: Métallurgie extractive Québec, 1998).

20. B. M. Dweik, C. C. Liu, R. F. Savinell, C. D. Zhou, E. J. Taylor, E. Stortz, and R. P. Renz. Circulating particulate bed electrode: Electrochemical extraction of copper ions from dilute aqueous solutions. In *Electrochemistry in Mineral and Metal Processing IV*, ed. R. Woods, F. M. Doyle, and P. Richardson (Pennington, NJ: The Electrochemical Society, 1996), pp. 416–428.

21. D. McKay, C. Hayes, and C. Oloman. Electrowinning on a spouted bed. Presented at *32nd Canadian Chemical Engineering Conference* (Vancouver, BC, Canada, 1982).

22. De Nora Elettrodi S. P. A., Falling bed cathode cell for metal electrowinning. D. J. Robinson, S. A. MacDonald, and F. Todaro (Inventors), U.S. Patent 0102302 (A1) (2007).

23. J. Salas, S. Siu, and J. W. Evans. Particulate electrodes for the electrowinning of copper. Presented at Copper '95 (Santiago, Chile, 1995).

24. J. W. Evans, A. Roy, and C. Allen. Spouted bed electrowinning of zinc from chloride electrolytes. Presented at Lead-Zinc 2000 Symposium (Pittsburgh, PA, 2000).

25. V. Jiricny, A. Roy, and J. W. Evans. Spouted bed electrowinning in the recovery of zinc from scrap galvanized steel. Presented at EPD Congress 1998, TMS Annual Meeting (San Antonio, TX, 1998).

26. V. Jiricny, A. Roy, and J. W. Evans. Electrodeposition of zinc from sodium zincate/hydroxide electrolytes in a spouted bed electrode. *Metal. Mat. Trans. B—Proc. Metal. Mat. Proc. Sci.*, **31** (2000), 755–766.

27. V. Jiricny, S. Siu, A. Roy, and J. W. Evans. Regeneration of zinc particles for zinc-air fuel cells in a spouted-bed electrode. *J. App. Electrochem.*, **30** (2000), 647–656.

28. University of California, Efficient electrowinning of zinc from alkaline electrolytes. S. C. Siu and J. W. Evans (Inventors), U.S. Patent 5958210 (A) (1999).

29. K. Juttner, U. Galla, and H. Schmieder. Electrochemical approaches to environmental problems in the process industry. *Electrochim. Acta*, **45** (2000), 2575–2594.

30. V. Stankovic. Metal removal from effluents by electrowinning and a new design concept in wastewater purification technology. Presented at 4th Croatian Symposium on Electrochemistry (Primosten, Croatia: 2006).

31. V. D. Stankovic and S. Stankovic. An investigation of the spouted bed electrode cell for the electrowinning of metal from dilute-solutions. *J. Appl. Electrochem.*, **21** (1991), 124–129.

32. K. Scott. A consideration of circulating bed electrodes for the recovery of metal from dilute-solutions. *J. Appl. Electrochem.*, **18** (1988), 504–510.

33. Eltron Research, Inc., Three dimensional electrode for the electrolytic removal of contaminants from aqueous waste streams, E. F. Spiegel and A. F. Sammells (Inventors), US6298996 (B1), October 9, 2001.

34. Eveready Battery Company, Inc., Alkaline electrochemical cell with reduced gassing, J. L. Stimits and J. S. Dreger (Inventors), US2008102360 (A1), September 18, 2008.

35. B. M. Dweik, C. C. Liu, and R. F. Savinell. Hydrodynamic modelling of the liquid-solid behaviour of the circulating particulate bed electrode. *J. Appl. Electrochem.*, **26** (1996), 1093–1102.

17 Scaleup, slot-rectangular, and multiple spouting

John R. Grace and C. Jim Lim

17.1 Introduction

Scaleup of test results from smaller to larger equipment is an important aspect in the design and operation of spouted bed units for physical and chemical processes of practical importance. A key need is the ability to use data obtained on smaller units in the design of full-scale equipment. Similar considerations pertain to the application of results obtained at atmospheric pressure and room temperature to columns to be operated at elevated pressures and/or temperatures. Despite the inclusion of words such as "scaleup" and "scaling" in the titles of a number of articles dealing with spouted beds, there are no established procedures for scaleup and considerable uncertainty about how best to achieve it. The question of the maximum practical size of spouted beds is also unresolved. As noted with reference to fluidized beds,[1] scaleup is "not an exact science, but remains the province of that mixture of mathematics, witchcraft, history and common sense which we call engineering."

This chapter considers a number of interrelated questions and issues:

- Is there a maximum practical size of spouted beds, and if so, what is it?
- What is the effect of column diameter on spouting behavior? What are the effects of pressure and temperature?
- Can one use small-scale results reliably to predict spouting behavior in larger columns? In particular, can one use dimensional similitude to scale up (or scale down) hydrodynamics and other experimental results obtained in equipment of a given size to predict with confidence behavior and performance of a unit of a different size but similar geometry?
- Can multiple spouts, slot-rectangular spouted beds, or some combination of the two (rectangular vessels with multiple gas-entry slots) facilitate scaleup?
- How does scaling of spouted beds compare with scaleup of fluidized beds?

In this chapter, we consider only cases in which the spouting fluid is a gas. In addition, we consider only cases in which the containing vessel is vertical at the spouted bed surface (i.e., we do not cover the scaleup of conical beds [Chapter 5]). Although one of the claims sometimes made for adding draft tubes to spouted beds is to improve

Spouted and Spout-Fluid Beds: Fundamentals and Applications, eds. Norman Epstein and John R. Grace. Published by Cambridge University Press. © Cambridge University Press 2011.

scaleup, we do not treat draft tubes here, as they are covered in Chapter 7. We barely touch on scaleup of spout-fluid beds. In addition, specific processes such as drying, combustion, and gasification are treated in Chapters 11, 12, and 15, so they are not dealt with specifically in this chapter. Finally, we note that, just as for fluidized beds,[1] serious operability challenges (e.g., related to agglomeration, attrition, and vibration) are often encountered in scaleup, but are not treated in this chapter.

17.2   Maximum size of spouted beds

Spouted bed and spout-fluid bed studies have been performed predominantly on relatively small units, $\lesssim 0.3$ m in diameter. In applications of spouted and spout-fluid beds, the diameter is normally less than 1 m. This compares with fluidized beds, for which there are many applications in which the containing vessels are tens of meters in diameter. Key questions with respect to spouted beds are, therefore, how they can be scaled up (and scaled down for test purposes) and whether there is any upper limit on spouted bed diameter.

Consider a cylindrical or conical-cylindrical column of diameter D with a single central orifice of diameter D_i at the bottom. For stable spouting over the entire column, the optimum range of D/D_i is said[2] to be 6 to 10, and the maximum is likely to be ~ 12 to avoid substantial dead regions. For stable spouting, it has been shown[3] that D_i/d_p should not exceed 25. For a single-orifice spouted bed, to have steady coherent spouting that covers the entire cross-sectional area of the column, this suggests that

$$\frac{D}{d_p} = \frac{D}{D_i} \times \frac{D_i}{d_p} \leq 300. \tag{17.1}$$

This is similar to the maximum ratio of 200 proposed by Nemeth et al.[2] Hence ~ 300 particle diameters is at or near the upper limit of what one should adopt as the diameter of single-orifice spouted beds of circular cross-section for optimal hydrodynamics. Since most particles processed in spouted beds are approximately 4 mm in size or smaller, this then corresponds to a maximum column diameter of the order of 1 m. If columns of similar single-orifice geometry, but larger diameter, are provided, they are likely to operate in unsteady and suboptimal modes. Operating with larger equipment requires either multiple orifices or alternative equipment configurations, as will be discussed later.

17.3   Influence of column diameter on hydrodynamics

The column diameter is included as a parameter in a number of the theoretical, empirical, and semiempirical correlations and equations used for predicting the behavior of spouted beds (see Chapter 3). If column geometry and such operating variables as D_i, d_p, particle density, and bed depth (H) are held constant, then, for example, the well-known Mathur-Gishler[4] equation predicts that the minimum spouting velocity, U_{ms}, $\propto D^{-4/3}$, based on small columns, although, as indicated in Chapter 3, the dependence decreases toward a 0-power for columns of $D > 0.5$ m. The maximum spoutable bed depth, H_m, $\propto D^{8/3}$, according to the correlation of McNab and Bridgwater.[5] There is a much lesser, though still appreciable, effect of D on average spout diameter, with exponents[6,7] of 0.68 and 0.59. On the other hand, neither the total pressure drop nor the pressure drop at minimum spouting are expected to be affected by D, providing that the other specified variables are maintained constant. In cases in which there are "dead regions" around the lower outer part of the column, there is evidence[8,9] that the volume of the dead zone relative to the bed volume is likely to be larger as the column diameter and bed depth are increased. Given these very different dependencies on D, the effect of column diameter is clearly complex.

Relatively few spouted bed columns of diameter or width exceeding 0.61 m have been reported in the open literature. Those in which there was a single inlet orifice are:

- A dryer of $D = 0.914$ m at the National Research Council of Canada, reported in a personal communication from W.S. Peterson to Mathur and Epstein.[10]
- Green and Bridgwater[11,12]: 30°-sector column of radius 0.78 m.
- Fane and Mitchell[13]: full column of $D = 1.1$ m.
- Lim and Grace[8]: half column of $D = 0.91$ m with a flat base.
- He et al.[9]: same half column of $D = 0.91$ m as in the previous entry, but now with a conical base, and operated as both a spouted bed and a spout-fluid bed.
- Kalwar et al.[14]: rectangular column, 0.75 m wide, with dimensions up to 0.47 m in the orthogonal direction.
- Priolo granulator, Italy, 3.5 m diameter column sketched by Piccinini.[15]

Only the last of these is substantially larger than 1 m in diameter, and there is no indication of how well, or in what hydrodynamic mode, this unit operated.

17.4   Application of dimensional similitude to scaling of spouted beds

A powerful technique for simulating and scaling physical systems is to build a geometrically similar physical "cold" model in which all the important independent dimensionless groups match (i.e., are identical) for the model and prototype units. The set of dimensionless groups to be matched can be obtained in several different manners:

- By writing all the governing differential equations (e.g., equation of motion) in dimensionless form;
- By applying the well-known Buckingham Pi theorem, after intuitively listing all quantities likely to affect the phenomena of interest;
- When hydrodynamics alone are involved, by considering "force balances," such as balances of gravity and drag on particles, again including all forces likely to be important in the given problem.

Dimensional similitude methodology is widely employed in aircraft and ship design, and has become popular in scaling of fluidized beds.[16] He et al.[17] applied this approach

Table 17.1. Properties of the four columns used in the scaling study of He et al.[17]

Diameter, mm	Temperature, °C	Pressure, kPa	Particles
0.051	25	101	Steel shot
0.076	25	135	Steel, glass
0.152	25–500	101–312	Glass, sand
0.914	25	101	Polystyrene

Table 17.2. Properties of particles used to test scaling criteria.[17]

Material	D_p, mm	ρ_p, kg/m^3	ε_0, –	ϕ_s, –	φ, °
Glass beads	2.18	2400	0.41	1	26
Glass beads	1.09	2450	0.42	1	27
Steel shot	1.09	7400	0.42	1	28
Steel shot	0.73	7400	0.42	1	29
Sand	2.18	2400	0.44	0.88	38
Sand	1.80	2490	0.45	0.88	39
Sand	0.54	2490	0.45	0.88	41
Polystyrene	3.25	1020	0.44	0.87	40

to scaling of the hydrodynamics of spouted beds, leading to the following dimensionless groups for a bed of fixed geometry:

$$\frac{gd_p}{U^2}, \frac{\rho d_p U}{\mu}, \frac{\rho_p}{\rho}, \frac{H}{d_p}, \frac{D_i}{d_p}, \phi_s, \varepsilon_0, \varphi, PSD, \tag{17.2}$$

where ϕ_s denotes the particle sphericity, φ is the angle of internal friction of the particulate material, and PSD is a dimensionless parameter (e.g., standard deviation divided by mean particle diameter) describing the particle size distribution. These groups are the same as those of Glicksman[16] for fluidized beds, except for the inclusion of the loose-packed bed voidage (ε_0) and φ. These extra terms are added because of more frequent particle–particle contacts and greater transmission of compression and friction forces in spouted beds relative to fluidized beds.

He et al.[17] also carried out experimental hydrodynamic tests with narrow size distributions of regular particles to test the sufficiency of these relations for four different semicylindrical columns, differing in diameter, as well as being operated at different temperatures and pressures. The diameters of these columns and operating temperature and pressure ranges are provided in Table 17.1. Properties of the particles tested appear in Table 17.2. Dependent variables compared were the maximum spoutable bed depth, fountain height, spout diameter, axial pressure profiles, and dead zone boundaries. When all the groups in (17.2) were very nearly matched, the dimensionless hydrodynamic behavior was nearly identical. Deliberately mismatching the dimensionless groups, one

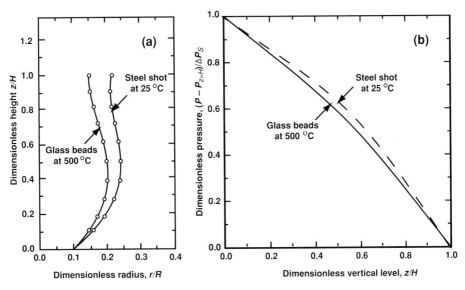

Figure 17.1. Dimensionless (a) spout diameter and (b) pressure profiles for two scaled columns: a 0.152-m diameter column with glass beads at 500 °C, and a 0.051-m diameter column with steel shot at room temperature, after He et al.[17]

or two at a time, led to significant lack of agreement. The authors found that all the dimensionless groups included in (17.2) were important for the range of conditions studied. This approach was also supported by experimental results for three similar slot-rectangular columns,[18] and by computational fluid dynamic (CFD) simulations.[19] The degree of agreement for matched columns is illustrated in Figures 17.1 and 17.2. This agreement suggests that the hydrodynamics of spouted beds can be scaled (upward or downward) by geometrically similar physical cold models, providing it is possible to maintain equality of all important independent dimensionless groups (geometric similarity implies equality of all groups such as H/D, D/D_i and D_i/d_p). Moreover, the approach can be employed to test the effects of operating pressure and temperature, in addition to the influence of scale (D).

Several CFD studies of spouted beds[20–24] have demonstrated that the coefficient of restitution for particle–particle collisions, η_p, should also be added to the set of dimensionless groups to be matched for spouted beds. This arises because interparticle collisions play an important role in the fountain and spout regions. With this addition, (17.2) becomes

$$\frac{gd_p}{U^2}, \frac{\rho d_p U}{\mu}, \frac{\rho_p}{\rho}, \frac{H}{d_p}, \frac{D_i}{d_p}, \phi_s, \varepsilon_0, \varphi, PSD, \eta_P. \tag{17.3}$$

It is clearly difficult in practice to match as many as 10 dimensionless groups, but if this can be done, coupled with geometric similarity, there is a sound basis for scaleup. It should be remembered in practice, however, that this approach may well fail in some cases, for example:

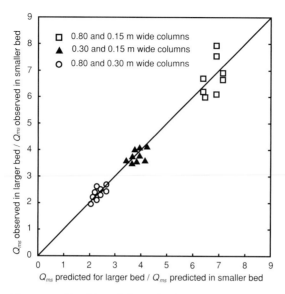

Figure 17.2. Matching of dimensionless minimum spouting velocities for three dimensionally similar units of slot-rectangular spouted bed geometry, after Costa and Taranto.[18]

- When particles of the same sphericity (a single parameter representing complex three-dimensional forms) have significantly different shapes.
- When more than one parameter is needed to describe particle size distributions.
- For "overdeveloped" fountains (those in which the particles bounce off the inner wall) of the column, so the particle wall coefficient of restitution is also important.
- For vessels with very rough inner surfaces that may behave very differently from smooth walls.
- If substantial pulsations are provided by the blower, then their amplitude, frequency and waveform may all play significant roles.
- If other forces, such as those caused by electrostatics or surface moisture, play major roles, additional dimensionless groups will be required.
- If physical properties change during the course of the operation – for example, as a result of particle attrition, agglomeration, or drying in batchwise operation – similarity between the model and the prototype may be destroyed.

It should also be remembered that cold modeling based on dimensional similitude is readily suited only to physical modeling of hydrodynamics. It may be extended to other physical phenomena such as convective heat transfer if it is also possible to match other key dimensionless groups such as the Prandtl number, but it is unlikely to be able to deal with situations in which there are other complications, such as substantial temperature or concentration gradients, significant radiant heat transfer, chemical reactions, or erosion (wear) of surfaces.

On the other hand, in some cases it may be possible to simplify the matching. For example, it may be possible on occasion[17] to replace the Reynolds number by U/U_{ms}, which is easier to match. Alternatively, it may be possible to use the minimum fluidization

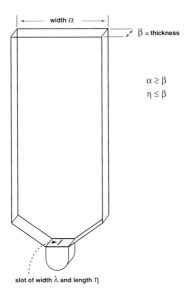

width α

β = thickness

$\alpha \geq \beta$
$\eta \leq \beta$

slot of width λ and length η

Figure 17.3. Schematic of slot-rectangular spouted bed geometry with a single slot.

velocity, U_{mf}, or the terminal free settling velocity in formulating a reduced set of dimensionless groups.[25] If particles are very uniform in size, the *PSD* parameter may be disregarded; the same applies to the sphericity if the particles are very nearly spherical.

17.5   Slot-rectangular spouted beds

In order to facilitate scaleup, Mujumdar[26] promoted the concept of two-dimensional spouted beds (2DSBs), in which planar symmetry replaces axial symmetry. Two facing walls are completely vertical and parallel, whereas the other two are vertical, with a sloping lower section so that the gas flow, which enters through an open slot at the bottom, diverges as it rises. This geometry is shown schematically in Figure 17.3. A "half-column" geometry is also possible,[26] in which one installs only one side of what is shown. In comparison with conventional (conical-cylindrical) spouted beds, which are limited in their volumetric processing capacity, it is stated[26,27] that the volumetric capacity of a 2DSB can be easily increased by extending the bed thickness. As a further advantage, it is proposed[27] that different flow regimes can be achieved by small changes in inlet slot width. If this geometry is adopted, it is claimed[28] that scaleup can be achieved by increasing the width and/or the thickness, with or without separating walls.

The implication of referring to the planar geometry as two-dimensional is that there would be negligible variations in the direction (referred to here as "thickness") normal to the column width, so scaleup could be achieved by simply increasing that dimension. However, tests with columns of different column thickness[29,30] have shown clear three-dimensional behavior – for instance, with two or more discrete jets or spouts forming along the slot length. In view of this three-dimensional behavior, Freitas et al.[29] suggested that the name "slot-rectangular spouted bed" would be more appropriate for this generic geometry; we adopt this terminology in the rest of this chapter.

Zhao et al.[31] suggest that the thickness of such columns should not be less than $5d_p$ to avoid excessive wall effects. However, the multiple of 5 is likely applicable only for narrow particle size distributions and smooth spherical particles in smooth-walled vessels, as experience with fluidized beds, in which particle size distributions tend to be broader and particle shapes less regular, suggests a more conservative ratio, for example, that the column thickness (or other gaps) not be less than about 20 particle diameters to prevent bridging.

A number of experimental studies have been performed on many of the same hydro-dynamic features (e.g., minimum spouting velocity, maximum spoutable bed depth) for slot-rectangular spouted beds, as are covered by several chapters of this book for the more conventional cone-cylindrical spouted bed geometry. Up to eight[32] or nine[30] sep-arate flow regimes have been identified. The greater number of flow regimes than for conventional conical-cylindrical beds can be attributed to the three-dimensionality of the geometry, as well as to the greater number of independent variables. Some hysteresis has been observed in the flow regimes, with regime boundaries differing for increasing and decreasing flow.[30] Hydrodynamic studies have generally shown that slot-rectangular vessels have similar qualitative behavior to conventional cone-cylindrical columns, but it is not possible to simply adapt relationships obtained for conical-cylindrical units to the slot-rectangular geometry. Instead, the experimental work on slot-rectangular columns has led to a series of separate empirical and semiempirical correlations for such proper-ties as minimum spouting velocity, maximum spoutable bed depth, maximum pressure drop, and flow regimes, specific to the slot-rectangular geometry. These studies have been summarized by Chen[30] in tabular form. The results are not summarized here because, in the judgment of the authors, they lack generality, given the sheer number of independent variables and the limited ranges of these covered in the reported experimental work.

Figure 17.4 shows a top view and side view of a slot at the base of a symmetrical slot-rectangular column to define the geometry. Chen[30] carried out an extensive study on the effects of slot geometry, including cases in which the slot length, η, < column thickness, β, and configurations in which the slot length η perpendicular to the column width is less than the slot width λ parallel to the column width, α. In all cases, the slot was symmetrically located at the center of the column base. Chen[30] also tested extensions of the slot into the windbox, where the depth, κ, was substantially greater than the plate thickness, as well as cases in which the slots converged or diverged along their lengths. Slots of greater κ, smaller λ, and smaller η/λ ratio provided more stable spouts. Stable spouting could be achieved if $\sqrt{\eta\lambda}/d_p \leq 21.3$ and either $\eta/\lambda \leq 15$ or $\kappa/d_p \geq 25$. Higher pressure drop across the slot and divergence of the flow through the slot gave more stable spouting.

Slot-rectangular columns are useful for testing multiphase CFD codes, with several different software packages tested in this manner, giving predictions that are generally in good agreement with experimental results.[19–25,32] Given this favorable agreement and the difficulties, discussed previously in correlating results for systems with so many

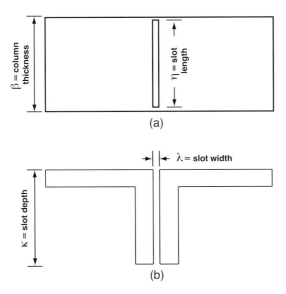

Figure 17.4. Slot geometry and definition of dimensions: (a) plan view; (b) side view.

variables, we recommend that CFD simulations be used as a primary vehicle for scaleup of columns of this geometry, with proper validation, whenever possible, of the particular software in spouted beds of similar geometry.

17.6   Multiple spout geometries

Another possible way to scale up spouted beds is to provide multiple discrete entry points for the incoming spouting gas, essentially dividing the overall system into modular spouted beds in parallel. This is likely to involve orifices of circular cross-section in a horizontal distributor plate (as in many fluidized beds), or multiple rectangular slots in parallel. The bottom plate may be flat[36] or dished above each orifice.[2,34,37] The multiple entry points can be fed from a common plenum chamber or "windbox," or each entry point may be connected separately to a common gas supply – for instance, served by a separate pipe and control valve from a common manifold. The overall vessel can then be rectangular with an aspect ratio of horizontal width and length of order unity,[2,33–35] thin,[38,39] or even annular[2,40] in cross-section. Draft plates or draft tubes may be installed above each gas-entry opening.[28,39] Gas can enter only at the major orifices or with auxiliary gas from surrounding smaller ports to provide a multiple-spout-fluid bed.[36] The most widely studied multiple-spout geometry is shown schematically in Figure 17.5.

When orifices are fed from a common plenum chamber, it is difficult to ensure uniformity of flow through the various orifices owing to instability.[30,38,41] Some of the entry points can even become inactive, that is, with no spout above them. When

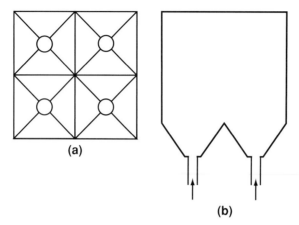

Figure 17.5. Geometry of a typical multiple spouted bed, adapted from Murthy and Singh[34]:
(a) plan view; (b) side view.

adjacent slots are fed from the same plenum chamber, instability is likely to occur, with
a substantial increment in flow needed after each spout becomes active for the next one to
be activated. This is easily explained, as when spouting starts at one orifice, its pressure
drop decreases relative to the one at which spouting has not yet started, resulting in
more gas going to the actively spouting orifice and less to the others. Ensuring a high
pressure drop through the distributor can help to prevent instabilities and keep all orifices
active.[41,42]

Full or partial vertical partitions may be installed at the boundaries between adjacent
geometrically similar compartments, or there may be no partitions. Vertical baffles may
also be installed in multiple spouted beds to reduce short-circuiting of particles, resulting
in residence time distributions that approach those for plug flow.[35] One of the problems
encountered with multiple spouted beds is interference among the spouts, sometimes
even leading to their merging. Partial baffles between modules that extend from the base
to the bed surface have not been found to be very helpful.[30,33] However, vertical plates
suspended from above, extending from approximately the top of the fountains to the top
of the dense bed, have been found[30] to be very helpful in isolating adjacent spouts and
fountains, while still allowing transfer of solids among adjacent modules.

When stable spouting is achieved with multiple orifices, results from single-orifice
spouted beds (e.g., from Chapter 3) can usually be employed to predict the most important
spouting properties such as minimum spouting velocity and maximum spoutable bed
depth.[33,35] If the modules are rectangular or square in cross-section, then the diameter,
D, needed in the correlations can be taken to be the area-equivalent diameter of the
cross-sectional area of the module.

Another option for multiple spouted beds is to use multiple slots, rather than orifices of
circular cross-section. It is then recommended[30] that the slots be located symmetrically
within each module, that the maximum module width be $225d_p$, and that the guidelines
provided in Section 17.5 be followed with respect to the length ratios for the slots.

17.7   Scaleup of spout-fluid beds

Spout-fluid beds have several extra degrees of freedom, compared with conventional spouted beds and the other geometries covered in this chapter. In particular, the ratio of auxiliary gas flow to primary (central orifice) gas flow can be varied, and there are many different possible configurations for the delivery of the auxiliary gas. As spout-fluid beds are covered in detail in Chapter 6, they are not dealt with explicitly here, except to note that the methodologies and many of the comments in the present chapter also apply to the design and scaleup of spout-fluid beds.

17.8   Final comments and recommendations related to scaleup

Scaleup is an area of uncertainty for spouted beds, in terms of both the changes in behavior as equipment size is varied and how best to configure and design units for commercial-scale operation. A number of methods are available for scaling up (or down) spouted beds:

- In some cases, such as spouted bed dryers,[43] specific design criteria and procedures are available.
- Building a series of columns of identical geometry, but different scale, for spouting of the same material is quite common when scaling up fluidized beds, and may prove to be useful for some complex spouted bed processes. However, this approach does not appear to have received much attention in the spouted bed literature.
- Empirical and semiempirical correlations and simplified mechanistic hydrodynamic models of the kind reviewed in Chapter 3, may be helpful in predicting the performance and behavior of columns of different geometry or the effect of changes in temperature or pressure. However, there are commonly too many variables for these correlations to be reliable beyond the range of variables covered in deriving them.
- CFD codes, discussed in detail in Chapter 4, provide potentially powerful tools for predicting the influence of spouted bed scale, geometry, and operating conditions. CFD is likely to be the primary tool for scaleup in the future.
- Scaleup based on dimensional similitude can provide useful information on hydrodynamics, but the number of dimensionless groups to be matched is large, so it is difficult to carry out tests in which similitude is ensured by strict adherence to matching of all important independent dimensionless groups. The task of matching is even more difficult if other variables, such as those related to heat transfer and chemical reaction, are also important in the particular application.
- Multiorifice spouted beds can be used to provide scaleup. However, instabilities and interference between adjacent spouts can lead to serious operability issues. Although these can be alleviated by high-pressure-drop distributors or separate control valves to each gas-entry point, such measures add to the operating and capital cost of the equipment.

- Slot-rectangular units, with or without baffle plates and auxiliary fluidizing gas, provide alternative geometries to the conventional cone-cylinder spouted bed geometry, which may be helpful in designing larger units. The two-dimensional approach,[26] whereby scaleup would be achieved by simply extending the thickness of a thin planar column, is oversimplified, as significant three-dimensional effects become evident as the thickness of slot-rectangular columns is varied. Suspended vertical baffles separating adjacent units appear to be useful to prevent instabilities while retaining simplicity of design and the ability of particles to transfer between adjacent compartments.

References

1. J. M. Matsen. Scale-up of fluidized bed processes. *Powder Technol.*, **88** (1996), 237–244.
2. J. Nemeth, E. Pallai, and E. Arabi. Scale-up examination of spouted bed dryers. *Can. J. Chem. Eng.*, **61** (1983), 419–425.
3. P. P. Chandnani and N. Epstein. Spoutability and spout destabilization of fine particles with a gas. In *Fluidization V*, ed. K. Ostergaard and K. Sorensen (New York: Engineering Foundation, 1986), pp. 233–240.
4. K. B. Mathur and P. E. Gishler. A technique for contacting gases with coarse solid particles. *AIChE J.* **1** (1955), 157–164.
5. G. S. McNab and J. Bridgwater. Spouted beds – estimation of spouting pressure drop and the particle size for deepest bed. In *Proceedings of the European Congress on Particle Technology* (Nuremberg, 1977), 17 pages.
6. G. S. McNab. Prediction of spout diameter. *Brit. Chem. Eng. Proc. Tech.*, **17** (1972), 532.
7. S. W. M. Wu, C. J. Lim, and N. Epstein. Hydrodynamics of spouted beds at elevated temperatures. *Chem. Eng. Comm.*, **62** (1987), 251–268.
8. C. J. Lim and J. R. Grace. Spouted bed hydrodynamics in a 0.91 m diameter vessel. *Can. J. Chem. Eng.*, **65** (1987), 366–372.
9. Y. L. He, C. J. Lim, and J. R. Grace. Spouted bed and spout-fluid bed behaviour in a column of diameter 0.91 m. *Can. J. Chem. Eng.*, **70** (1992), 848–857.
10. K. B. Mathur and N. Epstein. *Spouted Beds* (New York: Academic Press, 1974).
11. M. C. Green and J. Bridgwater. An experimental study of spouting in large sector beds. *Can. J. Chem. Eng.*, **61** (1983), 281–288.
12. M. C. Green and J. Bridgwater. The behaviour of sector spouted beds. *Chem. Eng. Sci.*, **38** (1983), 481–485.
13. A. G. Fane and R. A. Mitchell. Minimum spouting velocity of scaled-up beds. *Can. J. Chem. Eng.*, **62** (1984), 437–439.
14. M. I. Kalwar, G. S. V. Raghavan, and A. S. Mujumdar. Circulation of particles in two-dimensional spouted beds with draft plates. *Powder Technol.*, **77** (1993), 233–242.
15. N. Piccinini, University of Torino, Personal communication, 1991.
16. L. R. Glicksman. Scaling relationships for fluidized beds. *Chem. Eng. Sci.*, **39** (1984), 1373–1379.
17. Y. L. He, C. J. Lim, and J. R. Grace. Scale-up studies in spouted beds. *Chem. Eng. Sci.*, **52** (1997), 329–339.
18. M. de A. Costa and O. P. Taranto. Scale-up and spouting of two-dimensional beds. *Can. J. Chem. Eng.*, **81** (2003), 264–267.

19. R. Béttega, R. G. Corrêa, and J. T. Freire. Scale-up study of spouted beds using computational fluid dynamics. *Can. J. Chem. Eng.*, **87** (2009), 193–203.

20. P. A. Shirvanian and J. M. Calo. Hydrodynamic scaling of a rectangular spouted vessel with a draft duct. *Chem. Eng. J.*, **103** (2004), 29–34.

21. H. Lu, Y. He, W. Liu, D. Gidaspow, and J. Bouillard. Computer simulations of gas-solid flow in spouted beds using kinetic-frictional stress model of granular flow. *Chem. Eng. Sci.*, **59** (2004), 865–878.

22. W. Du, X. J. Bao, J. Xu, and W. S. Wei. Computational fluid dynamics modeling of spouted bed. *Chem. Eng. Sci.*, **61** (2006), 4558–4570.

23. J. Xu, Y. Je, W. S. Wei, X. J. Bao, and W. Du. Scaling relationship of gas-solid spouted beds. In *Fluidization XII*, ed. X. T. Bi, F. Berruti, and T. Pugsley (Brooklyn, NY: Engineering Conference International, 2007), pp. 537–544.

24. W. Du, J. Xu, Y. Ji, W. S. Wei, and X. J. Bao. Scale-up relationships of spouted beds by solid stress analyses. *Powder Technol.*, **192** (2009), 273–278.

25. Q. C. Wang, K. Zhang, S. Brandani, and J. C. Jiang. Scale-up strategy for the jetting fluidized bed using a CFD model based on two-fluid theory. *Can. J. Chem. Eng.*, **87** (2009), 204–210.

26. A. S. Mujumdar. Spouted bed technology – a brief review. In *Drying '84*, ed. A. S. Mujumdar (New York: Hemisphere, 1984), pp. 151–157.

27. M. L. Passos, A. S. Mujumdar, and V. S. G. Raghavan. Prediction of the maximum spoutable bed height in two-dimensional spouted beds. *Powder Technol.*, **74** (1993), 97–105.

28. M. I. Kalwar, G. S. V. Raghavan, and A. S. Mujumdar. Circulation of particles in two-dimensional spouted beds with draft plates. *Powder Technol.*, **77** (1993), 233–242.

29. L. A. P. Freitas, O. M. Dogan, C. J. Lim, J. R. Grace, and B. Luo. Hydrodynamics and stability of slot-rectangular spouted beds. II. Increasing bed thickness. *Chem. Eng. Comm.*, **181** (2000), 243–258.

30. Z. W. Chen. Hydrodynamics, stability and scale-up of slot-rectangular spouted beds. Ph.D. thesis, University of British Columbia (2007).

31. X. L. Zhao, S. Q. Li, G. Q. Liu, Q. Song, and Q. Yan. Flow patterns of solids in a two-dimensional spouted bed with draft plates: PIV measurement and DEM simulations. *Powder Technol.*, **183** (2008), 79–87.

32. O. M. Dogan, L. A. P. Freitas, C. J. Lim, J. R. Grace, and B. Luo. Hydrodynamics and stability of slot-rectangular spouted beds. I. Thin bed. *Chem. Eng. Comm.*, **181** (2000), 225–242.

33. S. K. Foong, R. K. Barton, and J. S. Ratcliffe. Characteristics of multiple spouted beds. *Mech. and Chem. Eng., Trans. Instn. Engrs. Aust.*, **11** (1975), 7–12.

34. D. V. R. Murthy and P. N. Singh. Minimum spouting velocity in multiple spouted beds. *Can. J. Chem. Eng.*, **72** (1994), 235–239.

35. C. Beltramo, G. Rovero, and G. Cavaglià. Hydrodynamic and thermal experimentation on square-based spouted beds for polymer upgrading and unit scale-up. *Can. J. Chem. Eng.*, **87** (2009), 394–402.

36. D. O. Albina. Emissions from multiple-spouted and spout-fluid fluidized beds using rice husks as fuel. *Renewable Energy*, **31** (2006), 2152–2163.

37. B. Taha and A. Koniuta. Hydrodynamics and segregation from the Cerchar FBC fluidization grid. Fluidization VI Poster Session, Banff, Alberta, Canada, 1999, 1–5.

38. C. C. Huang and C. S. Chyang. Multiple spouts in a two-dimensional bed with a perforated-plate distributor. *J. Chem. Eng. Japan*, **26** (1993), 607–614.

39. A. Verma, J. C. Salas-Morales, and J. W. Evans. Spouted bed electrowinning of zinc. II. Investigations of the dynamics of particles in large thin spouted beds. *Met. and Mat. Trans.*, **28B** (1997) 69–79.
40. G. X. Hu, X. W. Gong, B. N. Wei, and Y. H. Li. Flow pattern and transitions in a novel annular spouted bed with multiple air nozzles. *Ind. Eng. Chem. Res.*, **47** (2008), 9759–9766.
41. V. B. Kvasha. Multiple-spouted gas-fluidized beds and cyclic fluidization: operation and stability. In *Fluidization*, ed. J. F. Davidson, R. Clift, and D. Harrison (London: Academic Press, 1985), pp. 675–701.
42. S. Fakhimi, S. Sohrabi, and D. Harrison. Entrance effects at a multi-orifice distributor in gas-fluidised beds. *Can. J. Chem. Eng.*, **61** (1983), 364–369.
43. M. I. Passos, A. S. Mujumdar, and G. Massarani. Scale-up of spouted bed dryers: criteria and applications. *Drying Technol.*, **12** (1994), 351–391.

18 Mechanical spouting

Tibor Szentmarjay, Elizabeth Pallai, and Judith Tóth

18.1   Principle of mechanical spouting

One of the main advantages of the conventional spouted bed is the characteristic recirculation particle mixing provided by a high-velocity gas jet through a nozzle at the conical bottom of the equipment. This ensures very effective "quasi-countercurrent" gas–solid contact. Because of the circulation of the particles, local overheating within the bed can be avoided and thus uniform product quality can be effected.[1]

Disadvantages include fluid motive-power consumption that occurs especially at the start of operation, but also persists under stable conditions owing to the vertical particle transport in the spout and the high pressure drop of the nozzle. In addition, conditions for heat and mass transfer can be obtained only within a limited range of gas flowrate because the velocity of the gas, usually air, is determined mainly by the size and density of the particles.[2]

These disadvantages of the spouted bed can be eliminated, while keeping its advantages, by the mechanically spouted bed (MSB), in which the most important characteristics of conventional spouted beds can be found.[3] According to the developed prototype, the typical spouted circulating motion is ensured by an open conveyor screw, installed along the vertical axis of the device, independent of the airflow rate. The diameter of the screw is nearly equal to the diameter of the gas channel (spout), around which a similar dense sliding layer (annulus) is formed. Because of mechanical particle circulation, fluid motive-power consumption is lower by 20–25 percent than for conventional spouting,[4] but this gain is reduced some 5–10 percent by the power consumption of the screw.

Moreover, airflow rate can be chosen in quite a wide range, independent of the particle size or density. It depends mainly on the required operation (e.g., drying, coating, granulation). With the high gas velocity (20–30 m/s) that is favorable from the point of view of heat and mass transfer, air is injected into the bed tangentially through specially designed "whirling" rings at the bottom of the bed. The bed diameter-to-height ratio can be selected quite freely, and particle circulation time can be controlled within wide limits. The height of the screw is always greater than that of the bed, and the bed height can be reduced until the desired particle circulation by the screw against the tangential air jet is obtained.

Spouted and Spout-Fluid Beds: Fundamentals and Applications, eds. Norman Epstein and John R. Grace. Published by Cambridge University Press. © Cambridge University Press 2011.

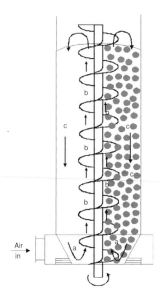

Figure 18.1. Principle of mechanical spouting, after Szentmarjay et al.[8]: (a) well-mixed drying zone, (b) mechanical spout, (c) annulus.

In the MSB one can distinguish three zones, which differ significantly from each other both spatially and in their flow pattern[5,6] (see Figure 18.1):

(1) a zone of intensive gas–solid contact with a characteristic turbulent particle flow pattern at the bottom of the bed in the vicinity of the gas inlet;
(2) a zone of particle transport vertically upward by the screw (mechanical spout) co-current to the gas stream; and
(3) a dense phase annular region sliding downward countercurrent to the airflow.

18.2   Mechanically spouted bed drying

In the beginning the field of applications focused only on drying of particulate solids, but the mentioned advantages have created very effective possibilities in drying of pastelike materials, pulps, suspensions, solutions, and heat-sensitive dispersions of high moisture content, which cannot be directly spouted. For such applications, the suspension is fed at several points into the annular region of the inert particles, which provide a large surface for contacting the gas. The suspension distributes itself on the surface of the inert particles sliding downward, and forms an almost uniform thin layer, with a mean thickness of a few microns. The wet coating in an optimum case is two to four times thicker than the primary particle size of the suspended material to be dried. Besides effective drying, the other goal of this process is usually reproduction in the dried product of the primary or

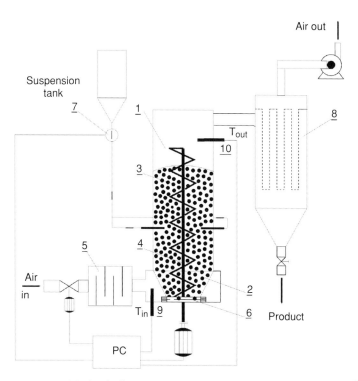

Figure 18.2. Mechanically spouted bed dryer, after Szentmarjay and Pallai[9]: (1) cylindrical column, (2) conical bottom, (3) inert particles, (4) houseless screw, (5) heat exchanger, (6) tangential air slots, (7) feeding pump, (8) bag filter, (9, 10) temperature and RH meters.

near-primary particle size of the suspension. The coating thickness can be influenced by diluting the suspension and by varying the bed height or the conveying rate of the screw – that is, by proper adjustment of the circulation time of the inert particles. At the bottom of the bed, the wet coating is contacted by the tangentially directed high-velocity hot air. In the wet filmlike coating, diffusion resistance can be considered negligible, so drying takes place in a very short time, even at relatively low temperature.[6–8] Because of the intensive friction between the inert particles and the screw, the dried fine coat wears off the surface of the particles in the screw; the fine product is then elutriated from the bed by the drying air, and it can be collected in an appropriate cyclone or bag filter. A sketch of an MSB dryer is shown in Figure 18.2.

Considering the overall drying process, the following sequential subprocesses have basic significance:

• Formation of wet coating on the surface of the inert particles,
• Drying of the coating,
• Erosion of the dried coating from the surface of the particles, and
• Elutriation of the product by the air stream.[6–8]

Table 18.1. Most important dimensions of mechanically spouted beds.

	Laboratory scale	Pilot plant	Industrial scale
D, m	0.12–0.14	0.38–0.42	600–1000
H, m	0.25–0.50	0.40–0.50	0.70–0.80
H/D	1.5–4.0	1.2–1.5	1.0–1.2
D_s (screw), m	0.040–0.05	0.12–0.15	0.20–0.35
s (pitch), m	0.028–0.032	0.090–0.095	0.145–0.250
D/D_s	2.8–3	2.8–3	3
s/D_s	0.65–0.75	0.72	0.72

18.3   Dimensions

The diameter D_s of the screw and the size of the inert particles largely determine the bed diameter. The bed is not practical if it is smaller than 120 mm in diameter, whereas, according to scaleup considerations (see Chapter 17), the upper limit of the diameter is about 1.2 m. The most important dimensions of MSB dryers are summarized in Table 18.1.

18.4   Inert particles

Spherical particles are generally preferred as the inert charge, but in some cases cylindrical bodies of equivalent diameter and height can be applied successfully. Their makeup depends on the field of application and hence on the physical, chemical, or biological properties of the wet material and on the applicable temperature range. Other important particle properties are their solidity (1 – internal porosity) and their heat and wear resistance. Adhesive properties are also important but, at the same time, the dried material must be erodable from the surface.

Many kinds of inert solids have been tested; it has been found that particles made of heat-resistant plastics, ceramic, or glass are mainly suitable. Effective erosion removal of the dried coating can be achieved only if the particles of the inert charge have near-uniform diameters. Because of the well-defined shape and size of the particles, the total surface of the inert bed can be calculated almost exactly. The most frequently used inert particles and their properties are summarized in Table 18.2.

18.5   Cycle time distribution

The residence time of the particles in the zones of the bed can be determined by measurement of cycle times. In one study, a single inert particle, tagged by Co-60 radioactive isotope, was traced in the bed for various bed depths, revolutions of the screw, and gas velocities.[6,7] The detector screened the whole cross-section of the bed.

Table 18.2. Properties of useful inert particles.

Particles	Glass beads	Al-oxide ceramic balls	Hostaform (polyformaldehyde)	Teflon
Shape		Spherical		Cylindrical
d_p, mm	5–8	6.6; 7.4	7.6; 12	6×6; 12×12
ρ_p, kg/m³	2400–2600	3520–3640	1340	2070
Max. allowable temp. (°C)	180	400	140	220

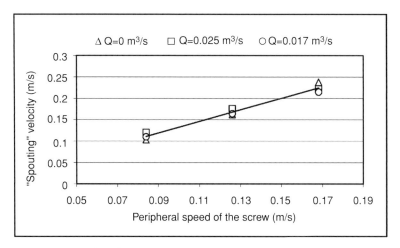

Figure 18.3. Velocity of particles upward in the screw at three volumetric flow rates, Q, of air: $D = 0.138$ m, $D_s = 0.04$ m, $s = 0.028$ m, $H = 0.4$ m, $\rho_p = 1340$ kg/m³, $d_p = 7.6$ mm.

Screening started at the top; when the detector was placed at a lower height, the path of the traced particle, both upward and downward, could be followed. With the detector at the top of the bed, only one peak appeared in the intensity-versus-time diagram during a cycle. At lower heights, however, two peaks were observed, and the time elapsed between the peaks was proportional to the distance the particle traveled from the detector to the top and back again. Thus, the particle passed the detector twice during one cycle, moving upward in the screw and downward in the annulus. Knowing the height of the bed and the geometry, the residence time of the tracer particle in selected sections of the bed could be obtained. It was found that a particle spent 70 percent to 80 percent of the cycle time in the cylindrical annulus, 5 percent to 10 percent in the screw, and 15 percent to 20 percent in the conical bottom. From the variances of the cycle time distributions and of the residence time distributions in the three zones, it was concluded that intensive particle mixing occurred in the vicinity of the air injection, whereas the flow pattern of the particles in the annulus could be characterized as plug flow. The particles traveling upward in the screw were surrounded by the annulus as a closed entity, and cross-mixing between the two sections was negligible. Furthermore, the particle velocity was independent of the gas velocity, both in the screw and in the annulus. In Figure 18.3, the "spouting" velocity of the tagged particle is plotted against the peripheral speed of the screw for different gas flowrates.

It follows from the foregoing that the velocity of the particles in both the screw and the annulus is determined essentially by the conveying rate of the screw. This was confirmed by means of a specially designed cylindrical screen basket with an orifice at the bottom, the diameter of which was identical to that of the screw. The basket was placed over the top of the bed; after a short operating time, the screw was stopped and the particles were weighed. It was proved that the mass flow rate of the particles is a function of the dimensions and revolution of the screw, as well as of the particle density and the voidage ε in the screw, but is independent of the gas velocity. Thus, for calculation of the mass flow rate $\dot{m}$ of the particles, the following expression can be used[9]:

$$\dot{m} = \frac{D_s^2 - d_s^2}{4} \pi s n \rho_p (1 - \varepsilon) \tag{18.1}$$

where s is the pitch, n is the speed of revolution of the screw, d_s is the screw's axle diameter, and ε is the loose-packed voidage.

From the mass flow rate and the bed volume, as well as from the volume of the characteristic zones, the residence time of the particles in each zone can be estimated and controlled; thus the drying process can also be well controlled. This information is necessary for scaleup calculations. Because of the mechanical spouting, the airflow rate can be chosen very freely, first considering the requirements for drying, given the moisture content and other properties of the solutions or slurries to be dried. To maintain the characteristic flow pattern of the MSB, the gas velocity should be between the elutriation velocity U_e of the fine product and the minimum fluidization velocity U_{mf} of the inert particles, that is:

$$U_e < U < U_{mf}. \tag{18.2}$$

18.6　Pressure drop

Gas velocity plays the primary role in determining the pressure drop across the bed, but some effect of the screw must also be taken into account. In the annulus, the gas velocity has been found to be mostly radially uniform, although a small increase has been observed from the column wall to the screw.[10] The pressure drop Δp across the bed in the MSB can be well approximated by the following modification of Δp_E, the pressure drop by Ergun's equation[11] for a packed bed of height H:

$$\Delta p = \Delta p_E (0.85 - 0.09 U_{ph}), \tag{18.3}$$

which is valid in the range of peripheral speed of the screw $0.4 < U_{ph} < 1.6$. The speed of rotation U_{ph} (m/s) depends on the inert particles and the dimensions of the screw, as well as on the drying task.

18.7   Drying mechanism

With mechanical spouting, not only can the efficiency of drying be improved vis-à-vis conventional spouting, but special drying tasks, such as gentle drying of pastelike, sticky, heat sensitive, and thermoplastic materials, are also made possible.[6,8,9]

The drying process takes place most intensively at the conical bottom of the bed, at a constant rate in a very short time. Steady-state conditions can be achieved only when the total operating time required by the successive subprocesses does not exceed the cycle time – in other words, the whole drying process must take place during one circulation. According to circulation measurements and drying experiments, the inert particles spend 10 percent to 15 percent of the cycle in the intensive drying zone, which means in practice that a particle can reside there for an average of 5 to 10 s. Naturally the subprocesses cannot be sharply separated from one another. Because of the relatively slow descent velocity of the particles in the annulus, sufficient time is available for formation of the wet coating. Moreover, the drying takes place in a bed height of a few centimeters. Therefore, the time required by the erosion process determines the total bed height and thereby the length, as well as the rotation speed, of the screw.

18.8   Scaleup

The optimum parameters for scaleup – the times required by the sequential subprocesses, the specific rate of water evaporation, the gas velocity, and the type and size of inert particles – can be obtained from laboratory-scale experiments. The height of the drying zone can be computed from the heat balance recommended by Mathur and Epstein,[1]

$$H = \frac{U d_p \rho c_p}{6\,(1 - \varepsilon)\, h_p} \ln \frac{T_{in} - T_p}{T_{out} - T_p}, \tag{18.4}$$

in which, for calculation of the fluid-particle heat transfer coefficient h_p at $Re_p > 1000$, the equation of Rowe and Claxton[12] can be used.

Knowing the height of the drying zone and the specific drying performance, as well as the amount of water to be evaporated, the total particle surface area and the volume of the drying zone can be obtained. From the bed volume and the time required by the drying process, the mass flow rate of the inert particles can be calculated based on Eq. (18.1). To ensure the required circulation time for the subprocesses, the cycle time divided by the bulk-volumetric flow rate of the particles yields the total volume of the bed. Finally, dimensions of the screw should be given by calculation from the peripheral speed of rotation in the laboratory tests.[9,13]

Several large scale MSBs currently operate for production of curatives and of trace elements for animal foods, as well as for production of basic materials for high-purity industrial ceramics.[6]

18.9   Developments

The bed height, and simultaneously the pressure drop across the bed, can be reduced without reducing the time and length required by the erosion subprocess by the following method: The upper section of the screw is surrounded by a tube, the length of which can be extended down to the feeding point of the suspension. Thereby, the height of the bed retaining the original annulus cross sectional area can be reduced by the length of the tube, whereas the screw can transport the inert particles upward so the time and length required by the erosion subprocess remain the same as before.

Another direction of recent developments is combination of the MSB dryer with microwave heating for drying and for heat treatment of grains. Laboratory-scale investigation has proved that very good drying efficiency can be achieved in this manner.[6]

Acknowledgment

The authors express their gratitude to Professor Norman Epstein for the detailed checking of this chapter.

References

1. K. B. Mathur and N. Epstein. *Spouted Beds* (New York: Academic Press, 1974).
2. A. S. Mujumdar. Spouted bed technology – a brief review. In *Drying '84*, ed. A. S. Mujumdar (New York: Hemisphere-McGraw-Hill, 1984), pp. 151–157.
3. Hungarian Pat. 176,030, U.S. Patent 4,203,226 (1977), French Patent 30,230 (1977).
4. T. Blickle, E. Aradi, and E. Pallai. Use of up-to-date processes for the drying of agricultural products. In *Drying '80*, ed. A. S. Mujumdar (New York: Hemisphere, 1980), pp. 265–271.
5. T. Szentmarjay and E. Pallai. Drying of suspensions in a modified spouted bed drier with inert packing. *Drying Technol.*, **7** (1989), 523–536.
6. E. Pallai, T. Szentmarjay, and A. S. Mujumdar. Spouted bed drying. In *Handbook of Industrial Drying*, ed. A. S. Mujumdar (London: CRC Press/Taylor and Francis Group, 2006), pp. 363–384.
7. T. Szentmarjay, E. Pallai, and A. Szalay. Drying process on inert particles in mechanically spouted bed dryer. *Drying Technol.*, **13** (1995), 1203–1219.
8. T. Szentmarjay, E. Pallai, and Zs. Regényi. Short-time drying of heat-sensitive biologically active pulps and pastes. *Drying Technol.*, **14** (1996), 2091–2115.
9. T. Szentmarjay and E. Pallai. Drying experiments with AlO(OH) suspension of high purity and fine particulate size to design an industrial scale dryer. *Drying Technol.*, **18** (2000), 759–776.
10. T. Szentmarjay, A. Szalay, and E. Pallai. Hydrodynamic measurements in mechanically spouted bed. *Hung. Ind. Chem.*, **20** (1992), 219–224.
11. S. Ergun. Fluid flow through packed columns. *Chem. Eng. Progr.*, **48** (1952), 89–94.
12. P. N. Rowe and K. T. Claxton. Heat and mass transfer from a single sphere to fluid flowing through an array. *Trans. Instn Chem. Engrs.*, **43** (1965), T321–T331.
13. T. Szentmarjay, A. Szalay, and E. Pallai. Scale-up aspects of the mechanically spouted bed dryer with inert particles, *Drying Technol.*, **12** (1994), 341–350.

19   Catalytic reactors and their modeling

Giorgio Rovero and Norberto Piccinini

In an earlier review on modeling of catalytic gas–solid fluidized bed reactors,[1] spouted beds were treated as a special case of fluidized beds, with the jet region extending to the upper free surface of the solids emulsion. The spout and the annulus are two well-distinguished zones, characterized by such different gas–solid contacting that they have been treated distinctly since the first approach[2] for modeling spouted bed chemical reactors. The spout zone acts as a dilute vertical transport system, whereas the peripheral annulus has many similarities with a countercurrent downflow packed bed, the major peculiarity being gas percolation into the dense emulsion from the spout. Therefore, solids motion in a spouted bed is a major factor affecting mass and heat transfer, mixing, contacting, and hence the choice of reactor model. The solids can react (e.g., in combustion, where they are depleted over time), constitute inerts (e.g., sand diluting a solid fuel and regulating the system hydrodynamics, as well as providing a heat buffer), or act as a catalyst.

Successful design and operation of a reactor depend on the ability to predict the system behavior, especially the hydrodynamics, mixing of individual phases, heat and mass transfer rates, and kinetics of the reactions involved. A model for spouted bed reactors must account for design equations (e.g., H_m, U_{ms}), basic hydrodynamics (e.g., D_s, $U_a(z)$, U_{mf}, U_t, distributed ΔP profiles), geometric and physical parameters (e.g., D, D_i, θ, d_p, ρ_p), solids circulation pattern and mixing, mass or mole balances, transfer between phases (spout and annulus, gas and catalyst particles), hydraulic assumptions and phenomenological observations (e.g., perfect mixing, plug flow, and radial or axial dispersion), transport mechanism hypotheses, heat and mass balances, and kinetic rate expressions.

19.1   Fundamental modeling

The earliest fundamental model to predict the chemical conversion in a spouted bed reactor, by Mathur and Lim,[2] and recapitulated by Mathur and Epstein,[3] established the basis both for subsequent theoretical studies and for experimental testing, and presented a general approach for cases in which the solid phase acts as a catalyst or heat carrier.

Spouted and Spout-Fluid Beds: Fundamentals and Applications, eds. Norman Epstein and John R. Grace. Published by Cambridge University Press. © Cambridge University Press 2011.

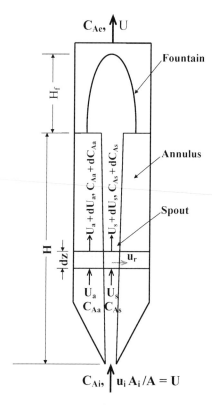

C_{Ae}, ↑U

Fountain

H_f

$U_a + dU_a$, $C_{Aa} + dC_{Aa}$

$U_s + dU_s$, $C_{As} + dC_{As}$

Annulus

Spout

H

dz

u_r

U_a U_s

C_{Aa} C_{As}

C_{Ai}, ↑ $u_i A_i / A = U$

Figure 19.1. Two-region model of a spouted bed catalytic reactor.[2]

The model assumes the existence of two regions, the spout and annulus; in both, the gas moves upward in "one-dimensional flow" according to the scheme presented in Figure 19.1. The model was developed for an isothermal constant-volume reaction. Mass balances in the two regions, together with continuity equations, provide a full flow description. A first-order reaction was promoted by a highly porous particulate catalyst, in which mass transfer and diffusional resistances can be neglected. The convective gas crossflow from the spout to the annulus satisfied the Mamuro and Hattori equation.[4] H_m was either derived from previous experiments or calculated for D in the range 0.15 to 0.61 m, with U_{ms} and D_s based on previous correlations. The spout voidage was set at a constant value of 0.95 for the largest column or matched to observed profiles for the smallest unit; in all cases the contribution to the overall conversion from the gas leaving the spout was predicted to be minimal. No contribution to the reaction was included for the catalyst in the fountain, even though the spout was extended to reach the highest elevation of the fountain itself. The conversion at the exit is given by the weighted average of the concentrations of the two regions, obtained by integrating the differential gas mass balance in the spout and the annulus:

$$\overline{U}_s \frac{dC_{As}}{dz} + k(1 - \varepsilon_s) C_{As} = 0 \qquad (19.1)$$

and

$$U_a \frac{dC_{Aa}}{dz} + \frac{1}{A_a} \cdot \frac{d(U_a A_a)}{dz}(C_{Aa} - C_{As}) + k(1 - \varepsilon_a)C_{Aa} = 0. \qquad (19.2)$$

The modeling predicted the reactor overall conversion with varying k, D, U, d_p, and H. Excluding the last parameter, which surprisingly generated a maximum conversion for a bed depth lower than H_m (caused by simplifying assumptions and a combination of hydrodynamic features), all other results were in line with expectations. The predicted conversion was compared with those for fixed and fluidized beds. The drawback of spouted beds was shown to be gas bypassing through the spout. The use of a spouted bed as a catalytic reactor appeared to be confined to relatively fast reactions, where the reaction rate is unaffected by the particle size. It was strongly recommended that studies be conducted to confirm the theoretical conclusions.[2]

Some modifications to the first theoretical account were introduced[5] to describe the performance of spouted beds (SBs) and spout-fluid beds (SFBs). After assuming that D_s is identical for the two configurations, the spout voidage was assumed to be linearly proportional to z. The velocity field in the SB annulus was modified to compensate for overestimation. As a result, the reactor conversion no longer showed its maximum value at $H < H_m$ for fast reactions. The overall conversion generated by the SFB is usually greater than for the SB because of greater flow of gas in the annulus.

Experimental results were later presented, together with modeling improvements.[6] Diffusional mass transfer between spout and annulus was added to the earlier two-region model. In addition, a novel representation of the annulus was proposed, the so-called streamtube model (see Figure 19.2): it is represented by a variable number of concentric annular pathlines of increasing length, radiating outward, each collecting gas crossflowing from the spout into the annulus; the integral of the ascending gas flowrate is consistent with the Mamuro and Hattori[4] velocity profile. The experiments were carried out in a 0.155-m ID vessel, adding ozone to the spouting air and decomposing it on an alumina-supported iron oxide catalyst, crushed to particle fractions in the 0.82 to 2.00 mm range. The agreement between the calculated and measured annulus and overall concentrations was good.

This project was continued[7] by scaling up the unit to 0.22 m ID and by refining the scrutiny scale of measurement at the top of the annulus. Sampling from the spout was accomplished by online ozone measurement. Because of the characteristics of the catalyst granules, it was possible to operate with spherical particles decreasing from 4.4 to 2.6 mm in diameter by progressive milling during the tests, while maintaining their original internal porosity and catalytic activity. The reaction rate constant k was varied from 1.5 to 63 s^{-1} by varying the temperature from 290 to 335 K. Within the ranges of the operating parameters explored, detailed investigation of the larger column shed light on the concentration profiles along the annulus radial coordinate. Figure 19.3 compares the predictions of both the one-dimensional and streamtube models with the experimental results; the experimental profile, which is intermediate between the predictions of the two models, suggests that the one-dimensional two-region description is oversimplified, whereas the streamtube representation requires some radial dispersion

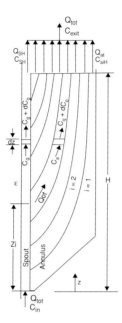

Figure 19.2. Section through spouted bed showing streamlines, concentrations, and flows used in streamtube model.[6]

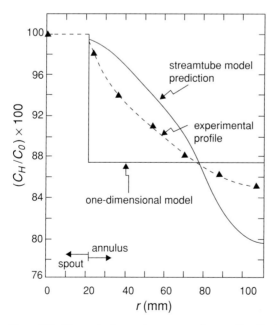

Figure 19.3. Dimensionless exit concentration profiles for 0.22 m column,[7] $k = 1.53$ s^{-1}. Overall C_H/C_0: experimental outlet value = 0.95, experimental integrated average = 0.90, predicted = 0.89.

between the streamtubes to make its prediction less steep radially. An alternative could be offered by a modified Mamuro and Hattori axial velocity profile in the annulus to account for gas recirculation at the bottom of spouted beds; such a modification could be described by a well-mixed region ahead of the streamlines, changing their respective lengths and receiving gas of more uniform concentration.

The mass balances for the reactant, written in dimensionless form, together with all the equations needed to evaluate the required quantities, led to a new complete theoretical model[8] for a first-order isothermal catalytic SB reactor. This model can apply to coarse spherical particles. Its outputs were compared to predictions from the earlier one-dimensional and streamtube models. Owing to a more favorable spout–annulus gas distribution, the new model predicts slightly higher conversion. However, the average deviation (11%, instead of 5% for the other models) was approximately double with respect to the experimental data in the 0.15-m unit.[5]

The first nonisothermal model[9] considered an adiabatic spouted bed catalytic unit for the dehydrogenation of ethylbenzene, an endothermic first-order irreversible reaction. Separate energy balances were required for the spout and annulus, interacting across their interface by bulk flows of gas and particles. For these conditions, axial and radial diffusional resistances within the phases were of negligible importance. Within the individual phases, no mass and heat transfer resistances were considered between the catalyst particles and gas. The model was developed by an a priori approach including all equations that provide the annulus–spout gas distribution, U_{mf}, U_{ms}, H_m, D_s, ε_s and a simplified description of the particle circulation velocities. Dynamic material balances were written for the spout and the annulus, respectively, as:

$$\frac{\partial C_{As}}{\partial t} = -u_s \frac{\partial C_{As}}{\partial z} - k_0 (1 - \varepsilon_s) exp(-E/R_g T_s) C_{As} \tag{19.3}$$

and

$$\frac{\partial C_{Aa}}{\partial t} = -u_a \frac{\partial C_{Aa}}{\partial z} + \frac{\partial u_a}{\partial z}(C_{As} - C_{Aa}) - k_0(1 - \varepsilon_a)exp(-E/R_g T_a)C_{Aa}. \tag{19.4}$$

Analogously the energy balances for the spout and annulus were written in the form:

$$\overline{C}_{ps} \frac{\partial T_s}{\partial t} = - \left[(\rho C_p)_g u_{gs} + (\rho C_p)_p v_{ps} \right] \frac{\partial T_s}{\partial z} + (\rho C_p)_p \frac{\partial v_{ps}}{\partial z}(T_a - T_s)$$
$$+ (-\Delta H) k_0 (1 - \varepsilon_s) exp\left(-E/R_g T_s\right) C_{As} \tag{19.5}$$

and

$$\overline{C}_{pa} \frac{\partial T_a}{\partial t} = \left[(\rho C_p)_p v_{pa} - (\rho C_p)_g u_{ga} \right] \frac{\partial T_a}{\partial z} + (\rho C_p)_p \frac{\partial u_{ga}}{\partial z}(T_s - T_a)$$
$$+ (-\Delta H) k_0 (1 - \varepsilon_a) exp(-E/R_g T_a) C_{Aa}. \tag{19.6}$$

As a first step, steady state was studied, erasing the transient terms and resulting in ordinary differential equations. Two cases, a flat-bottomed and a conical-bottomed vessel, were described, giving the same functional form to the annulus velocity and a cone-function of z to the cross-sectional area. The fractional exit conversion was evaluated as a function of D, H, θ, d_p, and U/U_{ms}. The sensitivity analysis of the last variable demonstrated that, by moderately increasing the gas velocity, additional solids circulation was obtained with more convective heat transfer to the annulus and an improved reaction rate, sufficient to compensate for increased gas bypassing in the spout.

A dynamic analysis[10] with 10 percent changes in temperature and inlet concentration demonstrated different responses for the spout and annulus, because of their different thermal capacity and particle/fluid interaction. New steady states were obtained after a 20- to 30-min transition. A moderate flow rate increase at the inlet initially caused an inverse response, followed by overall similar dynamics. The operability goals defined the control system design: the output concentration was selected as the control variable, with the inlet concentration as the main disturbance and the temperature or inlet flow rate as manipulated variables. Several control schemes were simulated and compared.

In a concise communication,[11] it was demonstrated that the "one-dimensional model" and "streamtube model" do not provide different overall conversions when a first-order reaction is considered, provided that the same hydrodynamic representations and the same mass transfer assumptions are included in both models. Based on general reactor engineering considerations, it was proved that the one-dimensional model predicts higher overall conversions for reactions of order less than unity, whereas the streamtube model generates higher conversions for reaction orders greater than one. It was noted that if the problem were tackled by a detailed experimental program, radial concentration profiles at different depths in the annulus would be helpful in discriminating between the models.

A further simple model was based on a phenomenological evaluation of the gas hydrodynamics, with the spout having well-defined plug flow, whereas some mixing was inferred in the annulus. This description[12] was defined as "semicompartmental," as the annulus was represented by two perfectly mixed regions in series. By assuming an annulus gas velocity profile as given by the Mamuro and Hattori equation,[4] evaluated at the dimensionless bed heights, z/H, of 0.25 and 0.75, the description of the two stages was straightforward. The predicted overall gas conversion was a function of d_p, k, U/U_{ms}, and a spout–annulus mass transfer coefficient. No maximum conversion was predicted with increasing bed depth, unlike the original model.[2] The experimental results available at that time were in satisfactory agreement, although the semicompartmental representation makes no allowance for radial variations in the reacting species concentration.

19.2   Applied studies

An exothermic reaction, CO oxidation over a $Co_3O_4/\alpha\text{-}Al_2O_3$ catalyst, was used to demonstrate the validity of a reactor model[13] for an adiabatic spouted bed. The theoretical description was based a priori on the definition of all variables acting in a spouted bed reactor. Considering a flat-based vessel, the model refers to an inlet region in which the gas expands before generating the actual spout, the peripheral annulus, a fountain core as an extension of the spout, and an axisymmetric downflowing fountain. The model predicted that the fountain contributed significantly to the reaction. Heat generated on the catalyst particles was then transferred to the gas by convection, as in a slowly moving

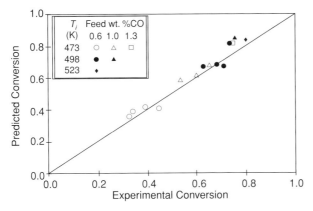

Figure 19.4. Comparison of experimental data with model predictions of overall reactor conversion.[13] Operating conditions: $D = 0.1$ m, $H = 0.17$ m, $D_i = 16$ mm. Reprinted with permission of John Wiley & Sons, Inc.

packed bed. These two conditions apply specifically to fast reactions and combustion. Separate energy balances were written for the solids and gaseous phases. All regions required voidage profiles and circulation rates, including a detailed description of the fountain, which had previously been neglected in spouted bed reactor models. The motion of particles in the annulus strictly followed streamlines, to satisfy both continuity with the spout loading and energy balances. The recursive numerical solution of the equation system required a sequence of steps:

(1) Read the input data.
(2) Calculate the hydrodynamic parameters.
(3) Calculate the annulus fluid flow field.
(4) Calculate the mass flow rate profiles and annulus particle velocity field.
(5) Calculate the annulus particle velocity balance.
(6) Calculate the spout mass and energy balance.
(7) Calculate the annulus particle energy balance.
(8) Calculate the annulus fluid mass and energy balance.
(9) Calculate the fountain mass and energy balances.
(10) Verify step 6.

The convergence criterion was a negligible change in temperature in the annulus, as this region provides a critical contribution to the overall reactant conversion. Model predictions were compared with the experimental data in a unit with $D = 0.11$ m, $H = 0.17$ m, $d_p = 3$ mm, and $D_i = 16$ mm, operating at 200 °C to 250 °C and about 210 kPa absolute pressure. It is seen in Figure 19.4 that the experimental results agree well with model predictions.

The catalytic disproportionation of propylene to ethylene and butylene under quasi-isothermal conditions was also investigated[14] in a small spouted bed ($D = 0.05$ m, $H = 0.12$ m, $D_i = 0.002$ m), operated with a fine WO_3-on-SiO_2 catalyst ($d_p = 0.14$ mm and $\rho_p = 740$ kg/m^3). Radial and axial conversions were measured at 673 K and 201 kPa

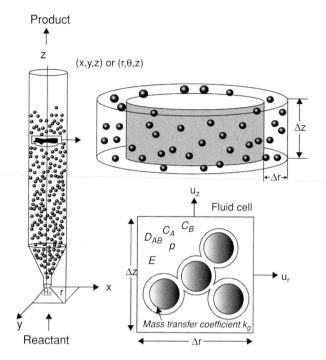

Figure 19.5. Axisymmetric representation of a spouted bed in cylindrical coordinates with fluid-particle flow field for a two-dimensional model cell.[15]

for gas flowrates covering an unusually broad range for spouted beds ($1.21 < U/U_{ms} < 3.21$). The reactant and product concentrations were measured by gas chromatography on samples from the spout, in the middle of the annulus, and at the wall; positive radial conversion gradients were confirmed. Because gas velocity in the annulus was not influenced by the overall gas flowrate, the experimental results suggest that the contacting efficiency between catalyst and gas could be improved by increasing the system turbulence. However, the conversion measured at the annulus top was always much lower than expected from the experimental profiles or calculated from the simple "one-dimensional," "streamtube," or "one-dimensional with axial dispersion" models. In the last case, the experimental and calculated axial profiles were compared, with the Peclet number, $Pe_D(z)$, varied from 0.1 to 1.0. Optimizing reactor models for spouted bed reactors should include axial and radial velocity profiles, solids mixing, and spout–annulus mass transfer, to consider mixing in the conical bottom and plug flow with some axial dispersion in the cylindrical part.

A computational fluid dynamic model based on equations of particle motion, gas motion, and mass conservation was developed[15] to predict the spatial particle distribution and the unconverted reactant distribution. The motion of particles was evaluated by a force balance that included the effects of gravitational, contact and drag forces. The model was based on the discrete element method (DEM) (see Chapter 4). Figure 19.5 shows the spouted bed unit, the axisymmetric geometry, and a model cell. A first-order irreversible reaction (catalyzed ozone decomposition) was chosen for the mass

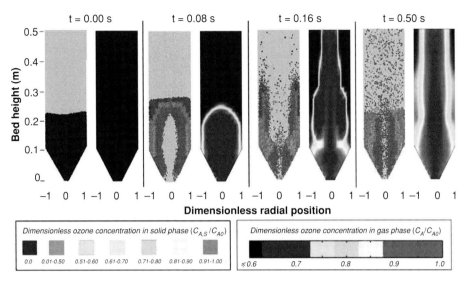

Figure 19.6. Predicted[15] particle distribution (left member of each pair) and unconverted ozone mole fraction (right member of each pair) distributions in gas and particle phases as functions of time with $U = 2.28$ m/s.

conservation equations of the unconverted reactant in the gas phase and within the porous particles. Three types of equations were solved simultaneously to give profiles of particle velocity and void fraction, gas flow field, and the conversion of the reactant in the system. The operating conditions reported in a previous experimental study[7] were fitted into the model to predict the ozone concentration and particle motion starting from a static initial condition. The system was predicted to reach steady state in about 0.5 s (see Figure 19.6). The predictions are compared with experimental results in Figure 19.7, demonstrating reasonably good agreement with the calculated profile at $z/H = 1$, but the earlier streamtube model[6] gives a somewhat better overall representation.

19.3 Conical spouted bed reactors

The features of a conical spouted bed (CcSB) reactor operating in a jet mode were studied by Olazar et al.[16] The reaction (polymerization of benzyl alcohol) was characterized by product sticking (because of temperature) and particle size heterogeneity (caused by growth of a polymer coating on the fine catalyst). An important feature of this kind of reactor, with respect to conventional spouted and bubbling fluidized beds, is that highly exothermic reactions can be carried out isothermally, without significant segregation in the solids phase.[17] Several aspects of CcSBs were investigated: (1) critical geometric factors, (2) design hydrodynamic correlations, (3) hydrodynamic model of the reactor, and (4) experimental model validation. An optimal cone angle in the range from 20° to 45° guarantees operability in terms of cyclic solid motion and gas residence time distribution. The D_i/D_o ratio influences the pressure drop and dead zone formation.

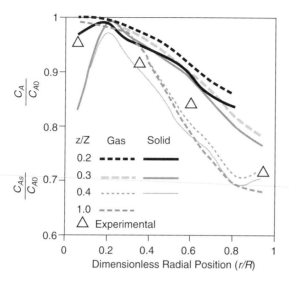

Figure 19.7. Radial profiles of unconverted ozone fraction at different heights for $t = 4$ s in gas and porous particle phases.[15] Comparison with the experiments[6] for $d_p = 4.4$ mm, catalyst loading: 3.93 kg (40,000 particles); $U = 2.44$ m/s.

D_i/d_p sets an operable reactor voidage. Previously proposed correlations for U_{ms}, ΔP and ΔP_M were verified. The reactor was divided into a number of conical streamtubes, each described by a one-dimensional unsteady-state mass conservation equation in plug flow, with longitudinal dispersion coefficient, D_z, obtained by fitting all the streamtubes for the gas phase with helium as tracer, for a range of experimental conditions. The polymer productivity was obtained by continuously running an automated laboratory reactor, changing the mean residence time of the catalyst and the partial pressure of benzyl alcohol.

In a subsequent paper,[18] the calculation steps for a CcSB simulation were presented after extending the governing mass conservation equation for an elemental volume of a streamtube to the reaction term. The polymerization rate derived from the literature also contained an expression for catalyst deactivation.[19] In principle, this simulation can apply to systems with catalyst circulation or other reactions. The calculation routine predicts the distribution activity of the catalyst, particle size distribution, flow rates of the gas phase and of the reactant, dispersion coefficient, radial and longitudinal profiles of gas velocity, reactant concentration profile, catalyst flow rate, and polymer production. Thanks to the simplified hydrodynamics, reactor scaleup is straightforward.

Continuous in situ pyrolysis of sawdust[20,21] was carried out for a CcSB, in which a small amount (10 g with $d_p = 0.7$ to 1.35 mm) of HZSM-5 zeolite catalyst was fluidized in a dilute mode. The biomass alone was treated thermally to obtain the yield and composition of the products. A conical spouted bed seems to offer an optimal geometric configuration in terms of handling heterogeneous materials, mixing of the various bed solids components (biomass and catalyst), and a very short gas residence

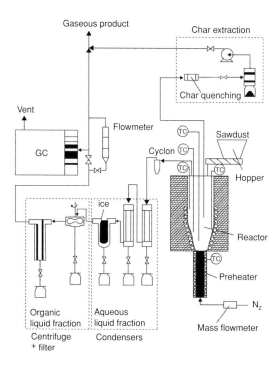

Figure 19.8. Schematic of continuous pyrolysis experimental unit.[20,21] Copyright © 2000 American Institute of Chemical Engineers (AIChE). Used with permission.

time. The geometric structure of the experimental unit (see Figure 19.8) had a total height of 0.34 m, $D = 0.12$ m, $H_c = 0.21$ m, $D_0 = 0.02$ m, $D_i = 0.01$ m, and a cone included angle of $28°$. The CcSB was operated at $400\,°C$, $450\,°C$, and $500\,°C$ with 10 to 14 L/min of nitrogen for as long as 5 h with pneumatic char extraction from the top. The bed was spouted at $U/U_{ms} = 1.2$ with a gas residence time of 50 ms in the bed and 20 ms in the spout. Typical results are shown in Figure 19.9: gaseous products reached higher yields at higher temperature owing to the catalytic effect. In addition, the catalyst modified the liquid phase, with the organic fraction converted to aqueous soluble products because of reduction reactions, leading to a more stable and less corrosive fuel.

In a related study, catalytic pyrolysis of biomass was carried out batchwise in a conical spouted bed[22] and compared with thermal pyrolysis: the kinetic scheme, kinetic constants, and yields of products in the gaseous, light liquid, and heavy liquid fractions were obtained. The goal of the process was to maximize the gas yield at the expense of the liquid products, which had limitations as bio-oils. The unit was the same as described in the previous work.[21] It operated at 673 K; 2 g of pine sawdust were dropped into 26 g of a sand/catalyst mixture, varying the active solids mass fraction from 0 to 100 percent. The sawdust was in a size range of 0.8 to 2 mm, and the catalyst was zeolite/bentonite/alumina in a 25/30/45 percent blend. The gas yields increased with a larger fraction of catalyst, with the ultimate effect of transforming heavy liquids into

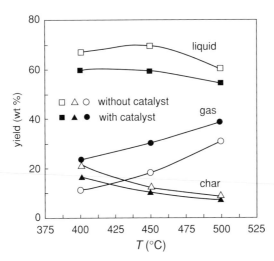

Figure 19.9. Effect of catalyst on distribution of products in pyrolysis of sawdust at different temperatures.[20,21] Copyright © 2000 American Institute of Chemical Engineers (AIChE). Used with permission.

gases, water, and less oxygenated liquid matter, which may undergo downstream steam reforming to generate syngas.

To obtain value from plastics residues, pyrolysis is one of the most practiced processes in fluidization studies, as well as being promising for implementation on a large scale. The use of acid catalysts offers advantages in shifting the process toward increased selectivity of products at lower temperatures. In this situation, conical spouted bed reactors are favorable because they operate in a diluted and well-mixed mode, efficiently preventing sticking and lump formation. An account[23] appeared in which a previously described[20,21] reactor was applied to HDPE pyrolysis (3 g of chips per batch) in 100 g of HZSM-5 zeolite catalyst. The operating temperature was set at 450 °C and 500 °C with N_2 as the spouting gas at a velocity 20 percent in excess of the minimum spouting value. Polymer decomposition was completed in 150 s and 120 s, with peak rates at 80 s and 50 s. About 55 percent of light olefins, 15 percent of light alkanes, 29 percent of gasoline fraction, and minimal heavy compounds and char residue were generated.

The catalytic partial oxidation of methane to syngas was investigated[24] in a CcSB with $D = 0.05$ m operated at 900 °C to 1000 °C using a $Ni/La/Al_2O_3$ catalyst ($d_p = 150$–200 μm and 600 μm). Experimental limitations, as well as process considerations, suggested particles significantly finer than those typically employed in spouted beds. Because of the lack of data, spouting was verified for hydrodynamic conditions simulating the actual process. The motion in the reactor appeared to be particularly favorable to preserve the catalytic activity over time, thanks to oxidation and reduction cycles while spouting with reaction. The hydrodynamics of the CcSB permitted a catalyst formulation (Ni concentration) more effective than that required by dense systems, leading to high CH_4 conversions and high selectivity to syngas.

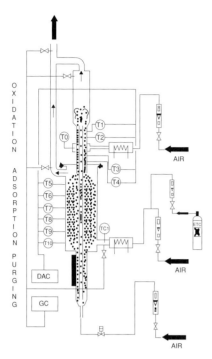

Figure 19.10. MSBDT pyrolysis plant configuration.[25]

19.4   Modified spouted bed reactors

A novel catalytic converter[25] (modified spouted bed with draft tube [MSBDT] reactor) was conceived after monitoring the adsorption/oxidation of ethylene oxide (EtO) on Pt/Al_2O_3 catalyst in a packed bed unit. Platinum was deposited on the exterior of 3.3-mm-diameter alumina beads. Tests in the packed bed defined optimal temperatures for adsorption and ignition. The reaction was demonstrated to be autothermal at EtO concentrations as low as 0.03 percent by volume, with careful regulation of the air (oxidant) flowrate. The adsorption was kinetically controlled at low temperatures ($\sim$80 °C). Gas–solid equilibrium prevailed at higher temperatures owing to the reaction exothermicity: temperature increases as high as $\sim$50 °C were detected, demonstrating adsorption on both the support and the platinum. The novel converter structure was derived from a spout-fluid configuration (essential for optimal control of flow rates and contact time) by adding an upper oxidation section and bottom purging, as illustrated in Figure 19.10. Solids circulation allowed the process to operate with cycled air cleaning by adsorption and catalyst regeneration by oxidation. In addition, to optimally match the sequence for catalyst heating, reaction, product desorption, and external transfer, pulsations were applied to the draft tube, leading to the temperature profiles shown in Figure 19.11. The process successfully withstood reasonable variations of the EtO concentration with time, thanks to the system heat capacity and easy regulation. Catalyst wear by attrition was investigated by monitoring the process efficiency during more than 500 h of operation.

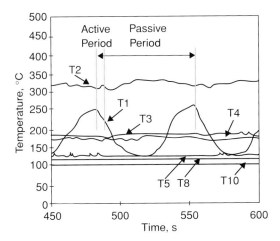

Figure 19.11. Changing temperature profiles along MSBDT reactor during self-sustained catalytic EtO incineration ($C_{EtO} = 0.1$ vol. %).[25] Locations of thermocouples are shown in Fig. 19.10.

Acknowledgment

The authors thank Ms. Marta Barberis Pinlung for her effective collaboration in editing.

Chapter-specific nomenclature

C	concentration, moles/m^3
C_p	volumetric heat capacity, J/m^{3}K
$\bar{C}_p$	weighted gas/particle volumetric heat capacity, J/m^{3}K
D_z	longitudinal dispersion coefficient, m^2/s
E	activation energy, J/mol
$\bar{G}$	productivity, tonnes m^{-2}h^{-1}, in ref. 14
k_0	pre-exponential factor, s^{-1}
$Pe_D(z)$	Peclet number $= wH/D_z$
T_i	gas inlet temperature, K
w	linear velocity of solid phase

Greek letters

ΔH	reaction enthalpy, J/mol
ζ	dimensionless height, z/H
ω_i	modified Arrhenius pre-exponential factor

Subscripts

A	species A
e	exit

References

1. L. Marmo, G. Rovero, and G. Baldi. Modelling of catalytic gas-solid fluidised bed reactors. *Catal. Today*, **52** (1999), 235–247.
2. K. B. Mathur and C. J. Lim. Vapour phase chemical reaction in spouted beds: a theoretical model. *Chem. Eng. Sci.*, **52** (1974), 789–797.
3. K. B. Mathur and N. Epstein. *Spouted Beds* (New York: Academic Press, 1974).
4. T. Mamuro and H. Hattori. Flow pattern of fluid in spouted beds. *J. Chem. Eng. Jap.*, **52** (1968), 1–5.
5. Dz. E. Hadzismajlovic, F. K. Zdanski, D. V. Vukovic, Z. B. Grbavcic, and H. Littman. A theoretical model of the first order isothermic catalytic reaction in spouted and spout-fluid bed. Presented at CHISA '78 *Congress* (Prague, 1978), Paper No C4.5.
6. N. Piccinini, J. R. Grace, and K. B. Mathur. Vapour phase chemical reaction in spouted beds: verification of theory. *Chem. Eng. Sci.*, **52** (1979), 1257–1263.
7. G. Rovero, N. Piccinini, J. R. Grace, N. Epstein, and C. M. H. Brereton. Gas phase solid-catalysed chemical reaction in spouted beds. *Chem. Eng. Sci.*, **52** (1983), 557–566.
8. H. Littman, P. V. Narayanan, A. H. Tomlins, and M. L. Friedman. A complete theoretical model for a first order isothermal catalytic reaction in a spouted bed. *AIChE Symp. Ser. No. 205*, **52** (1981), 174–183.
9. K. J. Smith, Y. Arkun, and H. Littman. Studies on modeling and control of spouted bed reactors – I. *Chem. Eng. Sci.*, **52** (1982), 567–579.
10. Y. Arkun, K. J. Smith, and G. Sawyer. Studies on modelling and control of spouted bed reactors – II. *Chem. Eng. Sci.*, **52** (1983), 897–909.
11. C. M. H. Brereton and J. R. Grace. A note on comparison of spouted bed reactor models. *Chem. Eng. Sci.*, **52** (1984), 1315–1317.
12. K. Viswanathan. Semicompartmental model for spouted bed reactors. *Can. J. Chem. Eng.*, **52** (1984), 623–631.
13. B. D. Hook, H. Littman, M. H. Morgan III, and Y. Arkun. A priori modelling of an adiabatic spouted bed catalytic reactor. *Can. J. Chem. Eng.*, **52** (1992), 966–968.
14. J. Dudas, O. Seitz, and L. Jelemensky. Chemical reaction in spouted beds. *Chem. Eng. Sci.*, **52** (1993), 3104–3107.
15. S. Limtrakul, A. Boonsrirat, and T. Vatanatham. DEM modeling and simulation of a catalytic gas-solid fluidized bed reactor: a spouted bed as a case study. *Chem. Eng. Sci.*, **52** (2004), 5225–5231.
16. M. Olazar, M. J. San José, G. Zabala, and J. Bilbao. New reactor in jet spouted bed regime for catalytic polymerizations. *Chem. Eng. Sci.*, **52** (1994), 4579–4588.
17. J. Bilbao, M. Olazar, A. Romero, and J. M. Arandes. Design and operation of a jet spouted bed reactor with continuous catalyst feed in the benzyl alcohol polymerization. *Ind. Eng. Chem. Res.*, **52** (1987), 1297–1304.
18. M. Olazar, J. M. Arandes, G. Zabala, A. T. Aguayo, and J. Bilbao. Design and operation of a catalytic polymerization reactor in a dilute spouted bed regime. *Ind. Eng. Chem. Res.*, **52** (1997), 1637–1643.
19. M. Olazar, G. Zabala, J. M. Arandes, A. G. Gayubo, and J. Bilbao. Deactivation kinetic model in catalytic polymerizations taking into account the initiation step. *Ind. Eng. Chem. Res.*, **52** (1996), 62–69.
20. M. Olazar, R. Aguado, M. J. San José, and J. Bilbao. Performance of a conical spouted bed in biomass catalytic pyrolysis. In *Récent Progrès en Génic des Procédes*, ed. G. Flamant,

D. Gauthier, M. Hemati, and D. Steinmetz (Toulouse, France: Lavoisier Technique et Documentation, 2000), **14**, 499–506.

21. M. Olazar, R. Aguado, and J. Bilbao. Pyrolysis of sawdust in a conical spouted-bed reactor with a HZSM-5 catalyst. *AIChE J.*, **52** (2000), 1025–1033.

22. A. Atutxa, R. Aguado, B. Valle, A. Gayubo, and J. Bilbao. Kinetic modelling of catalytic pyrolysis of biomass in a conical spouted bed reactor. In *CHISA '04 Congress* (Prague, 2004), Paper P 1.43.

23. G. Elordi, G. Lopez, R. Aguado, M. Olazar, and J. Bilbao. Catalytic pyrolysis of high density polyethylene on a HZSM-5 zeolite catalyst on a conical spouted bed reactor. *Int. J. Chem. Reactor Eng.*, **52** (2007), 1–9.

24. K. G. Marnasidou, S. S. Voutetakis, G. J. Tjatjopoulos, and I. A. Vasalos. Catalytic partial oxidation of methane to synthesis gas in a pilot-plant-scale spouted-bed-reactor. *Chem. Eng. Sci.*, **52** (1999), 3691–99.

25. Z. Lj. Arsenijevic, B. V. Grbic, Z. B. Grbavcic, N. D. Radic, and A. V. Terlecki-Baricevic. Ethylene oxide removal in combined sorbent/catalyst system. *Chem. Eng. Sci.*, **52** (1999), 1519–1524.

20 Liquid and liquid–gas spouting of solids

Željko B. Grbavčić, Howard Littman, and Morris H. Morgan III

The spouted bed technique permits agitation of particles too coarse for fluidizing with a gas when excellent heat and mass transfer characteristics and intimate fluid–particle contacting are important.[1] Liquid spouting has attracted much less interest, as coarse particles can be easily fluidized in this medium. However, recent advances in biotechnology and renewed interest in wastewater treatment have sparked new applications of liquid-spouted beds, particularly those incorporating a gas phase.

20.1   Liquid spouting

As discussed elsewhere in this book, a *spouted bed* can form when a fluid jet blows vertically upward along the center line of a vertical column, forming a spout in which fast-moving fluid and entrained particle mixing occur, surrounded by an annular region densely packed with particles moving slowly downward and inward. The spout is topped by a spillover fountain. Fluid percolates through the annulus from the spout. In a *spout-fluid bed* (see Chapter 6), additional fluid is introduced at the bottom of the annulus. Several fluid–particle patterns are possible, depending on the magnitude of the external annular fluid introduced to the annulus bottom[2–4]:

(1) Spouting with irrigation: beds in which the external annular fluid velocity, U_{a0}, is restricted to a velocity that keeps the annular velocity $U_{aH} \leq U_{mf}$.
(2) Spout-fluidization: beds in which the annulus is partly or completely fluidized; the level at which fluid velocity reaches U_{mf} depends on the external annular flowrate. If $U_{a0} = U_{mf}$, the annulus is completely fluidized.
(3) Jet-fluidized beds: beds in which the bed depth is deeper than the maximum spoutable bed height. When the fluid is a liquid, such beds exhibit two zones: a lower spouted bed region and an upper fluidized bed zone.

A typical regime map for a water spout-fluid bed system[3] is shown in Figure 20.1. The conventional spouted bed ($V_{a0} = 0$) falls between points E and D along the abscissa, whereas the fluidized bed is depicted along the ordinate between points G and A. Below the minimum spout-fluid line, GHE, the bed is fixed; the outer boundary curve, ABCD,

Spouted and Spout-Fluid Beds: Fundamentals and Applications, eds. Norman Epstein and John R. Grace. Published by Cambridge University Press. © Cambridge University Press 2011.

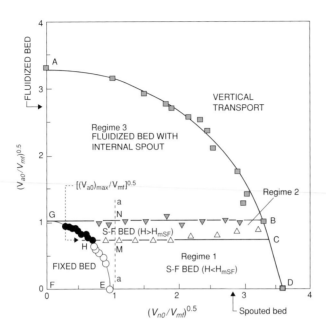

Figure 20.1. Flow regime map of a water spout-fluid bed of glass spherical particles ($D = 70$ mm, $D_i = 15$ mm, $d_p = 1.8$ mm, $H = 70$ mm, $H/H_m = 0.642$), adapted from Vuković et al.[3]

represents the locus of annulus and spout flowrates, whose sum equals V_T. One could also surmise from Figure 20.1 that because the experimental value of V_{ms} is approximately equal to V_{mf}, the actual bed height is close to H_m. Actual bed heights can be substantially less than H_m, however, even when (U_{ms}/U_{mf}) is close to unity.

A spout-fluid bed of height $H \leq H_{mSF}$ looks much the same as a spouted bed with $H < H_m$. As $(V_{a0})_{max}$ represents the inlet annulus flowrate required to fluidize the top of the annulus in a spout-fluid bed of height H, the annulus flowrate at point H is $(V_{a0})_{max}$. In the region EHCD, Regime I (item 1 in the preceding list), the total flowrate $> V_{mSF}$, with $V_{a0} \leq (V_{a0})_{max}$. The initial bed height is equal to or less than H_{mSF} and the bed is very similar in appearance to that of a conventional spouted bed. As V_{a0} is increased at constant V_{n0} along line a–a, the top of the annulus becomes incipiently fluidized at point M, as V_{a0} equals $(V_{a0})_{max}$. An increase in the external annulus flowrate, V_{a0} (along line a–a), results in the fluidization of the annulus, initiated at lower and lower levels. Finally, when V_{a0} reaches V_{mf} (point N on line a–a), the bottom of the annulus becomes just fluidized. These observations reflect the fact that H_{mSF} decreases as V_{a0} increases at constant V_{n0}. Along line HC, despite the fact that the spout diameter increases as V_{n0} is increased, the annulus height actually decreases, owing to the increased solids holdup in the spout and the fountain. Note that the data points lie above HC when $V_{n0} \gtrsim 9(V_{n0})_{mSF}$. The fountain height and spout diameter are large, and the annulus height is well below the initial bed height. In region HGBC, Regime 2 (item 2 in the preceding list), the bed forms two zones, in which a fluidized bed sits on top of a spout-fluid bed with a well-defined annulus and spout. This bed is very similar in appearance to a spouted bed with $H > H_m$ (i.e., to item 3 on the list). Along GB, U_{a0} equals U_{mf}, thus fluidizing the entire annulus, and the total volumetric flow rate is above V_{mf} except at point G. Regime 3 is bounded by region AGB, in which the fluid velocity $> U_{mf}$ everywhere in the annulus, and a liquid jet penetrates into the bed.

20.1.1   Pressure drop versus flow rate

The plot of pressure drop versus flow rate for liquid spouting is generally similar to that of a gas spouting system (see Chapter 2). With an increase in liquid superficial velocity, above U_{ms}, a constant pressure drop is established in the system. The difference between the peak pressure drop (ΔP_M) and the pressure drop at minimum spouting (ΔP_{ms}) decreases with increasing bed height. For gas phase systems at the minimum spouting velocity, a small reduction in the gas flowrate causes the spout and fountain to collapse, whereas in liquid spouting at V_{ms} the fountain is unexpanded with respect to the surface.

20.1.2   Minimum spouting velocity

In liquid-spouted beds the minimum spouting velocity at the maximum spoutable bed height is approximately equal to U_{mf}. Based on the assumption that $(U_s)_{Hm} = (U_a)_{Hm} = U_{mf}$ and that $A_s \ll A$, Grbavčić et al.[5] derived the following scaled equation for U_{ms}:

$$\frac{U_{ms}}{U_{mf}} = 1 - \left(1 - \frac{H}{H_m}\right)^3 . \tag{20.1}$$

Eq. (20.1) is based on the Mamuro-Hattori[6] equation for U_{aH}, assuming that at minimum spouting, $U_{aH} = U_{ms}$. The original Mathur-Gishler[7] equation, when scaled in this fashion, produces a different dependency:

$$\frac{U_{ms}}{U_{mf}} = \frac{U_{ms}}{U_m} = \left(\frac{H}{H_m}\right)^{0.5} . \tag{20.2}$$

This equation predicts lower values of U_{ms}/U_{mf} than Eq. (20.1) when $H/H_m \gtrsim 0.15$, and the converse when $H/H_m < 0.15$.

Littman and Morgan[8] developed a general correlation for U_{ms}/U_{mf} as a function of $(f_1/f_2 U_{mf})$, H/D and θ_f. That correlation was based on the following equation, derived from the annular pressure gradient at the top of the bed under minimum spouting conditions:

$$\frac{U_{ms}}{U_{mf}} = -\frac{f_1}{2 f_2 U_{mf}} + \left[\left(\frac{f_1}{2 f_2 U_{mf}}\right)^2 + \left(1 + \frac{f_1}{f_2 U_{mf}}\right) C_p\right]^{1/2};$$

$$\frac{H}{D} \geq \frac{H^*}{D} \quad \text{and} \quad A_f \cdot g(\phi_s) > 0.02, \tag{20.3}$$

where

$$C_p = 1 - Y - \frac{H}{D} X^2 \left[\frac{2Y + (X - 2) + (X - 0.2) - (3.24/\theta_f)}{2Y + 2(X - 0.2) - 1.8 + (3.24/\theta_f)}\right], \tag{20.4}$$

$$\theta_f = 7.18 \left[A_f \cdot g(\phi_s) - D_i/D\right] + 1.07, \tag{20.5}$$

$$X = 1/(1 + H/D), \tag{20.6}$$

$$Y = 1 - \Delta P_{ms}/\Delta P_{mf}, \tag{20.7}$$

and

$$A_f = \frac{\rho}{\rho_p - \rho} \cdot \frac{U_{mf} U_T}{g D_i}. \tag{20.8}$$

The dimensionless parameter, C_p, has an important effect on the U_{ms}/U_{mf} ratio and provides a connection to the viscous or inertial term in the Ergun[9] equation and bed geometry through the parameter θ_f. This model covers a wide range of experimental conditions, including water-spouted systems of spherical and nonspherical particles. For spherical particles, the $g(\phi_s)$ parameter of Eq. (20.5) approaches unity asymptotically.

Littman et al.[10,11] showed that the minimum spout-fluid flowrate in a liquid phase spout-fluid bed follows the simple linear relationship:

$$(V_{a0})_{mSF} = V_{mf} - \frac{V_{mf}}{V_{ms}}(V_{n0})_{mSF}. \tag{20.9}$$

As depicted in Figure 20.2 for such systems, the total minimum spout-fluid flowrate for $H/H_m \leq 1$ is given by

$$V_{mSF} = (V_{a0})_{mSF} + (V_{n0})_{mSF}. \tag{20.10}$$

For liquid spouting in a conical vessel, Legros et al.[12] proposed a model for the minimum spouting velocity based on the momentum transfer between the liquid jet and the bed. Beds consisting of different particle size distributions were used to substantiate this model. Good agreement was obtained, even when a large fraction of fine particles was present in the initial particle mixture.

20.1.3   Pressure drop at minimum spouting

ΔP_{ms} is commonly calculated by integrating the one-dimensional longitudinal pressure gradient in the annulus over the height of the bed using one of the annulus models. This

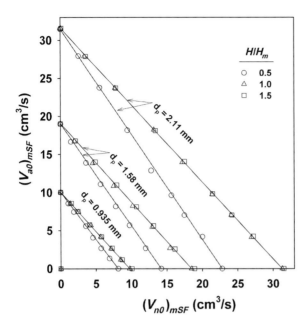

Figure 20.2. Relationship of spout and annular flows at the minimum spout-fluid flowrate, for water and glass beads in a 117×9.2-mm rectangular column with $D_i = 9.3$ mm, after Littman et al.[11]

procedure leads to quite reasonable results, although it ignores radial pressure gradients across the annulus and assumes that $\Delta P_S = \Delta P_{ms} = (\Delta P_a)_{ms}$. Equations for predicting $\Delta P_{ms}/\Delta P_{mf}$ have been proposed by Mamuro and Hattori,[6] Lefroy and Davidson[13] (for $H = H_m$), Epstein and Levine,[14] Grbavčić et al.,[5] and Morgan and Littman[15] (for $H \leq H_m$). The correlation of Morgan and Littman is

$$\Delta P_{ms}/\Delta P_{mf} = 1 - Y, \qquad (20.11)$$

where Y is obtained from:

$$Y^2 + [2(X - 0.2) - 1.8 + (3.24/\theta_f)]Y + [(X - 2)(X - 0.2) - (3.24X/\theta_f)] = 0. \qquad (20.12)$$

The ratio $\Delta P_{ms}/\Delta P_{mf}$ is a function of A_f, $g(\phi_s)$ and D_i/D, and was found to fit a wide range of experimental data involving both air- and water-spouted systems.

Based on their U_{ms}/U_{mf} model for spouted beds, Littman et al.[11] developed a relationship for the minimum spout-fluid bed pressure drop ratio, $\Delta P_{msf}/\Delta P_{mf}$. That model predicted a linear relationship between the spout-fluid pressure drop and the auxiliary velocity, U_{a0}.

20.1.4   Maximum spoutable bed depth

Littman et al.[16] also developed a model for predicting the maximum spoutable bed height (H_m) for coarse particles when the controlling mechanism was fluidization of the annulus. That model was based on a detailed axisymmetric analysis of the flow in the annulus, of the spouted bed employing interfacial pressure and velocity distributions, a fluid continuity equation, a vectorial Ergun equation[9] for the local pressure in the annulus, and appropriate boundary conditions. The following relationship was established between the maximum spoutable height, H_m, and the average spout diameter, D_s, for spherical particles:

$$\frac{H_m D_s}{D^2 - D_s^2} = 0.345 \left(\frac{D_s}{D}\right)^{-0.384}. \tag{20.13}$$

When evaluated with experimental values for D_s, predictions of H_m using Eq. (20.13) differed on average by 8.5 percent from experimental data for both air- and water-spouted beds. Assuming that H_m was proportional to the inlet fluid momentum, Littman et al.[17] subsequently developed an equation for predicting H_m for coarse spherical particles as a function of the inlet tube diameter, the column diameter, and the properties of the fluid–particle system:

$$\frac{H_m D_i}{D^2} = 0.218 + \frac{0.0050}{A_f}. \tag{20.14}$$

Eqs. (20.13) and (20.14) were combined to obtain a relationship for the D_s/D_i ratio as a function of D/D_i and parameter A_f.

Grbavčić et al.[5] presented the following simpler empirical correlation for predicting H_m in water-spouted beds:

$$\frac{H_m}{D} = 0.347 \left(\frac{D}{D_i}\right)^{0.41} \left(\frac{D}{d_p}\right)^{0.31}. \tag{20.15}$$

In spout-fluid bed systems, the maximum spoutable bed height decreases with increasing external annular flow. Grbavčić et al.[18] assumed that incipient fluidization of the solids at the top of the annulus is the limiting/controlling mechanism and proposed that $H_{mSF}/H_m = f(U_{a0}/U_{mf}, C)$, where the parameter C is the ratio of the fluid velocity at the top of the annulus at H_m or H_{mSF} to the minimum fluidization velocity. Their combined spout-fluid bed data for both air and water as the fluid gave a best-fit value of $C = 0.935$.

20.1.5   Fine particle systems

The spouting of fine particles ($d_p < 1$ mm) differs in two fundamental ways from large particle behavior:

1. Fine particles have a much smaller range of acceptable inlet diameter that result in stable spouting. Under operating conditions in which the inlet diameter exceeds the maximum stable inlet diameter, instabilities originate in the bed at either the spout inlet or outlet. Littman and Kim[19] characterized such particles at the minimum spouting conditions and examined the effect of both the inlet orifice diameter and the pressure distribution along the spout–annulus interface on the basic spouting parameters (U_{ms} and ΔP_{ms}).

2. Fine particles can cause a change in the spout inlet boundary condition. With gas-spouted systems the spout becomes unstable, bubble generation commences within the spout, and solid circulation is impaired. However, with liquid-phase spouting of fine particles, this instability manifests itself as a change in the inlet voidage. No longer is the inlet voidage equal to 1, but rather is a value less than 1. Dense transport is established throughout the spout, and $\Delta P_{ms}/\Delta P_{mf}$ exceeds 0.785. Morgan et al.[20] characterized such fine particle systems as low A_f systems when the values of this dimensionless parameter are less than 0.002 and thus indicative of a low inlet orifice momentum. In this regime, they found that a modified A_f parameter correlated the system dynamics better. Kim and Ha[21] studied the annulus flow of fine-particle water-spouted systems and found that the axisymmetric model of flow, which assumes Darcy flow in the annulus and uses the experimental spout–annulus interfacial condition, predicts the annulus fluid streamlines well.

20.1.6   Bed expansion

With an increase in liquid flow rate, a bed's spout and fountain expand, thereby increasing the average bed voidage even though the annular voidage increases minimally. Kmiec[22] investigated overall bed expansion to the top of the fountain using glass spheres, silica gel particles, ion-exchange resins, and sand spouted with water in an 88-mm-diameter conical-cylindrical column with included cone angles of 30°, 60°, and 180°. On a logarithmic plot, the voidage versus liquid superficial velocity relationship exhibited a change in slope at a voidage ≈ 0.85. Similar behavior has been reported by several investigators of liquid fluidized systems (Di Felice[23]). The following correlations were proposed by Kmiec[22] for low and- high-voidage regions:

For $\varepsilon < 0.85$,

$$\varepsilon = 0.838 \cdot Re^{0.182} Ar^{-0.0866}(H_0/D)^{-0.243}\theta^{-0.067}, \tag{20.16}$$

where $Re = d_p U \rho / \mu$ and $Ar = d_p{}^3 \rho(\rho_p - \rho)g/\mu$. For $\varepsilon > 0.85$,

$$\varepsilon = 1.102U^{0.0774}(H_0/D)^{-0.105}\theta^{-0.047}, \tag{20.17}$$

with U in m/s. Eqs. (20.16) and (20.17) are valid for $3.5 < Re < 350$, $2.1 \cdot 10^3 < Ar < 2.6 \cdot 10^6$, $0.19 < H_0/D < 1.55$, $\pi/6 < \theta < \pi$ radians, and $0.023 < U < 0.095$ m/s.

Ishikura et al.[24] investigated the maximum bed expansion in liquid-spouted and fluidized beds undergoing upward piston movement under conditions in which U exceeds the single particle terminal velocity.

20.1.7   Mass transfer

Hadžismajlović et al.[25] and Kim et al.[26] studied the liquid–solid mass transfer coefficients in liquid spouted and spout-fluid beds of ion exchange resins. They found that the traditional spouted bed is less effective than an equivalent fluidized bed. Such liquid spout-fluid beds can be successfully used to treat liquids contaminated with suspended solid particles, but the bed height should be significantly greater than H_m to obtain efficiency comparable with fluidized beds.

20.1.8   Spouting of binary mixtures and elutriation

Relatively little research has been done on liquid spouting of poly-disperse particle systems. Ishikura and Nagashima[27] investigated the spouting of binary particle mixtures with glass spheres of $d_p = 1.124$ mm as the coarse particles and glass spheres of diameters 233 and 474 μm as the finer component. The spouting fluids were water and aqueous sucrose solution. The addition of a small amount of the finer particles to the coarse ones produced a much lower minimum spouting velocity for the mixture than that for the coarse particles alone. An increase in the liquid viscosity led to a decrease of the minimum spouting velocity and hence the bed pressure drop. Ishikura et al.[28,29] also investigated the elutriation of the fine particles from a liquid spouted bed of binary solids in conical-based cylindrical columns of 66 and 100 mm diameter. These results were compared to similarly sized fluidized beds employing a perforated plate instead of an inlet nozzle. The initial fines entrainment velocity, U_{be}, was found to be smaller than the free-settling terminal velocity of the fines, but larger than the velocity required to entrain the same species from a liquid-fluidized bed. It was also found that U_{be} decreased with a reduction in freeboard height, making the particles more subject to elutriation. An empirical correlation for the elutriation coefficient was strongly dependent on a modified Froude number. Other variables – the column diameter, the initial total particle holdup, initial fines mass fractions, and nozzle diameter – were found to have little effect on this elutriation coefficient.

20.2   Liquid–gas spouting

Functionally, liquid–gas spouting systems are analogous to three-phase fluidization, and thus many expressions used to predict the dynamics of the latter hold for the former. Basically, two types of contactors have been investigated: contactors in which the gas is a dispersed phase, including liquid–gas spouted beds with draft tube, and contactors in which the liquid is a dispersed phase. The principal applications of these systems are similar to those for three-phase fluidized beds.

20.2.1   Gas as a dispersed phase

20.2.1.1   Liquid–gas spouted and spout-fluid beds

Nishikawa et al.[30] studied gas absorption in a liquid–gas spouted bed by monitoring oxygen dissolution into a copper-catalyzed sodium sulfite solution in a conical-based cylindrical column of diameter 150 mm and length 1400 mm. Air and water were introduced at the cone base through a nozzle whose diameter varied from 10 to 45 mm. Glass spheres of diameters 1.01, 2.59, 3.10, and 4.87 mm were the solid particles. Bed mass varied between 2 and 10 kg. For the largest solids mass loading, the estimated

H/D ratio was ~3. Experiments conducted at gas and liquid superficial velocities of 4.7 and 3.8 cm/s, respectively, showed that particles smaller than 3 mm were not effective because of channeling in the central portion of the bed. With particles larger than 3 mm, the gas–liquid volumetric mass transfer coefficient was more than 1.75 times larger than that of a column without particles because of efficient bubble breakage in both the spout region and in the fluidized bed region above the spout.

Wang et al.[31] proposed the use of a three-phase spouted bed with large particles and a downward annular liquid flow for gas–liquid reaction systems in which deposition and adhesion on the nozzle or the reactor wall limited effectiveness. Large particles were found to reduce fouling because of their high impact momentum. Glass beads of 10.5, 12.0, and 16.0 mm diameter were used as the solid phase. The column was 230 mm in diameter and was equipped with a slotted conical base. Water in the column leaked into a reservoir through the slots and was pumped back to the column for spouting the glass particles through a 16-mm-diameter nozzle. Air was introduced through a ring-type distributor equipped with six 8-mm-diameter gas injection tubes. Wang et al.[31] identified three characteristic flow regimes: a packed bed regime, a transition regime, and a spouting regime. The experimental minimum liquid spouting velocity was found to increase with increasing static bed height and to decrease slightly with increasing gas velocity. The spout was effective for bubble breakup, whereas frequent collisions of the particles with the reactor wall and the nozzles prevented fouling and promoted self-cleaning. Gas holdup increases accompanied corresponding increases of the superficial gas and liquid circulation velocities. Gas holdup varied between 0.1 and 0.5, depending on bed operating conditions.

Anabtawi et al.[32,33] investigated liquid-phase mass transfer from the dispersed gas in a three-phase spout-fluid bed at conditions above and below the minimum spout-fluid values. They followed oxygen absorption in carboxymethylcellulose solutions under varying rheological conditions. The gas-absorbing solution was introduced into the surrounding annular section and the spouting air through a central nozzle. Spherical glass particles of diameter 1.75 mm were the solids. These authors stated that the main advantage of this contacting system was the enhanced mixing associated with a vigorous circulatory motion caused by rising bubbles.

20.2.1.2 Liquid–gas spouted and spout-fluid beds with a draft tube

The gas–liquid–solid fluidized bed has emerged in recent years as one of the most promising devices for three-phase operations.[34] A new design with a spouting orientation incorporates a draft tube that is coaxially located inside the bed with a gas and liquid injector under the draft tube. The draft tube promotes bulk circulation of gas, liquid, and solids between the draft tube and annulus, thereby achieving intimate contacting between phases (Figure 20.3). If there are no particles flowing in the draft tube, the system is, in essence, an internal loop gas lift reactor. Fan et al.[34] conducted the most detailed study of this type of contacting system. They identified flow regimes and studied an array of variables: pressure profiles and pressure drops, bubble penetration depth in the annulus, overall gas holdup, apparent liquid circulation rate, and bubble size distribution

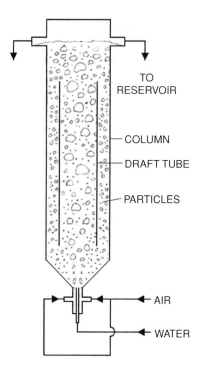

Figure 20.3. Liquid–gas spouted bed with a draft tube, adapted from Fan et al.[34]

in both the draft tube and annulus. Three flow regimes were identified: a packed bed mode, a fluidized bed mode, and a circulated bed mode. The circulated bed mode is of particular interest, as this bed mode generates both high gas holdup and efficient contacting between phases. The transition points between the respective regimes are a complex function of particle size, particle density, and particle loading.

The overall gas holdup increases with an increase in either gas or liquid superficial velocities. In all cases the overall gas holdup of a draft tube three-phase spouted bed is significantly higher than that for the corresponding three-phase fluidized bed system.

Different hydrodynamic aspects of liquid–gas spouted and spout-fluid beds with a draft tube have also been investigated by Karamanev et al.,[35] Hwang and Fan,[36] Vunjak-Novaković et al.,[37] Kundaković et al.,[38] Cecen Erbil,[39] Nitta and Morgan,[40] Olivieri et al.,[41] and Pironti et al.[42]

20.2.2   Liquid as a dispersed phase

Fluidized bed contactors containing large, low-density spheres considerably improve gas–liquid contacting in scrubbers, absorbers, distillation columns, and direct cooling towers.[43] They operate at much higher gas and liquid rates before flooding than conventional packed towers and have lower static bed heights. Lighter packing and higher fluid flowrates also make them efficient low-pressure-drop contactors. Movable packing

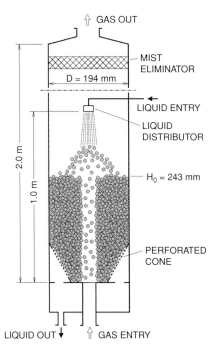

Figure 20.4. Three-phase spouted bed, adapted from Vuković et al.[44]

systems allow for the handling of gases and liquids containing particulate matter and precipitates, and, for all practical purposes, clogging is eliminated. The highly turbulent states induced in such contactors reveal transfer rates two orders of magnitude higher than those in packed beds.[43] These fluidized bed contactors do possess certain shortcomings – they tend to channel, and liquid backmixing makes true countercurrent operation impossible. Vuković et al.[44] developed a three-phase spouted bed contactor in which the solid particles are spouted in a countercurrent flow of gas and liquid. A schematic diagram of their system is shown in Figure 20.4. Hollow 10-mm-diameter polyethylene spheres ($\rho_p = 320$ kg/m^3) were spouted in a 194-mm-diameter column. A perforated 60° conical section, 86 mm high, served both as a bed support and water drain. Air was introduced axially through a converging nozzle 30 mm in diameter, and water was admitted through a distributor containing sixty 2-mm-diameter tubes.

    Two general flow regimes were observed in this three-phase spouted bed contactor as the gas flowrate was raised. In the higher-flowrate regime, the pressure drop, total liquid holdup, and bed expansion all increased with gas flowrate. The "active" holdup, given by the ratio of the measured bed pressure drop/pressure drop owing to the total weight of the bed, rises rapidly in this flow rate regime and it is likely that interphase transfer processes then occur at the highest rate. A spouted bed contactor with gas and liquid mass flowrates of 2.18 and 1.88 kg/m^{2}s, respectively, had similar pressure drop per unit area of particle surface, total holdup per unit of operating bed volume, and "active" holdup as a comparable fluidized bed contactor.

20.2.3   Processing in liquid–gas spouted beds

Several possible applications of liquid–gas spouted beds have been reported. Kecha-giopoulos et al.[45] investigated a spouted bed reactor system for hydrogen production via reforming of ethylene glycol, which served as a representative compound for aqueous phase bio-oil. An olivine–nickel alloy was a suitable catalyst with high reforming activity, excellent anticoking characteristics, and exceptional mechanical strength. Coke formation, a major problem in most reforming processes, was drastically reduced because of rapid and effective mixing of the hot solid particles and the cold reactants. Wright and Raper[46] investigated fluidized and spouted beds for the biological filtration of gases because of their high specific gas flowrate and vigorous mixing that facilitates enhanced gas–biomass contacting. Switching from a conventional fluidized bed to a spouted bed improved yields by 10 percent to 20 percent. Nieto et al.[47] and Tailleur[48] studied the butene–isobutane alkylation reaction on a super-acid solid catalyst in a three-phase spouted bed reactor. The main result was that the three-phase draft tube spouted bed reactor improved both gas–solid contact and liquid mixing because of internal and external recycling. Dabhade et al.[49] investigated the degradation of phenol by immobilized *Nocardia hydrocarbonoxydans* (actinomycetes) on granular activated carbon in a gas–liquid–solid three-phase spouted bed contactor. The effect of an array of variable flow rates, influent concentrations, and solid loadings on phenol degradation was examined. It was found that adsorption was dominant during the initial reaction phase, whereas biodegradation dominated after adsorption equilibrium was reached. In general, higher liquid flow rate increases shear between the spout and the annulus and enhances turbulence; unfortunately, in biofilm reactors, this turbulence caused biomass detachment, resulting in poor degradation of phenol. Elmaleh et al.[50] evaluated the oxygen transfer characteristics of a high compact multiphase reactor (HCMR) for wastewater treatment employing cells immobilized on spouting particles. The high turbulence levels caused significant particle–particle attrition, limited the biofilm thickness around the particles, and lowered the biomass holdup. Even though biomass holdup was relatively low in these HCMRs, they were effective low-energy and low-sludge-producing reactors.

Chapter-specific nomenclature

A_f	parameter defined by Eq. (20.8)
C_p	parameter defined by Eq. (20.4)
f_1	$= 150[(1-\varepsilon)^2/\varepsilon^3]\mu/d_p^2$
f_2	$= 1.75[(1-\varepsilon)/\varepsilon^3]\rho/d_p$
$g(\phi_s)$	particle sphericity function[8], $g(\phi_s) = 1$ for spherical particles
H_{mSF}	maximum spoutable bed height at the minimum spout-fluid condition, m
H^*	lowest bed height for a one-dimensional model based on Eq. (20.3), m
U_{a0}	superficial fluid velocity at the inlet to the annulus $(= V_{a0}/A_a)$, m/s
U_G	superficial gas velocity in three-phase bed, m/s
U_L	superficial liquid velocity in three-phase bed, m/s

U_s superficial fluid velocity in the spout, m/s

U_T terminal velocity of a single particle, m/s

V total fluid flow rate ($= V_{a0} + V_{n0}$), m³/s

V_{a0} inlet annulus flowrate, m³/s

V_{mf} minimum fluidizing flow rate, m³/s

V_{ms} minimum spouting flow rate, m³/s

V_{mSF} total fluid flow rate at the minimum spout-fluid condition, m³/s

V_{n0} fluid flow rate in spout inlet tube, m³/s

V_T $= U_T \cdot A$, m³/s

X $= 1/(1 + H/D)$

Y $= 1 - \Delta P_{ms}/\Delta P_{mf}$

Greek letters

ε_g gas holdup in three-phase bed

θ_f parameter defined by Eq. (20.5)

ϕ_s sphericity

Subscripts

a in the annulus

mf minimum fluidization

ms minimum spouting

mSF minimum spout-fluid condition

References

1. K. B. Mathur and N. Epstein. *Spouted Beds* (New York: Academic Press, 1974).
2. A. Nagarkatti and A. Chatterjee. Pressure and flow characteristics of a gas phase spout-fluid bed and the minimum spout-fluid condition. *Can. J. Chem. Eng.*, **52** (1974), 185–195.
3. D. V. Vuković, Dž. E. Hadžismajlović, Ž. B. Grbavčić, R. V. Garić, and H. Littman. Flow regimes for spout-fluid beds. *Can. J. Chem. Eng.*, **62** (1984), 825–829.
4. W. Sutanto, N. Epstein, and J. R. Grace. Hydrodynamics of spout-fluid beds. *Powder Technol.*, **44** (1985), 205–212.
5. Ž. B. Grbavčić, D. V. Vuković, F. K. Zdanski, and H. Littman. Fluid flow pattern, minimum spouting velocity and pressure drop in spouted beds. *Can. J. Chem. Eng.*, **54** (1976), 33–42.
6. T. Mamuro and H. Hattori. Flow pattern of fluid in spouted beds. *J. Chem. Eng. Japan*, **1** (1968), 1–5.
7. K. B. Mathur and P. E. Gishler. A technique for contacting gases with coarse solid particles. *AIChE J.*, **1** (1955), 157–164.
8. H. Littman and M. H. Morgan III. A general correlation for the minimum spouting velocity. *Can. J. Chem. Eng.*, **61**(1983), 269–273.
9. S. Ergun. Fluid flow through packed columns. *Chem. Eng. Progr.*, **48**:2 (1952), 89–94.

10. H. Littman, D. V. Vuković, F. K. Zdanski, and Ž. B. Grbavčić. Pressure drop and flowrate characteristics of liquid phase spout-fluid bed at the minimum spout-fluid flowrate. *Can. J. Chem. Eng.*, **52** (1974), 174–179.

11. H. Littman, D. V. Vuković, F. K. Zdanski, and Ž. B. Grbavčić. Basic relations for the liquid phase spout-fluid bed at the minimum spout fluid flowrate. In *Fluidization Technology*, Vol. 1, ed. D. L. Keairns (New York: Hemisphere and McGraw-Hill, 1976), pp. 373–388.

12. R. Legros, S. Charbonneau, and R. C. Mayer. Prediction of minimum spouting velocities in liquid-solids conical beds. In *Fluidization VIII*, ed. J. F. Large and C. Laguérie (New York: Engineering Foundation, 1998), pp. 639–646.

13. G. A. Lefroy and J. F. Davidson. The mechanics of spouted beds. *Trans. Instn. Chem. Engrs.*, **47** (1969), T120–T128.

14. N. Epstein and S. Levine. Non-Darcy flow and pressure distribution in a spouted bed. In *Fluidization*, ed. J. F. Davidson and D. L. Keairns (London: Cambridge University Press, 1978), pp. 98–103.

15. M. H. Morgan III and H. Littman. General relationships for the minimum spouting pressure drop ratio $\Delta P_{ms}/\Delta P_{mf}$ and the spout-annulus interfacial condition in spouted bed. In *Fluidization*, ed. J. R. Grace and J. M. Matsen (New York: Plenum Press, 1980), pp. 287–296.

16. H. Littman, M. H. Morgan III, D. V. Vuković, F. K. Zdanski, and Ž. B. Grbavčić. A theory for predicting maximum spoutable bed height in spouted beds. *Can. J. Chem. Eng.*, **55** (1977), 497–501.

17. H. Littman, M. H. Morgan III, D. V. Vuković, F. K. Zdanski, and Ž. B. Grbavčić. Prediction of the maximum spoutable height and the average spout to inlet tube diameter ratio in spouted beds of spherical particles. *Can. J. Chem. Eng.*, **57** (1979), 684–687.

18. Ž. B. Grbavčić, D. V. Vuković, Dž. E. Hadžismajlović, R. V. Garić, and H. Littman. Prediction of the maximum spoutable bed height in spout-fluid beds. *Can. J. Chem. Eng.*, **69** (1991), 386–389.

19. H. Littman and S. J. Kim. The minimum spouting characteristics of small glass particles spouted with water. In *Fluidization V*, ed. V. K. Ostergaard and A. Sorensen (New York: Engineering Foundation, 1988), pp. 257–264.

20. M. H. Morgan III, H. Littman, and B. Sastri. Jet penetration and pressure drops in water spouted beds of fine particles. *Can. J. Chem. Eng.*, **66** (1988), 735–739.

21. S. J. Kim and J. H. Ha. Flow in the annulus of a water spouted bed of small glass particles at minimum spouting. *J. Chem. Eng. Japan*, **19** (1986), 319–325.

22. A. Kmiec. Expansion of solid-liquid spouted beds. *Chem. Eng. J.*, **10** (1975), 219–223.

23. R. Di Felice. Hydrodynamics of liquid fluidization. *Chem. Eng. Sci.*, **50** (2005), 1213–1245.

24. T. Ishikura, I. Tanaka, and H. Shinohara. Length of particles bed in batch solid-liquid spouted and fluidized systems – experimental study for the region of transport bed. *J. Chem. Eng. Japan*, **12** (1979), 332–333.

25. Dž. E. Hadžismajlović, D. V. Vuković, F. K. Zdanski, Ž. B. Grbavčić, and H. Littman. Mass transfer in liquid spout-fluid beds of ion exchange resin. *Chem. Eng. J.*, **12** (1979), 227–236.

26. S. J. Kim, C. Y. Chung, S. Y. Cho, and R. J. Chang. Mass transfer in liquid-fluidized and spouted beds of ion exchange resin at low Reynolds number. *Korean J. Chem. Eng.*, **8** (1991), 73–79.

27. T. Ishikura and H. Nagashima. Flow characteristics of liquid-spouted beds with binary mixtures of particles. *Fukuoka Daigaku Kogaku Shuho*, **64** (2000), 153–161.

28. T. Ishikura, I. Tanaka, and H. Shinohara. Elutriation of particles from a batch spouted bed in solid-liquid system. *J. Chem. Eng. Japan*, **12** (1979), 148–151.

29. T. Ishikura. Behaviour and removal of fine particles in a liquid-solid spouted bed consisting of binary mixtures. *Can. J. Chem. Eng.*, **70** (1992), 880–886.

30. M. Nishikawa, K. Kosaka, and K. Hashimoto. Gas absorption in gas-liquid or solid-gas-liquid spouted vessel, 2nd *Pacific Chemical Engineering Conference (PAChEC '77)*, **2** (1977), 1389–1396.

31. J. F. Wang, T. F. Wang, L. Z. Liu, and H. Chen. Hydrodynamic behavior of a three-phase spouted bed with very large particles. *Can. J. Chem. Eng.*, **81** (2003), 861–866.

32. M. Z. Anabtawi, N. Hilal, and A. E. Al Muftah. Volumetric mass transfer coefficient in non-Newtonian fluids in spout fluid beds. *Chem. Eng. Technol.*, **26** (2003), 759–764.

33. M. Z. Anabtawi, N. Hilal, A. E. Al Muftah, and M. C. Leaper. Non-Newtonian fluids in spout-fluid beds: mass transfer coefficient at low Reynolds numbers. *Partic. Sci. & Technol.*, **22** (2004), 391–403.

34. L. S. Fan, S.-J. Hwang, and A. Matsuura. Hydrodynamic behavior of a draft tube gas-liquid-solid spouted bed. *Chem. Eng. Sci.*, **39** (1984), 1677–1688.

35. D. G. Karamanev, T. Nagamune, and I. Endo. Hydrodynamic and mass transfer study of a G-S-fluid-solid draft tube spouted bed bioreactor. *Chem. Eng. Sci.*, **47** (1992), 3581–3588.

36. S.-J. Hwang and L. S. Fan. Some design considerations of a draft tube gas-liquid-solid spouted bed. *Chem. Eng. J.*, **33** (1986), 49–56.

37. G. Vunjak-Novaković, G. Jovanović, Lj. Kundaković, and B. Obradović. Flow regimes and liquid mixing in a fluidized bed bioreactor with an internal draft tube. In *Fluidization VII*, ed. O. E. Potter and D. J. Nicklin (New York: Engineering Foundation, 1992), pp. 433–444.

38. Lj. Kundaković, B. Obradović, and G. Vunjak-Novaković. Fluid dynamic studies of a three-phase fluidized bed. *J. Serbian Chem. Soc.*, **61** (1996), 297–310.

39. A. Cecen Erbil. Effect of the annulus aeration on annulus leakage and particle circulation in a three-phase spout-fluid bed with a draft tube. *Powder Technol.*, **162**, (2006), 38–49.

40. B. V. Nitta and M. H. Morgan III. Particle circulation and liquid bypassing in three phase draft tube spouted beds. *Chem. Eng. Sci.*, **47** (1992), 3459–3466.

41. G. Olivieri, A. Marzocchella, and P. Salatino. Hydrodynamics and mass transfer in a lab-scale three-phase internal loop airlift. *Chem. Eng. J.*, **96** (2003), 45–54.

42. F. F. Pironti, V. R. Medina, R. Calvo, and A. E. Saez. Effect of draft tube position on the hydrodynamics of a draft tube slurry bubble column. *Chem. Eng. J. & Biochem. Eng. J.*, **60** (1995), 155–160.

43. B. K. O'Neill, D. J. Nicklin, N. J. Morgan, and L. S. Leung. The hydrodynamics of gas-liquid contacting in towers with fluidized packing. *Can. J. Chem. Eng.*, **50** (1972), 595–601.

44. D. V. Vukovic, F. K. Zdanski, G. V. Vunjak, Ž. B. Grbavčić, and H. Littman. Pressure drop, bed expansion, and liquid holdup in a three phase spouted bed contactor. *Can. J. Chem. Eng.*, **52** (1974), 180–184.

45. P. N. Kechagiopoulos, S. S. Voutetakis, A. A. Lemonidou, and I. A.Vasalos. Sustainable hydrogen production via reforming of ethylene glycol using a novel spouted bed reactor. *Catalysis Today*, **127** (2007), 246–255.

46. P. C. Wright and J. A. Raper. Investigation into the viability of a liquid-film three-phase spouted bed bio-filter. *J. Chem. Technol. & Biotech.*, **73** (1998), 281–291.

47. O. Nieto, M. Nino, R. Martinez, and R. G. Tailleur. Simulation of a spouted bed reactor for solid catalyst alkylation. *Fuel*, **86** (2007), 1313–1324.

48. R. G. Tailleur. Simulation of three-phase spouted bed reactor for solid catalyst alkylation. *Chem. Eng. & Proc.*, **47** (2008), 1384–1397.

49. M. A. Dabhade, M. B. Saidutta, and D. V. R. Murthy. Continuous phenol removal using *Nocardia hydrocarbonoxydans* in spouted bed contactor: shock load study. *African J. Biotech.*, **8** (2009), 644–649.

50. S. Elmaleh, S. Papaconstantinou, G. M. Rios, and A. Grasmick. Organic carbon conversion in a large-particle spouted bed. *Chem. Eng. J.*, **34** (1987), B29–B34.

Index